學習英檢中級單字不再囫圇吞棗，
只要這一本，
由時間淬煉出來的單字聖經！

學習有捷徑
夢想最接近

上場之前——
你真的了解全民英檢嗎？

🔍 測驗介紹

全民英檢（General English Proficiency Test全民英語能力分級檢定測驗，簡稱GEPT），在台灣已行之有年，從2000年開始，就是台灣學校、公家機關與民營企業對考生（受試人）英語程度的重要參考依據。

此試共分五級，分別是：初級Elementary、中級Intermediate、中高級High-Intermediate、高級Advanced、優級Superior，各包含「聽、讀（初試）」和「說、寫（複試）」四種考試類型，用以評量考生是否具備該級數的全方位英語能力。

🔍 全民英檢考試與國際標準CEFR能力對照

CEFR是歐洲官方專為歐洲人士設計、可以用來評斷民眾英文程度的一種量表，全名是Common European Framework of Reference for Languages: Learning, Teaching, Assessment（歐洲語言學習、教學、評量共同參考架構）。

語言學習不應只是閉門造車，透過與國際CEFR量表接軌，考生就能更清楚自己的定位，並規劃未來的努力目標。

CEFR C2	GEPT優級
CEFR C1+	GEPT高級說寫
CEFR C1	GEPT高級聽讀
CEFR B2+	GEPT中高級說寫
CEFR B2	GEPT中高級聽讀
CEFR B1+	GEPT中級說寫
CEFR B1	GEPT中級聽讀
CEFR A2+	GEPT初級說寫
CEFR A2	GEPT初級聽讀

資料來源：https://www.lttc.ntu.edu.tw/CEFRbyLTTC_tests.ht-m

關於中級測驗

通過全民英檢中級檢定，即代表考生具備能使用簡單英語進行日常生活溝通的能力，如：

 聽 在日常生活中，能聽懂一般的會話；能大致聽懂公共場所廣播、氣象報告及廣告等。在工作時，能聽懂簡易的產品介紹與操作說明。能大致聽懂外籍人士的談話及詢問。

 讀 在日常生活中，能閱讀短文、故事、私人信件、廣告、傳單、簡介及使用說明等。在工作時，能閱讀工作須知、公告、操作手冊、例行的文件、傳真、電報等。

 寫 能寫簡單的書信、故事及心得等。對於熟悉且與個人經歷相關的主題，能以簡易的文字表達。

 說 在日常生活中，能以簡易英語交談或描述一般事物，能介紹自己的生活作息、工作、家庭、經歷等，並可對一般話題陳述看法。在工作時，能進行簡單的答詢，並與外籍人士交談溝通。

職務參考：一般行政、業務、技術、銷售人員、護理人員、旅館／飯店接待人員、總機人員、警政人員、旅遊從業人員等，宜具備中級能力。

資料來源：https://www.gept.org.tw/Exam_Intro/t02_introduction.asp

中級測驗考試內容

通過全民英檢中級檢定,即代表考生具備能使用簡單英語進行日常生活溝通的能力,如:

	初試		複試	
測驗項目	聽力	閱讀	寫作	口說
總題數	45題	40題	2題	13~14題
總作答時間	約30分鐘	45分鐘	40分鐘	約15分鐘
滿分分數	120分	120分	100分	100分
測驗內容	•看圖辨義 15題 •問答15題 •簡短對話 15題	•詞彙和結構 15題 •段落填空 10題 •閱讀理解 15題	•中譯英40% •英文作文60%	•朗讀短文2篇 •回答問題 10題 •看圖敘述 1張圖
總測驗時間 (含考試說明)	兩項合計約2小時		約1小時	約1小時
通過標準	兩項測驗成績總和達160分,且其中任一項成績不低於72分		80分	80分

資料來源:https://www.gept.org.tw/Exam_Intro/t02_introduction.asp

依據全民英檢官方公告顯示,欲通過中級「聽、讀、寫、說」四類測試的字彙需求量為4,947個單字,但本書除了收錄此4,947個單字之外,又再精選了近400個常用單字,目的就是為了讓考生不只能過關,更能以滿分為目標,持續精進英文能力。

其他英檢相關資訊,如:報名費用、考試時間、採納英檢成績之學校/民營單位/公家機關名單……等,則以官方網站(https://www.gept.org.tw/index.asp)不定期公告的內容為準。

出擊準備——
本書教你必殺四招！

🔍 必殺第1招

全書採用英檢中心官方公佈單字，紮穩你的基礎馬步！

全書收錄財團法人語言訓練測驗中心公佈之全民英檢中級字彙 ＋ 教育部公佈之國中必備字彙 ＋ 名師嚴選試題最常出現重點單字，就是英檢中級必考5,300字！要打好基礎，就靠這一本！

🔍 必殺第2招

全方位單字小檔案＋片語＋各詞性例句，擴大你的守備範圍！

本書除了標注單字詞性、音標、自然發音法音節點，更適時補充延伸片語，甚至貼心標注該字彙為「英檢初級」或「英檢中級」程度，是難度較高的中級單字都會搭配例句讓考生熟悉用法；若是多種詞性的單字，則每個詞性都會搭配相關例句，讓考生更能加深印象！最全方位的學習，就靠這一本！

🔍 必殺第3招

例句編寫參考全民英檢中級出題範圍，加重你的出招勁道！

其實全民英檢考試最常出現的題目範圍，基本上都是換湯不換藥！像是「聽力」容易考廣播、氣象、廣告；「寫作」常考書信、心得……等。所以，本書的例句編寫並非毫無方向的造句發揮，而是參考全民英檢官方公佈的出題範圍寫成，讓你能一邊閱讀、一邊累積實戰招式！最有力道的學習，就靠這一本！

在日常生活中，能聽懂一般的會話；能大致聽懂公共場所廣播、氣象報告及廣告等。在工作時，能聽懂簡易的產品介紹與操作說明。能大致聽懂外籍人士的談話及詢問。例：

以下為書內呈現單字例句：

a·brupt [ə`brʌpt] **adj.** 突然的；意外的；唐突的；魯莽的 🎧 *Track 0002*
▶ We are sorry for the inconvenience and trouble that this abrupt change of schedule may have caused.
我們對這次行程突然的變更所可能造成的不便和困擾深感抱歉。

在日常生活中，能閱讀短文、故事、私人信件、廣告、傳單、簡介及使用說明等。在工作時，能閱讀工作須知、公告、操作手冊、例行的文件、傳真、電報等。例：

以下為書內呈現單字例句：

ad·ap·ta·tion [ˌædæp`teʃən] **n.** 改編 🎧 *Track 0005*
▶ This movie is an adaptation from a very popular book.
這部電影是從一本非常受歡迎的書改編而來的。

能寫簡單的書信、故事及心得等。對於熟悉且與個人經歷相關的主題，能以簡易的文字表達。例：

以下為書內呈現單字例句：

a·cad·e·my [ə`kædəmɪ] **n.** 學院 🎧 *Track 0006*
▶ I go to a local academy of arts. 我就讀於本地一所藝術學院。

在日常生活中，能以簡易英語交談或描述一般事物，能介紹自己的生活作息、工作、家庭、經歷等，並可對一般話題陳述看法。在工作時，能進行簡單的答詢，並與外籍人士交談溝通。例：

ac·com·pa·ny [ə`kʌmpənɪ] **v.** 陪伴 🎧 *Track 0012*
▶ I usually accompany my mom to the supermarket after school.
我放學後通常都會陪我媽媽去超級市場。

必殺第4招

　　真人發音MP3＋30回實戰雙CD，讓你在場上能眼觀四面、耳聽八方！

・以自然發音法錄音之關鍵單字MP3

　　本書的MP3完整收錄5,300的關鍵英文單字，以自然發音法的方式的錄音，先將單字拆解成音節後，再搭配一次完整複誦（如：ex‧per‧i‧men‧tal／experimental），讓你反覆聽、反覆記，印象度提升200%！

・30回模擬試題光碟

　　30回模擬實戰單字題庫光碟，題目均附詳細翻譯與解答，考前迅速瞭解自己的實力與學習成果，臨場對單字的記憶與熟練度便能自然發揮！

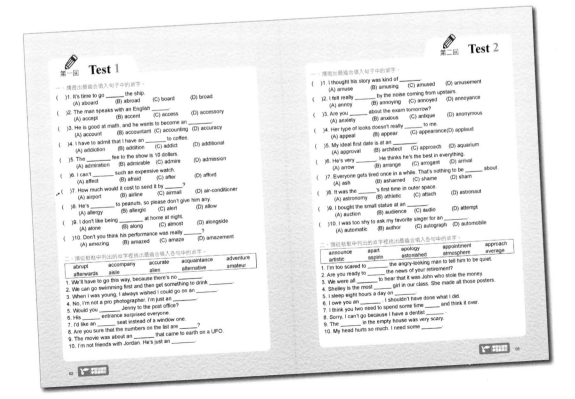

Preface 前言

　　全民英檢是現今許多學校都嚴格要求學生具備的語言能力門檻，甚至有些大專院校規定若無通過一定級數就無法畢業，面對這樣的規定而感到焦慮的考生大有人在，不知你是不是也有以下的擔憂呢？

★ 茫茫單字海，到底要撈什麼才對、背多少才夠？

　　很多考生擔心自己單字量不夠，考試題目有看沒有懂不說，面對口說與寫作測驗更是腦筋一片空白，壓根兒連一個字都生不出來。幸好，本書除了幫考生將官方公佈的英檢「初級」與「中級」所需的單字全數收錄之外，還加入了教育部公佈的國中必備字彙及名師嚴選試題最常出現重點單字，內容絕對完整又精準，相信考生只要熟悉本書中的單字，在考試時的答題能力與臨場快速反應肯定大幅精進！

★ 全民英檢到底怎麼考？有多少內容要準備？

　　很多考生因為考前未熟悉正式考試的題型與內容，導致實際面對考場的時候總因緊張而丟失應得的分數。考慮到這點，本書每個單字例句的編排並不是隨興造句，而是符合英檢官方公佈的常見出題範圍，如：聽力出題範圍多為「廣播」、「氣象」、「廣告」；寫作出題範圍多為「心得」、「故事」、「書信」……等。讓考生在閱讀本書例句時，同時還能熟悉考題，正式上場時才不會因驚慌而丟失分數。

★ 單字我會拼，但誰知道要怎麼唸？

　　許多考生很認真地把單字都背起來了，卻無法在考聽力時辨認出來，就更別提在考口說的時候能夠流暢地說了。為了幫助大家解決這個盲點，本書以自然發音法為出發點，把所有單字標上音節點，在錄音時除了幫大家拆解音節唸之外，還搭配兩次正常語速的完整單字唸誦。這種富有清楚節奏感的方式，絕對可以把每個單字都深深烙印在考生的腦海中，就連做夢都可以清楚講英文。

★ 一個單字有這麼多解釋，我怎麼可能背得完？

　　許多考生即使瞭解了單字的中文意思，但突然在題目中看到，還是會出現選擇障礙。事實上，英檢不但考的是你是否認得單字，更考你是否會活用，光是死板地背下每個單字的中文意思是不夠的，知道單字在句子中多是搭配哪些字詞、或是情境出現才是得分關鍵。所以，本書附上的題目光碟，以共30回的填空與選擇題，讓考生練習找出正確的單字，以累積實戰時所需的實力與直覺。（光碟共兩張，可別把試題光碟和錄音MP3光碟搞混囉！）

　　本書編排簡易、示例清楚、錄音也經過精心設計，只期能夠幫助考生的語言學習力大增、不會再因考試感到焦慮。祝大家在考場上都能一擊必殺！

Contents 目錄

在書中，你可能會看到以下代號。原來，它們是這個意思……

n. 名詞	adv. 副詞	aux. 助動詞
v. 動詞	prep. 介系詞	det. 限定詞
adj. 形容詞	pron. 代名詞	interj. 感嘆詞
art. 冠詞	abbr. 縮寫	conj. 連接詞

Aa

本書除包含官方公佈的中級4,947單字外，更精挑了近400個滿分必學的高手單字。同時，在片語的挑選、例句的使用上，皆依上述英檢官方公佈之能力範疇做設計，難度適中、不偏離考試主題。發音部分則是自然發音＆KK音標雙管齊下，搭配MP3以「分解／完整」方式錄音，給你最多元有效的學習手段，怎麼記都可以，想忘掉都好難！

通過中級英文檢定者的英文能力：

在日常生活中，能聽懂一般的會話；能大致聽懂公共場所廣播、氣象報告及廣告等。在工作時，能聽懂簡易的產品介紹與操作説明。能大致聽懂外籍人士的談話及詢問。

在日常生活中，能閱讀短文、故事、私人信件、廣告、傳單、簡介及使用説明等。在工作時，能閱讀工作須知、公告、操作手冊、例行的文件、傳真、電報等。

能寫簡單的書信、故事及心得等。對於熟悉且與個人經歷相關的主題，能以簡易的文字表達。

在日常生活中，能以簡易英語交談或描述一般事物，能介紹自己的生活作息、工作、家庭、經歷等，並可對一般話題陳述看法。在工作時，能進行簡單的答詢，並與外籍人士交談溝通。

---

a [ə]　　　　　　　🎧 *Track 0001*
art. 一；一（個）

A.M.＝a.m.
＝AM [e-εm]　🎧 *Track 0002*
adv. 午前

a·ban·don [ə`bændən]　🎧 *Track 0003*
v. 遺棄；丟棄；拋棄
▶ The old sofa was abandoned at the corner of the street. 那張舊沙發被遺棄在街角。
n. 放縱；放任
▶ She sang with abandon in the KTV.
她在KTV裡恣意高歌。

a·bil·it·y [ə`bɪləti]　🎧 *Track 0004*
n. 能力；能耐

a·ble [`ebḷ]　　🎧 *Track 0005*
adj. 有能力的、可以的、會的

ab·norm·al [æb`nɔrmḷ]　🎧 *Track 0006*
adj. 不正常的；異乎尋常的；例外的

▶ It is abnormal for a child to act so violently.
一個孩童有如此暴力的行為是不正常的。

a·board [ə`bord]　🎧 *Track 0007*
prep. 上（船、飛機、車）
▶ Passengers are waiting to go aboard the train. 旅客正在等著上火車。
adv. 在船（或飛機、車）上；上船（或飛機、車）
▶ All aboard! 請上車（船）！

ab·o·rig·i·nal　🎧 *Track 0008*
[͵æbə`rɪdʒənḷ]
adj. 土著的；原始的；原有的；原住民的
▶ Many aboriginal languages here are no longer used.
這裡的許多原住民語言已經不再使用了。

ab·o·rig·i·ne　🎧 *Track 0009*
[͵æbə`rɪdʒəni]
n. 土著居民；原住民

▶The aborigines here have great singing voices. 這裡的原住民有美妙的歌聲。

a·bout [ə`baʊt] 🎧 *Track 0010*
prep. 關於;在……附近;大約
adv. 到處;在附近;大約

a·bove [ə`vʌv] 🎧 *Track 0011*
prep. 在……之上;超過;勝過
adv. 在上面;高於、大於;以上的
adj. 以上的;前述的

a·broad [ə`brɔd] 🎧 *Track 0012*
adv. 在國外;到國外

a·brupt [ə`brʌpt] 🎧 *Track 0013*
adj. 突然的;意外的;唐突的;魯莽的
▶We are sorry for the inconvenience and trouble that this abrupt change of schedule may have caused. 我們對這次行程突然的變更所可能造成的不便和困擾深感抱歉。

ab·sence [`æbsns] 🎧 *Track 0014*
n. 不在;缺席

ab·sent [`æbsnt] 🎧 *Track 0015*
adj. 缺席的,不在場的

ab·so·lute [`æbsə͵lut] 🎧 *Track 0016*
adj. 絕對的;完全的
▶There is no absolute answer to this question. 這個問題沒有絕對的答案。

ab·so·lute·ly 🎧 *Track 0017*
[`æbsə͵lutlɪ]
adv. 絕對地;完全地
▶You are absolutely right. 你說的完全正確。

ab·sorb [əb`sɔrb] 🎧 *Track 0018*
v. 吸收
▶I can't absorb all the information at once. 我無法一次吸收所有的資訊。

ab·stract [`æbstrækt] 🎧 *Track 0019*
adj. 抽象的;深奧難懂的
▶The theory is far too abstract for me to understand. 這理論對我來說太過抽象難懂了。
n. 摘要;抽象派藝術作品;抽象概念;萃取物

▶This is an abstract of my term paper. 這是我學期研究報告的摘要。

(補充片語)
term paper 學期研究報告

(相關片語)
abstract painting 抽象畫
▶He decorated the wall with an abstract painting. 他用一幅抽象畫來裝飾這面牆。

a·buse [ə`bjus] 🎧 *Track 0020*
n. 濫用;虐待、傷害
▶The baby boy's death resulted from child abuse. 男嬰的死是受虐所造成的。

(補充片語)
child abuse 虐待兒童
v. 濫用;虐待
▶The baby boy was physically abused. 這男嬰遭到身體上的虐待。

ac·a·dem·ic [͵ækə`dɛmɪk] 🎧 *Track 0021*
adj. 大學的;學術的;學校的
▶Students nowadays suffer from great academic pressure.
現在的學生承受很大的學業壓力。

(相關片語)
academic year （大學）學年
▶The academic year begins in September and ends in the following June. 學年是於九月開始,到隔年六月結束。

a·cad·e·my [ə`kædəmɪ] 🎧 *Track 0022*
n. 學院
▶I go to a local academy of arts.
我就讀於本地一所藝術學院。

(相關片語)
Academy Award 奧斯卡金像獎
▶The actor won two Academy Awards for the same role. 這男演員以同一個角色贏得了兩座奧斯卡金像獎。

ac·cent [`æksɛnt] 🎧 *Track 0023*
n. 重音;口音、腔調
▶The man speaks in a British accent.
男子說著一口英國腔。

ac·cept [ək`sɛpt] 🎧 *Track 0024*
v. 接受

ac·cept·a·ble
🎧 *Track 0025*

[ək`sɛptəbḷ]

adj. 可接受的；還可以的

▶ This apple pie is acceptable, but it's not as good as mine. 這蘋果派味道還可以，但是沒有我做的好吃。

ac·cept·ance [ək`sɛptəns]
🎧 *Track 0026*

n. 接受；歡迎

▶ The new product has met wide acceptance with housewives. 新產品廣受家庭主婦歡迎。

(補充片語)

meet acceptance with 被接受；受歡迎

ac·cept·ed [ək`sɛptɪd]
🎧 *Track 0027*

adj. 公認的；被視為

▶ She has been accepted as a member of our family. 她已經被視為我們家的一份子。

ac·cess [`æksɛs]
🎧 *Track 0028*

n. 接近；接近的機會；進入的權利；通道、門路

▶ The bridge is the only access to the village. 這座橋是通往該村的唯一通道。

v. 使用；接近；取出（資料）

▶ Who gave you the right to access these files? 誰給你權利讀取這些檔案的？

ac·ces·so·ry [æk`sɛsərɪ]
🎧 *Track 0029*

n. 附件；配件；飾品；同謀、幫兇

▶ I'm going to shop for some accessories to go with my evening dress. 我要去逛街買些搭配我晚禮服的飾品。

adj. 附加的；附屬的；同謀的、幫兇的

▶ Accessory food factors, such as minerals, are essential for normal life. 附加食物因子如礦物質，對維持正常生命是不可或缺的。

ac·cid·ent [`æksədənt]
🎧 *Track 0030*

n. 意外

ac·ci·den·tal [ˌæksə`dɛntḷ]
🎧 *Track 0031*

adj. 偶然的；意外的

▶ I didn't make the mistake on purpose. It was purely accidental. 我不是故意犯錯的，純屬意外。

(相關片語)

accidental death 意外死亡

▶ The news of his accidental death astonished everyone. 他意外死亡的消息震驚了每一個人。

ac·com·mo·date
🎧 *Track 0032*

[ə`kamə,det]

v. 能容納；能提供……膳宿；可承載

▶ The school dorm can accommodate 1,000 students. 學校宿舍可容納1,000名學生住宿。

ac·com·mo·da·tion
🎧 *Track 0033*

[ə,kamə`deʃən]

n. 適應；調節；住處；膳宿

▶ Does this school offer accommodations for international students on campus? 這間學校有提供留學生校內住處嗎？

(補充片語)

on campus 校內

ac·com·pa·ny
🎧 *Track 0034*

[ə`kʌmpənɪ]

v. 陪伴；伴隨

▶ Do you want me to accompany you there? 你希望我陪你去嗎？

ac·com·plish
🎧 *Track 0035*

[ə`kamplɪʃ]

v. 完成；實現

▶ The mission has been accomplished. 任務已達成。

ac·com·plish·ment
🎧 *Track 0036*

[ə`kamplɪʃmənt]

n. 成就；成績；完成；實現

▶ Winning three gold medals is quite an accomplishment that you should be proud of. 贏得三面金牌是你應該感到驕傲的驚人成就。

ac·cord [ə`kɔrd]
🎧 *Track 0037*

v. 與……一致；符合；使一致、調解

▶ My opinion accords with yours. 我的意見與你的一致。

n. 一致；符合

※灰色單字為英檢初級必備單字

▶His view on this matter is in accord with mine. 他對這件事的看法跟我的是一致的。

(補充片語)

in accord with 與……一致

ac·cord·ing [ə`kɔrdɪŋ] 🎧 Track 0038
prep. 根據；按照

ac·cord·ing·ly [ə`kɔrdɪŋlɪ] 🎧 Track 0039
adv. 相應地；因此；於是
▶He was inadequate for his job. Accordingly, he was dismissed.
他無法勝任他的工作，因此，他被解僱了。

ac·count [ə`kaʊnt] 🎧 Track 0040
n. 帳戶；帳目；描述；解釋
▶I'd like to open an account in your bank.
我想在這家銀行開個帳戶。

v. 報帳；解釋、說明；對……負責；將……視為
▶How do you account for your absence from yesterday's meeting?
你要如何為你缺席昨天的會議解釋？

(相關片語)

take into account 一併考慮；考慮進去
▶I will take your advice into account.
我會將你的建議考慮進去。

ac·coun·tant [ə`kaʊntənt] 🎧 Track 0041
n. 會計師
▶Jenny is a certified public accountant.
珍妮是一個有合格證書的會計師。

ac·coun·ting [ə`kaʊntɪŋ] 🎧 Track 0042
n. 會計；會計學
▶I failed my accounting test again.
我會計學考試又考砸了。

ac·cu·ra·cy [`ækjərəsɪ] 🎧 Track 0043
n. 正確（性）；準確（性）
▶My boss emphasizes on accuracy instead of speed. 我的老闆強調正確性，而非速度。

ac·cu·rate [`ækjərɪt] 🎧 Track 0044
adj. 準確的；精確的

▶My boss asked me to report accurate data to him. 老闆要求我向他報告準確的數據。

ac·cu·sa·tion [,ækjə`zeʃən] 🎧 Track 0045
n. 控告；指責；罪名
▶The man says that it's a false accusation.
男子說這是不實的指控。

ac·cuse [ə`kjuz] 🎧 Track 0046
v. 控告；指控
▶He accused his roommate of stealing his money. 他控告他的室友偷他的錢。

ac·cus·tomed [ə`kʌstəmd] 🎧 Track 0047
adj. 通常的；習慣的；適應了的
▶I have become accustomed to city life.
我已經習慣了都市生活。

ace [es] 🎧 Track 0048
n. （骰子的）一點；發球得分；能手、佼佼者
▶He is an ace at acting. 他是個戲精。
adj. 第一流的
▶He is an ace film director.
他是個一流的電影導演。
v. 得分；在……做得好
▶I aced the finals. 我期末考考得很好。

ache [ek] 🎧 Track 0049
n. （持續的）疼痛
▶I've got an ache in my ear. 我耳朵會痛。
v. （持續性）疼痛
▶I am aching all over. 我全身都痛。

a·chieve [ə`tʃiv] 🎧 Track 0050
v. 完成、實現；達到

a·chieve·ment [ə`tʃivmənt] 🎧 Track 0051
n. 達成；成就、成績
▶For the shy boy, being able to dance on the stage is an achievement. 對那個害羞的男孩來說，能上台跳舞是個成就。

ac·id [`æsɪd] 🎧 *Track 0052*
n. （化）酸；有酸味的東西；尖酸刻薄
▶ You should be very careful when using strong acid to clean your bathroom or the toilet.
使用強酸來清潔浴室或馬桶時，要非常小心。

adj. 酸的；有酸味的；（化）酸性的；尖酸刻薄的
▶ Her acid comments were the reason she had no friends.
她刻薄的評論正是她沒有朋友的理由。

ac·ne [`ækni] 🎧 *Track 0053*
n. 痤瘡；粉刺；面皰；青春痘
▶ The acne on my face really bothers me.
我臉上的痘子真是讓我很困擾。

ac·quaint [ə`kwent] 🎧 *Track 0054*
v. 使認識；使了解；使熟悉
▶ I will acquaint myself with the new job as soon as possible. 我會儘快熟悉新工作。
（補充片語）
acquaint oneself with 使自己熟悉

ac·quaint·ance [ə`kwentəns] 🎧 *Track 0055*
n. （與人）相識；相識的人
▶ Tom and I are merely nodding acquaintances. 湯姆和我只是點頭之交。
（補充片語）
nodding acquaintance 點頭之交
（相關片語）
make the acquaintance of sb. 結識某人
▶ I made the acquaintance of the girl during my vacation in Hawaii.
我是在夏威夷度假時認識那女孩的。

ac·quire [ə`kwaɪr] 🎧 *Track 0056*
v. 取得；獲得；學到
▶ We go to school in order to acquire knowledge. 我們上學是為了求取知識。

a·cre [`ekɚ] 🎧 *Track 0057*
n. 英畝
▶ My grandfather owns 100 acres of farmland. 我的祖父擁有一塊100英畝的農田。

a·cross [ə`krɔs] 🎧 *Track 0058*
prep. 橫越、穿過　**adv.** 橫過；在對面

act [ækt] 🎧 *Track 0059*
n. 行為、行動；表現
v. 行動；做出……舉止；表演

ac·tion [`ækʃən] 🎧 *Track 0060*
n. 行動，行為

act·ive [`æktɪv] 🎧 *Track 0061*
adj. 活躍的；積極的；主動的

ac·tiv·it·y [æk`tɪvətɪ] 🎧 *Track 0062*
n. 活動

act·or [`æktɚ] 🎧 *Track 0063*
n. 男演員

ac·tress [`æktrɪs] 🎧 *Track 0064*
n. 女演員

ac·tu·al [`æktʃʊəl] 🎧 *Track 0065*
adj. 實際的；事實上的
▶ What is the actual cost of this product?
這項產品的實際成本為何？

ac·tual·ly [`æktʃʊəlɪ] 🎧 *Track 0066*
adv. 實際上、真的

a·dapt [ə`dæpt] 🎧 *Track 0067*
v. 適應；使適應
▶ I will try to adapt myself to the new environment as soon as I can.
我會試著盡快讓自己適應新環境。
（補充片語）
adapt oneself to 使自己適應

ad·ap·ta·tion [ˌædæp`teʃən] 🎧 *Track 0068*
n. 適應；適合；改編；改寫
▶ This film is an adaptation from a true story.
這部電影是由一個真人真事改編而成的。

add [æd] 🎧 *Track 0069*
v. 加、添加、增加

ad·dict [`ædɪkt] 🎧 *Track 0070*
n. 上癮的人

※灰色單字為英檢初級必備單字

▶He is a drug addict. 他是個吸毒成癮的人。

v. 使入迷；使沉溺；使成癮

▶He used to be addicted to alcohol in his youth. 他年輕時曾經沉迷於飲酒。

相關片語

selfie addict 自拍狂

▶My sister is an absolute selfie addict.
我姐是個不折不扣的自拍狂。

ad·dic·tion [ə`dɪkʃən] 🎧 *Track 0071*
n. 成癮；沉溺；入迷

▶Many female friends of mine have an addiction to Korean dramas.
我有很多女性友人都對韓劇上癮了。

ad·di·tion [ə`dɪʃən] 🎧 *Track 0072*
n. 加；增加的部分；加法

ad·di·tion·al [ə`dɪʃənl] 🎧 *Track 0073*
adj. 添加的；額外的

▶We can't afford additional expenses.
我們負擔不起額外的支出。

ad·dress [ə`drɛs] 🎧 *Track 0074*
n. 地址

ad·e·quate [`ædəkwɪt] 🎧 *Track 0075*
adj. 足夠的；適當的；可勝任的

▶Make sure we can provide adequate food and drinks for all our guests. 一定要確認我們能提供所有賓客足夠的食物和飲料。

ad·jec·tive=adj. 🎧 *Track 0076*
[`ædʒɪktɪv]

n. 形容詞

▶If you have to describe yourself with an adjective, what would it be? 如果你必須用一個形容詞來描述你自己，那會是什麼？

ad·just [ə`dʒʌst] 🎧 *Track 0077*
v. 調整；改變……以適應

▶Both of you have to adjust yourselves to marriage life. 你們兩人都必須改變自己，以適應婚姻生活。

ad·min·is·tra·tion 🎧 *Track 0078*
[əd͵mɪnə`streʃən]

n. 管理；經營

▶I major in Business Administration.
我主修企業管理。

ad·mi·ra·ble 🎧 *Track 0079*
[`ædmərəbl]

adj. 值得讚揚的；令人欽佩的；極好的

▶That's a very admirable achievement. Well done.
那是個非常令人敬佩的成就。做得好。

ad·mi·ra·tion 🎧 *Track 0080*
[͵ædmə`reʃən]

n. 欽佩；仰慕；讚美；引人讚美的人或事物

▶The woman looks at her husband with respect and admiration.
女子對丈夫十分敬愛。

ad·mire [əd`maɪr] 🎧 *Track 0081*
v. 欣賞；稱讚

ad·mis·sion [əd`mɪʃən] 🎧 *Track 0082*
n. （學校、會場、俱樂部等的）進入許可

▶I hope I can get the admission to the university.
我希望能得到那間大學的入學許可。

ad·mit [əd`mɪt] 🎧 *Track 0083*
v. 承認

ad·o·les·cent [͵ædl̩`ɛsnt] 🎧 *Track 0084*
n. 青少年

▶When I was an adolescent, my relationship with my parents was awful. 當我是個青少年時，我跟父母的關係很糟糕。

adj. 青春期的；青少年的；不成熟的

▶Such adolescent behavior is unacceptable considering you're forty. 這樣不成熟的行為很難以接受，你都已經四十歲了。

a·dopt [ə`dɑpt] 🎧 *Track 0085*
v. 採取；收養

a·dor·a·ble [ə`dorəbl] 🎧 *Track 0086*
adj. 值得敬重的；可愛的

▶Your baby is so adorable.
你的寶寶好可愛喲！

a·dore [ə`dor]　🎧 *Track 0087*
v. 崇敬；愛慕；極喜歡
▶ She adores her husband.
　她十分敬愛她的丈夫。

a·dult [ə`dʌlt]　🎧 *Track 0088*
n. 成年人

ad·ult·hood [ə`dʌlthʊd]　🎧 *Track 0089*
n. 成年；成年期
▶ Now that you have reached adulthood, you should take responsibility for yourself.
　既然你已經成年了，就應該為自己負責任。

(補充片語)

now that 既然；
take responsibility for 為……負責任

ad·vance [əd`væns]　🎧 *Track 0090*
n. 前進；發展
v. 前進；發展；將……提前

ad·vanced [əd`vænst]　🎧 *Track 0091*
adj. 在前面的；先進的；高級的；年邁的
▶ Mr. Franklin teaches English to advanced students.
　富蘭克林老師教高級程度的學生英文。

ad·vant·age [əd`væntɪdʒ]　🎧 *Track 0092*
n. 有利條件；優勢

ad·ven·ture [əd`vɛntʃə]　🎧 *Track 0093*
n. 冒險；冒險活動；激勵人心的經歷
▶ He loves to share his adventures on the ocean. 他很愛分享他在海上的冒險經歷。

(相關片語)

adventure novel 冒險小說
▶ I enjoy reading adventure novels.
　我很愛讀冒險小說。

ad·ver·tise
=ad·ver·tize [`ædvə.taɪz]　🎧 *Track 0094*
v. 做廣告；為……做宣傳
▶ We don't have the budget to advertise the product. 我們沒有幫產品打廣告的預算。

ad·ver·tise·ment
[`ædvə`taɪzmənt]　🎧 *Track 0095*
n. 廣告；宣傳；公告

▶ The advertisement says that the company is looking for an office assistant. 這廣告上說這家公司正徵求一名辦公室助理。

ad·ver·tis·er
[`ædvə.taɪzə]　🎧 *Track 0096*
n. 刊登廣告者；廣告商
▶ More and more advertisers use social network advertising to promote their products. 越來越多廣告商利用社群網路廣告來宣傳他們的產品。

ad·vice [əd`vaɪs]　🎧 *Track 0097*
n. 勸告，忠告；建議

ad·vise [əd`vaɪz]　🎧 *Track 0098*
v. 勸告，忠告；建議

ad·vi·ser=ad·vis·or　🎧 *Track 0099*
[əd`vaɪzə]
n. 顧問
▶ The company hired him to be their technical adviser.
　這家公司聘他做技術顧問。

af·fair [ə`fɛr]　🎧 *Track 0100*
n. 事情，事件

af·fect [ə`fɛkt]　🎧 *Track 0101*
v. 影響

af·fec·tion [ə`fɛkʃən]　🎧 *Track 0102*
n. 影響；感染；感情；鍾愛；愛慕之情
▶ She has great affection for Jimmy, but he knows nothing about it. 她對吉米有很深的愛慕之情，但他對此一無所知。

af·fec·tion·ate　🎧 *Track 0103*
[ə`fɛkʃənɪt]
adj. 充滿深情的；有愛心的
▶ They have been married for over twenty years, but are still affectionate towards each other.
　他們已經結縭超過二十年，但仍十分恩愛。

af·ford [ə`ford]　🎧 *Track 0104*
v. 提供；給予
▶ We can't afford a trip to Hawaii.
　我們付不起去夏威夷旅遊的費用。

※灰色單字為英檢初級必備單字

a·fraid [ə`fred] 🎧 *Track 0105*
adj. 害怕的；擔心的

aft·er [`æftə] 🎧 *Track 0106*
prep. 在……之後 **conj.** 在……之後

aft·er·noon [`æftə`nun] 🎧 *Track 0107*
n. 下午，午後

af·ter·wards [`æftəwədz] 🎧 *Track 0108*
adv. 之後；後來
▶ We went swimming and then had dinner afterwards. 我們去游泳，然後吃晚餐。

a·gain [ə`gɛn] 🎧 *Track 0109*
adv. 再次地

a·gainst [ə`gɛnst] 🎧 *Track 0110*
prep. 反對；逆著

age [edʒ] 🎧 *Track 0111*
n. 年紀；年齡 **v.** 變老

a·ged [`edʒɪd] 🎧 *Track 0112*
adj. 年老的；……歲的
▶ She lives together with her aged parents. 她與年邁的父母同住。

a·gen·cy [`edʒənsɪ] 🎧 *Track 0113*
n. 專業行政機構；代辦處；仲介
▶ Thanks to the employment agency, I've got a new job. 多虧了職業介紹所，我有新工作了。

[相關片語]
travel agency 旅行社
▶ You can have a travel agency book the tickets for you. 你可以請旅行社幫你訂票。

a·gent [`edʒənt] 🎧 *Track 0114*
n. 代理人；代理商；仲介
▶ Tammy is my agent when I am away from the office. 我不在辦公室時，譚美即是我的代理人。

ag·gres·sive [ə`grɛsɪv] 🎧 *Track 0115*
adj. 侵略的；挑釁的；有進取精神的；有企圖心的
▶ We prefer aggressive employees to obedient ones. 比起乖乖聽話的員工，我們比較喜歡有進取心的員工。

a·go [ə`go] 🎧 *Track 0116*
adv. 在……之前

a·gree [ə`gri] 🎧 *Track 0117*
v. 贊成，同意

a·gree·a·ble [ə`griəbl] 🎧 *Track 0118*
adj. 令人愉快的；欣然贊同的；一致的
▶ She has a very agreeable personality. 她的個性很令人愉快。

a·gree·ment [ə`grimənt] 🎧 *Track 0119*
n. 協議；同意

ag·ri·cul·ture [`ægrɪ‚kʌltʃə] 🎧 *Track 0120*
n. 農業
▶ More and more young farmers devote themselves to organic agriculture. 越來越多年輕的農夫致力於有機農業。

a·head [ə`hɛd] 🎧 *Track 0121*
adv. 在前；事前

aid [ed] 🎧 *Track 0122*
n. 幫助；救援 **v.** 幫助；救援

AIDS [edz] 🎧 *Track 0123*
n. 愛滋病（後天性免疫不全症候群）

aim [em] 🎧 *Track 0124*
v. 針對；瞄準；以……為目標 **n.** 瞄準的方向；目的、目標

air [ɛr] 🎧 *Track 0125*
n. 空氣

air-con·di·tioned [`ɛr-kən‚dɪʃənd] 🎧 *Track 0126*
adj. 裝有空氣調節設備的
▶ The whole office building is air-conditioned. 整棟辦公大樓是有空調設備的。

air-con·di·tion·er 🎧 *Track 0127*
[`ɛr-kən͵dıʃənə]

n. 冷氣；空氣調節裝置
▶ The air-conditioner needs to be fixed.
這冷氣需要修理了。

air·craft [`ɛr͵kræft] 🎧 *Track 0128*
n. 飛行器（如：飛機、直升機……等）

air·line [`ɛr͵laın] 🎧 *Track 0129*
n. 航線；航空公司

air·mail [`ɛr͵mel] 🎧 *Track 0130*
n. 航空郵件；航空郵政
▶ I sent her a postcard by airmail when I was traveling in Europe. 我在歐洲旅行時，以航空郵政寄了一張明信片給她。

air·plane [`ɛr͵plen] 🎧 *Track 0131*
n. =plane 飛機

air·port [`ɛr͵port] 🎧 *Track 0132*
n. 機場

air·way [`ɛr͵we] 🎧 *Track 0133*
n. （礦井的）風道；航空公司；航空路線
▶ British Airways has a good reputation.
英國航空風評很好。

aisle [aıl] 🎧 *Track 0134*
n. 走道；通道
▶ I prefer an aisle seat to a window seat when flying.
搭飛機時，我喜歡走道座位勝於靠窗座位。

a·larm [ə`lɑrm] 🎧 *Track 0135*
n. 警報；警報器；鬧鐘

al·bum [`ælbəm] 🎧 *Track 0136*
n. 相簿；集郵簿；唱片

al·co·hol [`ælkə͵hɔl] 🎧 *Track 0137*
n. 酒精
▶ I don't drink alcohol. 我不喝酒。

al·co·hol·ic [͵ælkə`hɔlık] 🎧 *Track 0138*
n. 酒精中毒者；酗酒的人

▶ My next-door neighbor is an alcoholic.
我隔壁鄰居是個酒鬼。

adj. 含酒精的；酗酒的
▶ Don't sell alcoholic beverages to those who are under 18.
不要把含酒精飲料賣給十八歲以下的人。

a·lert [ə`lɝt] 🎧 *Track 0139*
v. 使警覺；使注意；向……報警
▶ My neighbor saved my life by alerting me to a gas leak.
我鄰居提醒我注意瓦斯外漏，救了我一命。

adj. 警覺的
▶ She is alert when talking to strangers.
她在和陌生人說話時都很警覺。

n. 警戒；警戒狀態
▶ She's always on the alert for strangers in the neighborhood.
她對住家附近的陌生人總是保持警戒。

al·ge·bra [`ældʒəbrə] 🎧 *Track 0140*
n. 代數；代數學
▶ I have difficulty understanding algebra.
我無法理解代數。

a·li·en [`elıən] 🎧 *Track 0141*
adj. 外國的；外國人的；性質不同的；不相容的
▶ Alien fish species are a threat to native fish in this river. 外來的魚種對這條河的原生魚種是一種威脅。

n. 外國人；外僑；外星人
▶ People in this country are not friendly to aliens. 這個國家的人民對外國人不友善。

a·like [ə`laık] 🎧 *Track 0142*
adv. 一樣地；相似地
adj. 相同的；相像的

a·live [ə`laıv] 🎧 *Track 0143*
adj. 活著的

all [ɔl] 🎧 *Track 0144*
adj. 全部的；所有的
pron. 全部，一切 **adv.** 完全地，全然的

Aa
Bb
Cc
Dd
Ee

Ff
Gg
Hh
Ii
Jj

Kk
Ll
Mm
Nn
Oo

Pp
Qq
Rr
Ss
Tt

Uu
Vv
Ww
Xx
Yy
Zz

※灰色單字為英檢初級必備單字

al·ler·gic [ə`lɚdʒɪk]　🎧 *Track 0145*
adj. 過敏的；過敏性的；對……過敏的
▶ I'm allergic to peanuts. 我對花生過敏。

al·ler·gy [`ælɚdʒɪ]　🎧 *Track 0146*
n. 過敏症；反感
▶ I have an allergy to seafood.
我對海鮮過敏。

al·ley [`ælɪ]　🎧 *Track 0147*
n. 小巷，胡同
▶ The famous restaurant is located in a narrow alley.
那間有名的餐廳座落在一條狹窄的巷子裡。

（補充片語）
blind alley 死胡同；沒有前途的職業
▶ Our GPS led us into a blind alley.
我們的衛星導航把我們帶到一條死胡同裡。

al·li·ga·tor [`ælə,getɚ]　🎧 *Track 0148*
n. 短吻鱷
▶ Can you tell the difference between an alligator and a crocodile?
你能分辨出短吻鱷和鱷魚之間的差別嗎？

al·low [ə`laʊ]　🎧 *Track 0149*
v. 允許

al·low·ance [ə`laʊəns]　🎧 *Track 0150*
=poc·ket mo·ney
n. 津貼；零用錢
▶ My mother only gives me a monthly allowance of 200 NT dollars.
我媽媽一個月只給我兩百元零用錢。

al·mond [`amənd]　🎧 *Track 0151*
n. 杏仁；杏樹；杏仁色
adj. 杏仁色的；杏仁味的

al·most [`ɔl,most]　🎧 *Track 0152*
adv. 幾乎，差不多

a·lone [ə`lon]　🎧 *Track 0153*
adv. 獨自地　**adj.** 單獨的；只有、僅

a·long [ə`lɔŋ]　🎧 *Track 0154*
prep. 沿著……　**adv.** 向前；一起

a·long·side [ə`lɔŋ`saɪd]　🎧 *Track 0155*
prep. 在……旁邊；沿著……的邊；與……並排
▶ The two bookstores stand alongside each other. 兩間書店就開在彼此隔壁。
adv. 在旁邊；沿著；並排地
▶ The scores of the students are shown alongside their names.
學生們的成績就公布在他們的名字旁邊。

a·loud [ə`laʊd]　🎧 *Track 0156*
adv. 大聲地；出聲地

al·pha·bet [`ælfə,bɛt]　🎧 *Track 0157*
n. 字母系統；全套字母

al·read·y [ɔl`rɛdɪ]　🎧 *Track 0158*
adv. 已經

al·so [`ɔlso]　🎧 *Track 0159*
adv. 也，還

al·ter·na·tive　🎧 *Track 0160*
[ɔl`tɚnətɪv]
n. 供選擇的事物；選擇的餘地；選擇；二擇一
▶ If you don't want to cook, you have the alternative of ordering food delivery.
如果你不想煮飯，你可以選擇訂餐外送。

（補充片語）
food delivery 餐點外送
adj. 替代的；供選擇的；二擇一的
▶ In my opinion, solar energy is the best alternative energy to nuclear energy.
在我看來，太陽能是核能的最佳替代能源。

（補充片語）
alternative energy 替代能源

al·though [ɔl`ðo]　🎧 *Track 0161*
conj. 雖然，儘管

al·ti·tude [`æltə,tjud]　🎧 *Track 0162*
n. 高度；海拔；（等級、地位）高處
▶ The higher the altitude, the thinner the air.
海拔越高，空氣越稀薄。

al·to·geth·er
🎧 *Track 0163*

[ˌɔltəˈgɛðə]
adv. 完全，全然；全部

---

al·ways [ˈɔlwez]
🎧 *Track 0164*

adv. 總是；一直、永遠

---

am [æm]
🎧 *Track 0165*

v. 是（用在第一人稱單數現在式）

---

am·a·teur [ˈæməˌtʃʊr]
🎧 *Track 0166*

adj. 業餘的
▶ The song is played by an amateur orchestra.
這首曲子是由一個業餘交響樂團所演奏。

n. 業餘從事者
▶ The basketball team consists of amateurs.
這支籃球隊是由業餘選手組成的。

---

a·maze [əˈmez]
🎧 *Track 0167*

v. 使驚奇；使驚愕
▶ His answer amazed us all.
他的回答令我們眾人驚訝不已。

---

a·mazed [əˈmezd]
🎧 *Track 0168*

adj. 吃驚的；驚詫不已的
▶ I was amazed to know that he used to be a woman. 當我得知他過去其實是個女人時，感到非常驚訝。

---

a·maze·ment
🎧 *Track 0169*

[əˈmezmənt]
n. 驚奇；詫異
▶ To our amazement, these elephants can count. 讓我們感到驚奇的是，這些大象居然會數數。

---

a·maz·ing [əˈmezɪŋ]
🎧 *Track 0170*

adj. 驚人的；令人驚奇的
▶ It was amazing that the magician turned the paper into real money.
魔術師把紙變成真正的錢，真是令人驚奇。

---

am·bas·sa·dor
🎧 *Track 0171*

[æmˈbæsədə]
n. 大使；使節
▶ He is the current ambassador of the United States of America in Japan.
他是美國現任派駐日本的大使。

---

am·bi·tion [æmˈbɪʃən]
🎧 *Track 0172*

n. 雄心；抱負；追求的目標
▶ Her ambition is to set a world record.
她追求的目標是要創世界紀錄。

---

am·bi·tious [æmˈbɪʃəs]
🎧 *Track 0173*

adj. 有野心的；顯示雄心的；野心勃勃的
▶ He is an ambitious politician.
他是個野心勃勃的政客。

---

am·bu·lance
🎧 *Track 0174*

[ˈæmbjələns]
n. 救護車

A·mer·ic·a [əˈmɛrɪkə]
🎧 *Track 0175*

n. 美國；美洲

A·mer·i·can
🎧 *Track 0176*

[əˈmɛrɪkən]
adj. 美國的；美洲的
n. 美國人；美洲人

---

a·mid [əˈmɪd]
🎧 *Track 0177*

prep. 在……之間；在……之中；被……包圍
▶ The homeless man is used to sleeping amid piles of trash. 這無家可歸的男子已經習慣在一堆垃圾中睡覺了。

---

a·mong [əˈmʌŋ]
🎧 *Track 0178*

prep. 在……之中，在……之間

---

a·mount [əˈmaʊnt]
🎧 *Track 0179*

n. 總數，總額；數量

---

a·muse [əˈmjuz]
🎧 *Track 0180*

v. 使歡樂；逗……高興；為……提供娛樂
▶ He amused himself with a novel.
他看小說作為消遣。

---

a·muse·ment
🎧 *Track 0181*

[əˈmjuzmənt]
n. 樂趣；趣味；娛樂；消遣活動
▶ Playing chess used to be his favorite amusement.
下棋曾經是他最喜歡的消遣活動。

相關片語

amusement park 遊樂園

Aa
Bb
Cc
Dd
Ee

Ff
Gg
Hh
Ii
Jj

Kk
Ll
Mm
Nn
Oo

Pp
Qq
Rr
Ss
Tt

Uu
Vv
Ww
Xx
Yy
Zz

※灰色單字為英檢初級必備單字

▶ We had a great time at the amusement park. 我們在遊樂園玩得很開心。

a·mus·ing [ə`mjuziŋ] 🎧 *Track 0182*
adj. 有趣的；好玩的
▶ I don't find your bad joke amusing at all.
我一點都不覺得你那個笑話有多好玩。

an [æn] 🎧 *Track 0183*
art. 一個、一（用於以母音開頭的名詞之前）

a·nal·y·sis [ə`næləsɪs] 🎧 *Track 0184*
n. 分析；解析
▶ According to his analysis, the project is worth investing in.
根據他的分析，這企劃很值得投資。

an·a·lyst [`ænlɪst] 🎧 *Track 0185*
n. 分析師
▶ He works as a financial analyst in a big company. 他在一家大公司擔任財務分析師。

an·a·lyze [`ænl͵aɪz] 🎧 *Track 0186*
=an·a·lyse （英式英文）
v. 分析
▶ They are analyzing the data from the experiment. 他們正在分析實驗數據。

an·ces·tor [`ænsɛstə] 🎧 *Track 0187*
n. 祖宗，祖先
▶ He claimed that one of his ancestors was an American.
他聲稱他的祖先中有一個美國人。

an·chor [`æŋkə] 🎧 *Track 0188*
n. 新聞節目主播；靠山；錨
▶ My sister used to be a news anchor for BBC.
我姊姊曾經是英國廣播公司的新聞主播。

v. 主持（廣播節目）；拋錨泊船；固定
▶ She was very nervous when she anchored the morning news for the first time.
第一次播報晨間新聞時，她非常緊張。

an·cient [`enʃənt] 🎧 *Track 0189*
adj. 古老的；古代的

and [ænd] 🎧 *Track 0190*
conj. 和、及；然後

an·gel [`endʒl] 🎧 *Track 0191*
n. 天使；天使般的人

an·ger [`æŋgə] 🎧 *Track 0192*
n. 怒氣

an·gle [`æŋgl] 🎧 *Track 0193*
n. 角度
▶ A triangle has three angles.
一個三角形有三個角。

an·gry [`æŋgrɪ] 🎧 *Track 0194*
adj. 生氣的

an·i·mal [`ænəml] 🎧 *Track 0195*
n. 動物

an·kle [`æŋkl] 🎧 *Track 0196*
n. 足踝

an·ni·ver·sa·ry 🎧 *Track 0197*
[͵ænə`vɝsərɪ]
n. 週年紀念日；結婚紀念日
▶ We're giving a home party to celebrate our 20th anniversary.
我們將舉辦一個家庭派對，來慶祝我們的二十週年紀念日。

相關片語
wedding anniversary 結婚紀念日
▶ We never celebrate our wedding anniversary.
我們從不慶祝結婚紀念日。

an·nounce [ə`naʊns] 🎧 *Track 0198*
v. 發佈；宣布
▶ Peter announced that he and Jenny were engaged. 彼得宣佈他跟珍妮已經訂婚了。

an·nounce·ment 🎧 *Track 0199*
[ə`naʊnsmənt]
n. 通告；佈告
▶ Mr. Lin said that he was going to make an important announcement on the meeting.
林總說他將在會議上作重要的宣佈。

an·nounc·er [əˋnaʊnsɚ] 🎧 Track 0200
n. 宣布者；廣播員；播音員
▶ The radio announcer's voice is really comforting. 這收音機播音員的聲音真的讓人聽了很舒服。

an·noy [əˋnɔɪ] 🎧 Track 0201
v. 惹惱；使生氣；使不快；打擾
▶ Everything he does annoys me.
他不管做什麼都讓我很不爽。

an·noy·ance [əˋnɔɪəns] 🎧 Track 0202
n. 惱怒；使人討厭的事物；煩惱
▶ To her annoyance, the reporter kept asking awkward questions.
讓她很惱怒的是那個記者一直問讓人難以招架的問題。

an·noyed [əˋnɔɪd] 🎧 Track 0203
adj. 惱怒的；氣惱的
▶ I was annoyed with my girlfriend because she took forever to get ready. 我女友準備事情的動作總是很慢，讓我感到很火。

an·noy·ing [əˋnɔɪɪŋ] 🎧 Track 0204
adj. 令人不快的；令人氣惱的
▶ Could you stop making that annoying noise? 可以請你停止製造那種令人不快的噪音嗎？

an·nu·al [ˋænjʊəl] 🎧 Track 0205
adj. 一年的；一年一次的；每年的
▶ I'm taking my annual leave from October 11 to October 25.
我將在十月十一日至十月廿五日休年假。

(補充片語)
take leave 休假

n. 年刊；一年生植物
▶ *The Chicago Medicine* magazine is an annual. 《芝加哥醫學》雜誌是一本年刊。

a·non·y·mous [əˋnɑnəməs] 🎧 Track 0206
adj. 匿名的；無名氏的；來源不明的
▶ An anonymous letter disclosed this political scandal.
一封匿名信揭發了這一宗政治醜聞。

an·oth·er [əˋnʌðɚ] 🎧 Track 0207
pron. 另一個；再一個 **adj.** 另一的；另外的

an·swer [ˋænsɚ] 🎧 Track 0208
n. 答案 **v.** 回答

ant [ænt] 🎧 Track 0209
n. 螞蟻

An·tarc·tic [ænˋtɑrktɪk] 🎧 Track 0210
n. 南極地區
▶ The most common birds in the Antarctic are penguins. 南極最常見的鳥類就是企鵝。

adj. 南極的
▶ Penguins are one of the most common Antarctica animals.
企鵝是最常見的南極動物之一。

an·ten·na [ænˋtɛnə] 🎧 Track 0211
n. 天線；觸角
▶ Ants use their antennae to hear, smell, see and feel.
螞蟻利用牠們的觸角聽、聞、看及感覺。

an·them [ˋænθəm] 🎧 Track 0212
n. 聖歌；讚美詩；校歌；國歌
▶ He burst into tears when hearing his national anthem at the awards ceremony.
他在頒獎典禮上聽到國歌就突然哭了出來。

(補充片語)
burst into tears 突然哭泣；
national anthem 國歌；
awards ceremony 頒獎典禮

an·tique [ænˋtik] 🎧 Track 0213
adj. 古代的；年代久遠的；古董的；古風的
▶ I bought this antique cabinet at the flea market. 我在跳蚤市場上買了這個古董櫃。

n. 古董；古物
▶ He has a hobby of collecting antiques.
他有搜集古董的嗜好。

anx·i·e·ty [æŋˋzaɪətɪ] 🎧 Track 0214
n. 焦慮；掛念；令人焦慮的事
▶ My father's health condition is a great anxiety to me.
我父親的健康狀況是件讓我深感焦慮的事

※灰色單字為英檢初級必備單字

anx·ious [ˈæŋkʃəs] 🎧 *Track 0215*
adj. 焦慮的；令人焦慮的；掛念的；渴望的
▶ She couldn't sleep because she was anxious about the result of the exam.
她因為擔心考試的結果而睡不著。

an·y [ˈɛnɪ] 🎧 *Track 0216*
pron. 任何一人；任何一點
adv. 少許；稍微
adj. 任一；絲毫；所有的

an·y·bod·y [ˈɛnɪˌbadɪ] 🎧 *Track 0217*
pron. 任何人

an·y·how [ˈɛnɪˌhaʊ] 🎧 *Track 0218*
adv. 無論如何；總之

an·y·one [ˈɛnɪˌwʌn] 🎧 *Track 0219*
pron. 任何人

an·y·place [ˈɛnɪˌples] 🎧 *Track 0220*
adv. 任何地方

an·y·thing [ˈɛnɪˌθɪŋ] 🎧 *Track 0221*
pron. 任何事

an·y·time [ˈɛnɪˌtaɪm] 🎧 *Track 0222*
adv. 在任何時候；總是

an·y·way [ˈɛnɪˌwe] 🎧 *Track 0223*
adv. 無論如何，反正

an·y·where [ˈɛnɪˌhwɛr] 🎧 *Track 0224*
adv. 任何地方；無論何處

a·part [əˈpart] 🎧 *Track 0225*
adv. 分開地；相隔地
▶ We can't get along, so we'd better live apart.
我們相處不來，所以最好分開住。

adj. 分開的；單獨的
▶ When I was in Ethiopia, I felt like I was in a world apart. 當我在衣索比亞時，我認為自己就像是身處在一個被隔離的世界。

【相關片語】
apart from 除了
▶ Apart from the price, I like this product quite much. 除了價格之外，我相當喜歡這項產品。

a·part·ment 🎧 *Track 0226*
[əˈpartmənt]
n. 公寓

ape [ep] 🎧 *Track 0227*
n. 猿黑猩猩，大猩猩；模仿他人者
v. 模仿；學……的樣

a·pol·o·gize 🎧 *Track 0228*
[əˈpaləˌdʒaɪz]
v. 道歉；致歉

a·pol·o·gy [əˈpalədʒɪ] 🎧 *Track 0229*
n. 道歉
▶ Would you accept my apology?
你願意接受我的道歉嗎？

ap·par·ent [əˈpærənt] 🎧 *Track 0230*
adj. 表面的；明顯的；顯而易見的
▶ It is apparent that we can't afford the apartment. 我們顯然負擔不起這棟公寓。

ap·par·ent·ly 🎧 *Track 0231*
[əˈpærəntlɪ]
adv. 顯然地；顯而易見地
▶ This dress apparently doesn't fit me.
這件洋裝顯然不適合我穿。

ap·peal [əˈpil] 🎧 *Track 0232*
n. 懇求
▶ He made an appeal to his friend to lend him money. 他請求朋友借他錢。
v. 請求
▶ The least thing he would do is to appeal to his father for help.
向他父親求援是他最不可能會做的事。

ap·pear [əˈpɪr] 🎧 *Track 0233*
v. 出現；看來好像

ap·pear·ance 🎧 *Track 0234*
[əˈpɪrəns]
n. 出現，顯露；外表，外貌

ap·pe·tite [ˈæpəˌtaɪt] 🎧 *Track 0235*
n. 食慾；胃口

ap·plaud [əˋplɔd] 🎧 Track 0236
v. 鼓掌；向……喝彩；讚許
▶ The audience stood up to applaud the pianist for his excellent performance.
觀眾起立為這鋼琴家優異的表演鼓掌喝彩。

ap·plause [əˋplɔz] 🎧 Track 0237
n. 鼓掌歡迎；喝彩；嘉許
▶ Following his thirty-minute speech, cheers and applause went on for at least five minutes.
在他三十分鐘的演說之後，歡呼及掌聲持續了至少有五分鐘。

ap·ple [ˋæpl] 🎧 Track 0238
n. 蘋果

ap·pli·ance [əˋplaɪəns] 🎧 Track 0239
n. 器具；用具；裝置；設備
▶ All household appliances are on sale this week. 所有的家用電器這週都在特賣。

(補充片語)
household appliance 家電用品；家用電器

ap·pli·cant [ˋæpləkənt] 🎧 Track 0240
n. 申請人
▶ Jerry is the only applicant that meets all requirements for the position. 傑瑞是唯一符合該職務所有要求條件的求職者。

ap·pli·ca·tion 🎧 Track 0241
[ˏæpləˋkeʃən]
n. 應用、運用；申請、申請書
▶ Please fill out the application form and return it by this Friday.
請填妥申請表，並在本週五之前繳回。

(補充片語)
application form 申請表

ap·ply [əˋplaɪ] 🎧 Track 0242
v. 塗，敷；申請

ap·point [əˋpɔɪnt] 🎧 Track 0243
v. 指派
▶ He was appointed to manage the new branch office. 他被指派去管理新的分公司。

ap·point·ment 🎧 Track 0244
[əˋpɔɪntmənt]
n. 約定；約會
▶ I have an appointment with my dentist tomorrow night.
我明天晚上有預約看牙了。

ap·pre·ci·ate [əˋpriʃɪˏet] 🎧 Track 0245
v. 欣賞；感謝

ap·pre·ci·a·tion 🎧 Track 0246
[əˏpriʃɪˋeʃən]
n. 欣賞；感謝
▶ We wrote a letter to him to express our appreciation.
我們寫了一封信給他，表示我們的感謝。

ap·proach [əˋprotʃ] 🎧 Track 0247
n. 接近、靠近；通道、入口
▶ With the approach of the exam, he burned the midnight oil every night.
隨著考試越來越近，他每天晚上都開夜車。

(補充片語)
burn the midnight oil 開夜車、挑燈夜戰
v. 接近；與……商量、聯繫；著手處理
▶ Christmas is approaching.
聖誕節就要到了。

ap·pro·pri·ate 🎧 Track 0248
[əˋproprɪˏet]
adj. 適當的
▶ A bottle of wine would be an appropriate gift to bring to a housewarming party.
一瓶酒會是帶去喬遷派對的一份合適禮物。

ap·prov·al [əˋpruvl] 🎧 Track 0249
n. 批准
▶ We're not allowed to enter the generator room without Mr. Lu's approval.
沒有盧先生的同意我們不能進入機房。

ap·prove [əˋpruv] 🎧 Track 0250
v. 贊同；批准；認可
▶ My boss has approved of my leave.
我老闆已經同意讓我請假了。

※灰色單字為英檢初級必備單字

ap·prox·i·mate [əˋprɑksəmɪt] 🎧 *Track 0251*

adj. 接近的；近似的；大約的
▶ The approximate time of sunrise in November is 5:25 a.m. 十一月的日出大約時間是在上午五點廿五分。

v. 接近；近似；大致估計
▶ The distance between my apartment and my office is approximated as 10 kilos. 我的住處跟公司之間的距離大致估計為十公里。

A·pril [ˋeprəl] 🎧 *Track 0252*
n. 四月

a·pron [ˋeprən] 🎧 *Track 0253*
n. 圍裙；工作裙

a·quar·i·um [əˋkwɛrɪəm] 🎧 *Track 0254*
n. 魚缸；水族館
▶ There is a large, beautiful aquarium in the center of the hotel lobby.
飯店大廳中央有一個漂亮的大魚缸。

arch [artʃ] 🎧 *Track 0255*
n. 拱門；拱狀物
▶ The army marched through the arch.
軍隊行進穿過拱門。

v. 使成弧形；拱起；使成弓形
▶ My cat arches its back when he thinks he's in danger. 我的貓會在他認為自己有危險時拱起背來。

ar·chi·tect [ˋarkəˏtɛkt] 🎧 *Track 0256*
n. 建築師
▶ The building was designed by an Asian architect.
這棟建築物是由一位亞裔建築師所設計的。

ar·chi·tec·ture [ˋarkəˏtɛktʃə] 🎧 *Track 0257*
n. 建築學；建築風格；建築物
▶ The Taj Mahal is definitely an example of beautiful religious architecture.
泰姬瑪哈陵絕對是個標準的美麗宗教建築。

Arc·tic [ˋarktɪk] 🎧 *Track 0258*
n. 北極地帶；北極圈

▶ Scientists warn that climate changes in the Arctic could affect the climate in the rest of the world. 科學家警告，北極圈的氣候變化會影響世界其他地區的氣候。

adj. 北極的；極寒的
▶ Due to global warming, Arctic sea ice has decreased 14% since the 1970s.
由於地球暖化，北極的海冰自1970年代起已經減少了14%。

are [ar] 🎧 *Track 0259*
v. 是（第二人稱或第三人稱複數使用）

ar·e·a [ˋɛrɪə] 🎧 *Track 0260*
n. 地區

a·re·na [əˋrinə] 🎧 *Track 0261*
n. 競技場；（有觀眾席的）比賽場；圓形運動場
▶ People crowded into the arena to watch the World Cup finals.
人們湧進運動場觀賞世界盃決賽。

aren't [arnt] 🎧 *Track 0262*
abbr. 不是

ar·gue [ˋargjʊ] 🎧 *Track 0263*
v. 爭執；爭論

ar·gu·ment [ˋargjəmənt] 🎧 *Track 0264*
n. 爭執；論點

a·rise [əˋraɪz] 🎧 *Track 0265*
v. 升起；產生；出現
▶ Disagreements arise between us from time to time.
我們之間偶爾會出現意見不一的時候。

（補充片語）
from time to time 偶爾；有時

a·rith·me·tic [əˋrɪθmətɪk] 🎧 *Track 0266*
n. 算術
▶ She is very good at arithmetic.
她的算術很厲害。

adj. 算術的
▶ The boy solved the difficult arithmetic problem within five minutes. 這男孩在五分鐘之內就解開這道困難的算術題。

mental arithmetic 心算

▶Can you do mental arithmetic?
你會心算嗎？

arm [ɑrm] 🎧 *Track 0267*
n. 手臂

arm·chair [`ɑrm͵tʃɛr] 🎧 *Track 0268*
n. 扶手椅

armed [ɑrmd] 🎧 *Track 0269*
adj. 武裝的

▶Two armed men tried to rob the bank this
morning.
今天上午有兩名武裝男子企圖搶劫銀行。

ar·mour [`ɑrmɚ] 🎧 *Track 0270*
n. 盔甲；裝甲

▶The soldier wore armour to protect him
against being wounded.
士兵穿著盔甲，以保護自己不會受傷。

arms [ɑrmz] 🎧 *Track 0271*
n. 武器；戰爭

▶All farmers were up in arms against the
oppressors. 所有農人都奮起與壓迫者鬥爭。

相關片語

brothers in arms 戰友

▶Uncle Jamie and my father were brothers
in arms as well as friends in need. 傑米叔
叔跟我父親是戰友，也是有需要時會互相幫助
的真心朋友。

ar·my [`ɑrmɪ] 🎧 *Track 0272*
n. 軍隊

a·round [əˋraʊnd] 🎧 *Track 0273*
prep. 在……附近；環繞
adv. 到處、四處；周圍、附近；大約

a·rouse [əˋraʊz] 🎧 *Track 0274*
v. 喚起；叫醒

▶The movie aroused my childhood
memories. 這部電影喚起我兒時的記憶。

ar·range [əˋrendʒ] 🎧 *Track 0275*
v. 安排；整理

ar·range·ment 🎧 *Track 0276*
[əˋrendʒmənt]
n. 安排；準備工作

ar·rest [əˋrɛst] 🎧 *Track 0277*
v. 逮捕；拘留 n. 逮捕；拘留

ar·riv·al [əˋraɪvl] 🎧 *Track 0278*
n. 到來；到達；到達的人或物；新生兒

▶Everything in the store is on sale except
the new arrivals.
除了新到貨之外，店內所有商品都有特價。

ar·rive [əˋraɪv] 🎧 *Track 0279*
v. 抵達

ar·ro·gant [`ærəgənt] 🎧 *Track 0280*
adj. 傲慢自大的；自負的

▶He is so arrogant that he doesn't want
anyone's advice.
他非常傲慢自大，不想要任何人的意見。

ar·row [`æro] 🎧 *Track 0281*
n. 箭

art [ɑrt] 🎧 *Track 0282*
n. 藝術；美術

ar·ti·cle [`ɑrtɪkl] 🎧 *Track 0283*
n. 文章

ar·ti·fact [`ɑrtɪ͵fækt] 🎧 *Track 0284*
n. 手工藝品；加工品

▶This is a perfect artifact for our living room.
這是個很適合放在我們客廳的手工藝品。

ar·ti·fi·cial [͵ɑrtəˋfɪʃəl] 🎧 *Track 0285*
adj. 人工的；人造的；矯揉造作的

▶What I like about artificial flowers is that I
don't have to water them. 我喜歡人造花的
一點就是我不用幫它們澆水。

相關片語

artificial intelligence 人工智慧

▶Some scientists warn that artificial
intelligence may be a threat to human life
one day. 有些科學家警告，人工智慧有一天
可能會對人類生活造成威脅。

| Aa |
| Bb |
| Cc |
| Dd |
| Ee |
| Ff |
| Gg |
| Hh |
| Ii |
| Jj |
| Kk |
| Ll |
| Mm |
| Nn |
| Oo |
| Pp |
| Qq |
| Rr |
| Ss |
| Tt |
| Uu |
| Vv |
| Ww |
| Xx |
| Yy |
| Zz |

art·ist [`ɑrtɪst]　🎧 *Track 0286*
n. 藝術家

ar·tis·tic [ɑr`tɪstɪk]　🎧 *Track 0287*
adj. 藝術的
▶There are many artistic works in the museum. 博物館裡有很多藝術品。

as [æz]　🎧 *Track 0288*
conj. 像……一樣；當……時
prep. 像，如同；作為
adv. 一樣地，同樣地

as·cend [ə`sɛnd]　🎧 *Track 0289*
v. 登高；上升；登上
▶We sat on the grass watching the hot air balloons ascend to the sky.
我們坐在草地上看熱氣球升空。

as·cend·ing [ə`sɛndɪŋ]　🎧 *Track 0290*
adj. 上升的；向上傾斜的
▶The questions are listed in ascending order of difficulty.
這些問題是依難度提高的順序列出的。

ash [æʃ]　🎧 *Track 0291*
n. 灰燼；骨灰；廢墟
▶The whole building was completely burnt to ashes. 整棟建築物被徹底燒成灰了。
(相關片語)
rise from the ashes　東山再起；浴火重生
▶He believed that his business would rise from the ashes one day.
他相信他的事業總有一天能東山再起。

a·shamed [ə`ʃemd]　🎧 *Track 0292*
adj. 羞愧的；恥於……的
▶He was ashamed of making the same mistake over and over again.
他對自己不斷地犯同樣的錯誤而感到羞愧。

A·si·a [`eʃə]　🎧 *Track 0293*
n. 亞洲

A·sian [`eʃən]　🎧 *Track 0294*
adj. 亞洲的；亞洲人的　**n.** 亞洲人

a·side [ə`saɪd]　🎧 *Track 0295*
adv. 在旁邊；到旁邊；離開、撇開
▶She put everything aside and focused on her book.
她把所有事情都擱在一邊，專心看書。
(補充片語)
put aside　擱在一邊；放在一邊

ask [æsk]　🎧 *Track 0296*
v. 問；要求

a·sleep [ə`slip]　🎧 *Track 0297*
adj. 睡著的

as·pect [`æspɛkt]　🎧 *Track 0298*
n. 方面；觀點；外觀
▶We should consider all aspects of the issue before we make any decisions.
在我們做任何決定之前，應該要考慮這件事情所有方面的問題。

as·pirin [`æspərɪn]　🎧 *Track 0299*
n. 阿斯匹靈
▶He takes aspirin every day in order to protect his heart.
他每天服用阿斯匹靈以保護他的心臟。

as·sas·sin·ate 　🎧 *Track 0300*
[ə`sæsɪnˌet]
v. 刺殺
▶They are planning to assassinate the president. 他們策劃要刺殺總統。

as·sem·ble [ə`sɛmbl̩]　🎧 *Track 0301*
v. 集合；召集；聚集
▶All students were assembled on the playground. 所有學生都到操場上集合。

as·sem·bly [ə`sɛmblɪ]　🎧 *Track 0302*
n. 與會者；集會
▶All students gathered in the assembly hall. 所有學生都聚集在學校集會禮堂。
(補充片語)
assembly hall　會館；禮堂

as·set [`æsɛt] 🎧 *Track 0303*
n. 財產；資產
▶ Employees are a company's greatest assets. 員工是公司最大的資產。

as·sign [ə`saɪn] 🎧 *Track 0304*
v. 分配；分派
▶ I cannot get off work until I finish the task my boss assigned me. 在完成老闆分派給我的工作前，我不能下班。
(補充片語)
get off work 下班

as·sist [ə`sɪst] 🎧 *Track 0305*
v. 支援；協助
▶ Can you send someone to assist in promoting the new product? 你可以派人來支援新產品的宣傳嗎？

as·sist·ance [ə`sɪstəns] 🎧 *Track 0306*
n. 援助
▶ He turned down his father's financial assistance. 他拒絕父親的經濟援助。
(補充片語)
turn down 拒絕

as·sis·tant [ə`sɪstənt] 🎧 *Track 0307*
n. 助手
adj. 助理的；有幫助的

as·so·ci·ate [ə`soʃɪɪt] 🎧 *Track 0308*
v. 聯想；使有聯繫；結交
▶ We associate moon cakes with the Mid Autumn Festival. 我們把月餅和中秋節聯繫在一起。
n. 夥伴；同事；合夥人
▶ Jack is one of my associates in the Research & Development Department. 傑克是我在研發部的一位同事。

as·so·ci·a·tion [ə`sosɪˌeʃən] 🎧 *Track 0309*
n. 協會；聯盟；公會；聯想；結交
▶ They used to be very close, but their association didn't last long. 他們曾經非常親近，但是他們的關係並沒有維持很久。

as·sume [ə`sjum] 🎧 *Track 0310*
v. 以為；假定為；認為
▶ I assumed that you had had dinner already. 我還以為你已經吃過晚餐了。

as·sur·ance [ə`ʃʊrəns] 🎧 *Track 0311*
n. 保證；保險

as·sure [ə`ʃʊr] 🎧 *Track 0312*
v. 向……保證；使放心、使確信
▶ We assure you that your orders will be delivered to you within 24 hours. 我們向您保證，您訂購的商品會在24小時內完成送貨。

asth·ma [`æzmə] 🎧 *Track 0313*
n. 氣喘；哮喘
▶ The little boy was diagnosed with asthma. 那小男孩被診斷出有氣喘病。

as·ton·ish [ə`stanɪʃ] 🎧 *Track 0314*
v. 使震驚；使驚訝
▶ The news of his sudden death astonished us all. 他驟逝的消息震驚了我們所有人。

as·ton·ished [ə`stanɪʃt] 🎧 *Track 0315*
adj. 感震驚的；大為驚奇的
▶ We were all astonished at the news. 我們都對這消息感到很震驚。

as·ton·ish·ing [ə`stanɪʃɪŋ] 🎧 *Track 0316*
adj. 驚人的；令人驚訝的
▶ It was astonishing to everyone when he announced his retirement. 當他宣布他退休的消息時，每個人都很驚訝。

as·tro·naut [`æstrəˌnɔt] 🎧 *Track 0317*
n. 太空人
▶ Neil Armstrong was the first astronaut to walk on the Moon. 尼爾阿姆斯壯是第一位在月球上走路的太空人。

as·tron·o·my [əs`tranəmɪ] 🎧 *Track 0318*
n. 天文學
▶ My father has a lot of knowledge about astronomy. 我父親在天文學方面的知識很淵博。

Aa
Bb
Cc
Dd
Ee
Ff
Gg
Hh
Ii
Jj
Kk
Ll
Mm
Nn
Oo
Pp
Qq
Rr
Ss
Tt
Uu
Vv
Ww
Xx
Yy
Zz

※灰色單字為英檢初級必備單字

a·sy·lum [ə`saɪləm]　🎧 *Track 0319*
n. 避難；政治庇護；收容所
▶ Germany granted asylum to nearly half of all Syrian refugees.
德國給予近乎一半的敘利亞難民庇護。

相關片語
political asylum　政治庇護
▶ Those refugees from Syria were seeking political asylum.
那些來自敘利亞的難民要尋求政治庇護。

at [æt]　🎧 *Track 0320*
prep. 在（某地點）；在（某時刻）；對著、向

ath·lete [`æθlit]　🎧 *Track 0321*
n. 運動員
▶ Both his brothers are athletes. One is a tennis player, and the other is a basketball player. 他的兩個哥哥都是運動員。一個是網球選手，另一個是籃球選手。

相關片語
athlete's foot　香港腳
▶ His athlete's feet bother him a lot.
他的香港腳讓他相當困擾。

ath·let·ic [æθ`lɛtɪk]　🎧 *Track 0322*
adj. 運動的
▶ He is an athletic coach.
他是一個運動教練。

at·mo·sphere [`ætməs‚fɪr]　🎧 *Track 0323*
n. 大氣；（某地區的）空氣；氣氛
▶ The atmosphere of the meeting was quite intense. 會議的氣氛相當緊張。

at·om [`ætəm]　🎧 *Track 0324*
n. 原子；微量、微粒
▶ Don't underestimate the power of the atoms. 不要低估原子的力量。

a·tom·ic [ə`tɑmɪk]　🎧 *Track 0325*
adj. 原子的
▶ The atomic bomb is a very dangerous weapon.
原子彈是一種很危險的武器。

at·tach [ə`tætʃ]　🎧 *Track 0326*
v. 貼上；使附屬；附加
▶ I have attached a route map to the invitation card.
我已經把路線地圖附在邀請函上了。

at·tack [ə`tæk]　🎧 *Track 0327*
n. 攻擊　**v.** 攻擊

at·tempt [ə`tɛmpt]　🎧 *Track 0328*
n. 企圖；嘗試
▶ His attempt to climb the summit of Mt. Everest failed.
他想攻頂聖母峰的嘗試失敗了。

補充片語
climb the summit　攻頂

v. 企圖；嘗試做……
▶ The man attempted to steal her money.
男子企圖偷她的錢。

at·tend [ə`tɛnd]　🎧 *Track 0329*
v. 參加；出席

at·tend·ance [ə`tɛndəns]　🎧 *Track 0330*
n. 到場；出席；出席人數；伺候
▶ Tom is the only student that has a perfect school attendance record.
湯姆是唯一有學校全勤記錄的學生。

相關片語
take attendance　點名
▶ Professor Lee never takes attendance.
李教授從不點名。

at·ten·tion [ə`tɛnʃən]　🎧 *Track 0331*
n. 注意；注意力

at·tic [`ætɪk]　🎧 *Track 0332*
n. 頂樓；閣樓
▶ I found some old pictures in the attic.
我在閣樓裡找到一些老照片。

at·ti·tude [`ætətjud]　🎧 *Track 0333*
n. 態度
▶ He will be fired soon if he doesn't change his attitude at work.
他如果不改變工作態度，很快就會被解僱。

相關片語

give attitude 耍脾氣
▶ Don't give me your attitude.
別跟我耍脾氣。

at·tract [ə`trækt] 🎧 *Track 0334*
v. 吸引
▶ Her beautiful voice attracted everyone's attention. 她美妙的歌聲吸引了所有人的注意。

at·trac·tion [ə`trækʃən] 🎧 *Track 0335*
n. 吸引力；受人喜歡的事物
▶ The nice-looking actors and actresses are the main attraction of Korean dramas. 俊男美女是韓劇受歡迎的主要原因。

at·trac·tive [ə`træktɪv] 🎧 *Track 0336*
adj. 有吸引力的；引人注意的；動人的
▶ The job offer is very attractive to me.
這個工作機會會非常吸引我。

auc·tion [`ɔkʃən] 🎧 *Track 0337*
n. 拍賣
▶ He bought this motorcycle at an auction.
他在拍賣會上買了這輛摩托車。

v. 拍賣
▶ I'm going to auction some of my designer handbags.
我要拍賣我的一些名牌手提包。

au·di·ence [`ɔdɪəns] 🎧 *Track 0338*
n. 觀眾；聽眾；讀者

au·di·o [`ɔdɪo] 🎧 *Track 0339*
adj. 聽覺的；聲音的
▶ He listened to the audio book.
他聽著有聲書。

au·di·to·ri·um 🎧 *Track 0340*
[ˏɔdə`torɪəm]
n. 觀眾席；會堂；禮堂
▶ The auditorium was filled with fans.
觀眾席坐滿了粉絲。

Au·gust [`ɔgəst] 🎧 *Track 0341*
n. =Aug. 八月

aunt [ænt] 🎧 *Track 0342*
n. =auntie=aunty 阿姨；姑姑；嬸嬸；舅媽

Aus·tral·i·a [ɔ`streljə] 🎧 *Track 0343*
n. 澳洲

Aus·tra·li·an 🎧 *Track 0344*
[ɔ`streljən]
adj. 澳洲的；澳洲人的 **n.** 澳洲人

au·then·tic [ɔ`θɛntɪk] 🎧 *Track 0345*
adj. 可信的；真正的；非假冒的
▶ Are you sure this information is authentic?
你確定這個消息是可靠的嗎？

au·thor [`ɔθɚ] 🎧 *Track 0346*
n. 作者
▶ He is the author of the novel.
他是這本小說的作者。

au·thor·i·ty [ə`θɔrɛtɪ] 🎧 *Track 0347*
n. 權；權力
▶ I have no authority to make the decision.
我無權做決定。

au·to·bi·og·ra·phy 🎧 *Track 0348*
[ˏɔtəbaɪ`ɑgrəfɪ]
n. 自傳
▶ I just finished reading Steve Jobs' autobiography. 我剛讀完賈伯斯的自傳。

au·to·graph [`ɔtəˏgræf] 🎧 *Track 0349*
n. 親筆簽名；親筆稿
▶ He showed us the author's autograph.
他給我們看作者的親筆簽名的小說。

v. 親筆簽名於
▶ He asked the actress to autograph her photo. 他請女星在她的照片上簽名。

au·to·mat·ic [ˏɔtə`mætɪk] 🎧 *Track 0350*
adj. 自動的
▶ The automatic door opened. 自動門打開了。

au·to·mo·bile [`ɔtəməˏbil] 🎧 *Track 0351*
=au·to
n. 汽車
▶ The man is reading an automobile magazine. 男子正在閱讀一本汽車雜誌。

au·tumn [`ɔtəm] 🎧 *Track 0352*
n. 秋天

※灰色單字為英檢初級必備單字

au·xil·i·a·ry [ɔg`zɪljərɪ] 🎧 *Track 0353*
=aux.

n. 輔助者；輔助物；附屬組織；助動詞
▶ I need at least two auxiliaries to help me.
我需要至少兩名助手來幫我。

adj. 輔助的；附屬的
▶ The child's bicycle has auxiliary wheels.
這兒童腳踏車裝有輔助輪。

a·vail·a·ble [ə`veləbl] 🎧 *Track 0354*
adj. 可用的；可取得的；有空的；有效的

av·e·nue [`ævə͵nju] 🎧 *Track 0355*
n. 大道、林蔭大道；途徑、方法
▶ The shopping mall is located on the First Avenue. 這家購物中心位在第一大道上。

av·e·rage [`ævərɪdʒ] 🎧 *Track 0356*
adj. 一般的；平均的；中等的
▶ This country has the lowest average working hours per week at 25.6 hours.
這個國家有每週25.6小時的最低平均工時。

n. 平均；平均數
▶ She is quite a bit above average in weight.
她的體重高出平均相當多。

v. 算出平均數；平均
▶ Our expenses averaged 30,000 dollars per month. 我們一個月的開銷平均為三萬元。

a·void [ə`vɔɪd] 🎧 *Track 0357*
v. 避免

a·wait [ə`wet] 🎧 *Track 0358*
v. 等候；等待
▶ The huge prize awaits you.
大獎在等著你呢！

a·wake [ə`wek] 🎧 *Track 0359*
adj. 醒著的
▶ It is two o'clock, and I am still awake.
現在已經是兩點，而我依然醒著。

v. 喚醒；使覺醒；醒來；覺醒；意識到
▶ He finally awoke after we shook him hard.
在我們用力搖他之後，他終於醒來。

a·wak·en [ə`wekən] 🎧 *Track 0360*
v. 醒；覺醒；喚醒；喚起；意識到

▶ I awakened from a nightmare.
我從惡夢中醒來。

a·ward [ə`wɔrd] 🎧 *Track 0361*
n. 獎品；獎狀
▶ The role earned him an Academy Award.
這個角色為他贏得一座金像獎。

v. 給予；授予
▶ He was awarded a silver medal.
他獲頒銀牌獎。

a·ware [ə`wɛr] 🎧 *Track 0362*
adj. 知道的；察覺的

a·way [ə`we] 🎧 *Track 0363*
adv. 離開；不在；離……多遠；消失

awe [ɔ] 🎧 *Track 0364*
n. 敬畏
▶ They looked at the amazing art piece with awe. 他們敬畏地看著那傑出的藝術作品。

awe·some [`ɔsəm] 🎧 *Track 0365*
adj. 可怕的；有威嚴的；使人驚歎的
▶ He finally came up with an awesome idea. 他終於想出了超棒的點子。

aw·ful [`ɔfʊl] 🎧 *Track 0366*
adj. 可怕的；嚇人的；糟糕的
▶ The food in that restaurant was awful.
那間餐廳的食物很糟糕。

a·while [ə`hwaɪl] 🎧 *Track 0367*
adv. 片刻；一會兒
▶ Let's rest awhile. 我們休息一會兒吧。

awk·ward [`ɔkwəd] 🎧 *Track 0368*
adj. 笨拙的；棘手的；尷尬的
▶ He didn't answer awkward questions.
他沒有回答那些尷尬的問題。

ax [æks]**=axe**（英式英文） 🎧 *Track 0369*
n. 斧頭；解僱、退學
▶ The man split the wood with an ax.
男子用斧頭劈柴。

v. 用斧劈；解僱；撤銷、削減
▶ We had to ax our travel budget.
我們不得不削減我們的旅遊預算。

Bb

通過中級英文檢定者的英文能力：

 在日常生活中，能聽懂一般的會話；能大致聽懂公共場所廣播、氣象報告及廣告等。在工作時，能聽懂簡易的產品介紹與操作說明。能大致聽懂外籍人士的談話及詢問。

 在日常生活中，能閱讀短文、故事、私人信件、廣告、傳單、簡介及使用說明等。在工作時，能閱讀工作須知、公告、操作手冊、例行的文件、傳真、電報等。

 能寫簡單的書信、故事及心得等。對於熟悉且與個人經歷相關的主題，能以簡易的文字表達。

 在日常生活中，能以簡易英語交談或描述一般事物，能介紹自己的生活作息、工作、家庭、經歷等，並可對一般話題陳述看法。在工作時，能進行簡單的答詢，並與外籍人士交談溝通。

本書除包含官方公佈的中級4,947單字外，更精挑了近400個滿分必學的高手單字。同時，在片語的挑選、例句的使用上，皆依上述英檢官方公佈之能力範疇做設計，難度適中、不偏離考試主題。發音部分則是自然發音＆KK音標雙管齊下，搭配MP3以「分解／完整」方式錄音，給你最多元有效的學習手段，怎麼記都可以，想忘掉都好難！

B.C. [bi-si]　🎧 *Track 0370*
=Be·fore Christ
abbr. 西元前
▶The construction of the Great Wall of China was started in around 220 B.C. 中國萬里長城的建造大約起始於西元前220年。

ba·by [ˋbebɪ]　🎧 *Track 0371*
n. 嬰兒

ba·by·sit [ˋbebɪsɪt]　🎧 *Track 0372*
=ba·by·sit
v. 當臨時保姆
▶I can babysit your children while you're away. 我可以在你出門時幫你照顧小孩。

ba·by·sit·ter [ˋbebɪsɪtə]　🎧 *Track 0373*
=ba·by·sit·ter
n. 臨時保姆

bach·e·lor [ˋbætʃələ]　🎧 *Track 0374*
n. 單身男子；學士

▶He finally earned a bachelor's degree in Business Administration last year.
他終於在去年拿到了企業管理的學士學位。

相關片語
bachelor party （結婚典禮前為新郎辦的）單身派對
▶We are planning to give a bachelor party for Jamie.
我們正計劃要幫傑米辦一場單身派對。

back [bæk]　🎧 *Track 0375*
adv. 向後；以前；原處；回覆
n. 背部；後面　**v.** 後退；支持
adj. 後面的

back·ground [ˋbækˌgraʊnd]　🎧 *Track 0376*
n. 背景；出身背景；學經歷；背景資料
▶We never hire a person without checking his background first. 我們從不在未審查背景經歷的情況下就雇用一個人。

back·pack [`bæk͵pæk] 🎧 *Track 0377*
n. 登山；遠足用的背包
▶ Make sure you put all necessary supplies into your backpack.
你務必要將所有必需用品都放進背包。

v. 把……放入背包；背負簡便行李旅行
▶ We made friends with people from all over the world while backpacking around Europe. 我們在歐洲背包旅行時，結交了來自世界各地的朋友。

back·ward [`bækwəd] 🎧 *Track 0378*
adv. 向後；倒回
adj. 向後的；落後的、發展遲緩的

back·wards 🎧 *Track 0379*
[`bækwɚdz]
adv. 向後，逆著

bac·te·ri·a [bæk`tırıə] 🎧 *Track 0380*
n. 細菌（單數形式：**bacterium**）
▶ Bacteria are not visible to the naked eye.
肉眼是看不到細菌的。

bad [bæd] 🎧 *Track 0381*
adj. 壞的；惡劣的

badge [bædʒ] 🎧 *Track 0382*
n. 徽章；證章；標誌
▶ You cannot enter the office building without your employee badge.
沒有員工證，你是不能進入辦公大樓的。

bad·ly [`bædlı] 🎧 *Track 0383*
adv. 壞地；不利地；嚴重地；非常
▶ She was badly hurt. 她傷得很重。
相關片語
badly off 境況不佳的；處境糟糕的；窮困的
▶ He was badly off before he found a job.
他在找到工作之前，過得很窮困。

bad·min·ton 🎧 *Track 0384*
[`bædmıntən]
n. 羽毛球

bag [bæg] 🎧 *Track 0385*
n. 袋子

bag·gage [`bægıdʒ] 🎧 *Track 0386*
n. 行李
▶ I'm afraid that your baggage is overweight.
你的行李恐怕超重了。

bag·gy [`bægı] 🎧 *Track 0387*
adj. 袋狀的；寬鬆下垂的
▶ Wearing a baggy T-shirt is comfortable.
穿寬鬆的T恤很舒服。

bait [bet] 🎧 *Track 0388*
n. 餌；引誘物
▶ We use earthworms as fishing bait.
我們用蚯蚓當魚餌。

v. 置餌於……；引誘
▶ They baited the mouse with a piece of bacon.
他們為了抓老鼠，拿一塊培根當誘餌。

bake [bek] 🎧 *Track 0389*
v. 烘焙；烘烤

bak·er·y [`bekərı] 🎧 *Track 0390*
n. 烘焙坊；麵包店

bal·ance [`bæləns] 🎧 *Track 0391*
n. 平衡；均衡；和諧
▶ The boy lost his balance and fell off the bike. 男孩失去平衡，從腳踏車上摔了下來。

v. 使平衡；保持平衡；使相稱
▶ It's not easy for a working mother to balance work and family. 一個職業母親要保持工作和家庭的平衡並不容易。

bal·co·ny [`bælkənı] 🎧 *Track 0392*
n. 陽台

bald [bɔld] 🎧 *Track 0393*
adj. 禿頭的；無毛的；露骨的
▶ He is only thirty but he is nearly bald.
他才三十歲，頭就快要禿了。

ball [bɔl] 🎧 *Track 0394*
n. 球；球狀物

bal·let [`bæle] 🎧 *Track 0395*
n. 芭蕾舞；芭蕾舞音樂

▶ We enjoyed a great ballet show on TV.
我們在電視上欣賞了一場絕佳的芭蕾舞表演。

bal·loon [bə`lun]
🎧 *Track 0396*
n. 氣球

bal·lot [`bælət]
🎧 *Track 0397*
n. 選票；投票權；（不記名）投票
▶ The result of the ballot will be announced in two hours.
投票的結果將在兩小時後宣布。

v. 以不記名投票表決；投票選舉
▶ The factory workers balloted on whether to have a strike or not.
工廠工人投票決定是否要罷工。

bam·boo [bæm`bu]
🎧 *Track 0398*
n. 竹子

ban [bæn]
🎧 *Track 0399*
v. 禁止；取締
▶ In Taiwan, smoking is banned in public places. 在台灣，公共場所是禁止吸菸的。

n. 禁止；禁令
▶ We have put a ban on smoking in public places. 我們已經禁止在公共場所吸菸。

ba·na·na [bə`nænə]
🎧 *Track 0400*
n. 香蕉

band [bænd]
🎧 *Track 0401*
n. 帶；細繩；橡皮圈

ban·dage [`bændɪdʒ]
🎧 *Track 0402*
n. 繃帶
▶ The nurse applied a bandage over his wound on the arm.
護士在他手臂的傷口上包上繃帶。

v. 用繃帶包紮
▶ The nurse had his injured foot carefully bandaged.
護士將他受傷的腳仔細地用繃帶包紮好。

band-aid [`bænd͵ed]
🎧 *Track 0403*
n. 護創膠布；OK繃
▶ He put a band-aid on his cut wound.
他在割傷的傷口上貼了一塊OK繃。

ban·dit [`bændɪt]
🎧 *Track 0404*
n. 強盜；土匪；惡棍
▶ We met a group of bandits on our way.
我們在路上遇到了一幫土匪。

bang [bæŋ]
🎧 *Track 0405*
n. 猛擊；砰砰的聲音
▶ The book fell from the shelf and gave him a nasty bang on the head.
書從架子上掉下來，重重的擊中他的頭。

v. 猛擊；砰砰作響
▶ The drunk driver banged his car against the wire pole. 酒醉的駕駛砰地一聲將車子猛撞在電線桿上。

bank [bæŋk]
🎧 *Track 0406*
n. 銀行

bank·er [`bæŋkɚ]
🎧 *Track 0407*
n. 銀行家

bank·rupt [`bæŋkrʌpt]
🎧 *Track 0408*
adj. 破產的；完全失敗的
▶ His company was declared bankrupt.
他的公司已經被宣告破產了。

v. 使破產；使赤貧
▶ He admitted that his investment in the stock market was a failure that nearly bankrupted his company.
他承認他在股票市場的投資失敗，差點讓他的公司破產。

n. 破產者；（在某方面）完全喪失者
▶ He used to be a very successful businessman, but two years ago he was declared a bankrupt. 他曾是個非常成功的生意人，但兩年前他被宣告破產。

ban·ner [`bænɚ]
🎧 *Track 0409*
n. 旗幟；橫幅
▶ Where should I hang this welcoming banner?
我應該將這幅歡迎旗幟掛在哪裡？

ban·quet [`bæŋkwɪt]
🎧 *Track 0410*
n. 宴會；盛宴
▶ A banquet was given following the opening ceremony. 開幕儀式之後，有一場宴席。

Aa
Bb
Cc
Dd
Ee
Ff
Gg
Hh
Ii
Jj
Kk
Ll
Mm
Nn
Oo
Pp
Qq
Rr
Ss
Tt
Uu
Vv
Ww
Xx
Yy
Zz

v. 設宴款待

▶ We banqueted our guests after the wedding ceremony. 我們在結婚儀式完成之後，設宴款待我們的賓客。

bar [bɑr] 　　🎧 *Track 0411*
n. 酒吧；條狀物

bar·be·cue [`bɑrbɪkju] 　🎧 *Track 0412*
=Bar-B-Q
n. 烤肉；烤肉餐館　**v.**（在戶外）烤肉

bar·ber [`bɑrbɚ] 　　🎧 *Track 0413*
n. 理髮師

bar·ber·shop 　　🎧 *Track 0414*
[`bɑrbɚˌʃɑp]
n. 理髮店

▶ He went to the barbershop to get a haircut. 他去理髮店剪頭髮了。

bare [bɛr] 　　🎧 *Track 0415*
adj. 裸的；空的；無陳設的；勉強的

▶ The boy walked around with bare feet. 那男孩赤腳到處走路。

v. 使赤裸；露出；揭露

▶ He bared his arm to show us the scar. 他露出手臂，讓我們看他的傷疤。

bare·foot [`bɛrˌfʊt] 　🎧 *Track 0416*
adj. 赤腳的

▶ I was barefoot because I couldn't find my shoes.
我赤腳是因為我找不到我的鞋子。

adv. 赤腳地

▶ We walked barefoot on the sand.
我們赤著腳走在沙灘上。

相關片語

go barefoot 打赤腳

▶ I love to go barefoot inside the house.
我在屋子裡喜歡打赤腳。

bare·ly [`bɛrlɪ] 　　🎧 *Track 0417*
adv. 僅僅；勉強；幾乎沒有

▶ He can barely live on his slim income.
他微薄的收入僅夠勉強維生。

bar·gain [`bɑrgɪn] 　🎧 *Track 0418*
n. 協議；買賣、交易；特價商品

▶ The dress I bought in a sale was real bargain.
我在特賣會上買的這件洋裝真的好便宜。

v. 討價還價；達成協議

▶ She bought the dress without bargaining with the vendor.
她沒有跟小販討價還價就買了那件洋裝。

bark [bɑrk] 　　🎧 *Track 0419*
v.（狗等）吠叫　**n.** 吠叫聲

barn [bɑrn] 　　🎧 *Track 0420*
n. 穀倉；牛欄、馬舍

▶ The farmer gathered the wheat into his barn. 農夫將小麥聚集到穀倉裡。

bar·rel [`bærəl] 　　🎧 *Track 0421*
n. 大桶；一桶的量

▶ The cabin with a lot of beer barrels outside is a beer house.
那個外頭有很多啤酒桶的木屋是間啤酒屋。

相關片語

get sb. over a barrel 使某人聽從擺佈；束手無策

▶ They got me over a barrel because they knew I needed the money.
他們讓我不得不聽從他們的擺佈，因為他們知道我需要那些錢。

bar·ri·er [`bærɪr] 　　🎧 *Track 0422*
n. 障礙物；路障；柵欄；剪票口

▶ The police put up barriers to block the road. 警方設置路障，將道路封鎖起來。

base [bes] 　　🎧 *Track 0423*
v. 以……為基礎；將……建立在某種基礎上
n. 基礎；基本部分

base·ball [`besˌbɔl] 　🎧 *Track 0424*
n. 棒球

based [best] 　　🎧 *Track 0425*
adj. 有根基的；有基地的

▶ The film is based on a novel.
這部電影是以一本小說為基礎改編的。

base‧ment [`besmənt] 🎧 *Track 0426*
n. 地下室

ba‧sic [`besɪk] 🎧 *Track 0427*
adj. 基本的

ba‧sin [`besn] 🎧 *Track 0428*
n. 盆；洗滌槽；盆地
▶ There are piles of dirty dishes in the kitchen basin. 廚房洗滌槽有成堆的髒碗盤。

相關片語
hand basin 洗手槽
▶ Do you know how to install a hand basin by yourself? 你知道要怎麼自己安裝洗手槽嗎？

ba‧sis [`besɪs] 🎧 *Track 0429*
n. 基礎；根據

bas‧ket [`bæskɪt] 🎧 *Track 0430*
n. 籃子

bas‧ket‧ball 🎧 *Track 0431*
[`bæskɪt͵bɔl]
n. 籃球

bass [`bes] 🎧 *Track 0432*
n. 男低音；男低音歌手；低音樂器
▶ John sings bass in the choir.
約翰在合唱團中是唱男低音部。
adj. （聲音）低沉的；男低音的；（樂器）低音的
▶ The singer is known for his great bass voice.
這歌手因為其超好聽的低沉聲音而聞名。

bat [bæt] 🎧 *Track 0433*
n. 球棒；蝙蝠

batch [bætʃ] 🎧 *Track 0434*
n. 一批
▶ The whole batch of buns is completely sold out. 一整批小圓麵包全都賣光了。

bath [bæθ] 🎧 *Track 0435*
n. 沐浴

bathe [beð] 🎧 *Track 0436*
v. 浸洗；給……洗澡；使沈浸其中

bath‧room [`bæθ͵rum] 🎧 *Track 0437*
n. 浴室；洗手間

bat‧ter‧y [`bætərɪ] 🎧 *Track 0438*
n. 電池
▶ The battery is dead. 這電池沒電了。

相關片語
recharge one's batteries 使重新充電；使休息而重新得到活力
▶ You need a vacation to recharge your batteries. 你需要放個假，讓自己充個電。

bat‧tle [`bætl] 🎧 *Track 0439*
n. 戰鬥；戰役
v. 與……作戰；與……鬥爭

bay [be] 🎧 *Track 0440*
n. （海或湖泊的）灣
▶ They are going to build a resort hotel in the bay area.
他們將在海灣地區蓋一座度假飯店。

ba‧zaar [bə`zɑr] 🎧 *Track 0441*
n. 市場；商店街；市集；義賣市場
▶ We're going to the bazaar to buy some Christmas decorations.
我們要去市集買一些聖誕裝飾品。

be [bi] 🎧 *Track 0442*
v. 是；成為；正在（與現在分詞連用）；被（與過去分詞連用）

beach [bitʃ] 🎧 *Track 0443*
n. 海邊；海灘

bead [bid] 🎧 *Track 0444*
n. 有孔小珠；一串珠（念珠、淚珠、露珠、汗珠） **v.** 使成串珠狀、形成珠狀

beak [bik] 🎧 *Track 0445*
n. 鳥嘴；喙狀嘴
▶ Dolphins have beaks.
海豚有喙狀的嘴。

beam [bim] 🎧 *Track 0446*
n. 笑容、喜色、光束
▶ He shone a beam of light on the door.
他用一束光照射那扇門。

Aa
Bb
Cc
Dd
Ee

Ff
Gg
Hh
Ii
Jj

Kk
Ll
Mm
Nn
Oo

Pp
Qq
Rr
Ss
Tt

Uu
Vv
Ww
Xx
Yy
Zz

※灰色單字為英檢初級必備單字

v. 堆滿笑容、眉開眼笑

▶ My husband beamed with joy when I told him that I was pregnant. 我先生在聽到我告訴他我懷孕時，高興得眉開眼笑。

bean [bin]　　　　　🎧 *Track 0447*
n. 豆子

bear [bɛr]　　　　　🎧 *Track 0448*
n. 熊　**v.** 忍受；承擔；生（孩子）

beard [bɪrd]　　　　🎧 *Track 0449*
n. 山羊鬍；下巴上的鬍鬚

beast [bist]　　　　🎧 *Track 0450*
n. 野獸；粗暴的人；畜生；獸性

▶ Anger brought out the beast in him.
憤怒激發出了他心中的野獸。

(補充片語)
bring out the beast in sb. 激怒某人；激發某人的獸性

beat [bit]　　　　　🎧 *Track 0451*
v. 打；跳動
n. 敲打；心跳聲；拍子、節奏

beau·ti·ful [`bjutəfəl]　🎧 *Track 0452*
adj. 美麗的；完美的

beau·ty [`bjutɪ]　　　🎧 *Track 0453*
n. 美；美人；美好的事物；優點

be·cause [bɪ`kɔz]　　🎧 *Track 0454*
conj. 因為

be·come [bɪ`kʌm]　　🎧 *Track 0455*
v. 成為；變得

bed [bɛd]　　　　　🎧 *Track 0456*
n. 床

bed·room [`bɛd͵rʊm]　🎧 *Track 0457*
n. 臥室

bed·time [`bɛd͵taɪm]　🎧 *Track 0458*
n. 就寢時間

▶ It's bedtime. Turn off the TV and go to sleep. 睡覺時間到了。把電視關掉，去睡覺吧！

adj. 睡前的

▶ The boy asked his mother to read him a bedtime story.
男孩要求媽媽念個睡前故事給他聽。

bee [bi]　　　　　🎧 *Track 0459*
n. 蜜蜂

beef [bif]　　　　　🎧 *Track 0460*
n. 牛肉

beep [bip]　　　　　🎧 *Track 0461*
v. 吹警笛；發出嗶嗶聲　**n.** 嗶聲

beer [bɪr]　　　　　🎧 *Track 0462*
n. 啤酒

bee·tle [`bitl]　　　🎧 *Track 0463*
n. 甲蟲

be·fore [bɪ`for]　　　🎧 *Track 0464*
prep. 在⋯⋯之前　**conj.** 在⋯⋯之前
adv. 以前

beg [bɛg]　　　　　🎧 *Track 0465*
v. 乞求

beg·gar [`bɛgɚ]　　🎧 *Track 0466*
n. 乞丐

▶ The man gave the beggar some coins.
男子給了那個乞丐一些硬幣。

be·gin [bɪ`gɪn]　　　🎧 *Track 0467*
v. 開始；著手

be·gin·ner [bɪ`gɪnɚ]　🎧 *Track 0468*
n. 初學者；新手

be·gin·ning [bɪ`gɪnɪŋ]　🎧 *Track 0469*
n. 開始；起點　**adj.** 開始的

be·have [bɪ`hev]　　🎧 *Track 0470*
v. 做出⋯⋯舉止，表現；行為舉止

be·ha·vior [bɪ`hevjɚ]　🎧 *Track 0471*
=be·ha·viour（英式英文）
n. 行為；態度；舉止

▶ You are old enough to be responsible for your behavior.
你已經夠大了，能為自己的行為負責了。

be·hind [bɪˋhaɪnd] 🎧 *Track 0472*
prep. 在……之後
adv. 在背後；（留）在原處、在後；遲

be·ing [ˋbiɪŋ] 🎧 *Track 0473*
n. 生物；人；存在；生命
▶ He claimed that he had seen beings from another planet. 他聲稱自己看過外星人。

be·lief [bɪˋlif] 🎧 *Track 0474*
n. 信任；相信；信仰

be·liev·a·ble [bɪˋlivəbl] 🎧 *Track 0475*
adj. 可信的

be·lieve [bɪˋliv] 🎧 *Track 0476*
v. 相信

bell [bɛl] 🎧 *Track 0477*
n. 鈴；鐘

bel·ly [ˋbɛlɪ] 🎧 *Track 0478*
n. 肚子；腹部；胃；食慾
▶ The steak was delicious but my eyes were bigger than my belly today, so I didn't finish it.
牛排很美味，但我今天眼大肚子小（胃口很小），所以沒有吃完。

(補充片語)
eyes bigger than belly 眼大肚子小

be·long [bəˋlɔŋ] 🎧 *Track 0479*
v. 應被放置某處；屬於；適合

be·long·ings [bəˋlɔŋɪŋz] 🎧 *Track 0480*
n. 財物；攜帶物品
▶ Please don't forget to bring your personal belongings with you.
請不要忘記帶走您的個人物品。

be·lov·ed [bɪˋlʌvɪd] 🎧 *Track 0481*
adj. 心愛的；受鍾愛的
▶ I'm writing a letter to my beloved grandma. 我正在寫信給我親愛的奶奶。

n. （指丈夫、妻子或男女朋友等）心愛的人
▶ This necklace was a gift from my beloved.
這條項鍊是我心愛的人所送的禮物。

be·low [bəˋlo] 🎧 *Track 0482*
adv. 在下面；以下
prep. 在……下面；在……以下；低於

belt [bɛlt] 🎧 *Track 0483*
n. 帶狀物；腰帶

bench [bɛntʃ] 🎧 *Track 0484*
n. 長凳；長椅

bend [bɛnd] 🎧 *Track 0485*
v. 彎曲；使彎曲；使屈服；使致力於
n. 彎；轉彎處

be·neath [bɪˋniθ] 🎧 *Track 0486*
prep. 在……之下；向……下面；低於
▶ There's a trap door beneath the rug.
地毯下面有一扇活門。

ben·e·fi·cial [͵bɛnəˋfɪʃəl] 🎧 *Track 0487*
adj. 有益的；有幫助的
▶ Onions and garlic are both beneficial for our health.
洋蔥和大蒜對我們的健康都是有益的。

ben·e·fit [ˋbɛnəfɪt] 🎧 *Track 0488*
n. 益處
▶ A public garden will be a great benefit to our neighborhood.
一個公園會為我們社區帶來很大的益處。

v. 對……有益；有益於
▶ Taking vacations can benefit your brain's health.
休假能為你的大腦健康帶來益處。

ber·ry [ˋbɛrɪ] 🎧 *Track 0489*
n. 莓果
▶ The jam is made of various berries.
這果醬是用各種莓果做成的。

be·side [bɪˋsaɪd] 🎧 *Track 0490*
prep. 在……旁邊

Aa
Bb
Cc
Dd
Ee
Ff
Gg
Hh
Ii
Jj
Kk
Ll
Mm
Nn
Oo
Pp
Qq
Rr
Ss
Tt
Uu
Vv
Ww
Xx
Yy
Zz

※灰色單字為英檢初級必備單字

be·sides [bɪˋsaɪdz] 🎧 Track 0491
prep. 在⋯⋯之外;除⋯⋯之外
adv. 此外;而且

best [bɛst] 🎧 Track 0492
adv. 最好地;最適當地;最
adj. 最好的;最適當的

bet [bɛt] 🎧 Track 0493
n. 打賭;猜測 **v.** 打賭;敢斷言

be·tray [bɪˋtre] 🎧 Track 0494
v. 背叛;出賣;洩漏
▶ I trust no one after my best friend betrayed me.
在我被最好的朋友出賣之後,我就不相信任何人了。

bet·ter [ˋbɛtɚ] 🎧 Track 0495
adv. 更好地;更適當地;更
adj. 更好的;更適當的

be·tween [bɪˋtwin] 🎧 Track 0496
prep. 在⋯⋯之間

bev·er·age [ˋbɛvərɪdʒ] 🎧 Track 0497
n. 飲料
▶ Please help yourself to the beverages on the table. 請自己拿桌子上的飲料喝。

be·ware [bɪˋwɛr] 🎧 Track 0498
v. 當心;小心;提防
▶ Beware of pickpockets when traveling in the city.
在這城市旅遊時,要當心扒手。

(補充片語)
beware of 注意;小心

be·yond [bɪˋjɑnd] 🎧 Track 0499
prep. 在⋯⋯另一邊;超出
adv. 更遠處;此外

bi·as [ˋbaɪəs] 🎧 Track 0500
n. 偏心;偏見;偏愛
▶ Many people in this society have a bias against unmarried mothers.
這個社會上有很多人對未婚媽媽有偏見。

Bi·ble [ˋbaɪbl] 🎧 Track 0501
n. 聖經
▶ The Bible teaches us that if someone slaps you on one cheek, turn to them the other also. 聖經教導我們,如果有人打你的右臉,就把左臉也轉過來讓他打。

(補充片語)
slap on the cheek 打耳光

bi·cy·cle [ˋbaɪsɪkl] 🎧 Track 0502
n. =bike 自行車、單車、腳踏車

bid [bɪd] 🎧 Track 0503
n. 出價(投標);喊價
▶ He wanted the cabinet very badly, so he was determined to win the bid. 他實在太想要那個櫃子了,所以他決心要得標。

v. 命令;吩咐;喊價(投標)
▶ I can't believe you bid $10,000 for this old cabinet. 我不敢相信你竟然出價10,000元買這舊櫃子。

big [bɪg] 🎧 Track 0504
adj. 大的;年齡較長的

bike [baɪk] 🎧 Track 0505
n. 腳踏車
▶ My brother and I go to school by bike.
我跟哥哥騎腳踏車上學。

bill [bɪl] 🎧 Track 0506
n. 帳單

bil·lion [ˋbɪljən] 🎧 Track 0507
n. 十億;大量;無數
▶ The actress married a successful businessman whose net worth exceeded two billion dollars. 該女星嫁給一個身價超過二十億美元的成功實業家。

bin [bɪn] 🎧 Track 0508
n. 貯藏箱;(貯藏用的)容器
▶ She emptied a bag of rice into the bin.
她把一袋米倒入貯藏箱裡。

(相關片語)
trash bin 垃圾箱
▶ Please throw it into the trash bin.
請把它丟到垃圾箱裡去。

bind [baɪnd] 🎧 *Track 0509*
v. 綑；綁；紮；裝訂；黏合

bin·go [`bɪŋgo] 🎧 *Track 0510*
n. 賓果遊戲
▶ I like to play bingo with my family.
我喜歡跟家人玩賓果遊戲。

bi·noc·u·lars 🎧 *Track 0511*
[bɪ`nɑkjələ-s]
n. 雙筒望遠鏡
▶ He brings the binoculars with him when going bird watching.
他去賞鳥時，會帶著雙筒望遠鏡。

bi·og·ra·phy 🎧 *Track 0512*
[baɪ`ɑgrəfɪ]
n. 傳記
▶ I'm reading a biography of Steve Jobs.
我正在讀賈伯斯的傳記。

bi·o·lo·gi·cal 🎧 *Track 0513*
[ˌbaɪə`lɑdʒɪk]]
adj. 生物學的；生物的
▶ He was very shocked when he realized that his father and mother were not his biological parents. 當他知道他的爸爸媽媽不是親生父母時，十分的震驚。

(補充片語)
biological parents 親生父母

bi·ol·o·gy [baɪ`ɑlədʒɪ] 🎧 *Track 0514*
n. 生物；生物學

bird [bɝd] 🎧 *Track 0515*
n. 鳥

birth [bɝθ] 🎧 *Track 0516*
n. 出生；分娩；誕生

birth·day [`bɝθˌde] 🎧 *Track 0517*
n. 生日

bis·cuit [`bɪskɪt] 🎧 *Track 0518*
n. 小麵包；軟餅；（英）餅乾
▶ She made some biscuits for afternoon tea. 她為下午茶做了些餅乾。

bit [bɪt] 🎧 *Track 0519*
n. 小片；小塊；一點點

bite [baɪt] 🎧 *Track 0520*
v. 咬 **n.** 咬一口；（口）便餐

bit·ter [`bɪtə-] 🎧 *Track 0521*
adj. 苦的

bi·zarre [bɪ`zɑr] 🎧 *Track 0522*
adj. 古怪的；異乎尋常的
▶ He always comes up with bizarre ideas.
他總是會想出一些古怪的點子。

black [blæk] 🎧 *Track 0523*
adj. 黑色的；黑人的
n. 黑；黑色；（大寫時）指黑人

black·board [`blækˌbord] 🎧 *Track 0524*
n. 黑板

black·smith [`blækˌsmɪθ] 🎧 *Track 0525*
n. 鐵匠
▶ He earns his living as a blacksmith.
他以做鐵匠謀生。

(補充片語)
earn one's living 謀生

blade [bled] 🎧 *Track 0526*
n. 刀片；鋒刃
▶ Be careful with the blades of the food processor. 要小心食物調理機的刀片。

blame [blem] 🎧 *Track 0527*
v. 責怪；責罵 **n.** 指責；責備；責任

blank [blæŋk] 🎧 *Track 0528*
adj. 空白的；無表情的
n. 空白；空格處

blan·ket [`blæŋkɪt] 🎧 *Track 0529*
n. 毛毯；毯子

blast [blæst] 🎧 *Track 0530*
n. 疾風；爆破；突然吹奏（樂器）；猛然一擊；狂歡
▶ I heard the blast from two blocks away.
我在兩個街區以外都聽得到爆破的聲音。

※灰色單字為英檢初級必備單字

v. 炸開；吹奏；強烈譴責；轟擊
▶ Two armed men blasted open the gate with a shotgun and invaded the house. 兩個武裝的男子用霰彈槍轟開大門，並侵入房子。

blaze [blez] 　🎧 *Track 0531*
n. 火焰；強光；（情緒的）爆發；猛烈掃射
▶ He slapped his son in the face in a blaze of fury. 他在盛怒下打了他兒子一巴掌。

（補充片語）
slap sb. in the face 打某人耳光；
in a blaze of fury 盛怒之下

v. 燃燒；閃耀；迸發
▶ His eyes were blazing with anger. 他的眼睛燃燒著怒火。

bleach [blitʃ] 　🎧 *Track 0532*
v. 將……漂白；漂洗；使脫色
▶ Can you bleach this white dress for me? 你可以幫我漂洗這件白色洋裝嗎？

n. 漂白劑
▶ Can you remove the stain from the white shirt without using bleach? 你可以不用漂白劑，除掉這白襯衫上的污漬嗎？

bleak [blik] 　🎧 *Track 0533*
adj. 荒涼的；寒冷刺骨的；冷峻的；無希望的
▶ Our prospects of winning are bleak. 我們幾乎沒有勝利的希望。

bleed [blid] 　🎧 *Track 0534*
v. 流血；出血
▶ Oh no! You're bleeding! 不好了！你在流血！

blend [blɛnd] 　🎧 *Track 0535*
v. 混和；使混雜；使交融
▶ Please help me blend egg and sugar together. 請幫我把蛋和糖混在一起。

bless [blɛs] 　🎧 *Track 0536*
v. 為……祈福；保佑。
▶ May God bless this family. 願上帝保佑這一家人。

bless·ing [`blɛsɪŋ] 　🎧 *Track 0537*
n. 上帝的賜福；祝福；幸事；福氣
▶ It's a blessing to be alive. 能活著就是一種福氣。

blind [blaɪnd] 　🎧 *Track 0538*
adj. 盲的；視而不見的

blink [blɪŋk] 　🎧 *Track 0539*
v. 眨眼睛；（燈光）閃爍
▶ The boy started blinking his eyes because they were dry and itchy. 男孩因為眼睛乾癢而開始眨眼。

n. 一眨眼；一瞥；一瞬間
▶ Kids grow up in a blink of an eye. 孩子們一眨眼就長大了。

bliz·zard [`blɪzɚd] 　🎧 *Track 0540*
n. 大風雪；暴風雪；暴風雪似的一陣；大量
▶ All flights were canceled due to the blizzard. 因為暴風雪的關係，所有航班都已經取消了。

block [blɑk] 　🎧 *Track 0541*
n. 塊狀物；街區 **v.** 阻塞；堵住

blonde [blɑnd] 　🎧 *Track 0542*
adj. 金黃色的；金髮碧眼的
▶ She dyed her black hair blonde. 她把她烏黑的頭髮染成金色的。

n. 金髮碧眼的女子
▶ My new boss is a pretty blonde. 我的新主管是個金髮碧眼的漂亮女子。

（相關片語）
dumb blonde 漂亮無腦的金髮碧眼女子
▶ She proved to the world that she is not a dumb blonde. 她向世人證明自己並不是個只有臉蛋沒有頭腦的金髮女子。

blood [blʌd] 　🎧 *Track 0543*
n. 血

blood·y [`blʌdɪ] 　🎧 *Track 0544*
adj. 流血的；血淋淋的

bloom [blum] 　🎧 *Track 0545*
n. （觀賞的）花；開花

► The roses in our backyard are in full bloom. 我們後院的玫瑰盛開了。

(補充片語)

in full bloom 盛開

v. 開花
► The roses in the garden are beginning to bloom. 花園裡的玫瑰要開始開花了。

blos·som [`blɑsəm]　🎧 *Track 0546*
n. （果樹的）花；開花
► The red cotton trees are in blossom.
木棉樹正在開花。

v. 開花；生長茂盛
► The then little girl is blossoming into a graceful lady. 當時的小女孩正成長為一個亭亭玉立的女子。

blouse [blaʊz]　🎧 *Track 0547*
n. （婦女或孩童的）短上衣

blow [blo]　🎧 *Track 0548*
v. 吹
n. 吹氣；一擊；（口）強風；精神上的打擊

blue [blu]　🎧 *Track 0549*
adj. 藍色的；憂鬱的
n. 藍色；沮喪、憂鬱；藍調

blunt [blʌnt]　🎧 *Track 0550*
adj. 鈍的；不利的；耿直的、直率的；（頭腦或感覺）遲鈍的
► His blunt remarks offended his boss.
他直言不諱的言辭冒犯了他的上司。

blur [blɝ]　🎧 *Track 0551*
n. 模糊不清的事物；模糊；朦朧；污點
► Everything is a blur to me when I am not wearing my glasses.
當我沒有戴眼鏡時，所有東西在我看來都是模糊的。

v. 使模糊不清；使朦朧；弄髒
► My vision blurred as the alcohol took effect.
當酒精開始起作用，我的視線就模糊了。

blush [blʌʃ]　🎧 *Track 0552*
v. 臉紅；慚愧

► She blushed as she admitted that she had feelings for the young man.
她紅著臉承認自己對那年輕男子有好感。

n. 臉紅；羞愧
► His compliment brought a blush to her cheeks.
他的讚美使她臉紅了。

board [bord]　🎧 *Track 0553*
v. 上（船、車或飛機）　**n.** 板子

boast [bost]　🎧 *Track 0554*
v. 自吹自擂；吹噓；誇耀
► The woman is boasting about her genius son again.
那女人又在吹噓她的天才兒子了。

n. 自吹；大話；引以為豪的事物
► I'm so tired of listening to his boasts.
我聽膩他說大話了。

boat [bot]　🎧 *Track 0555*
n. 小船

bod·y [`bɑdɪ]　🎧 *Track 0556*
n. 身體

bod·y·guard　🎧 *Track 0557*
[`bɑdɪˌgɑrd]
n. 護衛者；保鏢
► He hired several bodyguards to protect him 24/7.
他請了幾名保鏢隨時隨地保護他。

boil [bɔɪl]　🎧 *Track 0558*
v. （水等）沸騰；烹煮；煮沸

bold [bold]　🎧 *Track 0559*
adj. 英勇的；無畏的；大膽的；厚顏無恥的
► He made a bold move to rescue the boy from the river. 他做了一個英勇的舉動，將男孩從河中救了出來。

bolt [bolt]　🎧 *Track 0560*
n. 門栓；門閂
► He slid the bolt into the socket to fasten the door.
他將門閂滑進插口內，把門拴住。

v. 拴上；閂上

▶Don't forget to bolt the door when you leave. 離開時別忘了把門栓上。

bomb [bɑm]　🎧 *Track 0561*
n. 炸彈

bond [bɑnd]　🎧 *Track 0562*
n. 聯繫；結合；羈絆
▶It's hard for me to form a bond with new people. 我很難和新認識的人產生羈絆。

v. 以……作保；使……黏合；團結在一起
▶The two kids bonded with each other immediately.
那兩個孩子立刻就產生了夥伴情誼。

bone [bon]　🎧 *Track 0563*
n. 骨頭

bo·nus [`bonəs]　🎧 *Track 0564*
n. 獎金；紅利；分紅；津貼
▶Our boss promised to give out a large year-end bonus this year.
我們老闆承諾今年會發出一大筆年終獎金。

(補充片語)
year-end bonus 年終獎金

bon·y [`bonɪ]　🎧 *Track 0565*
adj. 多骨的；瘦削的；骨瘦如柴的

book [bʊk]　🎧 *Track 0566*
n. 書；書本 **v.** 預訂；登記

book·case [`bʊk͵kes]　🎧 *Track 0567*
n. 書架；書櫥

book·let [`bʊklɪt]　🎧 *Track 0568*
n. 小冊子
▶You can get a booklet about the exhibition over there. 你可以在那邊拿一本和這場展覽有關的小冊子。

book·shelf [`bʊk͵ʃɛlf]　🎧 *Track 0569*
n. 書架
▶His bookshelf is filled with comic books.
他的書架上擺滿了漫畫書。

book·store [`bʊk͵stor]　🎧 *Track 0570*
=book·shop（英式英文）
n. 書店

▶This novel is the bestseller in our bookstore. 這本小說是本書店的暢銷書。

boom [bum]　🎧 *Track 0571*
v. 發出隆隆聲；激增；迅速發展
▶His business boomed as soon as the advertisement was launched.
那個廣告一推出，他的生意就爆增。

n. 隆隆聲；（商業）繁榮；（政治情況）好轉；激增、暴漲
▶We can expect a foreign investment boom in the following year. 我們可以預期未來的一年外來的投資會激增。

boost [bust]　🎧 *Track 0572*
n. 推動；促進；提高；增加
▶The employees are expecting a boost in their salary. 員工們期待薪水能有所增加。

v. 舉；推；抬；推動；促進；提高
▶Their encouragement boosted the boy's confidence.
他們的鼓勵增加了男孩的自信。

boot [but]　🎧 *Track 0573*
n. 靴子；一踢；解僱
▶Please take off your muddy boots before you come into the house.
請在進屋之前脫掉你泥濘的靴子。

v. 使穿靴；猛踢；趕走
▶He booted the dog out of the house.
他把狗趕出房子。

(相關片語)
give sb. the boot 解僱某人
▶My boss will give me the boot if I'm late for work again.
如果我上班再遲到，老闆會把我解僱。

booth [buθ]　🎧 *Track 0574*
n. 售貨棚；電話亭；（餐廳的）雅座；包廂
▶I'm looking for a telephone booth to give my friend a call.
我正在找電話亭要打電話給我朋友。

(補充片語)
look for 找；
telephone booth 電話亭；
give sb. a call 打電話給某人

bor·der [`bɔrdɚ] 🎧 *Track 0575*
n. 邊緣；邊界；國界
▶ The police captured the wanted criminal near the border between Mexico and the United States.
警方在美墨邊界逮捕到通緝犯。

v. 毗鄰；接界；與……接壤
▶ Mexico borders the United States.
墨西哥與美國接壤。

bore [bor] 🎧 *Track 0576*
v. 使無聊
▶ The movie really bores me.
這電影讓我覺得很無聊。

n. 令人討厭的人
▶ My new neighbor is really an awful bore.
我的新鄰居真是個討厭的人。

bore·dom [`bordəm] 🎧 *Track 0577*
n. 無聊；厭倦
▶ Sometimes I'll listen to music to fight off boredom at work. 有時候我會用聽音樂的方式擊退工作的厭倦感。

(補充片語)
fight off 抵抗；擊退

bor·ing [`borɪŋ] 🎧 *Track 0578*
adj. 無趣的；乏味的

born [bɔrn] 🎧 *Track 0579*
adj. 出生的；天生的

bor·row [`baro] 🎧 *Track 0580*
v. 借；向……借

boss [bɔs] 🎧 *Track 0581*
n. 老闆；主管

both [boθ] 🎧 *Track 0582*
adv. 並；又；兩者皆是 **adj.** 兩個都
pron. 兩者；雙方

both·er [`baðɚ] 🎧 *Track 0583*
v. 煩擾；打擾 **n.** 煩惱；麻煩

bot·tle [`batl̩] 🎧 *Track 0584*
n. 瓶子

bot·tom [`batəm] 🎧 *Track 0585*
n. 底部；底層 **adj.** 底部的；最底下的

bou·le·vard [`bulə,vard] 🎧 *Track 0586*
n. 林蔭大道；大道
▶ We took a walk down the boulevard.
我們沿著林蔭大道散步。

bounce [baʊns] 🎧 *Track 0587*
v. 彈起
▶ The ball didn't bounce up because it was deflated.
那球沒有彈起來，是因為沒氣了。

n. 彈；跳；彈性
▶ This basketball has lost its bounce.
這顆籃球已經沒有彈性了。

相關片語
get the bounce 被解僱
▶ Many of the employees got the bounce without any warning. 許多員工在沒有任何預警的情況下被解僱了。

bow [bo] 🎧 *Track 0588*
n. 船頭；前槳；蝴蝶結；鞠躬

bowl [bol] 🎧 *Track 0589*
n. 碗

bowl·ing [`bolɪŋ] 🎧 *Track 0590*
n. 保齡球

box [baks] 🎧 *Track 0591*
n. 盒子

box·ing [`baksɪŋ] 🎧 *Track 0592*
n. 拳擊；拳術
▶ The boxer started boxing at the age of 15.
這拳擊手十五歲時就開始打拳擊了。

boy [bɔɪ] 🎧 *Track 0593*
n. 男孩；兒子

boy·cott [`bɔɪ,kɑt] 🎧 *Track 0594*
v. 聯合抵制；拒絕參加；杯葛
▶ The group threatened to boycott the import of beef from the United States.
該團體威脅要聯合抵制美國牛肉的進口。

n. 聯合抵制；拒絕參加

▶The group threatened to organize a boycott of beef from the United States.
該團體威脅要籌劃抵制美國牛肉。

boy·friend [`bɔɪ,frɛnd] 🎧 Track 0595
n. 男朋友
▶She was surprised when her boyfriend proposed to her.
當她的男友向她求婚時，她非常驚訝。

boy·hood [`bɔɪhʊd] 🎧 Track 0596
n. 男子的童年；少年時代
▶I spent my boyhood by the lake surrounded by mountains.
我的童年是在群山環繞的湖邊度過的。

bra [brɑ] 🎧 Track 0597
=bras·siere
n. 胸罩
▶I was told not to wash my bras in a washing machine.
有人跟我說不要用洗衣機洗胸罩。

brace·let [`breslɪt] 🎧 Track 0598
n. 手鐲
▶My husband gave me a bracelet as our anniversary gift.
我老公送我一個手鐲作為結婚紀念日禮物。

braid [bred] 🎧 Track 0599
n. 辮子；髮辮
▶The girl with two braids is my sister.
那個綁著兩條辮子的女孩是我妹妹。
v. 將頭髮編成辮子；編織
▶The girl's hair is always neatly braided.
那個女孩的頭髮總是編著整齊的辮子。

brain [bren] 🎧 Track 0600
n. 腦；頭腦

brake [brek] 🎧 Track 0601
n. 煞車
▶The hand brake of this bike is broken.
這單車的手煞車壞了。
（補充片語）
hand brake 手煞車
v. 煞車

▶The bus braked to a stop just in time to avoid an accident.
這輛公車及時煞車，避免了一場意外。
（補充片語）
just in time 剛好及時

branch [bræntʃ] 🎧 Track 0602
n. 支線；分支；分店、分公司

brand [brænd] 🎧 Track 0603
n. 品牌；商標
v. 印商標於……；打烙印於……

brass [bræs] 🎧 Track 0604
n. 黃銅；銅器；銅管樂器
▶The vase is made of brass.
這花瓶是黃銅製的。
adj. 黃銅色的；黃銅製的；銅管樂器的
▶This is a brass vase.
這是個黃銅製的花瓶。
（相關片語）
as bold as brass 厚顏無恥的
▶Jeffery, as bold as brass, passed the buck to Andy. 傑佛瑞厚顏無恥地把過失都推到安迪身上。

brave [brev] 🎧 Track 0605
adj. 勇敢的

brav·e·ry [`brevərɪ] 🎧 Track 0606
n. 勇敢；勇氣
▶The teacher praised Peter for his bravery.
老師因為彼得的勇氣而讚揚他。

bread [brɛd] 🎧 Track 0607
n. 麵包

break [brek] 🎧 Track 0608
v. 打破；破壞 **n.** 休息

break·down 🎧 Track 0609
[`brek,daʊn]
n. （機器）故障；（精神）衰弱、崩潰；（體力）衰竭
▶My car had a breakdown on my way to work. 我的車在上班途中拋錨了。
（補充片語）
on one's way to... 往……的途中

nervous breakdown 精神崩潰
▶ Alice had a nervous breakdown when her boyfriend dumped her.
愛麗絲在男友甩掉她時精神崩潰了。

break·fast [`brɛkfəst] 🎧 Track 0610
n. 早餐

break·up [`brek`ʌp] 🎧 Track 0611
n. 中斷；中止；解體
▶ He started a new relationship soon after their breakup. 在他們分手之後不久，他便隨即展開新的戀情。

breast [brɛst] 🎧 Track 0612
n. 乳房；胸部
▶ The mother worried that she couldn't make enough breast milk to feed her baby. 那個媽媽擔心自己不能分泌足夠的母乳來餵養她的寶寶。

補充片語
breast milk 母乳

v. 挺胸面對；抵抗
▶ She was brave enough to breast harsh criticism. 她勇敢地挺起胸膛面對嚴厲的批評。

breath [brɛθ] 🎧 Track 0613
n. 呼吸
▶ You have to stop and take a deep breath.
你必須停下來，做個深呼吸。

補充片語
take a deep breath 深呼吸

breathe [brið] 🎧 Track 0614
v. 呼吸
▶ You can't breathe under the water without a snorkel. 沒有潛水用呼吸管，你在水下是無法呼吸的。

breed [brid] 🎧 Track 0615
n. （人工培育出來的動植物）品種
▶ This new breed of roses is easier to care for. 這新品種的玫瑰比較容易照顧。

v. 養殖；飼養；孕育
▶ Most milkfish are bred in the fish farms.
大部分虱目魚是在魚塭養殖的。

breeze [briz] 🎧 Track 0616
n. 微風；輕而易舉的事；
▶ The flowers are fluttering and dancing in the breeze. 花兒們在微風中輕舞飛揚。

v. 吹著微風；輕鬆地通過；輕盈地經過
▶ I saw a butterfly breezing through the garden. 我看見一隻蝴蝶輕舞過花園。

相關片語
shoot the breeze 閒聊；聊天
▶ We sat around the campfire and shot the breeze. 我們圍著營火坐著聊天。

bribe [braɪb] 🎧 Track 0617
n. 賄賂；行賄物
▶ The candidate admitted to offering bribes and had withdrawn from the election.
該候選人承認行賄，並已經退出選舉。

v. 賄賂；收買
▶ He bribed the cop to turn a blind eye to his doings. 他賄賂警察對他所做的事情視而不見。

補充片語
turn a blind eye to sth. 對某事視而不見；假裝沒看到

brick [brɪk] 🎧 Track 0618
n. 磚塊

bride [braɪd] 🎧 Track 0619
n. 新娘
▶ The bride looks very beautiful.
新娘看起來好美。

相關片語
bride-to-be 準新娘
▶ The bride-to-be will come to pick her wedding dress today.
準新娘今天會過來挑婚紗。

補充片語
wedding dress 婚紗

bride·groom 🎧 Track 0620
[`braɪd͵grʊm]
=groom
n. 新郎
▶ The bridegroom seemed very nervous before the wedding ceremony.
新郎在婚禮開始前顯得非常緊張。

※灰色單字為英檢初級必備單字

bridge [brɪdʒ] 　🎧 *Track 0621*
n. 橋

brief [brif] 　🎧 *Track 0622*
adj. 簡短的；短暫的

brief·case [`brif͵kes] 　🎧 *Track 0623*
n. 公事包
▶ Everything we need for the meeting is in my briefcase, but I left it in the taxi.
我們開會所需要的所有東西都在我的公事包裡，而我卻將它忘在計程車上了。

bright [braɪt] 　🎧 *Track 0624*
adj. 明亮的；晴朗的；聰明的

bril·liant [`brɪljənt] 　🎧 *Track 0625*
adj. 明亮的；優秀的；出色的；高明的
▶ He finally came up with a brilliant solution to the problem.
他終於想出一個解決問題的絕佳辦法。

bring [brɪŋ] 　🎧 *Track 0626*
v. 帶來

Brit·ain [`brɪtən] 　🎧 *Track 0627*
n. 英國

Brit·ish [`brɪtɪʃ] 　🎧 *Track 0628*
adj. 英國的；英國人的 n. 英國人

broad [brɔd] 　🎧 *Track 0629*
adj. 寬闊的；廣泛的；遼闊的

broad·cast [`brɔd͵kæst] 　🎧 *Track 0630*
n. 廣播；廣播節目 v. 播送；廣播

broke [brok] 　🎧 *Track 0631*
adj. 破產的；身無分文的
▶ You wouldn't have been broke if you had not invested all your money in the stock market. 如果你沒有把所有的錢都投資在股市，你現在就不會身無分文。

(相關片語)
go for broke　孤注一擲
▶ He decided to go for broke regardless of everyone's advice.
他決定不顧大家的勸告，孤注一擲。

brook [brʊk] 　🎧 *Track 0632*
n. 小河；小溪
▶ We often go fishing in the brook near our house. 我們常去我們家附近的小溪釣魚。

broom [brum] 　🎧 *Track 0633*
n. 掃把；掃帚
▶ Get a broom and give this room a good sweep. 拿支掃把來把這房間好好掃一掃。

broth·er [`brʌðɚ] 　🎧 *Track 0634*
n. 兄；弟

brow [braʊ] 　🎧 *Track 0635*
n. 額頭；眉毛；面容、表情
▶ Toby knitted his brows when he heard the bad news.
托比聽到壞消息時，緊皺著眉頭。

(補充片語)
knit one's brows　皺眉

brown [braʊn] 　🎧 *Track 0636*
adj. 褐色的；棕色的 n. 褐色；棕色

brown·ie [`braʊnɪ] 　🎧 *Track 0637*
n. 巧克力小方餅；果仁巧克力小方塊蛋糕；布朗尼
▶ Your dessert, a brownie with vanilla ice cream, is served. 現在為您端上您的甜點—布朗尼蛋糕佐香草冰淇淋。

browse [braʊz] 　🎧 *Track 0638*
v. 瀏覽；隨便翻閱；漫不經心地逛（商品）
▶ I browsed through the catalog to see if there was anything I need. 我翻閱了一下商品目錄，看看有沒有我需要的東西。

n. 瀏覽
▶ I had a browse through the items on the shelf and didn't see anything I needed. 我瀏覽了一下架子上的商品，並沒有看到我需要的東西。

bruise [bruz] 　🎧 *Track 0639*
n. 傷痕；青腫；擦傷；挫傷
▶ The teacher noticed some bruises on the boy's arms and legs.
老師發現男孩的手臂和腳上有幾處淤傷。

v. 使受瘀傷；使青腫；使碰傷；使（情感）受挫

▶He bumped into a tree and bruised his forehead.
他撞到一棵樹，把額頭給撞得瘀青了。

brunch [brʌntʃ] 🎧 *Track 0640*
n. 早午餐

brush [brʌʃ] 🎧 *Track 0641*
n. 刷子 **v.** 刷

bru·tal [`brutl̩] 🎧 *Track 0642*
adj. 殘忍的；野蠻的；粗暴的；嚴酷的；殘酷的
▶We had a very brutal winter last year.
我們去年度過了一個非常嚴酷的冬天。

bub·ble [`bʌbl̩] 🎧 *Track 0643*
n. 水泡；泡狀物；冒泡聲；泡影、虛幻之事
▶Taking a bubble bath is my favorite way to relax. 洗個泡泡浴是我最喜歡用來讓自己放鬆的方式。

(補充片語)
take a bath 泡澡、沐浴；
bubble bath 泡泡澡

v. 沸騰；冒泡；發出沸騰聲；充滿生氣
▶The soup is bubbling on the stove.
爐子上的湯已經煮沸了。

buck·et [`bʌkɪt] 🎧 *Track 0644*
n. =pail 水桶

buck·le [`bʌkl̩] 🎧 *Track 0645*
n. 帶釦；搭鉤
▶Where is the buckle of the seatbelt?
安全帶的釦子在哪兒？

v. 扣緊；扣住
▶Please buckle your seatbelt.
請扣上安全帶。

bud [bʌd] 🎧 *Track 0646*
n. 芽；花苞、花蕾；萌芽；未成熟的事物；小孩
▶The roses are now in bud.
玫瑰正含苞待放。

v. 發芽；開始生長
▶The roses I planted in the garden are budding. 我種在花園裡的玫瑰正在發芽。

Aa
Bb
Cc
Dd
Ee

Ff
Gg
Hh
Ii
Jj

Kk
Ll
Mm
Nn
Oo

Pp
Qq
Rr
Ss
Tt

Uu
Vv
Ww
Xx
Yy
Zz

(相關片語)
taste bud 味蕾
▶The meal totally satisfied my taste buds.
餐點完全地滿足了我的味蕾。

bud·get [`bʌdʒɪt] 🎧 *Track 0647*
n. 預算；經費
▶I like this apartment, but the rent is slightly over my budget. 我很喜歡這棟公寓，但是租金稍微超出我的預算。

v. 按預算計劃；編列預算；安排
▶Since we only live on one income, we need to budget our money very carefully.
因為我們只靠一份收入過活，所以我們需要非常謹慎地安排我們的錢。

buf·fa·lo [`bʌfl̩͵o] 🎧 *Track 0648*
n. 水牛；野牛；（美國城市）水牛城
▶I'll make some Buffalo chicken wings for appetizer. 我會做些水牛城雞翅來當開胃菜。

buf·fet [bʌ`fe] 🎧 *Track 0649*
n. 自助餐；快餐

bug [bʌg] 🎧 *Track 0650*
n. 蟲子；（口）故障

build [bɪld] 🎧 *Track 0651*
v. 興建；建立

build·ing [`bɪldɪŋ] 🎧 *Track 0652*
n. 建築物

bulb [bʌlb] 🎧 *Track 0653*
n. 電燈泡；球莖；球狀物
▶Can you change the broken light bulb for me? 你可以幫我換壞掉的燈泡嗎？

bull [bʊl] 🎧 *Track 0654*
adj. 雄的；公牛的；行情看漲的
▶He caught a bull frog in a ditch.
他在水溝裡抓到一隻牛蛙。

(相關片語)
bull in a china shop 魯莽闖禍的人
▶The new waitress is such a bull in a china shop. She breaks things all the time. 新來的女服務生真是個魯莽闖禍的人，一天到晚打破東西。

bul·let [`bʊlɪt］ 🎧 *Track 0655*
n. 子彈
▶The soldier committed suicide with his last bullet. 士兵用他最後一顆子彈自殺了。

相關片語
bullet train 高速火車（子彈列車）
▶It takes less than an hour to travel between the two cities by bullet train.
搭子彈列車往來這兩個城市，不用一小時的時間。

bul·le·tin [`bʊlətɪn］ 🎧 *Track 0656*
n. 公告；公報
▶The bulletin says that Jack has been promoted to manager of the Sales Department. 公告上寫説傑克已經被晉升為業務部的經理。

相關片語
bulletin board 佈告欄
▶The notice will be posted on the bulletin board today.
公告將在今天張貼於佈告欄上。

bul·ly [`bʊlɪ］ 🎧 *Track 0657*
n. 惡霸；特強凌弱者
▶The class bully has been expelled from school.
那個班上的惡霸已經被學校退學了。

v. 威嚇；特強凌弱；橫行霸道；霸凌
▶The boy didn't want to go to school because he was being bullied by his classmates. 男孩不想去上學，是因為遭到同班同學的霸凌。

bump [bʌmp］ 🎧 *Track 0658*
v. 碰；撞；重擊；撞傷
▶The truck bumped into a tree.
那台貨車撞到了一顆樹。

補充片語
bump into 撞到

n. 重擊；猛撞；凸塊
▶He stumbled over a bump on the road and twisted his ankle. 他被路上隆起的地面絆了一跤，扭傷了腳踝。

相關片語
goose bumps 雞皮疙瘩

▶I had goose bumps when listening to the ghost story.
我在聽鬼故事時，全身起雞皮疙瘩。

bun [bʌn］ 🎧 *Track 0659*
n. 小圓麵包

bunch [bʌntʃ］ 🎧 *Track 0660*
n. 一束；串；一群、一伙
▶He bought me a bunch of roses on my birthday. 他在我生日那天買了束玫瑰花送我。

bun·dle [`bʌndḷ］ 🎧 *Track 0661*
n. 綑；束；大堆、大量

bur·den [`bɝdn］ 🎧 *Track 0662*
n. 重擔；負擔；沉重的責任
▶Children are blessings, not burdens.
孩子是上帝的賜福，而非負擔。

v. 加負擔於；加負荷於
▶He was burdened with heavy debt.
他負擔著沉重的債務。

bu·reau [`bjʊro］ 🎧 *Track 0663*
n. 事務處；聯絡處；局，司，署，社
▶She had the travel bureau arrange for her accommodation in New York.
她請旅行社幫她安排紐約的住處。

補充片語
travel bureau 旅行社

burg·er [`bɝgɚ］ 🎧 *Track 0664*
n. 漢堡；漢堡牛肉餅；各種夾餅

bur·glar [`bɝglɚ］ 🎧 *Track 0665*
n. 夜賊；破門竊盜者
▶The burglar was caught red-handed last night. 這個夜賊昨晚犯行時當場被逮。

補充片語
catch sb. red-handed 當場抓獲；在某人犯案時逮獲

burn [bɝn］ 🎧 *Track 0666*
v. 燃燒；著火；燒傷；燒死

burst [bɝst］ 🎧 *Track 0667*
v. 爆炸；突然發生

bur·y [`bɛrɪ] 🎧 *Track 0668*
v. 埋葬；使專心
▶ After her cat died, she buried it in the backyard. 貓死後，她把牠埋在後院。
相關片語
bury oneself in 埋首於某事
▶ The scientist buried himself in his experiments.
科學家埋首於實驗中。

bus [bʌs] 🎧 *Track 0669*
n. 公車

bush [bʊʃ] 🎧 *Track 0670*
n. 灌木叢
▶ A bird in the hand is worth two in the bush. 二鳥在林，不如一鳥在手。
相關片語
beat around the bush 拐彎抹角地說
▶ Stop beating around the bush. Just tell me what happened. 不要再拐彎抹角了。儘管告訴我發生什麼事了。

busi·ness [`bɪznɪs] 🎧 *Track 0671*
n. 職業；商業；生意；公司

busi·ness·man 🎧 *Track 0672*
[`bɪznɪsmən]
n. 生意人；實業家

bus·y [`bɪzɪ] 🎧 *Track 0673*
adj. 忙碌的；繁忙的

but [bʌt] 🎧 *Track 0674*
conj. 但是；卻 **prep.** 除……以外

butch·er [`bʊtʃɚ] 🎧 *Track 0675*
n. 肉販；屠夫；劊子手
▶ I stopped by the butcher's shop to buy some pork.
我順道經過肉販店買了些豬肉。
v. 屠宰（牲口）；屠殺；蹧蹋
▶ Butchering cattle is a very tiring and hard job. 屠宰牛隻是一件非常累人且費力的工作。

but·ter [`bʌtɚ] 🎧 *Track 0676*
n. 奶油

but·ter·fly [`bʌtɚˏflaɪ] 🎧 *Track 0677*
n. 蝴蝶

but·ton [`bʌtn] 🎧 *Track 0678*
n. 鈕扣；按鈕 **v.** 扣上；扣住

buy [baɪ] 🎧 *Track 0679*
v. 買、購買

buzz [bʌz] 🎧 *Track 0680*
v. 嗡嗡叫；按機器使發出信號；嘰嘰喳喳；給……打電話
▶ I'm Lily. Can you buzz me in?
我是莉莉。可以幫我開門嗎？
補充片語
buzz sb. in 按（開門）鈕讓某人進入
n. 嗡嗡聲；機器噪音；電話
▶ Give me a buzz when you are free.
有空時打個電話給我。
補充片語
give sb. a buzz 打電話給某人

by [baɪ] 🎧 *Track 0681*
prep. 在……旁；在……（時間）之前；透過；被
adv. 經過；在旁邊

Aa
Bb
Cc
Dd
Ee

Ff
Gg
Hh
Ii
Jj

Kk
Ll
Mm
Nn
Oo

Pp
Qq
Rr
Ss
Tt

Uu
Vv
Ww
Xx
Yy
Zz

※灰色單字為英檢初級必備單字

Cc

通過中級英文檢定者的英文能力：

 在日常生活中，能聽懂一般的會話；能大致聽懂公共場所廣播、氣象報告及廣告等。在工作時，能聽懂簡易的產品介紹與操作說明。能大致聽懂外籍人士的談話及詢問。

 在日常生活中，能閱讀短文、故事、私人信件、廣告、傳單、簡介及使用說明等。在工作時，能閱讀工作須知、公告、操作手冊、例行的文件、傳真、電報等。

 能寫簡單的書信、故事及心得等。對於熟悉且與個人經歷相關的主題，能以簡易的文字表達。

 在日常生活中，能以簡易英語交談或描述一般事物，能介紹自己的生活作息、工作、家庭、經歷等，並可對一般話題陳述看法。在工作時，能進行簡單的答詢，並與外籍人士交談溝通。

本書除包含官方公佈的中級4,947單字外，更精挑了近400個滿分必學的高手單字。同時，在片語的挑選、例句的使用上，皆依上述英檢官方公佈之能力範疇做設計，難度適中、不偏離考試主題。發音部分則是自然發音＆KK音標雙管齊下，搭配MP3以「分解／完整」方式錄音，給你最多元有效的學習手段，怎麼記都可以，想忘掉都好難！

---

cab·bage [ˋkæbɪdʒ] 🎧 *Track 0682*
n. 甘藍菜；捲心菜

cab·in [ˋkæbɪn] 🎧 *Track 0683*
n. （船或飛機的）客艙；小木屋
▶ The man was locked in a cabin in the forest. 男子被鎖在森林裡的一棟小木屋裡。

相關片語

cabin crew 客機航班服務員
▶ The cabin crew had an ambulance waiting for the sick passenger at the gate.
客機航班服務員要一輛救護車在閘門等候該生病的乘客。

cab·i·net [ˋkæbənɪt] 🎧 *Track 0684*
n. 櫥；櫃

ca·ble [ˋkebl̩] 🎧 *Track 0685*
n. 電纜；有線電視

cac·tus [ˋkæktəs] 🎧 *Track 0686*
n. 仙人掌

▶ A recent study confirmed that cacti could not protect people from radiation.
最近的一項研究證實仙人掌無法保護人免受輻射傷害。

ca·fé [kəˋfe] 🎧 *Track 0687*
n. 咖啡廳；小餐館

caf·e·te·ri·a [͵kæfəˋtɪrɪə] 🎧 *Track 0688*
n. 自助餐廳

caf·feine [ˋkæfiɪn] 🎧 *Track 0689*
n. 咖啡因
▶ Excessive intake of caffeine can cause sleep problems.
過度的攝取咖啡因會導致睡眠問題。

cage [kedʒ] 🎧 *Track 0690*
n. 鳥籠；獸籠

cake [kek] 🎧 *Track 0691*
n. 蛋糕

cal·cu·late [`kælkjə͵let] 🎧 Track 0692
v. 計算；估計；推測；（以某種目的）計劃
▶ He calculated the total cost of the loan, and then decided not to borrow the money. 他計算了借貸的總成本，然後決定不要借這筆錢了。

cal·cu·lat·ing 🎧 Track 0693
[`kælkjə͵letɪŋ]
adj. 計算的；慎重的；工於心計的
▶ All the evidence showed that the man was a cold and calculating killer. 所有證據顯示這男子是個冷酷且工於心計的殺手。

cal·cu·la·tion 🎧 Track 0694
[͵kælkjə`leʃən]
n. 計算
▶ I started learning mental calculation since I was six. 我從六歲開始學心算。

(補充片語)

mental calculation 心算

cal·cu·la·tor 🎧 Track 0695
[`kælkjə͵letɚ]
n. 計算機；計算者
▶ I can't do mental calculation. Can I use a calculator? 我不會心算。可以用計算機嗎？

cal·en·dar [`kæləndɚ] 🎧 Track 0696
n. 月曆；行事曆

calf [kæf] 🎧 Track 0697
n. 小牛
▶ He had no option but to sell his calves for cash. 他別無選擇，只得賣掉小牛換點現金。

(相關片語)

calf love 年少的初戀
▶ A smile crept up her face when she recalled her calf love. 當她想起自己的初戀時，一抹微笑爬上了她的臉龐。

call [kɔl] 🎧 Track 0698
v. 喊叫；稱呼；打電話 **n.** 打電話

cal·lig·ra·phy 🎧 Track 0699
[kə`lɪgrəfɪ]
n. 書法；筆跡

▶ My grandfather is a master in Chinese calligraphy. 我的爺爺是個中國書法大師。

calm [kɑm] 🎧 Track 0700
adj. 冷靜的；鎮定的
v. 使冷靜；使鎮定

cal·o·rie [`kælərɪ] 🎧 Track 0701
n. 卡路里；（熱量單位）大卡
▶ It is recommended that a female adult should ingest at least 1,200 calories per day.
一般建議一個成人女性一天至少需要攝取1200大卡。

cam·el [`kæml̩] 🎧 Track 0702
n. 駱駝

cam·e·ra [`kæmərə] 🎧 Track 0703
n. 相機

camp [kæmp] 🎧 Track 0704
n. 露營活動 **v.** 露營

cam·paign [kæm`pen] 🎧 Track 0705
n. 戰役；活動；運動；競選活動
▶ The group is organizing a campaign against the use of animal furs and skins. 該團體正在籌劃一場反對使用動物毛皮的活動。

v. 從事運動；參加競選；出征
▶ He has decided to campaign for president. 他已經決定要參選總統。

camp·ing [`kæmpɪŋ] 🎧 Track 0706
n. 露營
▶ We go camping once every other week. 我們每兩周露營一次。

cam·pus [`kæmpəs] 🎧 Track 0707
n. 校園

can [kæn] 🎧 Track 0708
aux. 表示「可以；能夠；可能」的助動詞

Can·ad·a [`kænədə] 🎧 Track 0709
n. 加拿大

※灰色單字為英檢初級必備單字

Ca·na·di·an [kə`nedɪən] 🎧 *Track 0710*
adj. 加拿大的；加拿大人的
n. 加拿大人

ca·nal [kə`næl] 🎧 *Track 0711*
n. 運河；水道
▶ They are planning to dig a canal across Nicaragua, connecting the Pacific and Atlantic. 他們計劃鑿一條橫越尼加拉瓜，聯繫太平洋與大西洋的運河。

can·cel [`kænsl̩] 🎧 *Track 0712*
v. 取消

can·cer [`kænsə-] 🎧 *Track 0713*
n. 癌

can·di·date [`kændədet] 🎧 *Track 0714*
n. 候選人
▶ The candidate denied offering bribes. 該候選人否認行賄。

can·dle [`kændl̩] 🎧 *Track 0715*
n. 蠟燭

can·dy [`kændɪ] 🎧 *Track 0716*
=sweet（英式英文）
n. 糖果

cane [ken] 🎧 *Track 0717*
n. 藤條；手杖
▶ The old man walking with a cane is my grandpa. 那個拄著手杖走路的老人就是我爺爺。

can·non [`kænən] 🎧 *Track 0718*
n. 大砲
▶ The ship fired the cannon at another ship. 這艘船對另一艘船開砲。

can·not [`kænɑt] 🎧 *Track 0719*
abbr. 不能、不會

ca·noe [kə`nu] 🎧 *Track 0720*
n. 獨木舟
▶ We crossed the river in a canoe. 我們搭獨木舟過河。
v. 划獨木舟
▶ We had to canoe across the river. 我們必須得划獨木舟過河。

相關片語
paddle one's own canoe 自力更生；獨立自主
▶ He started paddling his own canoe after graduating from college. 他在大學畢業之後，就開始自力更生了。

can't [kænt] 🎧 *Track 0721*
abbr. 不能、不會

can·vas [`kænvəs] 🎧 *Track 0722*
n. 帆布；油畫；風帆
▶ She carried a canvas bag on her shoulder. 她肩上背了個帆布包。

can·yon [`kænjən] 🎧 *Track 0723*
n. 峽谷
▶ The Grand Canyon is a famous tourist attraction in America. 大峽谷是美國著名的觀光景點。

補充片語
tourist attraction 觀光景點

cap [kæp] 🎧 *Track 0724*
n. 無邊便帽；制服帽

ca·pa·bil·i·ty [ˌkepə`bɪlətɪ] 🎧 *Track 0725*
n. 能力；才能；性能；潛力
▶ Tom proved to us that he had the capability to manage a branch office. 湯姆向我們證明他有管理一間分公司的能力。

ca·pa·ble [`kepəbl̩] 🎧 *Track 0726*
adj. 有能力做……的；能夠做……的；能幹的；有才華的
▶ He is capable of managing a branch office. 他有能力管理一間分公司。

ca·pac·i·ty [kə`pæsətɪ] 🎧 *Track 0727*
n. 容量；能量；生產力；能力；資格
▶ The arena has a capacity of 20,000. 這個巨蛋體育場能容納兩萬名觀眾。
adj. 達到最大限度的
▶ The diva singer's farewell concert drew capacity attendance. 那位天后歌手的告別演唱會當天是座無虛席。

cape [kep] 🎧 Track 0728
n. 披肩；斗篷
▶ Both Superman and Batman wear capes while Spiderman doesn't.
超人和蝙蝠俠都有穿披肩，但蜘蛛人沒有。

cap·i·tal [`kæpət!] 🎧 Track 0729
n. 資金；資本；本錢；首都
▶ We need more capital to expand our factory buildings.
我們需要更多資金來擴建廠房。

adj. 主要的；首位的；重要的
▶ I've made a decision of capital importance.
我做了一個至關重要的決定。

cap·i·tal·is·m 🎧 Track 0730
[`kæpət!͵ɪzəm]
n. 資本主義
▶ Property is privately owned under capitalism.
在資本主義制度下，財產是私有的。

cap·i·tal·ist [`kæpət!ɪst] 🎧 Track 0731
adj. 資本主義的；資本家的；擁有資本的
▶ The United States of America is a capitalist country.
美國是個不折不扣資本主義國家。

n. 資本主義者；資本家；有錢人
▶ Most capitalists are careful and clever investors.
大部份的資本家都是謹慎明智的投資者。

cap·tain [`kæptɪn] 🎧 Track 0732
n. 船長；機長；隊長；領隊

cap·tion [`kæpʃən] 🎧 Track 0733
n. 標題；字幕；說明
▶ The funny caption has attracted thousands of people to watch this video.
有趣的標題已經吸引數以千計的人來看這部影片。

v. 加標題於
▶ You can caption this video to attract more people to watch it.
你可以為這個影片加上標題，吸引更多人來看。

cap·ture [`kæptʃɚ] 🎧 Track 0734
v. 捕獲；佔領；奪得；引起（注意）；（用照片）捕捉
▶ Her beautiful voice captured the audience's attention.
她美妙的聲音擄獲觀眾的注意力。

n. 俘虜；佔領；捕獲物；戰利品
▶ The man played dead to escape capture.
男子裝死，以避免被逮。

car [kɑr] 🎧 Track 0735
n. 汽車

car·bon [`kɑrbən] 🎧 Track 0736
n. 碳
▶ By walking or riding a bike, we can avoid carbon emissions completely.
透過走路或騎單車，我們可以完全避免碳排放。

（補充片語）
carbon emissions 碳排放

card [kɑrd] 🎧 Track 0737
n. 卡片

card·board [`kɑrd͵bord] 🎧 Track 0738
n. 硬紙板
▶ I was surprised to know that this table is made of cardboard. 知道這張桌子是用硬紙板做的，讓我很驚訝。

adj. 硬紙板的；虛構的
▶ He packed his old magazines in a cardboard box.
他將他的舊雜誌裝在一個硬紙板箱裡。

care [kɛr] 🎧 Track 0739
n. 看護；照料；所關心之事；用心
v. 關心；在意；喜歡

ca·reer [kə`rɪr] 🎧 Track 0740
n. 事業；（終身）職業

care·free [`kɛr͵fri] 🎧 Track 0741
adj. 無憂無慮的；輕鬆愉快的
▶ We had a carefree vacation in Bali.
我們在峇里島度過了一個輕鬆愉快的假期。

care·ful [`kɛrfəl] 🎧 Track 0742
adj. 小心的；注意的

Aa
Bb
Cc
Dd
Ee

Ff
Gg
Hh
Ii
Jj

Kk
Ll
Mm
Nn
Oo

Pp
Qq
Rr
Ss
Tt

Uu
Vv
Ww
Xx
Yy
Zz

※灰色單字為英檢初級必備單字

care·less [`kɛrlɪs`] 🎧 *Track 0743*
adj. 粗心的

car·go [`kargo`] 🎧 *Track 0744*
n. （裝載的）貨物
▶ This truck can carry up to 1000 pounds of cargo.
這輛卡車可以載重高達1000磅的貨物。

car·na·tion [kar`neʃən`] 🎧 *Track 0745*
n. 康乃馨
▶ He bought a bunch of carnations for his mother on Mother's Day. 他在母親節這天買了一束康乃馨送給他的媽媽。

car·ni·val [`karnəvl`] 🎧 *Track 0746*
n. 嘉年華會
▶ This year we must grab a good spot to watch the carnival parade.
今年我們一定要佔一個可以觀賞嘉年華遊行的好位子。
(補充片語)
carnival parade 嘉年華會遊行

car·pen·ter [`karpəntɚ`] 🎧 *Track 0747*
n. 木匠
▶ Mr. Peterson is a very skillful carpenter.
皮特森先生是個技藝非常高超的木匠。

car·pet [`karpɪt`] 🎧 *Track 0748*
n. 地毯

car·riage [`kærɪdʒ`] 🎧 *Track 0749*
n. 四輪馬車；火車車廂；嬰兒車；運費
▶ How much do you charge for carriage?
你們運費要收多少？
(相關片語)
baby carriage 嬰兒車
▶ I'd like to check in this baby carriage.
我想要託運這個嬰兒車。

car·ri·er [`kærɪɚ`] 🎧 *Track 0750*
n. 運送人；送信者；從事運輸事業者；（車上的）置物架；帶菌者
▶ Mosquitoes are main carriers of various viruses such as dengue fever.
蚊子是各種病毒如登革熱的主要媒介物。

(相關片語)
mail carrier 郵差；郵車
▶ The mail carrier always comes around 9 a.m.
郵差大概都是早上九點時會來。

car·rot [`kærət`] 🎧 *Track 0751*
n. 紅蘿蔔

car·ry [`kæri`] 🎧 *Track 0752*
v. 扛、抱、拿、背、提、搬等

cart [kart] 🎧 *Track 0753*
n. 推車 **v.** 用運貨車裝運

car·ton [`kartn`] 🎧 *Track 0754*
n. 紙盒；紙板箱
▶ He bought a few cartons of cigarettes at the duty free shop.
他在免稅商店買了幾條香菸。

v. 用紙盒裝；製作紙盒
▶ He took out the cartoned milk from the fridge.
他從冰箱拿出盒裝牛奶。

car·toon [kar`tun`] 🎧 *Track 0755*
n. 卡通

carve [karv] 🎧 *Track 0756*
v. 雕刻；切開；開拓
▶ The old carpenter carved a bird from a piece of wood.
老木匠用一塊木頭雕出一隻鳥。

case [kes] 🎧 *Track 0757*
n. 箱子、盒子；事件、案例

cash [kæʃ] 🎧 *Track 0758*
n. 現金 **v.** 兌現

cash·ier [kæ`ʃɪr`] 🎧 *Track 0759*
n. 出納；出納員
▶ Lillian works in the supermarket as a cashier.
莉莉安在那間超市當出納員。

cas·sette [kə`sɛt`] 🎧 *Track 0760*
n. 卡式錄音帶或錄影帶

cast [kæst] 🎧 *Track 0761*

n. 拋；擲；班底、演員陣容

▶I want to see that movie because I am really attracted by its cast.
我想去看那部電影，因為它的演員陣容實在很吸引我。

v. 丟，擲；投射（光影或視線）；鑄造

▶He cast the net into the sea, hoping to catch some fish.
他把網子拋到海中，希望能捕到一些魚。

cas·tle [`kæsl] 🎧 *Track 0762*

n. 城堡

cas·u·al [`kæʒʊəl] 🎧 *Track 0763*

adj. 偶然的；隨便的；不拘禮節的；非正式的

▶It's a casual party. Just wear whatever you feel comfortable in. 這是個非正式的派對。穿你覺得舒服的衣服就行了。

cas·u·al·ty [`kæʒʊəltɪ] 🎧 *Track 0764*

n. 傷亡人員；傷亡人數；受害者

▶Both sides suffered heavy casualties.
雙方傷亡都很慘重。

cat [kæt] 🎧 *Track 0765*

n. 貓

cat·al·og [`kætəlɔg] 🎧 *Track 0766*
=cat·al·ogue (英式英文)

n. 目錄；型錄

▶I browsed through the catalog but nothing really captured my eyes.
我瀏覽了一下型錄，但是沒有東西能真正吸引我的注意。

v. 編目錄；登記

▶The new products are being cataloged.
新產品正在編入型錄中。

ca·tas·tro·phe 🎧 *Track 0767*
[kə`tæstrəfɪ]

n. 大災難；慘敗；天翻地覆的事件

▶The earthquake in Nepal was a major natural catastrophe.
尼泊爾的地震是一場重大的天災。

catch [kætʃ] 🎧 *Track 0768*

v. 抓、接；趕上 **n.** 抓、接

cat·e·go·ry [`kætə,gorɪ] 🎧 *Track 0769*

n. 種類；類目；範疇

▶This book should be put in the sci-fi category. 這本書應該歸在科幻類。

cat·er·pil·lar 🎧 *Track 0770*
[`kætə,pɪlə]

n. 毛毛蟲

▶The caterpillar has turned into a beautiful butterfly.
毛毛蟲已經變成一隻美麗的蝴蝶了。

cat·tle [`kætl] 🎧 *Track 0771*

n. 牛；牲畜

▶There are over a hundred cattle on the farm. 這個農場上有超過一百頭牛。

cause [kɔz] 🎧 *Track 0772*

v. 引起、導致 **n.** 原因、起因；理由

cave [kev] 🎧 *Track 0773*

n. 洞穴；洞窟 **v.** 塌陷；屈服

cav·i·ty [`kævətɪ] 🎧 *Track 0774*

n. 洞；穴；（身體的）腔室；（牙的）蛀洞

▶The dentist found a few cavities in my teeth. 牙醫在我牙齒上找到幾個蛀洞。

CD [si-di] 🎧 *Track 0775*
=comp·act disk

n. 光碟

cease [sis] 🎧 *Track 0776*

v. 停止；終止；結束

▶My love for you will never cease.
我對你的愛是永遠不會停止的。

n. 停止

▶They prayed for his recovery without cease. 他們不停地為他的康復而祈禱。

(補充片語)

without cease 不停地

cei·ling [`silɪŋ] 🎧 *Track 0777*

n. 天花板

Aa
Bb
Cc
Dd
Ee
Ff
Gg
Hh
Ii
Jj
Kk
Ll
Mm
Nn
Oo
Pp
Qq
Rr
Ss
Tt
Uu
Vv
Ww
Xx
Yy
Zz

※灰色單字為英檢初級必備單字

cel·e·brate [ˈsɛləˌbret]　🎧 *Track 0778*
v. 慶祝

cel·e·bra·tion　🎧 *Track 0779*
[ˌsɛləˈbreʃən]
n. 慶祝
▶ The party is held in celebration of his recovery.
這派對是為了慶祝他恢復健康而舉辦的。

ce·leb·ri·ty [sɪˈlɛbrətɪ]　🎧 *Track 0780*
n. 名流；名人
▶ Even celebrities need privacy.
就算是名人，也需要隱私。

cell [sɛl]　🎧 *Track 0781*
n. 細胞

cel·lar [ˈsɛlə]　🎧 *Track 0782*
n. 地下室；地窖；酒窖
▶ We have a cellar in this house.
我們這房子裡有個地窖。

cel·lo [ˈtʃɛlo]　🎧 *Track 0783*
n. 大提琴
▶ She started taking cello lessons when she was five.
她五歲就開始上大提琴課了。

cell-phone [sɛl-fon]　🎧 *Track 0784*
n. 行動電話
▶ Cell-phones are commonplace today.
行動電話現在是很普遍的。

ce·ment [səˈmɛnt]　🎧 *Track 0785*
n. 水泥
▶ The cement is fully mixed.
水泥已經充分攪拌好了。
v. 用水泥塗；用水泥接合
▶ He cemented bricks to concrete to build a wall. 他將磚頭用水泥接合，使之凝固以造一面牆。

cem·e·tery [ˈsɛməˌtɛrɪ]　🎧 *Track 0786*
n. 墓地
▶ He doesn't know his friend was buried in which cemetery.
他不知道他的朋友被埋在哪一個墓地。

cent [sɛnt]　🎧 *Track 0787*
n. 一分（美元）

cent·er [ˈsɛntə]　🎧 *Track 0788*
=cent·re（英式英文）
n. 中心點；中央
v. 以……為中心；使集中

cen·ti·met·er [ˈsɛntəˌmitə]　🎧 *Track 0789*
=cen·ti·met·re（英式英文）
n. 公分

cen·tral [ˈsɛntrəl]　🎧 *Track 0790*
adj. 中心的；中央的

cen·tu·ry [ˈsɛntʃʊrɪ]　🎧 *Track 0791*
n. 世紀

ce·re·al [ˈsɪrɪəl]　🎧 *Track 0792*
n. 麥片；穀類加工食品

cer·e·mo·ny [ˈsɛrəˌmonɪ]　🎧 *Track 0793*
n. 儀式；典禮
▶ Everyone was dressed to the nines for the awards ceremony.
每個人都穿得非常講究地來參加頒獎典禮。
（補充片語）
be dressed to the nines 穿著講究

cer·tain [ˈsɝˌtən]　🎧 *Track 0794*
adj. 確信的；某……；某種程度的

cer·tain·ly [ˈsɝˌtənlɪ]　🎧 *Track 0795*
adv. 無疑地；當然

cer·tif·i·cate　🎧 *Track 0796*
[səˈtɪfəkɪt]
n. 證書；執照；憑證
▶ He didn't know that he was not his parents' biological son until he saw his birth certificate.
一直到他看到自己的出生證明，才知道自己不是父母的親生兒子。
（補充片語）
biological son 親生兒子；
birth certificate 出生證明

chain [tʃen] 🎧 *Track 0797*

n. 鏈條；項圈；一連串；連鎖店

▶ The burglar was finally arrested and ended up in chains.
那個夜賊終於落網，最後被囚禁了。

(補充片語)

end up 以……為結局；
in chains （囚犯）被鏈鎖住的；被囚禁的

v. 用鏈拴住；拘禁

▶ He chained his dog to a streetlight pole.
他把狗用鏈拴在路燈桿上。

(相關片語)

chain smoker 一根接著一根抽煙的人

▶ I can't stand living with a chain smoker.
我不能忍受跟一個菸抽個不停的人住在一起。

chair [tʃɛr] 🎧 *Track 0798*

n. 椅子

chair·man [`tʃɛrmən] 🎧 *Track 0799*

n. 主席；議長；（大學）系主任

chalk [tʃɔk] 🎧 *Track 0800*

n. 粉筆

chal·lenge [`tʃælɪndʒ] 🎧 *Track 0801*

n. 挑戰；艱鉅的事；異議、質疑

▶ To manage a team of thirty people is a real challenge to me.
管理一個三十個人的團隊，對我來說的確是個挑戰。

v. 向……挑戰；對……提出異議；激發

▶ Professor Lee always encourages his students to challenge conventional wisdom.
李教授總是鼓勵他的學生們對一般人對事物的看法提出質疑。

cham·ber [`tʃembɚ] 🎧 *Track 0802*

n. 房間；寢室；會場；會議廳；（體內的）腔室

▶ The human heart is a muscular organ with four chambers.
人類的心臟是有四個腔室的肌肉器官。

cham·pagne [ʃæm`pen] 🎧 *Track 0803*

n. 香檳；香檳酒

▶ The waiter filled my glass with champagne.
侍者在我的杯子裡斟滿香檳酒。

cham·pi·on [`tʃæmpɪən] 🎧 *Track 0804*

n. 冠軍；優勝者

▶ Jack practiced very hard because he wanted to become the champion.
傑克很努力地練習，是因為他想要成為冠軍。

v. 擁護；支持；為……而戰

▶ They championed the cause of liberty. 他們為了自由而戰。

cham·pi·on·ship 🎧 *Track 0805*
[`tʃæmpɪənˌʃɪp]

n. 優勝；冠軍地位；錦標賽

▶ The young player is very likely to win the World Cup Tennis Championships.
該年輕選手很有希望贏得世界盃網球錦標賽。

chance [tʃæns] 🎧 *Track 0806*

n. 機會

change [tʃendʒ] 🎧 *Track 0807*

n. 改變；變化 **v.** 改變；變動

change·a·ble 🎧 *Track 0808*
[`tʃendʒəbl]

adj. 易變的；不定的

▶ Peter is difficult to get along with because his temper is quite changeable.
彼得很難相處，因為他的脾氣陰晴不定。

chan·nel [`tʃænl] 🎧 *Track 0809*

n. 水道；航道；頻道

chant [tʃænt] 🎧 *Track 0810*

n. 歌；曲子；詠唱

▶ I've never heard this chant before.
我以前沒聽過這首曲子。

v. 吟誦；反覆地唱

▶ The kids are chanting the Rules for Students. 孩子們在吟誦弟子規。

cha·os [`keɑs] 🎧 *Track 0811*

n. 混亂；雜亂的一團

▶ The flood caused chaos throughout the village. 洪水讓這村莊各處混亂成一團。

※灰色單字為英檢初級必備單字

chap·ter [ˈtʃæptə] 🎧 *Track 0812*
n. （書籍的）章；回

char·ac·ter [ˈkærɪktə] 🎧 *Track 0813*
n. （人的）性格；（事物的）特質；（戲劇或小說的）人物角色

char·ac·ter·is·tic 🎧 *Track 0814*
[ˌkærəktəˈrɪstɪk]
n. 特性；特徵；特色
▶ Excellent service is a key characteristic of a successful hotel.
出色的服務是一間成功的飯店的關鍵特色。

adj. 特有的；表示特性的
▶ Indecision is characteristic of my husband.
猶豫不決是我老公的特性。

charge [tʃɑrdʒ] 🎧 *Track 0815*
n. 費用；掌管 **v.** 索費；指控

char·i·ty [ˈtʃærətɪ] 🎧 *Track 0816*
n. 慈悲；慈善；施捨；善舉；慈善事業
▶ The old man donated all his money to charities before he died.
老翁在死前將所有的錢都捐給慈善團體了。

charm [tʃɑrm] 🎧 *Track 0817*
n. 魅力；符咒、護身符
▶ Those fans are dazzled by his charm and good looks, not his acting skills.
那些粉絲是被他的魅力和俊美的外表所迷惑，而非他的演技。

v. 使陶醉；吸引；對……施魔法
▶ Kids were charmed by the puppet show.
孩子們都被木偶戲給迷住了。

(相關片語)
work like a charm 十分奏效地；迅速地成功
▶ The painkillers worked like a charm.
這止痛藥一吃就有效。

charm·ing [ˈtʃɑrmɪŋ] 🎧 *Track 0818*
adj. 迷人的；有魅力的
▶ Our new office assistant is a charming young lady.
我們的新辦公室助理是個迷人的年輕小姐。

chart [tʃɑrt] 🎧 *Track 0819*
n. 圖表

chase [tʃes] 🎧 *Track 0820*
v. 追逐；追求

chat [tʃæt] 🎧 *Track 0821*
n. 聊天
▶ He likes to have a chat with his students after class. 他下課後喜歡跟學生聊天。

v. 聊天
▶ The girls are chatting about the latest Korean dramas. 女孩們在聊著最新的韓劇。

(補充片語)
water cooler chat 辦公室閒聊

cheap [tʃip] 🎧 *Track 0822*
adj. 便宜的；廉價的

cheat [tʃit] 🎧 *Track 0823*
v. 欺騙；行騙；作弊
n. 騙子；欺詐；作弊

check [tʃɛk] 🎧 *Track 0824*
=cheque （英式英文）
n. 支票

check·out [ˈtʃɛkˌaʊt] 🎧 *Track 0825*
n. 結帳離開；付款櫃台
▶ The checkout time is 11 a.m.
結帳退房的時間是上午十一點。

cheek [tʃik] 🎧 *Track 0826*
n. 臉頰；腮幫子；傲慢態度；厚臉皮
▶ Tears streamed down her cheeks.
眼淚汩汩落下她的臉頰。

(相關片語)
have the cheek to do sth. 厚者臉皮做某事
▶ She had the cheek to pass the buck to me. 她竟有臉把責任都推到我身上。

(補充片語)
pass the buck to sb. 將責任或過失推給某人

cheer [tʃɪr] 🎧 *Track 0827*
v. 歡呼；使振奮、高興
n. 歡呼；喝彩；鼓勵

cheer·ful [ˈtʃɪrfəl] 　🎧 *Track 0828*
adj. 興高采烈的；使人愉快的；樂意的
▶ Whenever I feel down, I listen to a cheerful song to cheer myself up.
每當我感到情緒低落時，我就會聽一首開心的歌讓自己高興起來。

cheese [tʃiz] 　🎧 *Track 0829*
n. 乳酪；乾酪

chef [ʃɛf] 　🎧 *Track 0830*
n. （餐館的）主廚；廚師；大廚師
▶ It is every chef's dream to win three Michelin stars.
贏得米其林三星是每一個廚師的夢想。

chem·i·cal [ˈkɛmɪkl] 　🎧 *Track 0831*
n. 化學製品；化學藥品
adj. 化學的；化學上的

chem·ist [ˈkɛmɪst] 　🎧 *Track 0832*
n. 化學家
▶ The chemist buries himself in all kinds of chemistry experiments all day. 這化學家整天都埋首於各種化學實驗中。

（補充片語）
bury oneself in sth. 埋首致力於某事物

chem·is·try [ˈkɛmɪstrɪ] 　🎧 *Track 0833*
n. 化學；化學作用
▶ He accidentally burnt himself when he was doing a chemistry experiment.
他在做一個化學實驗時，不小心燒傷自己了。

cher·ish [ˈtʃɛrɪʃ] 　🎧 *Track 0834*
v. 珍惜
▶ I cherish every moment I spend with the people I love.
我珍惜與我所愛的人所度過的每一刻。

cher·ry [ˈtʃɛrɪ] 　🎧 *Track 0835*
n. 櫻桃；櫻桃樹；櫻桃色
▶ The cherries on the tree are ripe enough to pick.
樹上的櫻桃已經夠熟，可以摘了。

chess [tʃɛs] 　🎧 *Track 0836*
n. 西洋棋

chest [tʃɛst] 　🎧 *Track 0837*
n. 胸口、胸膛；五斗櫃
▶ I feel a pain in my chest.
我感覺胸口疼痛。

相關片語
get sth. off one's chest 將某事傾吐出來
▶ You might feel better if you get your sorrow off your chest. 如果你將心中的悲傷說出來，可能就會舒服一點。

chew [tʃu] 　🎧 *Track 0838*
v. 嚼；咀嚼；嚼碎；深思細想
▶ You need to chew before you swallow.
吞嚥之前要先咀嚼一下。

相關片語
chew the fat 閒聊；發牢騷
▶ Come over and chew the fat with us.
過來跟我們一起閒聊。

chick [tʃɪk] 　🎧 *Track 0839*
n. 小雞；少女；小妞

chick·en [ˈtʃɪkɪn] 　🎧 *Track 0840*
n. 小雞；雞肉

chief [tʃif] 　🎧 *Track 0841*
adj. 主要的；等級最高的
n. 首長；長官

child [tʃaɪld] 　🎧 *Track 0842*
n. 孩子；孩童

child·birth [ˈtʃaɪld͵bɝθ] 　🎧 *Track 0843*
n. 分娩；生產
▶ Mr. Johnson's wife died during childbirth three years ago.
強森先生的妻子三年前生產時死了。

child·hood [ˈtʃaɪld͵hʊd] 　🎧 *Track 0844*
n. 童年

child·ish [ˈtʃaɪldɪʃ] 　🎧 *Track 0845*
adj. 孩子般的；幼稚的

child·like [ˈtʃaɪld͵laɪk] 　🎧 *Track 0846*
adj. 孩子般的；天真的；單純的

chill [tʃɪl] 　🎧 *Track 0847*
n. 寒冷；寒氣；風寒；掃興

Aa Bb Cc Dd Ee
Ff Gg Hh Ii Jj
Kk Ll Mm Nn Oo
Pp Qq Rr Ss Tt
Uu Vv Ww Xx Yy Zz

※灰色單字為英檢初級必備單字

▶ A nice down coat is what you need to beat the winter chill. 一件好的羽絨衣正是你需要用來擊退冬日寒氣的東西。

(補充片語)

down coat 羽絨衣

adj. 冷颼颼的；冷淡的；使人寒心的；冷靜的

▶ He's very chill. Nothing makes him excited. 他很冷靜，沒什麼事能讓他興奮。

(相關片語)

catch a chill 著涼

▶ I feel under the weather today. I might have caught a chill. 我今天覺得不太舒服。我大概是著涼了。

chill·y [`tʃɪlɪ]　🎧 *Track 0848*

adj. 冷颼颼的；冷淡的；使人寒心的

▶ It's pretty chilly today. We should turn on the heater. 今天蠻冷的。我們應該要開暖氣。

chim·ney [`tʃɪmnɪ]　🎧 *Track 0849*

n. 煙囪

▶ The kids are wondering how Santa is going to get into the house if we don't have a chimney. 孩子們在想，如果我們沒有煙囪，聖誕老人要怎麼進到屋子裡來。

chim·pan·zee 🎧 *Track 0850*
[ˌtʃɪmpæn`zi]

n. 黑猩猩

▶ The teacher explained the differences between a chimpanzee and a gorilla to the students. 老師向學生解釋黑猩猩和大猩猩之間的差異。

chin [tʃɪn]　🎧 *Track 0851*

n. 下巴

chi·na [`tʃaɪnə]　🎧 *Track 0852*

n. 瓷器；陶瓷器

▶ Please be careful with these china cups. 請務必小心輕放這些瓷杯。

Chi·nese [`tʃaɪ`niz]　🎧 *Track 0853*

adj. 中國的；中國人的　**n.** 中國人

chip [tʃɪp]　🎧 *Track 0854*

n. 碎片；炸洋芋片；瑣碎之物

▶ I can't believe I ate up a whole bag of chips. 我不敢相信我竟然把一整包洋芋片都吃光了。

v. 削；鑿；把……切成薄片

▶ He chipped a hole in the wall. 他在牆上鑿了一個洞。

(相關片語)

chip in for 為……而湊錢

▶ Let's chip in for a pizza, shall we? 咱們一起湊錢買個比薩，好嗎？

chirp [tʃɝp]　🎧 *Track 0855*

v. 發出啾啾聲；唧唧喳喳地說話

▶ I heard the birds chirping in the tree. 我聽到樹上的小鳥啾啾地叫著。

n. 啾啾聲；唧唧聲

▶ I was woken by the chirps of the birds this morning. 我今天早上是被小鳥的啾啾聲吵醒的。

cho·co·late [`tʃɑkəlɪt]　🎧 *Track 0856*

n. 巧克力；巧克力糖；巧克力飲料

choice [tʃɔɪs]　🎧 *Track 0857*

n. 選擇

choir [kwaɪr]　🎧 *Track 0858*

n. 合唱團；唱詩班

▶ She's a soprano in the choir. 她在合唱團裡唱女高音。

choke [tʃok]　🎧 *Track 0859*

v. 使窒息；掐住脖子；哽住；說不出話來；塞住

▶ I thought I would be choked to death until he let go of me. 在他放開我之前，我還以為我會被掐死。

(補充片語)

choke sb. to death 把某人掐死；
let go of 鬆開、釋放

n. 窒息；噎

▶ She told us what happened with a choke in her voice. 她語帶哽咽地告訴我們發生了什麼事。

cho·les·te·rol 🎧 *Track 0860*
[kə`lɛstə,rol]
n. 膽固醇
▶ Not all cholesterol is bad for health.
並非所有的膽固醇都是有害健康的。

choose [tʃuz] 🎧 *Track 0861*
v. 選擇

chop [tʃɑp] 🎧 *Track 0862*
v. 砍；劈；切細、剁碎
▶ Could you chop up these onions for me?
你可以幫我把這些洋蔥剁碎嗎？

n. 砍；劈；剁；肋骨肉、排骨
▶ I'd like to have Japanese fried pork chops
with rice. 我想吃日式炸豬排配飯。

chop·stick [`tʃɑp,stɪk] 🎧 *Track 0863*
n. 筷子

chore [tʃor] 🎧 *Track 0864*
n. 家庭雜務；日常瑣碎而例行的工作
▶ Everyone in the house should share the
chores. 屋子裡的每一個人都應該要一起分擔
家庭雜務。

cho·rus [`korəs] 🎧 *Track 0865*
n. 合唱團；合唱曲；副歌
▶ My favorite part of the song is the chorus.
我在這首歌中最喜歡的地方就是副歌。

Chris·tian [`krɪstʃən] 🎧 *Track 0866*
adj. 基督教的
▶ Christmas is a Christian festival
celebrated on December 25 around the
world.
聖誕節是一個全世界在十二月二十五日一起慶
祝的基督教節慶。

n. 基督教徒
▶ Christmas is a holiday celebrated by
Christians around the world.
聖誕節是一個全世界的基督徒共同慶祝的節
日。

Christ·mas [`krɪsməs] 🎧 *Track 0867*
=X·mas
n. 聖誕節

chub·by [`tʃʌbɪ] 🎧 *Track 0868*
adj. 豐腴的；圓胖的

church [tʃɝtʃ] 🎧 *Track 0869*
n. 教堂

ci·gar [sɪ`gɑr] 🎧 *Track 0870*
n. 雪茄煙
▶ The old cowboy lit a cigar and smoked
it. 老牛仔點了一支雪茄煙抽了起來。

cig·a·rette [,sɪgə`rɛt] 🎧 *Track 0871*
n. 香菸
▶ He smokes at least two packs of cigarettes
a day.
他一天至少要抽兩包菸。

cin·e·ma [`sɪnəmə] 🎧 *Track 0872*
n. 電影院；一部電影
▶ Let's go to the cinema this weekend,
shall we? 我們這週末去看電影，好嗎？

（補充片語）
go to the cinema 去看電影

cir·cle [`sɝkl̩] 🎧 *Track 0873*
n. 圓圈

cir·cu·lar [`sɝkjələ] 🎧 *Track 0874*
adj. 圓的；迂迴的；拐彎抹角的
▶ All twelve of us sat around the circular
table. 我們十二個人全都圍著圓桌而坐。

cir·cu·late [`sɝkjə,let] 🎧 *Track 0875*
v. 循環；傳播；流通
▶ The rumor was rapidly circulated through
the office.
流言很快就在辦公室裡傳開了。

cir·cu·la·tion 🎧 *Track 0876*
[,sɝkjə`leʃən]
n. 循環；（貨幣或消息的）傳播；（報刊
的）發行
▶ Gingers and garlic are both healthy foods
that help improve blood circulation. 薑和
蒜頭都是可以幫助促進血液循環的健康食物。

（補充片語）
blood circulation 血液循環

※灰色單字為英檢初級必備單字

cir·cum·stance [ˋsɝkəmˏstæns]
🎧 *Track 0877*

n. 情況；環境

▶ Under no circumstances should you hurt your wife. 無論在什麼樣的情況下，你都不應該傷害老婆。

(補充片語)

under no circumstances 在任何情況下都不⋯⋯

cir·cus [ˋsɝkəs]
🎧 *Track 0878*

n. 馬戲團；馬戲表演

▶ We went to the circus last weekend. 我們上週末去看馬戲團表演。

cit·i·zen [ˋsɪtəzn]
🎧 *Track 0879*

n. 市民；居民；公民

cit·y [ˋsɪtɪ]
🎧 *Track 0880*

n. 城市

civ·il [ˋsɪvḷ]
🎧 *Track 0881*

adj. 市民的；民用的；民事的；文明的；國內的

▶ People in that country suffered a great deal during the four years of civil war. 那個國家的人民在四年內戰期間受了很多苦。

(補充片語)

civil war 內戰

ci·vil·ian [sɪˋvɪljən]
🎧 *Track 0882*

adj. 平民的；百姓的

▶ The civil war resulted in thousands of civilian casualties. 這場內戰造成數以千計的老百姓傷亡。

n. 平民；百姓

▶ The civilians were beat up by the bandits. 那些老百姓被劫匪打了。

civ·i·li·za·tion [ˏsɪvḷəˋzeʃən]
🎧 *Track 0883*

n. 文明；文明國家；文明世界；文明設施；開化

▶ Ancient Egypt was one of the oldest civilizations on earth. 古埃及是世界上最古老的文明之一。

civ·i·lize [ˋsɪvəˏlaɪz]
🎧 *Track 0884*

v. 使文明；使開化；教化；熏陶；使有教養

▶ He doesn't behave like a civilized person. 他表現得並不像是個有教養的人。

claim [klem]
🎧 *Track 0885*

v. 要求；主張；聲稱

n. 要求；主張；斷言

clap [klæp]
🎧 *Track 0886*

v. 拍（手）；鼓（掌）**n.** 拍手鼓掌；喝彩

clar·i·fy [ˋklærəˏfaɪ]
🎧 *Track 0887*

v. 澄清；闡明

▶ If he had clarified the misunderstanding earlier, we wouldn't have got divorced. 如果他有早一點澄清誤會，我們就不會離婚了。

clash [klæʃ]
🎧 *Track 0888*

n. 碰撞聲；衝突；不協調

▶ The negotiation ended up in a violent clash. 談判在激烈的衝突中結束。

(補充片語)

end up in 以⋯⋯結束

v. 碰地相撞；發生衝突；抵觸

▶ The color of my jacket clashed with that of my jeans. 我外套和牛仔褲的顏色相衝了。

class [klæs]
🎧 *Track 0889*

n. 班級；課；（社會）階級、等級

clas·sic [ˋklæsɪk]
🎧 *Track 0890*

adj. 典型的；經典的

n. 典型事物；著名事件；經典名著

clas·si·cal [ˋklæsɪkḷ]
🎧 *Track 0891*

adj. 經典的，古典的

clas·si·fi·ca·tion [ˏklæsəfəˋkeʃən]
🎧 *Track 0892*

n. 分類；類別

▶ Biographies and literature are books of different classifications. 傳記和文學作品是不同類別的書。

clas·si·fy [ˋklæsəˌfaɪ]　🎧 *Track 0893*
v. 將……分類；將……歸類
▶ This document has been classified confidential.
這份文件已經被歸類為機密文件。

class·mate [ˋklæsˌmet]　🎧 *Track 0894*
n. 同班同學

class·room [ˋklæsˌrʊm]　🎧 *Track 0895*
n. 教室
▶ The teacher decorated the classroom with the students' paintings.
老師用學生們的畫作來佈置教室。

claw [klɔ]　🎧 *Track 0896*
n. 爪子；手
v. 用爪子抓、撕、挖；費力奪回

clay [kle]　🎧 *Track 0897*
n. 黏土；泥土

clean [klin]　🎧 *Track 0898*
v. 清潔　**adj.** 乾淨的

clean·er [ˋklinɚ]　🎧 *Track 0899*
n. 清潔工；乾洗店；清潔劑

cleanse [klɛnz]　🎧 *Track 0900*
v. 清乾淨
▶ You can cleanse your face with this cream.
你可以用這個乳霜清洗你的臉。

clear [klɪr]　🎧 *Track 0901*
adj. 清楚的；清澈的
v. 清除；收拾；使乾淨；使清楚

clear·ance [ˋklɪrəns]　🎧 *Track 0902*
n. 清除；出空；清倉大拍賣
▶ Everything in the store is 70% off during the clearance sale.
店內所有商品在清倉特賣期間都打三折。

(補充片語)
clearance sale　清倉特賣；出清特賣

clerk [klɝk]　🎧 *Track 0903*
n. 店員；辦事員

clev·er [ˋklɛvɚ]　🎧 *Track 0904*
adj. 聰明的；靈巧的

click [klɪk]　🎧 *Track 0905*
v. 發出咔嗒聲；按壓滑鼠以點選
▶ He clicked the icon and opened the document file.
他點了一下電腦圖示，打開了文件夾。

n. 咔嗒聲；按一下滑鼠
▶ You will hear a click when it is firmly in place.
當它緊緊地裝好時，你會聽到咔嗒的一聲。

cli·ent [ˋklaɪənt]　🎧 *Track 0906*
n. 客戶
▶ I'm going downtown to visit a client this afternoon.
我今天下午要到市區去拜訪一位客戶。

cliff [klɪf]　🎧 *Track 0907*
n. 懸崖
▶ He must be crazy to take a selfie on the edge of the cliff.
他一定是瘋了，才會在懸崖邊緣自拍。

cli·mate [ˋklaɪmɪt]　🎧 *Track 0908*
n. 氣候

cli·max [ˋklaɪmæks]　🎧 *Track 0909*
n. 頂點；最高點
▶ His career reached a climax when he was appointed as CEO of the company. 他的事業在他被任命為公司的總裁時達到最高峰。

climb [klaɪm]　🎧 *Track 0910*
v. 爬；攀爬

climb·er [ˋklaɪmɚ]　🎧 *Track 0911*
n. 攀登者；登山者
▶ The climbers trapped in the mountain are still waiting for rescue.
困在山裡頭的登山者仍在等待救援。

climb·ing [ˋklaɪmɪŋ]　🎧 *Track 0912*
n. 攀登
▶ Mountain climbing is really not my thing.
爬山真的不是我愛做的事。

※灰色單字為英檢初級必備單字

clin·ic [ˋklɪnɪk]
🎧 *Track 0913*
n. 診所；臨床授課；會診
▶I'm taking my son to the eye clinic.
我要帶我兒子去眼科診所。

clip [klɪp]
🎧 *Track 0914*
n. 夾；迴紋針
▶She fastened all the handouts with a paper clip. 她用迴紋針將所有講義夾緊。
v. 用夾子夾緊；用迴紋針夾住
▶She clipped the coupons together.
她把折價優惠券都用夾子夾在一起。

clock [klɑk]
🎧 *Track 0915*
n. 時鐘

clock·wise [ˋklɑk͵waɪz]
🎧 *Track 0916*
adj. 順時針方向的
▶She slowly stirred the soup in a clockwise direction while adding the eggs. 她一邊以順時針方向慢慢地攪拌著湯一邊把蛋加進去。
adv. 順時針方向地
▶Do you stir your coffee clockwise or counterclockwise? 你是以順時針方向或反時針方向攪拌你的咖啡？

clone [klon]
🎧 *Track 0917*
n. 翻版；複製人；複製品；一味仿效的人
▶The scientist tried to create a clone of himself from his own skin cells.
該科學家企圖用自己的皮膚細胞製作一個自己的複製人。

close [klos]
🎧 *Track 0918*
v. 關起；關閉；結束 **n.** 結束；末尾
adj.（距離）近的；（關係）親近的
adv. 接近地；緊密地

clos·et [ˋklɑzɪt]
🎧 *Track 0919*
n. 衣櫃

cloth [klɔθ]
🎧 *Track 0920*
n. 布；織物；衣料

clothe [kloð]
🎧 *Track 0921*
n. 為……穿衣；為……提供衣服

clothed [kloðd]
🎧 *Track 0922*
adj. 穿……衣服的
▶The man was fully clothed when he was found dead.
男子被發現死亡時，身上衣著完整。

clothes [kloz]
🎧 *Track 0923*
n. 衣服

cloth·ing [ˋkloðɪŋ]
🎧 *Track 0924*
n. 衣服；衣著

cloud [klaʊd]
🎧 *Track 0925*
n. 雲
▶Look at the dark clouds in the sky. Soon it's gonna rain.
你看天空的烏雲。馬上就要下雨了。
v.（煙霧）籠罩；瀰漫；使模糊；使混濁
▶Don't let love cloud your judgment.
別讓愛情擾亂了你的判斷力。

相關片語
on cloud nine 欣喜若狂；樂上雲霄
▶Jack was on cloud nine when his wife was pregnant again.
傑克在妻子再度懷孕時欣喜若狂。

cloud·y [ˋklaʊdɪ]
🎧 *Track 0926*
adj. 多雲的；陰天的

clo·ver [ˋklovɚ]
🎧 *Track 0927*
n. 紅花草；苜蓿；三葉草
▶Clovers are very common here.
三葉草在這裡很普遍。

相關片語
live in clover 生活優逸
▶After twenty years of hard work, they finally can live in clover.
在二十年的努力工作後，他們終於能過著安逸舒適的生活。

clown [klaʊn]
🎧 *Track 0928*
n. 小丑 **v.** 扮小丑；開玩笑；裝傻

club [klʌb]
🎧 *Track 0929*
n.（運動、娛樂等的）俱樂部；會所

clue [klu] 🎧 *Track 0930*
n. 線索；提示；跡象
▶ I don't have a clue what this button is for.
我不知道這個按鈕是要幹嘛用的。

clum·sy [`klʌmzɪ] 🎧 *Track 0931*
adj. 笨拙的
▶ The clumsy waitress poured coffee on the customer. 那個笨拙的女服務生把咖啡倒在客人身上了。

coach [kotʃ] 🎧 *Track 0932*
n. （運動隊的）教練；巴士；長途公車

coal [kol] 🎧 *Track 0933*
n. 煤；煤塊；木炭

coarse [kors] 🎧 *Track 0934*
adj. 粗的；粗糙的；粗劣的；粗俗的
▶ That joke was very coarse and was not fun at all.
那個笑話很粗俗，而且一點都不好笑。

coast [kost] 🎧 *Track 0935*
n. 海岸

coat [kot] 🎧 *Track 0936*
n. 外套；（動物的）皮毛

cock [kɑk] 🎧 *Track 0937*
n. 公雞

cock·roach [`kɑk͵rotʃ] 🎧 *Track 0938*
=roach
n. 蟑螂

cock·tail [`kɑk͵tel] 🎧 *Track 0939*
n. 雞尾酒
▶ A cocktail party will be given after the ceremony. 典禮之後會有一場雞尾酒會。

co·coa [`koko] 🎧 *Track 0940*
n. 可可粉

co·co·nut [`kokə͵nət] 🎧 *Track 0941*
n. 椰子；椰子肉
▶ A coconut fell out of the tree and hit him on the head.
一顆椰子從樹上掉下來，擊中他的頭。

相關片語
coconut milk 椰奶
▶ I always add some coconut milk in my Thai curry to balance the spice.
我通常會在泰式咖哩中加一些椰奶，以平衡香料的辣味。

code [kod] 🎧 *Track 0942*
n. 規則；代碼
▶ Business Formal is the standard dress code for a job interview.
商務正式服裝是工作面試的標準服裝規則。

補充片語
dress code 服裝規定

v. 為……編碼
▶ They are coding the new arrivals.
他們正在為新進商品編碼。

cof·fee [`kɔfɪ] 🎧 *Track 0943*
n. 咖啡

cof·fin [`kɔfɪn] 🎧 *Track 0944*
n. 棺材
▶ The man's body had been put in a coffin.
男子的屍體已經被放入棺材。

v. 入殮；將……放進棺材
▶ The old man died seven years ago but hasn't been coffined yet.
該老先生七年前死亡，至今尚未入殮。

相關片語
drive a nail into one's coffin 促死某人早死；加速某人死亡
▶ You are driving a nail into your coffin if you keep smoking so many cigarettes every day.
如果你繼續每天抽那麼多香菸，就會讓自己提早見閻羅王。

coin [kɔɪn] 🎧 *Track 0945*
n. 錢幣

co·in·ci·dence 🎧 *Track 0946*
[ko`ɪnsɪdəns]
n. 巧合；同時發生的事；符合
▶ It was a coincidence that we live in the same apartment building.
我們住在同一棟公寓大樓，純屬巧合。

Aa
Bb
Cc
Dd
Ee

Ff
Gg
Hh
Ii
Jj

Kk
Ll
Mm
Nn
Oo

Pp
Qq
Rr
Ss
Tt

Uu
Vv
Ww
Xx
Yy
Zz

※灰色單字為英檢初級必備單字

Coke [kok]　　🎧 *Track 0947*
n. 可樂

cold [kold]　　🎧 *Track 0948*
adj. 冷的　**n.** 寒冷；感冒

col·lapse [kə`læps]　　🎧 *Track 0949*
v. 倒塌；崩潰；瓦解
▶ The whole building collapsed during the earthquake.
整棟樓在地震發生時倒塌了。
n. 倒塌；崩潰；突然失敗；（健康）衰竭、垮掉
▶ The collapse of his health resulted from overwork.
他身體會垮掉是過度勞累所造成的。

col·lar [`kɑlɚ]　　🎧 *Track 0950*
n. 衣領、領子；狗的項圈
▶ We tried to reach the dog's owner by the phone number on its collar.
我們打項圈上的電話號碼，試圖聯繫狗狗的主人。

相關片語
get hot under the collar　發怒
▶ Steven got hot under the collar when he realized that he was betrayed by his best friend. 史蒂文知道自己竟被最好的朋友給出賣時，勃然大怒。

col·league [kɑ`lig]　　🎧 *Track 0951*
n. 同事
▶ Tom is an ill-tempered person. Most of his colleagues don't want to work with him. 湯姆是個壞脾氣的人。他大部份的同事都不想跟他共事。

col·lect [kə`lɛkt]　　🎧 *Track 0952*
v. 收集；領取

col·lec·tion [kə`lɛkʃən]　　🎧 *Track 0953*
n. 收集；收藏品

col·lec·tor [kə`lɛktɚ]　　🎧 *Track 0954*
n. 收集者；收藏家；收費員；收票員
▶ My father is a collector of insect specimens. 我父親是個昆蟲標本收藏家。

col·lege [`kɑlɪdʒ]　　🎧 *Track 0955*
n. 大學

col·lide [kə`laɪd]　　🎧 *Track 0956*
v. 碰撞；相撞；衝突
▶ The two cars collided at the intersection.
兩輛汽車在十字路口發生碰撞。

col·o·ny [`kɑlənɪ]　　🎧 *Track 0957*
n. 殖民地；僑居地
▶ Taiwan was a Dutch colony for twenty years in the 17th century.
台灣在十七世紀時，有二十年的時間是荷蘭的殖民地。

col·or [`kʌlɚ]　　🎧 *Track 0958*
=col·our （英式英文）
n. 顏色；色彩　**v.** 著色；塗上顏色

col·ored [`kʌlɚd]　　🎧 *Track 0959*
adj. 有顏色的；彩色的；著色的；經渲染的；帶有偏見的
▶ He gave the little girl some colored pencils to draw with.
他給了小女孩一些彩色鉛筆讓她畫畫。

col·or·ful [`kʌlɚfəl]　　🎧 *Track 0960*
=col·our·ful （英式英文）
adj. 色彩豐富的；多彩多姿的

col·umn [`kɑləm]　　🎧 *Track 0961*
n. （報紙的）欄；（報紙、雜誌的）短評欄、專欄
▶ She only reads the gossip column in the newspapers.
她只看報紙上的八卦專欄。

comb [kom]　　🎧 *Track 0962*
n. 梳子；梳理　**v.** 梳頭

com·bi·na·tion [ˌkɑmbə`neʃən]　　🎧 *Track 0963*
n. 混合；混合體；組合
▶ She looked at him in a combination of curiosity and disgust.
她用混合著好奇與噁心的表情看著他。

com·bine [kəm`baɪn] 🎧 *Track 0964*
v. 使結合；兼有
▶ The film combines humor, sorrow and happiness.
這部片結合了幽默、悲傷和歡笑。

com·bined [kəm`baɪnd] 🎧 *Track 0965*
adj. 聯合的；共同的；多功能組合的
▶ This achievement is the result of the combined effort of every individual in my team. 這項成就是我的團隊中每一個人共同努力的成果。

come [kʌm] 🎧 *Track 0966*
v. 來

co·me·di·an [kə`mɪdɪən] 🎧 *Track 0967*
n. 喜劇演員；逗人開心的人
▶ I was very shocked to hear that my favorite comedian is actually depressed.
聽到我最喜歡的喜劇演員是個憂鬱症患者，讓我很震驚。

com·e·dy [`kɑmədɪ] 🎧 *Track 0968*
n. 喜劇
▶ I thought it was a comedy, but it turned out to be a sad movie. 我以為這是喜劇，結果卻是一部悲傷的電影。

(補充片語)
turn out 結果

com·et [`kɑmɪt] 🎧 *Track 0969*
n. 彗星
▶ The comet will get very close to us, but it is very unlikely to hit earth.
這顆彗星將會離我們非常近，但不太可能會撞到地球。

com·fort [`kʌmfət] 🎧 *Track 0970*
n. 安逸；舒適；使人舒服的設備；給予安慰的東西
▶ Is there anything we can do to bring comfort to her?
有什麼我們可以做來給她安慰的事嗎？

v. 安慰；慰問
▶ There's nothing we can do to comfort her. 我們做什麼都無法安慰她。

(相關片語)
comfort food 讓人感溫馨的食物
▶ Ice cream is the comfort food I want when I come home after a long tiring day. 冰淇淋是當我在漫長疲倦的一天回到家時，會想要吃的溫馨食物。

com·fort·a·ble [`kʌmfətəbl̩] 🎧 *Track 0971*
adj. 舒適的；自在的

com·fort·a·bly [`kʌmfətəblɪ] 🎧 *Track 0972*
adv. 舒適地；舒服地
▶ When I came home, I found my dog sleeping comfortably on my bed. 當我回到家時，我發現我的狗在我的床上睡得很舒服。

(相關片語)
comfortably off 生活寬裕
▶ We are not very rich, but we are comfortably off. 我們不是非常有錢，但生活也算寬裕了。

com·ic [`kɑmɪk] 🎧 *Track 0973*
adj. 喜劇般的；連環漫畫的
n. 連環漫畫；連環漫畫書

com·ing [`kʌmɪŋ] 🎧 *Track 0974*
adj. 即將到來的
▶ Have you planned for the coming long weekend?
你為即將到來的週末連假做計劃了嗎？

com·ma [`kɑmə] 🎧 *Track 0975*
n. 逗號；停頓
▶ The sentence is grammatically incorrect without a comma before "because". 這個句子的「因為」前面沒有逗號，在文法上是不正確的。

com·mand [kə`mænd] 🎧 *Track 0976*
v. 命令，指揮

com·mand·er [kə`mændə] 🎧 *Track 0977*
n. 指揮官；司令官
▶ My father-in-law is a commander in the United States Army.
我的公公是美軍的指揮官。

※灰色單字為英檢初級必備單字

com·ment [`kɑmɛnt`] 🎧 *Track 0978*
n. 批評；議論 **v.** 發表意見；評論

com·merce [`kɑmɝs`] 🎧 *Track 0979*
n. 商業；貿易；交易；（思想）交流
▶ My father works in commerce.
我父親是從事貿易工作的。

com·mer·cial 🎧 *Track 0980*
[kəˋmɝʃəl]
adj. 商業的；以營利為目的的；工業用的
▶ He opened a savings account in that commercial bank.
他在那間商業銀行開了個存款帳戶。

n. 商業廣告
▶ A convincing TV commercial can greatly improve the sales of your product.
一個有說服力的電視廣告能大大提升你的產品銷售額。

相關片語
commercial break 播廣告的空檔
▶ She went to the bathroom during the commercial break.
她趁播廣告的空檔去上廁所。

com·mis·sion 🎧 *Track 0981*
[kəˋmɪʃən]
n. 佣金；（權限或任務的）委託
▶ The salesman can earn a 5% commission from each item he sells.
業務員可從他售出的每件商品中賺取百分之五的佣金。

v. 委任；委託；任命
▶ Nick was commissioned to take charge of the Sales Department.
尼克被任命掌管業務部門。

相關片語
out of commission 退出現役；不工作
▶ I can't work because my computer is out of commission at present. 我的電腦現在壞掉不能用，所以我沒辦法工作。

com·mit [kəˋmɪt] 🎧 *Track 0982*
v. 做（錯事）；犯（罪）
▶ It's impossible to commit murder and get away with it.
犯下殺人罪之後，是不可能不受制裁的。

補充片語
get away with 不受懲罰
相關片語
commit suicide 自殺
▶ It never occurred to them that their daughter would commit suicide.
他們從沒想過他們的女兒會自殺。

com·mit·ment 🎧 *Track 0983*
[kəˋmɪtmənt]
n. 承諾
▶ He is a man afraid of making commitment.
他是個害怕做出承諾的男人。

com·mit·tee [kəˋmɪtɪ] 🎧 *Track 0984*
n. 委員會
▶ Mr. Miller refused to serve on the management committee.
米勒先生拒絕擔任管委會的委員。

補充片語
serve on a committee 擔任委員會委員；
management committee 管理委員會

com·mon [`kɑmən`] 🎧 *Track 0985*
adj. 一般的；共同的

com·mon·place 🎧 *Track 0986*
[`kɑmən‚ples`]
adj. 普通平凡的；陳腐的；平淡無味的
▶ Smart phones have become commonplace over the past few years.
智慧型手機在過去幾年變得非常普遍。

n. 司空見慣的事；老生常談
▶ Luxury camping is now a commonplace here.
豪華露營現在在這裡已經是很普通的事情。

com·mu·ni·cate 🎧 *Track 0987*
[kəˋmjunə‚ket]
v. 溝通
▶ She finds it difficult to communicate with her teenage kids.
她發現要跟她青春期的孩子溝通很困難。

com·mu·ni·ca·tion 🎧 *Track 0988*
[kə‚mjunəˋkeʃən]
n. 溝通

▶ Communication between parents and children is important.
父母子女間的溝通是很重要的。

com·mu·nist
[`kɑmjʊ͵nɪst]

Track 0989

adj. 共產主義的；共產黨的；支持共產主義的
▶ He was born and raised in a communist family. 他在一個共產主義的家庭出生長大。

n. 共產主義；共產黨員
▶ All of his family members are communists, and he is no exception. 他家所有的成員都是共產黨員，而他也不例外。

com·mu·ni·ty
[kə`mjunətɪ]

Track 0990

n. 社區；共同社會；（一般）社會大眾；（財產）共有
▶ He devoted himself to community service after retirement.
他在退休後致力於社區服務。

(補充片語)
devote oneself to 專心致力於某事；
community service 社區服務

com·pan·ion
[kəm`pænjən]

Track 0991

n. 同伴；伴侶；朋友
▶ The old dog is the old man's only companion.
這隻老狗是那老人唯一的同伴。

(相關片語)
travelling companion 旅伴
▶ Kevin is not only a good tour guide, but also a great travelling companion. 凱文不僅是一個很好的導遊，也是個很棒的旅伴。

com·pa·ny [`kʌmpənɪ]
n. 公司

Track 0992

com·par·a·tive
[kəm`pærətɪv]

Track 0993

adj. 比較的；用比較方法的；比較而言的；相對的
▶ The country has a comparative advantage in leather products.
該國家在皮革生產上佔有相對優勢。

com·pare [kəm`pɛr]
v. 比較；對照

Track 0994

com·pared [kəm`pɛrd]
adj. 比照的；對照的

Track 0995

▶ In my opinion, American food can't be compared with Chinese food. They're two different things.
對我來說，美式餐點和中式餐點不能拿來比，它們是不一樣的兩件事。

(補充片語)
not to be compared with 相差極遠；遠比不上

com·pa·ri·son
[kəm`pærəsn]

Track 0996

n. 比較
▶ Her beauty is beyond comparison.
她的美貌無與倫比。

(相關片語)
out of all comparison 無與倫比
▶ Her voice is out of all comparison.
她的歌聲無與倫比。

com·pass [`kʌmpəs]
n. 羅盤；指南針

Track 0997

▶ How do we know whether we're going in the correct direction without a compass?
沒有指南針，我們怎麼知道我們走的方向是否正確？

com·pete [kəm`pit]
v. 與……競爭；媲美、比得上

Track 0998

▶ This pie is good, but not good enough to compete with my grandmother's.
這個派很好吃，但還沒有好吃到可以比得上我奶奶做的。

com·pe·ti·tion
[͵kɑmpə`tɪʃən]

Track 0999

n. 競爭；比賽；競爭對手
▶ They are going to put on a cooking competition to find out the best student chef in the nation. 他們將舉行一場烹飪競賽，以找出全國最棒的學生主廚。

(補充片語)
put on 舉辦

Aa
Bb
Cc
Dd
Ee

Ff
Gg
Hh
Ii
Jj

Kk
Ll
Mm
Nn
Oo

Pp
Qq
Rr
Ss
Tt

Uu
Vv
Ww
Xx
Yy
Zz

※灰色單字為英檢初級必備單字

com·pet·i·tive
[kəmˈpɛtətɪv] 🎧 *Track 1000*

adj. 競爭的；競爭性的；好競爭的
▶ Emilie is a very competitive person. She cares a lot about winning. 艾蜜莉是個競爭心很強的人，她非常在乎輸贏。

com·pet·i·tor
[kəmˈpɛtətɚ] 🎧 *Track 1001*

n. 競爭者；對手
▶ You need to know who your competitors are before you start a business. 在你創業之前，你必須知道你的競爭對手是誰。

com·plain [kəmˈplen] 🎧 *Track 1002*
v. 抱怨

com·plaint [kəmˈplent] 🎧 *Track 1003*
n. 抱怨；投訴；怨言
▶ We received a lot of complaints about the new product.
我們收到很多關於新產品的投訴。

com·plete [kəmˈplit] 🎧 *Track 1004*
v. 完成；使完整
adj. 完整的；結束的

com·ple·tion 🎧 *Track 1005*
[kəmˈpliʃən]
n. 完整

com·plex [ˈkɑmplɛks] 🎧 *Track 1006*
adj. 錯綜複雜的；複合的、合成的
▶ The most complex organ in the human body is the brain.
人體中最複雜的器官就是腦。

n. 複合物；綜合體
▶ They are going to build a shopping complex that contains shops, restaurants, theaters and a gym.
他們將蓋一座包含商店、餐廳、電影院和一間健身房的複合式購物城。

com·pli·cate [ˈkɑmpləˌket] 🎧 *Track 1007*
v. 使複雜
▶ Your interference will only complicate the problem. 你的干涉只會使問題變得複雜。

com·pli·cat·ed 🎧 *Track 1008*
[ˈkɑmpləˌketɪd]
adj. 複雜的；難懂的
▶ This math problem is too complicated for elementary school students.
這道數學題對小學生來說太複雜難懂了。

com·pli·ment 🎧 *Track 1009*
[ˈkɑmpləmənt]
n. 讚美；恭維
▶ I don't know what it means, but I'll just take that as a compliment. 我不知道那是什麼意思，但我就當做是讚美了。

v. 讚美
▶ He complimented her new haircut.
他讚美她的新髮型。

com·pose [kəmˈpoz] 🎧 *Track 1010*
v. 作（詩曲）；構（圖）；組成、構成；使鎮靜
▶ The team is composed of highly trained and experienced engineers.
這個團隊是由經過高度訓練且具經驗的工程師所組成的。

(補充片語)

be composed of 由……組成

相關片語

compose oneself 使鎮定下來
▶ She tried to compose herself after hearing the bad news. 她在聽到壞消息之後，試圖讓自己冷靜下來。

com·pos·er [kəmˈpozɚ] 🎧 *Track 1011*
n. 作曲家；調停者
▶ The composer of the Fifth Symphony is Beethoven.
第五號交響曲的作曲者是貝多芬。

com·po·si·tion 🎧 *Track 1012*
[ˌkɑmpəˈzɪʃən]
n. 寫作；作曲；作文；構圖；成分；合成物
▶ The science teacher is explaining the composition of blood and its functions to the students. 科學老師正在向學生解釋血液的成分及其功能。

com·pound
[kɑm`paʊnd]

n. 混合物;化合物
▶ Water is a compound that contains hydrogen and oxygen.
水是一個含有氫及氧的化合物。

adj. 複合的
▶ Brunch is a compound word formed by two words: "breakfast" and "lunch".
早午餐是一個將「早餐」和「午餐」兩個字接合而成的複合字。

v. 使混合;用合成方法製作;加重
▶ They successfully compounded several ingredients into an effective organic solvent.
他們成功地將數種成分合成出一種有效的有機溶劑。

🎧 *Track 1013*

com·pre·hen·sion
[ˌkɑmprɪ`hɛnʃən]

n. 理解;理解力
▶ This mathematical theory is far beyond my comprehension.
這套數學理論遠遠超過我能理解的範圍。

(補充片語)
beyond one's comprehension 某人難以理解的

🎧 *Track 1014*

com·pute [kəm`pjut]

v. 計算;估算
▶ Your pay is computed on a daily basis.
你的酬勞是按日計算的。

🎧 *Track 1015*

com·put·er [kəm`pjutɚ]
n. 電腦

🎧 *Track 1016*

con·ceal [kən`sil]

v. 隱藏;隱瞞
▶ They concealed the truth from me.
他們對我隱瞞了真相。

🎧 *Track 1017*

con·cen·trate
[`kɑnsən‚tret]

v. 集中;聚集;全力以赴;全神貫注
▶ I can't concentrate on my homework with the TV on.
電視開著,我沒辦法專心寫作業。

🎧 *Track 1018*

con·cen·tra·tion
[ˌkɑnsən`treʃən]

n. 集中;專心
▶ All kids were listening to the teacher with great concentration.
所有的孩子都聚精會神地聽老師說話。

(補充片語)
with great concentration 聚精會神地

🎧 *Track 1019*

con·cept [`kɑnsɛpt]
n. 概念;觀念;思想
▶ The professor proposed a new concept of the universe.
該教授提出了一個宇宙的新概念。

🎧 *Track 1020*

con·cern [kən`sɝn]
n. 關心的事;掛念
v. 關於;關係到;使關心、使擔心、使不安

🎧 *Track 1021*

con·cern·ing
[kən`sɝnɪŋ]

prep. 關於
▶ This is a case concerning domestic violence.
這是一個跟家暴有關的案件。

🎧 *Track 1022*

con·cert [`kɑnsɚt]
n. 音樂會;演奏會
▶ Please turn off your cell phones before the concert.
請在音樂會開始前將您的手機關機。

🎧 *Track 1023*

con·clude [kən`klud]
v. 結束;推斷出;最後決定為
▶ I hope the meeting will be concluded by 5 p.m.
我希望會議會下午五點之前結束。

🎧 *Track 1024*

con·clu·sion
[kən`kluʒən]

n. 結論;結果;締結;議定
▶ Let's not jump to a conclusion before hearing from both sides. 在聽過兩邊的說法之前,我們不要先忙著下結論。

(補充片語)
jump to a conclusion/conclusions 匆匆下結論

🎧 *Track 1025*

※灰色單字為英檢初級必備單字

Aa
Bb
Cc
Dd
Ee

Ff
Gg
Hh
Ii
Jj

Kk
Ll
Mm
Nn
Oo

Pp
Qq
Rr
Ss
Tt

Uu
Vv
Ww
Xx
Yy
Zz

con·crete [`kɑnkrit] 🎧 *Track 1026*
adj. 有形的；具體的
▶ We welcome any concrete suggestions to improve work efficiency. 我們歡迎任何可以提高工作效率的具體建議。

n. 具體物；混凝土
▶ The house was built with reinforced concrete.
這房子是用鋼筋混凝土所建造的。

con·di·tion [kən`dɪʃən] 🎧 *Track 1027*
n. 狀況；條件；情況；環境、形式
▶ The patient's condition has gone from bad to worse.
病人的情況越來越糟糕了。

v. 決定；為⋯⋯的條件；使處於良好狀態
▶ Good sleep conditions your health.
良好的睡眠決定你的健康。

相關片語

in condition　身體健康
▶ You will be back in condition after a good rest. 好好休息過後，你就會恢復身體健康了

con·duct [kən`dʌkt] 🎧 *Track 1028*
v. 引導；帶領；管理；處理；指揮
▶ Ms. Chen will conduct the church choir.
陳小姐將會指揮教堂唱詩班。

n. 品行；行為
▶ Henry was awarded a Good Conduct Prize when he was in third grade.
亨利曾在三年級時獲頒品行優良獎。

con·duc·tor 🎧 *Track 1029*
[kən`dʌktɚ]
n. 領導人；（合唱團或樂隊）指揮
▶ The conductor cued the pianist to start.
樂隊指揮暗示鋼琴家開始彈奏。

cone [kon] 🎧 *Track 1030*
n. 圓錐體；錐形冰淇淋筒
▶ Would you like your ice cream in a cone or in a cup? 你想要把冰淇淋放在冰淇淋筒裡還是杯子裡？

con·fe·rence 🎧 *Track 1031*
[`kɑnfərəns]
n. 會議；會談

▶ I will be in Tokyo for the Asia Business Conference next week.
我下週會到東京參加亞洲商務會議。

相關片語

press conference　記者會
▶ The actor announced his retirement in the press conference.
該男星在記者會上宣布退隱。

con·fess [kən`fɛs] 🎧 *Track 1032*
v. 坦白；承認；懺悔告解
▶ He confessed that he had an affair with his secretary.
他承認跟他的秘書有外遇。

con·fi·dence 🎧 *Track 1033*
[`kɑnfədəns]
n. 自信；信心
▶ I don't have much confidence, but I'll try my best.
我沒有什麼信心，但我會盡力去做。

con·fi·dent [`kɑnfədənt] 🎧 *Track 1034*
adj. 自信的；有信心的

con·fine [kən`faɪn] 🎧 *Track 1035*
v. 限制；使侷限
▶ We'll confine this meeting to two hours.
我們會將會議限制在兩小時內開完。

con·firm [kən`fɝm] 🎧 *Track 1036*
v. 確定；確認

con·flict [`kɑnflɪkt] 🎧 *Track 1037*
n. 衝突

con·front [kən`frʌnt] 🎧 *Track 1038*
v. 面對
▶ Stay calm when confronting danger.
面臨危險時要保持冷靜。

con·fron·ta·tion 🎧 *Track 1039*
[ˌkɑnfrʌn`teʃən]
n. 對質；對抗；衝突
▶ The laborers had a confrontation with the management.
勞方與資方起了衝突。

Con·fu·ci·us [kənˋfjuʃəs] 🎧 *Track 1040*
n. 孔子

---

con·fuse [kənˋfjuz] 🎧 *Track 1041*
v. 使困惑；搞亂

---

con·fu·sion 🎧 *Track 1042*
[kənˋfjuʒən]

n. 混亂；困惑；混淆
▶ He tried to explain as clearly as possible in order to avoid confusion.
他試著盡可能地解釋清楚，以避免混淆。

---

con·grat·u·late 🎧 *Track 1043*
[kənˋgrætʃəˏlet]

v. 恭喜
▶ I would like to congratulate you on your newborn baby.
恭喜你的寶貝出生了。

---

con·grat·u·la·tion 🎧 *Track 1044*
[kənˏgrætʃəˋleʃən]

n. 恭喜

---

con·gress [ˋkaŋgrəs] 🎧 *Track 1045*
n. 正式會議；代表大會；立法機關；美國國會；聚會
▶ A congress on global warming will be held in Denmark on December 12.
一場有關球暖化的會議將在十二月十二日於丹麥舉行。

---

con·junc·tion 🎧 *Track 1046*
[kənˋdʒʌŋkʃən]

n. 連接詞；結合；連接；同時發生
▶ We have to work in conjunction with each other.
我們必須彼此配合地進行工作。

（補充片語）
in conjunction with 與……一起

---

con·nect [kəˋnɛkt] 🎧 *Track 1047*
v. 連接；聯想；接通電話
▶ Could you connect me with your manager, please?
可以請你幫我把電話接到你們經理那裡嗎？

---

con·nec·tion [kəˋnɛkʃən] 🎧 *Track 1048*
n. 關聯
▶ The police questioned those in connection with the suspect.
警方訊問了那些跟嫌犯有關的人。

（補充片語）
in connection with 與……有關

---

con·quer [ˏkaŋkɚ] 🎧 *Track 1049*
v. 攻克；佔領；征服；得勝
▶ Not everyone can conquer Mount Everest.
並非每個人都能征服聖母峰。

---

con·science [ˋkanʃəns] 🎧 *Track 1050*
n. 良心；道德心
▶ Those cold-blood killers have no conscience, no souls.
那些冷血的殺手是沒有良心，沒有靈魂的。

---

con·scious [ˋkanʃəs] 🎧 *Track 1051*
adj. 意識到的
▶ The woman wasn't conscious that someone was following her.
女子沒有意識到有人在跟蹤她。

---

con·se·quence 🎧 *Track 1052*
[ˋkansəˏkwɛns]

n. 結果；後果
▶ You can do as you please, but you have to take the consequences. 你想怎麼做就怎麼做，但是你必須要承擔後果。

（補充片語）
take the consequences 承擔後果

---

con·se·quent 🎧 *Track 1053*
[ˋkansəˏkwɛnt]

adj. 作為結果的；隨之發生的
▶ Your job is to prevent the patient from falling and having consequent injuries.
你的工作就是要預防病人跌倒以及隨之發生的傷害。

---

con·se·quent·ly 🎧 *Track 1054*
[ˋkansəˏkwɛntlɪ]

adv. 結果；因此；必然地
▶ He didn't study at all and consequently failed the finals.
他完全沒唸書，結果期末考考砸了。

---

con·ser·va·tive　🎧 *Track 1055*
[kənˈsɝ·vətɪv]

adj. 保守的；守舊的；傳統的

▶I grew up in a very conservative Chinese family.
我在一個非常傳統保守的中國家庭長大。

n. 保守者；守舊派

▶Both my parents are conservatives who are unwilling to change their ways of living. 我的雙親都是保守的人，不願意改變他們的生活方式。

con·sid·er [kənˈsɪdə·]　🎧 *Track 1056*
v. 考慮；認為

con·sid·er·a·ble　🎧 *Track 1057*
[kənˈsɪdərəb!]

adj. 相當大的；相當多的

▶We spent a considerable amount of money to update our home décor.
我們花了相當多錢將我們的房子重新裝潢。

con·sid·er·ate　🎧 *Track 1058*
[kənˈsɪdərɪt]

adj. 週到的

▶It's very considerate of you to make a reservation in advance.
你會想到要事先訂位真是太周到了。

con·sid·e·ra·tion　🎧 *Track 1059*
[kənsɪdəˈreʃən]

n. 考慮；需要考慮的事；體貼、關心

▶We will take your advice into consideration.
我們會將你的建議列入考慮。

(補充片語)
take sth. into consideration　考慮；將某事列入考慮

con·sist [kənˈsɪst]　🎧 *Track 1060*
v. 組成；構成；存在於；符合

▶A nuclear family consists of parents and their children. 一個核心家庭是由父母親和他們的孩子所組成的。

(補充片語)
nuclear family　小家庭、核心家庭；
consist of　由……組成

con·sis·tent　🎧 *Track 1061*
[kənˈsɪstənt]

adj. 始終如一的；前後一致的

▶As a parent, your actions should be consistent with your words. 身為一個家長，你的行為必須與你的言論一致。

(補充片語)
be consistent with　與……一致

con·so·nant　🎧 *Track 1062*
[ˈkɑnsənənt]

n. 子音

▶He can't pronounce the consonant "th" correctly.
他無法正確地做出「th」這個子音的發音。

con·stant [ˈkɑnstənt]　🎧 *Track 1063*
adj. 固定的；不停的、連續不斷的

▶It's been raining for a week. I'm so tired of the constant rain.
已經下一個星期的雨了。我對這下不停的雨感到好厭煩。

con·sti·tute　🎧 *Track 1064*
[ˈkɑnstəˌtjut]

v. 構成；形成；設立（機構）；制定（法律）

▶The man was arrested because his action constituted a threat to public security.
男子會遭到逮捕，是因為他的行為對社會治安已構成威脅。

con·sti·tu·tion　🎧 *Track 1065*
[ˌkɑnstəˈtjuʃən]

n. 憲法、章程；體格；（事物的）構造或組成方式

▶The constitution of this country allows each president to serve only two terms.
該國憲法規定，每位總統只能有兩次任期。

con·struct [kənˈstrʌkt]　🎧 *Track 1066*
v. 建造；構成；創立（學說）；構（詞）

▶They used wood to construct the bridge.
他們用木頭來建造這座橋。

n. （複數）構想；概念

▶ The constructs of this scientific theory are too complicated for me to understand.
這科學理論的概念對我來說太複雜難懂了。

con·struc·tion 🎧 *Track 1067*
[kən`strʌkʃən]

n. 建造；建設；建築物

▶ The new school dormitory is now under construction.
新的學校宿舍目前已在搭建中。

(補充片語)
under construction 在建造中

con·sult [kən`sʌlt] 🎧 *Track 1068*
v. 商量

▶ I would like to consult my teacher with the problem.
我想跟老師商量一下這個問題。

con·sul·tant 🎧 *Track 1069*
[kən`sʌltənt]

n. 顧問；諮詢者

▶ Let me discuss this with our legal consultant first.
讓我先跟我們的法律顧問討論一下這個問題。

(補充片語)
legal consultant 法律顧問

con·sume [kən`sjum] 🎧 *Track 1070*
v. 消耗；花費；吃完；喝光；揮霍；耗盡

▶ Humans are consuming the earth's natural resources faster than ever.
人類正比以往更快速地在消耗著地球的天然資源。

con·sum·er [kən`sjumɚ] 🎧 *Track 1071*
n. 消費者；顧客

▶ Housewives are our target consumers.
家庭主婦是我們的目標消費者。

con·tact [`kɑntækt] 🎧 *Track 1072*
n. 接觸；聯繫

v. 與……接觸；與……聯繫

con·ta·gious 🎧 *Track 1073*
[kən`tedʒəs]

adj. 接觸傳染性的；感染性的

▶ Ebola is a highly contagious and deadly virus. 伊波拉是一種高感染性且致命的病毒。

con·tain [kən`ten] 🎧 *Track 1074*
v. 包含

con·tain·er [kən`tenɚ] 🎧 *Track 1075*
n. 容器；貨櫃

▶ Can you find me a container for these cookies?
你可以找一個可以裝這些餅乾的容器嗎？

con·tem·po·ra·ry 🎧 *Track 1076*
[kən`tɛmpəˌrɛrɪ]

adj. 當代的；同時代的；同齡的

▶ My great-grandfather was contemporary of Abraham Lincoln.
我的曾祖父跟林肯是同個時代的人。

n. 同時代的人；同齡的人；同時期的東西；當代人

▶ It is a memory that you can share with your contemporaries only. 這是一個你只能跟同時代的人一起分享的回憶。

con·tent [kən`tɛnt] 🎧 *Track 1077*
adj. 滿足的；滿意的

▶ She seems content with her marriage life. 她看起來似乎對婚姻生活很滿意。

v. 使滿足；使滿意

▶ There was nothing to do, so he had to content himself with listening to music.
沒有什麼事可以做，所以他只能聽音樂來自我滿足。

n. 滿足；內容物

▶ His heart was filled with content when his son was born.
當他兒子出生時，他的心裡充滿了滿足感。

(相關片語)
to one's heart's content 盡情地
▶ Let's drink to our heart's content.
咱們盡情地喝吧！

con·test [`kɑntɛst] 🎧 *Track 1078*
n. 比賽；競賽；競爭

▶ She took part in the speech contest and won the first prize.
她參加演講比賽，得了第一名。

v. 競爭；角逐

▶ They are contesting for the big prize.
他們在競爭那個大獎。

con·tes·tant 🎧 *Track 1079*
[kən`tɛstənt]

n. 參賽者

▶ All our contestants have to pass the same difficult tests to enter the finals.
我們所有的參賽者都必須通過同樣困難的測試才能進入決賽。

con·text [`kantɛkst] 🎧 *Track 1080*

n. 上下文；（事件的）來龍去脈；背景

▶ Checking the context is the best way to figure out the meaning of a word.
要搞清楚一個字的意思，看上下文是最好的方法。

con·ti·nent [`kantənənt] 🎧 *Track 1081*

n. 大陸；陸地；洲

▶ The Earth is divided into seven continents, including Asia, Africa, North America, South America, Europe, Australia and Antarctica.
地球被分為七大洲，包含亞洲、非洲、北美洲、南美洲、歐洲、澳洲和南極洲。

con·tin·u·al 🎧 *Track 1082*
[kən`tɪnjʊəl]

adj. 多次重複的；連續的；不間斷的

▶ He still drinks a lot regardless of the continual warnings of his doctor.
他不顧醫生不斷的警告，還是喝很多的酒。

con·tin·ue [kən`tɪnjʊ] 🎧 *Track 1083*

v. 繼續

con·tin·u·ous 🎧 *Track 1084*
[kən`tɪnjʊəs]

adj. 連續不間斷的；持久不鬆懈的

▶ The well provides the villagers a continuous supply of water.
這口井為村民提供連續不間斷的水。

con·tract [kən`trækt] 🎧 *Track 1085*

n. 合約 **v.** 訂契約

con·tra·ry [`kantrɛrɪ] 🎧 *Track 1086*

adj. 相反的；對比的；逆向的

▶ My opinions are contrary to yours.
我的意見跟你相反。

con·trast [`kan͵træst] 🎧 *Track 1087*

n. 對比；對照

▶ In contrast to a diamond necklace, a crystal necklace is rather cheap.
跟鑽石項鍊比起來，水晶項鍊相當便宜。

(補充片語)

in contrast to 與……相比

v. 使對比；形成對照

▶ His personality contrasts sharply with that of his sister.
他的個性跟他姊姊形成鮮明的對照。

con·trib·ute 🎧 *Track 1088*
[kən`trɪbjut]

v. 貢獻；捐獻

▶ He contributed all his money to the charities.
他將所有的錢都捐給慈善機構。

con·tri·bu·tion 🎧 *Track 1089*
[͵kantrə`bjuʃən]

n. 貢獻；捐獻；捐獻的財物

▶ Alexander Graham Bell's greatest contribution was the invention of the telephone. 亞歷山大·貝爾最偉大的貢獻就是電話的發明。

con·trol [kən`trol] 🎧 *Track 1090*
n. 控制 **v.** 控制

con·trol·ler [kən`trolə] 🎧 *Track 1091*
n. 管理人；控制器；主計員

con·ve·ni·ence 🎧 *Track 1092*
[kən`vinjəns]

n. 便利；方便；便利設施

▶ The hostel has a laundry room on the ground floor for the guests' convenience.
為了房客的方便，青年旅社在一樓處設有一間洗衣房。

(相關片語)

convenience store 便利商店

▶ Most traditional grocery stores have been replaced by convenience stores. 大部分傳統的雜貨店已經被便利商店給取代了。

con·ve·ni·ent
🎧 *Track 1093*
[kən`vinjənt]
adj. 方便的;便利的

con·ven·tion·al
🎧 *Track 1094*
[kən`vɛnʃənl]
adj. 習慣的;慣例的;傳統式的;符合習俗的
▶ We had a very conventional wedding ceremony.
我們舉辦了一個非常傳統的婚禮儀式。

con·ver·sa·tion
🎧 *Track 1095*
[ˌkɑnvɚ`seʃən]
n. 對話;對談

con·verse
[kən`vɝs]
🎧 *Track 1096*
v. 交談;談話
▶ We conversed face to face for hours.
我們面對面談了好幾個小時。

con·vey
[kən`ve]
🎧 *Track 1097*
v. 運送;傳達
▶ Make sure the message is conveyed to all departments.
請務必將此訊息傳達給所有部門。

con·vince
[kən`vɪns]
🎧 *Track 1098*
v. 說服;使相信
▶ I didn't trust him at first, but he finally convinced me of his good intentions. 我一開始並不信任他,但他終於讓我相信他的善意。

cook
[kʊk]
🎧 *Track 1099*
v. 烹煮;做菜 **n.** 廚師

cook·er
[`kʊkɚ]
🎧 *Track 1100*
n. 炊具;爐灶;烹調器具

cook·ie
[`kʊkɪ]=cook·y
🎧 *Track 1101*
n. 甜餅乾

cook·ing
[`kʊkɪŋ]
🎧 *Track 1102*
n. 烹調;烹調術
▶ I'm going to take a cooking class.
我要去上烹飪課。

adj. 烹調用的
▶ Which kind of cooking oil do you use, olive oil or peanut oil?
你是用哪一種烹調用油,橄欖油還是花生油?

cool
[kul]
🎧 *Track 1103*
adj. 涼爽的;冷靜的;冷淡的;(口)極好的
v. 使涼快;使冷卻;使(情緒)平息

co·op·er·ate
[ko`ɑpəˌret]=co·op·er·ate
🎧 *Track 1104*
v. 合作;配合
▶ The suspect wouldn't cooperate with the police.
嫌犯不願與警方配合。

co·op·e·ra·tion
🎧 *Track 1105*
[ko.ɑpə`reʃən]
n. 協力;合作;配合
▶ We wouldn't have accomplished our goal without your full cooperation.
沒有你們全力的配合,我們就無法達成我們的目標。

co·op·e·rat·ive
🎧 *Track 1106*
[ko`ɑpəˌretɪv]
adj. 合作的;樂意配合的
▶ The suspect wasn't very cooperative.
嫌犯並不是非常地配合。

cope
[kop]
🎧 *Track 1107*
v. 對付;處理
▶ A three-year-old kid doesn't know how to cope with anger. 一個三歲的孩子不知道怎麼處理憤怒的情緒。

(補充片語)
cope with 處理;巧妙應付

cop·per
[`kɑpɚ]
🎧 *Track 1108*
n. 銅;銅製品;銅幣
▶ These coins were cast in copper.
這些錢幣是以銅鑄造的。

adj. 銅的;銅製的;紅銅色的
▶ The copper kettle caught my eye immediately.
那只銅製水壺立刻吸引了我的目光。

※灰色單字為英檢初級必備單字

cop·y [ˋkɑpɪ] 🎧 *Track 1109*
n. 抄本；複製品 **v.** 抄寫；抄襲；模仿

cop·y·right [ˋkɑpɪ͵raɪt] 🎧 *Track 1110*
n. 版權；著作權
▶ You can't use this photo in your book unless you have the copyright.
除非你擁有這相片的版權，否則不能將它放在你的書裡。

adj. 有版權的
▶ Copyright regulations can help to protect your creative work.
版權條例有助於保護你的創意作品。

v. 取得版權
▶ You will get into trouble if you use a copyrighted photo. 如果你使用了有版權的照片，是會惹上麻煩的。

cor·al [ˋkɔrəl] 🎧 *Track 1111*
n. 珊瑚；珊瑚製品；珊瑚色
▶ I was surprised when I learned that corals are in fact animals.
當我知道珊瑚原來是動物時，十分地驚訝。

adj. 珊瑚的；珊瑚製的
▶ The coral necklace looks lovely on you. 你戴那條珊瑚項鍊真是好看。

cord [kɔrd] 🎧 *Track 1112*
n. 細繩；粗線；絕緣電線
▶ He used a cord to tie up the old newspapers.
他用一條細繩將舊報紙綑起來。

(相關片語)
emergency cord （火車上的）緊急煞車繩
▶ He had no choice but to pull the emergency cord and jump off the train. 他別無他法，只得拉下緊急煞車繩並跳下火車。

core [kor] 🎧 *Track 1113*
n. 果核；核心
▶ When you eat an apple, you should eat the entire apple, including the core. 當你吃蘋果時，你應該吃一整顆蘋果，包含果核。

corn [kɔrn] 🎧 *Track 1114*
n. 小麥、穀物；玉米

cor·ner [ˋkɔrnə] 🎧 *Track 1115*
n. 角、角落

cor·po·ra·tion [͵kɔrpəˋreʃən] 🎧 *Track 1116*
n. 法人；社團法人；股份公司；大公司
▶ A large corporation provides better employee welfare, such as health insurance, retirement benefits and so on.
一間大公司會提供較好的員工福利，如健康保險、退休金等等。

cor·rect [kəˋrɛkt] 🎧 *Track 1117*
adj. 正確的 **v.** 糾正、訂正

cor·re·spond [͵kɔrɪˋspɑnd] 🎧 *Track 1118*
v. 符合；相應；一致
▶ As a teacher, your actions should correspond with your words.
身為一名老師，你應該要言行一致。

(補充片語)
correspond with 符合

cor·re·spon·dent [͵kɔrɪˋspɑndənt] 🎧 *Track 1119*
n. 對應物；特派員、通訊記者；客戶
▶ If you are a sports enthusiast and you enjoy writing, a sports correspondent may be a perfect job for you.
如果你對運動很有熱忱，而且喜歡寫作，那麼體育記者對你來説可能是個理想的工作。

cor·ri·dor [ˋkɔrɪdə] 🎧 *Track 1120*
n. 走廊；迴廊；通道
▶ Walk to the end of the corridor and you'll see the elevator.
這條通道走到底，你就會看到電梯了。

cos·met·ics [kɑzˋmɛtɪks] 🎧 *Track 1121*
n. 化妝品；美容品
▶ He wonders why women spend so much money on cosmetics. 他不知道為什麼女人要花那麼多錢買化妝品。

cost [kɔst] 🎧 *Track 1122*
n. 費用；成本；代價
v. 花費（時間、金錢、勞力等）

cost·ly [`kɔstlɪ]　　🎧 *Track 1123*
adj. 貴重的；昂貴的；代價高的

cos·tume [`kɑstjum]　　🎧 *Track 1124*
n. 服裝；戲服
▶We're holding a costume party on Halloween, and you are invited.
我們在萬聖節這天要舉辦一場變裝派對，你已經受邀了。

(補充片語)
hold a party 舉辦派對；
costume party 化妝舞會；變裝派對

cot·tage [`kɑtɪdʒ]　　🎧 *Track 1125*
n. 農舍；小屋；（度假）別墅
▶We usually spend our holidays in our cottage by the lake.
我們假日通常是在我們湖邊的小屋中度過。

cot·ton [`kɑtn]　　🎧 *Track 1126*
n. 棉；棉花

couch [kaʊtʃ]　　🎧 *Track 1127*
n. 長沙發

cough [kɔf]　　🎧 *Track 1128*
v. 咳嗽　**n.** 咳嗽；咳嗽聲

could [kʊd]　　🎧 *Track 1129*
aux. 助動詞can的過去式；表示假設語氣的「可以、但願」

coul·dn't [`kʊdnt]　　🎧 *Track 1130*
abbr. 不能（could not的縮寫）

coun·cil [`kaʊnsl]　　🎧 *Track 1131*
n. 會議；政務會；協調會；議事、商討
▶We will discuss this proposal in the council.
我們會在會議中討論這項提案。

count [kaʊnt]　　🎧 *Track 1132*
v. 數；算；將……計算在內；有意義；依賴
n. 計算；總數

coun·ter [`kaʊntɚ]　　🎧 *Track 1133*
n. 計數器；櫃台
▶He uses a counter to count how many steps he takes a day.
他用一台計數器來數他每天走幾步路。

v. 反抗；反擊
▶We must stand together to counter terrorism.
我們必須要站在同一陣線，反抗恐怖主義。

coun·ter·clock·wise 🎧 *Track 1134*
[ˌkaʊntɚˈklɑkˌwaɪz]
adj. 逆時針的
▶You need to drive around the circle in a counterclockwise direction.
你必須用逆時針的方向開過圓環。

coun·try [`kʌntrɪ]　　🎧 *Track 1135*
n. 國家；鄉下、郊外

coun·try·side 🎧 *Track 1136*
[`kʌntrɪˌsaɪd]
n. 鄉村；鄉間

coun·ty [`kaʊntɪ]　　🎧 *Track 1137*
n. 縣；郡

cou·ple [`kʌpl]　　🎧 *Track 1138*
n. 夫妻；一對

cou·pon [`kupɑn]　　🎧 *Track 1139*
n. 聯票；減價優惠券
▶This 10% off coupon is valid until September 30.
這張九折優惠券九月底前有效。

cour·age [ˈkɝɪdʒ]　　🎧 *Track 1140*
n. 勇氣

cou·ra·geous 🎧 *Track 1141*
[kəˈredʒəs]
adj. 英勇的；勇敢的
▶Standing up against bullies is a very courageous act.
站起來對抗霸凌是個非常勇敢的行為。

course [kors]　　🎧 *Track 1142*
n. 課程；習慣的程序；一道菜

court [kort]　　🎧 *Track 1143*
n. 法庭；場地

cour·te·ous [`kɝtjəs]　　🎧 *Track 1144*
adj. 慇懃的；謙恭的；有禮貌的

※灰色單字為英檢初級必備單字

▶The young man is courteous to everyone, especially the elderly. 這位年輕人對每個人都很謙恭有禮，尤其是老年人。

cour·te·sy [`kɜˋtəsɪ] 🎧 Track 1145
n. 禮貌；禮節
▶He gave a nod to his neighbor out of courtesy. 他出於禮貌向鄰居點了點頭。

(相關片語)
courtesy bus 免費接駁車
▶Our hotel provides courtesy bus service to and from Changi Airport.
本飯店提供來回樟宜機場的免費接駁車服務。

cous·in [`kʌzn] 🎧 Track 1146
n. 表或堂兄弟姐妹

cov·er [`kʌvɚ] 🎧 Track 1147
v. 覆蓋
n. 遮蓋物；書皮（封面或封底）

cow [kaʊ] 🎧 Track 1148
n. 母牛；奶牛

cow·ard [`kaʊɚd] 🎧 Track 1149
adj. 膽小的；怯懦的
▶Attacking a person who cannot defend himself is a coward act.
攻擊無法防禦自己的人是懦弱的行為。

n. 膽小鬼；懦夫
▶Only a coward would attack a person who cannot defend himself.
只有懦夫才會去攻擊無法防禦自己的人。

cow·ard·ly [`kaʊɚdlɪ] 🎧 Track 1150
adj. 膽小的；懦弱的；卑劣的
▶Attacking people who cannot defend themselves is a cowardly act. 攻擊無法防禦自己的人，是一種卑劣的行為。

adv. 膽小地；怯懦地；卑劣地
▶It didn't occur to them that their enemy would cowardly make a sneak attack at midnight.
他們沒想到敵人會卑劣地在午夜發動偷襲。

cow·boy [`kaʊbɔɪ] 🎧 Track 1151
n. 牛仔；牧牛人

co·zy [`kozɪ] 🎧 Track 1152
adj. 舒適的；愜意的
▶My apartment is small but cozy.
我的公寓很小，卻很舒適。

crab [kræb] 🎧 Track 1153
n. 螃蟹；蟹肉

crack [kræk] 🎧 Track 1154
n. 裂縫、裂痕；爆裂聲；猛烈一擊
▶There is a crack in the mirror.
這鏡子有條裂痕。

v. 裂開；砸開；猛擊；爆裂；斷裂
▶The glass bottle cracked when I poured hot water in it.
玻璃瓶在我把熱水倒進去時裂開了。

(相關片語)
a hard nut to crack 棘手的事；難對付的人
▶My new boss is a hard nut to crack. I don't think he will grant my leave. 我的新主管很難說話。我不覺得他會准我的假。

crack·er [`krækɚ] 🎧 Track 1155
n. 薄脆餅乾；鞭炮、爆竹
▶I just had some crackers, so I'm not very hungry. 我剛吃了一些餅乾，所以並不很餓。

cra·dle [`kredl] 🎧 Track 1156
n. 搖籃；嬰兒時期；發源地
▶The baby is sleeping tight in the cradle.
寶寶在搖籃內睡得很熟。

v. 把⋯⋯放在搖籃內
▶She gently cradled the baby after he fell asleep.
寶寶睡著之後，她輕輕地將他放在搖籃內。

(相關片語)
from cradle to grave 生老病死
▶The new health insurance policy will protect every citizen from cradle to grave. 新的健保政策會保護每個公民的生老病死。

craft [kræft] 🎧 Track 1157
n. 工藝；手藝
▶She owns a small shop that sells arts and crafts from Thailand.
她擁有一家賣泰國手工藝品的小店。

arts and crafts 手工藝品

cram [kræm] 🎧 *Track 1158*

v. 把……塞進；擠滿；塞滿；狼吞虎嚥地吃；死記硬背；填鴨式地教

▶ I hate to see students nowadays cram for tests and exams.
我很不喜歡看到現在的學生為了應付測驗和考試而死記硬背。

相關片語

cram school 補習班

▶ I don't let my kids go to cram school.
我不讓我的小孩上補習班。

cramp [kræmp] 🎧 *Track 1159*

v. 用夾鉗夾緊；限制；約束；妨礙

▶ They consider children a burden that will cramp their freedom.
他們把孩子視為會妨礙他們自由的負擔。

n. 鐵鉗；約束物；束縛；抽筋；痙攣

▶ My stomach cramps are killing me.
我的胃痙攣快把我痛死了。

crane [kren] 🎧 *Track 1160*

n. 鶴；起重機

v. 用起重機搬運；伸長脖子看

crash [kræʃ] 🎧 *Track 1161*

n. 相撞；墜毀；失敗；垮台

▶ All passengers were killed in the plane crash.
所有乘客都在這起飛機失事中喪生。

補充片語

plane crash 飛機失事；空難

v. 相撞；墜毀；（電腦）當機

▶ The car crashed into the traffic island. 車子猛地撞上安全島。

補充片語

traffic island 安全島

crawl [krɔl] 🎧 *Track 1162*

v. 爬行；蠕動；緩慢前進；爬滿

▶ The little boy watched the turtle crawling on the ground.
小男孩看著烏龜在地上緩慢爬行。

n. 爬行；緩慢前進

▶ The cars were moving at a crawl during the evening rush hour. 車子在夜晚尖峰時間以非常緩慢的速度前進。

cray·on [`kreən] 🎧 *Track 1163*

n. 蠟筆

cra·zy [`krezɪ] 🎧 *Track 1164*

adj. 瘋狂的；失常的

creak [krik] 🎧 *Track 1165*

v. 發出軋吱聲

▶ The bicycle creaked along.
腳踏車一路發出軋吱的聲音。

n. 軋軋吱吱聲

▶ The creaks are harsh to the ear.
這軋吱聲聽起來很刺耳。

補充片語

harsh to the ear 刺耳

cream [krim] 🎧 *Track 1166*

n. 奶油；乳脂食品；乳膏狀物

cre·ate [krɪ`et] 🎧 *Track 1167*

v. 創造；創作

cre·a·tion [krɪ`eʃən] 🎧 *Track 1168*

n. 創造；創立；宇宙；萬物

▶ Our teacher told us a story about the creation of the world.
老師跟我們說了一個關於世界之創造的故事。

cre·a·tive [krɪ`etɪv] 🎧 *Track 1169*

adj. 創意的；有創造力的

▶ James is a very creative fashion designer.
詹姆士是個非常有創造力的時裝設計師。

cre·a·tiv·i·ty [ˌkrie`tɪvətɪ] 🎧 *Track 1170*

n. 創造力

▶ His latest design lacks creativity.
他最新的設計作品缺乏創造力。

crea·ture [`kritʃɚ] 🎧 *Track 1171*

n. 生物；動物

▶ Blue whales are the largest creatures known to have lived on earth.
藍鯨是住在地球上已知最大的生物。

cred·it [`krɛdɪt】 🎧 Track 1172
n. 賒賬；信譽；銀行存款；信用
▶ He never buys anything on credit.
他從不以賒賬的方式買東西。

(補充片語)
on credit 以賒帳方式；憑信用卡

v. 相信；將……記入貸方；將……歸於；記學分
▶ He credited his success to his supportive wife.
他將他的成功歸功於支持他的妻子。

creep [krip] 🎧 Track 1173
v. 躡手躡腳地走；緩慢前進；爬行；蔓延；起雞皮疙瘩
▶ He didn't notice that a snake was creeping into his room.
他沒注意到一條蛇正爬進他的房間。

n. 爬；蠕動；毛骨悚然的感覺
▶ Thai horror movies always give me the creeps.
泰國的恐怖片總是能讓我感到毛骨悚然。

(補充片語)
give sb. the creeps 讓某人感到毛骨悚然；使人汗毛直豎

crew [kru] 🎧 Track 1174
n. 一組工作人員；全體船員或機組人員
▶ Before takeoff, the cabin crew must check if all passengers are seated properly with their seatbelts fastened.
在飛機起飛之前，航班空服員必須檢查所有乘客是否都有繫上安全帶坐好。

(補充片語)
cabin crew 航班空服人員

crib [krɪb] 🎧 Track 1175
n. 小兒床；有欄杆的嬰兒床
▶ The baby climbed out of his crib and fell.
寶寶從他的嬰兒床爬出來，摔倒了。

crick·et [`krɪkɪt] 🎧 Track 1176
n. 蟋蟀；板球；光明正大

▶ I can hear crickets chirping outside.
我可以聽到外面有蟋蟀在鳴叫。

crime [kraɪm] 🎧 Track 1177
n. 罪行；罪過

crim·i·nal [`krɪmənl] 🎧 Track 1178
adj. 犯罪的；犯法的；刑事上的
▶ It is our policy to not hire people with criminal records.
不雇用有犯罪記錄的人是本公司的政策。

(補充片語)
criminal record 犯罪記錄

n. 罪犯
▶ Several criminals are scheming to escape from prison.
數名罪犯正在密謀逃獄。

crip·ple [`krɪpl] 🎧 Track 1179
n. 跛子
▶ He proved to his parents that even a cripple could earn his own living.
他向父母親證明，即使是一個跛子也能自食其力。

(補充片語)
earn one's own living 自食其力

v. 使成跛子；使陷入癱瘓
▶ The car accident crippled the traffic for hours.
這起車禍意外使交通癱瘓了數小時。

cri·sis [`kraɪsɪs] 🎧 Track 1180
n. 危機；危險期

crisp [krɪsp] 🎧 Track 1181
adj. 脆的；酥的；脆嫩的；清爽的；乾脆俐落的
▶ These chips are not crisp enough.
這些洋芋片不夠酥脆。

crisp·y [`krɪspɪ] 🎧 Track 1182
adj. 酥脆的；清脆的；乾淨俐落的
▶ This roast duck with crispy skin is really delicious.
這有著酥脆鴨皮的烤鴨真是太美味了。

crit·ic [`krɪtɪk]　　🎧 *Track 1183*
n. 評論家；批評家；吹毛求疵的人
▶He is a famous chef as well as a food critic. 他是個名廚，也是個美食評論家。

crit·i·cal [`krɪtɪkl]　　🎧 *Track 1184*
adj. 緊要的；關鍵性的；批判的；愛挑剔的
▶You are too critical of your own work.
你對你自己的工作太吹毛求疵了。

crit·i·cis·m　　🎧 *Track 1185*
[`krɪtə‚sɪzəm]
n. 批評；評論；苛求；挑剔
▶The actress' clothing and hair were both beyond criticism.
該女星的服裝和髮型都無可挑剔。

(補充片語)

beyond criticism　無可挑剔；無從指責

crit·i·cize [`krɪtɪ‚saɪz]　🎧 *Track 1186*
v. 批評；非難；評論
▶She criticized him for his inappropriate comments about female workers. 她因為他對女性員工所做的不當評論而指責他。

croc·o·dile [`krɑkə‚daɪl]　🎧 *Track 1187*
n. 鱷魚；鱷魚皮革
▶The leather handbag is made from the skin of crocodiles.
這皮製手提包是用鱷魚皮做的。

(相關片語)

crocodile tears　鱷魚眼淚；假慈悲
▶That evil woman and her crocodile tears make me sick. 那個邪惡的女人和她虛情假意的眼淚讓我作嘔。

crook·ed [`krʊkɪd]　　🎧 *Track 1188*
adj. 歪曲的；變形的；不正當的
▶Stay away from those crooked people.
離那些不正派的人遠一點。

crop [krɑp]　　🎧 *Track 1189*
n. 作物；莊稼；收成
v. 剪短；種植、播種；收割

cross [krɔs]　　🎧 *Track 1190*
v. 穿越；橫過　**n.** 十字形；十字架

cross·road [`krɔs‚rod]　🎧 *Track 1191*
n. 十字路口；交叉點；轉折點
▶Most traffic accidents occur at crossroads.
大多數的交通意外都發生在十字路口。

crouch [`kraʊtʃ]　　🎧 *Track 1192*
adj. 蹲伏；彎腰；卑躬屈膝，諂媚
▶My dog is crouching by the sofa.
我的狗正蹲伏在沙發旁。

crow [kro]　　🎧 *Track 1193*
n. 烏鴉　**v.** （雞）報曉；啼

crowd [kraʊd]　　🎧 *Track 1194*
n. 人群

crowd·ed [`kraʊdɪd]　🎧 *Track 1195*
adj. 擁擠的

crown [kraʊn]　　🎧 *Track 1196*
n. 王冠；榮冠；王位
▶This crown belongs to the king of the kingdom. 這個王冠是屬於這個王國的國王。
v. 為……加冕；立……為王
▶He was crowned King of the kingdom when he was only 12 years old. 當他才十二歲時，就被加冕為這個王國的君主。

cru·cial [`kruʃəl]　　🎧 *Track 1197*
adj. 決定性的；嚴酷的
▶Give him some more time to deliberate. It is a crucial decision for him to make.
給他多一些時間仔細考慮。他要做的可是一個至關重要的決定。

cru·el [`kruəl]　　🎧 *Track 1198*
adj. 殘忍的；痛苦傷人的

cru·el·ty [`kruəltɪ]　🎧 *Track 1199*
n. 殘酷；殘忍；殘酷的行為
▶The cruelties of the terrorists are unforgivable.
恐怖份子的殘酷暴行是不可原諒的。

cruise [kruz]　　🎧 *Track 1200*
v. 巡航；航遊；緩慢巡行；乘船遊覽
▶The police car is cruising up and down the neighborhood.
警車正在鄰近地區到處巡邏。

Aa
Bb
Cc
Dd
Ee

Ff
Gg
Hh
Ii
Jj

Kk
Ll
Mm
Nn
Oo

Pp
Qq
Rr
Ss
Tt

Uu
Vv
Ww
Xx
Yy
Zz

※灰色單字為英檢初級必備單字

up and down 到處

n. 巡航；巡邏；乘遊輪航遊
▶ Going on a cruise through Europe sounds fun. 搭遊輪遊歐洲聽起來很好玩。

補充片語

go on a cruise 搭遊輪航遊

crumb [krʌm]　🎧 *Track 1201*
n. 麵包、糕餅屑；碎屑；少許
▶ Those cookie crumbs attracted a large amount of ants.
那些餅乾屑引來一大堆的螞蟻。

v. 捏碎；弄碎；把……裹上麵包屑
▶ He crumbed the toast and fed it to the pigeons in the park.
他把吐司捏碎，餵食公園裡的鴿子。

crunch·y [ˋkrʌntʃɪ]　🎧 *Track 1202*
adj. 鬆脆的；易碎的
▶ The fried chicken is crunchy, juicy and super delicious.
這炸雞又脆又多汁，而且超級美味。

crush [krʌʃ]　🎧 *Track 1203*
v. 壓碎；壓壞；摧毀；擠、塞
▶ He accidently crushed the box and ruined the cake inside.
他不小心壓壞了盒子，把裡面的蛋糕給毀了。

n. 壓碎；壓壞；極度擁擠；暗戀
▶ She seems to have a crush on you.
她好像暗戀你。

補充片語

have a crush on sb. 暗戀某人

crutch [krʌtʃ]　🎧 *Track 1204*
n. 拐杖
▶ Why are you walking on crutches?
你怎麼拄著枴杖走路？

cry [kraɪ]　🎧 *Track 1205*
v. 哭；哭泣；喊叫　**n.** 叫喊聲；哭

crys·tal [ˋkrɪstḷ]　🎧 *Track 1206*
n. 水晶；水晶飾品
▶ The vase is made of crystal.
這花瓶是水晶製的。

adj. 水晶的；水晶製的；水晶般的
▶ She wore a beautiful crystal necklace.
她戴了一個美麗的水晶項鍊。

cub [kʌb]　🎧 *Track 1207*
n. 幼獸（獅、虎、狼等）
▶ The tiger cub looks just like a big cat.
這隻幼虎看起來就像是一隻大貓咪。

cube [kjub]　🎧 *Track 1208*
n. 立方體；立方
▶ The cube of 5 is 125. 五的三次方是125。

v. 使成立方體；使成小方塊
▶ Would you cube this pork for me?
你可以幫我把這塊豬肉切成小丁嗎？

cu·cum·ber [ˋkjukʌmbɚ]　🎧 *Track 1209*
n. 黃瓜；胡瓜
▶ He added some cucumber into his salad.
他加了一些黃瓜到他的沙拉裡。

cue [kju]　🎧 *Track 1210*
n. 提示；暗示
▶ It's a cue for you to leave.
這是你該離開的暗示。

v. 給提示；給暗示
▶ The conductor cued the choir to begin.
指揮暗示合唱團開始唱。

cui·sine [kwɪˋzin]　🎧 *Track 1211*
n. 烹飪；烹調法；菜餚
▶ My husband and I love Italian cuisine.
我先生和我都很喜歡義大利菜。

cul·ti·vate [ˋkʌltəˌvet]　🎧 *Track 1212*
v. 耕種；栽培；陶冶；培養
▶ He cultivated his mind by practicing Chinese calligraphy.
他以練習中國書法來修身養性。

cul·tu·ral [ˋkʌltʃərəl]　🎧 *Track 1213*
adj. 文化的；人文的；修養的
▶ His cultural background has a great influence on his values.
他的文化背景對他的價值觀有很大的影響。

cul·ture [ˋkʌltʃɚ]　🎧 *Track 1214*
n. 文化

cun·ning [`kʌnɪŋ] 　🎧 *Track 1215*
adj. 狡猾的
▶ He is as cunning as a fox.
　他像狐狸一樣狡猾。

cup [kʌp] 　🎧 *Track 1216*
n. 杯子；（一）杯

cup·board [`kʌbəd] 　🎧 *Track 1217*
n. 食櫥；碗櫃
▶ Those glasses are in the cupboard.
　那些杯子被放在碗櫃裡面。

cure [kjʊr] 　🎧 *Track 1218*
n. 治療；痊癒；療法
v. 治癒；消除（弊病等）

cu·ri·os·i·ty 　🎧 *Track 1219*
[͵kjʊrɪ`ɑsətɪ]
n. 好奇；好奇心
▶ He opened the box out of curiosity.
　他出於好奇心地打開了盒子。

cu·ri·ous [`kjʊrɪəs] 　🎧 *Track 1220*
adj. 好奇的；渴望知道的

curl [kɝl] 　🎧 *Track 1221*
v. 捲曲；使捲起來
▶ He sat still with his legs curled under
　himself. 他盤著腿坐著不動。
(補充片語)
curl one's legs under oneself　盤腿而坐
n. 捲髮；捲狀物；捲曲
▶ I love her natural curls.
　我很愛她的自然捲髮。

cur·rent [`kɝənt] 　🎧 *Track 1222*
adj. 現在的；當前的
n. 流動；氣流；潮流

cur·ry [`kɝɪ] 　🎧 *Track 1223*
n. 咖哩；咖哩菜餚
▶ I prefer Indian curry to Japanese curry.
　我喜歡印度咖哩更勝於日式咖哩。

curse [kɝs] 　🎧 *Track 1224*
v. 詛咒；咒罵

▶ They cursed the person who murdered
　their son. 他們詛咒殺害兒子的兇手。
n. 咒罵人的話；咒語；禍害
▶ The witch put a curse on the prince.
　巫婆對王子下了咒語。
(補充片語)
put a curse on sb.　對某人下咒；

cur·tain [`kɝtn] 　🎧 *Track 1225*
n. 窗簾；門簾；（舞台上的）幕

curve [kɝv] 　🎧 *Track 1226*
n. 曲線；弧線 **v.** 彎曲

cush·ion [`kʊʃən] 　🎧 *Track 1227*
n. 墊子；靠墊
▶ He fell asleep on the couch cushion.
　他在沙發靠墊上睡著了。
v. 裝上靠墊；緩和衝擊
▶ The mat on the floor cushioned his fall.
　地上的蓆子緩和了他跌下的衝擊。

cus·tom [`kʌstəm] 　🎧 *Track 1228*
n. 習俗；習慣

cus·tom·er [`kʌstəmə] 　🎧 *Track 1229*
n. 顧客

cut [kʌt] 　🎧 *Track 1230*
v. 剪；切 **n.** 剪、切的傷口，割痕

cute [kjut] 　🎧 *Track 1231*
adj. 可愛的；漂亮的

cy·cle [`saɪkl̩] 　🎧 *Track 1232*
n. 週期；循環；腳踏車
▶ The 12 Chinese animal signs make a
　twelve-year cycle.
　中國十二生肖構成了一個十二年的循環週期。
v. 循環；輪轉；騎腳踏車
▶ We cycled around the island.
　我們騎腳踏車環島。

cy·clist [`saɪklɪst] 　🎧 *Track 1233*
n. 騎腳踏車的人；自行車騎士
▶ Some bike lanes are too rocky for cyclists.
　有些自行車道對自行車騎士來說太顛簸了。

※灰色單字為英檢初級必備單字

Dd

通過中級英文檢定者的英文能力：

 聽　在日常生活中，能聽懂一般的會話；能大致聽懂公共場所廣播、氣象報告及廣告等。在工作時，能聽懂簡易的產品介紹與操作說明。能大致聽懂外籍人士的談話及詢問。

 讀　在日常生活中，能閱讀短文、故事、私人信件、廣告、傳單、簡介及使用說明等。在工作時，能閱讀工作須知、公告、操作手冊、例行的文件、傳真、電報等。

 寫　能寫簡單的書信、故事及心得等。對於熟悉且與個人經歷相關的主題，能以簡易的文字表達。

 說　在日常生活中，能以簡易英語交談或描述一般事物，能介紹自己的生活作息、工作、家庭、經歷等，並可對一般話題陳述看法。在工作時，能進行簡單的答詢，並與外籍人士交談溝通。

本書除包含官方公佈的中級4,947單字外，更精挑了近400個滿分必學的高手單字。同時，在片語的挑選、例句的使用上，皆依上述英檢官方公佈之能力範疇做設計，難度適中、不偏離考試主題。發音部分則是自然發音＆KK音標雙管齊下，搭配MP3以「分解／完整」方式錄音，給你最多元有效的學習手段，怎麼記都可以，想忘掉都好難！

---

dad [dæd]＝**dad·dy**
＝**pap·a**＝**pa**＝**pop**　🎧 *Track 1234*
n. 爸爸

daf·fo·dil [`dæfədɪl]　🎧 *Track 1235*
n. 黃水仙
▶ She decorated her dining table with a large bunch of daffodils.
她用一大束黃色水仙花佈置餐桌。

dai·ly [`delɪ]　🎧 *Track 1236*
adj. 每天的；**adv.** 每天

dai·ry [`dɛrɪ]　🎧 *Track 1237*
n. 製酪場；乳品店；牛奶與乳品業
▶ We purchase fresh milk and cheese directly from a local dairy. 我們向一個本地的製酪場購買新鮮的牛奶和起司。

dam [dæm]　🎧 *Track 1238*
n. 水壩；水堤
▶ The dam is still under construction.
這水壩還在施工中。

v. 築壩於……
▶ The river was dammed two years ago.
這河是在兩年前築的壩。

dam·age [`dæmɪdʒ]　🎧 *Track 1239*
n. 損害；損失；**v.** 損害；毀壞

damn [dæm]　🎧 *Track 1240*
v. 咒罵；指責；罰……入地獄
▶ I damn those who bully the weak.
我詛咒那些恃強凌弱的人。

n. 詛咒；絲毫；一點點
▶ I do not give a damn about what people think.
我一點都不在乎別人怎麼想。

【相關片語】
damn the consequence　不顧一切
▶ Let's drink to our heart's content and damn the consequence.
咱們不顧一切地盡情喝個痛快吧！

damp [dæmp] 🎧 Track 1241

adj. 有濕氣的；潮濕的
▶ I'm not used to the damp weather in London. 我不習慣倫敦的潮濕天氣。

n. 濕氣；潮濕
▶ I can smell the damp in this room.
我在這房間聞到一股濕氣。

v. 使潮濕；弄濕
▶ She damped a towel and wiped her face.
她把一條毛巾弄濕，然後擦臉。

相關片語

something damp 一杯酒
▶ Would you like something damp?
你想不想喝一杯酒呢？

dance [dæns] 🎧 Track 1242

v./n. 跳舞

danc·er [`dænsɚ] 🎧 Track 1243

n. 舞者；舞蹈家
▶ My wife is world-famous ballet dancer.
我的太太是個世界知名的舞者。

danc·ing [`dænsɪŋ] 🎧 Track 1244

n. 跳舞；舞蹈
▶ She spends at least three hours practicing dancing every day.
她每天至少花三小時練舞。

dan·ger [`dendʒɚ] 🎧 Track 1245

n. 危險

dan·ger·ous [`dendʒɚrəs] 🎧 Track 1246

adj. 危險的

dare [dɛr] 🎧 Track 1247

aux. 敢；膽敢
▶ How dare you steal money from your mother?
你怎麼敢偷你媽媽的錢？

v. 敢；膽敢
▶ He dared not tell her the truth.
他不敢告訴她事實。

dark [dɑrk] 🎧 Track 1248

adj. 暗的；黑的；**n.** 黑暗

dark·en [`dɑrkn] 🎧 Track 1249

v. 使變暗

dar·ling [`dɑrlɪŋ] 🎧 Track 1250

n. 心愛的人；寵兒
▶ She's my darling. 她是我心愛的人。

adj. 親愛的；寵愛的；漂亮的
▶ I can't wait to see my darling mom.
我等不及要看到我親愛的媽咪了。

dart [dɑrt] 🎧 Track 1251

n. 標槍；投標遊戲；猛衝、飛奔
▶ Those guys are good at playing darts.
那些傢伙很會玩飛鏢。

v. 擲飛鏢；猛衝
▶ The police officer darted across the street to catch the thief.
警察衝過馬路，把小偷給逮住了。

dash [dæʃ] 🎧 Track 1252

v. 猛撞；急奔；潑灑；使（希望）破滅
▶ The students dashed out of the classroom as soon as the teacher dismissed the class. 老師一下課，學生們就急奔出教室。

n. 急衝；奔跑；短跑；破滅
▶ Ryan made a dash for the bathroom as soon as he got home.
萊恩一回到家就急奔廁所。

補充片語

make a dash for 急奔某處；衝向某物

da·ta [`detə] 🎧 Track 1253

n. 資料；數據

date [det] 🎧 Track 1254

n. 日期；約會；約會對象；
v. 確定年代；註明日期；和……約會

daugh·ter [`dɔtɚ] 🎧 Track 1255

n. 女兒

dawn [dɔn] 🎧 Track 1256

n. 黎明；破曉；**v.** 破曉；天亮

day [de] 🎧 Track 1257

n. 一天；日；白晝

Aa
Bb
Cc
Dd
Ee
Ff
Gg
Hh
Ii
Jj
Kk
Ll
Mm
Nn
Oo
Pp
Qq
Rr
Ss
Tt
Uu
Vv
Ww
Xx
Yy
Zz

※灰色單字為英檢初級必備單字

day·break [ˈde͵brek] 🎧 *Track 1258*
n. 黎明；破曉
▶ He went out to work before daybreak.
他破曉之前就出門工作了。

day·light [ˈde͵laɪt] 🎧 *Track 1259*
n. 日光；白晝
▶ My father always went out to work before daylight.
我爸爸總是在天亮前就出門工作了。

(補充片語)
before daylight 天亮前

(相關片語)
in broad daylight 大白天地；光天化日之下
▶ I can't believe they dared to kidnap young children in broad daylight. 我不敢相信他們竟敢在光天化日之下綁架小孩。

daz·zle [ˈdæzl] 🎧 *Track 1260*
v. 使目眩；使眼花；使迷惑
▶ Mike apparently was dazzled by Julie's beauty.
麥可很顯然地是被茱莉的美貌給迷住了。

n. 耀眼的光；令人讚歎或迷惑的東西
▶ The sun's dazzle is harsh to the eye.
太陽的奪目強光很刺眼。

dead [dɛd] 🎧 *Track 1261*
adj. 死的；無效的；已廢的

dead·line [ˈdɛd͵laɪn] 🎧 *Track 1262*
n. 截止期限；最後日期
▶ I promise you that I will get my job done by the deadline.
我答應你我會在截止時間之前把工作完成。

dead·ly [ˈdɛdlɪ] 🎧 *Track 1263*
adj. 致命的；不共戴天的；死一般的；非常的
▶ Ebola is a deadly virus transmitted by animals and humans. 伊波拉是一種會經由動物及人類傳播的致命病毒。

deaf [dɛf] 🎧 *Track 1264*
adj. 聾的

deal [dil] 🎧 *Track 1265*
v. 處理；對付；**n.** 交易

deal·er [ˈdilɚ] 🎧 *Track 1266*
n. 業者；商人；經銷商
▶ My father is a dealer in computer components.
我爸爸是個電腦零件的經銷商。

(相關片語)
drug dealer 毒販
▶ The drug dealer was arrested.
那個毒販已經被逮了。

dear [dɪr] 🎧 *Track 1267*
adj. 親愛的；**int.** （感歎詞）哎呀；
n. 親愛的（人）

death [dɛθ] 🎧 *Track 1268*
n. 死；死亡

de·bate [dɪˈbet] 🎧 *Track 1269*
n. 辯論；辯論會；**v.** 辯論；爭論

debt [dɛt] 🎧 *Track 1270*
n. 債；負債

dec·ade [ˈdɛked] 🎧 *Track 1271*
n. 十年
▶ It's been a decade since I last saw you.
我上次見你已經是十年前的事了。

de·cay [dɪˈke] 🎧 *Track 1272*
v. 腐朽；蛀蝕；腐爛；衰敗；使蛀壞
▶ This abandoned house decayed over time. 這棟廢棄的房子隨著時間而腐朽。

(補充片語)
over time 隨著時間

n. 腐朽；腐爛；蛀牙
▶ What can we do to stop or slow the decay of this ancient temple?
我們可以怎麼做來阻止或減緩這棟古老寺廟的朽壞？

de·ceive [dɪˈsiv] 🎧 *Track 1273*
v. 欺騙
▶ The man tried to deceive me into buying the fakes.
那男人想騙我買那些冒牌貨。

(補充片語)
deceive sb. into doing sth. 騙某人做某事

De·cem·ber [dɪˋsɛmbɚ] 🎧 *Track 1274*
=Dec.
n. 十二月

de·cide [dɪˋsaɪd] 🎧 *Track 1275*
v. 決定

de·ci·sion [dɪˋsɪʒən] 🎧 *Track 1276*
n. 決定

deck [dɛk] 🎧 *Track 1277*
n. 甲板
▶ It is quite windy on the deck.
甲板上風相當大。

相關片語
deck shoe 平底帆布鞋
▶ Her white deck shoes are totally worn out.
她的白色平底帆布鞋已經完全破舊不堪了。

補充片語
worn out 破損的

dec·la·ra·tion 🎧 *Track 1278*
[͵dɛkləˋreʃən]
n. 聲明
▶ I was asked to make a declaration of secrecy before I took the job.
在接這份工作前,我被要求要做出保密聲明。

補充片語
declaration of secrecy 保密聲明

de·clare [dɪˋklɛr] 🎧 *Track 1279*
v. 宣稱;宣告;申報(稅)
▶ The man declared himself not guilty.
男子宣稱自己無罪。

相關片語
declare war 宣戰
▶ The United States of America declared war on Japan on December 7, 1941.
美國在1941年十二月七日向日本宣戰。

de·cline [dɪˋklaɪn] 🎧 *Track 1280*
v. 婉拒;婉謝
▶ She had to decline their invitation because of a prior engagement. 因為有事先安排事情,她必須婉拒他們的邀請。

dec·o·rate [ˋdɛkə͵ret] 🎧 *Track 1281*
v. 裝飾;佈置

dec·o·ra·tion 🎧 *Track 1282*
[͵dɛkəˋreʃən]
n. 裝飾;裝潢;裝飾物
▶ Candles are very elegant table decorations.
蠟燭是非常優雅的餐桌裝飾物。

相關片語
interior decoration 室內裝潢
▶ They spent a large amount of money on interior decoration.
他們花了一大筆錢做室內裝潢。

de·crease [ˋdikris] 🎧 *Track 1283*
v./n. 減少;降低

ded·i·cate [ˋdɛdə͵ket] 🎧 *Track 1284*
v. 以……奉獻;獻(給);題獻(著作)
▶ The author dedicated his latest book to his wife. 作者將他的新書題獻給他的妻子。

deed [did] 🎧 *Track 1285*
n. 行為;行動
▶ I feel disdain for your dirty deeds.
我不屑你的卑鄙行為。

補充片語
dirty deed 卑鄙行為

deep [dip] 🎧 *Track 1286*
adj. 深的;**adv.** 深地

deer [dɪr] 🎧 *Track 1287*
n. 鹿

de·feat [dɪˋfit] 🎧 *Track 1288*
n. 失敗;挫折
▶ You may encounter many defeats in your life, but you must not be defeated.
你在人生中可能會遭遇許多挫折,但是你絕對不能被它們擊敗。

v. 戰勝;擊敗
▶ Good defeats evil. 邪不勝正。

de·fend [dɪˋfɛnd] 🎧 *Track 1289*
v. 防禦;保衛
▶ We need more weapons to defend our country. 我們需要更多的武器來保衛國家。

de·fense [dɪ`fɛns]　🎧 *Track 1290*
=defence（英式英文）
n. 防禦；抵禦
▶ We have to strengthen the defense of our country. 我們必須加強國家的防禦。

de·fen·sive [dɪ`fɛnsɪv]　🎧 *Track 1291*
adj. 防禦的
▶ A defensive person doesn't make friends easily.
一個防禦心強的人不太容易交到朋友。

（補充片語）
make friends 交朋友

def·i·cit [`dɛfɪsɪt]　🎧 *Track 1292*
n. 不足額；赤字
▶ The government will have to raise taxes in order to reduce the budget deficit.
政府將需要提高稅金以降低預算赤字。

de·fine [dɪ`faɪn]　🎧 *Track 1293*
v. 解釋；為……下定義；確定……的界限
▶ The boundary between the two countries is clearly defined in the treaty.
這兩個國家的疆界在條約中有清楚劃定。

def·i·nite [`dɛfənɪt]　🎧 *Track 1294*
adj. 明確的
▶ I need you to give me a definite answer.
我需要你給我一個明確的答案。

def·i·ni·tion [ˌdɛfə`nɪʃən]　🎧 *Track 1295*
n. 定義
▶ Everyone has his own definition of happiness.
每個人都有自己對幸福的定義。

de·gree [dɪ`gri]　🎧 *Track 1296*
n. 程度；度數；學位

de·lay [dɪ`le]　🎧 *Track 1297*
n./v. 延遲；耽擱

del·e·gate [`dɛləˌget]　🎧 *Track 1298*
n. 代表；會議代表；代表團團員
▶ The Chinese delegates were not pleased with some terms of the treaty.
中國代表團代表對條約的部分條款不滿意。

（補充片語）
be pleased with 對……感到滿意
v. 委派……為代表；委派某人做……；授權給……
▶ The manager has delegated Peter to take charge of the project.
經理已經委派彼得負責這個企劃案。

（補充片語）
take charge of 負責

de·lete [dɪ`lit]　🎧 *Track 1299*
v. 刪除；劃掉；刪去
▶ Amy deleted Peter and James from her guest list.
愛咪將彼得及詹姆士從她的賓客名單中刪除。

de·lib·e·rate [dɪ`lɪbərɪt]　🎧 *Track 1300*
adj. 深思熟慮的；謹慎的；蓄意的
▶ The man was accused of deliberate murder. 男子被控蓄意殺人。

v. 考慮；仔細思考
▶ We need a few more days to deliberate on this matter.
我們需要多幾天的時間來仔細思考這個問題。

del·i·cate [`dɛləkət]　🎧 *Track 1301*
adj. 精美的；精緻的；易碎的；需要小心處理的；鮮美的
▶ Please be careful with these delicate crystal wine glasses.
請小心這些精緻的水晶酒杯。

de·li·cious [dɪ`lɪʃəs]　🎧 *Track 1302*
adj. 美味的

de·light [dɪ`laɪt]　🎧 *Track 1303*
n. 欣喜；愉快；樂趣
▶ He told us the good news with delight.
他興高采烈地告訴我們這個好消息。

v. 使高興；使感欣喜
▶ The good news delighted everybody.
這個好消息令每個人都感到開心。

de·light·ed [dɪ`laɪtɪd]　🎧 *Track 1304*
adj. 高興的；快樂的
▶ I'm so delighted to hear from you.
我真高興能接到你的信。

hear from sb. 接到某人的信；從……得到消息

de·light·ful [dɪ`laɪtfəl] 🎧 *Track 1305*
adj. 令人高興的
▶ The result of the game was delightful.
比賽的結果是令人高興的。

de·lin·quent [dɪ`lɪŋkwənt] 🎧 *Track 1306*
adj. 怠忽職守的；有過失的
▶ He was fired for being delinquent.
他因為怠忽職守而被開除。

n. 違法者；有過失者
▶ These juvenile delinquents belong to the same gang. 這些少年犯都是同一個幫派的。

補充片語

juvenile delinquent 少年犯

de·liv·er [dɪ`lɪvɚ] 🎧 *Track 1307*
v. 運送；投遞

de·liv·er·y [dɪ`lɪvərɪ] 🎧 *Track 1308*
n. 遞送
▶ The contract will be sent to you by special delivery.
合約會以限時專送的方式郵遞給您。

補充片語

special delivery （郵件）限時專送

相關片語

delivery room 產房
▶ Husbands are encouraged to be with their wives in the delivery room.
我們鼓勵先生們進產房陪伴太太生產。

de·mand [dɪ`mænd] 🎧 *Track 1309*
n. 要求；請求
▶ The client made a demand for early delivery of his order.
該客戶提出將他訂購的物品早日交貨的要求。

補充片語

early delivery 早日交貨

v. 要求；請求
▶ The customer demanded that we should compensate for her loss.
那個顧客要求我們應賠償她的損失。

相關片語

in demand 非常需要的；受歡迎的

▶ Certificated accountants are in demand.
有執照的會計師是很多公司都需要的。

de·mand·ing [dɪ`mændɪŋ] 🎧 *Track 1310*
adj. 苛求的；高要求的；使人需吃力應付的
▶ He has to deal with many demanding clients every day.
他每天都必須應付許多要求很多的客戶。

de·moc·ra·cy [dɪ`mɑkrəsɪ] 🎧 *Track 1311*
n. 民主；民主政體；民主國家

dem·o·crat [`dɛmə͵kræt] 🎧 *Track 1312*
n. 民主主義者；（美國）民主黨人；民主黨支持者
▶ My father is a Democrat, but my mother is a Republican. 我爸是民主黨支持者，但我媽是共和黨支持者。

dem·o·crat·ic [͵dɛmə`krætɪk] 🎧 *Track 1313*
adj. 民主的；民主政體的

dem·on·strate [`dɛmən͵stret] 🎧 *Track 1314*
v. 論證；證明；示範
▶ The saleswoman demonstrated the bread machine for the customers.
女售貨員為顧客示範操作麵包機。

dem·on·stra·tion [͵dɛmən`streʃən] 🎧 *Track 1315*
n. 示範；論證；證明
▶ The instructor taught us the dance moves by demonstration.
指導員以示範的方式教我們舞蹈動作。

de·ni·al [dɪ`naɪəl] 🎧 *Track 1316*
n. 否認；否定；拒絕承認
▶ The actress issued a denial of her involvement in the sex scandal.
女星發表聲明否認與該性醜聞有所關聯。

補充片語

issue a denial of 發表否認聲明

dense [dɛns] 🎧 *Track 1317*
adj. 密集的；稠密的；濃密的

※灰色單字為英檢初級必備單字

► The fog was so dense that we couldn't see what was in front of us. 霧太濃密了，以至於我們無法看清前方有什麼。

den·tal [ˋdɛntl̩] 🎧 *Track 1318*
adj. 牙齒的；牙科
► He goes to the dental clinic for a teeth cleaning every six months.
他每六個月去牙科診所洗牙一次。

(補充片語)

dental clinic 牙科診所；teeth cleaning 洗牙

den·tist [ˋdɛntɪst] 🎧 *Track 1319*
n. 牙醫

de·ny [dɪˋnaɪ] 🎧 *Track 1320*
v. 否認

de·part [dɪˋpɑrt] 🎧 *Track 1321*
v. 分離；離開
► We expect to depart at six.
我們預計六點離開。

de·part·ment 🎧 *Track 1322*
[dɪˋpɑrtmənt]
n. 部門

de·par·ture [dɪˋpɑrtʃɚ] 🎧 *Track 1323*
n. 出發；離開；啟程
► When will you leave town? Let's meet before your departure. 你什麼時候要離開這裡？咱們在你出發前碰個面吧！

(相關片語)

departure lounge 候機室
► Passengers were waiting to board at the departure lounge.
旅客在候機室等候登機。

de·pend [dɪˋpɛnd] 🎧 *Track 1324*
v. 依賴；信賴；視……而定

de·pend·a·ble 🎧 *Track 1325*
[dɪˋpɛndəbl̩]
adj. 可靠的；可信任的
► Sadly, I don't have any dependable friends.
令人悲傷的是，我沒有任何可以信賴的朋友。

de·pen·dent [dɪˋpɛndənt] 🎧 *Track 1326*
adj. 依靠的；依賴的
► She became financially dependent on her husband after quitting her job.
她在辭去工作後，便成了在經濟上必須依賴丈夫的女人。

n. 受撫養者；受撫養親屬
► He claimed his parents and his three children as dependents on his tax return.
他聲請父母及三個孩子為受撫養親屬以辦理退稅。

de·pict [dɪˋpɪkt] 🎧 *Track 1327*
v. 描畫；描述；描寫
► The movie depicted the country's leader as a tyrant.
該電影將這位國家領導者描述為一個暴君。

de·pos·it [dɪˋpɑzɪt] 🎧 *Track 1328*
n. 存款；保證金、押金、訂金；沈澱物
► You have to pay a deposit to confirm your room reservation.
您必須付一筆訂金以確認訂房。

v. 放下；放置、寄存
► She deposited all her earnings in the bank.
她將她所有賺來的錢都存在銀行裡。

(相關片語)

safe deposit 保險箱
► You may keep your valuables in the safe deposit. 您可以將您的貴重物品放在保險箱裡。

de·press [dɪˋprɛs] 🎧 *Track 1329*
v. 使沮喪
► The result of the game depressed us all.
比賽的結果令所有人沮喪。

de·pressed [dɪˋprɛst] 🎧 *Track 1330*
adj. 消沉的、沮喪的、抑鬱的；蕭條的
► They were depressed to know that their father only had three months to live.
得知父親只剩三個月能活，他們感到很抑鬱。

de·press·ing [dɪˋprɛsɪŋ] 🎧 *Track 1331*
adj. 令人沮喪的
► I don't know how to tell her this depressing news.
我不知道該怎麼告訴她這個令人沮喪的消息。

de·pres·sion [dɪˋprɛʃən] 🎧 *Track 1332*
n. 沮喪、抑鬱；意志消沉；不景氣、蕭條
▶ Drinking will only worsen your depression.
喝酒只會讓你的抑鬱更嚴重。

相關片語

pregnancy depression 孕期憂鬱症
▶ My wife has all symptoms of pregnancy depression.
我太太有孕期憂鬱症的所有症狀。

depth [dɛpθ] 🎧 *Track 1333*
n. 深度；厚度
▶ The river is five feet in depth.
這條河深度有五呎。

相關片語

out of one's depth 非某人所能理解；非某人能力所及
▶ You asked the wrong person. Photography is totally out of my depth.
你問錯人了。我對攝影一竅不通。

de·scribe [dɪˋskraɪb] 🎧 *Track 1334*
v. 形容；描述

de·scrip·tion [dɪˋskrɪpʃən] 🎧 *Track 1335*
n. 描述；敘述；說明
▶ He gave a brief description of the job.
他對這份工作做了簡單的描述。

de·scrip·tive [dɪˋskrɪptɪv] 🎧 *Track 1336*
adj. 描寫的；記敘的
▶ The students were asked to write a descriptive article about a person they admired the most.
學生們被要求寫一篇有關一個他們最欽佩的人的記敘文。

des·ert [ˋdɛzət] 🎧 *Track 1337*
v. 逃跑；拋棄；遺棄；**n.** 沙漠

de·serve [dɪˋzɝv] 🎧 *Track 1338*
v. 應受；值得
▶ You deserve the promotion.
你是應該得到晉升的。

de·sign [dɪˋzaɪn] 🎧 *Track 1339*
n./v. 設計

de·sign·er [dɪˋzaɪnə] 🎧 *Track 1340*
n. 設計師
▶ It is her dream to become a fashion designer.
成為一名服裝設計師是她的夢想。

de·sire [dɪˋzaɪr] 🎧 *Track 1341*
n./v. 渴望

desk [dɛsk] 🎧 *Track 1342*
n. 書桌

de·spair [dɪˋspɛr] 🎧 *Track 1343*
n. 絕望
▶ The woman looked at the burnt house in despair.
婦人絕望地望著燒得焦黑的房子。

補充片語

in despair 絕望地

des·per·ate [ˋdɛspərɪt] 🎧 *Track 1344*
adj. 危急的；絕望的；極度渴望的
▶ Joseph was desperate when his wife left him.
當妻子離開他時，約瑟夫感到十分絕望。

de·spise [dɪˋspaɪz] 🎧 *Track 1345*
v. 鄙視；看不起
▶ I despise him for bullying the weak.
我因為他恃強凌弱而鄙視他。

補充片語

bully the weak 恃強凌弱；欺負弱者

de·spite [dɪˋspaɪt] 🎧 *Track 1346*
prep. 儘管
▶ She went shopping despite the heavy rain. 儘管雨很大，她還是去逛街了。

des·sert [dɪˋzɝt] 🎧 *Track 1347*
n. 甜點；餐後點心

des·ti·na·tion [ˌdɛstəˋneʃən] 🎧 *Track 1348*
n. 目的地；終點
▶ Please tag my luggage to my final destination.
請將我的行李標示要直接送到最終目的地。

※灰色單字為英檢初級必備單字

des·ti·ny [ˋdɛstənɪ] 🎧 *Track 1349*
n. 命運
▶ It was my destiny to become a nurse.
命運註定讓我成為一名護理師。

de·stroy [dɪˋstrɔɪ] 🎧 *Track 1350*
v. 破壞；摧毀
▶ Drugs destroyed his life.
毒品毀了他的人生。

de·struc·tion 🎧 *Track 1351*
[dɪˋstrʌkʃən]
n. 摧毀；破壞；毀滅
▶ The earthquake caused severe destruction to the city.
地震對這城市造成嚴重的破壞。

de·struc·tive [dɪˋstrʌktɪv] 🎧 *Track 1352*
adj. 破壞性的；毀滅性的；消極的、無幫助的
▶ Nuclear bombs are one of the most destructive weapons ever built. 核子彈是人類所建造出最具破壞性的武器之一。

de·tail [ˋditel] 🎧 *Track 1353*
n. 細節；詳情
▶ I want to hear all the details about your plan. 我想聽關於你這計劃的所有細節。
v. 詳述；詳細說明
▶ The witness detailed what he saw to the police.
目擊者將他所見到的事情詳細地告訴警方。

(相關片語)
in detail 詳細地
▶ Tell me what happened in detail.
詳細地告訴我發生了什麼事。

de·tailed [ˋdiˋteld] 🎧 *Track 1354*
adj. 詳細的
▶ More detailed information can be found in the manual.
更詳細的資料在手冊中可查到。

de·tect [dɪˋtɛkt] 🎧 *Track 1355*
v. 發覺；察覺；看穿
▶ She detected danger as the man came near. 男子走近時，她便察覺出危險。

de·tec·tive [dɪˋtɛktɪv] 🎧 *Track 1356*
n. 偵探
▶ She hired a private detective to investigate into the incident.
她雇了一名私家偵探去調查那件事。
adj. 偵探的；偵探用的
▶ She loves reading detective fictions.
她很愛閱讀偵探小說。

de·ter·gent [dɪˋtɝdʒənt] 🎧 *Track 1357*
n. 洗潔劑；去垢劑
▶ I can't do the laundry because we ran out of laundry detergent.
我沒辦法洗衣服，因為我們的洗衣劑用完了。

(補充片語)
do the laundry 洗衣服；
run out of 用完；
laundry detergent 洗衣劑

adj. 洗滌的
▶ We're running out of detergent powder.
我們的洗衣粉快用完了。

de·ter·mi·na·tion 🎧 *Track 1358*
[dɪˌtɝməˋneʃən]
n. 決心；堅定、果斷；決斷力
▶ I hope you have the determination to quit smoking this time.
我希望你這次能有戒菸的決心。

de·ter·mine [dɪˋtɝmɪn] 🎧 *Track 1359*
v. 決心；決定

de·ter·mined [dɪˋtɝmɪnd] 🎧 *Track 1360*
adj. 下定決心的
▶ He is determined to quit smoking.
他已經決心要戒菸了。

de·vel·op [dɪˋvɛləp] 🎧 *Track 1361*
v. 建立；發展

de·vel·op·ment 🎧 *Track 1362*
[dɪˋvɛləpmənt]
n. 發展；發育；進展；開發
▶ Too much junk food is not good for children's physical development.
吃太多垃圾食物對孩童的身體發育沒有好處。

(補充片語)
physical development 身體發育

de·vice [dɪ`vaɪs] 🎧 Track 1363
n. 設備；儀器；裝置
▶ The hardware device is not connected to the computer yet.
這個硬體裝置還沒有連上電腦。

dev·il [`dɛvl̩] 🎧 Track 1364
n. 撒旦；魔鬼；惡魔；惡棍
▶ Doing drugs is like having dealings with the devil. 吸毒就像是在跟魔鬼打交道。

(相關片語)
the very devil 棘手的事；難處理的事
▶ The task my boss just assigned me was the very devil. 我主管剛剛派給我的任務是件十分棘手的工作。

de·vise [dɪ`vaɪz] 🎧 Track 1365
v. 設計；發明
▶ He devised a new method to train dogs.
他設計了一種訓練狗狗的新方法。

de·vote [dɪ`vot] 🎧 Track 1366
v. 將……奉獻給
▶ She devoted herself to special education throughout her life.
她終其一生致力於特殊教育。

(補充片語)
devote oneself to 專心於；獻身於

de·vot·ed [dɪ`votɪd] 🎧 Track 1367
adj. 專心致志的；獻身的；摯愛的
▶ My father is devoted to community service after his retirement.
我父親在退休後便投身社區服務的工作。

de·vo·tion [dɪ`voʃən] 🎧 Track 1368
n. 獻身；奉獻
▶ He was awarded the Nobel Prize for his devotion to science.
他因為對科學的奉獻而獲頒諾貝爾獎。

dew [dju] 🎧 Track 1369
n. 露水；露

di·a·be·tes [ˌdaɪə`bitiz] 🎧 Track 1370
n. 糖尿病

▶ My friend has diabetes, though she says it's not serious.
我朋友有糖尿病，不過她說不嚴重。

di·ag·nose [`daɪəgnoz] 🎧 Track 1371
v. 診斷
▶ He was astonished when he was diagnosed with stomach cancer.
被診斷出胃癌時，他震驚不已。

di·ag·no·sis [ˌdaɪəg`nosɪs] 🎧 Track 1372
n. 診斷；診斷結果；診斷書
▶ The incorrect treatment resulted from the doctor's wrong diagnosis.
這錯誤的治療是醫生錯誤的診斷所造成的。

(補充片語)
result from 起因於

di·a·gram [`daɪəˌgræm] 🎧 Track 1373
n. 圖表；圖解
▶ This diagram shows the relationship between customer satisfaction and service quality. 這個圖表顯示了顧客滿意度與服務品質之間的關係。

v. 圖示；以圖解法表示
▶ Susie diagramed the procedure of the ceremony to show us how the wedding would proceed. 蘇西以典禮的流程圖表向我們說明婚禮的進行方式。

dial [`daɪəl] 🎧 Track 1374
v. 撥打；**n.** 表盤；鐘盤

di·a·lect [`daɪəlɛkt] 🎧 Track 1375
n. 方言
▶ Most people in China can speak at least two different dialects.
中國大部份的人都會說至少兩種不同的方言。

di·a·logue [`daɪəˌlɔg] 🎧 Track 1376
=di·a·log （英式英文）
n. 對話；交談
▶ The dialogue in the novel was not very realistic.
這本小說中寫的對話感覺不是很真實。

di·a·mond [`daɪəmənd] 🎧 Track 1377
n. 鑽石

※灰色單字為英檢初級必備單字

di·a·per [`daɪəpɚ] 🎧 *Track 1378*
n. 尿布
▶ It's quite inappropriate to change your baby's diaper in public.
公開幫寶寶換尿布是相當不合宜的舉動。

(補充片語)
in pubic 公開；公然地

di·a·ry [`daɪərɪ] 🎧 *Track 1379*
n. 日記

dic·tion·a·ry [`dɪkʃən͵ɛrɪ] 🎧 *Track 1380*
n. 字典

did·n't [`dɪdnt] 🎧 *Track 1381*
abbr. 未、沒有做（did not的縮寫）

die [daɪ] 🎧 *Track 1382*
v. 死；死去

di·et [`daɪət] 🎧 *Track 1383*
n./v. 飲食；特種飲食；
adj. 減重的；節食的

dif·fer [`dɪfɚ] 🎧 *Track 1384*
v. 不同；相異；分歧
▶ Our opinions always differ from each other. 我們的意見老是跟對方不同。

(補充片語)
differ from 與……不同

dif·fe·rence [`dɪfərəns] 🎧 *Track 1385*
n. 不同；差異

dif·fe·rent [`dɪfərənt] 🎧 *Track 1386*
adj. 不同的

dif·fi·cult [`dɪfə͵kəlt] 🎧 *Track 1387*
adj. 困難的；難處理的；難對付的

dif·fi·cul·ty [`dɪfə͵kʌltɪ] 🎧 *Track 1388*
n. 困難；難處

dig [dɪg] 🎧 *Track 1389*
v. 挖；掘

di·gest [daɪ`dʒɛst] 🎧 *Track 1390*
v. 消化；融會貫通

▶ My daughter cannot digest dairy products.
我女兒沒辦法消化乳製品。

n. 摘要；文摘
▶ This is this week's news digest.
這是這個星期的新聞摘要。

di·ges·tion [də`dʒɛstʃən] 🎧 *Track 1391*
n. 消化；消化能力
▶ Apples and bananas are both good foods for good digestion.
蘋果和香蕉都是對消化有益的好食物。

di·git [`dɪdʒɪt] 🎧 *Track 1392*
n. 數字；手指
▶ As a kindergarten teacher, your salary will never reach 6 digits.
做一個幼稚園老師，你的薪水永遠不會達到六位數。

di·gi·tal [`dɪdʒɪtl] 🎧 *Track 1393*
adj. 指狀的；數字的；數碼的
▶ A digital watch should be an appropriate present for a teenage boy.
一支數字電子錶應該會是適合一個十幾歲男孩的禮物。

dig·ni·ty [`dɪgnətɪ] 🎧 *Track 1394*
n. 尊嚴；莊嚴；高尚；尊貴
▶ Some men still believe that it is beneath their dignity to cook in the kitchen.
有些男人仍認為進廚房做菜是件有失尊嚴的事。

(補充片語)
beneath one's dignity 有失身分；有失尊嚴

di·lem·ma [də`lɛmə] 🎧 *Track 1395*
n. 進退兩難；困境
▶ I was caught in a dilemma of staying in this company or job-hopping to that one.
我陷入了是該繼續留在這間公司還是跳槽到那間公司的兩難局面。

(補充片語)
be caught in a dilemma 陷入兩難局面

dil·i·gent [`dɪlədʒənt] 🎧 *Track 1396*
adj. 勤勞的

dim [dɪm] 🎧 Track 1397

adj. 微暗的；暗淡的；朦朧的

▶ Reading in dim light will damage your eyesight.
在黯淡的光線中閱讀會損害你的視力。

v. 使變暗淡；使變模糊

▶ His eyesight dimmed with age.
他的視力隨著年紀而變模糊了。

dime [daɪm] 🎧 Track 1398

n. 一角硬幣

▶ The man tossed some dimes into the beggar's hat.
男子丟了幾個一角硬幣到乞丐的帽子裡。

dine [daɪn] 🎧 Track 1399

v. 進餐；用餐

▶ They dine out once in a while.
他們有時候會外出用餐。

(補充片語)

dine out 外出用餐；
once in a while 偶爾、有時

din·ner [ˋdɪnɚ] 🎧 Track 1400

n. 晚餐

di·no·saur [ˋdaɪnəˌsɔr] 🎧 Track 1401

n. 恐龍

dip [dɪp] 🎧 Track 1402

v. 浸染；浸洗

▶ She dipped the clothes in the bleach.
她把衣服浸泡在漂白劑裡。

n. 浸泡；凹地；蘸濕；蘸醬

▶ Watch out! There's a dip in the ground.
小心！地面有個凹陷。

(相關片語)

go for a dip 游個泳

▶ It's so hot today. Let's go for a dip.
今天好熱。我們去游個泳吧！

di·plo·ma [dɪˋplomə] 🎧 Track 1403

n. 畢業文憑

▶ I need my college diploma for a job interview.
我工作面試須要我的大學文憑。

dip·lo·mat [ˋdɪpləmæt] 🎧 Track 1404

n. 外交官

di·rect [daɪˋrɛkt] 🎧 Track 1405

adj. 直接的；**v.** 指揮；指導；指路

di·rec·tion [daɪˋrɛkʃən] 🎧 Track 1406

n. 方向

di·rec·tor [daɪˋrɛktɚ] 🎧 Track 1407

n. 主管；指揮；導演

dirt [dɝt] 🎧 Track 1408

n. 污物；泥土；爛泥

▶ He wiped off the dirt on his pants before getting into the car.
他在上車之前把褲子上的髒東西拍掉。

(相關片語)

treat sb. like dirt 待某人如糞土

▶ She treated her maid like dirt.
她對待她的女傭如糞土。

dirt·y [ˋdɝtɪ] 🎧 Track 1409

adj. 髒的；**v.** 弄髒

dis·a·bil·i·ty [dɪsəˋbɪlətɪ] 🎧 Track 1410

n. 無能；殘疾；不利條件

▶ He didn't let his physical disability affect his work performance.
他並未讓身體的殘疾影響他的工作表現。

(補充片語)

physical disability 身體殘疾

dis·a·bled [dɪsˋebl̩d] 🎧 Track 1411

adj. 有殘缺的；有殘疾的；殘廢的

▶ This bike is specifically designed for disabled people.
這款腳踏車是特別為殘障人士所設計的。

(相關片語)

learning-disabled 有學習障礙的

▶ The mother is very patient with her learning-disabled son.
這位母親對她有學習障礙的兒子非常有耐心。

dis·ad·van·tage 🎧 Track 1412
[ˌdɪsədˋvæntɪdʒ]

n. 缺點；不利條件；損害

※灰色單字為英檢初級必備單字

▶One disadvantage of hiring young people is their lack of experience.
雇用年輕人不利的一點就是他們缺乏經驗。

v. 使處不利地位；損害
▶Being addicted to social media may disadvantage your social life and interactions with humans.
對社群媒體上癮可能會有損你的社交生活及與人之間的互動。

dis·ad·van·taged 　🎧 *Track 1413*
[ˌdɪsəd`væntɪdʒd]

adj. 弱勢的；貧困的
▶Many students from disadvantaged families can't afford school lunches. 許多來自弱勢家庭的學生付不起學校的午餐費用。

dis·a·gree [ˌdɪsə`gri] 　🎧 *Track 1414*
v. 意見不和；爭論；不一致
▶They always disagree on what to eat.
他們總是為了要吃什麼而起爭執。

dis·a·gree·ment 　🎧 *Track 1415*
[ˌdɪsə`grimənt]
n. 意見不一；爭論；不符

dis·ap·pear [ˌdɪsə`pɪr] 　🎧 *Track 1416*
v. 消失；不見

dis·ap·point [ˌdɪsə`pɔɪnt] 🎧 *Track 1417*
v. 使失望
▶It disappointed me that he didn't remember our anniversary.
他不記得我們的週年紀念日，讓我很失望。

dis·ap·point·ed 　🎧 *Track 1418*
[ˌdɪsə`pɔɪntɪd]
adj. 失望的
▶I am very disappointed at your service.
我對你們的服務感到很失望。

dis·ap·point·ing 　🎧 *Track 1419*
[ˌdɪsə`pɔɪntɪŋ]
adj. 使人失望的
▶The service I received in that restaurant was very disappointing.
我在那餐廳得到的服務令人非常失望。

dis·ap·point·ment 　🎧 *Track 1420*
[ˌdɪsə`pɔɪntmənt]
n. 失望；掃興；令人失望、掃興的人或事
▶To my disappointment, I didn't get the job offer.
令我失望的是，我沒有得到那個工作機會。

(補充片語)
to one's disappointment 使某人失望的是……

dis·ap·prov·al 　🎧 *Track 1421*
[ˌdɪsə`pruvl]
n. 不贊成；不喜歡
▶My boss gave me a look of disapproval when I asked for three days' leave.
當我說要請三天假時，老闆給了我一個不贊成的表情。

dis·ap·prove [ˌdɪsə`pruv] 🎧 *Track 1422*
v. 不贊成；不同意
▶My boss disapproved my request for a week's annual leave.
我老闆不贊成我請一個星期的年假。

di·sas·ter [dɪ`zæstə] 　🎧 *Track 1423*
n. 災難；不幸
▶Earthquakes and tsunamis are both unpredictable natural disasters.
地震和海嘯都是不可預測的天災。

(補充片語)
natural disaster 天災；自然災難

dis·card [dɪs`kɑrd] 　🎧 *Track 1424*
v. 拋棄；摒棄；丟棄
▶I thought you have already discarded this old bicycle.
我還以為你早就把這輛舊單車給丟了。

n. 被拋棄的人；拋棄物
▶Get a big box and put all your discards in it.
拿個大箱子，把你所有不要的東西都放進來。

dis·ci·pline [`dɪsəplɪn] 　🎧 *Track 1425*
n. 紀律；風紀
▶An army without discipline is doomed to defeat.
一支缺乏紀律的軍隊注定是會被擊敗的。

v. 訓練；使有紀律；懲戒
▶ You have to discipline yourself and stop putting things off until the last minute. 你必須自律，並且不要再把事情拖到最後才做。

(補充片語)
put off 拖延；
the last minute 最後一刻

dis·co [`dɪsko] 　　🎧 *Track 1426*
=dis·co·theque
n. 小舞廳；迪斯可舞廳
▶ She often went to the disco with friends when she was in college.
她上大學時，常跟朋友一起去舞廳。

dis·com·fort [dɪs`kʌmfɚt] 🎧 *Track 1427*
n. 不適，不安，不舒服；使人不舒服的事物
▶ She suffered great discomfort during her pregnancy.
她在懷孕期間承受極大的身體不適。

v. 使不舒服；使不安
▶ He was discomforted by his illness.
他的病讓他很不舒服。

dis·con·nect [ˌdɪskə`nɛkt] 🎧 *Track 1428*
v. 使分離
▶ We will have to disconnect the telephone if you don't pay for your bill by this Friday.
如果你這星期五之前不付帳單的話，我們就必須切斷電話線。

dis·count [`dɪskaʊnt] 🎧 *Track 1429*
n. 折扣；不全信
▶ I won't consider buying it unless you give me a discount.
除非你給我個折扣，否則我不會考慮買。

v. 將……打折扣；懷疑地看待；不全相信
▶ This store doesn't discount throughout the year. 這家店全年不打折。

dis·cour·age [dɪs`kɝɪdʒ] 🎧 *Track 1430*
v. 使洩氣；使沮喪
▶ They tried to discourage him from taking that job. 他們勸他不要接受那份工作。

dis·cov·er [dɪs`kʌvɚ] 🎧 *Track 1431*
v. 發現

dis·cov·e·ry [dɪs`kʌvərɪ] 🎧 *Track 1432*
n. 發現
▶ Scientists are excited about the discovery of a nearly complete dinosaur fossil.
科學家們對於發現一個幾乎完整的恐龍化石感到興奮不已。

(補充片語)
dinosaur fossil 恐龍化石

di·scrim·i·na·tion 🎧 *Track 1433*
[dɪˌskrɪmə`neʃən]
n. 區別；歧視、不公平待遇
▶ Gender discrimination in the workplace still exists in today's world.
職場的性別歧視在今日世界仍是存在的。

(補充片語)
gender discrimination 性別歧視

di·scuss [dɪ`skʌs] 🎧 *Track 1434*
v. 討論

di·scus·sion [dɪ`skʌʃən] 🎧 *Track 1435*
n. 討論

dis·ease [dɪ`ziz] 🎧 *Track 1436*
n. 疾病
▶ AIDS is an incurable disease.
愛滋病是一種無法治癒的疾病。

dis·guise [dɪs`gaɪz] 🎧 *Track 1437*
n. 假裝；掩飾；喬裝
▶ The suspect got away from the building in disguise. 嫌犯變裝逃出了大樓。

v. 掩飾；隱瞞；把……喬裝起來
▶ The suspect disguised himself as an old lady so that no one could recognize him.
嫌犯將自己喬裝成一位老太太，因此沒有人能認得出他來。

dis·gust [dɪs`gʌst] 🎧 *Track 1438*
v. 使作嘔；使討厭
▶ The smell of his feet disgusted her.
他的腳臭味使她作嘔。

n. 作嘔；厭惡；憎惡
▶ She looked at the man in disgust.
她厭惡地看著那個男人。

※灰色單字為英檢初級必備單字

in disgust 厭惡地

dish [dɪʃ] 🎧 *Track 1439*
n. 盤;碟;菜餚

dis·hon·est [dɪs`ɑnɪst] 🎧 *Track 1440*
adj. 不誠實的

disk [dɪsk] =disc 🎧 *Track 1441*
n. 圓盤;盤狀物;光碟(電腦磁碟;唱片;影像圓盤)
▶Everything you need is saved in the disk.
你要的所有東西都存在光碟裡了。

dis·like [dɪs`laɪk] 🎧 *Track 1442*
v. 不喜歡
▶I dislike the decoration of this apartment.
我不喜歡這間公寓的裝潢。

n. 不喜歡
▶I have a dislike for eggplants.
我不喜歡茄子。

補充片語
have a dislike for 不喜歡

相關片語
likes and dislikes 好惡
▶She is familiar with all his likes and dislikes.
她對他所有的好惡一清二楚。

dis·miss [dɪs`mɪs] 🎧 *Track 1443*
v. 讓……離開;遣散
▶The teacher dismissed the class ahead of time. 老師提前下課。

dis·or·der [dɪs`ɔrdɚ] 🎧 *Track 1444*
n. 混亂;無秩序;失調;障礙
▶She has been suffering from sleep disorder for many years.
她多年來一直受睡眠障礙所苦。

補充片語
suffer from 受……所苦;
sleep disorder 睡眠障礙;睡眠失調

di·splay [dɪ`sple] 🎧 *Track 1445*
v. 陳列;展出;顯示
▶His paintings were displayed in the art museum. 他的繪畫作品在美術博物館展出。

n. 展覽;陳列;陳列品
▶Keep your hands off the displays in the museum. 請勿觸碰博物館內的展覽品。

補充片語
keep off 遠離;使不接近

dis·pos·a·ble [dɪ`spozəbl] 🎧 *Track 1446*
adj. 用完即丟的;一次性使用的;可任意處置、使用的
▶We no longer provide free disposable chopsticks.
我們不再提供免費的免洗筷。

補充片語
disposable chopsticks 免洗筷子

dis·pos·al [dɪ`spozl] 🎧 *Track 1447*
n. 處置;處理;自由處置權
▶Aside from the car, I also have 3000 dollars at my disposal.
除了這輛車外,我還有三千美元可以自由使用。

補充片語
aside from 除了;
at one's disposal 供任意使用,可自行支配

dis·pose [dɪ`spoz] 🎧 *Track 1448*
v. 配置;處理;處置
▶Man proposes, God disposes.
謀事在人,成事在天。

dis·pute [dɪ`spjut] 🎧 *Track 1449*
v. 爭論;爭執
▶They always dispute over money.
他們總是為了錢的事起爭執。

n. 爭論;爭執
▶Don't drag me into your disputes.
別把我扯進你們的爭執裡。

補充片語
drag in 把……扯進來;硬扯進

dis·sat·is·fac·tion [ˌdɪssætɪs`fækʃən] 🎧 *Track 1450*
n. 不滿;不平
▶I don't have any dissatisfaction with my life.
我對我的生活沒有任何的不滿。

dis·solve [dɪ`zɑlv] 🎧 *Track 1451*
v. 分解；使溶解；使融化；使終結；解（謎）；（會議）解散
▶ Now, we need to dissolve some sugar in the melted chocolate. 現在，我們必須將一些糖溶解在已經融化的巧克力裡。

dis·tance [`dɪstəns] 🎧 *Track 1452*
n. 距離

dis·tant [`dɪstənt] 🎧 *Track 1453*
adj. 遠的；遠離的；遠親的；冷淡、疏遠的
▶ He's just a distant relative of mine. 他只是我的一個遠房親戚。

dis·tinct [dɪ`stɪŋkt] 🎧 *Track 1454*
adj. 與其他不同的；清楚的
▶ Jeff's interests are distinct from his twin brother's. 傑夫的興趣跟他的雙胞胎兄弟不同。

dis·tinc·tion [dɪ`stɪŋkʃən] 🎧 *Track 1455*
n. 區別；區分；差別；不同點
▶ He loves all his children without distinction. 他無所差別地愛他所有的孩子。

dis·tin·guish [dɪ`stɪŋgwɪʃ] 🎧 *Track 1456*
v. 區別
▶ Even his father can hardly distinguish him from his twin brother. 即使是他父親也很難分辨他跟他雙胞胎哥哥之間的不同。

dis·tin·guished [dɪ`stɪŋgwɪʃt] 🎧 *Track 1457*
adj. 卓越的；著名的
▶ He is a distinguished photographer. 他是個名攝影師。

dis·tract [dɪ`strækt] 🎧 *Track 1458*
v. 轉移；岔開；使分心；使苦惱
▶ Don't distract me while I'm driving. 我在開車的時候不要讓我分心。

dis·tress [dɪ`strɛs] 🎧 *Track 1459*
n. 不幸；悲痛；貧困；引起痛苦的事物
▶ His father's death caused him great distress. 他父親的死為他帶來極大的痛苦。

v. 使悲痛；使苦惱；使憂傷
▶ Her parents' divorce distressed her greatly. 她父母的離婚使她非常痛苦。

dis·trib·ute [dɪ`strɪbjʊt] 🎧 *Track 1460*
v. 分發；分配
▶ The man distributed his money and property evenly to his three sons before he died. 男子在死前將他的錢和財產平均分給三個兒子。

dis·tri·bu·tion [ˌdɪstrə`bjuʃən] 🎧 *Track 1461*
n. 分配；配給物
▶ The three sons were not happy about the distribution of their father's property. 這三個兒子對他們父親財產的分配感到不滿。

dis·trict [`dɪstrɪkt] 🎧 *Track 1462*
n. 地區；行政區
▶ I'm looking for an apartment near the school district. 我正在找這個學區附近的套房。

(補充片語)
look for 尋找；
school district 學區

dis·trust [dɪs`trʌst] 🎧 *Track 1463*
v. 不信任
▶ I distrust my husband. 我不信任我的丈夫。

n. 不信任；懷疑
▶ She looked at him with distrust when he gave her the money back. 當他把錢還給她時，她用懷疑的目光看著他。

dis·turb [dɪs`tɝb] 🎧 *Track 1464*
v. 打擾
▶ I don't want to be disturbed when I am reading. 我閱讀時不想被打擾。

dis·turb·ance [dɪs`tɝbəns] 🎧 *Track 1465*
n. 打擾；擾亂；引起騷亂的事物
▶ The school library is where I can study without disturbance. 學校圖書館是我可以不受干擾讀書的地方。

※灰色單字為英檢初級必備單字

without disturbance 不受干擾地

ditch [dɪtʃ] 🎧 *Track 1466*
n. 溝；壕溝；水道
▶ The man didn't know there was a ditch at the side of the road until he fell into it.
男子一直到跌進去，才知道路邊有個壕溝。

v. 掘溝；用溝渠圍住；（車）開入溝裡、（飛機）水上迫降、（火車）脫軌；拋棄、擺脫、甩掉
▶ Instead of ditching your girlfriend, you should break up with her nicely.
與其拋棄你的女友，不如好好地跟她分手。

dive [daɪv] 🎧 *Track 1467*
v. 跳水
▶ The lifeguard dove into the swimming pool to save the drowning woman.
救生員跳入游泳池中，救了那個溺水的女子。

di·verse [daɪˋvɝs] 🎧 *Track 1468*
adj. 不同的；互異的；各式各樣的；多變化的
▶ Peter and his siblings have diverse personalities.
彼得和他的兄弟姐妹們的個性迥然不同。

di·vide [dəˋvaɪd] 🎧 *Track 1469*
v. 分；劃分

di·vine [dəˋvaɪn] 🎧 *Track 1470*
adj. 神性的；天賜的；神聖的；天才的；極好的
▶ The singer fascinated all the audience with her divine voice.
這歌手用她神賜的歌聲迷住了所有的觀眾。

di·vi·sion [dəˋvɪʒən] 🎧 *Track 1471*
n. 部門

di·vorce [dəˋvors] 🎧 *Track 1472*
n. 離婚
▶ Sadly, their marriage ended in divorce.
令人難過的是，他們的婚姻以離婚收場。

v. 與……離婚
▶ She decided to divorce her husband as soon as she found him cheating on her.
她一發現丈夫偷吃就決定跟他離婚。

diz·zy [ˋdɪzɪ] 🎧 *Track 1473*
adj. 暈的

do [du] 🎧 *Track 1474*
v. 做；**aux.** 構成疑問句、否定句、強調句或倒裝句的助動詞

dock [dɑk] 🎧 *Track 1475*
n. 碼頭；港區；船塢
▶ Our ship slowly began to move away from the dock.
我們的船開始慢慢地駛離碼頭。

v. 使靠碼頭
▶ The ship will be docked at Kaohsiung temporarily. 那艘船將會暫時停靠在高雄。

doc·tor [ˋdɑktɚ] 🎧 *Track 1476*
=doc.=phys·i·cian
=Dr （英式英文）
n. 醫生

doc·u·ment [ˋdɑkjəmənt] 🎧 *Track 1477*
n. 文件

doc·u·men·ta·ry [ˏdɑkjəˋmɛntərɪ] 🎧 *Track 1478*
adj. 文件的；記錄的
▶ She is a director of documentary films.
她是個拍紀錄片的導演。

documentary film 紀錄片；文獻片

n. 紀錄片；紀實節目
▶ I am watching a documentary about single mothers.
我正在看一部關於單親媽媽的紀實節目。

dodge [dɑdʒ] 🎧 *Track 1479*
v. 閃開；躲避；巧妙迴避
▶ The protesters started to throw eggs at the mayor, but he dodged.
抗議者開始朝市長丟雞蛋，但他躲開了。

n. 託詞；推託的妙計
He came up with many dodges to avoid punishment. 他使出各種詭計來避開刑罰。

does·n't [ˋdʌznt] 🎧 *Track 1480*
abbr. 不（does not的縮寫）

dog [dɔg]　🎧 *Track 1481*
n. 狗

doll [dɑl]　🎧 *Track 1482*
n. 洋娃娃

dol·lar [`dɑlɚ]=**buck**　🎧 *Track 1483*
n. 元；美元、加幣

dol·phin [`dɑlfɪn]　🎧 *Track 1484*
n. 海豚

dome [dom]　🎧 *Track 1485*
n. 圓頂屋；半球形物；蒼穹
▶ The opening and closing ceremony will both be held at the Tokyo Dome.
開幕及閉幕典禮都會在東京巨蛋舉行。

(補充片語)
Tokyo Dome　東京巨蛋；東京巨蛋形球場；東京巨蛋體育館

do·mes·tic [də`mɛstɪk]　🎧 *Track 1486*
adj. 家庭的；家事的；國內的
▶ Just let them take care of their own domestic affairs.
就讓他們去處理自己的家務事吧！

(補充片語)
take care of　處理；
domestic affair　家務事

(相關片語)
domestic violence　家庭暴力
▶ The woman and her children are all victims of domestic violence.
這位女子和她的孩子都是家庭暴力的受害者。

dom·i·nant [`dɑmənənt]　🎧 *Track 1487*
adj. 佔優勢的；具支配地位的；統治的
▶ Production cost is the dominant factor of our price determination.
生產成本是我們決定價格的最大因素。

dom·i·nate [`dɑmə‚net]　🎧 *Track 1488*
v. 支配；統治；處於支配地位；控制
▶ Don't try to dominate me.
你別想要控制我。

do·nate [`donet]　🎧 *Track 1489*
v. 捐獻；捐贈

▶ The little girl donated all money she saved in her piggy bank to help street dogs. 小女孩捐出她存在撲滿裡所有的錢來幫助流浪狗。

(補充片語)
piggy bank　（豬形）撲滿；存錢筒

do·na·tion [do`neʃən]　🎧 *Track 1490*
n. 捐贈物；捐獻；捐款
▶ We made a donation of NT$10,000 to the orphanage.
我們捐了一萬元新台幣給那間孤兒院。

(相關片語)
organ donation　器官捐贈
▶ He has signed up for organ donation.
他已經簽署器官捐贈同意書了。

don·key [`dɑŋkɪ]　🎧 *Track 1491*
n. 驢子；傻瓜

don't [dont]　🎧 *Track 1492*
abbr. 不（do not的縮寫）

doom [dum]　🎧 *Track 1493*
n. 厄運；毀滅；末日審判
He might be able to get away with it for a time, but he will meet his doom eventually. 他也許一時能逃過懲罰，但他最終還是會遭審判的。

(補充片語)
get away with　不應某事而受懲罰；
for a time　一時；
meet one's doom　面對審判、難逃厄運

v. 註定；命定；使失敗；使毀滅
▶ The expert predicted that the new health insurance policies were doomed to fail.
該專家預言新的健保政策註定會失敗。

door [dor]　🎧 *Track 1494*
n. 門

door·step [`dor‚stɛp]　🎧 *Track 1495*
n. 門階
▶ He opened the door and picked up the newspapers from his doorstep.
他打開門，並從門階上撿起報紙。

(相關片語)
on/at one's doorstep　很近

※灰色單字為英檢初級必備單字

▶The MRT station is practically on our doorstep. 捷運站差不多就在我們家門口。

door·way [ˋdor͵we]　🎧 *Track 1496*
n. 出入口；門口；門路；途徑
▶Education is a doorway to success.
教育是通往成功之門。

dorm [dɔrm]　🎧 *Track 1497*
n. 宿舍
▶The new school dorm is still under construction. 新的學校宿舍還在興建中。

dor·mi·to·ry　🎧 *Track 1498*
[ˋdɔrmə͵torɪ]＝**dorm**
n. 宿舍
▶My sister will move to the college dormitory before school begins.
我姊姊在開學前要搬到大學宿舍裡去住。

dos·age [ˋdosɪdʒ]　🎧 *Track 1499*
n. （藥的）劑量；服用方式
▶All drug dosages should be adjusted according to the weight of the patients. 所有的藥物劑量都是依病人的體重來做調整的。

dose [dos]　🎧 *Track 1500*
n. （藥物的）一劑；劑量
▶Let him take a dose after every meal and rest as much as possible. 讓他在每餐飯後服一次藥，並且盡可能地多休息。

相關片語
like a dose of salts　很快地；一下子
▶He was so hungry that he ate up everything on his plate like a dose of salts. 他實在是餓極了，一下子就把盤子裡的東西吃個精光。

dot [dɑt]　🎧 *Track 1501*
n. 點；小圓點

doub·le [ˋdʌbl̩]　🎧 *Track 1502*
adj. 兩倍的；成雙的；雙人的；**v.** 使加倍；增加一倍；**n.** 兩倍數量；加倍

doubt [daʊt]　🎧 *Track 1503*
n./v. 懷疑；疑慮

doubt·ful [ˋdaʊtfəl]　🎧 *Track 1504*
adj. 懷疑的；疑惑的
▶I am doubtful whether he is telling the truth. 我懷疑他說的是不是實情。

dough [do]　🎧 *Track 1505*
n. 生麵糰
▶We want to eat homemade pizza tonight, so I'm making pizza dough now.
我們今晚想要吃自己做的比薩，所以我現在正在做比薩麵糰。

相關片語
earn one's own dough　自己掙錢
▶You've got to earn your own dough from now on. 你從現在起得自己掙錢了。

dough·nut [ˋdo͵nʌt]　🎧 *Track 1506*
＝**donut**
n. 油炸圈餅；炸麵圈

dove [dʌv]　🎧 *Track 1507*
n. 鴿；溫和派人士
▶The dove is a symbol of peace and love.
鴿是和平與愛的象徵。

down [daʊn]　🎧 *Track 1508*
adv. 向下地；（程度、數量）減緩、減少地；**prep.** 在……下方；沿著；**n.** 下降；失敗；蕭條；**adj.** 向下的；（情緒）低落的

down·load [ˋdaʊn͵lod]　🎧 *Track 1509*
v. （電腦）下載
▶I never download illegal software.
我從不下載非法軟體。
n. 下載；下載的文件
▶I suggest you remove all files from your list of downloads first.
我建議你先把下載清單上所有的檔案都移除。

down·stairs [͵daʊnˋstɛrz]　🎧 *Track 1510*
adv. 在樓下；往樓下；**adj.** 樓下的

down·town [͵daʊnˋtaʊn]　🎧 *Track 1511*
adv. 往城市商業區；**adj.** 城市商業區的；**n.** 城市商業區；鬧區

down·wards 🎧 *Track 1512*

[`daʊnwɚdz]

adv. 向下地；朝下地

▶ I saw a man lying face downwards on the pavement. I was not sure if he was still breathing.
我看到一名男子臉部朝下地橫臥在人行道上，不確定他是否還有呼吸。

doze [doz] 🎧 *Track 1513*

v. 打瞌睡；打盹

▶ Gary dozed off during the meeting.
蓋瑞在開會時打瞌睡。

n. 瞌睡；假寐

▶ A lazy afternoon like this is perfect for a doze.
像這樣的一個懶洋洋的下午最適合打瞌睡了。

doz·en [`dʌzn] 🎧 *Track 1514*

n. 一打，許多

Dr. [`dɑktɚ]=**doc·tor** 🎧 *Track 1515*

n. 博士，醫生；大夫；學者；教師

draft [dræft] 🎧 *Track 1516*

n. 草稿，草圖

▶ He showed me the draft of his speech and asked for my advice.
他拿演講的草稿給我看，並詢問我的意見。

v. 起草；設計

▶ I drafted my speech for the opening ceremony on my way here.
我在來這裡的路上為開幕典禮的致辭起草。

drag [dræg] 🎧 *Track 1517*

v. 拉；拖；拖曳；慢吞吞地進行

▶ She dragged her heavy baggage out of the airport. 她將她沉重的行李拖出機場。

n. 拖曳；拉；累贅；拖後腿的事；令人厭倦的事

▶ I'm not taking Laura to the party. She's a drag. 我才不要帶蘿拉去派對。她是個累贅。

(相關片語)

drag one's feet 拖拖拉拉

▶ I wanted to set off earlier, but my wife was dragging her feet.
我想早點出發，但是我太太一直拖拖拉拉的。

drag·on [`drægən] 🎧 *Track 1518*

n. 龍

Drag·on-boat Fes·tiv·al [`drægən-bot-`fɛstəvl] 🎧 *Track 1519*

n. 端午節

drag·on·fly [`drægən͵flaɪ] 🎧 *Track 1520*

n. 蜻蜓

▶ A dragonfly just flew into our garden.
有隻蜻蜓剛剛飛進我們的花園了。

drain [dren] 🎧 *Track 1521*

v. 排出、排掉（液體）；喝乾；耗盡

▶ It took them two days to drain the water out from the house after the flood.
在洪水過後，他們花了兩天的時間才把水從房子裡排出來。

(補充片語)

drain out （把水等）排掉

n. 排水管

▶ Can you come over to check my kitchen drain?
你可以過來檢查一下我廚房的排水管嗎？

(相關片語)

laugh like a drain 放聲大笑

▶ He laughed like a drain when I told him the joke.
當我跟他說這個笑話時，他放聲大笑。

dra·ma [`drɑmə] 🎧 *Track 1522*

n. 戲劇；戲劇性

dra·mat·ic [drə`mætɪk] 🎧 *Track 1523*

adj. 戲劇的；劇本的；戲劇般的；戲劇性的；引人注目的

▶ Simon has made dramatic progress in English. 賽門在英文方面有戲劇般的進步。

drape [drep] 🎧 *Track 1524*

n. 簾；幔；**v.** 覆蓋；垂掛

draw [drɔ] 🎧 *Track 1525*

v. 畫

drawer [`drɔɚ] 🎧 *Track 1526*

n. 抽屜

※灰色單字為英檢初級必備單字

draw·ing [`drɔɪŋ] 🎧 *Track 1527*
n. 描繪;圖畫
▶The little boy made a drawing of robots and cars.
小男孩畫了一張機器人和車子的畫。

dread [drɛd] 🎧 *Track 1528*
n. 害怕;畏懼;恐怖
▶It's not normal for a boy to have a dread of his own father.
一個男孩會懼怕自己的父親,並不正常。

(補充片語)
have a dread of 對……懼怕

v. 害怕;擔心;畏懼
▶He dreads sleeping in the dark.
他害怕在黑暗中睡覺。

dread·ful [`drɛdfəl] 🎧 *Track 1529*
adj. 可怕的
▶It was really a dreadful traffic accident.
這真是一場可怕的交通意外。

dream [drim] 🎧 *Track 1530*
n. 夢;夢想;**v.** 做夢;夢到

dress [drɛs] 🎧 *Track 1531*
v. 給……穿衣;使穿著;穿衣;打扮;
n. 衣服;女裝;連身裙

dress·er [`drɛsə-] 🎧 *Track 1532*
n. 附有鏡子的衣櫥;附有抽屜的梳妝台

dress·ing [`drɛsɪŋ] 🎧 *Track 1533*
n. 服飾、打扮;梳理;敷藥包紮;醬料
▶I don't want any dressing on my salad.
我的沙拉上面不要加醬料。

drift [drɪft] 🎧 *Track 1534*
v. 漂流;漂泊;遊蕩;吹積成堆
▶The sailor had a glimpse of a human body drifting in the sea from the deck of the ship. 該船員從船上甲板瞥見一個人類的身體在海上漂流。

n. 漂流;漂移;漂流物;緩流
▶We lay on the grass, watching the drift of the clouds through the sky.
我們躺在草地上,看著雲朵在天空的漂移。

drill [drɪl] 🎧 *Track 1535*
n. 鑽頭;操練、訓練
▶Our school will conduct a fire drill next week. 我們學校下星期要實施消防演習。

(補充片語)
fire drill 消防演習;消防訓練

v. 鑽孔;操練、訓練
▶He drilled a hole in the wall.
他在牆上鑽了一個洞。

drink [drɪŋk] 🎧 *Track 1536*
v. 喝;**n.** 飲料

drink·ing [`drɪŋkɪŋ] 🎧 *Track 1537*
n. 喝,喝酒

drip [drɪp] 🎧 *Track 1538*
v. 滴下;滴落
▶Tears dripped down her face.
淚水從她的臉龐滴落下來。

n. 滴下;滴水聲;點滴;水滴
▶The drip of the water leaking from the faucet kept me awake all night.
從水龍頭傳出的水滴聲使我徹夜清醒沒睡。

drive [draɪv] 🎧 *Track 1539*
v. 開車;駕駛;**n.** 開車兜風;駕車旅行

driv·er [`draɪvə-] 🎧 *Track 1540*
n. 駕駛人;司機

drive·way [`draɪvˌwe] 🎧 *Track 1541*
n. 私人車道;馬路;車道
▶You can't park your car on the driveway.
你不能把你的車停在車道上。

drop [drɑp] 🎧 *Track 1542*
v. 滴下;丟下;下(車);**n.** 滴;落下;降落

drought [draʊt] 🎧 *Track 1543*
n. 乾旱;旱災
▶The country has been experiencing its worst drought since 2003.
這個國家正經歷自2003年以來最嚴重的乾旱。

drown [draʊn] 🎧 *Track 1544*
v. 溺死
▶ His son drowned in the swimming pool last year. 他兒子去年在游泳池溺死了。
相關片語
look like a drowned rat 濕得像落湯雞
▶ He looked like a drowned rat when he came home.
當他回到家時，全身濕得像隻落湯雞。

drow·sy [`draʊzɪ] 🎧 *Track 1545*
adj. 昏昏欲睡的；睏倦的；無活力的；呆滯的
▶ She felt drowsy after drinking a glass of wine. 她喝了一杯酒就覺得昏昏欲睡。

drug [drʌg] 🎧 *Track 1546*
n. 藥；毒品

drug·store [`drʌg͵stor] 🎧 *Track 1547*
n. 藥局

drum [drʌm] 🎧 *Track 1548*
n. 鼓

drunk [drʌŋk] 🎧 *Track 1549*
adj. 喝醉酒的
▶ He always beats his wife when he is drunk. 他總是喝醉了就打他太太。
n. 醉漢；酒鬼
▶ Her husband is a drunk. 她丈夫是個酒鬼。
相關片語
drunk driving 酒後駕駛
▶ He avoided drunk driving by taking a taxi home.
他以搭計程車回家的方式避免酒後開車。

dry [draɪ] 🎧 *Track 1550*
adj. 乾的；**v.** 弄乾；使乾燥

dry·er [`draɪɚ] 🎧 *Track 1551*
n. 乾燥器；吹風機；烘乾機

duck [dʌk] 🎧 *Track 1552*
n. 鴨子；鴨肉

duck·ling [`dʌklɪŋ] 🎧 *Track 1553*
n. 小鴨

▶ It turned out that the ugly duckling was actually a swan.
結果那隻醜小鴨其實是隻天鵝。

due [dju] 🎧 *Track 1554*
adj. 應支付的；到期的；預定應到的；應有的
▶ The bill is due today.
這張帳單的繳費日今天到期。
相關片語
due date 期限；到期日；預定日期；預產期
▶ The woman gave birth to her child two weeks ahead of her due date.
女子比預產期提前兩週便生下了她的寶寶。

dull [dʌl] 🎧 *Track 1555*
adj. 晦暗的；模糊的；陰沈的；乏味的、單調的
▶ The speech was so dull that most audience started to nod off. 這演講太乏味了，使得大部分的聽眾都開始打盹了。

dumb [dʌm] 🎧 *Track 1556*
adj. 啞的；不能說話的；沉默寡言的；愚笨的

dump [dʌmp] 🎧 *Track 1557*
v. 傾倒；拋棄
▶ Please don't dump your trash here.
請不要把垃圾倒在這裡。
n. 垃圾場
▶ This car is so worn-out that it should go to the dump. 這輛車已經破到不行，應該要丟到垃圾場去了。
相關片語
down in the dumps 沮喪的；抑鬱的
▶ She's been down in the dumps since she was dumped. 她被甩了之後就一直很抑鬱。

dump·ling [`dʌmplɪŋ] 🎧 *Track 1558*
n. 餃子；水煎包等

dur·a·ble [`djʊrəbl̩] 🎧 *Track 1559*
adj. 經久的；耐用的
▶ When purchasing durable goods, it is the quality that he takes into account.
當購買耐用品時，他所考慮的是品質。

※灰色單字為英檢初級必備單字

take into account 考慮

du·ra·tion [djʊˋreʃən] 🎧 *Track 1560*
n. （時間）持續；持久；持續時間
▶ The duration of the graduation ceremony will be approximately two hours.
畢業典禮的持續時間大約是兩小時。

dur·ing [ˋdjʊrɪŋ] 🎧 *Track 1561*
prep. 在……期間

dusk [dʌsk] 🎧 *Track 1562*
n. 薄暮；黃昏
▶ We will probably arrive at dusk.
我們可能會在黃昏時到達。

dust [dʌst] 🎧 *Track 1563*
n. 灰塵
▶ The books were all covered with dust.
這些書上蓋滿了灰塵。

v. 除去灰塵；打掃
▶ He dusted down the chair before sitting on it. 他揮去椅子上的灰塵之後，才坐上去。

補充片語
dust down 除去……的灰塵

相關片語
bite the dust 被拒絕；倒地而死；陣亡；掛點
▶ The man got shot and bit the dust.
男子中彈並倒地身亡。

dust·y [ˋdʌstɪ] 🎧 *Track 1564*
adj. 滿是灰塵的；塵狀的
▶ He pulled a book out from the dusty bookshelf and started to read. 他從滿是灰塵的書架上拉出一本書，並開始讀。

du·ty [ˋdjutɪ] 🎧 *Track 1565*
n. 職責；任務

dwarf [dwɔrf] 🎧 *Track 1566*
n. 侏儒；矮子；矮小的動物
My sister told me a story about Snow White and the seven dwarves. 我姊姊跟我說了一個關於白雪公主和七個小矮人的故事。

adj. 矮小的；發育不全的
▶ We'd like to remove all the dwarf trees from our yard.
我們想移除院子裡所有的矮樹。

v. 使矮小；萎縮；阻礙生長
▶ These children were dwarfed from poor nutrition.
這些孩子因為營養不良而長不高。

dye [daɪ] 🎧 *Track 1567*
n. 染料；染色
▶ Hair dye can damage your hair.
頭髮染料可能會損害你的頭髮。

v. 染髮
▶ The old man dyed his gray hair black.
老人把白髮染黑了。

dy·nam·ic [daɪˋnæmɪk] 🎧 *Track 1568*
adj. 動力的；力學的；動態的；有活力的；機能的
▶ Our team has recruited some dynamic young members this year. 我們的團隊今年增加了一些有活力的年輕成員。

dy·na·mite [ˋdaɪnəˌmaɪt] 🎧 *Track 1569*
n. 炸藥
▶ The man claimed that he had dynamite and threatened to blow up the plane.
男子聲稱自己持有炸藥，並威脅要炸掉飛機。

v. 用炸藥爆破；炸毀
▶ They are going to dynamite this dangerous building.
他們即將炸毀這棟危樓。

dyn·a·sty [ˋdaɪnəstɪ] 🎧 *Track 1570*
n. 王朝；朝代
▶ He claimed that he was the offspring of the imperial family of the Qing Dynasty.
他宣稱自己是清朝皇室的後裔。

Ee

通過中級英文檢定者的英文能力：

 在日常生活中，能聽懂一般的會話；能大致聽懂公共場所廣播、氣象報告及廣告等。在工作時，能聽懂簡易的產品介紹與操作説明。能大致聽懂外籍人士的談話及詢問。

 在日常生活中，能閱讀短文、故事、私人信件、廣告、傳單、簡介及使用説明等。在工作時，能閱讀工作須知、公告、操作手冊、例行的文件、傳真、電報等。

 能寫簡單的書信、故事及心得等。對於熟悉且與個人經歷相關的主題，能以簡易的文字表達。

 在日常生活中，能以簡易英語交談或描述一般事物，能介紹自己的生活作息、工作、家庭、經歷等，並可對一般話題陳述看法。在工作時，能進行簡單的答詢，並與外籍人士交談溝通。

本書除包含官方公佈的中級4,947單字外，更精挑了近400個滿分必學的高手單字。同時，在片語的挑選、例句的使用上，皆依上述英檢官方公佈之能力範疇做設計，難度適中、不偏離考試主題。發音部分則是自然發音＆KK音標雙管齊下，搭配MP3以「分解／完整」方式錄音，給你最多元有效的學習手段，怎麼記都可以，想忘掉都好難！

---

each [itʃ] *Track 1571*
pron. 每一個；**adj.** 每一的；各自的；
adv. 每一

ea·ger [`igɚ] *Track 1572*
adj. 熱心的；熱切的；渴望的；急切的
▶ She is eager to learn a skill to make a living. 她急著想學一個謀生技能。

ea·gle [`igl̩] *Track 1573*
n. 老鷹

ear [ɪr] *Track 1574*
n. 耳；聽力

ear·ly [`ɝlɪ] *Track 1575*
adj. 早的；**adv.** 早地

earn [ɝn] *Track 1576*
v. 賺得；贏得

ear·nest [`ɝnɪst] *Track 1577*
adj. 認真的

▶ Henry is an earnest student.
亨利是一個認真的學生。

n. 誠摯
▶ He made an apology to her in earnest.
他誠摯地向她道歉。

相關片語
earnest money deposit 保證金
▶ The buyer of the house will make the earnest money deposit this afternoon.
房子的買家今天下午會來付保證金。

earn·ings [`ɝnɪŋz] *Track 1578*
n. 收入；工資
▶ I give all my earnings to my wife.
我把所有的收入都交給我妻子。

ear·phone [`ɪr͵fon] *Track 1579*
n. 耳機；聽筒
▶ Listening to music on earphones constantly will permanently damage your hearing. 長期用耳機聽音樂會對你的聽力造成永久的損害。

ear·ring [ˋɪrˏrɪŋ] 🎧 *Track 1580*
n. 耳環
▶This pair of earrings was a gift from my husband on our 10th wedding anniversary.
這對耳環是我老公在我們十週年結婚紀念日時送我的禮物。

earth [ɝθ] 🎧 *Track 1581*
n. 地球；泥土

earth·quake [ˋɝθˏkwek] 🎧 *Track 1582*
n. 地震
▶I was just about to go to sleep when the earthquake occurred.
地震發生時，我正好要去睡。

ease [iz] 🎧 *Track 1583*
v. 減輕；緩和；使安心
▶He took a pill to ease his stomachache.
他服了顆藥來減輕胃痛。

n. 舒適；悠閒；容易；放鬆；自在
▶I always feel at ease when I'm with Jane.
當我跟珍在一起時，總是覺得很放鬆。

(補充片語)
feel at ease 感到舒適自在、無憂慮

eas·i·ly [ˋizɪlɪ] 🎧 *Track 1584*
adv. 容易地；輕易地
▶My boss loses his temper easily.
我老闆很容易發脾氣。

(補充片語)
lose one's temper 發脾氣

east [ist] 🎧 *Track 1585*
n. 東方；**adv.** 東邊地，往東邊地；**adj.** 東邊的

Eas·ter [ˋistɚ] 🎧 *Track 1586*
n. 復活節

east·ern [ˋistɚn] 🎧 *Track 1587*
adj. 東邊的

eas·y [ˋizɪ] 🎧 *Track 1588*
adj. 容易的；輕鬆的

eat [it] 🎧 *Track 1589*
v. 吃

ech·o [ˋɛko] 🎧 *Track 1590*
n. 回聲；共鳴；應聲蟲
▶David is an echo of his boss.
大衛是他老闆的應聲蟲。

v. 發出回聲；產生迴響；重複他人的話
▶Her laughter echoed across the empty room.
她的笑聲在空蕩蕩的房間裡迴蕩。

e·clipse [ɪˋklɪps] 🎧 *Track 1591*
n. （天）蝕；（聲望等）失色
▶There will be a lunar eclipse tonight.
今晚會有月蝕。

(補充片語)
lunar eclipse 月蝕

v. 蝕；遮蔽……的光；對……投下陰影
▶The sex scandal eclipsed his career in politics.
性醜聞對他的政治事業投下陰影。

ec·o·nom·ic [ˏikəˋnɑmɪk] 🎧 *Track 1592*
adj. 經濟上的
▶They sold their apartment for economic reasons.
由於經濟上的原因，他們賣掉了他們的公寓。

ec·o·nom·i·cal 🎧 *Track 1593*
[ˏikəˋnɑmɪkl]
adj. 經濟的；節約的；節儉的
▶Compared with driving a car, traveling by MRT is more economical.
跟開車比起來，搭捷運行動比較省。

ec·o·nom·ics 🎧 *Track 1594*
[ˏikəˋnɑmɪks]
n. 經濟學
▶I'm taking Professor Smith's economics this semester.
我這學期要修史密斯教授的經濟學。

e·con·o·mist [ɪˋkɑnəmɪst] 🎧 *Track 1595*
n. 經濟學者
▶Professor Smith is a world-famous economist.
史密斯教授是一個世界知名的經濟學家。

e·con·o·my [ɪˋkɑnəmɪ]　🎧 *Track 1596*
n. 節約；節省；經濟；經濟情況
▶ This country's economy has improved significantly.
這個國家的經濟已經顯著地改善。

edge [ɛdʒ]　🎧 *Track 1597*
n. 邊；邊緣

ed·i·ble [ˋɛdəbl̩]　🎧 *Track 1598*
adj. 可食的
▶ The mushrooms are not edible. They are poisonous. 這些蘑菇不能吃。它們有毒。

ed·it [ˋɛdɪt]　🎧 *Track 1599*
v. 編輯；校訂
▶ Jenny is in charge of editing this book.
珍妮負責編輯這本書。

e·di·tion [ɪˋdɪʃən]　🎧 *Track 1600*
n. 版本；發行數
▶ This is latest edition of the encyclopedia.
這是這套百科全書的最新版本。

ed·i·tor [ˋɛdɪtɚ]　🎧 *Track 1601*
n. 編輯
▶ The publishing house is looking for an experienced editor.
這家出版社正在徵求一名有經驗的編輯。

ed·i·to·ri·al [ˏɛdəˋtorɪəl]　🎧 *Track 1602*
adj. 編輯的；編者的
▶ It is our plan to expand our editorial team this year.
擴充我們的編輯團隊是我們今年的計劃。

n. （報刊的）社論；（電台、電視的）重要評論
▶ His editorials for the newspaper are well received by the public.
他為這家報紙所寫的社論廣受民眾歡迎。

ed·u·cate [ˋɛdʒəˏket]　🎧 *Track 1603*
v. 教育
▶ Both my brother and I were educated in the United States.
我和我哥哥都是在美國受教育的。

ed·u·ca·tion [ˏɛdʒʊˋkeʃən]　🎧 *Track 1604*
n. 教育

ed·u·ca·tion·al [ˏɛdʒʊˋkeʃənl̩]　🎧 *Track 1605*
adj. 有教育意義的；與教育有關的；教育的
▶ This TV program is entertaining as well as educational.
這個電視節有娛樂性，也富教育意義。

eel [il]　🎧 *Track 1606*
n. 鰻；鰻魚
▶ Most eels you eat in Japan are imported from Taiwan. 你在日本吃到的大部分鰻魚都是從台灣進口的。

ef·fect [ɪˋfɛkt]　🎧 *Track 1607*
n. 影響；作用
v. 造成；達到（目的）；產生

ef·fec·tive [ɪˋfɛktɪv]　🎧 *Track 1608*
adj. 有效的

ef·fi·cien·cy [ɪˋfɪʃənsɪ]　🎧 *Track 1609*
n. 效率
▶ My boss emphasizes work efficiency.
我的上司很強調工作效率。

ef·fi·cient [ɪˋfɪʃənt]　🎧 *Track 1610*
adj. 效率高的
▶ He is an efficient employee.
他是一個很有效率的員工。

ef·fort [ˋɛfɚt]　🎧 *Track 1611*
n. 努力

egg [ɛg]　🎧 *Track 1612*
n. 蛋

e·go [ˋigo]　🎧 *Track 1613*
n. 自我；自我意識；自尊心
▶ Not getting the promotion was definitely a blow to his ego.
沒有獲得晉升對他的自尊心絕對是個打擊。

(補充片語)
a blow to one's ego　對某人自尊心的一個打擊

Aa
Bb
Cc
Dd
Ee
Ff
Gg
Hh
Ii
Jj
Kk
Ll
Mm
Nn
Oo
Pp
Qq
Rr
Ss
Tt
Uu
Vv
Ww
Xx
Yy
Zz

※灰色單字為英檢初級必備單字

eight [et] 🎧 *Track 1614*
pron. 八個；**n.** 八；八個；
adj. 八的；八個的

eigh·teen [`e`tin] 🎧 *Track 1615*
pron. 十八（個）；**n.** 十八；十八個；
adj. 十八的；十八個的

eigh·ty [`etɪ] 🎧 *Track 1616*
pron. 八十（個）；**n.** 八十；八十個；
adj. 八十的；八十個的

ei·ther [`iðɚ] 🎧 *Track 1617*
adv. 也（用於否定句）；**pron.** （兩者中）
任一；**adj.** （兩者中）任一的；**conj.** 或者

e·lab·o·rate [ɪ`læbə͵ret] 🎧 *Track 1618*
adj. 精心製作的；精巧的；煞費苦心的
▶She made an elaborate costume for the
Halloween party.
她為了萬聖節派對製作了精巧的服裝。

v. 精心製作；詳盡闡述；詳細說明
▶My boss wants me to elaborate on my
proposal in today's meeting. 我老闆要我在
今天的會議上詳細說明我的企劃案。

(補充片語)
elaborate on 詳細說明

e·las·tic [ɪ`læstɪk] 🎧 *Track 1619*
adj. 有彈性的；可伸縮的；能恢復的
▶This skirt is not elastic at all.
這件裙子完全沒有彈性。

el·bow [`ɛlbo] 🎧 *Track 1620*
n. 肘；肘部；彎頭；（椅子的）扶手
▶This shirt has a hole in the elbow of the
right sleeve.
這件襯衫的右邊袖子手肘處有個破洞。

v. 用手肘推擠著前進
▶It was so crowded that he had to elbow
his way to the exit. 人實在太多了，以至於
他必須用手肘推擠才能到出口。

(相關片語)
up to one's elbows 非常忙
▶She was still up to her elbows in cleaning
up the house when the guests arrived.
客人到達時，她仍在忙著清理房子。

el·der [`ɛldɚ] 🎧 *Track 1621*
n. 長者；前輩；**adj.** 年紀較大的

el·der·ly [`ɛldɚlɪ] 🎧 *Track 1622*
adj. 年長的；年邁的
▶My grandfather is elderly, but he is still in
good health.
我爺爺年紀相當大了，但是身子仍很硬朗。

e·lect [ɪ`lɛkt] 🎧 *Track 1623*
v. 選舉；推選；選擇

e·lec·tion [ɪ`lɛkʃən] 🎧 *Track 1624*
n. 選舉；當選

e·lec·tric [ɪ`lɛktrɪk] 🎧 *Track 1625*
adj. 電的；導電的；電動的

e·lec·tri·cal [ɪ`lɛktrɪkl] 🎧 *Track 1626*
adj. 與電有關的；電器科學的；電的
▶My husband is engaged in importing
electrical appliances.
我先生是從事電器進口的。

(補充片語)
be engaged in 從事；
electrical appliance 電器

e·lec·tri·cian [͵ɪlɛk`trɪʃən] 🎧 *Track 1627*
n. 電工；電氣技師
▶He is a certificated electrician.
他是個有執照的電氣技師。

e·lec·tri·ci·ty 🎧 *Track 1628*
[͵ɪlɛk`trɪsətɪ]
n. 電；電流；電力；電學
▶I can't imagine life without electricity.
我沒辦法想像沒有電的生活。

e·lec·tron·ic [ɪlɛk`trɑnɪk] 🎧 *Track 1629*
adj. 電子的
▶He is an electronic engineer.
他是一個電子工程師。

e·lec·tron·ics 🎧 *Track 1630*
[ɪlɛk`trɑnɪks]
n. 電子學
▶There is a good possibility that I have to
retake Electronics next semester.
我下學期很可能要重修電子學。

el·e·gant [ˋɛləgənt] 🎧 Track 1631
adj. 雅緻的，優美的，優雅的
▶ She looked stunning in that elegant white evening dress. 她穿著那件優雅的白色晚禮服看起來真是太美了。

el·e·ment [ˋɛləmənt] 🎧 Track 1632
n. （化）元素；成分；要素

el·e·men·ta·ry [͵ɛləˋmɛntərɪ] 🎧 Track 1633
adj. 基本的
▶ My six-year-old son will go to elementary school next year.
我六歲的兒子明年要上小學了。

(補充片語)
elementary school 小學

el·e·phant [ˋɛləfənt] 🎧 Track 1634
n. 大象

el·e·va·tor [ˋɛlə͵vetə] 🎧 Track 1635
n. 電梯
▶ If you want to lose weight, take the stairs instead of the elevator.
如果你想減重，就以走樓梯代替搭電梯。

(補充片語)
lose weight 減重；
take the stairs 走樓梯；
instead of 代替

e·lev·en [ɪˋlɛvn] 🎧 Track 1636
pron. 十一（個）；**n.** 十一；十一個；
adj. 十一的；十一個的

e·lim·i·nate [ɪˋlɪmə͵net] 🎧 Track 1637
v. 排除；消除；（比賽中）淘汰
▶ It never occurred to him that he would be eliminated from the competition in the first round.
他從沒想過自己會在第一輪比賽就遭到淘汰。

else [ɛls] 🎧 Track 1638
adv. 其他；另外；**adj.** 其他的；另外的

else·where [ˋɛls͵hwɛr] 🎧 Track 1639
adv. 在別處；往別處；到別處

▶ This restaurant is fully booked tonight. Let's have dinner elsewhere. 這間餐廳今晚已經都被訂滿了。我們到其他地方吃晚餐吧。

e-mail [ˋiˋmel] 🎧 Track 1640
n. 電子郵件；
v. 用電子郵件發送；寄電子郵件給……

em·bar·rass [ɪmˋbærəs] 🎧 Track 1641
v. 使困窘

em·bar·rass·ment [ɪmˋbærəsmənt] 🎧 Track 1642
n. 窘；難堪；使人難堪的事物
▶ Falling down in front of someone you have a crush on is a real embarrassment.
在你暗戀的人面前跌倒真的是件很糗的事。

(補充片語)
fall down 跌倒；
have a crush on sb. 對某人迷戀

em·bas·sy [ˋɛmbəsɪ] 🎧 Track 1643
n. 大使館
▶ The embassy is heavily guarded 24 hours a day.
大使館一天二十四小時都是守衛森嚴的狀態。

e·merge [ɪˋmɝdʒ] 🎧 Track 1644
v. 浮現；（問題）發生；顯露；（事實）暴露；（從困境中）露頭
▶ China has emerged as a major global economic power in recent years.
在近幾年中，中國已經嶄露頭角，成為主要的世界經濟大國。

e·mer·gen·cy [ɪˋmɝdʒənsɪ] 🎧 Track 1645
n. 緊急情況
▶ Don't call 119 unless it is a real emergency.
除非是真正的緊急狀況，否則不要打119。

(相關片語)
emergency room 急診室
▶ The patient was sendt into the emergency room. 病人被送進了急診室。

e·mo·tion [ɪˋmoʃən] 🎧 Track 1646
n. 情緒；情感

e·mo·tion·al [ɪˈmoʃənl] 🎧 Track 1647

adj. 感情（上）的；易情緒激動的；感情脆弱的

▶ My sister always gets a little emotional during her period.
我姐姐生理期時總是有點情緒化。

em·pe·ror [ˈɛmpərə] 🎧 Track 1648

n. 皇帝

▶ Pu Yi was the last emperor of the Qing Dynasty. 溥儀是清朝最後一位皇帝。

em·pha·sis [ˈɛmfəsɪs] 🎧 Track 1649

n. 強調；重視

▶ My parents put emphasis on our table manners. 我的父母很重視我們的餐桌禮儀。

(補充片語)

put emphasis on 重視

em·pha·size [ˈɛmfəˌsaɪz] 🎧 Track 1650
=em·pha·sise （英式英文）

v. 強調

em·pire [ˈɛmpaɪr] 🎧 Track 1651

n. 帝國；皇權

▶ Hong Kong was once a colony of the British Empire.
香港曾經是大英帝國的殖民地。

em·ploy [ɪmˈplɔɪ] 🎧 Track 1652

v. 聘雇；雇用

em·ploy·ee [ˌɛmplɔɪˈi] 🎧 Track 1653

n. 員工

▶ Leading a company with nearly 5,000 employees is not an easy job. 領導一個有近五千名員工的公司並不是件容易的事。

em·ploy·er [ɪmˈplɔɪə] 🎧 Track 1654

n. 雇主

▶ The employer was accused of not paying the salary to 500 employees.
該雇主被控未付五百名員工薪水。

em·ploy·ment 🎧 Track 1655
[ɪmˈplɔɪmənt]

n. 雇用；職業、工作

▶ I am seeking employment at present.
我目前正在求職。

(補充片語)

seek employment 找工作、求職；
at present 現在

(相關片語)

employment agency 職業介紹所

▶ I got my current job via the employment agency.
我是透過職業介紹所找到目前這份工作的。

emp·ty [ˈɛmptɪ] 🎧 Track 1656

adj. 空的；未占用的；**v.** 使成為空的

en·a·ble [ɪnˈebl] 🎧 Track 1657

v. 使能夠

▶ Cellphones enable people to contact each other wherever they are.
手機讓人們無論在何地都能與彼此聯絡。

en·close [ɪnˈkloz] 🎧 Track 1658

v. 圍住；隨函附上

▶ The beautiful lake is enclosed by mountains.
這美麗的湖泊被群山環繞著。

en·closed [ɪnˈklozd] 🎧 Track 1659

adj. 與世隔絕的；封閉的

▶ We spent the whole summer in an enclosed peaceful village. 我們整個夏天都是在一個與世隔絕的寧靜村莊中度過的。

en·coun·ter [ɪnˈkaʊntə] 🎧 Track 1660

v. 遭遇（敵人）；偶然相遇

▶ Stay calm especially when you encounter danger.
保持冷靜，尤其是在你遭遇危險的時候。

n. 遭遇；衝突

▶ I had a chance encounter with an old acquaintance at the airport.
我在機場巧遇一個舊識。

(補充片語)

chance encounter 巧遇；
old acquaintance 舊識

en·cour·age [ɪnˈkɝɪdʒ] 🎧 Track 1661

v. 鼓勵

en·cour·age·ment 🎧 *Track 1662*
[ɪn`kɝɪdʒmənt]

n. 鼓勵；獎勵

► His encouragement gave me strength to keep on trying.
他的鼓勵給了我繼續努力的力量。

en·cy·clo·pe·di·a 🎧 *Track 1663*
[ɪn͵saɪklə`pidɪə]

n. 百科全書

► My parents bought me a full encyclopedia set as my birthday present on my 16th birthday. 我爸媽在我十六歲生日這天買給我一整套百科全書當做生日禮物。

(相關片語)

living encyclopedia 活百科全書；學識極為淵博的人

► Patrick is a living encyclopedia. He can answer any questions you have. 派屈克是部活百科全書。他能回答你任何問題。

end [ɛnd] 🎧 *Track 1664*
n. 結局；終點；盡頭；結束；
v. 結束；了結；作為……的結尾

en·dan·ger [ɪn`dendʒɚ] 🎧 *Track 1665*
v. 危及；危害

► Poisonous cooking oil will endanger our health. 有毒的烹飪用油會危害我們的健康。

end·ing [`ɛndɪŋ] 🎧 *Track 1666*
n. 結局；結尾

► I'm glad that the story has a happy ending.
我很高興這故事有個快樂的結局。

en·dur·ance [ɪn`djʊrəns] 🎧 *Track 1667*
n. 忍耐；耐久力

► You need to increase your endurance to run a full marathon.
你必須增加耐力才能跑全程馬拉松。

en·dure [ɪn`djʊr] 🎧 *Track 1668*
v. 忍耐；忍受；持久；持續

► I can't endure such ridiculous heat.
我忍受不了如此高的溫度。

en·e·my [`ɛnəmɪ] 🎧 *Track 1669*
n. 敵人

en·er·get·ic [͵ɛnɚ`dʒɛtɪk] 🎧 *Track 1670*
adj. 精力旺盛的；精神飽滿的

► The baby was still energetic but both his parents were completely tired out. 爸媽都已經累壞了，但這小寶寶依然精力旺盛。

(補充片語)

be tired out 疲憊不堪的

en·er·gy [`ɛnɚdʒɪ] 🎧 *Track 1671*
n. 精力；活力；能量

en·force [ɪn`fors] 🎧 *Track 1672*
v. 實施；執行；強制；強迫

► The police have the authority to enforce the law. 警察有執行法律的權力。

en·gage [ɪn`gedʒ] 🎧 *Track 1673*
v. 佔用；聘雇；使訂婚；使從事、忙於

► Both of my parents are engaged in the study of science.
我的雙親都從事科學研究。

(補充片語)

be engaged in 從事

en·gine [`ɛndʒən] 🎧 *Track 1674*
n. 引擎；發動機

en·gi·neer [͵ɛndʒə`nɪr] 🎧 *Track 1675*
n. 工程師

en·gi·neer·ing 🎧 *Track 1676*
[͵ɛndʒə`nɪrɪŋ]

n. 工程；工程學

► Mechanical engineering is my major.
我主修機械工程。

Eng·land [`ɪŋglənd] 🎧 *Track 1677*
n. 英國；英格蘭

En·glish [`ɪŋglɪʃ] 🎧 *Track 1678*
adj. 英文的；英國的；英國人的；
n. 英語；英國人

En·glish·man 🎧 *Track 1679*
[`ɪŋglɪʃmən]

n. 英國人

※灰色單字為英檢初級必備單字

en·hance [ɪn`hæns] 🎧 *Track 1680*
v. 提高;增加(價值、品質、吸引力等)
▶ The survey shows that reducing working hours can actually enhance work efficiency. 這調查顯示減少工作時數其實可以提高工作效率。

en·joy [ɪn`dʒɔɪ] 🎧 *Track 1681*
v. 喜愛;享受

en·joy·a·ble [ɪn`dʒɔɪəbl] 🎧 *Track 1682*
adj. 快樂的
▶ We had an enjoyable dinner last night. 我們昨晚吃了一頓愉快的晚餐。

en·joy·ment [ɪn`dʒɔɪmənt] 🎧 *Track 1683*
n. 樂趣;享受;令人愉快的事
▶ Taking a hot bath after a long tiring day is a great enjoyment to me. 在漫長疲累的一天之後泡個熱水澡,對我來說是一大享受。

en·large [ɪn`lɑrdʒ] 🎧 *Track 1684*
v. 擴大;擴展;放大;詳述
▶ I'd like to enlarge this photo to 8×12 inches. 我想把這張相片放大到8×12吋。

en·large·ment [ɪn`lɑrdʒmənt] 🎧 *Track 1685*
n. 擴大;擴展;擴充;增建;放大的照片
▶ She decorated their living room with an enlargement of their wedding photo. 她用他們婚紗照的放大照片佈置他們的客廳。

e·nor·mous [ɪ`nɔrməs] 🎧 *Track 1686*
adj. 巨大的;龐大的
▶ Their wedding cake was the most enormous one I've ever seen. 他們的結婚蛋糕是我看過最大的。

e·nough [ə`nʌf] 🎧 *Track 1687*
adv. 足夠地;**adj.** 足夠的;**pron.** 足夠的東西

en·roll [ɪn`rol] 🎧 *Track 1688*
=en·rol(英式英文)
v. 登記;註冊;使入會、入伍、入學;招生

▶ The public kindergarten only enrolls fifty new students this year. 這間公立幼稚園今年只招收五十名新生。

en·roll·ment [ɪn`rolmənt] 🎧 *Track 1689*
n. 登記;入會;入伍
▶ The private kindergarten has reached its full enrollment number. 這所私立幼稚園已經招生額滿了。

en·sure [ɪn`ʃʊr] 🎧 *Track 1690*
v. 保證;擔保
▶ If you don't pay the deposit, I can't ensure that we will still have rooms available for you on that day. 如果您沒有付訂金,我不能保證那天還會有空房給您。

en·ter [`ɛntɚ] 🎧 *Track 1691*
v. 進入

en·ter·prise [`ɛntɚ,praɪz] 🎧 *Track 1692*
n.(冒險性)事業;企業;公司
▶ You'd better have a clear idea of what you want to do before starting a new enterprise. 要開創一個新事業,你最好要清楚知道自己到底想做什麼。

相關片語
private enterprise 私人企業;民營企業
▶ Formosa Plastics Group is one of the largest private enterprises in Taiwan. 台塑集團是台灣最大的民營企業之一。

en·ter·tain [,ɛntɚ`ten] 🎧 *Track 1693*
v. 使歡樂;娛樂
▶ He hired a clown to entertain his guests at the party. 他雇了一個小丑在派對上娛樂賓客。

en·ter·tain·er [,ɛntɚtenɚ] 🎧 *Track 1694*
n. 款待者;請客者;表演者
▶ This versatile entertainer is very popular among young people. 這位全方位的藝人很受年輕人歡迎。

en·ter·tain·ment 🎧 *Track 1695*
[ˌɛntɚ`tenmənt]
n. 招待；款待；娛樂；消遣
▶She sang a song for the guests' entertainment. 她唱了一首歌來娛樂賓客。

(補充片語)
for sb's entertainment 為某人提供娛樂；給某人助興

en·thu·si·as·m 🎧 *Track 1696*
[ɪn`θjuzɪˌæzəm]
n. 熱心；熱情
▶I have a lot of enthusiasm for education. 我對教育很有熱情。

(相關片語)
brief period of enthusiasm 三分鐘熱度
▶He has only a brief period of enthusiasm for everything.
他對每件事都只有三分鐘熱度。

en·thu·si·as·tic 🎧 *Track 1697*
[ɪnˌθjuzɪ`æstɪk]
adj. 熱情的；熱心的
▶Our new neighbor seems to be very enthusiastic about community affairs.
我們的新鄰居似乎對社區事務相當熱心。

en·tire [ɪn`taɪr] 🎧 *Track 1698*
adj. 整個的；全部的

en·ti·tle [ɪn`taɪt!] 🎧 *Track 1699*
v. 給予權利；給予資格；為書題名；給稱號
▶Female employees are entitled to menstrual leave in our company.
本公司的女性員工有權利放生理假。

(補充片語)
be entitled to 給予權利、使有資格；
menstrual leave 生理假

en·trance [`ɛntrəns] 🎧 *Track 1700*
n. 入口；進入；入學

en·try [`ɛntrɪ] 🎧 *Track 1701*
n. 入場；出賽；進入權；入口；參賽者（作品）
▶Foreign visitors with infectious diseases will be denied entry to the country. 有傳染性疾病的外國旅客將會被該國拒絕入境。

(補充片語)
deny entry 拒絕入場；拒絕入境

en·ve·lope [`ɛnvəˌlop] 🎧 *Track 1702*
n. 信封

en·vi·ous [`ɛnvɪəs] 🎧 *Track 1703*
adj. 嫉妒的；羨慕的
▶There's no need to be envious of your own sister. 沒必要嫉妒自己的姐姐。

en·vi·ron·ment 🎧 *Track 1704*
[ɪn`vaɪrənmənt]
n. 環境

en·vi·ron·men·tal 🎧 *Track 1705*
[ɪnˌvaɪrən`mɛnt!]
adj. 環境的；有關環境的
▶Environmental pollution in this area is getting worse.
這個地區的環境污染越來越嚴重了。

(相關片語)
environmental protection 環境保護
▶Mr. Brown had devoted himself to environmental protection since his retirement.
布朗先生自從退休後就致力於環境保護。

en·vy [`ɛnvɪ] 🎧 *Track 1706*
n. 羨慕；妒忌；**v.** 羨慕；妒忌

e·qual [`ikwəl] 🎧 *Track 1707*
adj. 平等的；相等的；**v.** 等於；比得上；**n.** （地位或能力）相同的人；相等的事物

e·qual·i·ty [i`kwɑlətɪ] 🎧 *Track 1708*
n. 相等；平等；均等
▶Gender equality is an idea widely accepted around the world.
世界各地已經大大接受兩性平等的觀念。

(補充片語)
gender equality 兩性平等

e·quip [ɪ`kwɪp] 🎧 *Track 1709*
v. 裝備；配備
▶Our new office is well equipped.
我們的新辦公室設備十分完善。

※灰色單字為英檢初級必備單字

e·quip·ment [ɪˋkwɪpmənt] 🎧 Track 1710

n. 配備、裝備、設備；用具；才能知識

▶ It cost us nearly NT$200,000 to buy our camping equipment.
我們花了將近台幣二十萬買露營裝備。

e·quiv·a·lent 🎧 Track 1711
[ɪˋkwɪvələnt]

adj. 相等的；等同的；等價的；等效的

▶ According to the current exchange rate, one US dollar is equivalent to 30 NT dollars.
根據目前的匯率，一美元相當於新台幣30元。

(補充片語)

exchange rate 匯率

n. 相等物；等價物；對應詞

▶ What's the Chinese equivalent of the word "discrimination"?
「discrimination」這個字的中文對應字是什麼？

e·ra [ˋɪrə] 🎧 Track 1712

n. 時代；年代；紀元

▶ The invention of the personal computer led to a new era in the late 20th century.
個人電腦的發明開啟了二十世紀晚期的一個新時代。

e·rase [ɪˋres] 🎧 Track 1713

v. 擦去；抹掉；清除

▶ I wish there were a drug that could help people erase painful memories. 我希望有一種藥可以幫助人們忘卻痛苦的記憶。

e·ras·er [ɪˋresə] 🎧 Track 1714

n. 橡皮擦；板擦

e·rect [ɪˋrɛkt] 🎧 Track 1715

v. 豎立；使直立；建立；安裝

▶ The monument was erected in memory of the national hero.
這紀念碑是為了紀念這位民族英雄而豎立的。

(補充片語)

in memory of 為了紀念……；
national hero 民族英雄

er·rand [ˋɛrənd] 🎧 Track 1716

n. 差事；差使

▶ He hates running errands for his boss.
他很討厭幫他老闆跑腿辦事。

(補充片語)

run errands 跑腿辦事

er·ror [ˋɛrə] 🎧 Track 1717

n. 錯誤；失誤

e·rupt [ɪˋrʌpt] 🎧 Track 1718

v. 噴出；迸發；爆發；發疹

▶ The volcano erupted and buried hundreds of people alive.
火山爆發，並活埋了數百人。

es·ca·la·tor [ˋɛskəˌletə] 🎧 Track 1719

n. 電扶梯

▶ You mustn't allow your children to play on the escalator.
你絕不能讓你的孩子在手扶梯上玩耍。

es·cape [əˋskep] 🎧 Track 1720

v. 逃跑

▶ The police have put the prisoner who escaped from jail under arrest.
警方已經將逃獄的罪犯緝捕歸案。

(補充片語)

put sb. under arrest 將某人緝捕歸案

n. 逃跑；逃避

▶ The suspect successfully made his escape. 嫌犯成功地逃跑了。

(相關片語)

escape one's notice 疏忽；沒注意到

▶ It didn't escape my notice that she had had a new haircut.
我注意到她剪了個新髮型。

es·cort [ˋɛskɔrt] 🎧 Track 1721

n. 護衛隊

▶ The president is always guarded by a team of escorts.
總統總是由一整隊的護衛保護著。

v. 護航；護送

▶ The police officer escorted her all the way home. 警員一路護送她回到家。

es·pe·cial·ly [əˋspɛʃəlɪ] 🎧 Track 1722

adv. 尤其；特別是

es·say [ˈɛse] 🎧 Track 1723
n. 論說文；散文
► I have to finish my essay on Shakespeare by the end of this month. 我必須在這個月底前完成我這篇關於莎士比亞的論文。

es·sence [ˈɛsns] 🎧 Track 1724
n. 本質；要素；本體；精髓
► The essence of his speech was that we must conduct ourselves with dignity. 他演說的核心就是我們一定要自重。

（補充片語）
conduct oneself with dignity 自重

es·sen·tial [ɪˈsɛnʃəl] 🎧 Track 1725
adj. 必要的
► Protein is an essential nutrient to building up muscle or losing weight. 要增加肌肉或是減重，蛋白質是個必要的營養素。

es·sen·tial·ly [ɪˈsɛnʃəlɪ] 🎧 Track 1726
adv. 實質上；本來；本質上
► Socialism and communism are essentially the same things. 社會主義和共產主義在本質上是一樣的東西。

es·tab·lish [əˈstæblɪʃ] 🎧 Track 1727
v. 建立；設立；創辦
► The company was established in 1980. 這間公司是1980年創立的。

es·tab·lish·ment [ɪsˈtæblɪʃmənt] 🎧 Track 1728
n. 建立；創立；建立的機構
► They invested all their money in the establishment of their business. 他們將所有的錢都投資在他們事業的建立上了。

es·tate [ɪsˈtet] 🎧 Track 1729
n. 地產；財產；資產
► To everyone's surprise, he refused to inherit his father's estate valued at ten million dollars. 讓所有人吃驚的是，他竟然拒絕繼承他父親估計值一千萬元的財產。

（相關片語）
real estate 不動產
► Jack is a successful real estate agent. 傑克是個成功的不動產經紀人。

es·ti·mate [ˈɛstəˌmet] 🎧 Track 1730
v. 估計；估量
► The production cost is estimated to be ten million dollars. 生產成本預估要一千萬元。

n. 估計；估價；評斷；看法
► The real estate agent's estimate of my apartment's value was a bit higher than I expected. 不動產經紀人對我公寓價值的估計比我所預期高出一些。

etc. [ɛtˈsɛtərə]＝et cet·er·a 🎧 Track 1731
adv. 等等
► His collections include foreign coins, foreign stamps, foreign antiques, etc. 他的收藏品包含外國錢幣、外國郵票、外國古董等等。

e·ter·nal [ɪˈtɝnl] 🎧 Track 1732
adj. 永恆的；無窮的；無休止的
► I'm so tired of the girls' eternal gossip. 我厭倦女孩兒們永無休止的八卦聊天。

e·ter·ni·ty [ɪˈtɝnətɪ] 🎧 Track 1733
n. 永恆；不朽；來世；永恆的真理；無終止的一段時間
► His body will die, but his spirit will live for eternity. 他的肉體會死，但他的精神會永垂不朽。

Eu·rope [ˈjʊrəp] 🎧 Track 1734
n. 歐洲

Eu·ro·pe·an [ˌjʊrəˈpiən] 🎧 Track 1735
adj. 歐洲的；歐洲人的；**n.** 歐洲人

e·vac·u·ate [ɪˈvækjʊˌet] 🎧 Track 1736
v. 撤離；撤空；疏散；避難
► All villagers were evacuated from their homeland before the hurricane. 所有村民在暴風雨到來之前都已經自家園撤離了。

e·val·u·ate [ɪˈvæljʊˌet] 🎧 Track 1737
v. 估……的價；評估
► A good boss must be impersonal when evaluating an employee's work performance. 一個好主管在評估員工工作表現時，一定要保持客觀。

※灰色單字為英檢初級必備單字

eve [iv] 🎧 *Track 1738*
n. （節日的）前夕；（大事發生的）前一刻

e·ven [`ivən] 🎧 *Track 1739*
adj. 平坦的，平等的；一致的；對等的
▶ This dining table is not even.
這張餐桌不平整。

相關片語
break even 不賺不賠；收支平衡的
▶ Our restaurant finally started to break
even. 我們的餐廳終於開始收支平衡。

eve·ning [`ivnɪŋ] 🎧 *Track 1740*
n. 夜晚；晚上

e·vent [ɪ`vɛnt] 🎧 *Track 1741*
n. 事件；項目

e·ven·tu·al [ɪ`vɛntʃʊəl] 🎧 *Track 1742*
adj. 最終發生的；最後的；結果的
▶ Sooner or later, his arrogance will lead to
his eventual failure.
遲早，他的自大將導致他最終的失敗。

補充片語
sooner or later 遲早

e·ven·tu·al·ly 🎧 *Track 1743*
[ɪ`vɛntʃʊəlɪ]
adv. 最終地、最後
▶ Good will defeat evil eventually.
正義最終會戰勝邪惡的。

ev·er [`ɛvɚ] 🎧 *Track 1744*
adv. 從來；任何時候；究竟

ev·er·y [`ɛvrɪ] 🎧 *Track 1745*
adj. 每一個；一切的

ev·er·y·bod·y 🎧 *Track 1746*
[`ɛvrɪˌbɑdɪ]
pron. 每個人；人人；各人

ev·ery·day [`ɛvrɪˌde] 🎧 *Track 1747*
adj. 每日的，平常的
▶ It's totally OK to wear your everyday
clothes to the party.
你穿便服來派對是完全沒問題。

補充片語
everyday clothes 便裝

ev·er·y·thing [`ɛvrɪˌθɪŋ] 🎧 *Track 1748*
pron. 每件事；事事

ev·er·y·where 🎧 *Track 1749*
[`ɛvrɪˌhwɛr]
adv. 到處；處處；每個地方

ev·i·dence [`ɛvədəns] 🎧 *Track 1750*
n. 證據；證人；證詞
▶ He believed his father was murdered, but
he couldn't find any convincing evidence.
他認為他的父親是被謀殺的，但他找不到任何
有說服力的證據。

v. 證明；顯示；表明
▶ He is a great student, as evidenced by
his numerous certificates of award.
他是個好學生，從他許多的獎狀便可證明。

補充片語
as evidenced by 由……可證明；
certificate of award 獎狀

ev·i·dent [`ɛvədənt] 🎧 *Track 1751*
adj. 明顯的
▶ It is evident that the woman is suffering
from domestic violence.
顯然，這女人正遭受著家庭暴力。

e·vil [`ivl] 🎧 *Track 1752*
n. 邪惡；禍害；**adj.** 邪惡的；惡毒的

ev·o·lu·tion [ˌɛvə`luʃən] 🎧 *Track 1753*
n. 發展；進展；演化
▶ My essay is about the evolution of human
behavior.
我的論文內容跟人類行為發展有關。

e·volve [ɪ`vɑlv] 🎧 *Track 1754*
v. 使逐步成形；發展；進化；成長
▶ The teacher had the students observe
how a caterpillar evolved into a butterfly.
老師讓學生觀察一隻毛毛蟲是如何成長成一隻
蝴蝶。

ex·act [ɛg`zækt] 🎧 *Track 1755*
adj. 精確的；確切的

ex·act·ly [ɪgˋzæktlɪ] 🎧 *Track 1756*

adv. 正是；的確是

▶Thank you for the gift. A watch is exactly what I need most. 謝謝你的禮物。一隻手錶正是我現在最需要的東西。

ex·ag·ge·rate 🎧 *Track 1757*
[ɪgˋzædʒəˌret]

v. 誇張；誇大；言過其實

▶The salesman exaggerated this machine's functions and capabilities.
推銷員誇大了這機器的功能和性能了。

ex·ag·ge·ra·tion 🎧 *Track 1758*
[ɪgˌzædʒəˋreʃən]

n. 誇張；誇大；誇張的言語

▶His story sounds a bit of an exaggeration to me. 他的故事在我聽來有點誇張。

ex·am [ɛgˋzæm] 🎧 *Track 1759*

n. 考試；測驗

ex·am·i·na·tion 🎧 *Track 1760*
[ɪgˌzæməˋneʃən]

n. 考試

▶I'll have to burn the midnight oil for the coming final examination.
我得為即將到來的期末考試開夜車了。

(補充片語)

burn the midnight oil 開夜車

ex·am·ine [ɛgˋzæmɪn] 🎧 *Track 1761*

v. 檢查

ex·am·in·er [ɪgˋzæmɪnɚ] 🎧 *Track 1762*

n. 主考人；檢查人

▶He was caught cheating by the examiner.
他作弊被主考官逮個正著。

(相關片語)

medical examiner 驗屍官

▶According to the medical examiner, the man was choked to death.
根據驗屍官的說法，男子是被掐死的。

(補充片語)

choke to death 掐死；窒息而死

ex·am·ple [ɛgˋzæmpl̩] 🎧 *Track 1763*

n. 例子；榜樣

ex·cel [ɪkˋsɛl] 🎧 *Track 1764*

v. 勝過他人；優於；突出

▶Henry's academic achievements are just passable, but he excels in sports.
亨利的學習成績差強人意，但他在運動方面表現突出。

ex·cel·lence [ˋɛksl̩əns] 🎧 *Track 1765*

n. 優秀

▶If you keep practicing, you will achieve excellence.
如果你持續練習，你就會達到優異的境界。

ex·cel·lent [ˋɛksl̩ənt] 🎧 *Track 1766*

adj. 出色的；優秀的

ex·cept [ɛkˋsɛpt] 🎧 *Track 1767*

conj. 除了；要不是；**prep.** 除……之外

ex·cep·tion [ɪkˋsɛpʃən] 🎧 *Track 1768*

n. 例外

▶Everyone should follow the rule and you are no exception.
每個人都應該遵守規定，你也不例外。

ex·cep·tion·al 🎧 *Track 1769*
[ɪkˋsɛpʃənl̩]

adj. 例外的；特殊的；異常的

▶The teenager showed exceptional courage when saving the old lady's life.
這青少年展現了過人的勇氣，拯救了那位老太太的性命。

ex·change [ɪksˋtʃendʒ] 🎧 *Track 1770*

n. 交換；交流；交易所

▶There is an international exchange student from the United States in our class.
我們班上有一個來自美國的國際交換學生。

v. 交換；兌換；調換

▶I'd like to exchange these NT dollars into Japanese yen.
我想將這些新台幣兌換成日元。

(相關片語)

exchange angry words 爭吵

※灰色單字為英檢初級必備單字

▶ We exchanged angry words a few days ago, but we're good now. 我們前幾天吵了幾句，不過我們現在在已經沒事了。

ex·cite [ɛk`saɪt] 🎧 Track 1771
v. 刺激；使激動

ex·cit·ed [ɛk`saɪtɪd] 🎧 Track 1772
adj. 感到興奮的

ex·cit·ed·ly [ɪk`saɪtɪdlɪ] 🎧 Track 1773
adv. 興奮地；激動地
▶ The kids are excitedly talking about their plans for the summer vacation.
孩子們興奮地談論著他們的暑假計劃。

ex·cite·ment [ɪk`saɪtmənt] 🎧 Track 1774
n. 刺激；興奮；令人興奮的事
▶ To our excitement, our daughter gave birth to a healthy boy last night.
讓我們興奮的是，我們的女兒昨晚生下了一個健康的男孩。

ex·cit·ing [ɛk`saɪtɪŋ] 🎧 Track 1775
adj. 刺激的；令人激動的

ex·claim [ɪks`klem] 🎧 Track 1776
v. 呼喊；驚叫；（抗議地）大聲叫嚷；大聲說出
▶ "Wow, you haven't changed a bit!" Marie exclaimed.
「哇，你一點都沒變呢！」瑪麗驚呼。

ex·clu·sive [ɪk`sklusɪv] 🎧 Track 1777
adj. 除外的；唯一的；獨有的；獨家的
▶ The hotel charges NT$5,000 for a double room per night, exclusive of tax.
這飯店一個雙人房一晚要價五千，不含稅。

n. 獨家新聞；獨家產品
▶ The pineapple cheesecake is this bakery's exclusive.
這款鳳梨起司蛋糕是這間烘焙坊的獨家產品。

ex·cur·sion [ɪk`skɝʒən] 🎧 Track 1778
n. 遠足；短途旅行
▶ The kids are excited about their excursion tomorrow.
孩子們為了明天的遠足興奮得不得了。

ex·cuse [ɛk`skjuz] 🎧 Track 1779
n. 理由；藉口；**v.** 原諒；辯解

ex·ec·u·tive [ɪɡ`zɛkjʊtɪv] 🎧 Track 1780
n. 執行者；高級官員；經理；業務主管
▶ All executives are supposed to attend the meeting. 所有經理級主管都應該要出席會議。
adj. 執行的；經營管理的；行政的
▶ Peter Rogers was appointed the chief executive officer of the company this January. 彼得‧羅傑斯是在今年一月被任命為公司的執行長。

(補充片語)
chief executive officer =CEO 執行長；首席執行官

ex·er·cise [`ɛksɚ͵saɪz] 🎧 Track 1781
n. 運動；練習；習題；**v.** 做運動

ex·haust [ɪɡ`zɔst] 🎧 Track 1782
v. 用完；耗盡；使精疲力盡；使排出氣體
▶ Running the marathon exhausted him completely. 跑馬拉松讓他徹底精疲力盡。
n. 廢氣
▶ Car exhaust is a major contributor to air pollution in the city.
汽車廢氣是這城市空氣污染的一個主要因素。

(補充片語)
air pollution 空氣污染

ex·hib·it [ɪɡ`zɪbɪt] 🎧 Track 1783
v. 展示；陳列
▶ I was proud when seeing my artworks exhibited in the gallery. 看到我的作品被展示在美術館裡，我感到很驕傲。
n. 展示品；陳列品
▶ Please keep your hands off the exhibits.
請不要觸碰展示品。

(補充片語)
keep one's hands off sth. 不要用手觸碰某物

ex·hi·bi·tion [͵ɛksə`bɪʃən] 🎧 Track 1784
n. 展覽
▶ My father's first photographic exhibition will be held in the Modern Gallery next month. 我父親首次攝影展將在下個月於現代美術館舉辦。

ex·ile [ˋɛksaɪl] 🎧 *Track 1785*
n. 流亡;離鄉背井;被流放者;離鄉背井者
▶ The political exile finally returned to his homeland after sixty years. 這個政治流亡者在六十年後終於回到他的家鄉。

v. 流放;放逐;使離鄉背井
▶ The man was exiled from his own country for life. 男子被自己的國家終生放逐。

(相關片語)
live in exile 過流亡生活
▶ He has lived in exile since he sneaked out of the country.
他自從潛逃出國之後就過著流亡的生活。

ex·ist [ɛgˋzɪst] 🎧 *Track 1786*
v. 存在

ex·ist·ence [ɪgˋzɪstəns] 🎧 *Track 1787*
n. 存在;實在
▶ I don't believe in the existence of ghosts.
我不相信鬼的存在。

ex·it [ˋɛksɪt] 🎧 *Track 1788*
n. 出口;**v.** 出去;離去

ex·ot·ic [ɛgˋzɑtɪk] 🎧 *Track 1789*
adj. 異國情調的;奇特的;外國的
▶ There are many exotic restaurants on this street. 這條街上有很多異國餐廳。

ex·pand [ɪkˋspænd] 🎧 *Track 1790*
v. 展開;擴充;擴展
▶ They will expand their factory next year.
他們明年將會擴廠。

ex·pan·sion [ɪkˋspænʃən] 🎧 *Track 1791*
n. 擴展
▶ Since our business has just started, we can't afford the expansion of the factory.
因為事業才剛起步,我們無法負擔工廠擴充的費用。

ex·pect [ɛkˋspɛkt] 🎧 *Track 1792*
v. 期待;預期

ex·pec·ta·tion [ˌɛkspɛkˋteʃən] 🎧 *Track 1793*
n. 期待

▶ Against all expectations, our proposal was adopted.
出乎意料地,我們的提案被採納了。

(補充片語)
against all expectations 出乎意料地

ex·pe·di·tion [ˌɛkspɪˋdɪʃən] 🎧 *Track 1794*
n. 遠征;考察;探險隊
▶ The team went on an expedition to the Sahara Desert last November.
該團隊在去年十一月時到沙哈拉沙漠進行了一次遠征考察。

(補充片語)
go on an expedition 去探險、進行遠征考察

(相關片語)
go on a shopping expedition 上街購物
▶ The girls went on a shopping expedition while the boys went to the bar.
男生們到酒吧時,女生們上街購物去了。

ex·pel [ɪkˋspɛl] 🎧 *Track 1795*
v. 驅逐;趕走;排出(氣體等);把……除名、開除
▶ He abandoned himself to despair after being expelled from school.
他在被學校開除之後就自暴自棄。

(補充片語)
abandon oneself to despair 自暴自棄

ex·pense [ɪkˋspɛns] 🎧 *Track 1796*
n. 花費;費用
▶ Since we live on only one income, it is necessary that we cut down on our daily expenses. 既然我們只靠一份收入過日子,就有必要削減我們的日常開銷。

(補充片語)
cut down 削減;
daily expense 日常支出

ex·pen·sive [ɛkˋspɛnsɪv] 🎧 *Track 1797*
adj. 昂貴的;高價的

ex·pe·ri·ence [ɛkˋspɪrɪəns] 🎧 *Track 1798*
n. 經驗;經歷;**v.** 經歷;體驗

※灰色單字為英檢初級必備單字

ex·per·i·ment [ɪk`spɛrəmənt] 🎧 *Track 1799*

n. 實驗

▶We don't use any animals in our experiments.
我們的實驗過程中不使用任何的動物。

v. 做實驗

▶It is ruthless and brutal to experiment on animals.
在動物身上做實驗是很殘酷粗暴的行為。

ex·per·i·men·tal [ɪk`spɛrə`mɛntl] 🎧 *Track 1800*

adj. 實驗性的；根據實驗的；實驗用的

▶This anti-cancer drug is still in the experimental stage.
這個抗癌藥物仍在實驗階段。

(補充片語)

anti-cancer drug 抗癌藥；
in the experimental stage 處於試驗階段

ex·pert [`ɛkspɚt] 🎧 *Track 1801*

n. 專家；能手

ex·pir·a·tion [ˌɛkspɚ`reʃən] 🎧 *Track 1802*

n. 終結；期滿；吐氣；死亡

▶The expiration date of the instant noodles was three months ago.
這包泡麵的到期日是三個月前。

(補充片語)

expiration date 到期日；有效日期

ex·pire [ɪk`spaɪr] 🎧 *Track 1803*

v. 期滿；屆期；呼氣；斷氣

▶My passport will expire in two months.
我的護照兩個月後就到期了。

ex·plain [ɛk`splen] 🎧 *Track 1804*

v. 解釋；說明

ex·pla·na·tion [ˌɛksplə`neʃən] 🎧 *Track 1805*

n. 說明；解釋

▶You owe me an explanation for your absence from the meeting.
你必須向我解釋缺席會議的原因。

ex·plode [ɪk`splod] 🎧 *Track 1806*

v. 爆炸；使爆炸

▶The car exploded soon after it bumped into the tree. 汽車撞到樹之後不久就爆炸了。

ex·ploit [ɪk`splɔɪt] 🎧 *Track 1807*

v. 剝削；利用；開發；開拓

▶Mrs. Louise is accused of exploiting her foreign domestic worker.
路易斯太太被控剝削她的外籍家庭幫傭。

(補充片語)

be accused of 被控……；
foreign domestic worker 外籍家庭幫傭

ex·plore [ɪk`splor] 🎧 *Track 1808*

v. 探測；探勘；探討

▶At the meeting, we explored the possibilities of expanding our factory this year.
在會議上，我們探討了今年擴廠的可能性。

ex·plo·rer [ɪk`splorɚ] 🎧 *Track 1809*

n. 探險家；勘探者

▶Professor Norman is a mine explorer. 諾曼教授是個礦井勘探家。

ex·plo·sion [ɪk`sploʒən] 🎧 *Track 1810*

n. 爆發；爆炸

▶Many people died in the explosion.
很多人在這場爆炸中身亡。

ex·plo·sive [ɪk`splosɪv] 🎧 *Track 1811*

adj. 爆炸（性）的

▶Hydrogen is highly explosive. 氫具高度爆炸性。

n. 爆炸物

▶The police found a suitcase full of explosives. 警察發現一個裝滿炸藥的手提箱。

ex·port [ɛks`port] 🎧 *Track 1812*

n. 出口，出口產品；**v.** 出口

ex·pose [ɪk`spoz] 🎧 *Track 1813*

v. 使暴露於；使接觸到；揭露；揭發；

▶I don't want to expose my children to those violent programs on TV. 我不想讓我的孩子接觸那些電視上的暴力節目。

ex·po·sure [ɪk`spoʒɚ] 🎧 *Track 1814*

n. 暴露；曝曬；揭露；揭發；曝光
▶ X-ray exposure during pregnancy can cause harm to the unborn baby.
孕期的X光暴露可能對未出生嬰兒造成傷害。

ex·press [ɛk`sprɛs] 🎧 *Track 1815*

v. 表達；**n.** 特快車；**adj.** 特快的

ex·pres·sion [ɪk`sprɛʃən] 🎧 *Track 1816*

n. 表達
▶ She invited him to dinner as an expression of thanks. 她邀請他吃晚餐以表達感謝。

ex·tend [ɪk`stɛnd] 🎧 *Track 1817*

v. 延長
▶ I'd like to extend my stay for three days.
我想將停留時間延長三天。

ex·ten·sion [ɪk`stɛnʃən] 🎧 *Track 1818*

n. 延長；伸展；延期；增設部分
▶ The balcony is an illegal extension.
陽台是違法的增建部分。

ex·ten·sive [ɪk`stɛnsɪv] 🎧 *Track 1819*

adj. 廣大的；廣闊的；廣泛的；大規模的
▶ The best part we loved about our hotel room was its extensive bathroom. 我們最喜歡我們飯店房間的一點就是它寬闊的浴室。

ex·tent [ɪk`stɛnt] 🎧 *Track 1820*

n. 廣度；寬度；長度；程度；範圍
▶ I'm also responsible to some extent.
某個程度上，我也有責任。

ex·te·ri·or [ɪk`stɪrɪɚ] 🎧 *Track 1821*

adj. 外部的；外表的；外用的；對外的
▶ The ointment is for exterior use only.
這條藥膏只能外用。

n. 外部；外表
▶ You can't tell whether a person is good at singing by his exterior.
你沒辦法用一個人的外表看出他會不會唱歌。

ex·tinct [ɪk`stɪŋkt] 🎧 *Track 1822*

adj. 熄滅了的；已消亡的；絕種的；滅絕的
▶ How the dinosaurs became extinct is still a mystery. 恐龍究竟是如何滅絕的仍是個謎。

ex·tra [`ɛkstrə] 🎧 *Track 1823*

adj. 額外的

ex·traor·di·na·ry [ɪk`strɔrdn͵ɛrɪ] 🎧 *Track 1824*

adj. 異常的；非凡的
▶ The man showed extraordinary will to live.
男子展現了非凡的求生意志。

ex·treme [ɪk`strim] 🎧 *Track 1825*

adj. 末端的
▶ The arrival of the newborn baby brought the couple extreme happiness.
新生寶貝的到來帶給這對夫妻極度的快樂。

n. 極端
▶ She's very likely to go to extremes.
她很有可能會做出極端的事。

ex·treme·ly [ɪk`strimlɪ] 🎧 *Track 1826*

adv. 極度地；非常地
▶ All the workers were extremely exhausted.
所有的工人都極度地疲倦。

eye [aɪ] 🎧 *Track 1827*

n. 眼睛

eye·brow [`aɪ͵braʊ] 🎧 *Track 1828*

n. 眉；眉毛
▶ His rude behavior raised eyebrows.
他無禮的行為引起眾人的側目。

(補充片語)
raise eyebrows 引起側目、驚訝；招致不滿

eye·lash [`aɪ͵læʃ] 🎧 *Track 1829*

n. 睫毛
▶ The baby girl has beautiful long eyelashes.
這女寶寶有著美麗的長睫毛。

eye·lid [`aɪ͵lɪd] 🎧 *Track 1830*

n. 眼皮；眼瞼
▶ Jasmine is saving for a double eyelid surgery. 潔思敏正在為了雙眼皮手術而存錢。

eye·sight [`aɪ͵saɪt] 🎧 *Track 1831*

n. 視力；視野
▶ Keep all your belongings within eyesight.
將所有屬於你的物品都放在視線範圍之內。

※灰色單字為英檢初級必備單字

Ff

通過中級英文檢定者的英文能力：

 在日常生活中，能聽懂一般的會話；能大致聽懂公共場所廣播、氣象報告及廣告等。在工作時，能聽懂簡易的產品介紹與操作說明。能大致聽懂外籍人士的談話及詢問。

 在日常生活中，能閱讀短文、故事、私人信件、廣告、傳單、簡介及使用說明等。在工作時，能閱讀工作須知、公告、操作手冊、例行的文件、傳真、電報等。

 能寫簡單的書信、故事及心得等。對於熟悉且與個人經歷相關的主題，能以簡易的文字表達。

 在日常生活中，能以簡易英語交談或描述一般事物，能介紹自己的生活作息、工作、家庭、經歷等，並可對一般話題陳述看法。在工作時，能進行簡單的答詢，並與外籍人士交談溝通。

本書除包含官方公佈的中級4,947單字外，更精挑了近400個滿分必學的高手單字。同時，在片語的挑選、例句的使用上，皆依上述英檢官方公佈之能力範疇做設計，難度適中、不偏離考試主題。發音部分則是自然發音＆KK音標雙管齊下，搭配MP3以「分解／完整」方式錄音，給你最多元有效的學習手段，怎麼記都可以，想忘掉都好難！

---

fa·ble [ˈfebl̩]　🎧 *Track 1832*
n. 寓言；虛構的故事
▶ *The Lion and the Mouse* is one of my favorite tales in Aesop's Fables. 《獅子與老鼠》是我最喜歡的伊索寓言故事之一。
(補充片語)
Aesop's Fables　伊索寓言

fab·ric [ˈfæbrɪk]　🎧 *Track 1833*
n. 織品；布料
▶ Cotton is the most common fabric used for baby clothes.
棉是最常被使用來製作寶寶衣服的布料。

fab·u·lous [ˈfæbjələs]　🎧 *Track 1834*
adj. 驚人的；難以置信的；極好的
▶ My father has a fabulous collection of antiques. 我爸爸有驚人的古董收藏。

face [fes]　🎧 *Track 1835*
n. 臉；面子；**v.** 面對

fa·cial [ˈfeʃəl]　🎧 *Track 1836*
adj. 臉的；面部的
▶ I can't really talk or laugh with my facial mask on. 我戴著面膜不太能說話或笑。
(補充片語)
facial mask　面膜
(相關片語)
facial expression　面部表情
▶ He didn't know I was angry because he simply couldn't read facial expressions.
他不知道我在生氣，因為他根本不會看臉色。

fa·cil·i·ty [fəˈsɪlətɪ]　🎧 *Track 1837*
n. 能力、技能；設備、設施
▶ The department store lacks emergency assistance facilites.
這家百貨公司缺乏緊急服務設施。
(補充片語)
emergency assistance facility　緊急服務設施

fact [fækt] 　🎧 *Track 1838*
n. 事實，實情

fac·to·ry [`fæktərɪ] 　🎧 *Track 1839*
n. 工廠

fac·tion [`fækʃən] 　🎧 *Track 1840*
n. 派系；小集團；派系之爭；內鬨
▶ The board of directors has allegedly split into factions.
據説董事會已經分成好幾個派系了。

fac·tor [`fæktɚ] 　🎧 *Track 1841*
n. 因素；要素
▶ His health condition is the main factor that made him resign from his job.
健康狀況是他辭去工作的主要因素。

fac·ul·ty [`fæklti] 　🎧 *Track 1842*
n. （身體的）機能；技能；（大學的）全體教職員
▶ This university has 500 faculty members, including 350 professors and associate professors. 這所大學擁有五百名教職員，包含350名教授及副教授。

fad [fæd] 　🎧 *Track 1843*
n. 一時的流行；一時的風尚
▶ Sharing selfies on social media platforms has become the latest fad. 在社群平台上分享自拍照已經成為最新的時尚。

fade [fed] 　🎧 *Track 1844*
v. 凋謝；枯萎；褪去；逐漸消失
▶ Beauty fades, but dumbness is forever.
美貌會逐漸凋謝，但是愚蠢卻會跟著你一輩子。

Fah·ren·heit 　🎧 *Track 1845*
[`færən‚haɪt]
adj. 華氏溫度的；華氏的
▶ The temperature in the fridge is normally between 35 to 46 degrees Fahrenheit.
冰箱內的溫度正常情況下是在華氏35至46度之間。

fail [fel] 　🎧 *Track 1846*
v. 失敗；不及格

fail·ure [`feljɚ] 　🎧 *Track 1847*
n. 失敗

faint [fent] 　🎧 *Track 1848*
adj. 頭暈的；行將昏厥的；微弱的；虛弱的；軟弱無力的
▶ The woman's pulse suddenly became faint.
女子的脈搏突然變得很微弱。

v. 昏厥；暈倒
▶ All of a sudden, the woman fainted right in front of me.
那女人突然就在我面前昏倒了。

n. 昏厥
▶ Sally fell to the ground in a faint when hearing the bad news.
莎莉聽到這壞消息後就因為昏厥而倒在地上了。

fair [fɛr] 　🎧 *Track 1849*
adj. 公平的；公正的；
n. 集市；露天的娛樂集會；廟會

fair·ly [`fɛrlɪ] 　🎧 *Track 1850*
adv. 公平地；正當地；相當地；完全地
▶ He is a fairly good actor.
他是一個相當不錯的演員。

fai·ry [`fɛrɪ] 　🎧 *Track 1851*
n. 小妖精；仙女；仙子
▶ The tooth fairy came last night, took the tooth I put under my pillow and left the money.
牙齒仙子昨晚來了，拿走我放在枕頭下的牙齒，留下了錢。

adj. 仙女的；小妖精的；幻想中的
▶ Prince Charming only exists in fairy tales.
白馬王子只存在童話故事裡。

（補充片語）
fairy tale 童話故事
（相關片語）
fairy godmother （女）恩人
▶ Mrs. White is a fairy godmother to those homeless vagrants.
懷特太太是那些無家可歸的遊民的恩人。

※灰色單字為英檢初級必備單字

faith [feθ] 🎧 *Track 1852*
n. 信念；信任；信仰
▶I have to end our relationship because you broke faith with me.
因為你對我不忠誠，我必須結束我們的關係。
(補充片語)
break faith with sb. 對某人不忠誠；對某人沒信用

faith·ful [ˋfeθfəl] 🎧 *Track 1853*
adj. 忠誠的；忠貞的；忠實的
▶Helen was always faithful to her husband, even though he had been dead for many years. 海倫一直忠於她的丈夫，即使他已經死了很多年。

fake [fek] 🎧 *Track 1854*
adj. 假的；冒充的
▶The salesman deceived the old lady into buying the fake watch.
推銷員騙老太太買下那隻假錶。
(補充片語)
deceive sb. into doing... 哄騙某人做某事
n. 冒牌貨；仿冒品
▶The man claimed to be a doctor, but it turned out that he was a fake.
那男人自稱是個醫生，結果是個冒牌貨。
(補充片語)
turn out 結果
v. 假裝；做假動作；偽造；捏造；冒充
▶Peter faked my signature to get the contract.
彼得偽造我的簽名，拿到了那份合約。
(相關片語)
fake note 假鈔；偽鈔
▶The man was arrested for being in possession of fake notes.
男子因為持有偽鈔而遭逮捕。
(補充片語)
in possession of 持有；擁有

fall [fɔl]=**aut·umn** 🎧 *Track 1855*
n. 秋天；**v.** 落下；跌倒；下降

false [fɔls] 🎧 *Track 1856*
adj. 假的，不正確的

fame [fem] 🎧 *Track 1857*
n. 聲譽
▶Fame and gain are the things he cares about the least. 名利是他最不在乎的事情。
(相關片語)
come to fame 出名
▶The singer came to fame overnight.
這歌手一夜之間就成名了。

fa·mil·i·ar [fəˋmɪljɚ] 🎧 *Track 1858*
adj. 世所周知的；熟悉的；常見的；親近的
▶She looks familiar, but I have no idea who she is.
她看起來很眼熟，但我不知道她是誰。

fa·mil·i·ar·i·ty 🎧 *Track 1859*
[fə͵mɪlɪˋærətɪ]
n. 熟悉；通曉；親近；親暱
▶Most people here are shy and uncomfortable with too much familiarity.
這裡大部份的人都很羞澀，並且對太親暱的舉動感到不自在。

fam·i·ly [ˋfæməlɪ] 🎧 *Track 1860*
n. 家庭；家人

fa·mous [ˋfeməs] 🎧 *Track 1861*
adj. 有名的

fan [fæn] 🎧 *Track 1862*
n. 風扇；狂熱愛好者；粉絲

fa·nat·ic [fəˋnætɪk] 🎧 *Track 1863*
n. 狂熱者；極端分子；**adj.** 入迷的；狂熱的

fan·cy [ˋfænsɪ] 🎧 *Track 1864*
adj. 別緻的；花俏的；特級的

fan·tas·tic [fænˋtæstɪk] 🎧 *Track 1865*
adj. 極好的；了不起的

fan·ta·sy [ˋfæntəsɪ] 🎧 *Track 1866*
n. 空想；幻想；夢想
▶You can't have a real life if you keep living in a world of fantasy.
如果你繼續住在幻想的世界裡，你就不可能會擁有真實的人生。

far [fɑr] 🎧 *Track 1867*
adv. 遠地；**adj.** 遠的

fare [fɛr] 🎧 *Track 1868*
n. （交通工具的）票價；車（船）費
▶ How much is a full fare ticket?
一張全票多少錢？

相關片語

fare card 儲值卡
▶ Where can I add money to my fare card?
我可以在哪裡為我的儲值卡加值？

fare·well [`fɛr`wɛl] 🎧 *Track 1869*
n. 告別；送別演出
▶ He bade farewell to his family and friends from the departure lobby.
他從出境大廳向他的家人與朋友道別。

adj. 告別的
▶ We'll throw a farewell party for James.
我們會幫詹姆士辦一場餞別派對。

補充片語

throw a party 辦一場派對；
farewell party 歡送會

farm [fɑrm] 🎧 *Track 1870*
n. 農場

farm·er [`fɑrmɚ] 🎧 *Track 1871*
n. 農夫

far·ther [`fɑrðɚ] 🎧 *Track 1872*
adj. （距離、時間）更遠的，更往前的
▶ The gas station is at the farther end of the street. 加油站在街道更過去的那一頭。

adv. 更遠地，更進一步地
▶ I can't walk any farther. 我沒辦法再走更遠了。

fas·ci·nate [`fæsn͵et] 🎧 *Track 1873*
v. 迷住；使神魂顛倒
▶ Jerry was totally fascinated by the woman.
傑瑞已經完全被那女人給迷住了。

fas·ci·nat·ed [`fæsn͵etɪd] 🎧 *Track 1874*
adj. 著迷的
▶ I wonder why some women are particularly fascinated with married men. 我不知道為什麼有些女人會對已婚男子特別著迷。

fas·ci·nat·ing 🎧 *Track 1875*
[`fæsn͵etɪŋ]
adj. 迷人的；優美的；極好的
▶ Miranda is a fascinating young lady.
米蘭達是個迷人的年輕女子。

fash·ion [`fæʃən] 🎧 *Track 1876*
n. 時尚；流行；風行一時的人或事物
▶ She became a famous fashion model at the age of 16.
她在十六歲時就成了有名的時尚模特兒。

v. 使成形；把……塑造成
▶ He fashioned the cardboard into a temporary table.
他把紙板做成暫時用的桌子。

fash·ion·a·ble 🎧 *Track 1877*
[`fæʃənəbl]
adj. 流行的；時尚的；趕時髦的

fast [fæst] 🎧 *Track 1878*
adj. 快的；迅速的；**adv.** 快地

fas·ten [`fæsn] 🎧 *Track 1879*
v. 扣緊；閂住
▶ Please have your seatbelt fastened.
請將您的安全帶扣緊。

fat [fæt] 🎧 *Track 1880*
adj. 肥的；胖的；高脂的；**n.** 脂肪；油脂

fa·tal [`fetl] 🎧 *Track 1881*
adj. 命運的；命中註定的；無可挽回的；致命的
▶ The fatal head injury had permanently damaged his brain. 致命的頭部創傷已經對他的大腦造成永久性的損壞。

fate [fet] 🎧 *Track 1882*
n. 命運
▶ Everyone is a master of his own fate.
每個人都是自己命運的主人。

相關片語

as sure as fate 毫無疑問；千真萬確；命中注定
▶ My girlfriend will say yes to my proposal, as sure as fate.
我的女友會答應我的求婚，肯定會。

Aa
Bb
Cc
Dd
Ee
Ff
Gg
Hh
Ii
Jj
Kk
Ll
Mm
Nn
Oo
Pp
Qq
Rr
Ss
Tt
Uu
Vv
Ww
Xx
Yy
Zz

※灰色單字為英檢初級必備單字

fa·ther [`faðɚ]　🎧 *Track 1883*
n. 父親

fau·cet [`fɔsɪt]　🎧 *Track 1884*
n. 水龍頭

fault [fɔlt]　🎧 *Track 1885*
n. 缺點；錯誤

fault·y [`fɔltɪ]　🎧 *Track 1886*
adj. 有缺點的；不完美的；有缺陷的
▶ I'd like to return this faulty product.
我想退這件有瑕疵的產品。

fa·vor [`fevɚ]　🎧 *Track 1887*
=fa·vour（英式英文）
v. 贊同；偏愛、偏袒；
n. 贊成；偏愛；恩惠；幫忙

fa·vor·a·ble [`fevərəbl]　🎧 *Track 1888*
adj. 贊同的；順利的；適合的；討人喜歡的
▶ The weather today is favorable for a picnic. 今天的天氣很適合野餐。

fa·vor·ite [`fevərɪt]　🎧 *Track 1889*
=fa·vour·ite（英式英文）
adj. 最喜歡的；**n.** 最喜歡的人或事物

fax [fæks]**= fac·sim·il·e** 🎧 *Track 1890*
n. 傳真機；傳真通信
▶ You can send me the application form by fax. 你可以用傳真的方式把申請表傳給我。

v. 傳真
▶ Please fax me the application form as soon as possible.
請盡快將申請表傳真給我。

相關片語
junk fax 垃圾傳真（以傳真方式大量傳出的廣告資料）
▶ Stop sending me junk faxes!
不要再寄垃圾傳真給我了！

fear [fɪr]　🎧 *Track 1891*
n./v. 恐懼

fear·ful [`fɪrfəl]　🎧 *Track 1892*
adj. 可怕的；擔心的、害怕的

feast [fist]　🎧 *Track 1893*
n. 盛宴
▶ We always have a big feast on New Year's Eve. 我們在除夕夜這天總是會吃大餐。

v. 盛宴款待；盡情地吃；使感官得到享受
▶ The children feasted on chicken wings.
孩子們盡情地吃著雞翅。

相關片語
feast one's eyes on 欣賞某物之美；一飽眼福
▶ We feasted our eyes on the beauty of the sunset scenery at the beach.
我們在海邊飽覽夕陽美景。

feath·er [`fɛðɚ]　🎧 *Track 1894*
n. 羽毛
▶ Birds of a feather flock together. 鳥以群分，物以類聚（羽毛相同的鳥會聚在一起）。

補充片語
birds of a feather 有共同興趣的人，臭味相投的人

fea·ture [fitʃɚ]　🎧 *Track 1895*
n. 特徵；特色；面貌
▶ She couldn't see the robber's features very clearly in the dark.
她無法在黑暗中清楚地看見搶匪的容貌。

v. 以……為特色；以……為號召；起重要作用
▶ The Oscar-winning actress will feature in this biographical film. 這位得過奧斯卡的女演員將會主演這部傳記電影。

Fe·bru·a·ry [`fɛbrʊˏɛrɪ]　🎧 *Track 1896*
=Feb.
n. 二月

fed·e·ral [`fɛdərəl]　🎧 *Track 1897*
adj. 聯邦政府的，國家的
▶ The United States of America is a federal republic. 美國是個聯邦共和國。

n. 聯邦政府工作人員；（美國南北戰爭時）北部聯盟支持者
▶ He used to be a Federal, but he turned his coat in the end. 他曾經是個北部聯邦軍的支持者，但最後變節了。

turn one's coat 變節；改變立場

fee [fi]
🎧 *Track 1898*
n. 費用

fee·ble [ˋfibl]
🎧 *Track 1899*
adj. 衰弱無力的；（智力、性格）軟弱的；拙劣無效而站不住腳的；微弱的
▶ The firefighter heard a feeble cry for help from the basement.
消防員聽到從地下室傳來的微弱呼救聲。

feed [fid]
🎧 *Track 1900*
v. 餵食

feed·back [ˋfid͵bæk]
🎧 *Track 1901*
n. 反饋；反饋信息；一個人對某人或事物的反應
▶ We value our customers' feedback greatly because it helps us to improve our service. 我們相當重視顧客的回饋，因為它有助我們改進我們的服務。

feel [fil]
🎧 *Track 1902*
v. 感覺；覺得

feel·ing [ˋfilɪŋ]
🎧 *Track 1903*
n. 感覺；看法；預感

feel·ings [ˋfilɪŋz]
🎧 *Track 1904*
n. 感情；感性

fel·low [ˋfɛlo]
🎧 *Track 1905*
n. 男人；傢伙；同事；伙伴；
adj. 同伴的；同事的

fe·male [ˋfimel]
🎧 *Track 1906*
adj. 女的；雌的；**n.** 女性；雌性動物

fem·i·nine [ˋfɛmənɪn]
🎧 *Track 1907*
adj. 女性的；婦女的；女孩子氣的；陰性的
▶ The muscular man has a surprisingly feminine voice. 那個肌肉健壯的男子竟有著令人驚訝的女性嗓音。
n. 女性；陰性；陰性詞
▶ In this language, sun is a masculine while moon is a feminine. 在這個語言中，太陽是個陽性詞而月亮是個陰性詞。

fence [fɛns]
🎧 *Track 1908*
n. 柵欄；籬笆

fer·ry [ˋfɛrɪ]
🎧 *Track 1909*
n. 擺渡；渡輪
▶ The ferry service is provided only on weekdays. 渡輪服務僅在平日提供。
v. （乘渡輪）渡過
▶ The villagers have to ferry the river in order to go to town.
村民必須擺渡過河才能到城裡去。

fer·tile [ˋfɝtl]
🎧 *Track 1910*
adj. 多產的；繁殖力強的；富饒的；能生育的
▶ The humidity and warm temperatures provide a perfect fertile environment for bacteria to grow. 濕氣和高溫為細菌生長提供了絕佳的繁殖環境。

fer·ti·liz·er [ˋfɝtl͵aɪzɚ]
🎧 *Track 1911*
n. 肥料
▶ More and more farmers choose not to use any chemical fertilizers on their farms. 越來越多農夫選擇不在他們的農地上使用任何化學肥料。

fes·ti·val [ˋfɛstəvl]
🎧 *Track 1912*
n. 節慶；節日

fetch [fɛtʃ]
🎧 *Track 1913*
v. （去）拿來；去請……來；給……以
▶ Please fetch me my coat.
請去把我的外套拿來給我。

相關片語
fetch and carry 跑腿；做家務；當聽差；聽某人支使辦事
▶ I'm going to the supermarket to fetch and carry for my mom.
我正要去超市幫我媽跑腿。

fe·ver [ˋfivɚ]
🎧 *Track 1914*
n. 發燒；發熱

few [fju]
🎧 *Track 1915*
pron. 幾個；很少數；
adj. 幾個的；幾乎沒有的；少數的

※灰色單字為英檢初級必備單字

fi·an·cé [ˌfiənˋse] 🎧 *Track 1916*
n. 未婚夫
▶My fiancé and I are busy preparing for our wedding.
我的未婚夫跟我正忙著籌備婚禮。

fi·ber [ˋfaɪbɚ] 🎧 *Track 1917*
n. 纖維；纖維物質；性格、素質
▶A diet that lacks fiber can put your health at risk. 缺乏纖維的飲食會讓你健康不保。

fic·tion [ˋfɪkʃən] 🎧 *Track 1918*
n. 小說；虛構的事
▶I'm really into science fiction.
我真的很喜歡看科幻小說。

(補充片語)
science fiction 科幻小說

fid·dle [ˋfɪdl] 🎧 *Track 1919*
v. 拉小提琴；胡來；亂動；盲目擺動；浪費時間；遊蕩
▶Don't fiddle with the files on m desk.
不要亂動我書桌上的檔案。

n. 小提琴；瑣事；欺詐；騙局
▶I don't have time to waste on this fiddle.
我沒有時間浪費在這種小事上。

(相關片語)
fit as a fiddle 非常健康
▶I felt as fit as a fiddle after losing 25 kilos.
減去25公斤之後，我覺得自己身體非常健康。

field [fild] 🎧 *Track 1920*
n. 原野；運動場；領域

fierce [fɪrs] 🎧 *Track 1921*
adj. 兇猛的；好鬥的；狂熱的；激烈的；糟透的
▶They had a fierce argument last night.
他們昨晚發生了激烈的爭吵。

fif·teen [ˋfɪfˋtin] 🎧 *Track 1922*
pron. 十五（個）；**n.** 十五；十五歲；
adj. 十五的；十五個的

fif·ty [ˋfɪftɪ] 🎧 *Track 1923*
pron. 五十（個）；**n.** 五十；
adj. 五十的；五十個的

fight [faɪt] 🎧 *Track 1924*
v. 打架；搏鬥；爭吵；**n.** 打架；爭吵

fight·er [ˋfaɪtɚ] 🎧 *Track 1925*
n. 戰士；鬥士
▶Nelson Mandela was a world-famous fighter for freedom in South Africa.
曼德拉是個世界知名的南非自由鬥士。

(相關片語)
fire fighter 救火隊員
▶The fire fighter saved the old man's life at the risk of losing his own. 這救火隊員冒著自己的生命危險救了那個老人一命。

fig·ure [ˋfɪgjɚ] 🎧 *Track 1926*
n. 外形；體形；數字；人物；
v. 計算；認為；料到

file [faɪl] 🎧 *Track 1927*
n. 文件夾；檔案
▶It took him three days to read all the files on the case.
他花了三天的時間讀了這案子的所有檔案。

v. 把……歸檔；提出（申請）；提起（訴訟）
▶After being hit by her husband, she was determined to file for divorce. 在被丈夫毆打之後，她便決心要提出離婚訴訟。

(補充片語)
file for 提起訴訟

fill [fɪl] 🎧 *Track 1928*
v. 裝滿；充滿

film [film] 🎧 *Track 1929*
n. 影片；電影；底片

fil·ter [ˋfɪltɚ] 🎧 *Track 1930*
n. 濾（光、波等）器；多孔過濾材料
▶They made a simple filter to purify the water.
他們做了一個簡單的過濾器來淨化水。

v. 過濾；滲透；（消息等）走漏
▶Sunlight filtered through the blinds.
陽光透過了百葉窗。

fin [fɪn] 　🎧 *Track 1931*
n. 鰭；鰭狀物
▶ Our restaurant no longer serves any dishes with shark's fins in them.
本餐廳不再供應魚翅相關菜餚了。

(補充片語)
shark's fin 鯊魚鰭、魚翅

fi·nal [`faɪnl] 　🎧 *Track 1932*
adj. 最後的；確定的；**n.** 決賽；期末考

fi·nal·ly [`faɪnlɪ] 　🎧 *Track 1933*
adv. 最後地；終於

fi·nance [faɪ`næns] 　🎧 *Track 1934*
n. 財政；金融
▶ He was promoted to Finance Manager last month. 他上個月晉升為財務經理。

v. 籌措資金
▶ The railway construction had to be adequately financed to go forward. 鐵路建造工程必須要有充足的資金才能取得進展。

(補充片語)
go forward 行進；取得進展

fi·nan·cial [faɪ`nænʃəl] 　🎧 *Track 1935*
adj. 財政的
▶ Rumor has it that the company has encountered serious financial difficulties.
傳聞這間公司遇到重的財務困難。

find [faɪnd] 　🎧 *Track 1936*
v. 發現；找到

fine [faɪn] 　🎧 *Track 1937*
adj. 美好的；很好的；**v.** 處以罰金；**n.** 罰鍰

fin·ger [`fɪŋgɚ] 　🎧 *Track 1938*
n. 手指

fin·ish [`fɪnɪʃ] 　🎧 *Track 1939*
v. 結束；完成；**n.** 結束；終結；最後階段

fin·ished [`fɪnɪʃt] 　🎧 *Track 1940*
adj. 完成的；結束了的
▶ If we get caught, we're finished.
如果我們被逮到，我們就完蛋了。

fire [faɪr] 　🎧 *Track 1941*
n. 火；**v.** 開火射擊；解僱；起火燃燒

fire·crack·er [`faɪr,krækɚ] 　🎧 *Track 1942*
n. 鞭炮、爆竹
▶ It's illegal to set off firecrackers in a public place. 在公共場所燃放鞭炮是違法的。

fire·man [`faɪrmən] 　🎧 *Track 1943*
n. 消防隊員；救火隊員

fire·place [`faɪr,ples] 　🎧 *Track 1944*
n. 壁爐
▶ After dinner, we sat by the fireplace chatting and laughing till the midnight.
吃過晚飯後，我們坐在壁爐邊談笑直到深夜。

fire·proof [`faɪr,pruf] 　🎧 *Track 1945*
adj. 防火的、耐火的
▶ The vest is made from fireproof materials.
這件背心是用耐火材料製成的。

v. 使具防火性能；為……安裝防火設施
▶ This office building has been fireproofed.
這棟辦公大樓有安裝防火設施。

fire·wo·man [`faɪrwʊmən] 　🎧 *Track 1946*
n. 女消防員

fire·work [`faɪr,wɝk] 　🎧 *Track 1947*
n. 煙火
▶ Let's find a good spot to enjoy the fireworks.
我們找個好位置欣賞煙火吧！

firm [fɝm] 　🎧 *Track 1948*
n. 商行；公司；**adj.** 牢固的；堅定的

first [fɝst] 　🎧 *Track 1949*
adj. 第一的；最前面的；**adv.** 最先；首先；**pron.** 第一；第一個

fish [fɪʃ] 　🎧 *Track 1950*
n. 魚；**v.** 釣魚

fish·er·man [`fɪʃɚmən] 　🎧 *Track 1951*
n. 漁夫

Aa
Bb
Cc
Dd
Ee
Ff
Gg
Hh
Ii
Jj
Kk
Ll
Mm
Nn
Oo
Pp
Qq
Rr
Ss
Tt
Uu
Vv
Ww
Xx
Yy
Zz

※灰色單字為英檢初級必備單字

fish·ing [ˈfɪʃɪŋ]
🎧 *Track 1952*

n. 釣魚

▶ My father and I used to go fishing on the weekend when we lived in the countryside.
我們住在鄉下時，我爸跟我經常會在週末時去釣魚。

fist [fɪst]
🎧 *Track 1953*

n. 拳頭

▶ He couldn't help shaking his fist at that man. 他忍不住向那男人揮拳頭。

補充片語

shake one's fist at sb. 向某人揮拳

相關片語

make money hand over fist 賺大錢、發大財

▶ He daydreamed about making money hand over fist by selling clothes on the Internet.
他幻想可以靠著在網路上賣衣服發大財。

fit [fɪt]
🎧 *Track 1954*

n. 一陣；（病）發作

▶ She suddenly had a fit of dizziness.
她忽然感到一陣暈眩。

相關片語

in a fit of rage 一怒之下

▶ She slapped him in the face in a fit of rage.
她一怒之下賞了他一巴掌。

five [faɪv]
🎧 *Track 1955*

pron. 五（個）；**n.** 五；五歲；**adj.** 五的；五個的

fix [fɪks]
🎧 *Track 1956*

v. 修理；處理；安排

flag [flæg]
🎧 *Track 1957*

n. 旗子

flake [flek]
🎧 *Track 1958*

n. 小薄片

▶ The old paint on the wall is coming off in flakes. 牆上的舊油漆成片地掉落下來。

v. 成薄片；（成片）剝落

▶ The chef flaked the fish before frying it.
廚師在炸魚之前，先把魚切成薄片。

相關片語

flake out 累癱；入睡；昏倒

▶ I was so exhausted that I flaked out as soon as I hit the bed.
我實在是太累了，所以一上床就昏睡了。

flame [flem]
🎧 *Track 1959*

n. 火焰；火舌；光輝

▶ All of a sudden the car was in flames.
突然之間汽車就著火了。

補充片語

be in flames 著火；失火

v. 發出火焰；燃燒

▶ The campfire flamed brightly and intensely.
營火燃燒得明亮而熾烈。

flap [flæp]
🎧 *Track 1960*

v. 拍打；拍擊；振（翅）

▶ The wild goose flapped its wings and flew away.
雁子拍動牠的翅膀，然後飛走了。

n. 拍動；拍打聲；蓋口；激動慌亂（狀態）

▶ We were in a flap when we knew we got lost.
當我們知道自己迷路時，就整個慌亂了起來。

補充片語

be in a flap 處於慌亂之中

flare [flɛr]
🎧 *Track 1961*

v. （火焰）閃耀；燃燒；突然發怒

▶ The candle flared brightly in the breeze.
蠟燭在微風中明亮地燃燒著。

n. 閃耀的火光；閃光信號；照明燈；（怒氣的）爆發

▶ The flare of the candle lighted up the room. 蠟燭的火光照亮了房間。

相關片語

flare up （火）突然變旺；（人）突然發怒

▶ She flares up easily during her period.
她在生理期時很容易突然發怒。

flash [flæʃ]
🎧 *Track 1962*

n. 閃光；燈光的一閃；閃光燈

▶ Please don't use your camera flash inside the aquarium.
請勿在水族館內使用相機的閃光燈。

v. 使閃光；閃出；閃爍；（想法）閃現
▶ Don't flash your headlights at other road users.
不要對其他的道路使用者閃車前大燈。

相關片語
in a flash 很快；立刻
▶ The dinner will be ready in a flash.
晚餐立刻就會準備好了。

flash·light [`flæʃˌlaɪt] 🎧 *Track 1963*
n. 手電筒；閃光燈

flat [flæt] 🎧 *Track 1964*
n. =apartment一層樓；一層公寓；
adj. 平坦的；單調無聊的

flat·ter [`flætɚ] 🎧 *Track 1965*
v. 諂媚；奉承；使高興；
▶ He was good at flattering his boss.
他很擅長奉承自己的老闆。

補充片語
flatter oneself 自以為

fla·vor [`flevɚ] 🎧 *Track 1966*
=fla·vour （英式英文）
n. 味；味道
▶ I love the flavor of vanilla.
我喜歡香草的味道。

v. 給……調味
▶ He flavored the pork stew with soy sauce. 他以醬油為燉豬肉調味。

相關片語
flavor of the month 風靡一時的人或物；時尚
▶ It's just another flavor of the month.
這不過又是另一個風靡一時的東西罷了。

flaw [flɔ] 🎧 *Track 1967*
n. 缺點；瑕疵；裂縫
▶ It really embarrassed me when he pointed out my flaws in the presence of others. 當他在其他人面前指出我的缺失時，真的讓我很難堪。

v. 使破裂；使有缺陷
▶ The china cup flawed when I poured hot water in it. 在我注入熱水時，瓷杯就裂了。

flea [fli] 🎧 *Track 1968*
n. 跳蚤
▶ I found a flea on my dog.
我在我的狗狗身上發現一隻跳蚤。

相關片語
flea market 跳蚤市場
▶ I bought this antique dining table at the flea market.
我在跳蚤市場上買到這個古董餐桌。

flee [fli] 🎧 *Track 1969*
v. 逃；逃走
▶ The suspects had already fled before the police arrived.
警察來之前，嫌犯早就已經逃了。

flesh [flɛʃ] 🎧 *Track 1970*
n. 肉；肌肉；（供食用的）獸肉、果肉；肉體
▶ Don't worry. It's only a flesh wound.
別擔心。這只是個皮肉傷。

相關片語
flesh and blood 血肉之軀
▶ Soldiers are flesh and blood, just like everyone else.
軍人就跟每個人一樣，都是血肉之軀。

flex·i·ble [`flɛksəbl] 🎧 *Track 1971*
adj. 可彎曲的；有彈性的
▶ Our returns and refunds policies are quite flexible.
我們的退貨退款政策是相當有彈性的。

flight [flaɪt] 🎧 *Track 1972*
n. 班機；飛航

flip [flɪp] 🎧 *Track 1973*
v. 擲；輕拋；輕彈；快速翻（頁）
▶ He flipped through the magazine as he was waiting for boarding.
他在等候登機時，快速地翻閱了這本雜誌。

n. 輕彈；輕拋；（跳水或體操的）空翻
▶ They decided what to eat on the flip of a coin. 他們靠拋錢幣來決定要吃什麼。

相關片語
flip one's lid 發瘋；失去自制力

※灰色單字為英檢初級必備單字

▶I couldn't help flipping my lid at my roommate when he messed up the whole room. 當我室友把整個房間搞得一團亂時，我忍不住對他發飆了。

float [flot]　🎧 *Track 1974*
v. 浮；漂浮
▶They found a dead body floating on the sea. 他們發現一具屍體浮在海面上。

n. 漂流物；浮標；浮板
▶The kids are swimming with floats in the pool. 孩子們正在泳池裡用浮板游泳。

flock [flɑk]　🎧 *Track 1975*
n. 群；人群；群眾
▶Flocks of visitors crowded into the museum for the art exhibition.
成群的遊客湧進博物館看藝術展。

v. 聚集；成群
▶Hundreds of fans flocked around the singer. 成百的粉絲群繞著歌手。

flood [flʌd]　🎧 *Track 1976*
n. 洪水；水災
▶The flood has ruined our crops.
洪水毀了我們的作物。

v. 淹沒；使氾濫
▶Our home was flooded.
我們的家被淹沒了。

flood·ing [ˋflʌdɪŋ]　🎧 *Track 1977*
n. 氾濫；產後出血；水災
▶The weatherman warned that the hurricane might cause severe flooding. 氣象預報員警告說，颶風可能會帶來嚴重的水災。

floor [flor]　🎧 *Track 1978*
n. 地板；樓層

flour [flaʊr]　🎧 *Track 1979*
n. 麵粉；（穀類磨成的）粉

flour·ish [ˋflɝɪʃ]　🎧 *Track 1980*
v. （植物）茂盛；繁茂；（事業等）興旺；炫耀、誇耀
▶His business flourished under his leadership.
在他的領導下，他的生意非常興隆。

n. 揮舞；炫耀；華麗的詞藻
▶His article was full of flourish, but lacked sincerity. 他的文章充滿華麗的詞藻，但是缺乏真摯的感情。

flow [flo]　🎧 *Track 1981*
n. 流動；流暢；**v.** 流動；湧（進或出）

flow·er [ˋflaʊɚ]　🎧 *Track 1982*
n. 花

flu [flu]　🎧 *Track 1983*
n. 流行性感冒

flu·ent [ˋfluənt]　🎧 *Track 1984*
adj. 流利的
▶He speaks very fluent English.
他會說非常流利的英語。

flu·id [ˋfluɪd]　🎧 *Track 1985*
adj. 流動的；液體的；不固定的；易變的；流暢的
▶The ballerina's graceful and fluid movements captured the audience's attention. 芭蕾女伶優雅流暢的動作緊緊攫住了觀眾的注意。

n. 流體
▶Liquids and gases are both fluids.
液體和氣體都是流體。

flunk [flʌŋk]　🎧 *Track 1986*
v. 使不及格
▶You will flunk your finals if you don't study.
如果你不唸書，你的期末考會不及格的。

flush [flʌʃ]　🎧 *Track 1987*
v. 用水沖洗；（臉）發紅；漲紅；使興奮
▶Please don't forget to flush the toilet after use. 馬桶使用後請勿忘記沖水。

n. 沖洗；紅光；興奮、激動
▶They felt a flush of pride when their son received his award on the stage. 當他們的兒子在台上領獎時，他們感到一陣驕傲。

flute [flut]　🎧 *Track 1988*
n. 長笛；橫笛

flut·ter [`flʌtɚ] 🎧 *Track 1989*

v. 振翼；拍翅；（旗幟）飄揚；（脈搏）跳動；顫動、發抖

▶ Her voice fluttered with anger.
她的聲音因為憤怒而發抖。

n. 振翼；飄動；興奮；激動；（心臟）振顫

▶ The arrival of the celebrities caused a flutter at the restaurant.
名人的到來在餐廳內引起了一陣轟動。

fly [flaɪ] 🎧 *Track 1990*

v. 飛；駕駛飛機；搭飛機旅行；**n.** 蒼蠅

foam [fom] 🎧 *Track 1991*

n. 泡沫

▶ I use this brand of facial foam to wash my face.
我都適用這牌子的潔面泡沫來洗臉。

(補充片語)

facial foam 洗面乳

v. 起泡沫

▶ The man suddenly fell to the ground, foaming at the mouth.
男子突然倒在地上口吐白沫。

(補充片語)

foam at the mouth 口吐白沫

fo·cus [`fokəs] 🎧 *Track 1992*

v. 使集中；使聚焦；**n.** 焦點；重點

foe [fo] 🎧 *Track 1993*

n. 敵人；仇敵；危害物

▶ I'm your friend, not your foe.
我是你的朋友，不是你的敵人。

fog [fɑg] 🎧 *Track 1994*

n. 霧

fog·gy [`fɑgɪ] 🎧 *Track 1995*

adj. 有霧的；多霧的；朦朧的

▶ It's dangerous to drive on such a foggy day.
在這樣一個多霧的天氣開車是很危險的。

foil [fɔɪl] 🎧 *Track 1996*

n. 金屬薄片；箔紙

▶ She wrapped the chicken in foil before baking it in the oven.
她將雞肉用箔紙包起來後，便放入烤箱烤。

fold [fold] 🎧 *Track 1997*

v. 對折；摺疊

▶ The little girl folded a piece of paper into a heart and gave it to me. 小女孩將一張紙摺成一顆愛心，並將它送給了我。

n. 摺疊；摺痕

▶ Could you help me iron the shirt to get the folds out?
你可幫我熨這件襯衫，把上面的摺痕熨平嗎？

folk [fok] 🎧 *Track 1998*

n. 人們；各位；雙親

▶ I'd like to introduce you to my folks.
我想將你介紹給我雙親認識。

adj. 民間的；民眾的；通俗的

▶ What the girl is humming is a famous folk song. 那女孩正在哼唱的是一首有名的民謠。

(補充片語)

folk song 民謠

fol·low [`fɑlo] 🎧 *Track 1999*

v. 跟隨；跟著；接著

fol·low·er [`fɑlowɚ] 🎧 *Track 2000*

n. 追隨者；信徒；擁護者；侍從；部下

▶ My wife is a faithful follower of Korean dramas. 我太太是韓劇的忠實擁護者。

fol·low·ing [`fɑləwɪŋ] 🎧 *Track 2001*

adj. 接著的；其次的；下述的；**prep.** 在……以後；**pron.** 下列人員或事物；**n.** 追隨者

fond [fɑnd] 🎧 *Track 2002*

adj. 喜歡的；喜好的

▶ My brother is fond of extreme sports.
我哥哥喜歡極限運動。

(補充片語)

be fond of 喜歡；愛好

food [fud] 🎧 *Track 2003*

n. 食物

※灰色單字為英檢初級必備單字

139

fool [ful] 🎧 *Track 2004*
n. 笨蛋；傻瓜；v. 愚弄；鬼混

fool·ish [`fulɪʃ] 🎧 *Track 2005*
adj. 愚蠢的；荒謬可笑的

foot [fʊt] 🎧 *Track 2006*
n. 腳；英尺

foot·ball [`fʊt͵bɔl] 🎧 *Track 2007*
n. 足球

for [fɔr] 🎧 *Track 2008*
prep. 為了；conj. 因為；由於

for·bid [fɚ`bɪd] 🎧 *Track 2009*
v. 禁止；不許
▶ I forbid you to step into this house again.
我不許你再踏進這棟屋子一步。

force [fors] 🎧 *Track 2010*
n. 力量；武力；勢力
v. 強迫；迫使；強行攻佔

fore·cast [`for͵kæst] 🎧 *Track 2011*
n. 預測；預報；預料
▶ According to the weather forecast, the typhoon will directly hit southern Taiwan.
根據氣象預測，颱風將直接侵襲南台灣。

v. 預測；預報；預示；預言
▶ The weatherman forecasted that it would rain this afternoon.
氣象預報員預測今天下午會下雨。

fore·head [`for͵hɛd] 🎧 *Track 2012*
=brow （英式英文）
n. 額；前額；前部
▶ There was a scar on the robber's forehead.
搶匪的額頭上有個疤痕。

for·eign [`fɔrɪn] 🎧 *Track 2013*
adj. 外國的；外來的

for·eign·er [`fɔrɪnɚ] 🎧 *Track 2014*
n. 外國人

fore·see [for`si] 🎧 *Track 2015*
v. 預見；預知

▶ No one can foresee what will happen in the future.
沒有人可以預知未來會發生什麼事。

for·est [`fɔrɪst] 🎧 *Track 2016*
n. 森林

for·ev·er [fɚ`ɛvɚ] 🎧 *Track 2017*
adv. 永遠
▶ May our friendship last forever.
願我們的友誼能持續永遠。

for·get [fɚ`gɛt] 🎧 *Track 2018*
v. 忘記

for·get·ful [fɚ`gɛtfəl] 🎧 *Track 2019*
adj. 健忘的
▶ Women become forgetful when they are pregnant. 女人會在懷孕時變得健忘。

for·give [fɚ`gɪv] 🎧 *Track 2020*
v. 原諒

fork [fɔrk] 🎧 *Track 2021*
n. 叉子

form [fɔrm] 🎧 *Track 2022*
n. 外形；類型；表格；v. 形成；塑造；養成

form·al [`fɔrml] 🎧 *Track 2023*
adj. 正式的

for·ma·tion [fɔr`meʃən] 🎧 *Track 2024*
n. 形成；構成；構成物；結構
▶ Family life has a great influence on the formation of a child's character. 家庭生活對一個孩童的性格養成有很大的影響。

for·mer [`fɔrmɚ] 🎧 *Track 2025*
pron. 前者；adj. 從前的；前者的；前任的

for·mu·la [`fɔrmjələ] 🎧 *Track 2026*
n. 慣例；常規；配方；方程式
▶ Dr. Wang is the only person who possesses the formula of the medicine.
王醫師是唯一擁有這帖藥的處方的人。

fort [fort] 🎧 *Track 2027*
n. 堡壘；要塞

▶They disposed troops and arms at the fort. 他們在要塞配置了軍隊及軍備。

相關片語
hold the fort 代為照料
▶Vincent will hold the fort while I'm away from the office.
文森會在我不在辦公室時幫我代理工作。

forth [forθ] 🎧 *Track 2028*
adj. （空間）向前、向外；（時間）從……以後
▶From that day forth he made no trouble for his parents.
從那天以後他就不再給父母惹麻煩了。

補充片語
make trouble 惹麻煩

for·tu·nate [`fortʃənɪt] 🎧 *Track 2029*
adj. 幸運的
▶I feel fortunate to have met a good teacher.
我覺得自己能遇到一個好老師很幸運

for·tu·nate·ly [`fortʃənɪtlɪ] 🎧 *Track 2030*
adv. 幸運地
▶Fortunately, no one was hurt in the accident.
幸運地，沒有人在這場意外中受傷。

for·tune [`fortʃən] 🎧 *Track 2031*
n. 財產；財富
▶He made a fortune by investing in real estate. 他靠投資房地產致富。

補充片語
make a fortune 致富；發大財

for·ty [`fortɪ] 🎧 *Track 2032*
pron. 四十（個）；n. 四十；
adj. 四十的；四十個的

for·ward [`forwɚd] 🎧 *Track 2033*
adv. 向前；提前；今後；
adj. 前面的；早的；早熟的

for·wards [`forwɚdz] 🎧 *Track 2034*
adv. 往前的

fos·sil [`fasl] 🎧 *Track 2035*
n. 化石；頑固不化的人；守舊的事物

▶The scientists were excited when they discovered the fossils of a nearly complete dinosaur skeleton. 科學家們在發現一具近乎完整的恐龍骨骼化石時，都興奮得不得了。

adj. 化石的；成化石的
▶We still don't have enough renewable energy to replace fossil fuels at the moment. 此刻，我們仍沒有足夠的可再生能源來取代化石燃料。

補充片語
fossil fuel 化石燃料（天然氣、石油等）

相關片語
old fossil 頑固不化的人
▶An old fossil like him wouldn't change his mind. 像他這樣一個頑固不化的人，是不會改變心意的。

fos·ter [`fastɚ] 🎧 *Track 2036*
v. 養育；領養
▶We fostered the boy right after he was born. 我們在這男孩一出生就領養他了。

adj. 收養的；領養的
▶He lived with his foster son.
他跟他的養子住在一起。

補充片語
foster son 養子

foul [faʊl] 🎧 *Track 2037*
adj. 骯髒的；惡臭的；邪惡的；下流的；惡劣的；犯規的
▶There's a foul smell in the tap water.
自來水裡有種惡臭的氣味。

n. 犯規
▶The player was disqualified from the game after two technical fouls. 該選手在兩次技術性犯規之後被取消了比賽資格。

v. 弄髒；玷污；污染；使壅塞
▶Industrial waste from the factory has fouled the river.
來自工廠的工業廢料污染了這條河。

相關片語
through fair and foul 在任何情況下
▶I will not betray my friends through fair and foul.
不管在任何情況下，我都不會背叛我的朋友。

※灰色單字為英檢初級必備單字

found [faʊnd] 🎧 *Track 2038*
v. 建立；建造；創辦
▶ This elementary school was founded in 1984. 這所小學是在1984年創辦的。

foun·da·tion [faʊnˋdeʃən] 🎧 *Track 2039*
n. 建立；創辦；基礎；基金會；地基
▶ Education is the foundation of success. 教育是成功的基礎。

found·er [ˋfaʊndɚ] 🎧 *Track 2040*
n. 創立者；創建者；奠基者
▶ The monument was erected in memory of the founder of the hospital. 這紀念碑是為了紀念醫院的創辦人所豎立的。

foun·tain [ˋfaʊntɪn] 🎧 *Track 2041*
n. 噴水池；噴泉；噴泉式飲水器；（知識的）泉源
▶ In the middle of the square was a beautiful fountain. 在廣場的中央是一個美麗的噴水池。

相關片語
water fountain 飲水器
▶ There is a water fountain at the entrance of the park. 在公園的入口有個飲水器。

four [for] 🎧 *Track 2042*
pron. 四個；**n.** 四；四個；
adj. 四的；四個的

four·teen [ˋforˋtin] 🎧 *Track 2043*
pron. 十四（個）；**n.** 十四；**adj.** 十四個

fox [fɑks] 🎧 *Track 2044*
n. 狐狸；狡猾的人

fra·gile [ˋfrædʒəl] 🎧 *Track 2045*
adj. 易碎的；脆弱的；易損壞的
▶ There's nothing fragile in the box. 箱子裡沒有易碎的東西。

fra·grance [ˋfregrəns] 🎧 *Track 2046*
n. 芬芳；香氣；香味
▶ I don't wear perfume, because most fragrances give me a headache. 我不擦香水，因為大部分的香氣都會讓我頭痛。

frail [frel] 🎧 *Track 2047*
adj. 身體虛弱的；意志薄弱的；易損壞的
▶ The patient is still too frail to leave the hospital. 病人現在身體仍然太過虛弱而無法出院。

frame [frem] 🎧 *Track 2048*
v. 為……加框；塑造；製定；構想出
▶ I framed my five-year-old boy's painting and hung it on the wall. 我將我五歲兒子的畫作裱框，並將它掛在牆上。

n. 架構；框架；（人或動物的）骨骼；機構
▶ It's a perfect frame for the picture. 這對這張照片來說是一個完美的相框。

相關片語
frame of mind 心境；思想狀態；情緒
▶ Let's tell her about this when she's in a cheerful frame of mind. 我們等她心情愉快的時候再告訴這件事。

France [fræns] 🎧 *Track 2049*
n. 法國

frank [fræŋk] 🎧 *Track 2050*
adj. 老實的；坦白的

fraud [frɔd] 🎧 *Track 2051*
n. 欺騙；詐騙；騙局；騙子
▶ I thought the man was a lawyer, but he turned out to be a fraud. 我以為那個男人是個律師，結果他是個騙子。

相關片語
commit fraud 詐騙
▶ The man was arrested for committing insurance fraud. 那男子因為保險詐騙而被逮捕。

freak [frik] 🎧 *Track 2052*
n. 怪誕的舉動；畸形的人；反常現象；奇怪念頭；背離社會習俗的人
▶ My roommate is a freak who always walks around naked in the house. 我的室友是個怪胎，總是光著身子在屋子裡四處走動。

adj. 反常的；怪異的
▶ This series of freak accidents attracted the attention of the police. 這一連串怪異的意外事件引起了警方的注意。

freak of nature 不正常的事物；畸形的事物
▶ A frog with three heads is a freak of nature.
有三個頭的青蛙是畸形的。

free [fri] 🎧 *Track 2053*
adj. 自由的；免費的；不受限制的
v. 釋放；使自由

free·dom [ˋfridəm] 🎧 *Track 2054*
n. 自由

free·way [ˋfrɪˌwe] 🎧 *Track 2055*
=mo·tor·way （英式英文）
n. 高速公路
▶ My car broke down on the freeway.
我的車在高速公路上拋錨了。

補充片語

break down 拋錨；故障

freeze [friz] 🎧 *Track 2056*
v. 結冰；凝固
▶ Seawater actually freezes at a lower temperature than fresh water.
事實上海水結冰的溫度比淡水要來得低。

相關片語

freeze out 凍死
▶ The poor dog was frozen out on the street.
可憐的狗兒被凍死在路上了。

freez·er [ˋfrizɚ] 🎧 *Track 2057*
n. 冰箱；冷藏箱；冷凍櫃

freez·ing [ˋfrizɪŋ] 🎧 *Track 2058*
adj. 凍極的；極冷的
▶ It's freezing outside. I prefer staying home today.
外頭冷死了。我今天比較想要待在家。

相關片語

freezing point 冰點
▶ The freezing point of seawater is much lower than that of fresh water.
海水的冰點比淡水的低得多。

freight [fret] 🎧 *Track 2059*
n. 貨物；運費；貨運
▶ Your order will be delivered by freight.
您訂購的商品將以貨運方式寄送給您。

v. 裝貨於；運輸（貨物）；運貨
▶ How much does it cost to freight the sofa to Taiwan?
將這沙發運送到台灣要多少錢？

French [frɛntʃ] 🎧 *Track 2060*
adj. 法國的；法國人的；法語的；
n. 法國人；法語

fre·quen·cy [ˋfrikwənsɪ] 🎧 *Track 2061*
n. 頻繁；屢次；頻率；次數
▶ The survey shows that drunk-driving accidents occur with higher frequency during holidays.
調查顯示，放假期間酒駕意外發生頻率比較高。

fre·quent [ˋfrikwənt] 🎧 *Track 2062*
adj. 頻繁的；時常發生的；屢次的
▶ Mr. Miller is a frequent customer of our restaurant. 米勒先生是我們餐廳的常客。

v. 常到；時常出入
▶ No one likes to frequent hospitals.
沒有人喜歡時常出入醫院。

fresh [frɛʃ] 🎧 *Track 2063*
adj. 新鮮的

fresh·man [ˋfrɛʃmən] 🎧 *Track 2064*
n. （大學等的）一年級生；新生；新手；新人
▶ It's a welcoming party for the freshmen of the Business Administration Department.
這是企管系的新生歡迎會。

補充片語

welcoming party 歡迎會；
Business Administration Department 企業管理系

Friday [ˋfraɪˌde]=Fri. 🎧 *Track 2065*
n. 星期五

fridge [frɪdʒ] 🎧 *Track 2066*
=re·fri·ger·a·tor
n. 冰箱
▶ He didn't keep the milk in the fridge so the milk went bad.
他沒有把牛奶冰在冰箱裡，所以牛奶酸掉了。

※灰色單字為英檢初級必備單字

friend [frɛnd]　🎧 *Track 2067*
n. 朋友

friend·ly [ˈfrɛndlɪ]　🎧 *Track 2068*
adj. 友善的；友好的

friend·ship [ˈfrɛndʃɪp]　🎧 *Track 2069*
n. 友誼

fright [fraɪt]　🎧 *Track 2070*
n. 驚嚇；恐怖
▶ I nearly died of fright when I heard the ghost story. 我聽那鬼故事時差點嚇死。
相關片語
fright mail 恐嚇信件
▶ When I received the fright mail, I was so scared that I didn't know what to do.
收到恐嚇信時，我害怕得不知道該如何是好。

fright·en [ˈfraɪtn]　🎧 *Track 2071*
v. 使驚嚇；使害怕

fright·ened [ˈfraɪtnd]　🎧 *Track 2072*
adj. 受驚的，害怕的
▶ I'll never try bungee jumping because I am frightened of heights.
我永遠不會嘗試高空彈跳，因為我有懼高症。
補充片語
bungee jumping 高空彈跳

fright·en·ing [ˈfraɪtnɪŋ]　🎧 *Track 2073*
adj. 令人恐懼的，使人驚嚇的，駭人的
▶ It is the most frightening story I've ever heard. 這是我所聽過最駭人聽聞的故事。

fris·bee [ˈfrɪzbi]　🎧 *Track 2074*
n. 飛盤

frog [frɑg]　🎧 *Track 2075*
n. 青蛙

from [frɑm]　🎧 *Track 2076*
prep. 從

front [frʌnt]　🎧 *Track 2077*
n. 前方；**adj.** 前面的

frost [frɑst]　🎧 *Track 2078*
n. 霜；冰凍；（態度）冷淡；失敗

▶ I'm worried that the frost will ruin our crops. 我擔心寒霜會毀了我們的作物。
v. 結霜；凍壞；受凍
▶ It broke my heart to see that my plants were frosted.
看到我的植栽都結霜了，讓我心碎不已。

frost·y [ˈfrɔstɪ]　🎧 *Track 2079*
adj. 霜凍的；結霜的；嚴寒的
▶ We had a frosty winter.
我們度過了一個寒冬。

frown [fraʊn]　🎧 *Track 2080*
v. 皺眉；用皺眉表示不滿
▶ My boss always seemed to frown on me for some reason.
我老闆似乎總是為了某個原因對我不滿。
n. 皺眉；不悅之色
▶ She looked at her husband with a frown.
她面露不悅之色地看著她的丈夫。

fro·zen [ˈfrozn]　🎧 *Track 2081*
adj. 冷凍的；凍僵的；冷淡的；嚇呆的
▶ I don't eat frozen food. 我不吃冷凍食物。
補充片語
frozen food 冷凍食品；冷凍食物

fruit [frut]　🎧 *Track 2082*
n. 水果

frus·trate [ˈfrʌsˌtret]　🎧 *Track 2083*
v. 使挫敗；阻撓；使心煩
▶ It really frustrates me to not be able to get my work done.
工作都做不完，真的讓我感到很心煩。

fry [fraɪ]　🎧 *Track 2084*
v. 炸；煎；炒；**n.** 油炸物；薯條

fu·el [ˈfjʊəl]　🎧 *Track 2085*
n. 燃料
▶ Whatever you say will only add fuel to the fire. 不管你說什麼，都只是火上加油。
補充片語
add fuel to the fire 火上加油
v. 給……加油；提供燃料
▶ I have to fuel my car as soon as possible.
我得盡快幫車加油。

ful·fill [fʊl`fɪl]　🎧 *Track 2086*
=ful·fil （英式英文）
v. 執行（命令等）；服從；符合
▶ This applicant fulfills all our requirements.
這個應徵者符合我們所有的要求條件。

full [fʊl]　🎧 *Track 2087*
adj. 滿的；吃飽的

ful·ly [`fʊlɪ]　🎧 *Track 2088*
adv. 完全地；徹底地；充分地
▶ The restaurant is fully booked.
餐廳的訂位已經全滿了。

fun [fʌn]　🎧 *Track 2089*
n. 樂趣；**adj.** 有趣的；開心的

func·tion [`fʌŋkʃən]　🎧 *Track 2090*
n. 功能；**v.** 作用；運作

func·tion·al [`fʌŋkʃənl]　🎧 *Track 2091*
adj. 機能的；職務上的；功能上的；有起作用的；實用的
▶ The so-called functional drinks often contain high amounts of sugar. 那些所謂的功能性保健飲料通常含有高量的糖。

fund [fʌnd]　🎧 *Track 2092*
n. 資金；基金
▶ We raised funds for building a new library.
我們為了蓋一間新的圖書館募款。

v. 提供資金
▶ Peter convinced many of our shareholders to fund the project.
彼得說服我們許多股東為這計劃提供資金。

fun·da·men·tal　🎧 *Track 2093*
[ˌfʌndə`mɛntl]
adj. 基本的；根本的；關鍵的
▶ Their divorce resulted from fundamental differences between them.
他們的離婚是他們之間根本的分歧所造成的。

fu·ne·ral [`fjunərəl]　🎧 *Track 2094*
n. 喪葬；葬禮
▶ The man's funeral was held.
男子的葬禮舉行了。

fun·ny [`fʌnɪ]　🎧 *Track 2095*
adj. 有趣的；可笑的；古怪的

fur [fɝ]　🎧 *Track 2096*
n. 毛；皮毛
▶ People don't need to wear fur to make them look beautiful.
人們不需要穿皮草來讓自己看起來美麗。

fu·ri·ous [`fjʊərɪəs]　🎧 *Track 2097*
adj. 狂怒的；狂暴的；猛烈的
▶ The man was furious. 男子暴跳如雷。

fur·nish [`fɝnɪʃ]　🎧 *Track 2098*
v. 給（房間）配置傢俱；供應；提供
▶ We don't really have the budget to furnish our apartment.
我們其實並沒有為公寓購置傢俱的預算。

fur·nished [`fɝnɪʃt]　🎧 *Track 2099*
adj. 配有傢俱的
▶ We're looking for a fully furnished two-bedroom apartment.
我們正在找一間配備完整傢俱的兩房公寓。

fur·ni·ture [`fɝnɪtʃə]　🎧 *Track 2100*
n. 傢俱

fur·ther [`fɝðə]　🎧 *Track 2101*
adv. 進一步地；更遠地；
adj. 更遠的；更深層的；進一步的

fur·ther·more　🎧 *Track 2102*
[`fɝðə`mor]
adv. 而且；此外
▶ He is stubborn, and furthermore he is selfish. 他很頑固，除此之外他還很自私。

fuss [fʌs]　🎧 *Track 2103*
n. 忙亂；大驚小怪；異議；爭論
▶ She always makes a fuss over nothing.
她總是對一點也不重要的事情小題大做。

v. 忙亂；大驚小怪；過分講究；抱怨；為小事煩惱
▶ There's no need to fuss. 沒有必要大驚小怪的。

fu·ture [`fjutʃə]　🎧 *Track 2104*
n. 未來；**adj.** 未來的

Gg

通過中級英文檢定者的英文能力：

 聽 在日常生活中，能聽懂一般的會話；能大致聽懂公共場所廣播、氣象報告及廣告等。在工作時，能聽懂簡易的產品介紹與操作說明。能大致聽懂外籍人士的談話及詢問。

讀 在日常生活中，能閱讀短文、故事、私人信件、廣告、傳單、簡介及使用說明等。在工作時，能閱讀工作須知、公告、操作手冊、例行的文件、傳真、電報等。

 寫 能寫簡單的書信、故事及心得等。對於熟悉且與個人經歷相關的主題，能以簡易的文字表達。

說 在日常生活中，能以簡易英語交談或描述一般事物，能介紹自己的生活作息、工作、家庭、經歷等，並可對一般話題陳述看法。在工作時，能進行簡單的答詢，並與外籍人士交談溝通。

本書除包含官方公佈的中級4,947單字外，更精挑了近400個滿分必學的高手單字。同時，在片語的挑選、例句的使用上，皆依上述英檢官方公佈之能力範疇做設計，難度適中、不偏離考試主題。發音部分則是自然發音＆KK音標雙管齊下，搭配MP3以「分解／完整」方式錄音，給你最多元有效的學習手段，怎麼記都可以，想忘掉都好難！

---

gain [gen]　　　🎧 *Track 2105*
v. 贏得；得到；**n.** 獲得；獲利；收益

gal·ax·y [`gæləksɪ]　　🎧 *Track 2106*
n. 銀河
▶ This galaxy is observabl by naked eyes, even though it's distant from earth.
這個銀河系雖然距離地球非常遙遠，但仍是用肉眼就可以看得見的。

gal·le·ry [`gælərɪ]　　🎧 *Track 2107*
n. 畫廊，美術館
▶ My first photo exhibition will be held in the Modern Gallery in June. 我的第一場攝影展將在六月於現代美術館舉行。

gal·lon [`gælən]　　🎧 *Track 2108*
n. 加侖（液量單位；美制等於785升；英制等於546升）
▶ How many gallons of wine does the vineyard produce per year?
這葡萄園每年生產多少加侖的酒？

gal·lop [`gæləp]　　🎧 *Track 2109*
n. （馬）疾馳；騎馬奔馳
▶ They went for a gallop along the coast.
他們騎著馬沿著海岸奔馳了一番。
（補充片語）
go for a gallop　騎馬奔馳一番
（相關片語）
at a gallop　飛快地；以最快速度地
▶ The woman spoke at a gallop, so I didn't quite understand what she said. 那女人話說得好快，所以我不是很明白她說了什麼。

gam·ble [`gæmbl]　　🎧 *Track 2110*
v. 打賭
▶ I can't believe that you gambled away all your money.
我不敢相信你把所有錢都賭光了。
（補充片語）
gamble away　賭博輸掉某物；輸光

n. 賭博；打賭

▶ I'll take a gamble for my children.
我要為了孩子賭一把。

(補充片語)

take a gamble　冒險而為

gam·bler [`gæmblə]　🎧 *Track 2111*
n. 賭徒

▶ Her husband is not only an alcoholic, but also a gambler.
她先生不僅是個酒鬼，還是個賭徒。

gam·bling [`gæmblɪŋ]　🎧 *Track 2112*
n. 賭博

▶ After losing all his money on gambling, he lost his wife as well. 在他把所有的錢都拿去賭博輸掉後，他也失去了他的妻子。

(相關片語)

gambling man　賭徒

▶ Those gambling men were all under arrest. 那些賭徒都已經被捕了。

(補充片語)

under arrest　被捕的

game [gem]　🎧 *Track 2113*
n. 遊戲；比賽

gang [gæŋ]　🎧 *Track 2114*
n. （歹徒的）一幫；一群人、一夥人

▶ The police arrested a gang of robbers.
警方逮捕了一幫搶匪。

v. 使結成一夥；成群結隊

▶ The boys ganged up against the school bully. 男孩們結成一夥以對抗學校的惡霸。

gang·ster [`gæŋstə]　🎧 *Track 2115*
n. 歹徒、流氓

▶ I hope those gangsters can all be arrested. 我希望那些流氓能通通被抓起來。

gap [gæp]　🎧 *Track 2116*
n. 缺口；分歧；間斷；差距

▶ The widening gap between rich and poor in this country is a big headache to the new government.
這個國家越來越大的貧富差距對新政府來說是個令人頭痛的問題。

(補充片語)

gap between rich and poor　貧富差距

gar·age [gə`rɑʒ]　🎧 *Track 2117*
n. 車庫

gar·bage [`gɑrbɪdʒ]　🎧 *Track 2118*
n. 垃圾

gar·den [`gɑrdn]　🎧 *Track 2119*
n. 花園

gar·den·er [`gɑrdənə]　🎧 *Track 2120*
n. 園丁；花匠

▶ The man hired a gardener to take care of his flower garden.
男子請了一個園丁幫他打理花園。

gar·lic [`gɑrlɪk]　🎧 *Track 2121*
n. 大蒜；蒜頭

▶ Don't kiss me until you get rid of the smell of garlic from your mouth.
在你除掉口中的蒜頭味之前不要親我。

(補充片語)

get rid of　除去；擺脫

gas [gæs]　🎧 *Track 2122*
n. 氣體；瓦斯

gas·o·line [`gæsə͵lin] =gas=pe·trol　🎧 *Track 2123*
n. 汽油

gasp [gæsp]　🎧 *Track 2124*
v. 倒抽一口氣；喘氣；喘著氣說

▶ The man gasped out the murderer's name before he died.
男子在他死前喘著氣說出了兇手的名字。

n. 倒抽一口氣；喘息；喘氣

▶ The man said "I love you" to his wife at his last gasp. 男子在他剩下最後一口氣時，對妻子說了句「我愛你」。

(補充片語)

at one's last gasp　在奄奄一息時；在剩下最後一口氣時

※灰色單字為英檢初級必備單字

gate [get]　🎧 *Track 2125*
n. 大門；登機門

gath·er [`gæðɚ]　🎧 *Track 2126*
v. 聚集；收集；召集

gath·er·ing [`gæðərɪŋ]　🎧 *Track 2127*
n. 集會；聚會
▶ I met my husband at a social gathering.
我是在一個社交聚會上認識我先生的。

(補充片語)
social gathering　社交聚會

gay [ge]　🎧 *Track 2128*
adj. 同性戀的；快樂的；輕快的；尋歡作樂的
▶ The child was adopted by a gay couple.
那孩子被一對同性戀伴侶給領養了。

gaze [gez]　🎧 *Track 2129*
v. 凝視；注視；盯
▶ The groom gazed at his bride admiringly.
新郎欣賞地凝視著他的新娘。

n. 凝視；注視
▶ The groom turned his gaze to his bride.
新郎將目光移到他的新娘子身上。

gear [gɪr]　🎧 *Track 2130*
n. 齒輪；傳動裝置；工具；設備；家用器具
▶ I'm going to the store for some camping gear. 我要去那間店買些露營裝備。

v. 用齒輪使轉動；搭上齒輪；使適應；使準備好
▶ I'll have the factory workers gear up for the production.
我會要工廠員工為生產工作做好準備。

(補充片語)
gear up for sth. 為某事做好準備

gen·der [`dʒɛndɚ]　🎧 *Track 2131*
n. 性，性別
▶ Gender discrimination still exists in this society. 性別歧視仍然存在於這個社會。

gene [dʒin]　🎧 *Track 2132*
n. 基因；遺傳因子

▶ All my three children have music talent in their genes. 我三個孩子全都有音樂基因。

gen·er·al [`dʒɛnərəl]　🎧 *Track 2133*
adj. 一般的；普通的；大體的；全體的；大眾性的；**n.** 一般；一般情況

gen·er·al·ly [`dʒɛnərəlɪ]　🎧 *Track 2134*
adv. 通常；一般地；廣泛地；普遍地；大體而言
▶ Generally, he is a good boss.
大體而言，他是個好老闆。

gen·e·rate [`dʒɛnəˏret]　🎧 *Track 2135*
v. 產生；引起；生育
▶ Fire generates light and heat.
火會產生光和熱。

gen·e·ra·tion　🎧 *Track 2136*
[ˏdʒɛnəˈreʃən]
n. 世代

gen·e·ra·tor [`dʒɛnəˏretɚ]　🎧 *Track 2137*
n. 製造機；製造者；發電機
▶ The power is out so we have to use our backup generator.
停電了，所以我們得用備用的發電機。

gen·e·ros·i·ty　🎧 *Track 2138*
[ˏdʒɛnəˈrɑsətɪ]
n. 寬宏大量；慷慨
▶ I am impressed by his generosity.
他的寬宏大量讓我很感動。

gen·e·rous [`dʒɛnərəs]　🎧 *Track 2139*
adj. 慷慨的；大方的

ge·net·ics [dʒəˈnɛtɪks]　🎧 *Track 2140*
n. 遺傳學
▶ Professor Jones teaches genetics in a local college.
瓊斯教授在一所本地大學中教授遺傳學。

ge·nius [`dʒinjəs]　🎧 *Track 2141*
n. 天才；天賦才能

gen·tle [`dʒɛntl̩]　🎧 *Track 2142*
adj. 溫和的；輕柔的；有教養的；文靜的

gen·tle·man [ˈdʒɛntl̩mən] 🎧 *Track 2143*
n. 紳士；男士

gen·u·ine [ˈdʒɛnjʊɪn] 🎧 *Track 2144*
adj. 真的；非偽造的；名副其實的；真誠不造作的；由衷的
▶ This Monet's painting has been confirmed genuine. 這幅莫內的畫作被證實是真跡。

ge·og·ra·phy 🎧 *Track 2145*
[ˈdʒɪˈɑgrəfi]
n. 地理學；地勢；地形

ge·om·e·try [dʒɪˈɑmətrɪ] 🎧 *Track 2146*
n. 幾何學
▶ Geometry is beyond my comprehension. 我搞不懂幾何學。

germ [dʒɝm] 🎧 *Track 2147*
n. 微生物；細菌；起點；萌芽
▶ Don't share towels because they can spread germs.
不要共用毛巾，因為毛巾會傳播細菌。

Ger·man [ˈdʒɝmən] 🎧 *Track 2148*
adj. 德國的；德語的；德國人的
n. 德語；德國人

Germ·an·y [ˈdʒɝmənɪ] 🎧 *Track 2149*
n. 德國

ges·ture [ˈdʒɛstʃɚ] 🎧 *Track 2150*
n. 姿勢；手勢 **v.** 用手勢表示

get [gɛt] 🎧 *Track 2151*
v. 得到；理解；到達；有機會

ghost [gost] 🎧 *Track 2152*
n. 鬼

gi·ant [ˈdʒaɪənt] 🎧 *Track 2153*
adj. 巨大的；**n.** 巨人；偉人

gift [gɪft] 🎧 *Track 2154*
n. 禮物；天賦

gift·ed [ˈgɪftɪd] 🎧 *Track 2155*
adj. 有天資的；有天賦的

▶ He is a gifted pianist.
他是個有天份的鋼琴家。

gi·gan·tic [dʒaɪˈgæntɪk] 🎧 *Track 2156*
adj. 巨人的
▶ It's impossible for me to finish this gigantic hamburger all by myself. 要我獨自把這個巨大的漢堡吃完，是不可能的。

gig·gle [ˈgɪgl̩] 🎧 *Track 2157*
v. 咯咯地笑；咯咯笑著說
▶ His silly joke made her giggle.
他愚蠢的笑話使她咯咯地笑了起來。

n. 咯咯的笑；傻笑；可笑的人或事物；玩笑、趣事
▶ She burst into giggles at the sight of his new hairstyle.
她一看見他的新髮型就咯咯地笑了起來。

(補充片語)
burst into giggles 咯咯地笑起來；
at the sight of 一看見……就

gin·ger [ˈdʒɪndʒɚ] 🎧 *Track 2158*
n. 生薑
▶ I like to drink a cup of hot ginger tea in cold weather. 天氣冷我喜歡喝杯熱薑茶。

gi·raffe [dʒəˈræf] 🎧 *Track 2159*
n. 長頸鹿
▶ Giraffes are the tallest animals in the world. 長頸鹿是世界上最高的動物。

girl [gɝl] 🎧 *Track 2160*
n. 女孩；女兒

girl·friend [ˈgɝlˌfrɛnd] 🎧 *Track 2161*
n. 女朋友
▶ I'm introducing my girlfriend to my family tonight. 我今晚會將女友介紹給家人認識。

give [gɪv] 🎧 *Track 2162*
v. 給予；舉辦

gla·ci·er [ˈgleʃɚ] 🎧 *Track 2163*
n. 冰河

※灰色單字為英檢初級必備單字

▶ The scientists warned that rising global temperatures would speed the melting of glaciers. 科學家警告，不斷升高的地球溫度將會加速冰河的融化。

glad [glæd] 🎧 Track 2164
adj. 高興的

glance [glæns] 🎧 Track 2165
v. 粗略看一下；一瞥；掃視
▶ He glanced around the bus and recognized the boy who stole his money.
他掃視了公車，並認出了偷他錢的男孩。

n. 一瞥；掃視
▶ He only took a glance at the man and decided to hire him.
他只看了男子一眼，就決定要雇用他了。

glass [glæs] 🎧 Track 2166
n. 玻璃；玻璃杯

glas·ses [`glæsɪz] 🎧 Track 2167
n. 眼鏡
▶ I can't see anything without my glasses.
沒有眼鏡我什麼都看不見。

(相關片語)
field glasses 望遠鏡
▶ He used his field glasses to watch the birds on the trees.
他用他的望遠鏡觀察樹上的鳥。

glee [gli] 🎧 Track 2168
n. 快樂；歡欣
▶ Their anniversary was celebrated with glee. 他們興高采烈地慶祝結婚紀念日。

glide [glaɪd] 🎧 Track 2169
v. 滑動
▶ The small boat glided across the lake.
那條小船輕輕滑行過湖面。

n. 滑動；滑行
▶ They put on their skates and took a glide on the ice.
他們穿上溜冰鞋，並在冰上滑行一番。

(補充片語)
take a glide 滑行一番

glimpse [glɪmps] 🎧 Track 2170
n. 瞥見；一瞥；少許
▶ I caught a glimpse of my boyfriend in the crowd. 我在人群中瞥見我的男友。

(補充片語)
catch a glimpse of 一眼瞥見

v. 看一眼；瞥見
▶ I glimpsed my husband with a woman among the crowd.
我在人群中瞥見我先生和一個女子在一起。

glit·ter [`glɪtɚ] 🎧 Track 2171
v. 閃耀；閃亮
▶ Her clothes glitter in the dark. 她的衣服在黑暗中閃亮亮的。

glo·bal [`globl] 🎧 Track 2172
adj. 球狀的；全世界的；總體的
▶ Global warming is a serious threat to life on earth.
全球暖化對地球上的生物是嚴重的威脅。

globe [glob] 🎧 Track 2173
n. 球狀物；地球儀；地球
▶ He has travelled to most parts of the globe. 他已經旅行過地球上的大部分地方了。

gloom [glum] 🎧 Track 2174
n. 黑暗；陰暗；憂鬱的心情
▶ The death of the president has cast a gloom over the entire country.
總統的死訊讓整個國家籠罩在沮喪的氣氛中。

v. 變陰暗；顯得悶悶不樂；使憂鬱
▶ He gloomed over the bad news.
他因為這壞消息而悶悶不樂。

gloom·y [`glumɪ] 🎧 Track 2175
adj. 陰暗的；陰沉的；憂鬱的；陰鬱的
▶ We broke up on a gloomy winter day.
我們在一個陰沉的冬日分手。

glo·ri·ous [`glorɪəs] 🎧 Track 2176
adj. 光榮的；榮譽的；壯觀的；極好的
▶ Our school team had returned from a glorious victory.
我們的校隊帶著光榮的勝利歸來了。

glo·ry [ˋglorɪ]　🎧 *Track 2177*

n. 光榮；榮譽；可誇耀的事

▶ They are going to bring glory to their hometown. 他們將為家鄉帶來榮耀。

相關片語

morning glory　牽牛花；虎頭蛇尾的人

▶ Wild morning glories are growing everywhere in my garden.
野生牽牛花在我的花園裡長得到處都是。

glove [glʌv]　🎧 *Track 2178*

n. 手套

glow [glo]　🎧 *Track 2179*

v. 發熱、發光、發怒

▶ The man glowed with anger after reading the letter. 男子讀了信之後怒容滿面。

n. 白熱光；臉紅；發熱；激情；興高采烈；心滿意足

▶ There's a strange glow outside the window.
窗外有奇怪的光芒。

glue [glu]　🎧 *Track 2180*

n. 膠水；黏著劑；

v. 黏牢；緊附；如用黏著劑固定

go [go]　🎧 *Track 2181*

v. 去；離去；行走；從事（活動）；

n. 輪到的機會；嘗試；進行

goal [gol]　🎧 *Track 2182*

n. 目標

goat [got]　🎧 *Track 2183*

n. 山羊

god [gɑd]　🎧 *Track 2184*

n. 上帝；造物主；神祇

god·dess [ˋgɑdɪs]　🎧 *Track 2185*

n. 女神；受尊崇或仰慕的女子

▶ Anita is my goddess. I would do anything for her.
艾尼塔是我的女神。我願意為她做任何事。

gold [gold]　🎧 *Track 2186*

n. 金；金色；金幣；金牌

gold·en [ˋgoldn]　🎧 *Track 2187*

adj. 金的；金色的；黃金般的；絕好的；珍貴的

golf [gɑlf]　🎧 *Track 2188*

n. 高爾夫球運動

good [gʊd]　🎧 *Track 2189*

adj. 好的；愉快的；令人滿意的；擅長的；

n. 利益；好處；善事

good-bye [gʊdˋbaɪ]　🎧 *Track 2190*

n. 再見；道別

good·ness [ˋgʊdnɪs]　🎧 *Track 2191*

n. 良善；仁慈；美德；精華

▶ Please have the goodness to lend me some money.
請你大發慈悲，借一點錢給我吧。

補充片語

have the goodness to do sth.　懇請做某事

goods [gʊdz]　🎧 *Track 2192*

n. 商品

▶ They're going to have a garage sale to sell their old household goods. 他們將舉辦一場車庫拍賣，出售他們舊的家用品。

goose [gus]　🎧 *Track 2193*

n. 鵝；鵝肉

gor·geous [ˋgɔrdʒəs]　🎧 *Track 2194*

adj. 燦爛的；華麗的；令人愉快的；極好的

▶ The bride looks gorgeous in that white wedding dress.
新娘穿著那件白色結婚禮服看起來美極了。

go·ril·la [gəˋrɪlə]　🎧 *Track 2195*

n. 大猩猩；彪形大漢

▶ The boy was abandoned in the forest when he was three, and was raised by gorillas afterwards. 那男孩在三歲時被丟在森林裡，之後是被大猩猩養大的。

gos·sip [ˋgɑsəp]　🎧 *Track 2196*

n. 閒話；流言蜚語；小道新聞

※灰色單字為英檢初級必備單字

▶I overheard their gossip about me in the ladies' room.
我無意間在女廁所聽到他們在說我的閒話。

v. 閒聊；說長道短
▶The girls are gossiping about their boss.
女孩子們在聊老闆的八卦。

gov·ern [`gʌvə·n] 🎧 *Track 2197*
v. 統治；管理；控制
▶He is the King but he doesn't really govern the country.
他是國王，但是他並不真正統治這個國家。

gov·ern·ment 🎧 *Track 2198*
[`gʌvə·nmənt]
n. 政府

gov·er·nor [`gʌvə·nə·] 🎧 *Track 2199*
n. 州長；地方行政長官；總督；主管；（公共機構的）董事；老闆
▶The prison governor should be responsible for the prison break.
典獄長應該要為這次的越獄事件負責。

(補充片語)
prison governor 典獄長
be responsible for 為……負責；
prison break 越獄

gown [gaʊn] 🎧 *Track 2200*
n. 女晚禮服
▶Jenny looked stunning in her wedding gown.
珍妮穿著她的結婚晚禮服看起來真是美極了。

grab [græb] 🎧 *Track 2201*
v. 攫取；抓取；奪取；匆忙地做
▶Let's just grab something to eat at the food stand.
我們在那個小吃攤趕緊吃點什麼就好了。

n. 抓住；奪取之物
▶He made a grab for the knife before the burglar did. 他搶在搶匪之前抓住那把刀子。

grace [gres] 🎧 *Track 2202*
n. 優美；通情達理；風度；恩惠
▶They received us with a good grace.
他們欣然地招呼我們。

(補充片語)
with a good grace 欣然地

v. 使優美；使增光
▶The awarding ceremony was graced with the presence of the mayor.
這場頒獎典禮因為市長的蒞臨而增光不少。

grace·ful [`gresfəl] 🎧 *Track 2203*
adj. 優美的；得體的
▶The ballet dancer is always so graceful.
那名芭蕾舞者總是非常優雅。

gra·cious [`greʃəs] 🎧 *Track 2204*
adj. 親切的
▶Mrs. Lin is a gracious old lady living next to me.
林太太是個住在我隔壁的親切老婆婆。

grade [gred] 🎧 *Track 2205*
n. 分數；年級；等級

grad·u·al [`grædʒʊəl] 🎧 *Track 2206*
adj. 逐漸的；逐步的
▶The patient is making gradual progress towards recovery.
病患的身體狀況正朝著康復逐漸的進步中。

grad·u·al·ly [`grædʒʊəlɪ] 🎧 *Track 2207*
adv. 逐漸地
▶I am gradually getting used the weather here. 我逐漸地習慣這兒的天氣了。

grad·u·ate [`grædʒʊ͵et] 🎧 *Track 2208*
n. 畢業生
▶He's a Harvard graduate.
他是哈佛大學的畢業生。

v. 畢業
▶Many of my classmates started job-hunting before they graduated.
我班上許多同學在畢業前就開始找工作了。

grad·u·a·tion 🎧 *Track 2209*
[͵grædʒʊ`eʃən]
n. 畢業
▶Congratulations on your graduation!
恭喜你畢業了。

grain [gren] 🎧 *Track 2210*

n. 穀粒；穀類；細粒；一點

▶ You shouldn't waste a grain of rice.
你一粒米都不應該浪費。

相關片語

with a grain of salt 有保留地；不完全相信地

▶ The police took his testimony with a grain of salt. 警方對他的證詞有所保留。

gram [græm] 🎧 *Track 2211*

n. 克

gram·mar [ˋgræmə] 🎧 *Track 2212*

n. 文法

▶ My father employed a tutor to teach me English grammar.
我爸請了個家教來教我英文文法。

grand [grænd] 🎧 *Track 2213*

adj. 雄偉的；偉大的；重要的

grand·child 🎧 *Track 2214*
[ˋgrændˏtʃaɪld]

n. 孫子（女）；外孫（女）

▶ The 102-year-old man has more than 200 grandchildren.
這102歲的老人家有超過兩百個內外孫。

grand·daugh·ter 🎧 *Track 2215*
[ˋgrænˏdɔtə]

n. 孫女；外孫女

grand·fa·ther 🎧 *Track 2216*
[ˋgrændˏfɑðə]

n. 祖父；外祖父

grand·moth·er 🎧 *Track 2217*
[ˋgrændˏmʌðə]

n. 祖母；外祖母

grand·par·ent 🎧 *Track 2218*
[ˋgrændˏpɛrənt]

n. 祖父母；外祖父母

▶ Both of my grandparents are still living and in good health. 我的祖父母都還健在。

補充片語

live in good health 健康地活著；健在

grand·son [ˋgrændˏsʌn] 🎧 *Track 2219*

n. 孫子；外孫

grant [grænt] 🎧 *Track 2220*

v. 同意

▶ My boss didn't grant my personal leave.
我的老闆沒有同意讓我請事假。

n. 授與物；獎學金；助學金；補助金；同意；承認

▶ The professor received a grant for the project from the government.
教授獲得政府針對這企劃案所發的補助金。

grape [grep] 🎧 *Track 2221*

n. 葡萄

grape·fruit [ˋgrepˏfrut] 🎧 *Track 2222*

n. 葡萄柚

▶ She drinks a glass of grapefruit juice every morning in order to lose weight.
為了減重，她每天早上都喝一杯葡萄柚汁。

graph [græf] 🎧 *Track 2223*

n. 曲線圖；圖表；標繪圖

▶ The graph shows the variation of temperature with time.
這曲線圖顯示了溫度隨時間不同的變化。

v. 用圖表表示

▶ The professor graphed the effects of economic stress on crime.
該教授以圖表表示經濟壓力對犯罪的影響。

graph·ic [ˋgræfɪk] 🎧 *Track 2224*

adj. 生動的；寫實的；繪畫的；平面藝術的

▶ He gave a graphic description of what he had witnessed.
他對他所目擊的情況作了生動的描述。

grasp [græsp] 🎧 *Track 2225*

v. 抓牢；握緊；領會

▶ He grasps at any opportunity that might help him achieve success.
他抓住任何一個可以幫助他成功的機會。

n. 緊握；抓；理解；控制

▶ She held his hands in a grateful grasp.
她感激地緊緊握住他的手。

※灰色單字為英檢初級必備單字

grass [græs] 🎧 Track 2226
n. 草；草地

grass·hop·per 🎧 Track 2227
[`græs͵hɑpɚ]
n. 蚱蜢
▶ I saw a grasshopper hopping in the grass.
我看見一隻蚱蜢在草叢間跳躍。

gras·sy [`græsɪ] 🎧 Track 2228
adj. 長滿草的；草綠色的；有草味的

grate·ful [`gretfəl] 🎧 Track 2229
adj. 感謝的
▶ I am grateful for what she has done for me. 我很感謝她為我做的事情。

grat·i·tude [`grætə͵tjud] 🎧 Track 2230
n. 感激之情
▶ We'd like to invite you to dinner to express our gratitude.
我們想邀你們吃晚餐以表達感激。

grave [grev] 🎧 Track 2231
n. 墓穴；埋葬處
▶ You are digging your own grave if you do drugs. 如果你吸毒，就等於是在自掘墳墓。

(補充片語)
dig one's own grave 自掘墳墓、自取滅亡；
do drugs 吸毒

adj. 嚴肅的；認真的；嚴重的
▶ She rejected his request with a grave look on her face.
她面帶嚴肅神情地拒絕了他的要求。

grav·i·ty [`grævətɪ] 🎧 Track 2232
n. 地心引力；重量；嚴重性；嚴肅
▶ He tried to keep his gravity during the ceremony.
在典禮進行過程中，他試著保持嚴肅。

gray [gre] 🎧 Track 2233
adj. 灰色的；灰的；蒼白的；頭髮灰白的；
n. 灰色；灰色衣服

grease [gris] 🎧 Track 2234
n. 動物脂；油脂；賄賂

▶ Her hair is very fluffy so she has to put grease on her hair every day.
她的頭髮非常蓬鬆，所以她每天都必須在頭髮上抹髮油。

v. 塗油脂於；賄賂
▶ Robert greased his bike chain carefully.
羅伯特仔細地為他的腳踏車鏈上油。

(相關片語)
grease sb.'s palm 賄賂某人；打點
▶ I will grease the police officer's palm if necessary.
如果必要的話，我會去賄賂那個警員。

greas·y [`grizɪ] 🎧 Track 2235
adj. 油污的；油膩的；油滑奉承的
▶ My hair gets greasy within a day, so I have to wash it every day.
我的頭髮一天內就會變得油膩膩的，所以我每天都得洗頭。

(相關片語)
greasy spoon 廉價小飯館
▶ He took me to a greasy spoon for dinner on our first date.
我們第一次約會時，他帶我到一家廉價小飯館吃晚餐。

great [gret] 🎧 Track 2236
adj. 棒的；極好的；偉大的

great·ly [`gretlɪ] 🎧 Track 2237
adv. 極其；大大地；非常
▶ We were greatly impressed by their warm hospitality.
他們溫暖的款待讓我們非常感動。

greed·y [`gridɪ] 🎧 Track 2238
adj. 貪婪的；貪吃的

green [grin] 🎧 Track 2239
adj. 綠色的；（臉色）發青的；**n.** 綠色

green·house [`grin͵haʊs] 🎧 Track 2240
n. 溫室
▶ These vegetables are grown in the greenhouse. 這些蔬菜是在溫室種植的。

(相關片語)
greenhouse effect 溫室效應

▶ The greenhouse effect has led to global warming and climate change.
溫室效應已經導致地球暖化及氣候變遷。

greet [grit] 🎧 *Track 2241*
v. 迎接；問候；打招呼

greet·ing [`gritɪŋ] 🎧 *Track 2242*
n. 問候
▶ I received a greeting card from an old friend. 我收到一個老朋友寄來的問候卡片。

grief [grif] 🎧 *Track 2243*
n. 悲痛
▶ He buried his dog with grief.
他悲慟地埋葬他的狗。

相關片語
come to grief 終歸失敗；以失敗告終；出事故
▶ Our production plan came to grief due to the lack of funds.
我們的生產計劃因為缺乏資金而失敗了。

grieve [griv] 🎧 *Track 2244*
v. 悲傷
▶ We were grieved to learn that he didn't survive the car crash. 得知他未能在車禍中倖免於難，讓我們非常哀傷。

grill [grɪl] 🎧 *Track 2245*
v. （用烤架）烤；拷問；被炙烤
▶ The pork ribs have to be grilled for at least two hours. 豬肋排至少要烤兩小時。

n. 烤架；燒烤的肉類食物
▶ Let's put the chicken on the grill first.
我們先把雞肉放在烤架上。

grim [grɪm] 🎧 *Track 2246*
adj. 無情的；嚴厲的；殘酷的；猙獰的；可怕的
▶ The grim look on the man's face scared the little girl.
男子臉上可怕的表情把小女孩嚇壞了。

grin [grɪn] 🎧 *Track 2247*
v. 露齒而笑
▶ He grinned from ear to ear when his wife told him that she was pregnant.
當妻子告訴他她懷孕時，他咧開嘴笑了。

補充片語
grin from ear to ear 咧著嘴笑

n. 露齒的笑
▶ She held the baby in her arms with a broad grin on her face.
她滿臉笑容地將寶寶抱在懷裡。

相關片語
grin and bear it 逆來順受
▶ I wouldn't grin and bear it if I were you.
如果我是你，我絕不會逆來順受。

grind [graɪnd] 🎧 *Track 2248*
v. 磨碎；用力擠壓；磨光；咬牙
▶ He grinds his teeth in his sleep.
他睡覺的時候會磨牙。

n. 磨；苦差事
▶ Doing housework is a grind for me. I'd rather go to work.
做家事對我來說是件苦差事。我寧可去上班。

相關片語
have an axe to grind 有私心；另有企圖
▶ I bet she is helping us because she has an axe to grind.
我敢說她幫我們是另有企圖。

groan [gron] 🎧 *Track 2249*
n. 呻吟聲；哼聲；抱怨聲
▶ The patient's groan was so loud that it could be heard even outside the ward.
病人的呻吟聲太大聲了，甚至在病房外都聽得到。

v. 呻吟；抱怨；呻吟著說
▶ The patients groaned in pain.
病人痛苦地呻吟著。

gro·cer·y [`grosərɪ] 🎧 *Track 2250*
n. 食品；雜貨
▶ I do grocery shopping once a week.
我一星期做一次食品雜貨的採買。

相關片語
grocery store 雜貨店
▶ Could you stop by the grocery store and buy some milk and eggs?
你可以順道經過雜貨店，買些牛奶和雞蛋嗎？

Aa
Bb
Cc
Dd
Ee
Ff
Gg
Hh
Ii
Jj
Kk
Ll
Mm
Nn
Oo
Pp
Qq
Rr
Ss
Tt
Uu
Vv
Ww
Xx
Yy
Zz

※灰色單字為英檢初級必備單字

groom [grum] 🎧 *Track 2251*
n. 新郎
▶ The groom was nervous before the wedding ceremony.
新郎在婚禮開始前很緊張。

gross [gros] 🎧 *Track 2252*
adj. 總的；顯著的；粗俗的；令人討厭的
▶ Moldy bread is gross. 發霉的麵包很噁心。

ground [graʊnd] 🎧 *Track 2253*
n. 地面

group [grup] 🎧 *Track 2254*
n. （一）群；群；類；組

grow [gro] 🎧 *Track 2255*
v. 生長；成長；種植

growl [graʊl] 🎧 *Track 2256*
v. 咆哮；嗥叫；咆哮著說；（雷、砲等）轟鳴
▶ I heard Mr. Lee growling at his secretary when I passed by his office.
當我經過李經理的辦公室時，聽到他正在對秘書咆哮。

n. 咆哮聲；轟鳴聲；嗥叫
▶ He answered my question with a growl.
他用咆哮的聲音回答我的問題。

grown-up [ˈgronˌʌp] 🎧 *Track 2257*
n. 成年人
▶ Now that you are a grown-up, you should act like one. 既然你已經是個成年人，就應該表現得像個成年人。

growth [groθ] 🎧 *Track 2258*
n. 成長；發育；生長物；種植

grum·ble [ˈgrʌmbl̩] 🎧 *Track 2259*
v. 發牢騷；抱怨；咕噥
▶ He never grumbles about his job to his wife. 他從未對妻子抱怨過他的工作。

n. 怨言；牢騷
▶ The woman is full of grumbles about her lazy husband.
這女子對她懶惰的老公可是有滿腹牢騷。

guar·an·tee [ˌgærənˈti] 🎧 *Track 2260*
v. 保證
▶ It is guaranteed to rain whenever I have my car washed.
無論何時，我洗車之後，保證一定會下雨。

（補充片語）
be guaranteed to do sth. 必定做某事

n. 保證
▶ The bread machine has two years' guarantee. 這台麵包機有兩年的保固期。

（補充片語）
money-back guarantee 退款保證

guard [gɑrd] 🎧 *Track 2261*
n. 警衛；看守員；護衛隊；**v.** 保衛；防衛

guard·i·an [ˈgɑrdɪən] 🎧 *Track 2262*
n. 保護員；守護員；管理員；（律）監護人
▶ She became the legal guardian of these children after their parents died. 她在孩子們的父母死後，成了他們的法定監護人。

（補充片語）
legal guardian 法定監護人

gua·va [ˈgwɑvə] 🎧 *Track 2263*
n. 芭樂

guess [gɛs] 🎧 *Track 2264*
v./n. 猜；猜想

guest [gɛst] 🎧 *Track 2265*
n. 客人；賓客

guid·ance [ˈgaɪdns] 🎧 *Track 2266*
n. 指導
▶ I'll never accomplish my paper without your guidance.
沒有您的指導，我永遠也無法完成論文。

guide [gaɪd] 🎧 *Track 2267*
n. 導遊；嚮導；指導者；
v. 領路；帶領；引導

guide·line [ˈgaɪdˌlaɪn] 🎧 *Track 2268*

n. 指導方針
▶ The guidelines are for reference only.
這指導方針僅供參考。

guilt [gɪlt]   🎧 *Track 2269*
n. 有罪；過失；內疚
▶ He was filled with guilt for cheating on his wife. 他因為對妻子不忠而充滿罪惡感。

guilt·y [ˋgɪltɪ]   🎧 *Track 2270*
adj. 有罪的；有罪惡感的；內疚的
▶ He felt guilty about lying to his mother.
對媽媽說謊讓他深感罪惡。

gui·tar [gɪˋtɑr]   🎧 *Track 2271*
n. 吉他

gulf [gʌlf]   🎧 *Track 2272*
n. 海灣；巨大分歧、鴻溝
▶ A widening gulf between them finally led to their divorce. 他們之間越來越大的分歧終於導致他們的離異。

gulp [gʌlp]   🎧 *Track 2273*
v. 狼吞虎嚥地吃；大口地飲；喘不過氣；哽住
▶ He gulped down the sandwich and left in a hurry.
他狼吞虎嚥地吃下三明治後就匆匆離開了。

n. 吞嚥；一大口
▶ He took a gulp of water and proceeded with his speech.
他吞了一大口水後，便繼續他的演說。

gum [gʌm]   🎧 *Track 2274*
n. 樹脂；黏合劑；口香糖
▶ It's very inappropriate to talk to someone while having gum in your mouth.
跟別人說話時，一邊嚼著口香糖，是一件非常不得體的事。

gun [gʌn]   🎧 *Track 2275*

n. 槍

gut [gʌt]   🎧 *Track 2276*
n. 腸子；內臟；膽量
▶ At least he had the guts to go for what he wanted. 至少他有勇氣爭取自己想要的。

(補充片語)
at least 至少；
have the guts 有膽量、有勇氣；
go for 爭取

v. 取出內臟；損毀（屋內）裝置
▶ I asked the fishmonger to gut the fish for me. 我請魚販幫我取出魚的內臟。

(相關片語)
sweat one's guts out 拼命工作
▶ The child worker sweats his guts out for $10 a day.
那個童工為了一天賺十塊錢而拼命工作。

guy [gaɪ]   🎧 *Track 2277*
n. 傢伙；朋友；人

gym [dʒɪm]   🎧 *Track 2278*
n. 體育館；健身房

gyp·sy [ˋdʒɪpsɪ]   🎧 *Track 2279*
n. 吉普賽人；吉普賽語；流浪者
▶ The pickpocket was a gypsy.
那個扒手是個吉普賽人。

adj. 吉普賽人的；吉普賽的
▶ A gypsy woman tried to steal my wallet.
一個吉普賽女子企圖偷我的錢包。

Aa
Bb
Cc
Dd
Ee
Ff
Gg
Hh
Ii
Jj
Kk
Ll
Mm
Nn
Oo
Pp
Qq
Rr
Ss
Tt
Uu
Vv
Ww
Xx
Yy
Zz

※灰色單字為英檢初級必備單字

Hh

通過中級英文檢定者的英文能力：

 聽 在日常生活中，能聽懂一般的會話；能大致聽懂公共場所廣播、氣象報告及廣告等。在工作時，能聽懂簡易的產品介紹與操作說明。能大致聽懂外籍人士的談話及詢問。

 讀 在日常生活中，能閱讀短文、故事、私人信件、廣告、傳單、簡介及使用說明等。在工作時，能閱讀工作須知、公告、操作手冊、例行的文件、傳真、電報等。

 寫 能寫簡單的書信、故事及心得等。對於熟悉且與個人經歷相關的主題，能以簡易的文字表達。

 說 在日常生活中，能以簡易英語交談或描述一般事物，能介紹自己的生活作息、工作、家庭、經歷等，並可對一般話題陳述看法。在工作時，能進行簡單的答詢，並與外籍人士交談溝通。

本書除包含官方公佈的中級4,947單字外，更精挑了近400個滿分必學的高手單字。同時，在片語的挑選、例句的使用上，皆依上述英檢官方公佈之能力範疇做設計，難度適中、不偏離考試主題。發音部分則是自然發音＆KK音標雙管齊下，搭配MP3以「分解／完整」方式錄音，給你最多元有效的學習手段，怎麼記都可以，想忘掉都好難！

---

hab·it [`hæbɪt] 　🎧 *Track 2280*
n. 習慣

ha·bit·u·al [hə`bɪtʃʊəl] 　🎧 *Track 2281*
adj. 習慣的
▶ I was shocked to learn that my roommate was a habitual thief.
得知室友是個慣竊讓我很驚訝。

hack [hæk] 　🎧 *Track 2282*
v. 劈；砍；亂砍；當駭客；侵入
▶ The bank's website has been hacked.
這銀行的網站被入侵了。

hack·er [`hækɚ] 　🎧 *Track 2283*
n. 駭客；企圖不法侵入他人電腦系統的人
▶ Never use a password based on your birthdate, or the hackers will crack your password easily.
不要用出生日期來當你的密碼，否則駭客很容易就會破解你的密碼。

had·n't [`hædnt] 　🎧 *Track 2284*
abbr. 未曾、還沒（had not的縮寫）

hair [hɛr] 　🎧 *Track 2285*
n. 頭髮

hair·cut [`hɛr,kʌt] 　🎧 *Track 2286*
n. 剪髮

hair·dress·er 　🎧 *Track 2287*
[`hɛr,drɛsɚ]
n. 美髮師
▶ A skilled hairdresser takes years to train.
一個技術純熟的美髮師需要多年的訓練。

hair·style [`hɛr,staɪl] 　🎧 *Track 2288*
n. 髮型
▶ Your new hairstyle makes you look ten years younger.
你的新髮型讓你看起來年輕十歲了。

half [hæf] 　　　🎧 *Track 2289*
pron. 半；一半；二分之一
adj. 一半的；二分之一的
n. 半；二分之一；**adv.** 一半地；相當地

half·way [`hæf`we] 　🎧 *Track 2290*
adv. 在中途；到一半
▶Giving up halfway is not my style.
半途而廢不是我的作風。

hall [hɔl] 　　　🎧 *Track 2291*
n. 會堂；大廳

Hal·low·een [ˌhælo`in] 🎧 *Track 2292*
n. 萬聖節

hall·way [`hɔl`we] 　🎧 *Track 2293*
n. 玄關；門廳；走廊
▶She decorated the hallway of her house with a beautiful picture.
她用一幅美麗的圖片裝飾房子的玄關。

halt [hɔlt] 　　　🎧 *Track 2294*
v. 停止行進；停止；使終止
▶He halted for a few seconds and then proceeded with his speech.
他停了幾秒，然後繼續發表演說。

n. 停止；暫停；終止
▶The project has come to a halt due to the shortage of funds.
該企劃案因為經費短缺而陷入停頓。

(補充片語)
come to a halt　停止前進；陷入停頓

ham [hæm] 　　　🎧 *Track 2295*
n. 火腿

ham·bur·ger [`hæmbɝgɚ] 🎧 *Track 2296*
=bur·ger
n. 漢堡

ham·mer [`hæmɚ] 　🎧 *Track 2297*
n. 榔頭；鎚子

hand [hænd] 　　　🎧 *Track 2298*
n. 手；**v.** 遞交；傳遞

hand·bag [`hændˌbæg] 🎧 *Track 2299*
n. 手提包
▶The designer handbag cost her thirty thousand NT dollars.
這設計師名牌手提包花了她新臺幣三萬元。

hand·ful [`hændfəl] 　🎧 *Track 2300*
n. 一把；一握；少量
▶He gave the beggar a handful of coins.
他給了那乞丐一把硬幣。

hand·i·cap [`hændiˌkæp] 🎧 *Track 2301*
n. 障礙；不利條件；殘障
▶Lack of experience was surely a handicap to the applicants.
缺乏經驗對求職者來說當然是個不利條件。

v. 妨礙；使不利
▶The player was handicapped by his shoulder injury.
該選手的肩傷使他處於不利狀態。

hand·i·capped 　🎧 *Track 2302*
[`hændiˌkæpt]
adj. 有生理缺陷的；殘障的；智力低下的
▶Pregnancy over 35 increases the risk of having a handicapped baby.
超過三十五歲以上懷孕，會增加生出有缺陷的寶寶的風險。

hand·ker·chief 　🎧 *Track 2303*
[`hæŋkɚˌtʃɪf]
n. 手帕

han·dle [`hændl] 　🎧 *Track 2304*
v. 處理；對待；操作；
n. 把手；柄狀物；落人口實的把柄

hand·some [`hænsəm] 🎧 *Track 2305*
adj. 英俊的；可觀的

hand·writ·ing 　🎧 *Track 2306*
[`hændˌraɪtɪŋ]
n. 筆跡；筆法；書寫
▶This careless handwriting belongs to Jack. 這潦草的筆跡是傑克的。

hand·y [`hændi] 　🎧 *Track 2307*
adj. 手邊的；便利的；手巧的

※灰色單字為英檢初級必備單字

▶ It's quite handy for us to live near the supermarket.
住在超市附近對我們來說很便利。

相關片語

come in handy 遲早有用；派得上用場
▶ Rain or shine, an umbrella always comes in handy in summer.
無論下雨或放晴，夏天帶著一把雨傘，總是派得上用場。

---

hang [hæŋ] 🎧 *Track 2308*
v. 懸掛；吊起

---

hang·er [`hæŋɚ] 🎧 *Track 2309*
n. 衣架；掛鉤

---

hap·pen [`hæpən] 🎧 *Track 2310*
v. 發生

---

hap·pi·ly [`hæpɪlɪ] 🎧 *Track 2311*
adv. 快樂地
▶ They got married, and lived happily ever after.
他們結婚了，並從此過著幸福快樂的生活。

---

hap·py [`hæpɪ] 🎧 *Track 2312*
adj. 高興的；樂意的；滿意的

---

har·ass·ment [`hærəsmənt] 🎧 *Track 2313*
n. 煩擾；騷擾
▶ It is important to know how to protect yourself from sexual harassment at the workplace. 知道該如何保護自己不在工作場所受到性騷擾是很重要的。

---

har·bor [`harbɚ] 🎧 *Track 2314*
n. 港灣；避難所
▶ All ships stayed in the harbor during the typhoon. 颱風期間所有船隻都停在港內。

v. 庇護；藏匿；（船）入港停泊；躲藏
▶ He denied harboring the suspect.
他否認藏匿嫌犯。

---

hard [hard] 🎧 *Track 2315*
adj. 堅硬的；困難的；努力的
adv. 努力地；困難地；猛烈地

---

hard·en [`hardn] 🎧 *Track 2316*
v. 使變硬；變堅固；變得冷酷；變麻木
▶ He hardened his heart against his ex-wife. 他硬起心腸對待他的前妻。

---

hard·ly [`hardlɪ] 🎧 *Track 2317*
adv. 幾乎不；簡直不

---

hard·ship [`hardʃɪp] 🎧 *Track 2318*
n. 艱難
▶ I hope he is strong enough to face the hardships throughout his life.
希望他夠堅強以面對人生中的艱難。

---

hard·ware [`hard͵wɛr] 🎧 *Track 2319*
n. 五金器具；武器、軍事裝備；（電腦）硬體；裝備、設備
▶ The school's educational hardware is up to date. 這學校的教學設備是最新的。

---

hard-work·ing 🎧 *Track 2320*
[͵hard`wɝkɪŋ]
adj. 勤勉的；努力的
▶ He is the most hardworking employee in the company.
他是公司最勤勉的員工。

---

har·dy [`hardɪ] 🎧 *Track 2321*
adj. 能吃苦耐勞的；強壯的；堅強的
▶ Traditional Chinese women are very hardy.
傳統的中國婦女都很能吃苦耐勞。

---

harm [harm] 🎧 *Track 2322*
n. 傷害
▶ Reading without enough light will do harm to your eyes.
在光線不足的情況下閱讀會對你的眼睛造成傷害。

補充片語

do harm to 對……造成傷害

v. 傷害
▶ I will harm my child under no circumstances.
無論在什麼情況下，我都不會傷害我的孩子。

補充片語

under no circumstances 無論在什麼情況下都不……

harm·ful [ˋhɑrmfəl] 🎧 *Track 2323*
adj. 有害的
▶ Gutter oil is harmful to our health for sure.
地溝油肯定對我們的健康有害。

（補充片語）

gutter oil 地溝油；
for sure 肯定

har·mon·i·ca 🎧 *Track 2324*
[hɑrˋmɑnɪkə]
n. 口琴
▶ He took out his harmonica from his pocket and played a song for us. 他從口袋拿出他的口琴，並為我們吹奏了一首曲子。

har·mo·ny [ˋhɑrmənɪ] 🎧 *Track 2325*
n. 和睦；融洽；一致
▶ Most people have the ability to live in harmony with their external environment.
大部分的人都有協調外在環境，與之和平共處的能力。

（補充片語）

in harmony with 與……協調一致

harsh [hɑrʃ] 🎧 *Track 2326*
adj. 粗糙的；刺耳的；刺鼻的；澀口的；刺眼的；嚴厲的；惡劣的
▶ She received a very harsh comment that hurt her feelings badly.
她受到一個非常嚴厲的批評，讓她傷得很重。

har·vest [ˋhɑrvɪst] 🎧 *Track 2327*
n. 收獲；收成；成果
▶ We can expect a great harvest this year.
我們今年應該會有個大豐收。

v. 收獲；收割；獲得
▶ The farmers harvested the fruits in a hurry before the typhoon arrived.
農人們急忙在颱風到來之前採收水果。

has·n't [ˋhæznt] 🎧 *Track 2328*
abbr. 還沒、未曾（has not的縮寫）

has·sle [ˋhæsl] 🎧 *Track 2329*
n. 激烈爭論；口角；困難；麻煩
▶ It's a real hassle to apply for leave without pay in this company. 在這間公司申請留職停薪是一件很麻煩的事情。

v. 找麻煩
▶ Let me know immediately if the school bully hassles you again. 如果那個學校惡霸再找你麻煩，就趕快告訴我。

haste [hest] 🎧 *Track 2330*
n. 急忙；迅速；慌忙
▶ Haste makes waste. 一忙就會出亂子。

hast·y [ˋhestɪ] 🎧 *Track 2331*
adj. 匆忙的，倉促的；輕率的
▶ Their hasty marriage turned out to be a mistake. 他們的閃婚證明是個錯誤。

（補充片語）

turn out to be 原來是；結果是；證明是

hat [hæt] 🎧 *Track 2332*
n. 帽子

hatch [hætʃ] 🎧 *Track 2333*
v. 孵出；孵化
▶ Don't count your chickens before they're hatched. 別太早打如意算盤。（小雞孵出之前，別算你有幾隻雞。）

n. （蛋的）孵化；（小雞等）一窩
▶ There are more than ten ducklings in this hatch. 這一窩有超過十隻小鴨。

hate [het] 🎧 *Track 2334*
v. 厭惡；討厭；**n.** 仇恨；厭惡；反感

hate·ful [ˋhetfəl] 🎧 *Track 2335*
adj. 可憎的；討厭的

ha·tred [ˋhetrɪd] 🎧 *Track 2336*
n. 憎恨；敵意
▶ Her hatred for her stepfather grew stronger with each passing day.
她對繼父的敵意與日俱增。

（補充片語）

grow with each passing day 與日俱增

haunt [hɔnt] 🎧 *Track 2337*
v. （鬼魂）常出沒於；（思想）縈繞心頭；使困擾；纏住某人
▶ The abandoned house is said to be haunted by ghosts.
那幢荒廢的房子據說有鬼魂出沒。

※灰色單字為英檢初級必備單字

n. 常去的地方

▶The Internet café is one of my brother's haunts. 那家網咖是我哥常去的地方。

have [hæv]　🎧 *Track 2338*
v. 有；吃；使做……
aux. 已經（完成式的助動詞）

have·n't [`hævnt]　🎧 *Track 2339*
abbr. 還沒、未曾（**have not**的縮寫）

hawk [hɔk]　🎧 *Track 2340*
n. 鷹，隼；貪婪的傢伙；騙子

▶My boss has eyes like a hawk. He will catch every mistake you made.
我的老闆目光犀利如鷹，能抓出你所有的錯誤。

hay [he]　🎧 *Track 2341*
n. （飼料用的）乾草

▶I was a little hesitant, but he told me to make hay while the sun shines.
我有一點猶豫，但他提醒我要趁太陽大的時候曬乾草（把握時機）。

相關片語

hit the hay 去睡覺

▶When I arrived home, my husband had already hit the hay.
當我到家時，我老公早就去睡覺了。

haz·ard [`hæzəd]　🎧 *Track 2342*
n. 危險；危害物

▶Drug use during pregnancy will cause serious hazards to your baby.
在懷孕期間使用毒品將會對你的寶寶造成嚴重的危害。

v. 冒險做出；大膽嘗試；冒……的危險；使冒危險

▶Doing drugs will hazard your life.
吸毒會危害你的生命。

he [hi]　🎧 *Track 2343*
pron. 他

head [hɛd]　🎧 *Track 2344*
n. 頭；**v.** 前往

head·ache [`hɛd͵ek]　🎧 *Track 2345*
n. 頭痛；令人頭痛的事

head·line [`hɛd͵laɪn]　🎧 *Track 2346*
n. 標題；頭條新聞

▶The political scandal has been in the headlines for days.
這則政治醜聞已經上了好幾天的頭條新聞。

v. 給……加標題；使成頭條；使注意焦點

▶All newspapers headlined the celebrity's affair. 所有的報紙都以那名人的風流韻事作為頭條新聞。

相關片語

hit the headlines 上頭條

▶This bribery scandal will definitely hit the headlines. 這宗行賄醜聞絕對會上頭條。

head·mas·ter　🎧 *Track 2347*
[`hɛd`mæstə]
n. 美國私立學校校長

▶Rumor has it that the headmaster will resign from his position soon.
傳聞這位私立學校的校長即將辭去他的職務。

head·phones [`hɛd͵fonz] 🎧 *Track 2348*
n. 頭戴式耳機

▶Listening to loud music on headphones will damage your hearing.
用頭戴式耳機聽大聲的音樂會損害你的聽力。

head·quar·ters　🎧 *Track 2349*
[`hɛd`kwɔrtəz]
n. 總部；總公司

▶The Headquarters of the United Nations is located in New York.
聯合國的總部位於紐約。

head·set [`hɛd͵sɛt]　🎧 *Track 2350*
n. 戴在頭上的收話器；雙耳式耳機

▶When I drive, I always talk on the cellphone via headsets.
當我開車時，我都是用頭戴式收話器講手機。

heal [hil]　🎧 *Track 2351*
v. 治癒；使恢復健康；（傷口）癒合；痊癒

▶You cannot play basketball until your wound on the shoulder heals.
在你肩膀上的傷痊癒之前，你都不能打籃球。

health [hɛlθ] 🎧 *Track 2352*
n. 健康

health·y [`hɛlθɪ] 🎧 *Track 2353*
adj. 健康的

heap [hip] 🎧 *Track 2354*
n. 一堆；堆積；大量
▶ The teacher assigned us heaps of homework today.
老師今天派了一大堆的回家作業給我們。

v. 堆積；積聚；裝滿
▶ The kitchen sink was heaped with dirty dishes. 廚房流理台堆滿了髒碗盤。

hear [hɪr] 🎧 *Track 2355*
v. 聽到；聽見

heart [hɑrt] 🎧 *Track 2356*
n. 心；心臟

heart·break [`hɑrt͵brek] 🎧 *Track 2357*
n. 心碎；難忍的悲傷或失望
▶ He has just suffered a heartbreak and is not ready for a new relationship. 他才剛經歷過一次心碎，還沒準備好要展開新的戀情。

heat [hit] 🎧 *Track 2358*
n. 熱；熱氣；高溫；**v.** 加熱；使變熱

heat·er [`hitɚ] 🎧 *Track 2359*
n. 暖氣機；加熱器

heav·en [`hɛvən] 🎧 *Track 2360*
n. 天國；極樂之地；天堂
▶ Not everyone goes to heaven after they die. 不是所有人死後都會上天堂。
（相關片語）
seventh heaven 極樂；歡天喜地
▶ He was in seventh heaven the day when his daughter was born.
他女兒出生那天，他高興得不得了。

heav·en·ly [`hɛvənlɪ] 🎧 *Track 2361*
adj. 天空的；天堂般的；極好的；美好的
▶ We spent our vacation in a heavenly village. 我們在一個天堂般美好的村莊度過了我們的假期。

heav·y [`hɛvɪ] 🎧 *Track 2362*
adj. 沉重的；大的；繁忙的

he'd [hid] 🎧 *Track 2363*
abbr. 他會（he would、he had的縮寫）

heed [hid] 🎧 *Track 2364*
v. 留心；注意
▶ He didn't heed the doctor's warnings at all. 他完全不留意醫生的警告。
（補充片語）
not at all 一點也不

n. 留心；注意
▶ He paid no heed to the doctor's warnings.
他不把醫生的警告放在心上。
（補充片語）
pay heed to 留心；注意

heel [hil] 🎧 *Track 2365*
n. 腳後跟；高跟鞋
▶ I can't run with my high heels.
我沒辦法穿著高跟鞋跑步。
（相關片語）
down at heel 衣衫襤褸的；穿著寒酸的
▶ She looked quite down at heel when I met her the other day. 我前幾天遇到她時，她看起來衣著非常邋遢。

height [haɪt] 🎧 *Track 2366*
n. 高；高度

heir [ɛr] 🎧 *Track 2367*
n. 繼承人；嗣子；（性格、技能等的）繼承者
▶ The prince is the only heir to the throne.
王子是王位的唯一繼承人。

hel·i·cop·ter [`hɛlɪkɑptɚ] 🎧 *Track 2368*
n. 直升機

hell [hɛl] 🎧 *Track 2369*
n. 地獄、冥府；人間煉獄；極大困境；悲慘境地；（加強語氣）究竟
▶ To some students, school was worse than hell. 對一些學生來說，學校比地獄更糟。
（相關片語）
give sb. hell 怒斥某人；騷擾某人；困擾某人

※灰色單字為英檢初級必備單字

►My boss gave me hell for being late for the meeting today. 因為開會遲到，我老闆今天把我狠狠數落了一頓。

he'll [hil] 🎧 Track 2370
abbr. 他會（he will的縮寫）

hel·lo [hə`lo] 🎧 Track 2371
n. 表示問候的招呼；哈囉；
interj. 喂；你好；哈囉

hel·met [`hɛlmɪt] 🎧 Track 2372
n. 頭盔；安全帽
►Wearing a helmet can protect your head from harm.
戴安全帽可以保護你的頭受到傷害。

help [hɛlp] 🎧 Track 2373
v./n. 幫助

help·ful [`hɛlpfəl] 🎧 Track 2374
adj. 有幫助的

hen [hɛn] 🎧 Track 2375
n. 母雞

hence [hɛns] 🎧 Track 2376
adv. 因此；從現在起
►She lost three kilos and hence became more attractive.
她瘦了三公斤，因此更漂亮了。

her [hɝ] 🎧 Track 2377
pron. 她

herb [hɝb] 🎧 Track 2378
n. 草本植物；藥草
►She has an herb garden in back of the house. 她在房子後面有個香草花園。

herd [hɝd] 🎧 Track 2379
n. 畜群；牧群；放牧人
►We saw a herd of cattle grazing on the meadow. 我們看到一群牛隻在牧場上吃草。
v. 放牧；把……趕在一起；聚在一起；成群
►This dog is trained to herd sheep.
這隻狗是被訓練來牧羊的。

here [hɪr] 🎧 Track 2380
adv. 這裡

her·mit [`hɝmɪt] 🎧 Track 2381
n. 隱士；遁世者
►He became a hermit after he retired.
他在退休後變成了隱士。

he·ro [`hɪro] 🎧 Track 2382
n. 英雄；受崇拜的人

he·ro·ic [hɪ`roɪk] 🎧 Track 2383
adj. 英勇的；英雄的；記述英雄及其事跡的
►His selfless heroic act won our respect.
他無私的英勇表現贏得了我們的尊敬。

her·o·in [`hɛro,ɪn] 🎧 Track 2384
n. 海洛因
►The man was arrested for possessing heroin. 男子因為持有海洛因而被逮。

her·o·ine [`hɛro,ɪn] 🎧 Track 2385
n. 女英雄；女傑；受崇拜的女子
►Joan of Arc was a national heroine of France. 貞德是法國的民族女英雄。

hers [hɝz] 🎧 Track 2386
pron. 她的

her·self [hɝ`sɛlf] 🎧 Track 2387
pron. 她自己

he's [hiz] 🎧 Track 2388
abbr. 他是、他已（he is、he has的縮寫）

hes·i·tate [`hɛzə,tet] 🎧 Track 2389
v. 躊躇；猶豫
►Please don't hesitate to let me know if you need anything.
需要任何東西請不要猶豫，儘管跟我說。

hey [he] 🎧 Track 2390
interj. 嘿

hi [haɪ] 🎧 Track 2391
interj. 嗨（招呼語）

hid·den [`hɪdn] 🎧 *Track 2392*
adj. 隱藏的；隱秘的
▶I'm sure he is a good friend with no hidden agenda.
我相信他是一個並未藏有心機的好朋友。

(補充片語)
hidden agenda 隱藏的議程；未公開的計劃；引申為別有心機、有幕後動機

hide [haɪd] 🎧 *Track 2393*
v. 藏；躲藏

high [haɪ] 🎧 *Track 2394*
adj. 高的；（價值）高的；高速的
adv. 高地

high·light [`haɪ͵laɪt] 🎧 *Track 2395*
v. 用強光照射；用強光突出；使顯著；使突出
▶He highlighted the fact that roughly 805 million people in the world are starving on a daily basis.
他特別強調世界上大約有八億零五百萬人是每天都處在饑餓狀態的事實。

n. 強光（效果）；最精彩的部分；最重要的部分
▶The sex scenes were the highlights of the entire movie.
床戲是整部電影最精彩的部分。

(補充片語)
sex scene 床戲

high·ly [`haɪlɪ] 🎧 *Track 2396*
adv. 非常
▶He is highly interested in your proposal.
他對你的提案非常有興趣。

high-rise [`haɪ`raɪz] 🎧 *Track 2397*
n. 高樓
▶Our head office is located in a high-rise in downtown.
我們的總公司為在市區的一棟高樓內。

high·way [`haɪ͵we] 🎧 *Track 2398*
n. 公路；道路

hi·jack [`haɪ͵dʒæk] 🎧 *Track 2399*
v. 劫持；攔路搶劫
▶Three armed men hijacked a school bus this morning.
三名持槍男子今天上午劫持了一輛校車。

hi·jack·er [`haɪ͵dʒækɚ] 🎧 *Track 2400*
n. 強盜；劫機者；劫持者；劫盜
▶The hijacker took three students as hostages. 劫機犯挾持了三名學生作人質。

(補充片語)
take sb. hostage 把某人當人質

hi·jack·ing [`haɪdʒækɪŋ] 🎧 *Track 2401*
n. 攔路搶劫；劫持
▶The man was sentenced to death penalty for aircraft hijacking.
這男子因為犯下劫機案而被判處死刑。

(補充片語)
death penalty 死刑；
aircraft hijacking 劫機

hike [haɪk] 🎧 *Track 2402*
n./v. 徒步旅行

hik·er [`haɪkɚ] 🎧 *Track 2403*
n. 徒步旅行者；遠足者
▶I often have to run or walk fast so as to catch up with other hikers. 我常必須要跑或是快走，才能趕上其他健行者。

(補充片語)
so as to 為了；
catch up with 趕上

hik·ing [`haɪkɪŋ] 🎧 *Track 2404*
n. 徒步旅行
▶I often go hiking with family on the weekend.
我週末常常跟家人一起徒步旅行。

hill [hɪl] 🎧 *Track 2405*
n. 小山；丘陵

him [hɪm] 🎧 *Track 2406*
pron. 他

him·self [hɪm`sɛlf] 🎧 *Track 2407*
pron. 他自己

Aa
Bb
Cc
Dd
Ee
Ff
Gg
Hh
Ii
Jj
Kk
Ll
Mm
Nn
Oo
Pp
Qq
Rr
Ss
Tt
Uu
Vv
Ww
Xx
Yy
Zz

※灰色單字為英檢初級必備單字

hint [hɪnt]　🎧 Track 2408

n. 暗示；建議；指點；少許、微量

▶ My girlfriend dropped a hint to me that we should get married.
我女友暗示我們應該要結婚了。

(補充片語)

drop a hint to sb. 給予某人暗示

v. 暗示；示意

▶ She hinted that I should take the job offer. 她暗示我應該要接受這個工作機會。

(相關片語)

take a hint 領會別人的暗示；看眼色

▶ That guy just couldn't take a hint and kept talking endlessly. 那傢伙就根本不明白別人的暗示，還一直滔滔不絕講個不停。

hip [hɪp]　🎧 Track 2409

n. 臀部；屁股

hip·po·pot·a·mus [ˌhɪpəˈpɑtəməs] = hip·po　🎧 Track 2410

n. 河馬

hire [haɪr]　🎧 Track 2411

v./n. 雇用；租用

his [hɪz]　🎧 Track 2412

det. 他的；他的東西

hiss [hɪs]　🎧 Track 2413

v. 發出嘶嘶聲；發出噓聲（表示不滿）；以噓聲表示；嘶嘶地說出

▶ He was hissed at wherever he went after the scandal broke.
爆出醜聞後，他不管走到哪就被噓到哪。

n. 嘶嘶聲；噓聲

▶ I knew a tire of my bike was leaking because I could hear the faint hiss of escaping air.
我知道我的腳踏車有個輪胎在漏氣，因為我能聽到微弱的漏氣嘶嘶聲。

his·to·ri·an [hɪsˈtorɪən]　🎧 Track 2414

n. 歷史學家

▶ Professor Lee is a respectable historian.
李教授是位值得尊敬的歷史學家。

his·tor·ic [hɪsˈtɔrɪk]　🎧 Track 2415

adj. 歷史上著名的；具重大歷史意義的

▶ The 911 attacks were one of the most important historic events that changed the world forever.
911攻擊事件是永遠地改變了世界，最重要的歷史事件之一。

his·tor·i·cal [hɪsˈtɔrɪkl]　🎧 Track 2416

adj. 歷史的；史學的；有關歷史的

▶ The Romance of the Three Kingdoms is a great historical novel.
《三國演義》是一部偉大的歷史小說。

(補充片語)

historical novel 歷史小說

his·to·ry [ˈhɪstərɪ]　🎧 Track 2417

n. 歷史；由來；過去的經歷；故事

hit [hɪt]　🎧 Track 2418

v. 打；打擊；碰撞；

n. 打擊；碰撞；成功而風行一時的事物

hive [haɪv]　🎧 Track 2419

n. 蜂窩；蜂巢；熱鬧的場所；蜂群；喧嚷的人群

▶ The night market is a hive of various delicious snacks.
夜市是充滿各種美味小吃的熱鬧場所。

hoarse [hors]　🎧 Track 2420

adj. 嘶啞的；嗓子粗啞的

▶ My voice is hoarse because of my sore throat. 我因為喉嚨痛，所以聲音很沙啞。

hob·by [ˈhɑbɪ]　🎧 Track 2421

n. 嗜好

hock·ey [ˈhɑkɪ]　🎧 Track 2422

n. 曲棍球

▶ I seldom see people play hockey in Taiwan. 我很少在台灣看到人打曲棍球。

hold [hold]　🎧 Track 2423

v. 握住；抓住；舉行；**n.** 抓住；支撐

hold·er [ˈholdə]　🎧 Track 2424

n. 持有者；保有者；支托物

hole [hol] 🎧 *Track 2425*
n. 洞

hol·i·day [`hɑlə‚de] 🎧 *Track 2426*
n. 假日；節日；休假日

hol·low [`hɑlo] 🎧 *Track 2427*
adj. 中空的；凹陷的；空洞的；空虛的
▶ His hollow speech made me doze off.
他空洞的演說讓我打瞌睡。

n. 窪地；洞；坑；山谷
▶ Our laughter echoed in the hollow.
我們的笑聲在山谷中迴響。

holy [`holɪ] 🎧 *Track 2428*
adj. 神聖的；虔誠的；獻身於宗教的；聖潔的
▶ Practicing medicine is one of the holiest jobs in the world.
行醫是世界上最神聖的工作之一。

home [hom] 🎧 *Track 2429*
n. 家；**adv.** 在家；回家；到家
adj. 家庭的；本國的；總部的

home·land [`hom‚lænd] 🎧 *Track 2430*
n. 祖國；家鄉
▶ It has been twenty years since I left my homeland. 我已經離開家鄉20年了。

home·sick [`hom‚sɪk] 🎧 *Track 2431*
adj. 想家的

home·work [`hom‚wɝk] 🎧 *Track 2432*
n. 回家作業

hon·est [`ɑnɪst] 🎧 *Track 2433*
adj. 誠實的；用正當手段取得的；坦白的

hon·est·ly [`ɑnɪstlɪ] 🎧 *Track 2434*
adv. 誠實地；老實說；實在
▶ Honestly, it's the worst movie I've ever seen. 老實說，這是我看過最糟的一部電影。

hon·es·ty [`ɑnɪstɪ] 🎧 *Track 2435*
n. 誠實

hon·ey [`hʌnɪ] 🎧 *Track 2436*
n. 蜂蜜

hon·ey·moon [`hʌnɪ‚mun] 🎧 *Track 2437*
n. 蜜月；蜜月假期
▶ The newlyweds are on their honeymoon trip. 這對新婚夫妻正在蜜月旅行。

v. 度蜜月
▶ We honeymooned in the Maldives.
我們是在馬爾地夫度蜜月的。

Hong Kong [hɔŋ-kɔŋ] 🎧 *Track 2438*
n. 香港

honk [hɔŋk] 🎧 *Track 2439*
n. 汽車喇叭聲
▶ The man got a loud honk from a car when he tried to cross the road during the red light. 男子企圖闖紅燈過馬路時，被一輛汽車大聲地按喇叭。

v. 鳴（汽車）喇叭
▶ I honked the horn at the car running the red light. 我對一輛闖紅燈的車按喇叭。

hon·or [`ɑnɚ] 🎧 *Track 2440*
=hon·our（英式英文）
n. 榮譽；面子；光榮的人或事；禮儀；敬意
▶ We are taught to show honor to our elders. 我們被教導要尊敬長輩。

v. 使增光；給……以榮譽；尊敬
▶ I honor my father. 我很尊敬我的父親。

相關片語
in honor of 紀念；以表敬意；以慶祝
▶ We threw a party in honor of our 20th anniversary. 我們為了慶祝二十週年結婚紀念而舉辦了一場派對。

hon·or·a·ble [`ɑnərəbl] 🎧 *Track 2441*
adj. 可尊敬的；高尚的；光榮的；榮譽的；表示尊敬的；體面的
▶ My mother is an honorable person who provided for the whole family on her own after my father died.
我母親是個可敬的人，她在我父親死後，便獨自養活全家人。

hood [hʊd] 🎧 *Track 2442*
n. 頭巾；兜帽；風帽；罩；車蓋

Aa
Bb
Cc
Dd
Ee
Ff
Gg
Hh
Ii
Jj
Kk
Ll
Mm
Nn
Oo
Pp
Qq
Rr
Ss
Tt
Uu
Vv
Ww
Xx
Yy
Zz

※灰色單字為英檢初級必備單字

▶ I bought a coat with a removable hood.
我買了一件有可拆風帽的外套。

v. 罩上風帽；裝上車篷；覆蓋
▶ Snow hooded the treetops.
雪覆蓋著樹梢。

hoof [huf] 🎧 *Track 2443*
n. （馬）蹄；人的腳
▶ One of the horse's hooves was injured.
這匹馬的其中一隻蹄受傷了。

v. 用腳踢；步行
▶ My office is only two blocks from my place so I hoof to work every day.
我公司離家裡只有兩個紅綠燈，所以我每天都走路上班。

相關片語
on the hoof 即興地；事先無準備地
▶ Many of his popular songs were written on the hoof. 他有許多受歡迎的歌都是在即興地情況下寫出來的。

hook [huk] 🎧 *Track 2444*
n. 鉤；掛鉤
▶ Why don't you hang your coat on the hook？你為何不把外套掛在鉤子上？

v. 用鉤子鉤住；引人上鉤
▶ That woman aimed to hook a rich husband.
那女人目標就是要釣到一個有錢老公。

相關片語
by hook or by crook 不擇手段
▶ He will take revenge on the murderer by hook or by crook.
他會不擇手段，報復那個殺人兇手。

補充片語
take revenge on 向……報復

hop [hɑp] 🎧 *Track 2445*
v. （人）單足跳；（動物）齊足跳；跳舞
n. 跳躍

hope [hop] 🎧 *Track 2446*
v./n. 希望

hope·ful [`hopfəl] 🎧 *Track 2447*
adj. 抱有希望的；充滿希望的

▶ I was hopeful about getting the job offer.
我對得到這個工作機會充滿希望。

hope·ful·ly [`hopfəlɪ] 🎧 *Track 2448*
adv. 希望地
▶ Hopefully we can get there on time.
希望我們能準時到那裡。

ho·ri·zon [hə`raɪzn] 🎧 *Track 2449*
n. 地平線；（知識、經驗）眼界、視野
▶ Travelling broadens my mind and horizon. 旅行開拓了我的心和視野。

相關片語
a cloud on the horizon 預期未來可能發生的困難或關卡；大難臨頭
▶ Everyone was having fun while Helen saw a cloud on their horizon.
當海倫知道他們就要大難臨頭時，所有人還都玩得很開心。

hor·mone [`hɔrmon] 🎧 *Track 2450*
n. 荷爾蒙；激素
▶ Children with growth hormone deficiency are often smaller.
缺乏生長激素的孩童通常體形比較小。

補充片語
growth hormone 生長激素

horn [hɔrn] 🎧 *Track 2451*
n. 角；喇叭；管樂器；小號、號角
▶ They hunted the rhinos for their horns.
他們是為了犀牛的角而獵捕牠們。

相關片語
blow one's own horn 吹噓
▶ Don't listen to him. He's only blowing his own horn. 別聽他的。他只是在吹噓罷了。

hor·ri·ble [`hɔrəbl] 🎧 *Track 2452*
adj. 可怕的；糟透的

hor·ri·fy [`hɔrəˌfaɪ] 🎧 *Track 2453*
v. 使恐懼；使驚訝；使反感
▶ We were horrified by the series of terrorist attacks in France.
我們對於發生在法國的一連串恐怖攻擊事件感到震驚恐懼。

hor·ror [`hɔrɚ]
🎧 *Track 2454*

n. 恐怖

▶ I always have bad dreams after watching horror movies.
我看恐怖片之後總是會做惡夢。

(補充片語)

horror movie 恐怖片

horse [hɔrs]
🎧 *Track 2455*

n. 馬

hose [hoz]
🎧 *Track 2456*

n. 水管

▶ Our shower hose is too short. We need to replace it with a longer one.
我們的淋浴水管太短了。我們得換個長一點的。

v. 用軟管淋澆或沖洗

▶ I was hosing my flowerbed when the postman came.
郵差來的時候，我正在用軟管幫花圃澆水。

hos·pi·tal [`hɑspɪtl]
🎧 *Track 2457*

n. 醫院

hos·pi·tal·ize [`hɑspɪtl͵aɪz]
🎧 *Track 2458*

v. 使住院治療

▶ Fred had a car accident in Los Angeles and has been hospitalized in a local hospital there since then.
佛烈德在洛杉磯發生車禍，之後便一直在當地一間醫院住院治療。

host [host]
🎧 *Track 2459*

n. 主人；東道主；主持人

v. 主持；主辦；以主人身分招待

hos·tage [`hɑstɪdʒ]
🎧 *Track 2460*

n. 人質；抵押品

▶ The man hijacked the bus, and took all passengers as hostages.
男子劫持了公車，並將所有乘客當作人質。

(補充片語)

take sb. hostage/hold sb. hostage 抓住某人當作人質

hos·tel [`hɑstl]
🎧 *Track 2461*

n. 旅社；青年旅社

▶ We're trying to find a hostel for the night.
我們試著找一間旅社過夜。

host·ess [`hostɪs]
🎧 *Track 2462*

n. 女主人；旅館女老闆；女服務員

▶ The hostess waited at the door to greet her guests.
女主人在門口等候著迎接她的賓客。

hos·tile [`hɑstɪl]
🎧 *Track 2463*

adj. 敵人的，敵方的；懷敵意的、不友善的

▶ The children were hostile to their stepmother. 孩子們對他們的繼母懷有敵意。

hot [hɑt]
🎧 *Track 2464*

adj. 熱的；辣的

ho·tel [ho`tɛl]
🎧 *Track 2465*

n. 飯店

hound [haʊnd]
🎧 *Track 2466*

n. 獵犬；卑劣的人；有癮的人、瘋狂追求某事的人

▶ Most girls I know are gossip hounds.
我認識的大部分女孩子都是八卦迷。

hour [aʊr]
🎧 *Track 2467*

n. 小時

hour·ly [`aʊrlɪ]
🎧 *Track 2468*

adj. 每小時的

▶ Most of our hourly employees are college students.
我們大部分的時薪人員都是大學生。

(補充片語)

hourly employee 鐘點工；時薪人員

adv. 每小時地；頻繁地

▶ The nurse took the boy's temperature hourly. 護士每小時幫男孩量一次體溫。

house [haʊs]
🎧 *Track 2469*

n. 屋子；房子；

v. 給……房子住；將……收藏在屋內

house·hold [`haʊs͵hold]
🎧 *Track 2470*

n. 一家人；家庭；戶

▶ The whole household was deeply grieved by his death.
全家人對他的死都感到萬分地悲痛。

adj. 家庭的;家用的
▶ All household appliances in this store are on sale now.
這家店的所有家電用品都在特價優惠中。

補充片語
household appliance 家電產品;家用電器

house·keep·er 🎧 *Track 2471*
[ˈhaʊsˌkipɚ]
n. 管家;傭人領班
▶ We hired a housekeeper to take care of all housework for us.
我們請了一個管家幫我們打理所有的家事。

house·wife [ˈhaʊsˌwaɪf] 🎧 *Track 2472*
n. 家庭主婦
▶ My mother is a full-time housewife.
我媽媽是個全職的家庭主婦。

house·work [ˈhaʊsˌwɜˑk] 🎧 *Track 2473*
n. 家事
▶ I insist that my husband and I should share the housework equally.
我堅持先生與我應該要平均分擔家事。

hous·ing [ˈhaʊzɪŋ] 🎧 *Track 2474*
n. 住房供給;房屋;住宅
▶ Housing shortage is the first difficulty that the new mayor should deal with.
住房短缺是新市長應該要面對的第一個難題。

how [haʊ] 🎧 *Track 2475*
adv. 怎樣;多麼;為何;**conj.** 如何;怎麼

how·ev·er [haʊˈɛvɚ] 🎧 *Track 2476*
adv. 無論如何;不管用什麼方法
conj. 然而

howl [haʊl] 🎧 *Track 2477*
v. 嗥叫;怒吼;吼叫著說,狂喊
▶ We didn't sleep well last night because the dogs in the neighborhood howled all night.
我們昨晚沒睡好,因為附近的狗徹夜嗥叫。

n. 嗥叫;怒吼;號啕大哭;大笑
▶ The patient let out a howl of pain when the nurse changed his dressing.
病人在護士幫他換藥時發出痛苦的叫喊聲。

補充片語
let out a howl 發出喊叫;
change dressing 換藥

how's [haʊz] 🎧 *Track 2478*
abbr. 如何(how is的縮寫)

Hua·lian [ˈhwɑˈliɛn] 🎧 *Track 2479*
n. 花蓮

hug [hʌg] 🎧 *Track 2480*
n. 擁抱
▶ The little girl gave her mother a hug and said goodnight.
小女孩給了媽媽一個擁抱後便道晚安。

v. 擁抱
▶ They hugged each other when they finally met.
他們在終於見到對方時,緊緊地互相擁抱。

huge [hjudʒ] 🎧 *Track 2481*
adj. 巨大的;龐大的

hum [hʌm] 🎧 *Track 2482*
v. 發嗡嗡聲;發哼聲;哼曲子
▶ She hummed as she cooked dinner in the kitchen.
她一邊在廚房做晚飯一邊哼著歌。

n. 哼聲;哼曲子的聲音;嗡嗡聲
▶ The hum in my ears bothers me a lot.
我耳裡的嗡嗡聲讓我非常困擾。

hu·man [ˈhjumən] 🎧 *Track 2483*
adj. 人的;人類的;有人性的;**n.** 人;人類

hu·man·i·ty [hjuˈmænətɪ] 🎧 *Track 2484*
n. 人性;人道;人類
▶ He treated the boy with humanity, even though he's the son of his enemy.
即使那男孩是他仇家的兒子,他仍以人道的方式對待他。

hum·ble [ˈhʌmbl] 🎧 *Track 2485*
adj. 謙遜的;卑微的;簡陋的

hu·mid [ˈhjumɪd] 🎧 *Track 2486*
adj. 潮濕的

hu·mid·i·ty [hjuˋmɪdətɪ] 🎧 *Track 2487*
n. 濕氣；濕度
▶ The combination of humidity and high temperature here made me ill for days.
這裡的濕氣結合高溫，讓我病了好幾天。

hu·mil·i·ate [hjuˋmɪlɪˌet] 🎧 *Track 2488*
v. 羞辱；使蒙恥辱；使丟臉
▶ How could you humiliate me in front of all my friends?
你怎麼能在我所有朋友面前羞辱我？

hu·mor [ˋhjumə] 🎧 *Track 2489*
n. 幽默

hu·mor·ous [ˋhjumərəs] 🎧 *Track 2490*
adj. 幽默的；詼諧的

hunch [hʌntʃ] 🎧 *Track 2491*
n. 預感；直覺
▶ I have a hunch that he is in trouble.
我直覺他有麻煩了。

v. 弓起；聳起；隆起；彎成弓狀
▶ A cat will hunch its body when it's in pain.
貓在痛苦的時候會弓起身體。

hun·dred [ˋhʌndrəd] 🎧 *Track 2492*
n. 一百；
pron. 一百個；一百
adj. 一百的；一百個的

hun·ger [ˋhʌŋgə] 🎧 *Track 2493*
n. 饑餓；渴望

hun·gry [ˋhʌŋgrɪ] 🎧 *Track 2494*
adj. 餓的；饑餓的；渴望的

hunt [hʌnt] 🎧 *Track 2495*
v. 追獵；獵取；尋找；追求；**n.** 打獵；搜索

hunt·er [ˋhʌntə] 🎧 *Track 2496*
n. 獵人；追求者；搜尋者

hur·ri·cane [ˋhɝ ɪ ˌken] 🎧 *Track 2497*
n. 颶風；暴風雨
▶ Our flight has been cancelled due to the coming hurricane.
我們的班機因為即將來臨的颶風而取消了。

hur·ry [ˋhɝ ɪ] 🎧 *Track 2498*
v. 使趕快；催促；趕緊；匆忙
n. 急忙；倉促

hurt [hɝt] 🎧 *Track 2499*
v. 傷害；使疼痛；疼痛

hus·band [ˋhʌzbənd] 🎧 *Track 2500*
n. 丈夫；老公

hush [hʌʃ] 🎧 *Track 2501*
v. 使沉默；使安靜；安靜下來；沉默
▶ The host hushed the uproarious audience.
主持人要鼓譟的觀眾安靜下來。

n. 靜寂；沉默
▶ The moment the singer started to sing, a hush fell over the audience.
歌手一開始唱歌，觀眾便頓時安靜了下來。

相關片語
hush money 遮口費
▶ He finally admitted to paying the woman hush money to keep their affair a secret.
他終於承認有付該女子遮口費，為他們的風流韻事保密。

hut [hʌt] 🎧 *Track 2502*
n.（簡陋的）小屋
▶ The old man lived in a hut in the forest by himself. 老人獨自居住在森林裡的小屋中。

hy·dro·gen [ˋhaɪdrədʒən] 🎧 *Track 2503*
n. 氫
▶ A hydrogen bomb, the most powerful type of nuclear bomb, is the most destructive weapon by far.
氫彈—核彈中最具威力的一種，是目前最具破壞性的武器。

hyp·o·crite [ˋhɪpəkrɪt] 🎧 *Track 2504*
n. 偽君子；偽善者
▶ I disdain to make friends with hypocrites.
我不屑跟偽善者做朋友。

Aa
Bb
Cc
Dd
Ee
Ff
Gg
Hh
Ii
Jj
Kk
Ll
Mm
Nn
Oo
Pp
Qq
Rr
Ss
Tt
Uu
Vv
Ww
Xx
Yy
Zz

※灰色單字為英檢初級必備單字

Ii

通過中級英文檢定者的英文能力：

 聽 在日常生活中，能聽懂一般的會話；能大致聽懂公共場所廣播、氣象報告及廣告等。在工作時，能聽懂簡易的產品介紹與操作說明。能大致聽懂外籍人士的談話及詢問。

 讀 在日常生活中，能閱讀短文、故事、私人信件、廣告、傳單、簡介及使用說明等。在工作時，能閱讀工作須知、公告、操作手冊、例行的文件、傳真、電報等。

 寫 能寫簡單的書信、故事及心得等。對於熟悉且與個人經歷相關的主題，能以簡易的文字表達。

 說 在日常生活中，能以簡易英語交談或描述一般事物，能介紹自己的生活作息、工作、家庭、經歷等，並可對一般話題陳述看法。在工作時，能進行簡單的答詢，並與外籍人士交談溝通。

本書除包含官方公佈的中級4,947單字外，更精挑了近400個滿分必學的高手單字。同時，在片語的挑選、例句的使用上，皆依上述英檢官方公佈之能力範疇做設計，難度適中、不偏離考試主題。發音部分則是自然發音＆KK音標雙管齊下，搭配MP3以「分解／完整」方式錄音，給你最多元有效的學習手段，怎麼記都可以，想忘掉都好難！

I [aɪ] 🎧 *Track 2505*
pron. 我

ice [aɪs] 🎧 *Track 2506*
n. 冰

ice·berg [`aɪsˌbɝg] 🎧 *Track 2507*
n. 冰山
▶ The ship hit an iceberg and sank to the bottom of the Atlantic Ocean. 那艘船撞上了一座冰山，並沉到大西洋底去了。

ic·y [`aɪsɪ] 🎧 *Track 2508*
adj. 多冰的；結滿冰的；覆蓋著冰的；冰冷的
▶ The roads are icy and slippery.
路面結冰，很滑。

ID [aɪ-di] 🎧 *Track 2509*
n. 身分證明；身分證
▶ Show me your ID, please.
請讓我看你的身分證。

I'd [aɪd] 🎧 *Track 2510*
abbr. 我會、我已（I would或I had的縮寫）

i·de·a [aɪ`diə] 🎧 *Track 2511*
n. 想法；主意；計劃；打算；概念

i·deal [aɪ`diəl] 🎧 *Track 2512*
adj. 理想的；完美的
▶ He is an ideal husband.
他是一個理想的老公。

i·den·ti·cal [aɪ`dɛntɪkl̩] 🎧 *Track 2513*
adj. 完全相同的；完全相似的
▶ I have a dress which is exactly identical to yours.
我有一件跟你的一模一樣的洋裝。

相關片語
identical twin 同卵雙生
▶ Most identical twins look exactly alike.
大部分的同卵雙胞胎看起來一模一樣。

i·den·ti·fi·ca·tion 🎧 *Track 2514*
[aɪ͵dɛntəfəˋkeʃən]

n. 認出；識別；身分證明；身分證

▶ You need at least two forms of identification to open a bank account. 你需要至少兩種形式的身分證件才能開一個銀行帳戶。

i·den·ti·fy [aɪˋdɛntə͵faɪ] 🎧 *Track 2515*

v. 確認；識別；鑑定

▶ I cannot identify this handwriting. 我無法確認這是誰的筆跡。

i·den·ti·ty [aɪˋdɛntətɪ] 🎧 *Track 2516*

n. 身份；特點；特性

▶ The police guaranteed the informant that they would protect his identity. 警方向線民保證他們會保密他的身分。

id·i·om [ˋɪdɪəm] 🎧 *Track 2517*

n. 慣用語；成語；（個人特有）用語

▶ Idioms are commonly used in Americans' everyday conversations. 美國人的生活對話中經常使用慣用語。

id·i·ot [ˋɪdɪət] 🎧 *Track 2518*

n. 白癡；傻瓜；笨蛋

▶ Don't think you can fool me. I'm not an idiot. 別想耍我。我不是白癡。

i·dle [ˋaɪdḷ] 🎧 *Track 2519*

adj. 不工作的；閒置的；無所事事的；無目的的

▶ He wants to live an idle life after retirement. 他想在退休之後過閒散無事的生活。

v. 無所事事；閒逛；閒混；虛度（光陰）

▶ If you don't make a plan in advance, you're very likely to idle away the whole summer vacation. 如果你不事先做計劃，你很可能會虛度整個暑假。

<u>補充片語</u>

in advance 事先；
idle away 虛度（時光）

idol [ˋaɪdḷ] 🎧 *Track 2520*

n. 偶像；受崇拜的人；紅人

▶ As an idol of young people, you should set a good example for your fans. 身為年輕人的偶像，你應該要為你的粉絲樹立好榜樣。

<u>補充片語</u>

set an example 樹立榜樣

if [ɪf] 🎧 *Track 2521*

conj. 如果；是否

ig·no·rance [ˋɪgnərəns] 🎧 *Track 2522*

n. 無知

▶ Her parents were in complete ignorance of her interpersonal relationships. 她的父母對她的交友狀況一無所知。

<u>補充片語</u>

be in ignorance of 對……不知情；
interpersonal relationship 人際關係

ig·no·rant [ˋɪgnərənt] 🎧 *Track 2523*

adj. 無知的，不學無術的；沒有受教育的；無知造成的

▶ Mistakes are always forgivable, especially ignorant ones. 錯誤總是可以被原諒的，尤其是無知所造成的錯誤。

ig·nore [ɪgˋnor] 🎧 *Track 2524*

v. 不顧；忽視

I'll [aɪl] 🎧 *Track 2525*

abbr. 我會（I will 的縮寫）

ill [ɪl] 🎧 *Track 2526*

adj. 病的；不健康的；壞的；邪惡的

il·le·gal [ɪˋligḷ] 🎧 *Track 2527*

adj. 不合法的，違法的

▶ It is illegal to leave your young children home alone. 把年幼的孩子獨自留在家裡是違法的行為。

ill·ness [ˋɪlnɪs] 🎧 *Track 2528*

n. 病；患病（狀態）；身體不適

▶ I hope you will recover from your illness soon. 我希望你很快就能從病中康復。

il·lus·trate [ˋɪləstret] 🎧 *Track 2529*

v. （用圖、實例等）說明；插圖於，圖解說明

▶ Julia illustrated her proposal with some diagrams. 朱莉亞用一些圖表來說明她的企劃案。

Aa
Bb
Cc
Dd
Ee
Ff
Gg
Hh
Ii
Jj
Kk
Ll
Mm
Nn
Oo
Pp
Qq
Rr
Ss
Tt
Uu
Vv
Ww
Xx
Yy
Zz

※灰色單字為英檢初級必備單字

il·lus·tra·tion 🎧 *Track 2530*

[ɪˌlʌsˋtreʃən]

n. 說明，圖解，圖示，插圖，圖表，圖案

▶Children's storybooks are always full of illustrations. 孩子的故事書通常充滿了插圖。

I'm [aɪm] 🎧 *Track 2531*

abbr. 我是（I am的縮寫）

im·age [ˋɪmɪdʒ] 🎧 *Track 2532*

n. 肖像；形象；印象；概念

i·ma·gi·na·ble 🎧 *Track 2533*

[ɪˋmædʒɪnəbl]

adj. 能想像的；可想像得到的

▶This client is the most difficult person imaginable.

這個客戶是你能想像的最難搞的人。

i·ma·gi·na·ry 🎧 *Track 2534*

[ɪˋmædʒəˌnɛrɪ]

adj. 想像中的；虛構的；幻想的

▶Dragons and phoenixes are imaginary animals. 龍與鳳是虛構的動物。

i·ma·gi·na·tion 🎧 *Track 2535*

[ɪˌmædʒəˋneʃən]

n. 想像力；空想；幻想；妄想

▶Instead telling me the ending, he left it to my imagination. 他並沒有告訴我結局，而是把它留著讓我自己想像。

i·ma·gi·na·tive 🎧 *Track 2536*

[ɪˋmædʒəˌnetɪv]

adj. 虛構的；幻想的；有想像力的

▶This imaginative advertisement has successfully attracted the customers' attention. 這支極富想像力的廣告成功地吸引了消費者的注意。

i·ma·gine [ɪˋmædʒɪn] 🎧 *Track 2537*

v. 想像

im·i·tate [ˋɪməˌtet] 🎧 *Track 2538*

v. 模仿；以……做為範例，仿效

▶He made false documents by imitating his brother's signature.

他模仿他哥哥的簽名偽造文書。

(補充片語)

false documents 偽造文書

im·i·ta·tion [ˌɪməˋteʃən] 🎧 *Track 2539*

n. 模仿，模擬；仿造；偽造；仿製品；贗品

▶He got a tattoo on his arm in imitation of his idol.

他為了模仿他的偶像，在手臂上刺了青。

(補充片語)

in imitation of 為了仿效

im·me·di·ate [ɪˋmidɪɪt] 🎧 *Track 2540*

adj. 立即的

▶I'm looking forward to your immediate response to my question.

期待您針對我的問題給予立即的回覆。

im·me·di·ate·ly 🎧 *Track 2541*

[ɪˋmidɪtlɪ]

adv. 立刻地

▶Your father is on the danger list. You need to come back immediately.

你的父親病危了。你必須立刻回來。

(補充片語)

be on the danger list 病危；在病危名單上

im·mi·grant [ˋɪməgrənt] 🎧 *Track 2542*

n. （外來）移民

▶All illegal immigrants will be sent back to their countries.

所有的非法移民都會被遣返回國。

(補充片語)

illegal immigrant 非法移民

im·mi·grate [ˋɪməˌgret] 🎧 *Track 2543*

v. 遷居；遷入；從外地移居

▶I immigrated to Argentina with my family when I was five.

我五歲時就跟我家人移居到阿根廷了。

im·mi·gra·tion 🎧 *Track 2544*

[ˌɪməˋgreʃən]

n. 移居；移民入境；（總稱）外來移民

▶The government hopes the new investment immigration policy can attract more foreign capital.

政府希望新的投資移民政策可以吸引更多的外國資金。

補充片語

investment immigration 投資移民

im·mune [ɪ`mjun]　Track 2545
adj. 免疫的；不受影響的；有免疫力的
▶ A team of scientists found that a group of women in West Africa appear to be immune to the Ebola virus.
一個科學家團隊發現西非的一群女性顯然對伊波拉病毒有免疫力。

相關片語

immune system 免疫系統
▶ Poor nutrition or poor diet will weaken your immune system.
營養不良或飲食欠佳會削弱你的免疫系統。

im·pact [ɪm`pækt]　Track 2546
n. 衝擊；對……產生影響
▶ The invention of the cellphone has had a revolutionary impact on the world.
手機的發明對世界產生了極大的影響。

v. 衝擊；產生影響
▶ It is obvious that the invention of the cellphone has impacted on our life greatly.
手機的發明很明顯地對我們生活產生極大的影響。

im·pa·tient [ɪm`peʃənt]　Track 2547
adj. 沒耐心的；不耐煩的
▶ He's been very impatient with those kids.
他對那些孩子很沒耐心。

im·pe·ri·al [ɪm`pɪrɪəl]　Track 2548
adj. 帝國的；帝王的；威嚴宏大的
▶ It never occurred to Diana that she would marry into the imperial family one day.
戴安娜從沒想過她有一天會嫁入帝王之家。

im·per·son·al [ɪm`pɝsn̩l]　Track 2549
adj. 非個人的；非針對人的；客觀的；無人情味的；不具人格的
▶ The layoff was impersonal, so don't let it destroy your confidence. 裁員是對事不對人的，所以不要讓它毀了你的自信。

im·ple·ment [`ɪmpləmənt]　Track 2550
v. 執行；實施

▶ We need to raise funds to implement the program.
我們需要募集資金來執行這個計劃。

im·pli·ca·tion [ˌɪmplɪ`keʃən]　Track 2551
n. 牽連；含義；言外之意；暗示
▶ The actress acknowledged the rumor by implication. 女星含蓄地承認了傳言。

補充片語

by implication 含蓄地；暗示地

im·ply [ɪm`plaɪ]　Track 2552
v. 暗指；暗示；意味著
▶ His frown implied that he was not pleased with the answer.
他的皺眉暗示著他對此回答並不滿意。

im·po·lite [ˌɪmpə`laɪt]　Track 2553
adj. 無禮的

im·port [`ɪmport]　Track 2554
n. 進口；輸入；進口商品
v. 進口；輸入；引進

im·por·tance [ɪm`pɔrtn̩s]　Track 2555
n. 重要性

im·por·tant [ɪm`pɔrtn̩t]　Track 2556
adj. 重要的

im·pose [ɪm`poz]　Track 2557
v. 徵（稅）；加負擔於……；把……強加於
▶ The government is planning to impose a heavy tax on cigarettes and alcohol.
政府正計劃要對煙酒課以重稅。

im·pos·si·ble [ɪm`pɑsəbl̩]　Track 2558
adj. 不可能的

im·press [ɪm`prɛs]　Track 2559
v. 給……極深的印象
▶ I want to make a dinner on my own to impress my boyfriend.
我想要自己做一頓晚餐，讓我男友印象深刻。

im·pres·sion [ɪm`prɛʃən]　Track 2560
n. 印象

※灰色單字為英檢初級必備單字

▶He wanted to make a good impression on his future mother-in-law.
他想要給未來丈母娘留下好印象。

(補充片語)
make a good impression on sb. 給某人留下好印象

(相關片語)
first impression 第一印象
▶My first impression of my boyfriend was not very good.
我男友給我的第一印象並不是很好。

im·pres·sive [ɪm`prɛsɪv] 🎧 Track 2561
adj. 予人深刻印象的；令人欽佩的
▶His speech was pretty impressive.
他的致詞相當令人印象深刻。

im·prove [ɪm`pruv] 🎧 Track 2562
v. 進步；改進；改善

im·prove·ment 🎧 Track 2563
[ɪm`pruvmənt]
n. 改進；改善
▶There isn't much improvement in his acting. 他的演技沒什麼進步。

im·pulse [`ɪmpʌls] 🎧 Track 2564
n. 衝動；一時的念頭
▶My wife bought a designer bag on an impulse. 我老婆一時衝動買了個名牌包。

(補充片語)
on (an) impulse 一時衝動

in [ɪn] 🎧 Track 2565
prep. 在……裡；在……方面；穿著
adv. 進；在裡頭；adj. 在裡面的；流行的

in·ad·e·quate 🎧 Track 2566
[ɪn`ædəkwɪt]
adj. 不充分的；貧乏的；不適當的；不能勝任的
▶He may be a successful businessman, but he is definitely an inadequate father.
他也許是個成功的實業家，但他絕對是個不夠格的父親。

in·cense [`ɪnsɛns] 🎧 Track 2567
n. 香；焚香時的煙；香味；香氣

▶We don't burn incense at home in case we start a fire.
我們不在家裡燒香，以免引發火災。

v. 焚香；向……敬香；用香薰；激怒；使憤怒
▶I was incensed by his rude attitude.
我被他無禮的態度給激怒了。

inch [ɪntʃ] 🎧 Track 2568
n. 英吋

in·ci·dent [`ɪnsədnt] 🎧 Track 2569
n. 事件
▶Let's not mention the incident in the presence of others.
我們不要在其他人面前提到這件事。

in·clude [ɪn`klud] 🎧 Track 2570
v. 包含；包括

in·clud·ed [ɪn`kludɪd] 🎧 Track 2571
adj. 包含的；被包括的
▶The 10% service charge is already included in the bill.
百分之十的服務費已經被包含在帳單裡了。

in·clud·ing [ɪn`kludɪŋ] 🎧 Track 2572
prep. 包含

in·come [`ɪn͵kʌm] 🎧 Track 2573
n. 收入

in·com·plete [͵ɪnkəm`plit] 🎧 Track 2574
adj. 不完全的；不完整的；未結束的
▶Some people believe that life is incomplete without children.
有些人認為沒有孩子的人生是不完整的。

in·con·ve·ni·ent 🎧 Track 2575
[͵ɪnkən`vinjənt]
adj. 不方便的；不便的
▶It's quite inconvenient to live without electricity.
生活中沒有電是相當不方便的。

in·crease [ɪn`kris] 🎧 Track 2576
v./n. 增加；增長

in·creas·ing·ly
🎧 *Track 2577*

[ɪnˋkrisɪŋlɪ]

adv. 漸漸地；越來越多地

▶ It seems to be increasingly difficult to find time for myself.

要擁有自己的時間看來是越來越困難了。

in·deed [ɪnˋdid]
🎧 *Track 2578*

adv. 真正地；確實；更確切地

▶ I am very sorry indeed.

我真的覺得很遺憾。

in·de·pen·dence
🎧 *Track 2579*

[͵ɪndɪˋpɛndəns]

n. 獨立；自立

▶ Ireland gained its independence from England in 1921.

愛爾蘭在1921年從英格蘭取得獨立。

in·de·pen·dent
🎧 *Track 2580*

[͵ɪndɪˋpɛndənt]

adj. 獨立的

in·dex [ˋɪndɛks]
🎧 *Track 2581*

n. 索引；標誌；跡象；指示符號；指數；指標

▶ The index is normally in the back of a book.

索引通常是放在一本書的最後。

v. 將……編入索引；表明；指示

▶ A person's complexion often indexes his health.

一個人的氣色通常反映著他的健康狀態。

(相關片語)

index finger 食指

▶ It's rude to point at others with your index finger. 用食指指著別人是很沒有禮貌的。

In·di·a [ˋɪndɪə]
🎧 *Track 2582*

n. 印度

▶ It's not safe for a woman to travel in India alone.

一個女子要單獨到印度旅遊是不安全的。

In·di·an [ˋɪndɪən]
🎧 *Track 2583*

adj. 印度的；印第安的

▶ Indian curry is too spicy for me.

印度咖哩對我來說太辣了。

n. 印度人；印第安人

▶ All the Indians I know are very smart.

我所認識的印度人每個都很聰明。

in·di·cate [ˋɪndə͵ket]
🎧 *Track 2584*

v. 指示；指出；表明

in·di·ca·tion [͵ɪndəˋkeʃən]
🎧 *Track 2585*

n. 指示；跡象、徵兆

▶ There is every indication that the child has been abused.

所有的跡象都表示這孩子有受到虐待。

(補充片語)

there is every indication that... 所有跡象表明……

in·dif·fer·ent [ɪnˋdɪfərənt]
🎧 *Track 2586*

adj. 冷淡的

▶ The man is indifferent to his stepson.

男子對他的繼子很冷淡。

in·di·vid·u·al
🎧 *Track 2587*

[͵ɪndəˋvɪdʒʊəl]

adj. 個人的；個體的；特有的

n. 個人；個體

in·door [ˋɪn͵dor]
🎧 *Track 2588*

adj. 室內的

▶ There is an indoor basketball court in our school. 我們學校裡有一座室內籃球場。

in·doors [ˋɪnˋdorz]
🎧 *Track 2589*

adv. 在室內

▶ If it rains, the party will be held indoors instead. 如果下雨，派對就會改在室內舉行。

in·dulge [ɪnˋdʌldʒ]
🎧 *Track 2590*

v. 沉迷於；滿足；使高興；使享受一下；縱容；遷就

▶ I like to indulge myself with a hot bath after a long day's work. 我喜歡在一天漫長的工作後，泡個熱水澡享受一下。

in·dus·tri·al [ɪnˋdʌstrɪəl]
🎧 *Track 2591*

adj. 工業的

▶ Our headquarters is in Taipei while our factory is located in Tainan Technology Industrial Park. 我們的公司總部在台北，但我們的工廠位於台南科學工業園區。

industrial park 工業園區

in·dus·tri·al·ize 🎧 *Track 2592*
[ɪnˈdʌstrɪəlˌaɪz]
v. 使工業化
▶ South Korea is one of the most industrialized countries in the world.
南韓是世界上最工業化的國家之一。

in·dus·try [ˈɪndəstrɪ] 🎧 *Track 2593*
n. 工業；企業；行業

in·ev·i·ta·ble [ɪnˈɛvətəbl] 🎧 *Track 2594*
adj. 不可避免的
▶ The failure of his business was inevitable.
他的生意會失敗是必然的。

in·fant [ˈɪnfənt] 🎧 *Track 2595*
n. 嬰兒
▶ The infant is sleeping in his cradle.
嬰兒在搖籃裡睡覺。

in·fect [ɪnˈfɛkt] 🎧 *Track 2596*
v. 傳染；感染；使受影響；污染
▶ His enthusiasm for community service infected all of his family.
他對社區服務的熱忱感染了他所有的家人。

in·fec·tion [ɪnˈfɛkʃən] 🎧 *Track 2597*
n. 傳染；感染；傳染病
▶ A severe blood infection can result in organ failure and death.
嚴重的血液感染會導致器官衰竭和死亡。

補充片語
blood infection 血液感染；
result in 導致；
organ failure 器官衰竭

in·fer [ɪnˈfɝ] 🎧 *Track 2598*
v. 推斷；推論；意味著
▶ I inferred from what the doctor said that he's not doing well.
我從醫生所說的話推斷出他的情況不太樂觀。

in·fer·ence [ˈɪnfərəns] 🎧 *Track 2599*
n. 推論；推斷
▶ They have been late for two hours, and my inference is that they must have got lost.
他們已經遲到兩小時了，我推斷他們一定是迷路了。

in·fe·ri·or [ɪnˈfɪrɪə] 🎧 *Track 2600*
adj. （地位、品質）低等的；較差的；次於的
▶ Keep in mind that you are inferior to no one. 記住，你並不比任何人差。

補充片語
keep in mind 記住

n. （地位等）低於他人者；部下；次級品
▶ Mr. Williams is generous to his inferiors.
威廉斯先生對他的部下很寬厚。

in·fla·tion [ɪnˈfleʃən] 🎧 *Track 2601*
n. 通貨膨脹
▶ The government is urged to take measures to restrain inflation.
政府被催促為遏制通貨膨脹採取措施。

in·flu·ence [ˈɪnfluəns] 🎧 *Track 2602*
n. 影響；作用；影響力；**v.** 影響

in·flu·en·tial [ˌɪnfluˈɛnʃəl] 🎧 *Track 2603*
adj. 有影響力的；有權勢的
▶ He believed that his influential father would get him out of jail.
他相信他那有權勢的父親會將他弄出監獄。

in·form [ɪnˈfɔrm] 🎧 *Track 2604*
v. 通知
▶ Please inform me of any changes in your schedule.
如果您的行程有任何異動請通知我。

in·for·mal [ɪnˈfɔrml] 🎧 *Track 2605*
adj. 非正式的
▶ It's an informal party. Just wear your casual clothes.
這是個非正式的派對。穿輕便的衣服就好。

in·for·ma·tion 🎧 *Track 2606*
[ˌɪnfəˈmeʃən]
n. 資料；資訊；消息

in·for·ma·tive 🎧 *Track 2607*
[ɪnˈfɔrmətɪv]
adj. 情報的；教育性的
▶ Their children are only allowed to watch informative TV programs.
他們的小孩只能看教育性的電視節目。

in·formed [ɪnˈfɔrmd] 🎧 *Track 2608*
adj. 消息靈通的；根據情報的；有教養或見識的；收到通知的
▶ I wasn't informed of the cancellation of the meeting.
我沒有收到會議取消的通知。

in·gre·di·ent [ɪnˈgridɪənt] 🎧 *Track 2609*
n. 組成部分；原料；（構成）要素
▶ All dishes in our restaurant are cooked with natural, organic and fresh ingredients.
我們餐廳所有的菜餚都是以天然、有機且新鮮的原料烹煮的。

in·hab·i·tant 🎧 *Track 2610*
[ɪnˈhæbətənt]
n. 居民；居住者；棲息的動物
▶ The earliest inhabitants of this place are Indians. 這裡最早的居民是印第安人。

in·her·it [ɪnˈhɛrɪt] 🎧 *Track 2611*
v. 繼承；遺傳；成為繼承人；獲得遺傳
▶ My baby inherited his father's double eyelids and my tall nose. 我的寶寶遺傳了他爸爸的雙眼皮和我的高鼻子。

i·ni·tial [ɪˈnɪʃəl] 🎧 *Track 2612*
adj. 開始的，最初的
▶ They finally took the initial step toward formal negotiation.
他們終於踏出正式協商的第一步。

n. 首字母
▶ The painter signed his initials on each of his paintings. 畫家在他每一幅畫作上都簽下他名字的首字母。

v. 簽姓名的首字母於
▶ The painter initialed the painting T.W.Y.
畫家在畫作上簽下姓名的首字母T.W.Y。

in·ject [ɪnˈdʒɛkt] 🎧 *Track 2613*
v. 注射；插話；投入

▶ The nurse is injecting the patient with antibiotics. 護士正在為病患注射抗生素。

in·jec·tion [ɪnˈdʒɛkʃən] 🎧 *Track 2614*
n. 注射；注射劑；引入；投入；（人造衛星）射入軌道
▶ We will give you an injection to reduce inflammation. 我們會幫你打消炎針。

in·jure [ˈɪndʒɚ] 🎧 *Track 2615*
v. 使受傷
▶ The man was seriously injured in the car accident. 男子在車禍中受了重傷。

in·jured [ˈɪndʒɚd] 🎧 *Track 2616*
adj. 受傷的
▶ I can't play the piano with my injured fingers. 我無法用受傷的手指彈鋼琴。

in·ju·ry [ˈɪndʒɚrɪ] 🎧 *Track 2617*
n. 傷害；損害

ink [ɪŋk] 🎧 *Track 2618*
n. 墨水

inn [ɪn] 🎧 *Track 2619*
n. 小旅館
▶ He stayed in an old inn in the middle of nowhere last night.
他昨晚睡在偏遠地區的一間老舊的小旅館裡。

in·ner [ˈɪnɚ] 🎧 *Track 2620*
adj. 內部的；裡面的；核心的；精神的；內心的；隱晦的
▶ An inner voice warned him against trusting that man.
一個內在的聲音警告他不要相信那個男人。

in·no·cence [ˈɪnəsns] 🎧 *Track 2621*
n. 無罪
▶ He tried to convince me of his innocence.
他試圖讓我相信他是清白的。

in·no·cent [ˈɪnəsnt] 🎧 *Track 2622*
adj. 無辜的；無罪的；清白的；天真的；單純的；無害的
▶ The suspect claimed himself innocent.
嫌犯聲稱自己是無辜的。

※灰色單字為英檢初級必備單字

in·put [`ɪn͵pʊt]　🎧 Track 2623
n. 投入；輸入
▶ To reach our goals, we need more input from all of you. 為了達到我們的目標，我們需要你們所有人更多的投入。

v. 將⋯⋯輸入
▶ I have to input the latest data into the computer.
我必須將最新的數據資料輸入電腦。

in·quire [ɪn`kwaɪr]　🎧 Track 2624
=en·quire
v. 訊問；查問；調查
▶ The police promised to inquire into the incident. 警方承諾會調查這件事。

in·quir·y [ɪn`kwaɪrɪ]　🎧 Track 2625
=en·quir·y
n. 詢問；打聽；質詢；調查；探索
▶ Should you have any questions, please call our customer service center to make your inquiries.
萬一您有任何問題，請致電我們的顧客服務中心詢問。

in·sect [`ɪnsɛkt]　🎧 Track 2626
n. 昆蟲

in·sert [ɪn`sɝt]　🎧 Track 2627
v. 插入；嵌入
▶ You have to insert the key card to open the door. 你必須插入鑰匙卡才能打開門。

in·side [`ɪn`saɪd]　🎧 Track 2628
prep. 在⋯⋯裡面；**adv.** 在裡面；往裡面
n. 裡面；內部；內側

in·sist [ɪn`sɪst]　🎧 Track 2629
v. 堅持

in·spect [ɪn`spɛkt]　🎧 Track 2630
v. 檢查；審查；檢閱；進行檢查
▶ The mobile mechanic carefully inspected the tires for leaks.
汽車維修員仔細地檢查輪胎，看看是否有漏隙。

in·spec·tor [ɪn`spɛktɚ]　🎧 Track 2631
n. 檢查員；視察員；督察員
▶ The tax inspectors found that the bank had helped their wealthy clients dodge taxes.
稅務稽察員發現該銀行幫他們有錢的客戶逃漏稅。

（補充片語）

tax inspector　稅務稽察員

in·spi·ra·tion [͵ɪnspə`reʃən]　🎧 Track 2632
n. 靈感；鼓舞人心的人事物；吸入、吸氣
▶ A sudden inspiration came to him, so he quickly sat down and started writing.
他突然有了一個靈感，於是很快地坐下來開始寫作。

in·spire [ɪn`spaɪr]　🎧 Track 2633
v. 鼓舞；激勵

in·stall [ɪn`stɔl]　🎧 Track 2634
v. 安裝；設置；安頓
▶ The software you need is already installed.
你需要的軟體已經安裝好了。

in·stance [`ɪnstəns]　🎧 Track 2635
n. 例子；實例

in·stant [`ɪnstənt]　🎧 Track 2636
adj. 立即的；緊迫的；速食的
n. 剎那；頃刻

in·stead [ɪn`stɛd]　🎧 Track 2637
adv. 作為替代；反而；卻
▶ He didn't go to the office, but went to the Internet café instead.
他沒有去公司，反而去了網咖。

in·stinct [`ɪnstɪŋkt]　🎧 Track 2638
n. 本能；天性；直覺
▶ I decided to follow my instincts and take the job.
我決定要跟隨我的直覺，接受那份工作。

in·sti·tute [`ɪnstətjut]　🎧 Track 2639
n. 學會；協會；（專科性的）學校；（教師的）講習會；機構

▶My brother will graduate from the Massachusetts Institute of Technology next year. 我哥哥明年將從麻省理工學院畢業。

(補充片語)

the Massachusetts Institute of Technology 麻省理工學院

in·sti·tu·tion 🎧 *Track 2640*
[ˌɪnstəˋtjuʃən]

n. 公共團體；機構；制度；習俗

▶Today, the institution of slavery still exists in some countries, such as Yemen.
現在有些國家，如葉門，仍存在著奴隸制度。

in·struc·tion [ɪnˋstrʌkʃən] 🎧 *Track 2641*

n. 教學；講授；教導；命令；指示；用法說明

▶Please follow the instructions in the manual when operating the machine.
操作本機器時請遵循手冊上的指令。

in·struc·tor [ɪnˋstrʌktɚ] 🎧 *Track 2642*

n. 教員；教練；指導者；大學講師

▶Angus is a computer instructor in our college. 安古斯是我們大學的電腦講師。

in·stru·ment 🎧 *Track 2643*
[ˋɪnstrəmənt]

n. 儀器；器具；樂器

in·sult [ɪnˋsʌlt] 🎧 *Track 2644*

n. 辱罵；侮辱

▶You shouldn't throw insults at your parents.
你不該辱罵自己的父母。

v. 侮辱；羞辱

▶The woman's husband always insults her in the presence of all.
那女人的先生總是當眾羞辱她。

(補充片語)

in the presence of all 當眾；在眾人面前

in·sur·ance [ɪnˋʃʊrəns] 🎧 *Track 2645*

n. 保險；保險契約；保險業；保險金；預防措施；安全保證

▶Everyone in this country needs health insurance because the medical costs are extremely high.
這個國家的每個人都需要健康保險，因為醫療費用極高。

in·tel·lec·tual 🎧 *Track 2646*
[ˌɪntlˋɛktʃʊəl]

adj. 智力的；理智的；需要智力的；智力發達的

▶People with intellectual disabilities may have difficulty in learning and functioning in everyday life.
有智力障礙的人可能在學習和日常生活運作上會有困難。

(補充片語)

intellectual disability 智力障礙；
have difficulty in... 在……有困難

n. 高智力的人；知識份子

▶Intellectuals are the eyes of our society.
知識份子是我們社會的眼睛。

in·tel·li·gence 🎧 *Track 2647*
[ɪnˋtɛlədʒəns]

n. 智慧；智能；理解力；情報

▶You're insulting my intelligence if you think I'll believe your lies.
如果你以為我會相信你的謊話，就是在污辱我的智慧。

in·tel·li·gent [ɪnˋtɛlədʒənt] 🎧 *Track 2648*

adj. 有才智的；聰明的；有理性的

in·tend [ɪnˋtɛnd] 🎧 *Track 2649*

v. 想要；打算

▶He intended to take revenge on the man who killed his father.
他打算報復那個殺害他父親的男子。

(補充片語)

take revenge on 對……報復

in·tense [ɪnˋtɛns] 🎧 *Track 2650*

adj. 強烈的；劇烈的；極度的

▶The intense backache is killing me.
劇烈的背痛簡直快要了我的命。

in·ten·si·fy [ɪnˋtɛnsəˌfaɪ] 🎧 *Track 2651*

v. 加強；增強；加劇

▶The failure intensified his desire to succeed.
失敗加強了他想成功的渴望。

in·ten·sive [ɪnˋtɛnsɪv] 🎧 *Track 2652*

adj. 加強的；密集的；特別護理的；集約栽培的

Aa
Bb
Cc
Dd
Ee
Ff
Gg
Hh
Ii
Jj
Kk
Ll
Mm
Nn
Oo
Pp
Qq
Rr
Ss
Tt
Uu
Vv
Ww
Xx
Yy
Zz

▶ The patient needs intensive care.
這個病患需要重病特別護理。

in·ten·tion [ɪnˈtɛnʃən] 🎧 *Track 2653*
n. 意圖
▶ I had no intension to overhear your conversation.
我無意偷聽妳們的談話。

in·ter·act [ˌɪntəˈrækt] 🎧 *Track 2654*
v. 互動；互相作用；互相影響；交流
▶ Many parents have no idea how to interact with their teenage children. 很多父母不知道該怎麼跟他們十幾歲的孩子互動。

in·terest [ˈɪntərɪst] 🎧 *Track 2655*
n. 興趣；愛好；**v.** 使感興趣；使發生興趣

in·terest·ed [ˈɪntərɪstɪd] 🎧 *Track 2656*
adj. 感興趣的

in·terest·ing [ˈɪntərɪstɪŋ] 🎧 *Track 2657*
adj. 有趣的
▶ She's a very interesting person. I like spending time with her.
她是個很有趣的人。我很喜歡跟她在一起。

in·ter·fere [ˌɪntəˈfɪr] 🎧 *Track 2658*
v. 妨礙；干預；干涉
▶ Please don't interfere in our family affairs.
請不要干涉我們的家務事。

in·ter·fer·ence [ˌɪntəˈfɪrəns] 🎧 *Track 2659*
n. 阻礙；抵觸；干擾；干預
▶ Leave them alone. Our interference will just make things worse.
別管他們。我們的干預只會讓事情變得更糟。

(補充片語)

leave alone 避免擾亂；不干涉

in·ter·me·di·ate [ˌɪntəˈmidɪet] 🎧 *Track 2660*
adj. 居中的；中等程度的；中型的
▶ I need to rent an intermediate car during my stay in Paris.
我在停留巴黎的期間需要租用一台中型車。

in·ter·nal [ɪnˈtɜnl] 🎧 *Track 2661*
adj. 內部的；內在的；固有的；國內的；內政的；體內的
▶ Untreated internal bleeding may result in death. 未經治療的的內出血可能會導致死亡。

in·ter·na·tion·al [ˌɪntəˈnæʃənl] 🎧 *Track 2662*
adj. 國際的

In·ter·net [ˈɪntəˌnɛt] 🎧 *Track 2663*
n. 網路

in·ter·pret [ɪnˈtɜprɪt] 🎧 *Track 2664*
v. 解釋；說明；理解；口譯；做翻譯
▶ I was introduced to a master who specialized in interpreting dreams.
有人向我介紹一個專門解夢的大師。

in·ter·pre·ta·tion [ɪnˌtɜprɪˈteʃən] 🎧 *Track 2665*
n. 解釋；說明；翻譯；口譯；詮釋
▶ If it weren't for your interpretation, I wouldn't be able to get the contract from the foreign client. 要不是有你的翻譯，我是不可能拿到這外國客戶的合約的。

in·ter·pret·er [ɪnˈtɜprɪtə] 🎧 *Track 2666*
n. 口譯員；翻譯員
▶ Our company is looking for an English-French interpreter.
我們公司正在找一名英法文口譯員。

in·ter·rupt [ˌɪntəˈrʌpt] 🎧 *Track 2667*
v. 打斷

in·ter·val [ˈɪntəvl] 🎧 *Track 2668*
n. 間隔；距離；（音樂會等的）中場休息時間
▶ You must wait outside until the interval.
你在中場休息時間之前都必須在外面等候。

in·ter·view [ˈɪntəˌvju] 🎧 *Track 2669*
n. 訪談；面談；接見；**v.** 會見；訪談；採訪

in·ti·mate [ˈɪntəmɪt] 🎧 *Track 2670*
adj. 親密的；熟悉的；氣氛融洽的；精通的；私密的
▶ They seem to be very intimate.
他們看起來似乎很親密。

n. 至交；密友
▶ Jennifer is the only intimate that I have.
珍妮佛是我所擁有的唯一個至交。

in·to [`ɪntu] 🎧 *Track 2671*
prep. 到……裡；進入到；成為

in·tro·duce [ˌɪntrə`djus] 🎧 *Track 2672*
v. 介紹

in·tro·duc·tion [ˌɪntrə`dʌkʃən] 🎧 *Track 2673*
n. 介紹；正是引見；
▶ I was asked to make a self-introduction.
我被要求做自我介紹。

in·trude [ɪn`trud] 🎧 *Track 2674*
v. 侵入；闖入；打擾
▶ Please do not intrude into other people's property. 請不要闖入別人的地盤。

in·trud·er [ɪn`trudə] 🎧 *Track 2675*
n. 侵入者；闖入者；干擾者
▶ Two intruders broke into their house.
兩名武裝入侵者闖入他們的房子。

in·vade [ɪn`ved] 🎧 *Track 2676*
v. 侵入；侵略；侵犯；大批進入；侵襲
▶ You're no right to invade my privacy.
你無權侵犯我的隱私。

in·va·sion [ɪn`veʒən] 🎧 *Track 2677*
n. 入侵；侵略；侵犯；侵佔
▶ I would not tolerate any invasion of my privacy. 我不容許任何侵犯我隱私的行為。

in·vent [ɪn`vɛnt] 🎧 *Track 2678*
v. 發明

in·ven·tion [ɪn`vɛnʃən] 🎧 *Track 2679*
n. 發明；創造；發明物；發明才能
▶ Necessity is the mother of invention.
需要是發明之母。

in·ven·tor [ɪn`vɛntə] 🎧 *Track 2680*
n. 發明者
▶ The inventor of the cellphone must be a genius. 發明手機的人一定是個天才。

in·vest [ɪn`vɛst] 🎧 *Track 2681*
v. 投資
▶ It is unwise to invest all your money in the stock market.
把所有的錢都拿來投資股票是很不明智的。

in·ves·ti·gate [ɪn`vɛstə.get] 🎧 *Track 2682*
v. 調查

in·vest·ment [ɪn`vɛstmənt] 🎧 *Track 2683*
n. 投資；投資額；投資物；（時間、精神的）投入
▶ His father made a large investment.
他的父親做了巨額的投資。

in·vest·or [ɪn`vɛstə] 🎧 *Track 2684*
n. 投資者；出資者
▶ We have found 20 investors.
我們已經找到二十個投資者。

in·vis·i·ble [ɪn`vɪzəbl] 🎧 *Track 2685*
adj. 看不見的
▶ Germs are invisible to our naked eyes.
用我們的肉眼是看不到細菌的。

in·vi·ta·tion [ˌɪnvə`teʃən] 🎧 *Track 2686*
n. 邀請；邀請函；請帖

in·vite [ɪn`vaɪt] 🎧 *Track 2687*
v. 邀請

in·volve [ɪn`vɑlv] 🎧 *Track 2688*
v. 使捲入；連累；牽涉；需要；包含
▶ Please don't involve me in your dispute.
請不要把我牽扯入你們的爭端裡。

in·volved [ɪn`vɑlvd] 🎧 *Track 2689*
adj. 複雜的；有關的
▶ I am not involved in that bribery scandal.
我跟那件行賄醜聞沒有關係。

IQ [`aɪ`kju] 🎧 *Track 2690*
n. 智力商數
▶ Galileo Galilei had an IQ of 185.
伽利略擁有185的智商。

※灰色單字為英檢初級必備單字

i·ron [ˈaɪɚn] 🎧 *Track 2691*
n. 鐵；鐵質；熨斗；**v.** 用熨斗燙平

i·ron·y [ˈaɪrənɪ] 🎧 *Track 2692*
n. 反語；冷嘲；諷刺
▶ The great irony was that the marriage expert's marriage ended in divorce. 最諷刺的是，那個婚姻專家的婚姻以離婚終結。

ir·reg·u·lar [ɪˈrɛgjələ] 🎧 *Track 2693*
adj. 不規則的
▶ Irregular bowel movements are a warning sign of colon cancer.
不規律的排便是大腸癌的警訊。

ir·ri·tate [ˈɪrəˌtet] 🎧 *Track 2694*
v. 使惱怒；使煩躁；使難受
▶ Those comments did irritate me a bit.
那些評論的確讓我有點不爽。

is [ɪz] 🎧 *Track 2695*
v. 是（用於第三人稱單數現在式）

is·land [ˈaɪlənd] 🎧 *Track 2696*
n. 島；島嶼

isle [aɪl] 🎧 *Track 2697*
n. 小島
▶ The isle is uninhabited. 這小島已經無人居住。

is·n't [ˈɪznt] 🎧 *Track 2698*
abbr. 不是（is not的縮寫）

i·so·late [ˈaɪsḷˌet] 🎧 *Track 2699*
v. 使孤立
▶ Patients infected with Ebola were supposed to be completely isolated.
感染伊波拉病毒的病患都應受到完全的隔離。

i·so·la·tion [ˌaɪsḷˈeʃən] 🎧 *Track 2700*
n. 隔離；孤立；脫離
▶ Those who were infected with MERS had been taken off to the isolation wards.
那些感染MERS的人已經被送到隔離病房了。

is·sue [ˈɪʃʊ] 🎧 *Track 2701*
n. 發行物；發行量；問題；爭議
▶ It has been an issue for years.
這多年來一直是個爭議。

v. 發行；發佈；由……產生；使流出；核發
▶ If you have been issued a Working Holiday visa before, you can't apply again.
如果你過去曾被核發過打工度假簽證，你就永遠不能再次申請。

it [ɪt] 🎧 *Track 2702*
pron. 它；牠

itch [ɪtʃ] 🎧 *Track 2703*
v. 發癢；渴望
▶ My nose itches all the time.
我的鼻子總是發癢。

n. 癢；渴望
▶ I have an itch on my back. 我背很癢。

i·tem [ˈaɪtəm] 🎧 *Track 2704*
n. 項目；品項

it'll [ˈɪtl] 🎧 *Track 2705*
abbr. 它會（it will的縮寫）

its [ɪts] 🎧 *Track 2706*
det. 它的；牠的

it's [ɪts] 🎧 *Track 2707*
abbr. 它是（it is的縮寫）

it·self [ɪtˈsɛlf] 🎧 *Track 2708*
pron. 它自己；牠自己

I've [aɪv] 🎧 *Track 2709*
abbr. 我已、我有（I have的縮寫）

i·vo·ry [ˈaɪvərɪ] 🎧 *Track 2710*
n. 象牙；象牙色；象牙製品
▶ Elephants were killed for their ivory.
大象因為象牙而遭殺害。

adj. 象牙的；象牙製的；象牙色的
▶ The bride was in her ivory wedding dress.
新娘穿著她象牙色的結婚禮服。

i·vy [ˈaɪvɪ] 🎧 *Track 2711*
n. 常春藤
▶ The house is completely covered in ivy.
那棟房子完全被常春藤包覆住。

Jj

通過中級英文檢定者的英文能力：

 聽　在日常生活中，能聽懂一般的會話；能大致聽懂公共場所廣播、氣象報告及廣告等。在工作時，能聽懂簡易的產品介紹與操作說明。能大致聽懂外籍人士的談話及詢問。

 讀　在日常生活中，能閱讀短文、故事、私人信件、廣告、傳單、簡介及使用說明等。在工作時，能閱讀工作須知、公告、操作手冊、例行的文件、傳真、電報等。

 寫　能寫簡單的書信、故事及心得等。對於熟悉且與個人經歷相關的主題，能以簡易的文字表達。

 說　在日常生活中，能以簡易英語交談或描述一般事物，能介紹自己的生活作息、工作、家庭、經歷等，並可對一般話題陳述看法。在工作時，能進行簡單的答詢，並與外籍人士交談溝通。

本書除包含官方公佈的中級4,947單字外，更精挑了近400個滿分必學的高手單字。同時，在片語的挑選、例句的使用上，皆依上述英檢官方公佈之能力範疇做設計，難度適中、不偏離考試主題。發音部分則是自然發音＆KK音標雙管齊下，搭配MP3以「分解／完整」方式錄音，給你最多元有效的學習手段，怎麼記都可以，想忘掉都好難！

---

jack·et [`dʒækɪt]　🎧 *Track 2712*
n. 夾克；上衣

jade [dʒed]　🎧 *Track 2713*
n. 翡翠；玉；玉製品；綠玉色
▶ The bracelet is made of jade.
這只手環是玉製的。

adj. 玉的；玉製的；綠玉色的
▶ My mother bought me a jade bracelet.
我媽買了一個玉鐲子給我。

jail [dʒel]　🎧 *Track 2714*
n. 監獄
▶ His son is in jail for stealing money.
他兒子因為偷錢而坐牢。

v. 監禁
▶ He will be jailed for the rest of his life.
他一輩子都得被關在牢裡了。

jam [dʒæm]　🎧 *Track 2715*
v. 塞進；塞住；堵住；使擠滿

▶ Hundreds of people jammed into the store on the first day of the sale. 好幾百人在拍賣的第一天就把商店擠得水洩不通。

jan·i·tor [`dʒænɪtə]　🎧 *Track 2716*
n. 門警；看門人；門房；照看房屋的工友
▶ According to the curfew policy, the janitor of the school dorm will lock the gate at 12 a.m.
根據宵禁規定，學校宿舍的門房會在凌晨十二點鎖上大門。

Ja·nu·ar·y [`dʒænjʊˏɛrɪ]　🎧 *Track 2717*
=Jan
n. 一月

Ja·pan [dʒə`pæn]　🎧 *Track 2718*
n. 日本

Jap·a·nese [ˏdʒæpə`niz]　🎧 *Track 2719*
n. 日語；日本人
adj. 日本的；日本人的；日語的

jar [dʒɑr] 🎧 *Track 2720*
n. 罐；罈（寬口的）瓶
▶ She gave us a jar of homemade jam as a present.
她送我們一罐自製的果醬作為禮物。

jas·mine [`dʒæsmɪn] 🎧 *Track 2721*
n. 茉莉花；茉莉花茶；淡黃色
▶ Drinking a cup of jasmine tea before bed can help you sleep better.
在上床前喝一杯茉莉花茶能幫助你睡得更好。

jaw [dʒɔ] 🎧 *Track 2722*
n. 下巴；頜；顎
▶ My jaw dropped when the president showed up in our restaurant.
當總統出現在我們的餐廳時，我吃驚地下巴都掉下來了。

(補充片語)

one's jaw drop （因吃驚而）下巴掉下來

v. 閒聊；嘮叨；數落
▶ The girls can jaw with each other all day if you don't stop them. 如果你不阻止那些女孩子的話，她們可以聊上一整天。

(相關片語)

wag one's jaw 喋喋不休
▶ Could you stop wagging your jaw for a few minutes?
你可以安靜幾分鐘不要嘮叨嗎？

jazz [dʒæz] 🎧 *Track 2723*
n. 爵士樂；爵士舞

jeal·ous [`dʒɛləs] 🎧 *Track 2724*
adj. 妒忌的；吃醋的

jeal·ous·y [`dʒɛləsɪ] 🎧 *Track 2725*
n. 妒忌；猜忌
▶ We tolerate no jealousy in this house.
我們家不容許互相猜忌。

jeans [dʒinz] 🎧 *Track 2726*
n. 牛仔褲

jeep [dʒip] 🎧 *Track 2727*
n. 吉普車

jel·ly [`dʒɛlɪ] 🎧 *Track 2728*
n. 果凍；果醬；膠狀物
▶ He spread some grape jelly on his bread.
他在麵包上抹了一些葡萄果醬。

jet [dʒɛt] 🎧 *Track 2729*
n. 噴射機；噴射器；噴出物
▶ It is quite common to travel by jet nowadays.
現在搭飛機旅行是很普通的一件事。

v. 噴出；射出；搭飛機旅行
▶ How long does it take to jet from Tokyo to New York?
從東京搭飛機到紐約要多久？

(相關片語)

jet lag 時差
▶ I have just returned home from Los Angeles and I'm still suffering from jet lag.
我才剛從洛杉磯回來，現在還在受時差所苦。

jew·el [`dʒuəl] 🎧 *Track 2730*
n. 寶石；寶石飾物；首飾
▶ Everything in my jewel case was gone.
我珠寶盒裡所有的東西都不見了。

(補充片語)

jewel case 珠寶盒

jew·el·ery [`dʒuəlrɪ] 🎧 *Track 2731*
n. 珠寶
▶ You look beautiful even without jewelry.
即使不戴珠寶首飾，妳看起來還是很美。

jin·gle [`dʒɪŋgl] 🎧 *Track 2732*
v. 發出叮噹聲
▶ The wind chimes jingled in the breeze.
風鈴在微風中發出叮叮噹噹的聲音。

n. 叮噹聲
▶ The jingle of the bells woke me from my sleep.
鈴鐺的叮鈴聲把我從睡夢中喚醒。

job [dʒɑb] 🎧 *Track 2733*
n. 工作；分內事情；成果

jog [dʒɑg] 🎧 *Track 2734*
v. 慢跑

join [dʒɔɪn]　🎧 *Track 2735*
v. 加入；參加

joint [dʒɔɪnt]　🎧 *Track 2736*
adj. 聯合的；連接的；合辦的
n. 接合點；關節

joke [dʒok]　🎧 *Track 2737*
n. 笑話；玩笑；**v.** 開玩笑

jol·ly [`dʒɑlɪ]　🎧 *Track 2738*
adj. 快活的；高興的；令人愉快的；歡樂的
▶ We had a jolly evening.
　我們度過了愉快的一晚。

v. 用好話哄勸；用好話使高興；開玩笑；戲弄
▶ We jollied Mom into going shopping with us.
　我們哄媽媽跟我們一起去逛街。

jour·nal [`dʒɝnl]　🎧 *Track 2739*
n. 日誌；日報；雜誌；期刊
▶ He kept a journal of his travels across Europe, and published it when he returned.
　他將在歐洲各處旅行的經歷寫成日誌，並在回國後出版。

相關片語
medical journal　醫學期刊
▶ I read a research report about the Ebola virus in a medical journal.
　我在一本醫學期刊上讀到一篇關於伊波拉病毒的研究報告。

jour·nal·ist [`dʒɝnəlɪst]　🎧 *Track 2740*
n. 新聞工作者；新聞記者

jour·ney [`dʒɝnɪ]　🎧 *Track 2741*
n. 旅行；旅程；行程
▶ I am planning for our two-day journey to Kenting this weekend.
　我正在為我們這週末兩天的墾丁之旅做計劃。

v. 旅行
▶ He journeys a lot.
　他經常旅行。

相關片語
break one's journey　中途下車

▶ We'll break our journey at York.
　我們將在約克中途下車。

joy [dʒɔɪ]　🎧 *Track 2742*
n. 歡樂；樂趣

joy·ful [`dʒɔɪfəl]　🎧 *Track 2743*
adj. 高興的
▶ I have something joyful to share with you.
　我有件高興的事情要跟你分享。

judge [dʒʌdʒ]　🎧 *Track 2744*
n. 法官；裁判；**v.** 判決；判斷；評斷

judge·ment [`dʒʌdʒmənt]　🎧 *Track 2745*
n. 審判；判斷；判斷力；看法
▶ Don't let your feelings influence your judgment.
　不要讓感情影響你的判斷。

jug [dʒʌg]　🎧 *Track 2746*
n. 水罐；甕；壺
▶ He gulped down a jug of beer.
　他一口喝光一整罐啤酒。

juice [dʒus]　🎧 *Track 2747*
n. 果汁

juic·y [`dʒusɪ]　🎧 *Track 2748*
adj. 多汁的
▶ The fried chicken was so juicy and delicious that I just couldn't stop eating.
　那炸雞非常多汁美味，我吃得停不下來。

Ju·ly [dʒu`laɪ]　🎧 *Track 2749*
n. 七月

jump [dʒʌmp]　🎧 *Track 2750*
v. 跳；**n.** 跳躍；跳一步的距離

June [dʒun]　🎧 *Track 2751*
n. 六月

jun·gle [`dʒʌŋgl]　🎧 *Track 2752*
n. 叢林
▶ The lion is the king of the jungle.
　獅子是叢林之王。

※灰色單字為英檢初級必備單字

ju·ni·or [`dʒunjɚ]　🎧 Track 2753

adj. 年紀較輕的；資淺的；地位較低的；大學三年級的

▶ Uncle John is junior to my father by three years.
約翰叔叔比我父親小三歲。

n. 較年少者；較資淺者；等級較低者；晚輩；大學三年級生

▶ My son is a college junior.
我兒子是大學三年級生。

junk [dʒʌŋk]　🎧 Track 2754

n. 廢棄的舊物；垃圾

▶ I never eat junk food.
我從不吃垃圾食物。

相關片語

junk mail　垃圾郵件

▶ All junk mails will go straight to trash.
所有的垃圾郵件都會直接進入垃圾桶。

ju·ry [`dʒʊrɪ]　🎧 Track 2755

n. 陪審團

▶ The jury didn't believe what he said.
陪審團不相信他所說的話。

just [dʒʌst]　🎧 Track 2756

adv. 僅；只是；正好

jus·tice [`dʒʌstɪs]　🎧 Track 2757

n. 正義；公平；正當的理由；合法；司法；審判

▶ Anyone who commits a crime should be subjected to justice.
罪人就應受法律制裁。

相關片語

bring sb. to justice　使某人受到制裁；使某人歸案受審

▶ The police promised her that they would bring the murder to justice.
警方向她承諾，會將兇手緝捕歸案。

jus·ti·fy [`dʒʌstə͵faɪ]　🎧 Track 2758

v. 證明無罪；證明……為正當；為……辯駁

▶ His lawyer tried to justify his homicide.
他的律師企圖要辯駁他殺人是有正當理由的。

✦Note

Kk

通過中級英文檢定者的英文能力：

 聽
在日常生活中，能聽懂一般的會話；能大致聽懂公共場所廣播、氣象報告及廣告等。在工作時，能聽懂簡易的產品介紹與操作說明。能大致聽懂外籍人士的談話及詢問。

 讀
在日常生活中，能閱讀短文、故事、私人信件、廣告、傳單、簡介及使用說明等。在工作時，能閱讀工作須知、公告、操作手冊、例行的文件、傳真、電報等。

 寫
能寫簡單的書信、故事及心得等。對於熟悉且與個人經歷相關的主題，能以簡易的文字表達。

 說
在日常生活中，能以簡易英語交談或描述一般事物，能介紹自己的生活作息、工作、家庭、經歷等，並可對一般話題陳述看法。在工作時，能進行簡單的答詢，並與外籍人士交談溝通。

本書除包含官方公佈的中級4,947單字外，更精挑了近400個滿分必學的高手單字。同時，在片語的挑選、例句的使用上，皆依上述英檢官方公佈之能力範疇做設計，難度適中、不偏離考試主題。發音部分則是自然發音＆KK音標雙管齊下，搭配MP3以「分解／完整」方式錄音，給你最多元有效的學習手段，怎麼記都可以，想忘掉都好難！

---

kan·ga·roo [ˌkæŋɡəˋru]　🎧 *Track 2759*
n. 袋鼠

Kaoh·siung [ˋkaʊˋʃɔŋ]　🎧 *Track 2760*
n. 高雄

keen [kin]　🎧 *Track 2761*
adj. 熱衷的；渴望的，極想的
▶ He is keen to set off as soon as possible.
他很渴望及早出發。

keep [kip]　🎧 *Track 2762*
v. 保持；持有；繼續不斷

keep·er [ˋkipɚ]　🎧 *Track 2763*
n. 飼養人；保管者；看守人
▶ The keeper was killed by the tiger when he was trying to feed it.
保育員在正要餵食老虎時，被老虎給咬死了。

ketch·up [ˋkɛtʃəp]　🎧 *Track 2764*
n. 番茄醬

ket·tle [ˋkɛtl̩]　🎧 *Track 2765*
n. 水壺
▶ There is no water in the kettle.
水壺裡面沒有水。

相關片語
a fine kettle of fish 一蹋糊塗、亂七八糟；一團糟
▶ It's my birthday party, but you have made a fine kettle of fish of it.
這是我的生日派對，但你卻把它搞得一團糟。

key [ki]　🎧 *Track 2766*
n. 鑰匙；關鍵；**adj.** 主要的；關鍵的

key·board [ˋkiˌbord]　🎧 *Track 2767*
n. 鍵盤
▶ I would like to buy a wireless keyboard.
我想要買一個無線鍵盤。

kick [kɪk]　🎧 *Track 2768*
v. 踢；**n.** 踢；一時的愛好或狂熱

189

kid [kɪd] 🎧 *Track 2769*
n. 小孩；年輕人

kid·nap [`kɪdnæp] 🎧 *Track 2770*
v. 誘拐；綁架
▶ It turned out that the boy was kidnapped by his uncle.
結果那男孩竟是被他自己的叔叔所綁架的。

kid·ney [`kɪdnɪ] 🎧 *Track 2771*
n. 腎臟
▶ He saved his father's life by donating one of his kidneys to him.
他捐了一個腎臟給父親，救了父親一命。

kill [kɪl] 🎧 *Track 2772*
v. 殺死；引起死亡

kil·o·gram [`kɪlə‚græm] 🎧 *Track 2773*
n. 公斤

kil·o·me·ter [`kɪlə‚mitə] 🎧 *Track 2774*
n. 公里

kin [kɪn] 🎧 *Track 2775*
n. 家族；親戚；同類
▶ I am no kin to that person.
我跟那個人沒有親屬關係。
adj. 有親屬關係的
▶ They are my stepfather's children. They are not kin to me.
他們是我繼父的孩子，跟我沒有親屬關係。

kind [kaɪnd] 🎧 *Track 2776*
adj. 親切的；有同情心的；**n.** 種類

kin·der·gar·ten [`kɪndə‚gɑrtn] 🎧 *Track 2777*
n. 幼稚園

kin·dle [`kɪndl] 🎧 *Track 2778*
v. 激起；點燃；煽動
▶ The history teacher kindled the students' interest in Ancient Egypt.
歷史老師激起了學生們對古埃及的興趣。

kind·ly [`kaɪndlɪ] 🎧 *Track 2779*
adj. 親切的；和藹的；善良的；宜人的

▶ His kindly smile relieved my discomforts.
他親切的笑容緩解了我的不安。
adv. 親切地；和藹地；好心地；令人愉快地
▶ A police officer kindly offered his help when I got lost.
我迷路時，一個警察好心地來幫助我。

kind·ness [`kaɪndnɪs] 🎧 *Track 2780*
n. 仁慈；好意；友好的行為；好心
▶ My mother always taught us to treat people with kindness and respect.
我母親總是教我們要待人以仁慈及尊敬。

king [kɪŋ] 🎧 *Track 2781*
n. 國王；某領域中最有勢力的人；大王

king·dom [`kɪŋdəm] 🎧 *Track 2782*
n. 王國

kiss [kɪs] 🎧 *Track 2783*
v./n. 親吻

kit [kɪt] 🎧 *Track 2784*
n. 工具箱；成套工具
▶ The plumber came with his kit.
水電工帶著他的工具箱來了。
相關片語
first aid kit 急救藥箱
▶ Every household should have a first aid kit.
每個家庭都應該要有一個急救藥箱。

kitch·en [`kɪtʃɪn] 🎧 *Track 2785*
n. 廚房

kite [kaɪt] 🎧 *Track 2786*
n. 風箏

kit·ten [`kɪtn] 🎧 *Track 2787*
n. 小貓

kit·ty [`kɪtɪ] 🎧 *Track 2788*
n. 小貓；貓咪

knee [ni] 🎧 *Track 2789*
n. 膝蓋；膝關節

kneel [nil] 🎧 *Track 2790*
v. 跪（下）

▶He knelt down in front of his girlfriend and proposed marriage.
他在女友面前跪下來，並向她求婚。

(補充片語)

kneel down 跪下；
propose marriage 求婚

knife [naɪf] 　🎧 *Track 2791*
n. 刀；刀子

knight [naɪt] 　🎧 *Track 2792*
n. 武士
▶The two knights were fighting each other in order to win the woman's heart.
兩位騎士為了贏得女子芳心而與對方搏鬥。

knit [nɪt] 　🎧 *Track 2793*
v. 編織
▶She is knitting a sweater for her son.
她正在為兒子織毛衣。

n. 編織衣物；編織法
▶I like sweater knits.
我喜歡穿編織毛衣。

knob [nɑb] 　🎧 *Track 2794*
n. 門把
▶He turned the knob and found the door was locked. 他轉動門把，發現門是鎖著的。

knock [nɑk] 　🎧 *Track 2795*
v. 敲；擊打

knot [nɑt] 　🎧 *Track 2796*
n. 結
▶It is amazing that you can tie a knot with your tongue.
你竟然會用舌頭打結，真是神奇。

v. 打結；綑綁
▶He could knot the shoelaces on his own when he was only three.
他在年僅三歲的時候就會自己綁鞋帶了。

know [no] 　🎧 *Track 2797*
v. 知道；認識

knowl·edge [`nɑlɪdʒ] 　🎧 *Track 2798*
n. 知識；學問；了解

knowl·edge·a·ble 　🎧 *Track 2799*
[`nɑlɪdʒəbl]
adj. 有知識的；博學的；有見識的
▶My father is knowledgeable about astronomy.
我父親對天文學有淵博的知識。

knuck·le [`nʌkl] 　🎧 *Track 2800*
n. 指（根）關節；（四足動物的）膝關節
▶He's got a minor cut over a knuckle.
他的指關節處有個小傷口。

(相關片語)

rap on the knuckle 責備；訓斥
▶My mother gave me a rap on the knuckle for being rude.
我媽因為我沒禮貌訓斥了我一頓。

ko·a·la [ko`ɑlə] 　🎧 *Track 2801*
n. 無尾熊

Ko·re·a [ko`riə] 　🎧 *Track 2802*
n. 韓國

Ko·re·an [ko`riən] 　🎧 *Track 2803*
adj. 韓國的；韓語的；韓國人的
n. 韓語；韓國人

KTV [ke-ti-vi] 　🎧 *Track 2804*
n. 卡拉OK

Aa
Bb
Cc
Dd
Ee
Ff
Gg
Hh
Ii
Jj
Kk
Ll
Mm
Nn
Oo
Pp
Qq
Rr
Ss
Tt
Uu
Vv
Ww
Xx
Yy
Zz

※灰色單字為英檢初級必備單字

Ll

通過中級英文檢定者的英文能力：

 在日常生活中，能聽懂一般的會話；能大致聽懂公共場所廣播、氣象報告及廣告等。在工作時，能聽懂簡易的產品介紹與操作說明。能大致聽懂外籍人士的談話及詢問。

 在日常生活中，能閱讀短文、故事、私人信件、廣告、傳單、簡介及使用說明等。在工作時，能閱讀工作須知、公告、操作手冊、例行的文件、傳真、電報等。

 能寫簡單的書信、故事及心得等。對於熟悉且與個人經歷相關的主題，能以簡易的文字表達。

 在日常生活中，能以簡易英語交談或描述一般事物，能介紹自己的生活作息、工作、家庭、經歷等，並可對一般話題陳述看法。在工作時，能進行簡單的答詢，並與外籍人士交談溝通。

本書除包含官方公佈的中級4,947單字外，更精挑了近400個滿分必學的高手單字。同時，在片語的挑選、例句的使用上，皆依上述英檢官方公佈之能力範疇做設計，難度適中、不偏離考試主題。發音部分則是自然發音&KK音標雙管齊下，搭配MP3以「分解／完整」方式錄音，給你最多元有效的學習手段，怎麼記都可以，想忘掉都好難！

---

lab [læb] 🎧 Track 2805
n. 實驗室
▶ The students are still working in the lab.
學生們還在實驗室裡工作。

la·bel [`lebḷ] 🎧 Track 2806
n. 貼紙；標籤
▶ All items with red labels are sold at 50% off.
所有貼有紅色標籤的商品都是以五折出售。

v. 貼標籤
▶ Young people nowadays are labeled as the "Strawberry Generation".
現在的年輕人被貼上「草莓族」的標籤。

la·bor [`lebɚ] 🎧 Track 2807
=la·bour（英式英文）
n. 勞工
▶ Labor shortage is the main problem that we should solve.
勞工短缺是我們主要應該要解決的問題。

v. 勞動；努力幹活；費力前進
▶ My father labored on the farm for the entire life. 我爸一輩子都在田裡辛苦地工作。

la·bora·tor·y [`læbrə‚tɔrɪ] 🎧 Track 2808
=lab
n. 實驗室
▶ The professor has been doing experiments in the chemistry laboratory all day.
教授已經在化學實驗室做實驗一整天了。

lace [les] 🎧 Track 2809
n. 鞋帶；帶子
▶ He squat down and tied his laces.
他蹲下來綁鞋帶。

v. 繫上；束緊
▶ He is already six, but he still can't lace his shoes.
他已經六歲了，卻還不會綁鞋帶。

lack [læk] 🎧 Track 2810
n. 缺少；不足；**v.** 缺乏，沒有

lad [læd] 🎧 *Track 2811*
n. 男孩，少年；小伙子；老弟，伙伴
▶ What's up, lad?
嘿，老弟！

lad·der [`lædə] 🎧 *Track 2812*
n. 梯子
▶ The man fell off the ladder while he was washing the windows.
男子在洗窗戶時，從梯子上摔了下來。

la·dy [`ledɪ] 🎧 *Track 2813*
n. 女士；小姐

la·dy·bird [`ledɪ‚bɜd] 🎧 *Track 2814*
n. 瓢蟲（英）

lad·y·bug [`ledɪ‚bʌg] 🎧 *Track 2815*
n. 瓢蟲（美）
▶ A ladybug just flew into my room.
有隻瓢蟲剛剛飛進我的房間了。

lag [læg] 🎧 *Track 2816*
v. 走得慢；落後；延遲
▶ The runner was getting tired and began to lag in the race.
跑者漸漸感到疲累，於是開始在賽程中落後。

n. 落後；遲滯；衰退
▶ I just returned from London and am still suffering from jet lag.
我才剛從倫敦回來，現在還在受時差所苦。

(補充片語)
suffer from 受……所苦；
jet lag 時差感（因時差所造成的生理遲滯現象）

lake [lek] 🎧 *Track 2817*
n. 湖

lamb [læm] 🎧 *Track 2818*
n. 小羊；羔羊

lame [lem] 🎧 *Track 2819*
adj. 跛腳的，瘸的；站不住腳的，沒有說服力的
▶ He made a lame excuse for his absence from work.
他為他的曠職編了一個很瘸腳的藉口。

(補充片語)
make an excuse 編造藉口；
absence from work 曠職

v. 使跛腳；使無力
▶ The terrible traffic accident lamed the young man for life. 那場可怕的交通意外讓這年輕男子終身殘廢了。

lamp [læmp] 🎧 *Track 2820*
n. 燈；燈具

land [lænd] 🎧 *Track 2821*
n. 陸地；土地；**v.** 登陸；降落

land·la·dy [`lænd‚ledɪ] 🎧 *Track 2822*
n. 女房東；女地主
▶ My landlady won't allow me to keep a pet in her apartment. 我的女房東不會答應讓我在她的公寓裡養寵物的。

land·lord [`lænd‚lɔrd] 🎧 *Track 2823*
n. 房東；地主
▶ My landlord raised my rent last month.
我的房東上個月調漲我的房租了。

land·mark [`lænd‚mɑrk] 🎧 *Track 2824*
n. 地標
▶ The building is the most famous landmark of the city. 這座大樓是這城市最有名的地標。

land·scape [`lænd‚skep] 🎧 *Track 2825*
n.（陸上的）風景；景色
▶ We enjoyed the beautiful landscape from the ferry.
我們從渡輪上欣賞美麗的路上風景。

v. 在陸上造景；從事景觀美化工作
▶ He hired an expert to have his front yard landscaped.
他請了一個專家來為他的前院造景。

land·slide [`lænd‚slaɪd] 🎧 *Track 2826*
n. 山崩；坍方；（選舉）壓倒性大勝利
▶ The candidate won the election by a landslide.
該候選人以壓倒性的勝利贏得選舉。

(相關片語)
mudflows and landslides 土石流

▶Residents in mountain areas need to be on guard against mudflows and landslides during the typhoon.
住在山區的民眾在颱風期間應留意土石流。

lane [len] 🎧 *Track 2827*
n. 小路；巷；車道；跑道
▶The café is located on a quiet lane.
那間咖啡館位於一個安靜的巷弄內。

lan·guage [`læŋgwɪdʒ] 🎧 *Track 2828*
n. 語言

lan·tern [`læntə-n] 🎧 *Track 2829*
n. 燈籠；提燈
▶The Lantern Festival is celebrated on the 15th day of the first lunar month.
元宵節是在農曆一月的第十五天。

Lant·ern Fes·tiv·al 🎧 *Track 2830*
[`læntə-n-`fɛstəv]
n. 元宵節

lap [læp] 🎧 *Track 2831*
n. （跑場的）一圈；（泳池的）一個來回
▶He fell behind on the first lap, but caught up with other runners soon after.
他在第一圈落後，但是不久之後就追上其他跑者了。

(補充片語)
fall behind 落後；
catch up 趕上；
soon after 不久之後

large [lardʒ] 🎧 *Track 2832*
adj. 大的

large·ly [`lardʒlɪ] 🎧 *Track 2833*
adv. 大部份的；主要地；大量地
▶J. K. Rowling is a British novelist largely known for her *Harry Potter* series.
J. K. 羅琳是個主要因其《哈利波特》系列著作而知名的英國小說家。

la·ser [`lezə-] 🎧 *Track 2834*
n. 雷射

▶She is undergoing laser surgery to remove the tattoo on her arm.
她將接受雷射手術以移除她手臂上的刺青。

(補充片語)
laser surgery 雷射外科手術

last [læst] 🎧 *Track 2835*
v. 持續
▶Their marriage didn't last long.
他們的婚姻並沒有持續很久。

late [let] 🎧 *Track 2836*
adj. 晚的；遲的；**adv.** 晚地

late·ly [`letlɪ] 🎧 *Track 2837*
adv. 近來
▶How have you been lately? 近來如何？

lat·er [`letə-] 🎧 *Track 2838*
adv. 較晚地；以後

lat·est [`letɪst] 🎧 *Track 2839*
adj. 最新的；最近的；最遲的

lat·i·tude [`lætə‚tjud] 🎧 *Track 2840*
n. 緯度
▶Taiwan has the same latitude as Macau.
台灣跟澳門是在同一個緯度。

lat·ter [`lætə-] 🎧 *Track 2841*
adj. 後面的；後半的；後者的；最近的
▶He remained single in his latter years.
他的後半生維持單身狀態。

laugh [læf] 🎧 *Track 2842*
v. 笑
n. 笑；笑聲；樂趣；令人發笑的人事物

laugh·ter [`læftə-] 🎧 *Track 2843*
n. 笑；笑聲
▶Laughter is the best medicine.
大笑是最好的藥劑。

launch [lɔntʃ] 🎧 *Track 2844*
v. 發射；使（船）下水；發動；開始從事；出版；投放市場
▶They plan to launch their new product next week.
他們計畫下週要讓新產品問世。

n. 發射；（船）下水；發行；投放市場

▶ The spokesman of the company just announced that they would put off the launch of their new product. 該公司的發言人剛剛宣布，他們將延遲新產品的上市。

（補充片語）

put off 延遲

laun·dry [`lɔndrɪ]　🎧 *Track 2845*
n. 洗衣店；待洗的衣服；洗好的衣服

▶ I have a lot of laundry to do today.
我今天有好多衣服要洗。

（相關片語）

do the laundry 洗衣服

▶ I do the laundry every other day.
我每兩天洗一次衣服。

la·va [`lɑvə]　🎧 *Track 2846*
n. 熔岩

▶ Lava from the volcano buried the whole village. 火山噴出的熔岩把整座村子都掩埋了。

la·va·tor·y [`lævə͵torɪ]
=toi·let　🎧 *Track 2847*
n. 廁所

▶ The lavatory is currently occupied.
廁所現在有人在用。

law [lɔ]　🎧 *Track 2848*
n. 法律

law·ful [`lɔfəl]　🎧 *Track 2849*
adj. 合法的

▶ Is it lawful to sell cigarettes to teenagers in your country?
在你們國家，賣菸給青少年是合法的嗎？

lawn [lɔn]　🎧 *Track 2850*
n. 草坪

▶ We need a mower to mow the lawn.
我們需要一台割草機來割草。

law·yer [`lɔjɚ]　🎧 *Track 2851*
n. 法律

lay [le]　🎧 *Track 2852*
v. 放；鋪設；產卵

lay·er [`leɚ]　🎧 *Track 2853*
n. 層；階層；地層

▶ The ozone layer above Earth serves as a shield from the harmful radiation emitted by the sun. 地球上方的臭氧層能有效阻隔太陽所發出的有害輻射。

（補充片語）

ozone layer 臭氧層

la·zy [`lezɪ]　🎧 *Track 2854*
adj. 懶惰的；懶洋洋的

lead [lid]　🎧 *Track 2855*
n. 鉛

▶ Long-term exposure to lead can cause fatal health problems. 長期暴露在鉛害的環境下會造成致命的健康問題。

lead·er [`lidɚ]　🎧 *Track 2856*
n. 領導者；領袖

lead·er·ship [`lidɚ͵ʃɪp]　🎧 *Track 2857*
n. 領袖特質

lead·ing [`lidɪŋ]　🎧 *Track 2858*
adj. 領導的；主要的；飾演主角的

▶ Giant is a Taiwanese bicycle manufacturer occupying the leading position in the cycle industry in the world.
捷安特是在全世界腳踏車工業執牛耳地位的台灣腳踏車製造商。

（補充片語）

occupy a leading position 執牛耳地位

leaf [lif]　🎧 *Track 2859*
n. 葉子

leaf·let [`liflɪt]　🎧 *Track 2860*
n. 傳單；單張印刷品

▶ Each leaflet contains five buy 1 get 1 free coupons.
每張傳單上都包含五張買一送一的優惠券。

league [lig]　🎧 *Track 2861*
n. 同盟；聯盟；聯合會；社團

▶ He was found to be privately in league with their enemy. 他被發現私下與敵人有勾結。

※灰色單字為英檢初級必備單字

補充片語
in league with 與……聯盟；與……勾結

leak [lik]　🎧 *Track 2862*
v. 滲漏；洩漏
▶ The bathroom faucet is leaking.
　浴室水管在漏水。

n. 漏洞；裂縫；漏出（水、電、瓦斯等）；
（秘密）洩漏
▶ A small leak will sink a great ship.
　一個小漏洞就能弄沉一艘大船。

lean [lin]　🎧 *Track 2863*
v. 傾斜；傾身；倚靠；依賴
▶ She felt a bit dizzy so she leaned her
　head against the window.
　她感到有點暈眩，所以把頭靠在窗上。

adj. 無脂肪的；精瘦的；貧瘠的；收益差的
▶ A lean dog shames his master.
　狗瘦主人羞。

leap [lip]　🎧 *Track 2864*
v. 跳；跳躍；迅速進行；立即著手
▶ Look before you leap.
　三思而後行（先看清楚再跳）。

n. 跳；跳躍；飛躍；躍進
▶ Their productivity has increased by leaps
　and bounds.
　他們的生產力快速地躍進。

補充片語
by leaps and bounds 快速地，非常迅速地

learn [lɝn]　🎧 *Track 2865*
v. 學習

learn·ed [`lɝnɪd]　🎧 *Track 2866*
adj. 有學問的；博學的；學術性的；透過學
習而獲得的
▶ He is a very learned man, yet he is rather
　modest.
　他是一個非常博學的人，但是卻相當謙虛。

learn·er [`lɝnɚ]　🎧 *Track 2867*
n. 學習者
▶ I don't have much work experience, but I
　am a quick learner.
　我沒有太多工作經驗，但我學得很快。

learn·ing [`lɝnɪŋ]　🎧 *Track 2868*
n. 學習；學問；學識
▶ A little learning is a dangerous thing.
　一知半解是件危險的事情。

least [list]　🎧 *Track 2869*
adv. 最少；最不；**adj.** 最少的；最不重要
的；**pron.** 最少；最少的東西；**n.** 最少；最
小

leath·er [`lɛðɚ]　🎧 *Track 2870*
n. 皮革；皮革製品
▶ This designer handbag is made of cow
　leather.
　這個設計師名牌手提包是牛皮製成的。

adj. 皮革製的；皮的
▶ He gave his leather shoes a polish before
　he put them on.
　他將皮鞋擦一擦才穿上它們。

leave [liv]　🎧 *Track 2871*
v. 離開；留下；**n.** 休假

lec·ture [`lɛktʃɚ]　🎧 *Track 2872*
n. 授課；演講；冗長的訓話；告誡；責備
▶ He was invited to give a lecture on modern
　art. 他受邀做一場關於現代藝術的演説。

v. 演講；講課；教訓；訓斥
▶ My father lectured me for not doing well
　on my tests.
　我爸因為我考試沒考好而把我訓了一頓。

補充片語
lecture sb. for sth. 為……訓斥某人
相關片語
read sb. a lecture 訓斥某人一頓
▶ My father read me a lecture for failing the
　test. 我爸因為我考試考砸了而訓了我一頓。

lec·tur·er [`lɛktʃərɚ]　🎧 *Track 2873*
n. 演講者；講師
▶ My father-in-law is a lecturer in English
　Literature.
　我的岳父是一位英國文學講師。

left [lɛft]　🎧 *Track 2874*
adj. 左邊的；**n.** 左邊；左側；**adv.** 向左地

leg [lɛg] 　🎧 *Track 2875*
n. 腳

le·gal [ˋligl] 　🎧 *Track 2876*
adj. 合法的

le·gend [ˋlɛdʒənd] 　🎧 *Track 2877*
n. 傳說；傳奇故事；傳奇人物
▶ Legend has it that thousands of years ago, there were ten suns shining in the sky at the same time. 傳說好幾千年以前，天空曾經有十個太陽同時照耀著。

le·gen·da·ry 　🎧 *Track 2878*
[ˋlɛdʒənd‚ɛrɪ]
adj. 傳說的；傳奇的；赫赫有名的
▶ After waiting in line for six hours, I finally got to taste the legendary cheesecake. 在排了六個小時的隊之後，我終於得以嚐到傳說中的起司蛋糕。

lei·sure [ˋliʒɚ] 　🎧 *Track 2879*
n. 閒暇；空閒時間；悠閒；安逸
▶ Please give me a call at your leisure. 有空的時候請打個電話給我。

（補充片語）
at one's leisure 有空時；方便時

adj. 空暇的；有閒的；不以工作為主的
▶ The famous actress has been spotted on the MRT in her leisure wear many times. 該知名女演員多次被目擊穿著家居服搭捷運。

（補充片語）
leisure wear 便服，家居服

lei·sure·ly [ˋliʒɚlɪ] 　🎧 *Track 2880*
adj. 從容不迫的；悠閒的；慢慢的
▶ We love enjoying a leisurely brunch on Saturday morning. 我們很愛在星期六早上享用悠閒的早午餐。

adv. 從容不迫地；悠閒地
▶ The old lady is knitting a sweater leisurely in her armchair. 老太太正在她的扶手椅上慢慢地織著毛衣。

lem·on [ˋlɛmən] 　🎧 *Track 2881*
n. 檸檬

lem·on·ade [‚lɛmənˋed] 　🎧 *Track 2882*
n. 檸檬水
▶ I drink a glass of honey lemonade before breakfast every morning. 每天早上，我都會在早餐前喝一杯蜂蜜檸檬水。

lend [lɛnd] 　🎧 *Track 2883*
v. 借予；借出

length [lɛŋθ] 　🎧 *Track 2884*
n. （距離或時間的）長度

length·en [ˋlɛŋθən] 　🎧 *Track 2885*
v. 使加長；使延長
▶ You can lengthen the baby's nighttime sleep by shortening his day naps. 你可以藉由縮短寶寶的日間小睡時間來延長他的夜晚睡眠時間。

length·y [ˋlɛŋθɪ] 　🎧 *Track 2886*
adj. 長的；冗長的；囉唆的
▶ He dozed off during the Mayor's lengthy speech. 他在市長冗長的演說中打了瞌睡。

lens [lɛnz] 　🎧 *Track 2887*
n. 透鏡；鏡片
▶ My contact lenses are disposable. 我的隱形眼鏡是拋棄式的。

leop·ard [ˋlɛpɚd] 　🎧 *Track 2888*
n. 豹；美洲豹
▶ Which animal runs faster, a leopard or a lion? 哪一種動物跑得比較快，美洲豹還是獅子？

less [lɛs] 　🎧 *Track 2889*
adv. 較少地；不如
pron. 較少部分；較少量

les·son [ˋlɛsn] 　🎧 *Track 2890*
n. 課；教訓

let [lɛt] 　🎧 *Track 2891*
v. 使；讓

let's [lɛts] 　🎧 *Track 2892*
abbr. 讓我們來⋯⋯（let us的縮寫）

※灰色單字為英檢初級必備單字

let·ter [ˈlɛtə-]　　🎧 *Track 2893*
n. 信

let·tuce [ˈlɛtɪs]　　🎧 *Track 2894*
n. 萵苣

lev·el [ˈlɛvl]　　🎧 *Track 2895*
n. 水平面；程度；級別；**adj.** 水平的；同高度的；同程度的；平穩冷靜的

li·ar [ˈlaɪə-]　　🎧 *Track 2896*
n. 說謊的人
▶ He is an absolute liar. I don't believe a word he says. 他是個不折不扣的撒謊大王。我不相信他說的任何一句話。

lib·e·ral [ˈlɪbərəl]　　🎧 *Track 2897*
adj. 心胸寬闊的，寬容的，開明的；允許變革的，不守舊的；通才教育的
▶ They are liberal in their children's sexual orientation.
他們對孩子們的性別取向持開明的態度。

n. 自由主義者
▶ Both my parents are liberals. It makes no difference to them whether I am gay or not.
我的父母都是很開明的人。我是不是同性戀對他們來說都沒有差別。

lib·e·rate [ˈlɪbəˌret]　　🎧 *Track 2898*
v. 解放；使獲自由
▶ They liberated all their captives before they surrendered.
他們在投降之前釋放了所有的俘虜。

lib·er·ty [ˈlɪbə-tɪ]　　🎧 *Track 2899*
n. 自由；自由權；許可；自由活動或使用某物的權利；特權
▶ You are at liberty to do whatever you want. 你有自由想做什麼都可以。

(補充片語)
at liberty 自由的

li·brar·i·an [laɪˈbrɛrɪən]　🎧 *Track 2900*
n. 圖書館員
▶ He asked the librarian to find a book for him. 他請那名圖書館員幫他找一本書。

li·bra·ry [ˈlaɪˌbrɛrɪ]　　🎧 *Track 2901*
n. 圖書館

li·cense [ˈlaɪsns]　　🎧 *Track 2902*
=li·cence（英式英文）
v. 許可；特許；發許可證給
▶ That so-called doctor is not licensed to practice medicine.
那個所謂的醫生並沒有行醫的許可證。

n. 許可；特許；許可證；執照
▶ Peter's driver's license was suspended for drunk driving.
彼得的駕駛執照因為喝酒開車而被暫時吊銷。

(補充片語)
driver's license 駕駛執照

lick [lɪk]　　🎧 *Track 2903*
v. 舔；**n.** 舔一口

lid [lɪd]　　🎧 *Track 2904*
n. 蓋子

lie [laɪ]　　🎧 *Track 2905*
v. 躺；說謊；欺騙；**n.** 謊言

life [laɪf]　　🎧 *Track 2906*
n. 生命；性命；生活（狀態）；人生

life·time [ˈlaɪfˌtaɪm]　🎧 *Track 2907*
n. 一生；終身的
▶ Don't rush to get married. It's a decision of a lifetime.
別急著結婚。這是關乎一輩子的決定。

(相關片語)
the chance of a lifetime 千載難逢的機會
▶ I wouldn't miss this chance of a lifetime if I were you. 如果我是你，就絕不會錯過這個千載難逢的機會。

lift [lɪft]　　🎧 *Track 2908*
v. 舉起；提高；升起；**n.** 提；升；振奮；（英）電梯；順便搭載

light [laɪt]　　🎧 *Track 2909*
n. 燈；光線；**v.** 照亮；點燃；**adj.** 亮的；淺色的；**adv.** 輕便地；少負擔地

light·en [`laɪtn̩] 🎧 Track 2910
v. 變亮、發亮；減輕重量
▶He lit a candle to lighten the gloomy cellar.
他點了一支蠟燭，照亮陰暗的地窖。

light·house [`laɪt,haʊs] 🎧 Track 2911
n. 燈塔
▶This lighthouse is worn down by the years without repair.
這座燈塔已經年久失修了。

(補充片語)
worn down by the years without repair 年久失修

light·ning [`laɪtnɪŋ] 🎧 Track 2912
n. 閃電
▶Lightning always comes before thunder.
閃電總是在打雷前出現。

like [laɪk] 🎧 Track 2913
prep. 像；如；和……一樣；**v.** 喜歡

like·ly [`laɪklɪ] 🎧 Track 2914
adj. 很可能的；**adv.** 很可能地

lil·y [`lɪlɪ] 🎧 Track 2915
n. 百合；百合花
▶The lilies in our garden are in full bloom.
我們花園裡的百合盛開了。

(補充片語)
in full bloom 開花；盛開

limb [lɪm] 🎧 Track 2916
n. 肢；臂；腳
▶The girl was born without limbs.
這女孩生下來就沒有四肢。

(相關片語)
out on a limb 處於困境；處於孤立無援的境地
▶The boy's mother remarried after his father died and left him out on a limb.
男孩的母親在他父親死後便改嫁，棄他於不顧。

lim·it [`lɪmɪt] 🎧 Track 2917
v. 限制；**n.** 限制；界限；限度

lim·i·ta·tion [,lɪmə`teʃən] 🎧 Track 2918
n. 限制；限制因素；侷限
▶In here, you can do whatever you want without any limitations.
在這裡，你可以不受任何限制地愛做什麼就做什麼。

limp [lɪmp] 🎧 Track 2919
v. 一瘸一拐地走；跛行
▶The injured man limped to the hospital on his own.
那個受傷的男子自己一瘸一拐地到醫院去。

line [laɪn] 🎧 Track 2920
n. 線；排；路線；行列；**v.** 排隊

lin·en [`lɪnən] 🎧 Track 2921
n. 亞麻布；亞麻布製品
▶How often do you change your bed linen?
你多久換一次床單？

(補充片語)
bed linen 床單、枕套等床上織物用品

(相關片語)
dirty linen 家醜
▶Don't wash your dirty linen in the public.
家醜不要外揚。

link [lɪŋk] 🎧 Track 2922
n. 環節；連結；**v.** 結合；連接；勾住

li·on [`laɪən] 🎧 Track 2923
n. 獅子

lip [lɪp] 🎧 Track 2924
n. 嘴唇

lip·stick [`lɪp,stɪk] 🎧 Track 2925
n. 口紅
▶She often goes out without any make-up or lipstick.
她時常不化任何妝或擦口紅就出門。

liq·uid [`lɪkwɪd] 🎧 Track 2926
n. 液體；**adj.** 液體的；流動的

※灰色單字為英檢初級必備單字

Aa Bb Cc Dd Ee Ff Gg Hh Ii Jj Kk **Ll** Mm Nn Oo Pp Qq Rr Ss Tt Uu Vv Ww Xx Yy Zz

li·quor [ˋlɪkɚ]　🎧 *Track 2927*
=spir·its（英式英文）
n. 含酒精飲料
▶ We don't provide liquor for customers under 18.
我們不提供十八歲以下的顧客含酒精飲料。

list [lɪst]　🎧 *Track 2928*
n. 名冊；清單；**v.** 列舉

lis·ten [ˋlɪsn]　🎧 *Track 2929*
v. 聽

lis·ten·er [ˋlɪsnɚ]　🎧 *Track 2930*
n. 傾聽者；收聽者；（一位）聽眾
▶ A good listener does not interrupt.
一個好的傾聽者是不會打斷人說話的。

li·ter [ˋlitɚ]　🎧 *Track 2931*
=li·tre（英式英文）
n. 公升

lit·e·ra·ry [ˋlɪtəˏrɛrɪ]　🎧 *Track 2932*
adj. 文學的
▶ I don't know much about literary theory.
我對文學理論不太懂。

lit·e·ra·ture [ˋlɪtərətʃɚ]　🎧 *Track 2933*
n. 文學
▶ He is very interested in classic literature.
他對古典文學很有興趣。

lit·ter [ˋlɪtɚ]　🎧 *Track 2934*
n. 垃圾；廢棄物；雜亂
▶ My apartment was in a litter so I didn't invite him in.
我的公寓一團雜亂，所以我沒有邀請他進來。

v. 把……弄得亂七八糟；亂丟（雜物或廢棄物）
▶ Please do not litter here.
請勿在此處亂丟垃圾。

（相關片語）
litter bin 街上的垃圾箱
▶ Please throw your garbage into the litter bin.
請把你的垃圾丟到垃圾箱裡去。

lit·tle [ˋlɪtl]　🎧 *Track 2935*
adj. 小的；少的；年幼的；**pron.** 沒有多少；少許；一點（東西）；**adv.** 少；毫不

live [lɪv]　🎧 *Track 2936*
adj. 活的；實況的；即時的；現場的
▶ It's very cruel to experiment on live animals.
在活的動物身上做實驗是非常殘忍的。

live·ly [ˋlaɪvlɪ]　🎧 *Track 2937*
adj. 精力充沛的；愉快的
▶ Mrs. Gilbert is a lively old lady living next to me. 吉伯特太太是住在我隔壁的一位精力充沛的老太太。

liv·er [ˋlɪvɚ]　🎧 *Track 2938*
n. 肝；肝臟
▶ He was extremely shocked when he was diagnosed with terminal liver cancer.
被診斷出罹患末期肝癌時，他極度地震驚。

（補充片語）
terminal liver cancer　末期肝癌

liz·ard [ˋlɪzɚd]　🎧 *Track 2939*
n. 蜥蜴；類蜥蜴爬行動物
▶ She screamed at the sight of the lizard.
她一看見蜥蜴就尖叫。

（補充片語）
at the sight of　一看見……就

load [lod]　🎧 *Track 2940*
n. 裝載；重擔；裝載量；（一車或一船）貨物；工作量
▶ We need to recruit more engineers to lighten the load of our current employees.
我們需要招募更多工程師來減輕我們現有員工的工作量。

v. 裝載；裝貨；（把彈藥）裝入；使充滿；大量給予
▶ Be careful with the gun. It's loaded.
小心拿槍。它已經裝上子彈了。

（相關片語）
be a load off one's mind　使如釋重負
▶ Finally passing the finals was a huge load off my mind.
終於通過期末考試，真是讓我如釋重負。

loaf [lof]　🎧 *Track 2941*
n. 一條

loan [lon]　🎧 *Track 2942*
n. 借出；貸款
▶ No banks are willing to make a loan to his company.
沒有銀行願意貸款給他的公司。

(補充片語)
make a loan to 借貸給某人

v. 借出；貸與
▶ The bank loaned our company two million dollars.
銀行貸給我們公司兩百萬元。

lob·by [`labɪ]　🎧 *Track 2943*
n. 門廊；大廳
▶ I'll be waiting at the hotel lobby.
我會在飯店大廳等你。

lob·ster [`labstɚ]　🎧 *Track 2944*
n. 龍蝦
▶ The lobster is cooked perfectly.
▶ 這龍蝦烹煮得恰到好處。

lo·cal [`lokḷ]　🎧 *Track 2945*
adj. 地方性的；當地的；本地的；**n.** 當地居民；本地人

lo·cate [lo`ket]　🎧 *Track 2946*
v. 使……座落於；找出……所在位置；定居
▶ The shopping mall is located in the center of the city.
購物中心位於市中心。

lo·ca·tion [lo`keʃən]　🎧 *Track 2947*
n. 位置；場所；所在地
▶ We haven't decided on the location of our wedding banquet.
我們還沒選定舉行喜宴的地點。

(補充片語)
decide on 考慮後決定、選定；
wedding banquet 喜宴

lock [lak]　🎧 *Track 2948*
v. 鎖；鎖住；**n.** 鎖

lock·er [`lakɚ]　🎧 *Track 2949*
n. 衣物櫃
▶ There are lockers in the changing room for your personal belongings.
更衣室裡有置物櫃可以放你私人的物品。

(補充片語)
changing room （運動場內的）更衣室

lodge [ladʒ]　🎧 *Track 2950*
n. 守衛室；旅社；山林小屋
▶ The guard was found dead in the lodge.
警衛被發現死在守衛室裡。

v. 供……臨時住所；租房間給……住；暫住；投宿
▶ Is it convenient for you to lodge us for the night?
你方便讓我們暫住一宿嗎？

log [lɔg]　🎧 *Track 2951*
n. 原木；木料
▶ He bought a log coffee table at the garage sale.
他在車庫拍賣會上買了一個原木咖啡桌。

v. 伐木；採伐林木
▶ These trees will be logged next week.
這些樹木下個星期就會被砍掉。

(相關片語)
sleep like a log 睡得很熟
▶ I didn't want to wake him because he slept like a log.
因為他睡得很熟，所以我不想把他叫醒。

lo·gic [`ladʒɪk]　🎧 *Track 2952*
n. 邏輯；道理；理由
▶ His argument against capitalism completely lacks logic.
他反對資本主義的論點完全缺乏邏輯。

lo·gic·al [`ladʒɪkḷ]　🎧 *Track 2953*
adj. 合邏輯的；合理的；（邏輯上）當然的、必然的
▶ It is logical to assume that she will say yes to my proposal.
按理說她是會答應我的求婚的。

Aa
Bb
Cc
Dd
Ee
Ff
Gg
Hh
Ii
Jj
Kk
Ll
Mm
Nn
Oo
Pp
Qq
Rr
Ss
Tt
Uu
Vv
Ww
Xx
Yy
Zz

lo·go [`logo]
🎧 *Track 2954*

n. 標識

▶ Don't forget to apply for a patent for the logo design.
別忘了幫你的標識設計申請專利。

lol·li·pop [`lɑlɪ,pɑp]
🎧 *Track 2955*

n. 棒棒糖

▶ Most kids love lollipops.
大部分的孩子都愛吃棒棒糖。

Lond·on [`lʌndən]
🎧 *Track 2956*

n. 倫敦

lone [lon]
🎧 *Track 2957*

adj. 孤單的；無伴的；單一的

lone·li·ness [`lonlɪnɪs]
🎧 *Track 2958*

n. 孤獨；寂寞

▶ It was during the holidays that I felt my loneliness most keenly.
放假期間是我最感到孤寂的時候。

lone·ly [`lonlɪ]
🎧 *Track 2959*

adj. 孤單的；寂寞的

long [lɔŋ]
🎧 *Track 2960*

v. 期盼；渴望

▶ He longed for his family when he was studying abroad.
他在國外讀書時，非常想念他的家人。

long·ing [`lɔŋɪŋ]
🎧 *Track 2961*

n. 渴望

▶ He gazed at the giant pizza with longing.
他面帶渴望地看著那個巨大的披薩。

long-term [`lɔŋ,tɝm]
🎧 *Track 2962*

adj. 長期的

▶ It's difficult and heartbreaking to end a long-term relationship.
要結束一段長久的關係是困難且令人心碎的。

look [lʊk]
🎧 *Track 2963*

v. 看；看著；看起來；**n.** 看；臉色；外表；面容

loop [lup]
🎧 *Track 2964*

n. 圈，環，環狀物；環路，環線

▶ Their son has been bullied for years but they were totally out of the loop.
他們的兒子多年來一直被霸凌，但他們完全毫不知情。

（補充片語）

out of the loop 處在圈外；對事情內幕完全不知情

v. 打成環，使成圈；用環扣住；纏繞；使（飛機）翻筋斗

▶ The man looped his arms around his wife's waist from the back.
男子從背後用手環抱住妻子的腰。

loose [lus]
🎧 *Track 2965*

adj. 鬆的

▶ The loose tooth finally fell off after two weeks.
那顆鬆掉的牙齒在兩星期後終於掉了。

（相關片語）

at loose ends 無事可做；不知做什麼好

▶ You can help me mop the floor if you find yourself at loose ends.
如果你不知道自己該做什麼，可以幫我拖地板。

loos·en [`lusn]
🎧 *Track 2966*

v. 解開；鬆開；放鬆（限制）

▶ A glass of wine can loosen his tongue.
一杯酒就能讓他鬆口了。

（補充片語）

loose one's tongue 使某人鬆口；使人無拘束地說話

lord [lɔrd]
🎧 *Track 2967*

n. 統治者；君王

▶ The African elephant is the lord of the jungle. 那隻非洲象是叢林之王。

（相關片語）

as drunk as a lord 酩酊大醉

▶ Two glasses of wine and he was as drunk as a lord. 喝了兩杯酒，他就酩酊大醉了。

lor·ry [`lɔrɪ]
🎧 *Track 2968*

=**truck** （美式英文）

n. 卡車；運貨車

▶ The factory is looking for a certificated lorry driver. 這家工廠正在徵求一名合格證照的卡車司機。

lose [luz] 🎧 *Track 2969*
v. 丟；失去；輸掉；損失

los·er [`luzɚ] 🎧 *Track 2970*
n. 失敗者；失主

loss [lɔs] 🎧 *Track 2971*
n. 損失；喪失

lot [lɑt] 🎧 *Track 2972*
n. 很多；一塊地；**pron.** 很多
adv. 很多地；非常

lo·tion [`loʃən] 🎧 *Track 2973*
n. 化妝水；塗劑；護膚液
▶ Suntan lotion can protect your skin from the sun's UV rays. 防曬油可以保護你的皮膚免受太陽的紫外線傷害。

(補充片語)
suntan lotion 防曬油

loud [laʊd] 🎧 *Track 2974*
adj. 大聲的；**adv.** 大聲地

loud·speak·er 🎧 *Track 2975*
[`laʊd͵spikɚ]
n. 擴聲器；揚聲器；喇叭
▶ The teacher used a loudspeaker to announce the result of the game.
老師用揚聲器宣布比賽結果。

lounge [laʊndʒ] 🎧 *Track 2976*
v. 懶洋洋地倚靠；懶散地消磨時間；閒蕩；閒逛
▶ We lounged the night away chatting in the piano bar.
我們在鋼琴酒吧聊天消磨了這個夜晚。

(補充片語)
lounge away 閒散地消磨時間

n. 閒蕩；（飯店、旅館的）休息室、會客廳；（機場的）候機室；客廳
▶ We were asked to assemble at the hotel lounge at 7 a.m. tomorrow.
我們被要求明天七點在飯店大廳集合。

lou·sy [`laʊzɪ] 🎧 *Track 2977*
adj. 糟透的
▶ That's the lousiest movie that I have ever seen. 那是我看過最爛的一部電影。

love [lʌv] 🎧 *Track 2978*
v. 愛；喜好；**n.** 愛

love·ly [`lʌvlɪ] 🎧 *Track 2979*
adj. 可愛的；令人愉快的；美好的

lov·er [`lʌvɚ] 🎧 *Track 2980*
n. 戀人；情人（尤指男性）；愛好者

low [lo] 🎧 *Track 2981*
adj. 低的；矮的；情緒低落的

low·er [`loɚ] 🎧 *Track 2982*
v. 放下；降低
▶ She refused to lower her standards for anyone. 她拒絕為任何人降低自己的標準。

loy·al [`lɔɪəl] 🎧 *Track 2983*
adj. 忠誠的；忠心的
▶ Dogs are loyal to their owners.
狗對自己的主人很忠心。

loy·al·ty [`lɔɪəltɪ] 🎧 *Track 2984*
n. 忠誠；忠心
▶ My loyalty to my country never wavered in the least.
我對國家的的忠誠從未有絲毫動搖。

luck [lʌk] 🎧 *Track 2985*
n. 運氣；好運
▶ Wish you the best of luck.
祝你好運。

(相關片語)
hard luck 真不走運
▶ I heard you missed your idol's concert. Hard luck!
我聽說你錯過你偶像的演唱會。真是不走運啊！

luck·i·ly [`lʌkɪlɪ] 🎧 *Track 2986*
adv. 幸運地
▶ He was hit by a truck, but luckily he wasn't hurt.
他被一輛卡車撞到，但很幸運地並沒受傷。

luck·y [ˋlʌkɪ]　🎧 *Track 2987*
adj. 幸運的

lug·gage [ˋlʌgɪdʒ]　🎧 *Track 2988*
n. 行李
▶I don't have any luggage to check in.
我沒有需要託運的行李。

(補充片語)
check in 登記託運

lul·la·by [ˋlʌlə͵baɪ]　🎧 *Track 2989*
n. 催眠曲；搖籃曲
▶She sang her baby to sleep with a lullaby.
她唱搖籃曲哄寶寶睡覺。

v. 唱搖籃曲使入睡
▶The baby wouldn't fall asleep until his mother lullabied him.
寶寶一直到媽媽唱搖籃曲哄他才睡覺。

lu·nar [ˋlunɚ]　🎧 *Track 2990*
adj. 月球上的；月的；按月球的運轉測定的；陰曆的
▶Lunar New Year is the most important festival for Chinese people.
農曆新年對華人來說是最重要的節日。

(補充片語)
lunar New Year 農曆新年

lunch [lʌntʃ]　🎧 *Track 2991*
n. 午餐

lung [lʌŋ]　🎧 *Track 2992*
n. 肺，肺臟
▶The chest X-ray revealed a white spot on his lung.
胸部X光片顯示他的肺部有個白點。

(相關片語)
at the top of one's lungs 聲嘶力竭地
▶The fans cheered on their favorite team at the top of their lungs.
球迷們聲嘶力竭地為他們最喜歡的隊伍加油。

lux·u·ri·ous [lʌgˋʒʊrɪəs]　🎧 *Track 2993*
adj. 奢侈的
▶We dined at a luxurious restaurant last night. 我們昨晚到一間豪華餐廳用餐。

lux·u·ry [ˋlʌkʃərɪ]　🎧 *Track 2994*
n. 奢侈
▶She has been living in luxury since she inherited a large amount of money.
她自從繼承了一大筆錢之後就過著奢華的生活。

(補充片語)
live in luxury 過奢華的生活

ly·chee [ˋlaɪtʃi]= **lit·chi** 🎧 *Track 2995*
n. 荔枝
▶Lychees are a seasonal fruit only available in summer.
荔枝是一種只在夏天才吃得到的季節性水果。

lyr·ic [ˋlɪrɪk]　🎧 *Track 2996*
adj. 抒情的；熱情奔放的；適於演奏的
▶I wrote a lyric poem to express my love for you.
我寫了一首抒情詩來表達我對你的愛。

n. 抒情作品；歌詞
▶I don't remember the lyrics of the song, but I'm familiar with its melody.
我不記得這首歌的歌詞，但是很熟悉它的旋律。

Mm

通過中級英文檢定者的英文能力：

在日常生活中，能聽懂一般的會話；能大致聽懂公共場所廣播、氣象報告及廣告等。在工作時，能聽懂簡易的產品介紹與操作說明。能大致聽懂外籍人士的談話及詢問。

在日常生活中，能閱讀短文、故事、私人信件、廣告、傳單、簡介及使用說明等。在工作時，能閱讀工作須知、公告、操作手冊、例行的文件、傳真、電報等。

能寫簡單的書信、故事及心得等。對於熟悉且與個人經歷相關的主題，能以簡易的文字表達。

在日常生活中，能以簡易英語交談或描述一般事物，能介紹自己的生活作息、工作、家庭、經歷等，並可對一般話題陳述看法。在工作時，能進行簡單的答詢，並與外籍人士交談溝通。

本書除包含官方公佈的中級4,947單字外，更精挑了近400個滿分必學的高手單字。同時，在片語的挑選、例句的使用上，皆依上述英檢官方公佈之能力範疇做設計，難度適中、不偏離考試主題。發音部分則是自然發音＆KK音標雙管齊下，搭配MP3以「分解／完整」方式錄音，給你最多元有效的學習手段，怎麼記都可以，想忘掉都好難！

---

ma·am [`mæəm]　🎧 *Track 2997*
n. 閣下；女士（對女性的禮貌稱謂）

ma·chine [mə`ʃin]　🎧 *Track 2998*
n. 機器

ma·chin·e·ry [mə`ʃinərɪ]　🎧 *Track 2999*
n. 機器
▶ Most food products are made by machinery rather than by hand. 大部分的食品都是用機器做的，而不是手工做的。

mad [mæd]　🎧 *Track 3000*
adj. 發狂的；惱火的

mad·am [`mædəm]　🎧 *Track 3001*
n. （對婦女的恭敬稱呼）夫人，太太，小姐
▶ What would you like to eat today, madam? 夫人，您今天想吃什麼呢？

mag·a·zine [ˌmæɡə`zin]　🎧 *Track 3002*
n. 雜誌

ma·gic [`mædʒɪk]　🎧 *Track 3003*
adj. 魔術的；有魔力的；不可思議的
n. 魔法；巫術；神奇的力量

ma·gic·al [`mædʒɪkl̩]　🎧 *Track 3004*
adj. 魔術的，有魔力的，用魔法的；迷人的
▶ We enjoyed a magical ballet performance last night.
我們昨晚享受了一場迷人的芭蕾舞表演。

ma·gi·cian [mə`dʒɪʃən]　🎧 *Track 3005*
n. 魔術師

mag·net [`mæɡnɪt]　🎧 *Track 3006*
n. 磁鐵；磁石；有吸引力的人或物
▶ The sunrise scenery at Alishan is a magnet for visitors.
阿里山的日出景色對遊客來說深具吸引力。

[相關片語]

gossip magnet 話題人物；焦點話題
▶ Celebrities' private life is always a gossip magnet. 名人的私生活永遠都是焦點話題。

mag·net·ic [mæg`nɛtɪk] 🎧 *Track 3007*
adj. 磁鐵的；有磁性的；地磁的；有吸引力的；有魅力的
▶The Sun Moon Lake is one of the most magnetic tourist attractions here.
日月潭是這裡最具吸引力的觀光景點之一。

mag·nif·i·cent 🎧 *Track 3008*
[mæg`nɪfəsənt]
adj. 壯麗的；宏偉的；華麗的
▶The Great Wall of China is one of the most magnificent constructions in the world.
中國萬里長城是世界上最宏偉的建築之一。

maid [med] 🎧 *Track 3009*
n. 少女，未婚女子；侍女，女僕
▶The maid must have the breakfast ready before 7 a.m.
女僕必須在早上七點之前將早餐準備好。

mail [mel] 🎧 *Track 3010*
n. 郵件；**v.** 郵寄

mail·man [`mel‚mæn] 🎧 *Track 3011*
=post·man
n. 郵差

main [men] 🎧 *Track 3012*
adj. 主要的

main·land [`menlənd] 🎧 *Track 3013*
n. 大陸；本土
▶He immigrated to the island from the mainland when he was a teenager.
他十幾歲時就從大陸移居到島上來了。

main·ly [`menlɪ] 🎧 *Track 3014*
adv. 主要地
▶They speak to each other mainly in English, not Chinese.
他們主要是用英文和對方說話，而非中文。

main·tain [men`ten] 🎧 *Track 3015*
v. 維持；維修；保養；繼續

ma·jes·tic [mə`dʒɛstɪk] 🎧 *Track 3016*
adj. 雄偉的；壯觀的；莊嚴的；威嚴的
▶If you go to India, you must visit the majestic Taj Mahal. 如果你去印度，一定要去參觀雄偉的泰姬瑪哈陵。

ma·jor [`medʒɚ] 🎧 *Track 3017*
adj. 主要的；較多的；主修的；
n. 主修科目；主修學生；
v. 主修

ma·jor·i·ty [mə`dʒɔrətɪ] 🎧 *Track 3018*
n. 多數；過半數；大多數
▶The majority of the voters belong to the middle class.
大多數的選民都屬於中產階級。

make [mek] 🎧 *Track 3019*
v. 做；製造；使

mak·er [`mekɚ] 🎧 *Track 3020*
n. 製作者；製造廠；製造業者
▶My little brother is an absolute trouble maker. 我的弟弟是個不折不扣的麻煩製造者。

make-up [`mek‚ʌp] 🎧 *Track 3021*
n. 構成；化妝；補考
▶I don't like wearing make-up.
我不喜歡化妝。

相關片語
make-up test 補考
▶I failed my English midterm, so I have to take a make-up test.
我的英語期中考考砸了，所以我得補考。

male [mel] 🎧 *Track 3022*
adj. 男性的；雄的；公的；
n. 男子；雄性動物

mall [mɔl] 🎧 *Track 3023*
n. 大規模購物中心

mam·mal [`mæml] 🎧 *Track 3024*
n. 哺乳動物
▶Whales are the largest mammals on earth. 鯨魚是世界上最大的哺乳動物。

man [mæn] 🎧 *Track 3025*
n. （成年的）男人；人

man·age [ˋmænɪdʒ] 🎧 *Track 3026*
v. 管理；經營；控制；駕馭；設法做到
▶ He is too young to manage a company.
他太年輕，還無法管理一間公司。

man·age·a·ble 🎧 *Track 3027*
[ˋmænɪdʒəbl]
adj. 易辦的；可管理的；可控制的
▶ Short hair is much more manageable than long hair.
短髮比長髮要容易整理得多了。

man·age·ment 🎧 *Track 3028*
[ˋmænɪdʒmənt]
n. 管理；經營
▶ They have adopted a new method to improve their quality management system.
他們已經採用一個新方法來改善他們的品質管理系統。

(補充片語)
quality management　品質管理

man·ag·er [ˋmænɪdʒɚ] 🎧 *Track 3029*
n. 經理；經理人；負責人

Man·da·rin [ˋmændərɪn] 🎧 *Track 3030*
n. 中文

man·go [ˋmæŋgo] 🎧 *Track 3031*
n. 芒果

man·kind [ˋmænˏkaɪnd] 🎧 *Track 3032*
n. 人類；男人；男子
▶ The teacher introduced the evolution of mankind to the students in 12 pictures.
老師以十二張圖片向學生介紹人類的演化。

man-made [ˋmænˏmed] 🎧 *Track 3033*
adj. 人造的；人工的；人為的
▶ It is believed that the explosion was a man-made disaster.
大家都認為這起爆炸是人為的災禍。

man·ner [ˋmænɚ] 🎧 *Track 3034*
n. 態度；方式；禮貌；舉止

man·sion [ˋmænʃən] 🎧 *Track 3035*
n. 大廈；大樓；公寓；公寓大樓
▶ We live in the same mansion, so I run into him all the time.
我們住在同一棟大樓，所以我老是會碰到他。

(補充片語)
run into　偶然碰到

man·u·al [ˋmænjʊəl] 🎧 *Track 3036*
n. 手冊，簡介
▶ You can find more detailed information in this manual.
您可以在手冊中找到更詳細的資料。

adj. 手的；手工的；用手操作的；用體力的
▶ My parents are manual workers, not office workers.
我的父母是體力勞動者，而非辦公室上班族。

(補充片語)
manual worker　體力勞動者、手工勞動者；
office worker　辦公室上班族

man·u·fac·ture 🎧 *Track 3037*
[ˏmænjəˋfæktʃɚ]
v. 製造
▶ Our company has engaged in manufacturing household appliances for 20 years.
本公司致力於家電用品的生產已有二十年。

n. 製造；製造業；製品
▶ The company has engaged in the manufacture of bikes for over half a century.
這家公司已經從事自行車製造超過半世紀了。

man·u·fac·tur·er 🎧 *Track 3038*
[ˏmænjəˋfæktʃərɚ]
n. 製造業者；廠商
▶ The manufacturer promised to recall all defective products.
該製造商承諾召回所有瑕疵商品。

man·y [ˋmɛnɪ] 🎧 *Track 3039*
adj. 很多的；許多的；**pron.** 許多人；很多（事物）

map [mæp] 🎧 *Track 3040*
n. 地圖

Aa Bb Cc Dd Ee Ff Gg Hh Ii Jj Kk Ll Mm Nn Oo Pp Qq Rr Ss Tt Uu Vv Ww Xx Yy Zz

※灰色單字為英檢初級必備單字

ma·ple [`mepl̩] 🎧 *Track 3041*
n. 楓樹，楓樹
▶ Leaves on the maple trees in our backyard have all turned red.
我們後院楓樹的葉子都已經轉紅了。

[相關片語]
maple syrup　楓糖漿
▶ He likes to eat his pancakes with maple syrup. 他喜歡吃薄餅淋淋楓糖漿。

mar·a·thon [`mærəˌθɑn] 🎧 *Track 3042*
n. 馬拉松賽跑
▶ He's been training for months to run a marathon.
他已經接受了好幾個月跑馬拉松的訓練。

mar·ble [`mɑrbl̩] 🎧 *Track 3043*
n. 大理石
▶ The dining table is made of marble.
這張餐桌是大理石做的。

march [mɑrtʃ] 🎧 *Track 3044*
v. 前進；行軍
▶ All competitors marched into the stadium for the opening ceremony. 所有的參賽選手都行進至體育館參加開幕典禮。

n. 行軍，行進；進行曲
▶ The bride walked in as the band started playing the wedding march.
新娘在樂隊奏起結婚進行曲時，走了進來。

[相關片語]
steal a march on sb./sth.　搶在某人或某事之前
▶ We planned to steal a march on our rivals by launching the product a week beforehand.
我們計劃搶在競爭對手之前一星期推出這項產品。

mar·gin [`mɑrdʒɪn] 🎧 *Track 3045*
n. 邊，邊緣；頁邊空白；極限；餘地，餘裕
▶ Their log cabin locates in the margin of the woods. 他們的小木屋位在森林的邊緣。

[相關片語]
by a narrow margin　勉強
▶ We won the game by a narrow margin.
我們以些微之差的比數贏得比賽。

mark [mɑrk] 🎧 *Track 3046*
v. 做記號；打分數；**n.** 記號；符號

mark·er [`mɑrkɚ] 🎧 *Track 3047*
n. 記號筆；馬克筆

mar·ket [`mɑrkɪt] 🎧 *Track 3048*
n. 市場；股票市場；**v.** 在市場上銷售

mar·riage [`mærɪdʒ] 🎧 *Track 3049*
n. 婚姻；婚姻生活

mar·ried [`mærɪd] 🎧 *Track 3050*
adj. 已婚的；婚姻的

mar·ry [`mærɪ] 🎧 *Track 3051*
v. 嫁；娶；和……結婚；嫁女兒

mar·ve·lous [`mɑrvələs] 🎧 *Track 3052*
=mar·vel·lous （英式英文）
adj. 令人驚歎的；極好的

mask [mæsk] 🎧 *Track 3053*
n. 面具；口罩

mass [mæs] 🎧 *Track 3054*
n. 團；塊；大量；**adj.** 大眾的

mas·sage [mə`sɑʒ] 🎧 *Track 3055*
n. 按摩，推拿
▶ I need a full body massage to release my stress and soothe my aching muscles.
我需要來個全身按摩，以抒解壓力和減輕痠痛的肌肉。

v. 給……按摩，為……推拿
▶ Can you massage my neck and shoulders?
你可以幫我按摩一下頸部和肩膀嗎？

mas·sive [`mæsɪv] 🎧 *Track 3056*
adj. 大而重的；厚實的；魁偉的；大量的，大規模的
▶ The highway has been blocked by a massive traffic jam for hours.
這條路已經被大規模的交通擁塞給堵住好幾個小時了。

mas·ter [`mæstɚ] 🎧 *Track 3057*
n. 主人

mas·ter·piece
Track 3058

[`mæstɚˌpis]

n. 傑作;名作

▶ Victor Hugo's Les Misérables is one of the greatest masterpieces of European literature. 雨果的《悲慘世界》是歐洲文學最偉大的名作之一。

mat [mæt]
Track 3059

n. 草蓆

match [mætʃ]
Track 3060

n. 火柴;配對;**v.** 配對;搭配

mate [met]
Track 3061

n. 同伴;伙伴;配偶

▶ Jack is not only my husband, but also my soul mate.

傑克不僅是我的丈夫,也是我的靈魂伴侶。

（補充片語）

soul mate 靈魂相契、性情相投的人

v. 使成配偶;使配對;使交配;成配偶;成伙伴;交配

▶ My kitten is only three months old. She is not ready to mate with a male cat.

我的小貓才三個月大。她還不能跟公貓交配。

ma·te·ri·al [mə`tɪrɪəl]
Track 3062

n. 材料;材質

math [mæθ]
Track 3063

=math·e·mat·ics

n. 數學

math·e·mat·i·cal
Track 3064

[ˌmæθə`mætɪkl]

adj. 數學的

▶ Can you explain this mathematical formula for me?

可以請你解釋這一道數學公式給我聽嗎?

mat·ter [`mætɚ]
Track 3065

n. 事情;問題;毛病;**v.** 要緊;有關係;重要

mat·tress [`mætrɪs]
Track 3066

n. 褥墊,床墊

▶ She kept her personal savings under the mattress. 她把她的私房錢藏在床墊下。

ma·ture [mə`tjʊr]
Track 3067

adj. 成熟的

▶ Please behave in a mature way.

拜託你表現得成熟一點。

ma·tu·ri·ty [mə`tjʊrətɪ]
Track 3068

n. 成熟

▶ Tom is a man with a great deal of maturity although he's still quite young.

湯姆是個年紀雖輕,卻相當成熟穩重的男子。

max·i·mum [`mæksəməm]
Track 3069

adj. 最大的;**n.** 最大數;最大限度;最高極限;**adv.** 最多

may [me]
Track 3070

aux. （表示可能性）也許;（表示允許）可以;**n.** 五月（首字大寫）

may·be [`mebɪ]
Track 3071

adv. 大概;可能;或許

may·on·naise [ˌmeə`nez]
Track 3072

n. 美乃滋,蛋黃醬

▶ Mayonnaise is delicious but it is very high in calories. 美乃滋很美味,但是熱量很高。

may·or [`meɚ]
Track 3073

n. 市長;鎮長

▶ Our opening ceremony was graced with the presence of the mayor.

我們的開幕典禮因為市長的蒞臨而蓬蓽生輝。

（補充片語）

grace sth. with the presence of sb. 因某人的出現而增光

me [mi]
Track 3074

pron. 我

mead·ow [`mɛdo]
Track 3075

n. 草地

▶ There are flocks of sheep and cattle grazing on the meadow.

羊群和牛群在牧場上吃草。

meal [mil]
Track 3076

n. 一餐;進餐

※灰色單字為英檢初級必備單字

mean [min] 　🎧 *Track 3077*
adj. 吝嗇的；低劣的
▶ That is the meanest thing that I've ever heard. 那是我聽過最惡毒的話。

mean·ing [`minɪŋ] 　🎧 *Track 3078*
n. 意義；含義；重要性

mean·ing·ful [`minɪŋfəl] 🎧 *Track 3079*
adj. 意味深長的
▶ The time we spent together was short but meaningful.
我們一起度過的時光很短暫卻很有意義。

means [minz] 　🎧 *Track 3080*
n. 方法；手段；工具

mean·time [`min͵taɪm] 🎧 *Track 3081*
n. 其間，其時，同時
▶ I'll look after the baby. In the meantime, you can get something to eat.
我會照顧寶寶。在這期間你可以去吃點東西。

mean·while [`min͵hwaɪl] 🎧 *Track 3082*
adv. 其間，同時
▶ My wife fed the baby; meanwhile, I did the dishes.
我太太在餵寶寶吃飯，而同時我在洗碗。

mea·su·ra·ble 　🎧 *Track 3083*
[`mɛʒərəbl]
adj. 可測量的；可預見的；顯著的
▶ With our effort, I am confident that we can achieve measureable progress towards our goals.
透過我們的努力，我相信我們能夠朝著目標，得到顯著的進展。

mea·sure [`mɛʒɚ] 　🎧 *Track 3084*
n. 度量單位；尺寸；分量；**v.** 測量；計量

mea·sure·ment 　🎧 *Track 3085*
[`mɛʒɚmənt]
n. 尺寸、測量

meat [mit] 　🎧 *Track 3086*
n. 肉

me·chan·ic [mə`kænɪk] 🎧 *Track 3087*
n. 技工；修理工

me·chan·i·cal 　🎧 *Track 3088*
[mə`kænɪkl]
adj. 機械的；機械學的；機器驅動的；似機械的；無感情的
▶ I major in mechanical engineering in the university. 我在大學裡主修機械工程。
(補充片語)
mechanical engineering 機械工程（學）

med·al [`mɛdl] 　🎧 *Track 3089*
n. 獎章；紀念章
▶ He won a silver medal in the competition.
他在比賽中得到銀牌。

med·i·cal [`mɛdɪkl] 🎧 *Track 3090*
adj. 醫學的
▶ My son is a medical school student.
我兒子是一個醫學院的學生。
(補充片語)
medical school 醫學院

me·di·cine [`mɛdəsn] 🎧 *Track 3091*
n. 藥

med·i·tate [`mɛdə͵tet] 🎧 *Track 3092*
v. 沉思，深思熟慮；計劃，打算
▶ They are meditating a second honeymoon trip. 他們正在計劃做第二次的蜜月旅行。

me·di·um [`midɪəm] 🎧 *Track 3093*
（複數為mediums/media）
n. 中間；媒介物；手段；工具；傳播媒介
adj. 中間的；中等的

meet [mit] 　🎧 *Track 3094*
v. 遇見；認識；迎接

meet·ing [`mitɪŋ] 🎧 *Track 3095*
n. 會議；聚會

mel·low [`mɛlo] 🎧 *Track 3096*
adj. 成熟的；香醇的；圓潤的；柔和的；老練的；肥沃的；極好的
▶ The audience was captivated by the old singer's warm mellow voice.
聽眾被老歌手溫暖圓潤的聲音給深深迷住了。

mel·o·dy [ˋmɛlədɪ]
🎧 *Track 3097*
n. 旋律；悅耳的聲音；曲調
▶He took out his bamboo flute and played an old Chinese melody. 他拿出他的竹笛，吹奏了一首古老的中國曲調。

mel·on [ˋmɛlən]
🎧 *Track 3098*
n. 甜瓜

melt [mɛlt]
🎧 *Track 3099*
v. 使融化；使熔化；使溶解
▶He melted the chocolate in the warm milk. 他讓巧克力在溫熱的牛奶中融化。

mem·ber [ˋmɛmbɚ]
🎧 *Track 3100*
n. 成員；會員

mem·ber·ship
🎧 *Track 3101*
[ˋmɛmbɚˌʃɪp]
n. 會員身份；會員資格；會員人數
▶You can sign up for gym membership for free today.
您今天可以免費加入健身房的會員。

(補充片語)
sign up for 註冊參加；登記參加（俱樂部或課程學習）

mem·o·ra·ble
🎧 *Track 3102*
[ˋmɛmərəbl̩]
adj. 值得懷念的
▶Your father and I had a memorable honeymoon trip in Africa. 你的父親和我在非洲度過了一個難忘的蜜月旅行。

mem·o·ran·dum
🎧 *Track 3103*
[ˌmɛməˋrændəm]
n. 備忘錄；記錄；聯絡便條；（公司的）章程
▶The meeting memorandum will be sent to every participant by Friday.
會議備忘錄會在週五之前寄給所有的與會者。

me·mo·ri·al [məˋmorɪəl]
🎧 *Track 3104*
n. 紀念物；紀念碑；紀念館；紀念活動
▶It's a memorial to the victims of the 911 attacks.
這是一個紀念911攻擊事件罹難者的紀念碑。

adj. 紀念的；追悼的；記憶的
▶Uncle Joe, my dad's best friend, gave a memorial speech on my dad's funeral. 我爸最好的朋友喬伊叔叔，在他的葬禮上致悼詞。

(補充片語)
memorial speech 悼詞

mem·o·rize [ˋmɛməˌraɪz]
🎧 *Track 3105*
v. 記住
▶Memorizing English words is never a problem to me.
背英文單字對我來說從不是個問題。

mem·o·ry [ˋmɛmərɪ]
🎧 *Track 3106*
n. 記憶；記憶力；回憶

mend [mɛnd]
🎧 *Track 3107*
v. 修理；修正、改善
▶Would you mend my shirt for me?
你可以幫我補襯衫嗎？

相關片語
mend one's ways 改過、改正自己的缺點；改過自新
▶He deserves a chance to mend his ways.
他應該得到一個改過自新的機會。

men·tal [ˋmɛntl̩]
🎧 *Track 3108*
adj. 精神的；心理的
▶It's a difficult and exhausting task to raise a child with mental disabilities.
養育一個智能障礙的孩子是件艱難且令人耗盡心力的任務。

(補充片語)
mental disability 心智障礙

men·tion [ˋmɛnʃən]
🎧 *Track 3109*
v. 提到；說起
▶Don't you mention his name in front of me. 你別在我面前提到他的名字。

n. 提及；說起
▶She didn't make any mention of being pregnant. 她完全沒有提到懷有身孕的事情。

men·u [ˋmɛnju]
🎧 *Track 3110*
n. 菜單

※灰色單字為英檢初級必備單字

mer·chant [`mɚtʃənt] 🎧 *Track 3111*
n. 商人；零售商
▶ Mr. Robinson is a successful cloth merchant in our town.
羅賓森先生是我們鎮上一位成功的布商。

mer·cy [`mɚsɪ] 🎧 *Track 3112*
n. 慈悲；仁慈；憐憫；仁慈行為；寬容
▶ Having mercy on the children who lost their parents, Mr. Jones donated all his money to the orphan home.
因為憐憫那些失去父母的孩子，瓊斯先生將他所有的錢都捐給了孤兒院。

mere [mɪr] 🎧 *Track 3113*
adj. 僅僅的；只不過的
▶ The mere thought of the boy made her smile. 光是想著那男孩就讓她笑容滿面。

mer·it [`mɛrɪt] 🎧 *Track 3114*
n. 價值
▶ Everyone has his merits.
每個人都有自己的長處。

mer·maid [`mɚ,med] 🎧 *Track 3115*
n. 美人魚；女游泳健將
▶ I don't believe in the existence of mermaids.
我不相信人魚的存在。

mer·ry [`mɛrɪ] 🎧 *Track 3116*
adj. 歡樂的
▶ It was a simple, merry and unforgettable wedding.
那是一個簡單、歡樂又令人難忘的婚禮。

mess [mɛs] 🎧 *Track 3117*
n. 混亂；凌亂的狀態；髒亂的東西
▶ Don't make a mess of the living room.
別把客廳搞得一團亂。

(補充片語)
make a mess of 把……弄糟

v. 弄亂；弄糟；弄髒；毀壞
▶ He messed everything up.
他把所有的一切都搞砸了。

(補充片語)
mess up 搞砸；弄糟

mes·sage [`mɛsɪdʒ] 🎧 *Track 3118*
n. 訊息；口信；消息

mes·sen·ger [`mɛsndʒɚ] 🎧 *Track 3119*
n. 送信者；信差
▶ Homing pigeons had been used as messengers for centuries in the past.
過去有好幾世紀的時間，傳信鴿都被當作信差來用。

(補充片語)
homing pigeon 傳信鴿

mess·y [`mɛsɪ] 🎧 *Track 3120*
adj. 混亂的
▶ You're not going anywhere until you clean up your messy room. 在你把你凌亂的房間整理好之前，你哪裡都不能去。

met·al [`mɛtl] 🎧 *Track 3121*
n. 金屬

me·ter [`mitɚ] 🎧 *Track 3122*
v. 計量；用儀表測量
▶ The taxi fare is metered and charged for.
計程車費是用照表計價的。

meth·od [`mɛθəd] 🎧 *Track 3123*
n. 方法；方式

me·tro [`mɛtro]=Me·tro 🎧 *Track 3124*
n. 地下鐵道；捷運；地鐵
▶ You don't have to worry about traffic jams if you're traveling by metro. 如果你是搭地鐵移動，就不用擔心交通阻塞的問題。

mi·cro·phone [`maɪkrə,fon] 🎧 *Track 3125*
=mike
n. 擴音器；麥克風
▶ It was my turn to sing, but he wouldn't let go of the microphone.
輪到我唱歌了，但他不願意放開麥克風。

mi·cro·scope 🎧 *Track 3126*
[`maɪkrə,skop]
n. 顯微鏡
▶ Only with the aid of a microscope can we observe cells.
唯有借助顯微鏡，我們才能夠觀察細胞。

mi·cro·wave
Track 3127

[`maɪkro͵wev]

n. 微波爐；**v.** 微波

mid·day [`mɪd͵de]
Track 3128

n. 正午，中午，日正當中

▶The experts suggest that we should go out at the midday for Vitamin D. 專家建議我們應該為了攝取維他命D，在正中午出門。

(補充片語)

at the midday　在正午

mid·dle [`mɪdḷ]
Track 3129

adj. 中間的；中等的；**n.** 中部；中途

mid·night [`mɪd͵naɪt]
Track 3130

n. 午夜；**adj.** 半夜的

might [maɪt]
Track 3131

n. 力量；力氣

▶I will definitely fight back with all my might if someone tries to put a slur on me.
如果有人惡意中傷我，我一定會全力反擊。

(補充片語)

cast/put a slur on sb./sth. 中傷，詆毀，誹謗某人／某事

(相關片語)

with might and main　盡全力

▶I'm working with might and main to finish the job before the deadline.
我正盡全力在最後期限之前完成這份工作。

might·n't [`maɪtnt]
Track 3132

abbr. 可能不會（**might not**的縮寫）

might·y [`maɪtɪ]
Track 3133

adj. 強大的；強而有力的

▶The pen is mightier than the sword.
筆比劍更有力。（筆墨勝刀劍。）

(相關片語)

high and mighty　神氣活現

▶Larry has become high and mighty since he got promoted.
賴瑞自從獲得晉升就變得神氣活現的。

mild [maɪld]
Track 3134

adj. 溫和的

▶I prefer mild coffee. 我喜歡不濃的咖啡。

(相關片語)

meek and mild　逆來順受的

▶Traditional Chinese women were meek and mild. 傳統的中國婦女總是逆來順受。

mile [maɪl]
Track 3135

n. 英里；哩

mil·i·ta·ry [`mɪlə͵tɛrɪ]
Track 3136

adj. 軍事的；軍用的；軍人的；**n.** 軍人；軍隊

milk [mɪlk]
Track 3137

n. 奶

milk·shake [͵mɪlkˋʃek]
Track 3138

n. 奶昔

▶The boy ordered a chocolate milkshake.
男孩點了一杯巧克力奶昔。

mill [mɪl]
Track 3139

n. 磨坊；麵粉廠；工廠

▶He is a worker in a steel mill.
他是一家煉鋼廠的員工。

v. 碾碎；將……磨成粉

▶The machine can mill coffee beans into coffee powder.
這機器能把咖啡豆磨成咖啡粉。

(相關片語)

go through the mill　接受磨練

▶He is ready to go through the mill.
他已經準備好要接受磨練了。

mil·lion [`mɪljən]
Track 3140

pron. 百萬個；**n.** 百萬；百萬元；無數

adj. 百萬的

mind [maɪnd]
Track 3141

n. 頭腦；智力；意向；主意；**v.** 在意；介意

mine [maɪn]
Track 3142

n. 礦；礦井；寶庫

▶Southeast Asia has the largest gold mine in the world. 東南亞有世界上最大的金礦。

v. 採礦

▶He became rich by mining gold.
他靠挖金礦致富。

mine of information　知識的寶庫
▶ My father is a mine of information about photography. 我爸爸是個攝影知識的寶庫。

min·er [`maɪnɚ]　🎧 *Track 3143*
n. 礦工
▶ Unfortunately, all the coal miners died in the pit.
很不幸地，所有的煤礦工人都死在礦坑裡了。

min·e·ral [`mɪnərəl]　🎧 *Track 3144*
n. 礦物
▶ Africa has the richest minerals in the world. 非洲擁有全世界最多的礦藏。

adj. 礦物的，礦物質的
▶ Africa is rich in mineral resources.
非洲的礦物資源很豐富。

mineral water　礦泉水
▶ I drink mineral water instead of tap water.
我喝礦泉水，而非自來水。

min·i·mum [`mɪnəməm]　🎧 *Track 3145*
adj. 最小的，最少的，最低的
▶ The minimum monthly wage here is $20,008.
這裡的法定最低月薪為兩萬零八元。

min·is·ter [`mɪnɪstɚ]　🎧 *Track 3146*
n. 部長，大臣，公使
▶ He was appointed the Minister of Foreign Affairs in 2004.
他在2004年被任命為外交部長。

Minister of Foreign Affairs/foreign minister
外交部長

min·is·try [`mɪnɪstrɪ]　🎧 *Track 3147*
n. 全體閣員；部
▶ The Ministry shall resign at the end of the month. 內閣將在本月底總辭。

mi·nor [`maɪnɚ]　🎧 *Track 3148*
adj. 較少的；較小的；次要的；不重要的；年幼的；副修的；**n.** 未成年人；副修科目；**v.** 副修；兼修

mi·nor·i·ty [maɪ`nɔrətɪ]　🎧 *Track 3149*
n. 少數，少數派；少數民族；未成年
▶ Islam is a religious minority here.
伊斯蘭在這裡是宗教上的少數派。

mint [mɪnt]　🎧 *Track 3150*
n. 薄荷；薄荷糖
▶ I bought a jar of mints. 我買了一罐薄荷糖。

adj. 薄荷的
▶ He gave me a slice of mint chocolate.
他給了我一片薄荷巧克力。

mi·nus [`maɪnəs]　🎧 *Track 3151*
prep. 減去；**adj.** 負的；**n.** 負號、減號；負數；不利

min·ute [`mɪnɪt]　🎧 *Track 3152*
adj. 極細微的，細瑣的；詳細的，精密的
▶ He was the only person that noticed the minute problem.
他是唯一一個注意到這個細瑣的問題的人。

mir·a·cle [`mɪrəkl]　🎧 *Track 3153*
n. 奇蹟，奇蹟般的人或物；驚人的事跡
▶ It's a miracle that the man woke up from a 19-year coma.
那男子竟然能在昏迷十九年之後醒過來，真是個奇蹟。

mir·ror [`mɪrɚ]　🎧 *Track 3154*
n. 鏡子

mis·chief [`mɪstʃɪf]　🎧 *Track 3155*
n. 頑皮；惡作劇；淘氣鬼
▶ Peter is a mischief in my class.
彼得是我班上的一個淘氣鬼。

make mischief　挑撥離間
▶ Making mischief among friends is not something he would do.
在朋友之中挑撥離間不是他會做的事。

mis·e·ra·ble [`mɪzərəbl]　🎧 *Track 3156*
adj. 悲慘的，痛苦的；不幸的
▶ He revealed that he had a miserable childhood in the interview.
他在訪談中透露自己有個悲慘的童年。

mis·e·ry [ˈmɪzərɪ] 🎧 *Track 3157*
n. 痛苦
▶ Misery loves company. 同病相憐。

mis·for·tune [mɪsˈfɔrtʃən] 🎧 *Track 3158*
n. 不幸；惡運；不幸的事；災難
▶ The tsunami was a great misfortune for tens of thousands of people in Fukushima.
這場海嘯對福島數以萬計的人來說是個極不幸的災難。

mis·lead [mɪsˈlid] 🎧 *Track 3159*
v. 把……帶錯方向；把……引入歧途，把……帶壞
▶ The mother worried that her son would be misled by his companions.
那個母親擔心他兒子會被他的朋友帶壞。

mis·lead·ing [mɪsˈlidɪŋ] 🎧 *Track 3160*
adj. 使人誤解的；騙人的；引入歧途的
▶ The TV commercial was banned for giving misleading information. 這隻電視廣告因為提供使人誤解的資訊而被禁播了。

miss [mɪs] 🎧 *Track 3161*
v. 錯過；想念；**n.** （首字大寫）小姐；女士（對未婚女子的稱謂）

mis·sile [ˈmɪsl̩] 🎧 *Track 3162*
n. 飛彈
▶ The boundary of the country is strongly armed with missiles.
該國的疆界備有堅實的飛彈武力。

miss·ing [ˈmɪsɪŋ] 🎧 *Track 3163*
adj. 缺掉的；失蹤的

mis·sion [ˈmɪʃən] 🎧 *Track 3164*
n. 外交使團；使命，任務；傳教團；天職
▶ I'll accomplish this mission with all my might. 我會盡全力完成這個任務。

mist [mɪst] 🎧 *Track 3165*
n. 薄霧；靄；霧狀物；噴霧；朦朧；模糊不清
▶ A mist suddenly came over my eyes when I heard the sad song.
當我聽到這首悲傷的歌時，眼鏡突然模糊了起來。

v. 被蒙上薄霧；使變得模糊
▶ Tears misted my eyes as I read his letter.
當我讀著他的信時，淚水模糊了我的眼睛。

mis·take [mɪˈstek] 🎧 *Track 3166*
n. 錯誤；失誤；**v.** 弄錯，誤解

mis·ter [ˈmɪstɚ] 🎧 *Track 3167*
n. 先生（常縮寫為**Mr.**）
▶ Mr. Brown is a knowledgeable scholar.
布朗先生是一位知識淵博的學者。

相關片語
Mr. Right 真命天子
▶ She thought Henry was her Mr. Right, but he turned out to be a fraud. 她以為亨利是她的真命天子，結果他卻是個騙子。

mis·tress [ˈmɪstrɪs] 🎧 *Track 3168*
n. 女主人，主婦；女能手；女教師；女主管；情婦
▶ Everyone knows her husband has a mistress in China except her. 除了她之外，每個人都知道她老公在中國有個情婦。

mis·un·der·stand 🎧 *Track 3169*
[ˌmɪsʌndɚˈstænd]
v. 誤會，誤解
▶ You misunderstood his good intentions.
你誤解他的好意了。

mix [mɪks] 🎧 *Track 3170*
v. 混合；拌和；**n.** 混合；混合物；調配好的材料

mix·ture [ˈmɪkstʃɚ] 🎧 *Track 3171*
n. 混合，混合物，混合料
▶ The dough is a mixture of flour, sugar, and melted butter.
這麵團是麵粉、糖和融化奶油的混合體。

moan [mon] 🎧 *Track 3172*
n. 呻吟聲；（風或樹葉的）蕭蕭聲；悲歎，發牢騷
▶ The patient let out a moan when he turned his body over.
病人翻身時發出了一聲呻吟。

補充片語
let out a moan 發出呻吟聲；
turn one's body over 翻身

※灰色單字為英檢初級必備單字

v. 呻吟；發出蕭蕭聲；悲歎，抱怨
▶The woman always moans about her selfish and irresponsible husband.
婦人總是抱怨她那自私又不負責任的丈夫。

mob [mɑb] 🎧 *Track 3173*
n. 暴民；烏合之眾；（貶）人群，民眾
▶The mob threw eggs at the Mayor.
那群暴民對著市長丟雞蛋。

v. 成群襲擊，圍攻
▶The suspect was mobbed by the family members of the victim as soon as he stepped out of the court.
嫌犯一走出法院就遭到被害人家屬的圍攻。

相關片語
flash mob 快閃族
▶We enjoyed a fantastic performance of Beethoven's 9th Symphony by a flash mob in the station today.
我們今天在車站欣賞了一場精采的貝多芬第九號交響曲快閃演出。

mo·bile [`mobɪl] 🎧 *Track 3174*
adj. 可動的；移動式的
▶If you want to take a leak, there is a mobile toilet behind the tree.
如果你想要尿尿，樹後面有一個移動式廁所。

補充片語 take a leak 【俚】尿尿
相關片語
mobile phone 手機
▶Mobile phones are commonplace today.
手機現在很普遍。

mock [mɑk] 🎧 *Track 3175*
v. 嘲笑；（為取笑而）模仿；使無效，挫敗
▶I don't like those people because they always mock at my accent.
我不喜歡那些人，因為他們老是嘲笑我的口音。

n. 嘲弄，愚弄；笑柄；贗品
▶I was very angry when the disrespectful guy made a mock of my native accent.
那個失禮的傢伙嘲笑我的鄉音時，讓我非常生氣。

補充片語
make a mock of 嘲弄、嘲笑

mod·el [`mɑdl] 🎧 *Track 3176*
n. 模型；模範；模特兒；**v.** 做……的模型；當模特兒

mod·e·rate [`mɑdərɪt] 🎧 *Track 3177*
adj. 中等的，適度的，不過分的
▶She follows a moderate diet and exercise program. 她遵循有節制的飲食和運動計劃。

mod·ern [`mɑdən] 🎧 *Track 3178*
adj. 現代的；近代的；現代化的

mod·est [`mɑdɪst] 🎧 *Track 3179*
adj. 謙虛的，審慎的；適度的；有節制的
▶Although he is very successful, he is rather modest about his achievements.
雖然他非常成功，卻對自己的成就相當謙虛。

mod·es·ty [`mɑdɪstɪ] 🎧 *Track 3180*
n. 謙遜
▶His modesty makes him a popular person in our office.
他的謙遜使他成為公司受歡迎的人。

moist [mɔɪst] 🎧 *Track 3181*
adj. 潮濕的，微濕的；多雨的
▶Applying a facial mask once a week keeps your skin moist during the winter. 一週使用一次面膜能讓你的皮膚在冬天保持濕潤。

補充片語
facial mask 面膜

mois·ture [`mɔɪstʃə] 🎧 *Track 3182*
n. 濕氣，潮氣；水分；水汽
▶I turned on the dehumidifier to remove excess moisture from the air in the house.
我將除溼機打開，以除去房子內空氣中多餘的濕氣。

mo·ment [`momənt] 🎧 *Track 3183*
n. 瞬間；片刻

mom·my [`mɑmɪ] 🎧 *Track 3184*
n. 媽媽

Mon·day =Mon. [`mʌnde] 🎧 *Track 3185*
n. 星期一

mon·ey [ˋmʌnɪ] 🎧 *Track 3186*
n. 錢;金錢

mon·i·tor [ˋmɑnətɚ] 🎧 *Track 3187*
v. 監控;監聽
▶ The police monitored the suspect's movements through the mobile tracking system.
警方透過移動式追蹤系統監控嫌犯的行動。

n. 監聽員;監聽器;監測器;班長、級長;（電腦）顯示器;螢幕
▶ Her eyes got tired after staring at the monitor for hours.
她的眼睛在盯著螢幕好幾個小時後感到疲倦。

monk [mʌŋk] 🎧 *Track 3188*
n. 僧侶
▶ He chose to enter into religion and became a monk. 他選擇出家,成為一名僧侶。

mon·key [ˋmʌŋkɪ] 🎧 *Track 3189*
n. 猴子

mon·ster [ˋmɑnstɚ] 🎧 *Track 3190*
n. 怪獸;怪物

month [mʌnθ] 🎧 *Track 3191*
n. 月;月份

month·ly [ˋmʌnθlɪ] 🎧 *Track 3192*
adj. 每月的;每月一次的;**adv.** 每月;每月一次;**n.** 月刊;生理期

mon·u·ment 🎧 *Track 3193*
[ˋmɑnjəmənt]
n. 紀念碑;紀念館;歷史遺跡
▶ They erected a monument in the center of the square in memory of their revolutionary war heroes.
他們在廣場中央設立了一座紀念碑,以紀念他們的革命戰爭英雄。

補充片語
in memory of 以紀念

mood [mud] 🎧 *Track 3194*
n. 心情;心境;情緒
▶ I am not in the mood to go shopping with you. 我沒心情跟你去逛街。

補充片語
in the mood to 有做……的心情

moon [mun] 🎧 *Track 3195*
n. 月亮;月球

moon·light [ˋmun͵laɪt] 🎧 *Track 3196*
n. 月光
▶ We took a walk arm in arm in the moonlight.
我們在月光下挽著手臂散步。

補充片語
take a walk 散步;
arm in arm 挽著手臂

mop [mɑp] 🎧 *Track 3197*
n. 拖把;**v.** 用拖把拖;擦乾

mor·al [ˋmɔrəl] 🎧 *Track 3198*
adj. 道德上的;品行端正的;精神上的;道義上的
▶ I can give you nothing more than moral support. 我僅能給你精神上的支持。

補充片語
nothing more than 僅僅……而已;
moral support 精神上的支持

n. 道德;品行;道德寓意;道德規範
▶ Those who produce and sell tainted food to the public have no business morals at all.
那些生產並販售黑心食品給民眾的人毫無商業道德可言。

補充片語
tainted food 黑心食品;
business moral 職業道德

more [mor] 🎧 *Track 3199*
adv. 更多;更大程度地;再;**pron.** 更多的數量;更多的人或事物;**adj.** 更多的

more·o·ver [morˋovɚ] 🎧 *Track 3200*
adv. 並且;此外
▶ He is a doctor; moreover, he is a writer.
他是醫生,而且也是個作家。

morn·ing [ˋmɔrnɪŋ] 🎧 *Track 3201*
n. 早晨;上午

※灰色單字為英檢初級必備單字

mort·gage [`mɔrgɪdʒ] 🎧 *Track 3202*

n. 抵押；抵押借款

▶ He could barely feed himself with his minimum wages but he still managed to pay off his education mortgage.
他掙的最低薪資僅勉強能養活他自己，但他仍設法還清大學助學貸款。

(補充片語)

pay off 還清；
education mortgage 大學助學貸款

v. 抵押；以……做擔保

▶ He mortgaged their apartment to the bank without telling his wife.
他沒告訴妻子就將他們的公寓抵押給銀行。

mos·qui·to [məs`kito] 🎧 *Track 3203*

n. 蚊子

moss [mɔs] 🎧 *Track 3204*

n. 苔蘚

▶ A rolling stone gathers no moss.
滾石不生苔，轉業不聚財。

most [most] 🎧 *Track 3205*

adv. 最；最大程度地；非常；**pron.** 最大量；最多數；大部分；**adj.** 最多的；多數的

most·ly [`mostlɪ] 🎧 *Track 3206*

adv. 大部分地，大多數地，主要地

▶ The actor's fans, mostly women, don't want him to get married. 這男演員的粉絲，主要是女性，都不希望他結婚。

mo·tel [mo`tɛl] 🎧 *Track 3207*

n. 汽車旅館

▶ Let's find a motel to stay tonight.
我們今晚找間汽車旅館過夜吧。

moth [mɔθ] 🎧 *Track 3208*

n. 蛾；蠹，蛀蟲

▶ Moths are attracted to lights.
蛾會受燈光吸引。

mo·the·r [`mʌðɚ] 🎧 *Track 3209*
=mom·my=mom
=mom·ma=mam·ma

n. 媽媽；母親；**v.** 像母親般照料；生下

Mo·ther's Day 🎧 *Track 3210*
[`mʌðɚz-de]

n. 母親節

mo·tion [`moʃən] 🎧 *Track 3211*

n. （物體的）移動、運行；動作、姿態
v. 打手勢；做動作示意

mo·ti·vate [`motə͵vet] 🎧 *Track 3212*

v. 給……動機；刺激；激發

▶ He was motivated to become a doctor after the accident.
意外之後他便有了想成為醫生的動機。

mo·ti·va·tion 🎧 *Track 3213*
[͵motə`veʃən]

n. 刺激；推動

▶ The student lacks motivation towards learning. 那個學生缺少學習的動機。

mo·tor [`motɚ] 🎧 *Track 3214*

n. 馬達；發動機；電動機

▶ The boat is driven by an electric motor.
這艘船是靠馬達啟動的。

mo·tor·cy·cle [`motɚ͵saɪkl] 🎧 *Track 3215*
=mo·tor·bike （英式英文）

n. 摩托車

moun·tain [`mauntn] 🎧 *Track 3216*

n. 山

moun·tain·ous 🎧 *Track 3217*
[`mauntənəs]

adj. 多山的

▶ The holiday resort is located in a mountainous area. 那個度假勝地位於山區。

mouse [maus] 🎧 *Track 3218*

n. 鼠；膽小如鼠的人

mous·tache [məs`tæʃ] 🎧 *Track 3219*
=mus·tache

n. 髭，小鬍子

▶ Your moustache does make you look sexier, but it also makes you look older.
你的小鬍子的確讓你看起來更性感，但是也讓你看起來比較老。

mouth [maʊθ] 🎧 *Track 3220*
n. 嘴

mov·a·ble [`muvəbḷ] 🎧 *Track 3221*
adj. 可動的；可移動的
▶ The doll's arms and legs are movable.
這洋娃娃的手和腳是可以動的。

move [muv] 🎧 *Track 3222*
v. 移動；搬動；遷移；搬家；**n.** 移動；措施

move·ment [`muvmənt] 🎧 *Track 3223*
n. 運動；活動；行動

mo·vie [`muvɪ]=**film** 🎧 *Track 3224*
=**cin·em·a**=**pic·ture**
n. 電影

mow [mo] 🎧 *Track 3225*
v. （用鐮刀等）刈（草等）
▶ We need to mow the lawn this weekend.
我們這個週末要把草給除一除。

Mr. [`mɪstɚ]=**Mr** 🎧 *Track 3226*
n. 先生（用於男士稱謂）

Mrs. [`mɪsɪz]=**Mrs** 🎧 *Track 3227*
n. 太太；夫人（用於已婚女性稱謂）

MRT [ɛm-ɑr-ti] 🎧 *Track 3228*
=**mass rap·id tran·sit**
=**sub·way**=**un·der·ground**
=**me·tro**
n. 大眾捷運系統

Ms. [mɪz]=**Ms** 🎧 *Track 3229*
n. 女士（用於婚姻狀態不明的女性稱謂）

MTV [ɛm-ti-vi] 🎧 *Track 3230*
n. 音樂電視

much [mʌtʃ] 🎧 *Track 3231*
pron. 許多；大量的事物；**adv.** 非常；很；
adj. 許多；大量的

mud [mʌd] 🎧 *Track 3232*
n. 泥；泥漿

mud·dy [`mʌdɪ] 🎧 *Track 3233*
adj. 泥濘的；多泥的；渾濁的；糊塗的

▶ Please take off your muddy shoes before you step into the house.
請在踏入屋子前把你泥濘的鞋子脫下來。

mug [mʌg] 🎧 *Track 3234*
n. 大杯子，馬克杯；鬼臉，怪相；嘴臉
▶ I hate him so much that I don't even want to see his ugly mug. 我好討厭他，我甚至不想看到他那張醜陋的嘴臉。
v. 扮鬼臉，做怪相；給……拍照
▶ The naughty boy mugged at me and ran away. 那頑皮的男孩對我做了個鬼臉，然後就跑走了。

mule [mjul] 🎧 *Track 3235*
n. 騾子；固執的人

mul·ti·ple [`mʌltəpḷ] 🎧 *Track 3236*
adj. 複合的，多樣的
▶ The man suffered serious multiple injuries. 男子身上有多處嚴重的傷口。

mul·ti·ply [`mʌltəplaɪ] 🎧 *Track 3237*
v. 乘；相乘；使成倍增加；繁殖
▶ Mosquitoes multiply quickly.
蚊子繁殖速度是很快的。

mur·der [`mɝdɚ] 🎧 *Track 3238*
v. 殺害，謀殺
▶ He believed his father was murdered.
他認為他的父親是被殺害的。
n. 謀殺，殺害
▶ She was determined to accuse her ex-husband of premeditated murder.
她決心告她前夫蓄意謀殺。

mur·der·er [`mɝdərɚ] 🎧 *Track 3239*
n. 謀殺犯；兇手
▶ It is unbelievable that the murderer is still at large.
兇手至今仍逍遙法外，真是讓人難以相信。

mur·mur [`mɝmɚ] 🎧 *Track 3240*
n. 低語聲；低聲抱怨；輕柔而持續的聲音；心臟雜音
▶ The employees made no murmur.
員工並沒有表示不滿。

Aa Bb Cc Dd Ee Ff Gg Hh Ii Jj Kk Ll Mm Nn Oo Pp Qq Rr Ss Tt Uu Vv Ww Xx Yy Zz

※灰色單字為英檢初級必備單字

v. 輕聲細語；私語；小聲說話
▶ The audience started murmuring to each other. 觀眾開始彼此竊竊私語起來。

mus·cle [ˋmʌsḷ] 🎧 *Track 3241*
n. 肌，肌肉；體力；實力
▶ We can develop our muscles.
我們可以鍛鍊肌肉。

muse [mjuz] 🎧 *Track 3242*
v. 沉思，冥想；若有所思地說
▶ He mused over what to do next.
他沉思著下一步該怎麼做。

mu·se·um [mjuˋzɪəm] 🎧 *Track 3243*
n. 博物館

mush·room [ˋmʌʃrʊm] 🎧 *Track 3244*
n. 蘑菇，蕈
▶ These mushrooms are not edible.
這些蘑菇不能吃。

v. 採蘑菇；雨後春筍般迅速增長
▶ Mansions mushroomed all over the city.
城市裡的高樓像雨後春筍般不斷出現。

mu·sic [ˋmjuzɪk] 🎧 *Track 3245*
n. 音樂

mu·sic·al [ˋmjuzɪkḷ] 🎧 *Track 3246*
adj. 音樂的
▶ I cannot play any musical instruments.
我不會彈奏任何樂器。

n. 歌舞劇；音樂片
▶ I'm not really into musicals.
我不是很喜歡看歌舞劇。

mu·si·cian [mjuˋzɪʃən] 🎧 *Track 3247*
n. 音樂家

must [mʌst] 🎧 *Track 3248*
aux. 必定；必須；一定要

mus·tache [ˋmʌstæʃ] 🎧 *Track 3249*
n. 小鬍子
▶ He's extremely proud of his own mustache.
他很為自己的小鬍子感到驕傲。

must·n't [ˋmʌsnt] 🎧 *Track 3250*
abbr. 不可（must not的縮寫）

mute [mjut] 🎧 *Track 3251*
adj. 沉默的；啞的，不會說話的
▶ The boy was born mute.
那男孩生來就是啞的。

n. 啞巴；靜音
▶ Please put your cell phone on mute.
請把你的手機轉至靜音。

v. 消音；降低、減輕（聲音）
▶ Please mute your cell phone.
請將您的手機關靜音。

mut·ter [ˋmʌtɚ] 🎧 *Track 3252*
v. 低聲嘀咕；低聲抱怨
▶ I overheard some employees muttering.
我無意聽到有些員工在抱怨。

n. 咕噥，抱怨
▶ Some customers muttered complaints.
有些顧客在抱怨。

mu·tu·al [ˋmjutʃʊəl] 🎧 *Track 3253*
adj. 相互的
▶ We don't have any mutual friends.
我們沒有共同的朋友。

my [maɪ] 🎧 *Track 3254*
det. 我的

my·self [maɪˋsɛlf] 🎧 *Track 3255*
pron. 我自己

mys·te·ri·ous [mɪsˋtɪrɪəs] 🎧 *Track 3256*
adj. 神秘的；故弄玄虛的；詭異的
▶ His mysterious smile gave me the creeps.
他詭異的笑容讓我毛骨悚然。

mys·te·ry [ˋmɪstərɪ] 🎧 *Track 3257*
n. 神秘的事物；難以理解的事物，謎
▶ How exactly dinosaurs vanished from the earth has remained a mystery.
恐龍究竟是如何從地球上消失，至今仍是個難解的謎團。

myth [mɪθ] 🎧 *Track 3258*
n. 神話；虛構的人事物；無事實根據的觀點
▶ The story of this movie is a myth.
這部電影的劇情純屬虛構。

Nn

通過中級英文檢定者的英文能力：

在日常生活中，能聽懂一般的會話；能大致聽懂公共場所廣播、氣象報告及廣告等。在工作時，能聽懂簡易的產品介紹與操作說明。能大致聽懂外籍人士的談話及詢問。

在日常生活中，能閱讀短文、故事、私人信件、廣告、傳單、簡介及使用說明等。在工作時，能閱讀工作須知、公告、操作手冊、例行的文件、傳真、電報等。

能寫簡單的書信、故事及心得等。對於熟悉且與個人經歷相關的主題，能以簡易的文字表達。

在日常生活中，能以簡易英語交談或描述一般事物，能介紹自己的生活作息、工作、家庭、經歷等，並可對一般話題陳述看法。在工作時，能進行簡單的答詢，並與外籍人士交談溝通。

本書除包含官方公佈的中級4,947單字外，更精挑了近400個滿分必學的高手單字。同時，在片語的挑選、例句的使用上，皆依上述英檢官方公佈之能力範疇做設計，難度適中、不偏離考試主題。發音部則是自然發音＆KK音標雙管齊下，搭配MP3以「分解／完整」方式錄音，給你最多元有效的學習手段，怎麼記都可以，想忘掉都好難！

---

nail [nel]　　🎧 *Track 3259*
n. 釘子；指甲；**v.** 釘；釘牢；固定；集中於

na‧ïve [nɑˋiv]　　🎧 *Track 3260*
adj. 天真的，幼稚的
▶ Helen is so naïve that she still believes in the existence of Santa Claus.
海倫仍然相信聖誕老人的存在，真是太天真了。

na‧ked [ˋnekɪd]　　🎧 *Track 3261*
adj. 裸身的；光禿禿的；赤裸裸的
▶ He was all naked in the picture.
他在照片中全身赤裸。

(相關片語)
get naked 開心地玩
▶ Let's get naked at the party.
我們在派對開心地玩吧！

name [nem]　　🎧 *Track 3262*
n. 名字；**v.** 命名；為……取名

name‧ly [ˋnemlɪ]　　🎧 *Track 3263*
adv. 即；那就是
▶ I fear nothing but one person, namely my wife.
我什麼都不怕，就怕一個人，那就是我太太。

nan‧ny [ˋnænɪ]　　🎧 *Track 3264*
n. 母山羊；保姆
▶ We need to hire a full-time nanny to look after our baby.
我們必須請一個全職保姆來照顧我們的寶寶。

(補充片語)
look after 照顧

nap [næp]　　🎧 *Track 3265*
n. 打盹兒，午睡
▶ Grandpa always takes a nap after lunch.
爺爺總是在吃過中飯後午睡。

v. 打盹兒，午睡
▶ Grandpa is napping in his armchair.
爺爺在他的扶手椅上打盹兒。

catch sb. napping 發現某人未盡職；使某人措手不及

▶ I was caught napping when the teacher gave us a pop quiz today.
當老師今天給我們隨堂測驗時，真是讓我措手不及。

nap·kin [`næpkɪn] 🎧 *Track 3266*
n. 餐巾

nar·ra·tor [næ`retɚ] 🎧 *Track 3267*
n. 解說員，講述者，旁白

▶ The narrator vividly explained the hatching process of a chicken.
解說員生動地解釋一隻雞的孵化過程。

nar·row [`næro] 🎧 *Track 3268*
adj. 窄的；狹窄的；**v.** 使變窄；縮小、限制（範圍等）

nas·ty [`næstɪ] 🎧 *Track 3269*
adj. 齷齪的；使人難受的；淫猥的，下流的；惡劣的；難處理的；惡意的

▶ His nasty comments on my presentation really upset me. 他對我的報告所做的惡毒評論真的讓我很惱火。

na·tion [`neʃən] 🎧 *Track 3270*
n. 國家

na·tion·al [`næʃən!] 🎧 *Track 3271*
adj. 全國性的；國家的；國有的

na·tion·al·i·ty [ˌnæʃə`nælətɪ] 🎧 *Track 3272*
n. 國籍；民族

▶ There are more than 55 different nationalities in China.
中國有超過五十五個不同的民族。

na·tive [`netɪv] 🎧 *Track 3273*
adj. 天生的；出生地的；祖國的；家鄉的；土著的；天然的

▶ I am a native speaker of French. I was born and grew up in France, and finally moved to China when I was twenty-two.
我的母語是法文。我在法國土生土長，直到22歲時搬到了中國。

native speaker 說母語的人

n. 本地人；本國人；土著，原住民

▶ The foreigner's Chinese is as fluent as a native's.
那個外國人的中文就跟一個本地人一樣的流暢。

nat·u·ral [`nætʃərəl] 🎧 *Track 3274*
adj. 自然的

nat·u·ral·ist [`nætʃərəlɪst] 🎧 *Track 3275*
n. 自然主義者；博物學家

▶ He is a naturalist so he doesn't believe in the existence of hell.
他是個自然主義者，所以不相信地獄的存在。

nat·u·ral·ly [`nætʃərəlɪ] 🎧 *Track 3276*
adv. 自然地，天生地；當然

▶ I am your wife. Naturally you have to discuss this with me before you make any decision.
我是你的妻子。你當然必須要跟我討論這件事才能做決定。

na·ture [`netʃɚ] 🎧 *Track 3277*
n. 自然（狀態）；自然界；天性、本質

naugh·ty [`nɔtɪ] 🎧 *Track 3278*
adj. 頑皮的；淘氣的

na·val [`nevl] 🎧 *Track 3279*
adj. 海軍的，軍艦的，船的

▶ My father is a naval architect.
我父親是個造船工程師。

na·vy [`nevɪ] 🎧 *Track 3280*
n. 海軍

▶ My brother is now on active duty in the Navy. 我哥哥現在正在海軍服役。

on active duty 服役

near [nɪr] 🎧 *Track 3281*
prep. 在……附近；**adj.** 近的；**adv.** 近；接近；幾乎；**v.** 靠近

near·by [ˋnɪrˏbaɪ]　🎧 *Track 3282*
adj. 附近的
▶We always eat at a nearby Chinese restaurant.
我們總是在一間附近的中式餐館吃飯。

adv. 在附近
▶He asked a man standing nearby for directions.
他向站在附近的一位男子問路。

near·ly [ˋnɪrlɪ]　🎧 *Track 3283*
adv. 幾乎；差不多

near·sight·ed　🎧 *Track 3284*
[ˋnɪrˋsaɪtɪd]
adj. 近視的，近視眼的；目光短淺的，短視的
▶Two-thirds of students in my class are nearsighted.
我班上有三分之二的學生是近視的。

neat [nit]　🎧 *Track 3285*
adj. 整齊的；工整的；整潔的
▶Her bedroom is always clean and neat.
她的臥室總是乾淨又整潔。

ne·ces·sar·i·ly　🎧 *Track 3286*
[ˋnɛsəˏsɛrɪlɪ]
adv. 必定，必然地；必須地，必要地
▶You don't necessarily have to move out.
你不一定要搬出去。

ne·ces·sa·ry [ˋnɛsəˏsɛrɪ]　🎧 *Track 3287*
adj. 必須的；必要的

ne·ces·si·ty [nəˋsɛsətɪ]　🎧 *Track 3288*
n. 需要
▶Smart phones are necessities to many people nowadays.
智慧型手機對現今很多人來說是個必需品。

neck [nɛk]　🎧 *Track 3289*
n. 脖子；頸

neck·lace [ˋnɛklɪs]　🎧 *Track 3290*
n. 項鍊

neck·tie [ˋnɛkˏtaɪ]　🎧 *Track 3291*
n. 領帶
▶I don't know how to tie a necktie.
我不知道怎麼打領帶。

need [nid]　🎧 *Track 3292*
v. 需要；**n.** 需要；貧窮；困窘；**aux.** 必須

nee·dle [ˋnidl]　🎧 *Track 3293*
n. 針；指針；**v.** 用針縫；用針刺；用話刺激

need·y [ˋnidɪ]　🎧 *Track 3294*
adj. 貧窮的
▶They raised funds to help those needy people. 他們募款以幫助那些貧困的人。

neg·a·tive [ˋnɛgətɪv]　🎧 *Track 3295*
adj. 否定的；負面的、消極的
n. 否定；否定的回答；拒絕

ne·glect [nɪgˋlɛkt]　🎧 *Track 3296*
v. 忽視；忽略；忘了做；疏於照管
▶He neglected his duty, and consequently got the sack. 他怠忽職守，結果被解僱了。

（補充片語）
neglect one's duty 怠忽職守；
get the sack 被解僱，被開除

ne·go·ti·ate [nɪˋgoʃɪˏet]　🎧 *Track 3297*
v. 談判
▶The police had no choice but to negotiate with the hijackers.
警方別無選擇，只得跟劫匪談判。

ne·go·ti·a·tion　🎧 *Track 3298*
[nɪˏgoʃɪˋeʃən]
n. 談判，協商
▶The government refused to open negotiations with the rebel forces.
政府拒絕與叛軍展開和談。

（補充片語）
open negotiations with sb. 開始與某人進行談判；
rebel forces 叛軍

Aa
Bb
Cc
Dd
Ee

Ff
Gg
Hh
Ii
Jj

Kk
Ll
Mm
Nn
Oo

Pp
Qq
Rr
Ss
Tt

Uu
Vv
Ww
Xx
Yy
Zz

※灰色單字為英檢初級必備單字

neigh·bor [`nebɚ] 🎧 *Track 3299*
=neigh·bour （英式英文）
n. 鄰居；**v.** 住在附近；與……為鄰

neigh·bor·hood 🎧 *Track 3300*
[`nebɚ͵hʊd]
n. 鄰近地區
▶ There is no hospital in the neighborhood.
這附近沒有醫院。

nei·ther [`niðɚ] 🎧 *Track 3301*
adv. 也不；**pron.** 兩個中沒有一個；**adj.** 兩者都不；**conj.** 既不……，也不……

neph·ew [`nɛfju] 🎧 *Track 3302*
n. 姪兒；外甥

nerve [nɝv] 🎧 *Track 3303*
n. 神經；神經過敏；憂慮；勇敢；膽量；厚顏，無恥
▶ David wanted to argue with his boss, but lost his nerve when standing in his boss's office.
大衛想要跟他老闆理論，但是站在老闆辦公室裡卻失去了勇氣。

（補充片語）
lose one's nerve 失去勇氣，變得慌張

v. 鼓勵，激勵
▶ He nerved himself to ask her out.
他鼓起勇氣約她出去。

（補充片語）
nerve oneself 鼓足勇氣

ner·vous [`nɝvəs] 🎧 *Track 3304*
adj. 緊張的

nest [nɛst] 🎧 *Track 3305*
n. 巢；窩；穴；**v.** 築巢

net [nɛt] 🎧 *Track 3306*
n. 網狀物；網
▶ They tried to catch the butterflies with the nets. 他們試圖用網子抓蝴蝶。

v. 用網捕
▶ The kids were netting butterflies in the garden. 孩子們在花園裡用網子抓蝴蝶。

net·work [`nɛt͵wɝk] 🎧 *Track 3307*
n. 網；網狀物；網狀系統；廣播網，電視網；電腦網路
▶ Our marketing network is well developed.
我們的銷售網路已經建立得很好了。

v. 用網覆蓋；在廣播網聯播；建立關係網
▶ He didn't neglect to network with his past clients when he job-hopped to another company.
他在跳槽到另一家公司時，並未忽略要與過去的客戶建立關係網。

nev·er [`nɛvɚ] 🎧 *Track 3308*
adv. 從不；永不；絕不

nev·er·the·less 🎧 *Track 3309*
[͵nɛvɚðə`lɛs]
adv. 仍然
▶ I don't like him; nevertheless, I invited him to the party.
我不喜歡他，但是我還是請他來參加派對。

new [nju] 🎧 *Track 3310*
adj. 新的

New Year's Day 🎧 *Track 3311*
[nju-jɪrz-de]
n. 元旦

New Year's Eve 🎧 *Track 3312*
[nju-jɪrz-iv]
n. 除夕

New York [nju-jɔrk] 🎧 *Track 3313*
n. 紐約

new·com·er [`nju`kʌmɚ] 🎧 *Track 3314*
n. 新手，新到者，新生
▶ We're throwing a welcoming party for the newcomers.
我們將為新來的職員舉辦一場歡迎派對。

（補充片語）
welcoming party 迎新派對，歡迎派對

news [njuz] 🎧 *Track 3315*
n. 新聞；消息

news·cast·er   🎧 *Track 3316*
[`njuz͵kæstɚ]

n. 新聞廣播員

▶ A slip of the tongue made the newscaster say "fart" instead of "part". 新聞廣播員一時口誤，將「部分」說成了「放屁」。

(補充片語)

a slip of the tongue　口誤

news·pa·per [`njuz͵pepɚ] 🎧 *Track 3317*
n. 報紙

next [`nɛkst]   🎧 *Track 3318*
adj. 緊鄰的；接下來的；居次的；**adv.** 接下來；次於

nice [naɪs]   🎧 *Track 3319*
adj. 好的；美好的；好心的

nick·name [`nɪk͵nem] 🎧 *Track 3320*
n. 暱稱，小名，綽號

▶ "Nini" was the nickname my mother used to call me when I was a little girl.
「妮妮」是我媽媽在我小時候稱呼我的小名。

v. 給……起綽號

▶ He was nicknamed "Yes Man" because he always said yes to everyone.
因為他總是對每個人有求必應，所以被取了個「好好先生」的綽號。

niece [nis]   🎧 *Track 3321*
n. 姪女；外甥女

night [naɪt]   🎧 *Track 3322*
n. 夜晚

night·mare [`naɪt͵mɛr] 🎧 *Track 3323*
n. 噩夢，夢魘

▶ The murderer has had nightmares every night since he killed the little girl. 殺人兇手在殺害那個小女孩之後每晚都做噩夢。

nine [naɪn]   🎧 *Track 3324*
pron. 九個；**n.** 九；**adj.** 九的；九個的

nine·teen [`naɪn`tin] 🎧 *Track 3325*
pron. 十九個；**n.** 十九；十九歲；**adj.** 十九的；十九個的

nine·ty [`naɪntɪ]   🎧 *Track 3326*
pron. 九十；九十個；**n.** 九十；九十歲；**adj.** 九十的；九十個的

no [no]   🎧 *Track 3327*
adv./adj. 沒有；**n.** 不；沒有；拒絕

no·ble [`nobl̩]   🎧 *Track 3328*
adj. 高尚的；貴族的；顯貴的；崇高的

▶ Although he is from a noble family, he is modest and courteous.
雖然他出身貴族家庭，但是他非常的謙遜有禮

n. 貴族

▶ None of his schoolmates knew he was a noble.
他的學校同學中沒有一個人知道他是個貴族。

no·bod·y [`nobɑdɪ]   🎧 *Track 3329*
pron. 沒有人；無人；**n.** 無足輕重的小人物

no·bod·y's [`nobɑdɪz] 🎧 *Track 3330*
abbr. 沒有人的、沒有人是（**nobody**的所有格，或**nobody is**的縮寫）

nod [nɑd]   🎧 *Track 3331*
v. 點頭；打盹；**n.** 點頭；打瞌睡

noise [nɔɪz]   🎧 *Track 3332*
n. 噪音

nois·y [`nɔɪzɪ]   🎧 *Track 3333*
adj. 吵鬧的；喧鬧的；充滿噪聲的；嘈嚷的

none [nʌn]   🎧 *Track 3334*
pron. 一個也無；沒有任何人或物；無一人；**adv.** 毫不；絕不；一點也不

none·the·less   🎧 *Track 3335*
[͵nʌnðə`lɛs]

adv. 但是，仍然；儘管如此

▶ She was tired; nonetheless, she fixed a sandwich for her husband.
她很累，但還是幫她的丈夫做了個三明治。

non·sense [`nɑnsɛns] 🎧 *Track 3336*
n. 胡說；無意義的廢話

▶ Stop talking nonsense!
別胡說八道了！

※灰色單字為英檢初級必備單字

non-stop [`nɑn-stɑp]   Track 3337
adj. 直達的
▶This non-stop train is bound for Taipei.
這班直達車是開往臺北的。

(補充片語)
non-stop train 直達列車；
be bound for （準備）前往

adv. 不停地
▶It has been raining non-stop since last week.
從上星期開始就一直不停地下雨。

noo·dle [`nudl]   Track 3338
n. 麵

noon [nun]   Track 3339
n. 中午；正午

nor [nɔr]   Track 3340
conj. 也不

nor·mal [`nɔrml]   Track 3341
adj. 正常的
▶This night cream is for the normal type of skin.
這款晚霜是給正常膚質的人使用的。

nor·mal·ly [`nɔrmlɪ]   Track 3342
adv. 正常地；按照慣例地；通常
▶Normally, the kids are all asleep when I arrive home at night.
通常當我晚上回到家時，孩子們都在睡了。

north [nɔrθ]   Track 3343
n. 北方；**adj.** 北部的；北方的；**adv.** 向北；在北方；自北方

north-east [`nɔrθ`ist]   Track 3344
n. 東北，東北方；東北部
▶The cold air mass is from the northeast.
這波冷氣團是從東北方來的。

adv. 在東北；向東北；來自東北
▶The airplane turned northeast and disappeared from radar screens a few minutes later.
飛機轉向東北方，並在幾分鐘之後從雷達螢幕上消失。

adj. 東北的；來自東北的；朝東北的
▶It is expected that the northeast monsoon will bring us plenty of rain.
這個東北季風可望能為我們帶來豐沛的雨水。

nor·thern [`nɔrðə-n]   Track 3345
adj. 北方的

north-west [`nɔrθ`wɛst]   Track 3346
n. 西北，西北方；西北部
▶Taoyuan is in the northwest of Taiwan.
桃園位在台灣的西北部。

adv. 在西北；向西北；來自西北
▶The river turns northwest near the woods and then flows into the Atlantic Ocean.
這條河在樹林附近轉向西北方，接著便流入大西洋。

adj. 西北的；來自西北的；朝西北的
▶The northwest wind will keep us chilly all through the week.
這西北風會讓我們一整個星期都冷颼颼。

nose [noz]   Track 3347
n. 鼻子

nos·tril [`nɑstrɪl]   Track 3348
n. 鼻孔
▶Picking your nose constantly will increase the size of your nostrils.
時常挖鼻孔會讓你的鼻孔變大噢。

(補充片語)
pick one's nose 挖鼻孔

not [nɑt]   Track 3349
adv. 不

note [not]   Track 3350
n. 筆記；便條；**v.** 注意；提到；記下

note·book [`not,bʊk]   Track 3351
n. 筆記本；筆記型電腦

noth·ing [`nʌθɪŋ]   Track 3352
pron. 沒什麼；什麼事物都沒有；**n.** 微不足道的事或物

no·tice [`notɪs]   Track 3353
n. 公告；通知；注意；察覺；**v.** 注意；注意到

no·to·ri·ous [no`torɪəs] 🎧 *Track 3354*
adj. 惡名昭彰的，聲名狼藉的
▶ The company is notorious for producing and selling tainted foods.
這間公司因為製造並販賣黑心食品而聲名狼藉。

noun [naʊn] 🎧 *Track 3355*
n. 名詞
▶ The word "money" is an uncountable noun.
「錢」這個字是個不可數名詞。

nour·ish [`nɝɪʃ] 🎧 *Track 3356*
v. 養育，滋養；培育；鼓勵；施肥於
▶ Normally, a mother is able to produce enough milk to nourish her baby.
通常一個媽媽是能夠生產足夠的乳汁來養育她的寶寶。

nov·el [`nɑvl̩] 🎧 *Track 3357*
n. （長篇）小說；**adj.** 新奇的；新穎的

nov·el·ist [`nɑvl̩ɪst] 🎧 *Track 3358*
n. 小說家
▶ He is a very well-known novelist in his country.
他在國內是非常知名的小說家。

No·vem·ber [no`vɛmbɚ] 🎧 *Track 3359*
n. 十一月

now [naʊ] 🎧 *Track 3360*
adv. 現在；此刻；馬上；**n.** 現在；目前；此刻

now·a·days [`naʊə‚dez] 🎧 *Track 3361*
adv. 今日，現在
▶ Students nowadays are less diligent.
現在的學生比較不那麼勤勉了。

no·where [`no‚hwɛr] 🎧 *Track 3362*
adv. 任何地方都不
▶ I went back to the restaurant to look for my cellphone, but it was nowhere to be found.
我回餐廳去找我的手機，但是到處都找不到。

相關片語
middle of nowhere　偏遠的某地

▶ We got lost in the middle of nowhere.
我們在一個雞不生蛋、鳥不拉屎的地方迷路了。

nu·cle·ar [`njuklɪɚ] 🎧 *Track 3363*
adj. 核心的，中心的；原子彈的，原子核的
▶ Replacing nuclear power with renewable energies is very important.
以可再生能源來取代核能是很重要的一件事。

相關片語
nuclear family　核心家庭
▶ A nuclear family consists of a pair of parents and their children.
核心家庭是一對父母和他們的小孩所組成的。

num·ber [`nʌmbɚ] 🎧 *Track 3364*
n. 數字；數量；**v.** 編號；給號碼；算入

nu·me·rous [`njumərəs] 🎧 *Track 3365*
adj. 許多的；為數眾多的
▶ I found numerous grammatical mistakes in this article.
我在這篇文章中找到許多文法上的錯誤。

nun [nʌn] 🎧 *Track 3366*
n. 修女，尼姑
▶ She used to be a nun, but resumed secular life two years ago.
她曾經是個尼姑，但兩年前還俗了。

補充片語
resume secular life　還俗

nurse [nɝs] 🎧 *Track 3367*
n. 護士；**v.** 看護；護理

nur·se·ry [`nɝsərɪ] 🎧 *Track 3368*
n. 托兒所
▶ I have to pick up my kids at the nursery before six. 我得在六點前到托兒所去接小孩。

nurs·ing [`nɝsɪŋ] 🎧 *Track 3369*
n. 看護，護理
▶ Nursing is not just a job. It's an honorable career.
看護不只是一份工作。它是一份高尚的職業。

adj. 看護的，護理病人的

※灰色單字為英檢初級必備單字

► My grandpa lives with us instead of living in a nursing home.
我爺爺是跟我們住在一起，而不是住在養老院。

(補充片語)

nursing home 養老院；照料老人或病患的地方

nut [nʌt]　　🎧 *Track 3370*
n. 堅果；核果；難事；難對付的人；腦袋

► Eating nuts every day is good to your heart.
每天吃堅果對你的心臟有好處。

(相關片語)

do one's nut 發怒；氣炸

► My mom will do her nut when she sees the messy house.
我媽看到這亂七八糟的房子會氣死。

nu·tri·ent [`njutrɪənt]　🎧 *Track 3371*
n. 營養物，滋養物

► Breast milk contains all the nutrients a newborn baby requires.
母乳含有一個新生嬰兒所需要的所有營養。

nu·tri·tion [nju`trɪʃən]　🎧 *Track 3372*
n. 營養，滋養；營養物，滋養物

► Poor nutrition can negatively impact a child's normal growth and development.
營養不良會對一個孩童的正常成長與發展帶來負面的影響。

ny·lon [`naɪlɑn]　　🎧 *Track 3373*
n. 尼龍

► This raincoat is made from nylon.
這件雨衣是尼龍製成的。

♕Note

Oo

通過中級英文檢定者的英文能力：

 在日常生活中，能聽懂一般的會話；能大致聽懂公共場所廣播、氣象報告及廣告等。在工作時，能聽懂簡易的產品介紹與操作說明。能大致聽懂外籍人士的談話及詢問。

 在日常生活中，能閱讀短文、故事、私人信件、廣告、傳單、簡介及使用說明等。在工作時，能閱讀工作須知、公告、操作手冊、例行的文件、傳真、電報等。

 能寫簡單的書信、故事及心得等。對於熟悉且與個人經歷相關的主題，能以簡易的文字表達。

 在日常生活中，能以簡易英語交談或描述一般事物，能介紹自己的生活作息、工作、家庭、經歷等，並可對一般話題陳述看法。在工作時，能進行簡單的答詢，並與外籍人士交談溝通。

本書除包含官方公佈的中級4,947單字外，更精挑了近400個滿分必學的高手單字。同時，在片語的挑選、例句的使用上，皆依上述英檢官方公佈之能力範疇做設計，難度適中、不偏離考試主題。發音部分則是自然發音＆KK音標雙管齊下，搭配MP3以「分解／完整」方式錄音，給你最多元有效的學習手段，怎麼記都可以，想忘掉都好難！

---

oak [ok] Track 3374
n. 橡樹
▶ There is an old oak tree in front of our house.
我們房子前有棵老橡樹。

o·a·sis [oˋesɪs] Track 3375
n. （沙漠中的）綠洲；（困境中）令人寬慰的事物或地方
▶ The small village is like an oasis of peace in this troubled world.
這個小村莊就像是這個紛擾世界裡的一個寧靜的綠洲。

o·be·di·ent [əˋbidjənt] Track 3376
adj. 順從的，服從的
▶ He wants his subordinates to be completely obedient to what he says.
他希望他的部下對他說的話百分之百服從。

o·bey [əˋbe] Track 3377
v. 遵守；服從

ob·ject [ˋabdʒɪkt] Track 3378
n. 物體；對象；目標；目的
v. 反對；反對說

ob·jec·tion [əbˋdʒɛkʃən] Track 3379
n. 反對；異議；阻礙；反對的理由
▶ My parents have no objection to my international marriage.
我的父母親不反對我的異國婚姻。

ob·jec·tive [əbˋdʒɛktɪv] Track 3380
n. 目標，目的；受格
▶ My objective is to save enough money for a trip to Europe.
我的目標是要存到足夠到歐洲旅遊的錢。

adj. 客觀的，無偏見的；客觀存在的
▶ He gave us some objective advice.
他給了我們一些客觀的建議。

ob·ser·va·tion [ˌabzɚˋveʃən] Track 3381
n. 觀察；觀測力；監視；（觀察後的）意見或看法

229

▶The man's every movement is under observation by the police.
此人的一舉一動都受到警方嚴密監視。

ob·serve [əb`zɝv] 🎧 Track 3382
v. 注意；觀察；監視
▶She observed the way he treats his family and confirmed that he was a good man. 她觀察他對待家人的方式，確定他是個好男人。

ob·sta·cle [`ɑbstəkl] 🎧 Track 3383
n. 障礙物，妨礙
▶His arrogance is an obstacle to his success. 他的自負是他成功的阻礙。

ob·tain [əb`ten] 🎧 Track 3384
v. 獲得，得到
▶We are so grateful to have obtained financial support from all circles.
我們對於能得到來自各界的財務支援感到十分感謝。

ob·vi·ous [`ɑbvɪəs] 🎧 Track 3385
adj. 明顯的
▶It is obvious that he is inadequate to the job. 很明顯地，他並不勝任這份工作。

ob·vi·ous·ly [`ɑbvɪəslɪ] 🎧 Track 3386
adv. 明顯地，顯然地
▶Obviously, we can't afford to hire a full-time nanny. 我們顯然請不起全職保姆。

oc·ca·sion [ə`keʒən] 🎧 Track 3387
n. 場合；時機
▶Everyone was dressed to the nines for the special occasion.
大家都為了這個特別的場合盛裝打扮。

(補充片語)
be dressed to the nines 盛裝打扮

(相關片語)
have a sense of occasion 有場合觀念
▶He wouldn't wear his T-shirt and jeans to the wedding if he had any sense of occasion.
他如果有一丁點場合觀念，就不會穿著T恤和牛仔褲去參加婚禮。

oc·ca·sion·al [ə`keʒənl] 🎧 Track 3388
adj. 偶爾的；特殊場合的；臨時的
▶I don't like to drink alcohol, but I don't mind an occasional glass of wine.
我不喜歡喝酒，但是並不介意偶爾來一杯。

oc·cu·pa·tion [ˌɑkjə`peʃən] 🎧 Track 3389
n. 工作，職業；日常事務；佔領
▶He is a salesman by occupation.
他的職業是業務員。

oc·cu·py [`ɑkjəˌpaɪ] 🎧 Track 3390
v. 佔領，佔據
▶Work occupies most of his time.
工作佔了他大部份的時間。

oc·cur [ə`kɝ] 🎧 Track 3391
v. 發生

o·cean [`oʃən] 🎧 Track 3392
n. 海洋

o'clock [ə`klɑk] 🎧 Track 3393
adv. ⋯⋯點鐘

Oc·to·ber [ɑk`tobə] =Oct. 🎧 Track 3394
n. 十月

oc·to·pus [`ɑktəpəs] 🎧 Track 3395
n. 章魚
▶An octopus has eight arms.
一隻章魚有八隻腳。

odd [ɑd] 🎧 Track 3396
adj. 古怪的
▶He often comes up with odd ideas.
他總是會想出一些奇怪的點子。

(相關片語)
odd job 零工
▶He couldn't find a decent job, so he had to earn his living by doing odd jobs.
他找不到像樣的工作，只好靠打零工唯生。

of [ɑv] 🎧 Track 3397
prep. 屬於；⋯⋯的；因為

off [ɔf]　🎧 *Track 3398*
adv. 離開；隔開；關掉；**prep.** 在……下方；往……下面；離開；**adj.** 偏離的；較遠的；不正常的

of·fend [ə`fɛnd]　🎧 *Track 3399*
v. 冒犯，觸怒，使不舒服
▶She was offended by his insulting remarks.
他侮辱人的評論讓她感到很不舒服。

of·fense [ə`fɛns]　🎧 *Track 3400*
=of·fence
n. 罪過；觸怒
▶You don't need to take offense at that small trifle. 你無須為那種小事發怒。
(補充片語)
take offense at　因……發怒

of·fen·sive [ə`fɛnsɪv]　🎧 *Track 3401*
adj. 冒犯的；討厭的；進攻的
▶His inappropriate jokes were highly offensive to his female colleagues.
他不適當的笑話讓女同事們大為反感。

n. 進攻，攻勢
▶He is still waiting for the occasion to take the offensive. 他還在等待發動攻勢的時機。
(補充片語)
take the offensive　發動攻勢

of·fer [`ɔfɚ]　🎧 *Track 3402*
v. 提供；提議；給予；**n.** 提議；機會

of·fice [`ɔfɪs]　🎧 *Track 3403*
n. 辦公室；公司

of·fi·cer [`ɔfəsɚ]　🎧 *Track 3404*
n. 官員（軍官；警官）；公務員；高級職員

of·fi·cial [ə`fɪʃəl]　🎧 *Track 3405*
n. 官員；公務員；**adj.** 官方的；正規的

of·ten [`ɔfən]　🎧 *Track 3406*
adv. 時常

oh [o]　🎧 *Track 3407*
interj. （表示驚訝，恐懼）哦，噢，哎呀
▶Oh, that's too bad.
噢，那真是太可惜了。

oil [ɔɪl]　🎧 *Track 3408*
n. 油；**v.** 給……上油；塗油

OK [`o`ke]=**O.K.**　🎧 *Track 3409*
=ok=o.k.=o·kay
adj. 可以的；不錯的；**adv.** 尚可；**n.** 認可；**v.** 批准；認可

old [old]　🎧 *Track 3410*
adj. 老的；舊的

O·lym·pic [o`lɪmpɪk]　🎧 *Track 3411*
adj. 奧林匹克（競賽）的
▶It is all athletes' dream to win an Olympic medal.
贏得一面奧林匹克獎牌是所有運動員的夢想。

o·mit [o`mɪt]　🎧 *Track 3412*
v. 遺漏；省略；忽略不做

on [ɑn]　🎧 *Track 3413*
prep. 在……上；**adv.** 繼續；（穿）上；開著

once [wʌns]　🎧 *Track 3414*
adv. 一次；曾經；**conj.** 一旦；一……便……；**pron.** 一次；一回

one [wʌn]　🎧 *Track 3415*
pron. 一個；**n.** 一；一歲；**adj.** 一的；一個的

one·self [wʌn`sɛlf]　🎧 *Track 3416*
pron. 自己
▶Working on something by oneself is often more time-consuming than working with a team.
自己做某件事往往比跟一個團隊一起做來得耗時。

one-sid·ed [`wʌn`saɪdɪd]　🎧 *Track 3417*
adj. 單側的；片面的；一面倒的
▶We can't jump to conclusions based on one-sided information.
我們不能只憑片面資訊就驟然作出結論。

on·ion [`ʌnjən]　🎧 *Track 3418*
n. 洋蔥

Aa
Bb
Cc
Dd
Ee
Ff
Gg
Hh
Ii
Jj
Kk
Ll
Mm
Nn
Oo
Pp
Qq
Rr
Ss
Tt
Uu
Vv
Ww
Xx
Yy
Zz

※灰色單字為英檢初級必備單字

on·ly [ˈonlɪ] 🎧 *Track 3419*
adv. 僅；只；**adj.** 唯一的；**conj.** 可是；不過

on·to [ˈɑntu] 🎧 *Track 3420*
prep. 到⋯⋯之上；（口）對⋯⋯熟悉
▶ Everyone stood up to applaud as the prize-winner walked onto the stage.
在得獎人走上台時，所有人都站起來鼓掌。

o·pen [ˈopən] 🎧 *Track 3421*
v. 開；打開；**adj.** 開放的；打開的

o·pen·er [ˈopənɚ] 🎧 *Track 3422*
n. 開啟的工具；開端；開啟者
▶ I can't open the can without a can opener.
沒有開罐器我沒辦法打開這個罐頭。

（補充片語）
can opener 開罐器

（相關片語）
eye opener 使人瞠目結舌的事件
▶ The gutter oil scandal is a real eye opener to many people.
地溝油醜聞對許多人來說真是大開眼界。

o·pen·ing [ˈopənɪŋ] 🎧 *Track 3423*
n. 開幕
▶ To celebrate our grand opening, everything in the store is 20% off until September 30.
為了慶祝我們的盛大開幕，店裡所有商品在九月三十日之前都有八折優惠。

adj. 開幕的，開始的
▶ We invited many celebrities and over a hundred VIP customers to the opening ceremony of our branch restaurant.
我們邀請了許多名流以及超過一百名貴賓顧客來參加我們餐廳分店的開幕典禮。

op·e·ra [ˈɑpərə] 🎧 *Track 3424*
n. 歌劇
▶ We went to an opera but had no idea what it was about. 我們去看了一場歌劇，但完全不知道它在演什麼。

（相關片語）
soap opera 肥皂劇

▶ Watching soap operas is a waste of time.
看肥皂劇很浪費時間。

op·e·rate [ˈɑpəˌret] 🎧 *Track 3425*
v. 運轉；營運；操作；動手術

op·e·ra·tion [ˌɑpəˈreʃən] 🎧 *Track 3426*
n. 操作；運轉；經營；手術

op·e·ra·tor [ˈɑpəˌretɚ] 🎧 *Track 3427*
n. 操作者；經營者；施行手術的醫生
▶ The factory is looking for skilled machine operators.
這家工廠正在徵求有技術的機器操作員。

o·pin·ion [əˈpɪnjən] 🎧 *Track 3428*
n. 意見；看法

op·po·nent [əˈponənt] 🎧 *Track 3429*
n. 對手，敵手
▶ He defeated all his opponents in the competition and won the championship.
他在競賽中打敗所有的對手，贏得了冠軍。

op·por·tu·ni·ty 🎧 *Track 3430*
[ˌɑpɚˈtjunətɪ]
n. 機會

op·pose [əˈpoz] 🎧 *Track 3431*
v. 反對
▶ The villagers opposed having the nuclear power plant built in their village.
村民反對在村裡興建核電廠。

op·po·site [ˈɑpəzɪt] 🎧 *Track 3432*
adj. 相反的，對立的；對面的，相對的
▶ My husband and I have opposite points of view on this matter.
我先生與我對這個問題的看法是相反的。

n. 對立面，對立物
▶ My point of view on this matter is the opposite of his.
我對這件事的看法跟他的相反。

prep. 在⋯⋯對面
▶ We live opposite each other.
我們住在彼此對面。

adv. 在對面

▶ We sat opposite at the table.
我們面對面坐在餐桌旁。

op·po·si·tion [ˌɑpə`zɪʃən] 🎧 *Track 3433*
n. 反對，反抗，敵對，對立
▶ I don't have anything to say in opposition.
我沒有反對意見要說。

op·tion [`ɑpʃən] 🎧 *Track 3434*
n. 選擇
▶ He had no option but to accept his offer.
他不得不接受他的提議。

(補充片語)

have no option but to 不得不

or [ɔr] 🎧 *Track 3435*
conj. 或者；否則

o·ral [`orəl] 🎧 *Track 3436*
adj. 口頭的，口述的
▶ I have no idea how to prepare for the oral test. 我不知道該怎麼準備口試。
n. 口試
▶ I passed the written test, but failed the orals. 我通過了筆試，但口試沒過。

or·ange [`ɔrɪndʒ] 🎧 *Track 3437*
n. 柳橙；橙色；**adj.** 橙色的；柳橙的

or·bit [`ɔrbɪt] 🎧 *Track 3438*
n. 運行軌道
▶ Every star has its own orbit.
每顆星星都有自己的運行軌道。
v. 環繞（天體等）的軌道運行
▶ The moon orbits the earth.
月球繞著地球運行。

or·chard [`ɔrtʃəd] 🎧 *Track 3439*
n. 果園
▶ We picked these strawberries directly from the orchard.
我們直接從果園採收這些草莓。

or·ches·tra [`ɔrkɪstrə] 🎧 *Track 3440*
n. 管弦樂團
▶ My brother is the concert-master of that orchestra. 我哥哥是該管弦樂團的樂團首席。

or·der [`ɔrdə] 🎧 *Track 3441*
n. 次序；命令；訂購；**v.** 命令；訂購；點菜

or·der·ly [`ɔrdəlɪ] 🎧 *Track 3442*
adj. 整齊的，有條理的，守秩序的
▶ The demonstrators at the square were leaderless but orderly.
廣場上的示威者雖然沒有領袖，但是卻很有秩序。
n. （醫院的）護理員；勤務兵，傳令兵
▶ The orderly on duty immediately reported the patient's unusual symptoms to the doctor in charge.
值班的護理員立刻將病人不尋常的症狀報告給主治醫師。

(補充片語)

on duty 值班；
the doctor in charge 主治醫師

or·di·na·ry [`ɔrdnˌɛrɪ] 🎧 *Track 3443*
adj. 平凡普通的；平常的

or·gan [`ɔrgən] 🎧 *Track 3444*
n. 器官
▶ Skin is our largest organ.
皮膚是我們最大的器官。

or·gan·ic [ɔr`gænɪk] 🎧 *Track 3445*
adj. 有機的
▶ This multiple supermarket sells organic food and organic food products only.
這家連鎖超市只賣有機食物和有機食品。

or·gan·i·za·tion 🎧 *Track 3446*
[ˌɔrgənə`zeʃən]
=or·gan·i·sa·tion （英式英文）
n. 組織；機構

or·gan·ize [`ɔrgəˌnaɪz] 🎧 *Track 3447*
=or·gan·ise （英式英文）
v. 組織；安排；籌劃；使有條理

or·i·gin [`ɔrədʒɪn] 🎧 *Track 3448*
n. 起源
▶ The origin of life is still a mystery.
生命的起源仍是一團謎。

※灰色單字為英檢初級必備單字

o·rig·i·nal [əˈrɪdʒənl] 🎧 *Track 3449*

adj. 最初的，原始的；有獨創性的；原作的

▶ The selling price of this dress was 30 percent off the original price.
這件洋裝的售價是原價的七折。

---

or·na·ment [ˈɔrnəmənt] 🎧 *Track 3450*

n. 裝飾品；裝飾；增添光彩的人或事物

▶ We're going to shop for some ornaments for our Christmas tree.
我們要去為我們的聖誕樹採購一些裝飾品。

v. 美化；裝飾

▶ They ornamented the hall with colored ribbons and balloons.
他們以彩帶和氣球裝飾大廳。

---

or·phan [ˈɔrfən] 🎧 *Track 3451*

n. 孤兒

▶ The poor boy became an orphan after the fire accident.
這可憐的小男孩在一場火災意外後成了孤兒。

---

or·phan·age [ˈɔrfənɪdʒ] 🎧 *Track 3452*

n. 孤兒院；孤兒身份；孤兒（總稱）

▶ They raised funds to build an orphanage for abandoned children and orphans.
他們招募資金要為被拋棄的孩童或孤兒們蓋一間孤兒院。

---

os·trich [ˈɑstrɪtʃ] 🎧 *Track 3453*

n. 鴕鳥；鴕鳥般的人（以為不正視危險就能躲開危險的人）

▶ The ostrich is a bird that cannot fly.
鴕鳥是一種不會飛的鳥。

---

oth·er [ˈʌðɚ] 🎧 *Track 3454*

adj. 其他的；其餘的；（兩者中）另一個的；**pron.** （兩者中的）另一方；其餘的人或事物

---

oth·er·wise [ˈʌðɚˌwaɪz] 🎧 *Track 3455*

adv. 否則，不然；用別的方法；在其他方面

▶ I'm not going in the same direction; otherwise I'll give you a ride.
我不順路，否則我就會送你一程了。

---

ought [ɔt] 🎧 *Track 3456*

aux. （表示義務、責任等）應當；應該

▶ You ought to be faithful to your significant other. 你應該要忠於你的另一半。

(補充片語)
significant other 重要的另一位

---

ounce [aʊns] 🎧 *Track 3457*

n. 盎司，英兩；一點點，少量

▶ He had not an ounce of regret for what he did to the victims.
他對他被害者所做的事沒有絲毫的後悔。

---

our [aʊr] 🎧 *Track 3458*

det. 我們的

---

ours [aʊrz] 🎧 *Track 3459*

pron. 我們的（東西）

---

our·selves [ˌaʊrˈsɛlvz] 🎧 *Track 3460*

pron. 我們自己

▶ No one can help us but ourselves.
除了我們自己之外，沒人會幫我們的。

---

out [aʊt] 🎧 *Track 3461*

adv. 出外；向外；在外；**adj.** 外側的；向外的；用完的；不流行的；**prep.** 通過……而出

---

out·come [ˈaʊtˌkʌm] 🎧 *Track 3462*

n. 結果

▶ The outcome is quite satisfactory.
這結果讓人相當滿意。

---

out·door [ˈaʊtˌdor] 🎧 *Track 3463*

adj. 戶外的

▶ I am really into outdoor activities.
我很喜歡戶外活動。

---

out·doors [ˈaʊtˈdorz] 🎧 *Track 3464*

adv. 在戶外

▶ These boys like to play outdoors.
這些男孩子喜歡在戶外玩。

---

out·er [ˈaʊtɚ] 🎧 *Track 3465*

adj. 在外的，外圍的，外面的，遠離中心的

▶ The little boy's birthday wish is to take a trip to outer space.
小男孩的生日願望是能夠到外太空去旅行。

(補充片語)
outer space 外太空

out·fit [`aʊt͵fɪt] 🎧 *Track 3466*
n. 全套服裝；全套裝備
▶ I haven't decided on my party outfit.
我還沒決定好我的派對服裝。

v. 裝備，配備；獲得裝備
▶ All the firefighters were outfitted with up-to-date firefighting equipment.
所有的消防員都配備有最新的消防裝備。

out·go·ing [`aʊt͵goɪŋ] 🎧 *Track 3467*
adj. 外向的，活潑的；離開的，外發的
▶ Outgoing people make friends easily.
外向的人很容易交朋友。

out·let [`aʊt͵lɛt] 🎧 *Track 3468*
n. 出口；排氣口；（感情）發洩途徑；銷路，商店
▶ They are planning to build the largest outlet mall in Asia.
他們計劃蓋一座亞洲最大的購物商場。

out·line [`aʊt͵laɪn] 🎧 *Track 3469*
n. 外形，輪廓；提綱，概要
▶ He is drafting an outline of a business-restructuring plan.
他正在草擬一份企業改造計劃的大綱。

v. 畫出……的輪廓；概述
▶ He outlined his plans to reorganize the corporation.
他概述了他企業重組的計劃。

out·put [`aʊt͵pʊt] 🎧 *Track 3470*
n. 出產，生產；輸出；作品；產量
▶ The output of the factory has dropped significantly for the past two years.
過去兩年，工廠的產量顯著地下降。

out·side [`aʊt͵saɪd] 🎧 *Track 3471*
prep. 在……之外；**adv.** 在外面；**adj.** 外面的；外部的；**n.** 外面；外部；外觀

out·stand·ing 🎧 *Track 3472*
[`aʊt`stændɪŋ]
adj. 顯著的，傑出的；未解決的，未償還的
▶ There are some outstanding bills to be paid by the end of this month.
有幾張本月底要繳的未繳帳單。

out·ward [`aʊtwɚd] 🎧 *Track 3473*
adj. 向外的；外面的，外表的；可見的；肉體的
▶ He never judges people by their outward appearances.
他從不以外在容貌評斷人。

adv. 向外；（船）出海，出港；顯而易見地
▶ The ship was bound outward as we came into the harbor.
當我們回到港口時，那艘船正要出港。

o·val [`ovl] 🎧 *Track 3474*
adj. 卵形的
▶ The woman told the plastic surgeon that she wanted to have an oval face.
女子告訴整形醫生她想要有一張鵝蛋臉。

n. 卵形物
▶ The actress's face is a perfect oval.
這女星的臉是個完美的鵝蛋形。

ov·en [`ʌvən] 🎧 *Track 3475*
n. 爐；烤箱

o·ver [`ovɚ] 🎧 *Track 3476*
adv. 在上方；在上空；超過；遍及；**adj.** 結束了的；**prep.** 在上方；在上空；越過上方

o·ver·all [`ovɚ͵ɔl] 🎧 *Track 3477*
adj. 從頭到尾的；總的，全部的
▶ The overall length of the film is 120 minutes.
這部片的總長度是120分鐘。

adv. 從頭到尾；大體上，總的來說
▶ It was a successful concert performance overall.
大體來說，這是一場成功的音樂會表演。

n. 工作褲；罩衫
▶ The man in the green overalls is a plastic surgeon.
那個穿著綠色工作褲的男子是位整形外科醫生。

o·ver·coat [`ovɚ͵kot] 🎧 *Track 3478*
n. 外套
▶ He put on his overcoat and left for work.
他穿上外套，就出門上班了。

※灰色單字為英檢初級必備單字

o·ver·come [ˌovɚˈkʌm] 🎧 *Track 3479*
v. 得勝；克服
▶ She overcame her disability.
她克服了身體的殘疾。

o·ver·eat [ˈovɚˈit] 🎧 *Track 3480*
v. 吃得過飽
▶ I overate at dinner. 我晚餐吃過飽了。

o·ver·flow [ˌovɚˈflo] 🎧 *Track 3481*
v. 充滿，洋溢；氾濫；從……溢出
▶ His heart overflowed with guilt.
他心中充滿了罪惡感。
n. 溢出，過剩；氾濫
▶ The "one-child policy" in China was to solve the population overflow.
中國的一胎化政策是要解決人口過剩的問題。

o·ver·head [ˈovɚˈhɛd] 🎧 *Track 3482*
adj. 在頭頂上的；高架的；頭上的
▶ Please put your bag in the overhead compartment.
請將你的包包放在頭頂上的置物箱。
adv. 在頭頂上；在上頭；高高地
▶ The prizewinner held his cup overhead.
得獎者將他的獎杯舉得高高的。

o·ver·look [ˌovɚˈlʊk] 🎧 *Track 3483*
v. 眺望，俯瞰；看漏；寬容；監視；高聳於……之上
▶ Love enables them to overlook each other's faults. 愛讓他們寬容彼此的缺點。

o·ver·night [ˈovɚˈnaɪt] 🎧 *Track 3484*
adj. 通宵的，一整夜的；一夜間的，突然的
▶ Most overnight successes actually took a long time. 一夕間的成功大部分其實都是長時間的努力所換來的。
adv. 通宵，一整夜；一夜間，突然
▶ Stress turned his hair gray overnight.
壓力使他的頭髮一夕間變白。

o·ver·pass [ˌovɚˈpæs] 🎧 *Track 3485*
n. 天橋

o·ver·seas [ˈovɚˈsiz] 🎧 *Track 3486*
adj. 海外的；adv. 在海外

o·ver·sleep [ˈovɚˈslip] 🎧 *Track 3487*
v. 睡過頭
▶ Don't oversleep tomorrow. 明天不要睡過頭。

o·ver·take [ˌovɚˈtek] 🎧 *Track 3488*
v. 追上；趕上；超過；突然侵襲
▶ I took the shortcut to overtake them.
我為了趕上他們而抄近路。

o·ver·throw [ˈovɚθro] 🎧 *Track 3489*
v. 打倒；推翻；廢除
▶ The purpose of this revolution is to overthrow the government.
這次革命的目的是要推翻政府。
n. 打倒，推翻
▶ The overthrow of the corrupt government is no surprise to me.
我對這個腐敗的政府被推翻並不感到意外。

over-weight [ˈovɚˌwet] 🎧 *Track 3490*
adj. 體重過重的
▶ You are overweight. 你體重過重了。

owe [o] 🎧 *Track 3491*
v. 歸功於；欠；應給予
▶ You owe me an apology. 你應該向我道歉。

owl [aʊl] 🎧 *Track 3492*
n. 貓頭鷹；常熬夜的人
▶ Leo is a night owl. 李歐是個夜貓子。

own [on] 🎧 *Track 3493*
pron. 自己的（東西）；v. 擁有；adj. 自己的

own·er [ˈonɚ] 🎧 *Track 3494*
n. 所有人；物主

own·er·ship [ˈonɚˌʃɪp] 🎧 *Track 3495*
n. 所有權，物主身份
▶ This vacant land is under private ownership.
這塊空地是私有的。

ox [ɑks] 🎧 *Track 3496*
n. 牛；閹牛

ox·y·gen [ˈɑksədʒən] 🎧 *Track 3497*
n. 氧，氧氣
▶ The man died from lack of oxygen.
這男子因為缺氧而死。

Pp

通過中級英文檢定者的英文能力：

 在日常生活中，能聽懂一般的會話；能大致聽懂公共場所廣播、氣象報告及廣告等。在工作時，能聽懂簡易的產品介紹與操作說明。能大致聽懂外籍人士的談話及詢問。

 在日常生活中，能閱讀短文、故事、私人信件、廣告、傳單、簡介及使用說明等。在工作時，能閱讀工作須知、公告、操作手冊、例行的文件、傳真、電報等。

 能寫簡單的書信、故事及心得等。對於熟悉且與個人經歷相關的主題，能以簡易的文字表達。

 在日常生活中，能以簡易英語交談或描述一般事物，能介紹自己的生活作息、工作、家庭、經歷等，並可對一般話題陳述看法。在工作時，能進行簡單的答詢，並與外籍人士交談溝通。

本書除包含官方公佈的中級4,947單字外，更精挑了近400個滿分必學的高手單字。同時，在片語的挑選、例句的使用上，皆依上述英檢官方公佈之能力範疇做設計，難度適中、不偏離考試主題。發音部分則是自然發音＆KK音標雙管齊下，搭配MP3以「分解／完整」方式錄音，給你最多元有效的學習手段，怎麼記都可以，想忘掉都好難！

P.M. [`pi`ɛm]
=p.m.=PM 🎧 *Track 3498*
adv. 下午；午後

pace [pes] 🎧 *Track 3499*
n. 一步；步調；進度；步法
▶ The boy is making progress at a slow pace. 男孩以慢慢的步調在進步中。

v. 踱步；慢慢地走
▶ The man was pacing up and down in front of the operating room.
男子在手術室外面來回踱步。

[相關片語]

at a snail's pace 非常緩慢地
▶ The old lady is crossing the street at a snail's pace. 老太太以非常緩慢地速度在過馬路。

Pa·cif·ic [pə`sɪfɪk] 🎧 *Track 3500*
n. （大寫）太平洋
▶ The shipwreck was finally discovered on the bottom of the Pacific.
失事船隻的殘骸終於在太平洋底被發現。

adj. 太平洋的
▶ The Pacific Ocean covers about one third of the Earth's surface.
太平洋覆蓋約三分之一的地球表面。

pack [pæk] 🎧 *Track 3501*
v. 裝箱；打包；**n.** 包；綑；包裹；背包

pack·age [`pækɪdʒ] 🎧 *Track 3502*
n. 包裹

pack·et [`pækɪt] 🎧 *Track 3503*
n. 小包、小捆；小袋；一批（信）；一大筆（錢）
▶ He smokes at least two packets of cigarettes a day. 他一天至少抽兩包菸。

pad [pæd] 🎧 *Track 3504*
n. 低沉的腳步聲；輕拍聲
▶ I knew that my house had been broken in as I heard the pads downstairs.
當我聽到樓下的腳步聲時，就知道有人闖進我家了。

v. 步行;放輕腳步走
▶ She pads a long road to school every day.
她每天都走很長一段路上學。

page [pedʒ] 🎧 *Track 3505*
n. 頁

pain [pen] 🎧 *Track 3506*
n. 疼痛、痛苦;辛苦

pain·ful [`penfəl] 🎧 *Track 3507*
adj. 疼痛的、令人不快的

paint [pent] 🎧 *Track 3508*
v. 油漆;漆上顏色;畫;**n.** 油漆;塗料

paint·er [`pentə] 🎧 *Track 3509*
n. 油漆工;畫家

paint·ing [`pentɪŋ] 🎧 *Track 3510*
n. 上油漆;繪畫

pair [pɛr] 🎧 *Track 3511*
n. 一對;一雙

pa·ja·mas [pə`dʒæməs] 🎧 *Track 3512*
=py·ja·mas (英式英文)
n. 睡衣

pal [pæl] 🎧 *Track 3513*
n. 好朋友
▶ We have been pals since we were in high school. 我們從中學時代起就是好朋友了。

pal·ace [`pælɪs] 🎧 *Track 3514*
n. 宮殿
▶ The Buckingham Palace is a must-visit tourist spot.
白金漢宮是一個必遊的觀光景點。

pale [pel] 🎧 *Track 3515*
adj. 蒼白的

palm [pɑm] 🎧 *Track 3516*
n. 手掌;手心
▶ The man begged for money with an open palm on the street.
男人在街上張著手心討錢。

(相關片語)
have an itching palm 貪財,收賄
▶ He will definitely take the bribe as he has an itching palm.
他那麼貪財,肯定會收下這筆賄賂。

pan [pæn] 🎧 *Track 3517*
n. 平底鍋

pan·cake [`pæn͵kek] 🎧 *Track 3518*
n. 薄煎餅
▶ Mom made us some pancakes for breakfast. 媽媽做了一些薄餅給我們當早餐。

pan·da [`pændə] 🎧 *Track 3519*
n. 貓熊

pan·el [`pænl] 🎧 *Track 3520*
n. 專案小組,專題討論小組;嵌板,鑲板;儀表板
▶ A panel discussion on the issue was held the other day.
針對這個議題的小組討論會在隔天舉行。

(補充片語)
panel discussion 座談會,小組討論會

pan·ic [`pænɪk] 🎧 *Track 3521*
n. 驚慌
▶ The rumored layoffs started a panic in the office. 裁員的謠言在辦公室引起一陣恐慌。
v. 驚慌
▶ There's no need to panic. Everything is under control. 不需要驚慌。一切都在控制中。

(相關片語)
panic buying 瘋狂搶購
▶ Fears of price increases after the typhoon led to panic buying.
對颱風後物價上揚的恐懼導致民眾瘋狂搶購。

pants [pænts] 🎧 *Track 3522*
=trou·sers (英式英語)
n. 褲子

pa·pa [`pɑpə]**=fa·ther** 🎧 *Track 3523*
n. 爸爸

▶ He was thrilled when his son said "papa" for the first time.
當他兒子第一次叫爸爸時，他簡直欣喜若狂。

pa·pa·ya [pə`paɪə] 🎧 *Track 3524*
n. 木瓜

pa·per [`pepɚ] 🎧 *Track 3525*
n. 紙；報紙；試卷；報告

par·a·chute [`pærə,ʃut] 🎧 *Track 3526*
n. 降落傘
▶ He panicked when his parachute failed to open when he jumped off the helicopter.
在他從直升機上跳下來，降落傘卻無法打開時，他整個人都慌了。

v. 跳傘，跳傘降落；傘降
▶ He had to muster up his courage to parachute from 650 feet.
他得鼓足勇氣才能從650呎的高空跳傘降落。

pa·rade [pə`red] 🎧 *Track 3527*
n. 遊行，行進行列
▶ We found a perfect spot to watch the carnival parades.
我們發現一個可以觀賞嘉年華遊行的完美位置。

v. 在……遊行；炫耀，標榜；使列隊行進
▶ He grabs any chance to make a parade of his dancing skills.
他抓住任何可以炫耀舞技的機會。

(補充片語)
make a parade of 炫耀

par·a·dise [`pærə,daɪs] 🎧 *Track 3528*
n. 天堂，樂園，像天堂一樣的地方
▶ The amusement park is children's paradise.
遊樂園就是孩子的天堂。

par·a·graph [`pærə,græf] 🎧 *Track 3529*
n. （文章的）段，節
▶ This whole paragraph was lifted from an editorial published in *The New York Times*.
這整一段文字都是從刊登在紐約時代雜誌上的一篇社論抄襲來的。

par·al·lel [`pærə,lɛl] 🎧 *Track 3530*
adj. 平行的，同方向的；相同的
▶ His opinion exactly parallels mine.
他的看法跟我的完全相同。

n. 平行線；類似的人或事物；相似處
▶ *Along the River During the Qingming Festival* is a masterpiece without parallel.
《清明上河圖》是件難以比擬的傑作。

v. 與……平行；與……相比；與……相似
▶ The highway parallels the coastline.
這條公路與海岸線平行。

par·cel [`pɑrsḷ] 🎧 *Track 3531*
n. 小包，包裹
▶ The mail carrier handed me a parcel.
郵差遞給我一份包裹。

v. 分配，把……包起來
▶ We parceled some sandwiches for the picnic. 我們包了一些三明治要帶去野餐。

par·don [`pɑrdn] 🎧 *Track 3532*
n. 原諒；寬恕；**v.** 原諒；寬恕

par·ent [`pɛrənt] 🎧 *Track 3533*
n. 父親；母親

Par·is [`pærɪs] 🎧 *Track 3534*
n. 巴黎

park [pɑrk] 🎧 *Track 3535*
n. 公園；遊樂場；**v.** 停車

park·ing [`pɑrkɪŋ] 🎧 *Track 3536*
n. 停車，停車處
▶ There is no parking in front of my store.
我的店門口不准停車。

(相關片語)
parking space 停車位
▶ It's difficult to find a parking space in downtown. 要在市區找到一個停車位很難。

par·lia·ment [`pɑrləmənt] 🎧 *Track 3537*
n. 國會，議會
▶ The Parliament has approved the new tax policy.
國會已經核准了新的稅收政策。

par·rot [`pærət]　　🎧 *Track 3538*
n. 鸚鵡

part [pɑrt]　　🎧 *Track 3539*
v. 分開；告別；使分開
▶We have never seen each other again since we parted three years ago. 自從我們三年前分別之後，就再也沒有見過彼此。

par·tial [`pɑrʃəl]　　🎧 *Track 3540*
adj. 部分的，不完全的；偏袒的，不公平的
▶It is obvious that you are partial to your eldest son. 很明顯地你偏愛你的長子。

par·tic·i·pant 　　🎧 *Track 3541*
[pɑr`tɪsəpənt]
n. 參與者
▶All participants are required to comply with the rules and obey the instructions made by the referees. 所以參賽者都必須遵守比賽規則，並服從裁判的指示。

(補充片語)
comply with 遵守

par·tic·i·pate 　　🎧 *Track 3542*
[pɑr`tɪsə,pet]
v. 參與，參加
▶All employees were asked to participate in this annual sports meet.
所有員工都必須參加這一年一度的運動會。

par·ti·ci·ple [`pɑrtəsəp!]　🎧 *Track 3543*
n. 分詞
▶"Broken" is the past participle of "break".
broken是break的過去分詞。

par·tic·u·lar [pə`tɪkjələ]　🎧 *Track 3544*
adj. 特殊的；特定的

par·tic·u·lar·ly 　　🎧 *Track 3545*
[pə`tɪkjələlɪ]
adv. 特別，尤其；具體地；詳盡地
▶I don't particularly like country music.
我並沒有特別喜歡鄉村音樂。

part·ner [`pɑrtnə]　　🎧 *Track 3546*
n. 夥伴；拍檔；合夥人

part·ner·ship 　　🎧 *Track 3547*
[`pɑrtnə,ʃɪp]
n. 合夥；合作關係
▶Forming a good partnership with them will benefit our company. 與他們建立良好的夥伴關係將對我們公司有意。

par·ty [`pɑrtɪ]　　🎧 *Track 3548*
n. 派對；聚會；政黨

pass [pæs]　　🎧 *Track 3549*
v. 前進；通過；死亡；（考試）及格；**n.** 通行證

pas·sage [`pæsɪdʒ]　　🎧 *Track 3550*
n. 通道；通行；走廊；（文章或樂曲的）段落
▶The washroom is at the end of the passage.
洗手間在走道盡頭。

pas·sen·ger [`pæsndʒə]　🎧 *Track 3551*
n. 乘客；旅客

pas·sion [`pæʃən]　　🎧 *Track 3552*
n. 熱情
▶He had a passion for acting.
他十分愛好表演。

(相關片語)
passion fruit 百香果
▶Passion fruit is a tropical fruit.
百香果是一種熱帶水果。

pas·sive [`pæsɪv]　　🎧 *Track 3553*
adj. 被動的，消極的；順從的，服從的
▶The student took a passive attitude towards learning.
這個學生在學習上的態度是被動的。

pass·port [`pæs,port]　　🎧 *Track 3554*
n. 護照
▶Your passport expired two months ago.
你的護照兩個月前就到期了。

past [pæst]　　🎧 *Track 3555*
prep. 經過；通過；超過；**adv.** 經過；越過；**n.** 過去；昔日；往事；**adj.** 過去的；以前的

pas·ta [ˋpɑstə] 🎧 *Track 3556*
n. 義大利麵（細麵或通心粉等）
▶Let's have pasta for dinner tonight.
我們今晚晚餐吃義大利麵吧。

paste [pest] 🎧 *Track 3557*
n. 漿糊；麵糰 **v.** 用漿糊黏貼

pas·try [ˋpestrɪ] 🎧 *Track 3558*
n. 油酥麵團，酥皮點心
▶My mother is good at making pastry.
我媽媽很會做糕點。

pat [pæt] 🎧 *Track 3559*
v. 輕拍；輕撫
▶He patted the little boy on the head.
他輕輕拍了小男孩的頭。

n. 輕拍；輕打
▶She gave the student a pat on his back and gave him a few words of encouragement.
她輕拍學生的背，並說了幾句鼓勵的話。

path [pæθ] 🎧 *Track 3560*
n. 小徑；小路

pa·tience [ˋpeʃəns] 🎧 *Track 3561*
n. 耐心，耐性
▶I have no patience with little kids.
我對小孩子沒有耐心。

pa·tient [ˋpeʃənt] 🎧 *Track 3562*
adj. 有耐心的；有耐性的 **n.** 病人

pat·ri·ot·ic [ˌpetrɪˋɑtɪk] 🎧 *Track 3563*
adj. 愛國的
▶Dragon Boat Festival is celebrated in memory of the patriotic poet, Qu Yuan.
人們是為了紀念愛國詩人屈原而過端午節的。

pat·tern [ˋpætɚn] 🎧 *Track 3564*
n. 花樣；圖案

pause [pɔz] 🎧 *Track 3565*
v. 停頓；暫停 **n.** 停頓；中斷

pave [pev] 🎧 *Track 3566*
v. 鋪路；鋪設；鋪滿

▶We're going to pave our yard with roses.
我們將在院子裡種滿玫瑰。

相關片語
pave the way for... 為……鋪路，為……做準備
▶Education paves the way for a better future. 教育是為更好的未來做準備。

pave·ment [ˋpevmənt] 🎧 *Track 3567*
n. 人行道
▶It is illegal to park your car on the pavement.
將車子停在人行道上是違法的。

paw [pɔ] 🎧 *Track 3568*
n. 腳爪；【口】手
▶Get your paws off my son!
別用你的手碰我的兒子！

v. 用腳爪抓；笨拙地觸摸；翻找
▶The mother stopped the boy from pawing at everything he saw.
那個媽媽阻止男孩看到什麼都摸。

pay [pe] 🎧 *Track 3569*
v. 支付；付錢；償還 **n.** 薪水；報酬

pay·ment [ˋpemənt] 🎧 *Track 3570*
n. 支付；付款；支付的款項
▶Please make the payment by the end of this month. 請在月底之前完成付款。

PE [pi-i] 🎧 *Track 3571*
=phys·i·cal e·du·ca·tion
n. 體育；體能教育

pea [pi] 🎧 *Track 3572*
n. 豌豆
▶My mother is cooking pea soup.
我媽正在煮豌豆湯。

peace [pis] 🎧 *Track 3573*
n. 和平；平靜；治安

peace·ful [ˋpisfəl] 🎧 *Track 3574*
adj. 平靜的；和平的；寧靜的；安詳的

peach [pitʃ] 🎧 *Track 3575*
n. 桃子；桃樹；桃色

※灰色單字為英檢初級必備單字

pea·cock [`pikɑk]　🎧 *Track 3576*

n. 孔雀；愛炫耀的人，愛虛榮的人

▶ Look! The peacock is so beautiful!
你看！那隻孔雀真美！

---

peak [pik]　🎧 *Track 3577*

n. 山頂，山峰；高點

▶ The diva singer decided to retire from the stage at the peak of her singing career.
這位天后級歌手決定在她歌唱事業最高峰時退出舞台。

adj. 最高的

▶ It's nearly impossible to find a hotel room during the peak season. 要在旺季找到一間飯店房間是幾乎不可能的事。

v. 達到高峰

▶ The temperature peaked at over 36 degrees Celsius yesterday.
昨天氣溫已經飆高到攝氏三十六度以上了。

---

pea·nut [`pi͵nʌt]　🎧 *Track 3578*

n. 花生

▶ Mom made me a peanut butter sandwich.
媽媽幫我做了一個花生醬三明治。

(補充片語)

peanut butter　花生醬

---

pear [pɛr]　🎧 *Track 3579*

n. 洋梨；洋梨樹

---

pearl [pɝl]　🎧 *Track 3580*

n. 珍珠；珠狀物；珍珠色；珍品

▶ I benefited greatly by his pearls of wisdom.
他的金玉良言使我獲益良多。

(補充片語)

pearls of wisdom　智慧結晶；金玉良言

adj. 珍珠的，珍珠色的

▶ You look gorgeous in that pearl necklace.
你戴著這條珍珠項鍊真是美極了。

---

peas·ant [`pɛznt]　🎧 *Track 3581*

n. 農夫，小耕農；粗野人，鄉下人

▶ The peasants would labor in the fields from dawn to dusk.
農夫們從早到晚地在田裏勞動。

(補充片語)

from dawn to dusk　從早到晚，從日升到日落

---

peb·ble [`pɛbl]　🎧 *Track 3582*

n. 小卵石

▶ The path to the pond was paved with pebbles. 通往池塘的小徑是以鵝卵石鋪成的。

---

pe·cu·li·ar [pɪ`kjuljɚ]　🎧 *Track 3583*

adj. 奇怪的；乖僻的；獨特的，罕見的

▶ There is a peculiar smell in this room.
這個房間有個奇怪的味道。

---

ped·al [`pɛdl]　🎧 *Track 3584*

n. 踏板，腳蹬

▶ The little boy's legs are too short to reach the pedals.
小男孩的腳太短了，踩不到踏板。

v. 踩踏板；騎腳踏車

▶ I pedal twenty miles to work every day.
我每天騎二十英里的腳踏車去上班。

---

ped·dler [`pɛdlɚ]　🎧 *Track 3585*

n. 小販

▶ I'm glad that the drug peddler is now under arrest. 很高興那個毒販已經被逮捕了。

---

pe·des·tri·an [pə`dɛstrɪən]　🎧 *Track 3586*

adj. 步行的，行人的

▶ Please use the pedestrian crossing when crossing the road. 過馬路請走行人穿越道。

(補充片語)

pedestrian crossing　行人穿越道

n. 步行者，行人

▶ Two pedestrians were injured in the traffic accident. 這場車禍中有兩位行人受傷。

---

peek [pik]　🎧 *Track 3587*

v. 偷看，窺視

▶ Peter was caught peeking at Jerry's answer sheet during the test.
彼得被抓到在考試時偷看傑瑞的答案卷。

n. 偷看一下，一瞥

▶ I took a peek at his paycheck out of curiosity.
我出於好奇地偷偷地看了一眼他的薪資單。

peel [pil]　🎧 *Track 3588*
n. （果、菜的）皮
▶ He slipped on a banana peel.
他踩到一根香蕉皮滑倒了。

v. 剝皮、削皮、剝殼，脫去（衣服）
▶ I need a helping hand to peel these potatoes for me.
我需要一個幫手來幫我把這些馬鈴薯削皮。

(補充片語)
helping hand 幫手，援助，援手

peep [pip]　🎧 *Track 3589*
v. 窺視，偷看
▶ She peeped through the curtains to see what was going on outside.
她從窗簾縫窺視外面發生了什麼事。

n. 窺視，偷看
▶ I couldn't help but take a peep at his diary.
我忍不住偷看了他的日記。

peer [pɪr]　🎧 *Track 3590*
v. 與……相比，與……同等；凝視，盯著看
▶ She peered at herself in the mirror.
她凝視著鏡子中的自己。

n. 同輩的人，同事，同儕
▶ Many teenagers have trouble dealing with negative peer pressure.
很多青少年不知道怎麼處理負面的同儕壓力。

(補充片語)
peer pressure 同儕壓力

pen [pɛn]　🎧 *Track 3591*
n. 筆；鋼筆

pen·al·ty [`pɛnḷtɪ]　🎧 *Track 3592*
n. 懲罰
▶ The penalty for speeding is NT$3,000.
超速罰款新台幣三千元。

(相關片語)
death penalty 死刑
▶ Whether death penalty should be abolished has always been a huge controversy. 死刑是否應該廢除一直以來都是個極大的爭議。

pen·cil [`pɛnsḷ]　🎧 *Track 3593*
n. 鉛筆

pen·guin [`pɛngwɪn]　🎧 *Track 3594*
n. 企鵝
▶ Penguins are good swimmers.
企鵝都很會游泳。

pen·ny [`pɛnɪ]　🎧 *Track 3595*
n. 一分錢
▶ A penny saved is a penny gained.
省一分就是賺一分。

peo·ple [`pipḷ]　🎧 *Track 3596*
n. 人們；人民；民族

pep·per [`pɛpɚ]　🎧 *Track 3597*
n. 胡椒

per [pɚ]　🎧 *Track 3598*
prep. 每
▶ The entrance fee is $5 per person.
入場費每人五元。

per·cent [pɚ`sɛnt] =per cent　🎧 *Track 3599*
n. 百分之一；百分比
▶ Everything in the store is thirty percent off during the sale. 特賣期間店內所有東西都有百分之三十的折扣優惠。

per·cen·tage [pɚ`sɛntɪdʒ]　🎧 *Track 3600*
n. 百分率，百分比；比例
▶ A high percentage of elementary school students are overweight.
有很高比例的小學學童是體重過重的。

(相關片語)
no percentage 沒有好處，沒有利益
▶ There is no percentage in talking back to your boss.
跟你的上司頂嘴一點好處也沒有。

per·fect [`pɝfɪkt]　🎧 *Track 3601*
adj. 完美的；理想的

per·fec·tion [pɚ`fɛkʃən]　🎧 *Track 3602*
n. 完美
▶ She dressed herself to perfection.
她把自己打扮得完美無缺。

per·fect·ly [`pɝ·fɪktlɪ] 🎧 *Track 3603*
adv. 完美無缺地；完全地
▶ The chicken is cooked perfectly.
這雞肉烹調得恰到好處。

per·form [pɚ`fɔrm] 🎧 *Track 3604*
v. 演出；表演
▶ They have to rehearse several times before they perform on the stage.
上台演出前，他們必須排練好幾次。

per·form·ance 🎧 *Track 3605*
[pɚ`fɔrməns]
n. 表現；表演；演出
▶ We evaluate each employee's work performance every six months. 我們每半年為每位員工的工作表現做一次評估。

per·form·er [pɚ`fɔrmɚ] 🎧 *Track 3606*
n. 表演者，演奏者，演出者
▶ He is a lousy performer on the stage.
他在舞台上的表演糟糕透頂。

per·fume [pɚ`fjum] 🎧 *Track 3607*
n. 香水；香味，芳香
▶ I don't like to wear make-up, but I must wear perfume when I got out.
我不喜歡化妝，但我出門一定要噴香水。
v. 灑香水於，使充滿香氣；散發香氣
▶ She perfumed herself before going out.
她出門前在身上灑了些香水。

per·haps [pɚ`hæps] 🎧 *Track 3608*
adv. 也許；大概

pe·ri·od [`pɪrɪəd] 🎧 *Track 3609*
n. 時期；時代；週期；生理期

per·ma·nent [`pɝmənɛnt] 🎧 *Track 3610*
adj. 永久的；固定的
▶ He is a permanent employee of the company. 他是這家公司的正式職員。
n. 【口】燙髮
▶ I'm thinking to have a permanent because I'm tired of my straight hair.
我打算去燙個頭髮，因為我厭倦直髮了。

per·mis·sion [pɚ`mɪʃən] 🎧 *Track 3611*
n. 允許，許可，准許
▶ You can't take personal leave without your supervisor's permission.
沒有你直屬上司的許可，你不能休事假。
(補充片語)
personal leave 事假

per·mit [pɚ`mɪt] 🎧 *Track 3612*
v. 允許，許可，准許
▶ I don't think my boss will permit me to leave early. 我不認為我老闆會允許我早退。
n. 許可證，執照
▶ Have you got a permit to set up a stall in the night market?
你有在夜市擺攤的許可證嗎？
(補充片語)
set up a stall 擺攤

per·sist [pɚ`sɪst] 🎧 *Track 3613*
v. 堅持，固執；持續，存留
▶ The suspect persisted that he didn't kill the man. 嫌犯堅稱自己沒有殺害那個男子。

per·son [`pɝsn] 🎧 *Track 3614*
n. 人

per·son·al [`pɝsnl] 🎧 *Track 3615*
adj. 個人的；私人的；涉及私事的

per·son·al·i·ty 🎧 *Track 3616*
[ˌpɝsn`æləti]
n. 性格
▶ He has a stubborn personality.
他的性格很頑強。

per·suade [pɚ`swed] 🎧 *Track 3617*
v. 說服
▶ My father is very stubborn. It is almost impossible to persuade him into changing his mind. 我爸非常固執，要説服他改變心意幾乎是不可能的。
(補充片語)
persuade sb. into doing... 説服某人做某事；
change one's mind 改變某人的心意

per·sua·sion [pə`sweʒən] 🎧 *Track 3618*
n. 說服，勸說；信仰，信念
▶ The salesman used his persuasion to get the woman buy a subscription of the weekly magazine. 銷售員運用他的說服力，讓那女子訂購了那份週刊。

per·sua·sive [pə`swesɪv] 🎧 *Track 3619*
adj. 有說服力的
▶ The candidate's speech was persuasive. 該候選人的演說很有說服力。

pes·si·mis·tic 🎧 *Track 3620*
[,pɛsə`mɪstɪk]
adj. 悲觀的
▶ The patient was pessimistic about his condition. 病患對自己的病情很悲觀。

pest [pɛst] 🎧 *Track 3621*
n. 害蟲，有害的動植物；討厭的人，害人精
▶ Cockroaches are one of the most annoying household pests.
蟑螂是最討人厭的家庭害蟲之一。

pet [pɛt] 🎧 *Track 3622*
n. 寵物

pet·al [`pɛtl] 🎧 *Track 3623*
n. 花瓣
▶ My mom likes to use dried rose petals to make tea.
我媽媽喜歡用乾燥的玫瑰花瓣來泡茶。

pe·trol [`pɛtrəl] 🎧 *Track 3624*
=gas, gas·ol·ine （美式英文）
n. 汽油
▶ We need to stop at the petrol station to refuel. 我們必須在加油站停下來加油。

（補充片語）
petrol station 加油站

phar·ma·cy [`farməsɪ] 🎧 *Track 3625*
n. 藥局；藥房；配藥學
▶ Please go to the pharmacy to pick up your prescription medicine.
請到藥房去領取你的處方藥。

phe·nom·e·non 🎧 *Track 3626*
[fə`namə,nan]
n. 現象；稀有的事；非凡的人才
▶ Red rain is a unique natural phenomenon in India. 紅雨是印度獨有的自然現象。

Phil·ip·pines [`fɪlə,pinz] 🎧 *Track 3627*
n. 菲律賓

phi·los·o·pher 🎧 *Track 3628*
[fə`lasəfə]
n. 哲學家
▶ Socrates was a great philosopher.
蘇格拉底是一個偉大的哲學家。

phil·o·soph·i·cal 🎧 *Track 3629*
[,fɪlə`safɪkl]
adj. 達觀的
▶ My father takes a philosophical attitude toward life. 我父親擁有達觀的人生態度。

phi·los·o·phy [fə`lasəfɪ] 🎧 *Track 3630*
n. 人生觀
▶ Seize the day – that's my philosophy.
及時行樂是我的人生觀。

phone [fon] 🎧 *Track 3631*
=tel·e·phone
n. 電話；**v.** 打電話

pho·to [`foto] 🎧 *Track 3632*
n. 相片；照片

pho·to·graph 🎧 *Track 3633*
[`fotə,græf]
=pho·to
n. 相片；照片

pho·tog·ra·pher 🎧 *Track 3634*
[fə`tagrəfə]
n. 攝影師

pho·to·graph·ic 🎧 *Track 3635*
[,fotə`græfɪk]
adj. 攝影的；生動的，逼真的；極精確的
▶ His first photographic exhibition was a success. 他的第一次攝影展很成功。

※灰色單字為英檢初級必備單字

pho·tog·ra·phy
[fə`tɑgrəfɪ]

🎧 *Track 3636*

n. 攝影

▶ He is very interested in photography.
他對攝影很有興趣。

phrase [frez]

🎧 *Track 3637*

n. 片語；詞組；措辭，說法

▶ A good publicist must have a nice turn of phrase. 一個好的公關人員必須善於辭令。

(補充片語)

have a nice turn of phrase 善於辭令，很會說話

v. 用言詞表達

▶ He phrased his political standpoint tactfully. 他婉轉地表達了自己的政治觀點。

phys·i·cal [`fɪzɪkl]

🎧 *Track 3638*

adj. 身體的，肉體的；物質的；物理的；按自然法則的

▶ Despite his physical disabilities, David remains optimistic and confident.
雖然身體有缺陷，大衛仍然保持樂觀與自信。

n. 【口】身體檢查

▶ I have a physical once a year.
我每年都做身體檢查。

phy·si·cian [fɪ`zɪʃən]

🎧 *Track 3639*

n. （內科）醫生

▶ The patient told the physician that he had a severe headache.
病人告訴醫生他有劇烈頭痛。

phys·i·cist [`fɪzɪsɪst]

🎧 *Track 3640*

n. 物理學家

▶ Albert Einstein was one of the greatest physicists in the 20th century.
愛因斯坦是廿世紀最偉大的物理學家之一。

phys·ics [`fɪzɪks]

🎧 *Track 3641*

n. 物理學

pi·a·nist [pɪ`ænɪst]

🎧 *Track 3642*

n. 鋼琴家

▶ The pianist spends six hours a day practicing the piano.
那位鋼琴家每天花六個小時練琴。

pi·an·o [pɪ`æno]

🎧 *Track 3643*

n. 鋼琴

pick [pɪk]

🎧 *Track 3644*

v. 挑；撿；選；摘

pick·le [`pɪkl]

🎧 *Track 3645*

n. 醃過的醬菜

▶ I'd like a cheeseburger without pickles.
我要一個不加酸黃瓜的起司漢堡。

pick·pock·et [`pɪk͵pɑkɪt]

🎧 *Track 3646*

n. 扒手

▶ The pickpocket was caught red-handed.
這扒手當場被逮。

pic·nic [`pɪknɪk]

🎧 *Track 3647*

n./v. 野餐

pic·ture [`pɪktʃə]

🎧 *Track 3648*

n. 圖片；照片；**v.** 想像；畫；拍攝

pie [paɪ]

🎧 *Track 3649*

n. 餡餅；派（有餡的酥餅）

piece [pis]

🎧 *Track 3650*

n. 一片；一塊；一張；一件；破片

pig [pɪg]

🎧 *Track 3651*

n. 豬

pi·geon [`pɪdʒɪn]

🎧 *Track 3652*

n. 鴿子；鴿肉

pile [paɪl]

🎧 *Track 3653*

v. 堆積；堆放；**n.** 堆；一堆；大量

pil·grim [`pɪlgrɪm]

🎧 *Track 3654*

n. 香客，朝聖者

▶ All year round, Christian pilgrims flock to Jerusalem from all over the world.
一年到頭，基督教朝聖者都會從世界各地聚集在耶路撒冷。

pill [pɪl]

🎧 *Track 3655*

n. 藥丸，藥片

▶ Suffering from severe insomnia, she is unable to fall asleep without sleeping pills. 由於患有嚴重的失眠症，她沒有安眠藥就沒辦法入睡。

(補充片語)

sleeping pill 安眠藥

(相關片語)

bitter pill to swallow 不得不忍受的事
▶ Marrying off his daughter to his enemy was a bitter pill for him to swallow. 把女兒嫁給他的仇家對他來說是件難以忍受的事。

pil·low [`pɪlo] 🎧 Track 3656
n. 枕頭

pi·lot [`paɪlət] 🎧 Track 3657
n. （船的）領航員，（飛機的）駕駛員；領導人
▶ Being an airline pilot is his dream job. 當一名航空公司的飛機駕駛員是他夢想的工作。

v. 駕駛，領航，試用，引導
▶ You can't be nearsighted if you want to pilot an airplane.
如果你想要駕駛飛機，你就不能以近視。

pim·ple [`pɪmpl̩] 🎧 Track 3658
n. 丘疹；面皰；青春痘
▶ The big pimple on my nose bothers me a lot. 我鼻子上的大痘子讓我十分困擾。

pin [pɪn] 🎧 Track 3659
n. 大頭針；別針；胸針；**v.** （用別針）別住；（用大頭針）釘住

pine [paɪn] 🎧 Track 3660
n. 松樹，松木
▶ They enjoyed a forest bathing while taking a walk in the pine woods.
他們一邊在松樹林裡散步，一邊享受森林浴。

v. 渴望
▶ The boy pined for home and his family.
男孩渴望能夠回家，和家人在一起。

pine·ap·ple [`paɪn͵æpl̩] 🎧 Track 3661
n. 鳳梨

ping-pong [`pɪŋ͵pɑŋ] 🎧 Track 3662
=ta·ble ten·nis

n. 乒乓球；桌球
▶ He's really good at playing ping-pong.
他真的很會打乒乓球。

pink [pɪŋk] 🎧 Track 3663
adj. 粉紅的；桃紅的；**n.** 粉紅色；桃紅色

pint [paɪnt] 🎧 Track 3664
n. 品脫
▶ First of all, mix a pint of milk with 100 grams of sugar in the bowl. 首先，在碗裡混合一品脫的牛奶和一百克的糖。

(相關片語)

put a quart into a pint pot 做不可能做到的事
▶ Don't waste your time putting a quart into a pint pot. 不要浪費時間做不可能做到的事。

pi·o·neer [͵paɪə`nɪr] 🎧 Track 3665
n. 拓荒者，開拓者；先驅者
▶ They were the pioneers in this field.
他們是這個領域的開拓者。

v. 開創，開闢
▶ His grandfather was the one who pioneered the study of the brain.
他的祖父就是開創腦部研究的先驅。

pipe [paɪp] 🎧 Track 3666
n. 管；煙斗；管樂器

pi·rate [`paɪrət] 🎧 Track 3667
n. 海盜；掠劫者；海盜船；剽竊者；侵犯版權者
▶ It never occurred to these young sailors that they would encounter pirates.
這些年輕的水手從來沒想過會遇到海盜。

v. 掠奪；從事掠劫；剽竊；非法翻印；做海盜
▶ The composer accused the singer of pirating his copyright to the songs.
作曲家控告該歌手剽竊他的歌曲著作權。

adj. 海盜的；未經許可的
▶ The sailor turned his boat as soon as he spotted a pirate ship coming his way.
船員一發現有艘海盜船朝他駛來，便趕緊將船調頭。

Aa
Bb
Cc
Dd
Ee
Ff
Gg
Hh
Ii
Jj
Kk
Ll
Mm
Nn
Oo
Pp
Qq
Rr
Ss
Tt
Uu
Vv
Ww
Xx
Yy
Zz

※灰色單字為英檢初級必備單字

pit [pɪt]   🎧 *Track 3668*

n. 窪坑，凹處；地窖；陷阱；圈套；墓穴

▶ I knew he was trying to dig a pit for me, so I didn't tell him the truth. 我知道他在挖陷阱給我跳，所以我沒告訴他實情。

(補充片語)

dig a pit for sb. 給某人設圈套，挖陷阱給某人跳，算計某人

v. 挖坑；放入坑中；使掉入陷阱；留下凹痕

▶ The car was pitted with bullet scars. 這輛車彈痕累累。

pitch [pɪtʃ]   🎧 *Track 3669*

n. 投球；音樂聲調

▶ Tom hit the pitch as hard as he could. 湯姆用力地將球打擊出去。

v. 投球

▶ The coach is showing Tom how to pitch correctly. 教練正在為湯姆示範該如何正確地投球。

pit·y [ˋpɪtɪ]   🎧 *Track 3670*

n. 憐憫，同情；可惜的事

▶ It's a pity you missed the opportunity to meet your idol. 你錯過了可以見到你的偶像的機會，真是可惜。

v. 同情，憐憫

▶ There's no need to pity that person. 沒有必要同情那個人。

(相關片語)

take pity on 憐憫，同情

▶ She took pity on the poor girl and gave her some food and some money. 她很同情那個可憐的女孩，所以給了她一些食物和一些錢。

piz·za [ˋpitsə]   🎧 *Track 3671*

n. 比薩；義大利肉餡餅

place [ples]   🎧 *Track 3672*

n. 地方；居住的地方；**v.** 放置

plain [plen]   🎧 *Track 3673*

n. 平原；曠野；**adj.** 簡樸的；不攙雜的；清楚的；坦白的；**adv.** 清楚地；平易地；完全地

plan [plæn]   🎧 *Track 3674*

n. 計劃；**v.** 做計劃；規劃

plane [plen]   🎧 *Track 3675*

n. 飛機

plan·et [ˋplænɪt]   🎧 *Track 3676*

n. 行星

plant [plænt]   🎧 *Track 3677*

v. 種植；**n.** 植物；植栽

plas·tic [ˋplæstɪk]   🎧 *Track 3678*

n. 塑料，塑膠，塑膠製品

▶ The chair is made of plastic. 這把椅子是塑膠製的。

adj. 塑膠的，可塑的，易變的，易受影響的

▶ We don't provide free plastic bags any more. 我們已經不再提供免費的塑膠袋。

plate [plet]   🎧 *Track 3679*

n. 盤子

plat·form [ˋplæt͵fɔrm]   🎧 *Track 3680*

n. 講台；月台

play [ple]   🎧 *Track 3681*

v. 玩；遊戲；彈奏（樂器）；打（球類運動）；扮演（角色）；**n.** 遊戲；戲劇；活動

play·er [ˋpleə]   🎧 *Track 3682*

n. 選手；玩家

play·ful [ˋplefəl]   🎧 *Track 3683*

adj. 愛玩耍的；開玩笑的

play·ground   🎧 *Track 3684*
[ˋple͵graʊnd]

n. 遊樂場

plead [plid]   🎧 *Track 3685*

v. 辯護，抗辯；承認；以……為理由；懇求

▶ The pickpocket knelt down in front of the man and pleaded for mercy. 小偷跪在男子面前請求寬恕。

pleas·ant [ˋplɛzənt]   🎧 *Track 3686*

adj. 愉快的；欣喜的

please [pliz] 🎧 *Track 3687*
v. 使滿意；**adv.** 請

pleased [plizd] 🎧 *Track 3688*
adj. 高興的；滿意的

plea·sure [`plɛʒɚ] 🎧 *Track 3689*
n. 愉快；高興；樂事

plen·ti·ful [`plɛntɪfəl] 🎧 *Track 3690*
adj. 豐富的，充足的；富裕的；豐產的
▶ An overnight storm brought plentiful rain to ease the drought affecting the island.
一夜的暴風雨帶來了豐沛的雨水，紓解了島嶼的乾旱。

plen·ty [`plɛntɪ] 🎧 *Track 3691*
pron. 很多，大量
▶ Take your time. We have plenty of time.
慢慢來。我們有很多時間。

adv. 很多，綽綽有餘地；足夠地，充分地
▶ I think the apartment is plenty big enough for the three of us.
我想這個公寓大得夠我們三個人住了。

plot [plɑt] 🎧 *Track 3692*
n. 劇情，情節；陰謀，秘密計劃
▶ The plot of the film was completely fictitious. 這電影的情節純屬虛構。

v. 密謀，策劃；設計情節
▶ The novelist is plotting for his next novel.
這位小說家正在構思下一部小說的故事情節。

plug [plʌg] 🎧 *Track 3693*
n. 插頭；塞子，栓；消防栓
▶ Don't touch the live plug with a wet hand.
不要用潮濕的手觸碰通電的插頭。

v. 接通電源
▶ The printer is not working because it's not plugged in.
印表機不動是因為它沒插電。

plum [plʌm] 🎧 *Track 3694*
n. 洋李，梅子；紫紅色
▶ There is a plum tree in our yard.
我們的院子裡有一株李樹。

adj. 梅子的；紫紅色的
▶ I just drank a glass of fresh plum juice.
我剛喝了一杯新鮮的梅子汁。

plumb·er [`plʌmɚ] 🎧 *Track 3695*
n. 水電工
▶ She called the plumber to fix the leaking kitchen faucet.
她打電話叫水電工來修理漏水的廚房水龍頭。

plu·ral [`plʊrəl] 🎧 *Track 3696*
adj. 複數的；多元的
▶ The word "phenomena" is a plural noun.
Phenomena 這個字是一個複數名詞。

n. 複數；複數形
▶ "Phenomena" is the plural of phenomenon.
Phenomena是phenomenon的複數形。

plus [plʌs] 🎧 *Track 3697*
prep. 加上；**adj.** 正的，好處，高一點；**n.** 好處，附加物

pock·et [`pɑkɪt] 🎧 *Track 3698*
n. 口袋；財力；**adj.** 袖珍的；小型的；零星花用的；**v.** 把……裝入口袋內；侵吞；盜用

po·em [`poɪm] 🎧 *Track 3699*
n. 詩

po·et [`poɪt] 🎧 *Track 3700*
n. 詩人
▶ This poem was written by my favorite poet. 這首詩是我最喜歡的詩人所寫的。

po·et·ry [`poɪtrɪ] 🎧 *Track 3701*
n. （總稱）詩；詩歌；詩意
▶ The three-year-old boy is good at reciting Tang poetry.
這三歲小男孩很會背唐詩。

point [pɔɪnt] 🎧 *Track 3702*
v. 指；指出；
n. 尖端；要點；中心思想；得分

poi·son [`pɔɪzn̩] 🎧 *Track 3703*
n. 毒；毒藥；有害之物；**v.** 毒害；下毒

※灰色單字為英檢初級必備單字

poi·son·ous [ˈpɔɪznəs] 🎧 Track 3704
adj. 有毒的
▶ This mushroom is not edible because it's poisonous. 這蘑菇因為有毒，所以不能吃。

poke [pok] 🎧 Track 3705
v. 戳，捅；撥弄，攪動；向前突出，向前擠；激發；用拳打
▶ Please don't poke your head out of the window of a moving car.
請不要在車子移動時，將你的頭伸出窗外。

[相關片語]
poke into 探聽，干涉
▶ He was irritated when she tried to poke into his personal affairs.
當她企圖探聽他的私事時，他感到十分不悅。

pole [pol] 🎧 Track 3706
n. （地球的）極；極地區域；極地
▶ We are planning a trip to the North Pole to see the Northern Lights.
我們正在計劃一趟看北極光的北極之旅。

po·lice [pəˈlis] 🎧 Track 3707
n. 警察；警方

po·lice·man [pəˈlismən] 🎧 Track 3708
=cop
n. 警員；警察

pol·i·cy [ˈpɑləsɪ] 🎧 Track 3709
n. 政策；方針

pol·ish [ˈpɑlɪʃ] 🎧 Track 3710
n. 磨光；擦亮
▶ He let the boy give his shoes a polish.
他讓男孩幫他把鞋擦一擦。

v. 磨光；擦亮；磨光劑
▶ He made a living by polishing shoes.
他靠幫人擦鞋賺錢謀生。

[補充片語]
make a living 賺錢謀生
[相關片語]
polish the apple 拍馬屁
▶ He got the promotion by polishing the apple. 他靠逢迎拍馬才獲得拔擢。

po·lite [pəˈlaɪt] 🎧 Track 3711
adj. 禮貌的；有理的

po·lit·i·cal [pəˈlɪtɪkl] 🎧 Track 3712
adj. 政治上的
▶ My husband and I have opposite political views. 我和我丈夫的政治觀點是對立的。

pol·i·ti·cian [ˌpɑləˈtɪʃən] 🎧 Track 3713
n. 政治家
▶ Churchill was a respectable politician.
邱吉爾是一個可敬的政治家。

pol·i·tics [ˈpɑlətɪks] 🎧 Track 3714
n. 政治；政治學；政治手腕；政治活動
▶ He followed in his father's footsteps to go into politics. 他追隨父親的腳步從政。

poll [pol] 🎧 Track 3715
n. 民意測驗；投票；投票結果
▶ The result of the poll was contrary to our expectations. 投票的結果出乎我們的意料。

[補充片語]
contrary to one's expectations 出人意料

v. 對……進行民意測驗；使投票；獲得（票數）
▶ The candidate that I support polled 70 percent of the votes.
我支持的候選人獲得了百分之七十的選票。

pol·lute [pəˈlut] 🎧 Track 3716
v. 污染

pol·lu·tion [pəˈluʃən] 🎧 Track 3717
n. 污染

pond [pɑnd] 🎧 Track 3718
n. 池塘

po·ny [ˈponɪ] 🎧 Track 3719
n. 矮種馬，小馬；小型馬；小型（的東西）
▶ The girl rode her pony all over the grassland.
女孩騎著她的小馬在草原上到處跑。

pool [pul] 🎧 Track 3720
n. 池；水池

poor [pʊr] 🎧 *Track 3721*
adj. 可憐的；不幸的；貧窮的；粗劣的

pop [pɑp] 🎧 *Track 3722*
n. 砰的一聲，啪的一聲
▶ Jerry opened the champagne with a loud pop. 傑瑞砰地一聲打開了香檳。

v. 發出砰（或啪）的響聲；突然出現；迅速行動；開槍
▶ I was really surprised when he suddenly popped out from nowhere. 當他突然不知道從哪裡冒出來時，我真的被嚇到了。

pop·corn [`pɑp͵kɔrn] 🎧 *Track 3723*
n. 爆米花

pop·u·lar [`pɑpjələ] 🎧 *Track 3724*
adj. 流行的；普遍的；受歡迎的

pop·u·la·tion 🎧 *Track 3725*
[͵pɑpjə`leʃən]
n. 人口

pork [pɔrk] 🎧 *Track 3726*
n. 豬肉

port [port] 🎧 *Track 3727*
n. 港；港市；口岸
▶ This fishing village used to be an important port. 這個漁村過去曾是個重要的港口。

por·ta·ble [`portəbl] 🎧 *Track 3728*
adj. 便於攜帶的，手提式的；輕便的
▶ He carried his portable computer wherever he went. 他不管到哪裡都帶著他的手提電腦。

n. 手提式製品
▶ My computer is a portable.
我的電腦是手提式的。

por·ter [`portə] 🎧 *Track 3729*
n. （機場、車站的）搬運工人，腳夫；雜務工
▶ He tipped the porter who carried the luggage for him.
他給幫他搬行李的腳夫小費。

por·tion [`porʃən] 🎧 *Track 3730*
n. （一）部分；（食物等的）一份，一客；一份遺產
▶ I can't finish a large portion of roast beef by myself.
我沒辦法一個人吃完一大份的烤牛肉。

por·trait [`portret] 🎧 *Track 3731*
n. 畫像
▶ That's the painter's self-portrait.
這是那畫家的自畫像。

por·tray [por`tre] 🎧 *Track 3732*
v. 畫，描繪；扮演，表現；把……描繪成
▶ The author portrayed himself as an ignorant village idiot in his book.
作者在書中將他自己描繪成一個呆頭呆腦的無知鄉巴佬。

pose [poz] 🎧 *Track 3733*
v. 擺姿勢；裝腔作勢；使擺好姿勢
▶ She always knows how to pose for pictures.
她總是知道該怎麼擺照相姿勢。

n. 姿勢；姿態
▶ This yoga pose can help you sleep better.
這個瑜伽姿勢能幫助你睡得更好。

po·si·tion [pə`zɪʃən] 🎧 *Track 3734*
n. 位置；地方；姿勢；地位；身份；立場；職務；**v.** 把……放在適當位置

pos·i·tive [`pɑzətɪv] 🎧 *Track 3735*
adj. 確定的；確信的；積極的；肯定的；正面的

pos·sess [pə`zɛs] 🎧 *Track 3736*
v. 擁有
▶ We should cherish what we possess.
我們應珍惜我們所擁有的東西。

pos·ses·sion [pə`zɛʃən] 🎧 *Track 3737*
n. 擁有；所有物
▶ She carries all her possessions with her in an old suitcase.
她用一只皮箱隨身帶著她所有的財物。

※灰色單字為英檢初級必備單字

pos·si·bil·i·ty　🎧 *Track 3738*
[ˌpɑsə`bɪlətɪ]

n. 可能性；可能的事；發展前途

▶ If he did commit the murder, there is no possibility for him to get away with it.
如果他真的犯下殺人罪，他是不可能會逃得過制裁的。

（補充片語）

get away with 不因某事受懲罰

pos·si·ble [`pɑsəbl]　🎧 *Track 3739*
adj. 可能的；有可能的

pos·si·bly [`pɑsəblɪ]　🎧 *Track 3740*
adv. 也許，可能；盡全力地

▶ I'll be there as soon as I possibly can.
我會盡快趕到那裡去。

post [post]　🎧 *Track 3741*
n. 柱子；樁；杆

▶ He nailed the flyer on the post.
他將傳單釘在柱子上。

post·age [`postɪdʒ]　🎧 *Track 3742*
n. 郵資

▶ What is the postage for an airmail letter?
一封航空信要多少郵資？

post·al [`postl]　🎧 *Track 3743*
adj. 郵政的，郵局的，郵遞的

▶ Compared to other countries, postal services here are exceptionally reliable and efficient. 跟其他國家比起來，這裡的郵政服務極為可靠有效率。

post·card [`post͵kard]　🎧 *Track 3744*
n. 明信片

post·er [`postɚ]　🎧 *Track 3745*
n. 海報，廣告，招貼，佈告

▶ He hung his idol posters on the wall of his bedroom.
他把他的偶像海報掛在房間的牆上。

post·man [`postmən]　🎧 *Track 3746*
n. 郵差

▶ The postman collects the mail from the postbox once a day.
郵差一天收一次郵筒內的郵件。

post·pone [post`pon]　🎧 *Track 3747*
v. 使延期，延遲；延緩

▶ They postponed the opening ceremony to next Saturday because of the coming typhoon. 由於即將來臨的颱風，他們將開幕典禮給延到下週六了。

pot [pɑt]　🎧 *Track 3748*
n. 鍋子；一鍋

po·ta·to [pə`teto]　🎧 *Track 3749*
n. 馬鈴薯

po·ten·tial [pə`tɛnʃəl]　🎧 *Track 3750*
adj. 潛在的，可能的

▶ This TV commercial successfully prompted more of our potential customers to purchase our product. 這隻電視廣告成功地刺激我們更多的潛在客戶購買我們的產品。

n. 可能性，潛力；潛能

▶ She has singing potential; all she needs is some vocal training. 她有唱歌的潛力，她所需要的是一些發聲訓練。

pot·ter·y [`pɑtərɪ]　🎧 *Track 3751*
n. 陶器；陶器製造；陶器廠；製陶手藝；製陶行業

▶ We went to the museum for the pottery exhibition. 我們去博物館看陶器展。

poul·try [`poltrɪ]　🎧 *Track 3752*
n. 家禽，家禽肉

▶ Avian influenza is an infectious viral disease most commonly found among poultry. 禽流感是在家禽身上最常被發現的一種傳染性病毒疾病。

pound [paʊnd]　🎧 *Track 3753*
v. （連續）猛烈敲擊；（心臟）劇跳；搗碎；腳步沉重地行走；隆隆地行駛

▶ Her heart was pounding when the man approached her with a knife. 當男子持刀接近時，她的心臟怦怦跳得很厲害。

pour [por] 🎧 *Track 3754*

v. 倒，灌；傾注，大量投入；傾瀉，放射；傾吐

▶ For the ALS Ice Bucket Challenge, the celebrity poured a bucket of ice water over her head.
為了肌萎縮性脊髓側索硬化症的冰桶挑戰，這位名人往自己頭上倒了一桶冰水。

(補充片語)

ALS=Amyotrophic Lateral Sclerosis 肌萎縮性脊髓側索硬化症

pov·er·ty [`pɑvɚtɪ] 🎧 *Track 3755*

n. 貧困，貧窮

▶ No one wants to live in poverty.
沒有人想要過貧困的生活。

pow·der [`paʊdɚ] 🎧 *Track 3756*

n. 粉；粉狀物；化妝用粉；**v.** 擦粉；把粉撒在……上

pow·er [`paʊɚ] 🎧 *Track 3757*

n. 力量；能力；職權

pow·er·ful [`paʊɚfəl] 🎧 *Track 3758*

adj. 強而有力的；有權威的；有影響的

pow·er·less [`paʊɚlɪs] 🎧 *Track 3759*

adj. 無力量的，軟弱的；無能力的；無權力的，無影響力的

▶ The woman was powerless to protect herself and her children from the domestic violence. 婦人無力保護自己和孩子不受家暴。

prac·ti·cal [`præktɪkl] 🎧 *Track 3760*

adj. 實際的；實用的，有實用價值的；有實際經驗的

▶ We need a manager with at least five-year's practical experience in selling.
我們需要一個在銷售方面至少有五年實際經驗的經理人。

(相關片語)

practical joke 惡作劇，捉弄

▶ Those boys were punished for playing a practical joke on their teacher.
那些男孩子因為對老師惡作劇而被處罰。

prac·tice [`præktɪs] 🎧 *Track 3761*

n./v. 練習

praise [prez] 🎧 *Track 3762*

v. 讚美；表揚；**n.** 讚揚；稱頌

pray [pre] 🎧 *Track 3763*

v. 祈禱；祈求

prayer [prɛr] 🎧 *Track 3764*

n. 祈禱，禱告；祈禱文

▶ He says his prayers before every meal.
他每頓飯前都會禱告。

(補充片語)

say one's prayers 禱告，念禱文

pre·cious [`prɛʃəs] 🎧 *Track 3765*

adj. 貴重的；珍貴的

pre·cise [prɪ`saɪs] 🎧 *Track 3766*

adj. 精確的

▶ Please tell me the precise arrival time of your flight so that I can make arrangement for a pick-up service. 請告訴我你的班機準確的抵達時間，如此一來我才能安排接機服務。

pre·dict [prɪ`dɪkt] 🎧 *Track 3767*

v. 預測，預言，預料，預報

▶ No one can predict exactly when or where an earthquake will occur. 沒有人能夠準確地預測地震會在何時何地發生。

pre·dic·tion [prɪ`dɪkʃən] 🎧 *Track 3768*

n. 預測，預料，預報；預言的事

▶ His prediction about the earthquake came true. 他對地震的預言成真了。

pre·fer [prɪ`fɚ] 🎧 *Track 3769*

v. 寧願；更喜歡

pref·e·ra·ble [`prɛfərəbl] 🎧 *Track 3770*

adj. 更好的，更合適的；更可取的

▶ If you ask me, frozen food is preferable to fast food.
你要問我的話，我覺得冷凍食品比速食好。

※灰色單字為英檢初級必備單字

preg·nan·cy [ˋprɛgnənsɪ] 🎧 Track 3771

n. 懷孕；孕期

▶ Smoking during pregnancy will risk your baby's health.
懷孕時抽菸會使寶寶的健康遭受危險。

preg·nant [ˋprɛgnənt] 🎧 Track 3772

adj. 懷孕的，懷胎的；充滿的，富有的；意味深長的

▶ The woman is thirty weeks pregnant.
這女人已經懷孕三十週了。

prep·a·ra·tion 🎧 Track 3773
[͵prɛpəˋreʃən]

n. 準備；準備工作

▶ We didn't have much time to make preparations for our wedding.
我們沒有太多時間可以籌備我們的婚禮。

(補充片語)

make preparations for 籌備，為……做準備

pre·pare [prɪˋpɛr] 🎧 Track 3774

v. 準備

pre·pared [prɪˋpɛrd] 🎧 Track 3775

adj. 有準備的

▶ We must hope for the best, and meantime we should be prepared for the worst.
我們一定要抱最大的希望，同時也應該做好面對最壞情況的準備。

pres·ence [ˋprɛzns] 🎧 Track 3776

n. 出席；在場；面前

▶ He proposed to her in the presence of all of us. 他在我們所有人面前向她求婚。

pres·ent [ˋprɛznt] 🎧 Track 3777

adj. 出席的；在場的；現在的；當前的；
n. 禮物；現在

pre·sen·ta·tion 🎧 Track 3778
[͵prizɛnˋteʃən]

n. 報告，介紹，呈現，提出；上演；授予

▶ I spent three months to make preparations for the presentation.
我花了三個月的時間來準備這次的報告。

pres·ent·ly [ˋprɛzntlɪ] 🎧 Track 3779

adv. 現在，目前；不久，一會兒

▶ The concert will begin presently.
音樂會一會兒就要開始了。

pre·serve [prɪˋzɝv] 🎧 Track 3780

v. 保存，防腐；保護，維持，醃肉，把……製成果醬或蜜餞，把……製成罐頭食品

▶ It is of great urgency that we preserve our natural resources.
保護我們的天然資源是件刻不容緩的事。

n. 蜜餞，果醬；保護區；防護用品

▶ We're going to use these fresh strawberries to make strawberry preserves.
我們要用這些新鮮草莓來做草莓果醬。

pres·i·dent [ˋprɛzədənt] 🎧 Track 3781

n. 總統

pres·i·den·tial 🎧 Track 3782
[ˋprɛzədɛnʃəl]

adj. 總統的，總統制的，總統選舉的；總裁的，會長的

▶ According to the latest public opinion poll, he is the most promising presidential candidate. 根據最新的民調結果，他是最有希望的總統候選人。

(補充片語)

public opinion poll 民調

press [prɛs] 🎧 Track 3783

n. 新聞界；新聞輿論；壓、按；熨平、燙平；**v.** 按；擠；壓；催促

pres·sure [ˋprɛʃɚ] 🎧 Track 3784

n. 壓力，艱難；壓，按，擠

▶ We're looking for engineers who can work well under pressure.
我們要徵求在壓力下仍能順利工作的工程師。

v. 對……施加壓力；迫使

▶ The girl was pressured into marrying the man she didn't love.
女孩是受到壓力才嫁給她不愛的男人。

pre·tend [prɪˋtɛnd] 🎧 Track 3785

v. 假裝，佯裝；假扮，裝作

▶Stop pretending that you are innocent.
不要再裝無辜了。

pret·ty [ˋprɪtɪ] 🎧 *Track 3786*
adj. 漂亮的；**adv.** 非常；蠻；頗

pre·vent [prɪˋvɛnt] 🎧 *Track 3787*
v. 阻止；防止，預防
▶The sudden rain prevented them from going picnicking.
突來的雨讓他們無法去野餐。

pre·ven·tion [prɪˋvɛnʃən] 🎧 *Track 3788*
n. 預防
▶Prevention is better than cure.
預防勝於治療。

pre·view [ˋpriˌvju] 🎧 *Track 3789*
n. 預習，預看，預先審查；試映；預展；預告片
▶I saw the preview of the movie on the Internet.
我在網路上看過這部電影的預告片了。

v. 預習，預看，預先審查；試映；預告
▶The teacher asked us to preview the lesson before the class.
老師要我們上課前先預習課程。

pre·vi·ous [ˋpriviəs] 🎧 *Track 3790*
adj. 先前的，以前的
▶I had to decline their invitation because of a previous engagement.
因為有約在先，我必須婉拒他們的邀請。

price [praɪs] 🎧 *Track 3791*
n. 價錢；價格；**v.** 給……定價；為……標價

price·less [ˋpraɪslɪs] 🎧 *Track 3792*
adj. 貴重的，無價的
▶This handwritten manuscript of the novel is priceless.
這份小說的手抄本是無價的。

pride [praɪd] 🎧 *Track 3793*
n. 自豪；得意；引以為傲的人或事物；自尊心
▶He showed us his gold medal with pride.
他得意地向我們展示他的金牌。

v. 使得意，使自豪
▶He prided himself on owning a successful restaurant.
他為自己擁有一間成功的餐廳而自豪。

相關片語
take pride in 以……為傲
▶He took pride in his own singing skills
他為自己的歌藝感到驕傲。

priest [prist] 🎧 *Track 3794*
n. 牧師

pri·ma·ry [ˋpraɪˌmɛrɪ] 🎧 *Track 3795*
adj. 主要的；基本的
▶His stubbornness was the primary cause of his failure.
冥頑不靈是他失敗的主因。

prime [praɪm] 🎧 *Track 3796*
adj. 最初的，基本的；主要的，首位的；最好的
▶David Cameron, leader of the Conservative Party, was appointed to the Prime Minister of the United Kingdom in 2010. 保守黨領袖大衛・卡麥隆，在2010年被任命為英國首相。

補充片語
prime minister 首相

n. 初期；全盛時期；春天，黎明；精華，最好的部分
▶No one would have thought that such a good man like him would die in the prime of his life. 沒有人會想到像他這樣的一個好人竟然會英年早逝。

補充片語
die in the prime of one's life 英年早逝

v. 灌注，填裝；使準備好
▶Our troops were primed and ready for battle.
我們的軍隊已經準備好，可以作戰了。

prim·i·tive [ˋprɪmətɪv] 🎧 *Track 3797*
adj. 原始的，遠古的；粗糙的，未開化的；淳樸的，自然的
▶The painter is best known for his primitive style of painting.
這畫家因其淳樸的繪畫風格而為人所知。

prince [prɪns]   🎧 *Track 3798*
n. 王子

prin·cess [`prɪnsɪs]   🎧 *Track 3799*
n. 公主

prin·ci·ple [`prɪnsəpl]   🎧 *Track 3800*
n. 原則；原理；主義；信條

print [prɪnt]   🎧 *Track 3801*
v. 印；印刷；發行；出版，**n.** 印刷字體；印記；拷貝；印刷業

print·er [`prɪntə]   🎧 *Track 3802*
n. 印表機

pri·or·i·ty [praɪ`ɔrətɪ]   🎧 *Track 3803*
n. 優先，重點；優先考慮的事；優先權
▶ My family is always my top priority.
我的家人永遠是我優先考慮的對象。

pris·on [`prɪzn]   🎧 *Track 3804*
n. 監獄；拘留所

pris·on·er [`prɪznə]   🎧 *Track 3805*
n. 犯人；囚犯

priv·a·cy [`praɪvəsɪ]   🎧 *Track 3806*
n. 隱私
▶ Even my mother cannot invade my privacy by reading my emails or checking my phone. 就算是我媽也不能以看我的電子郵件或查我的手機來侵犯我的隱私權。

pri·vate [`praɪvɪt]   🎧 *Track 3807*
adj. 個人的；私下的

priv·i·lege [`prɪvl̩ɪdʒ]   🎧 *Track 3808*
n. 特權；（個人的）殊榮；議會特權；基本權利
▶ Our members enjoy the privilege to use all the hotel facilities for free. 我們的會員享有免費使用所有飯店設施的特權。

v. 給予……特權
▶ Passengers traveling with young kids are usually privileged to board before others.
帶著幼小孩童的乘客通常都會被給予比其他人優先登機的特權。

prize [praɪz]   🎧 *Track 3809*
n. 獎；獎品；獎金

prob·a·ble [`prɑbəbl]   🎧 *Track 3810*
adj. 很可能發生的；很可能成為事實的；很有希望的；可信的
▶ It is highly probable that he will be promoted to Export Sales Manager.
他非常有可能被升為外銷部經理。

prob·a·bly [`prɑbəblɪ]   🎧 *Track 3811*
adv. 可能；有可能地

prob·lem [`prɑbləm]   🎧 *Track 3812*
n. 問題；難題

pro·ce·dure [prə`sidʒə]   🎧 *Track 3813*
n. 手續；程序；步驟
▶ None of these problems would have occurred if you would just follow the procedure. 如果你有按照程序來做的話，這些問題根本就不會發生。

相關片語
standard operating procedure (SOP) 標準作業程序
▶ We follow a standard operating procedure to process our customers' complaints.
我們有一套處理顧客的投訴的標準作業程序。

pro·ceed [prə`sid]   🎧 *Track 3814*
v. 繼續進行；著手，開始；進行
▶ The worker put out his cigarette and proceeded with his work.
工人熄掉他的菸，並繼續工作。

pro·cess [`prɑsɛs]   🎧 *Track 3815*
n. 過程，進程；步驟，程序
▶ Your application is in the process of examination. 您的申請正在審核過程中。

v. 加工；處理；辦理
▶ It takes at least three working days process your visa application.
辦理簽證申請需要至少三個工作天。

pro·duce [prə`djus]   🎧 *Track 3816*
v. 生產；出產

pro·duc·er [prəˋdjusə·] 🎧 *Track 3817*
n. 生產者；製作人
▶ He became a film producer after he retired from the stage.
他從舞台退休之後，便成了一名電影製片人。

prod·uct [ˋprɑdəkt] 🎧 *Track 3818*
n. 產品

pro·duc·tion [prəˋdʌkʃən] 🎧 *Track 3819*
n. 生產；製作；產量；產物

pro·duc·tive [prəˋdʌktɪv] 🎧 *Track 3820*
adj. 生產的；多產的；富有成效的
▶ It's hard to keep the employees productive before the long holiday weekend.
要員工在放週休連假前保持工作成效，是很困難的一件事。

pro·fes·sion [prəˋfɛʃən] 🎧 *Track 3821*
n. （透過教育或訓練的）職業
▶ The girl dreams to make modeling her profession. 這女孩夢想以當模特兒為業。

pro·fes·sion·al 🎧 *Track 3822*
[prəˋfɛʃənl]
adj. 職業上的，職業性的；內行的，稱職的；擅長……的
▶ My wife is a professional musician.
我妻子是一名職業音樂家。

n. 職業選手，專家，行家
▶ The basketball player is a professional, not an amateur.
這位籃球選手是職業選手，而非業餘選手。

pro·fes·sor [prəˋfɛsə·] 🎧 *Track 3823*
n. 教授

prof·it [ˋprɑfɪt] 🎧 *Track 3824*
n. 利潤，盈利；收益；利益
▶ An orphanage is not a profit-making institution. 孤兒院並不是一個圖利的機構。

（補充片語）
profit-making institution 營利機構

v. 有益於，有利於；得益，獲益
▶ We profited greatly from your advice.
你的建議讓我們獲益良多。

prof·it·a·ble [ˋprɑfɪtəbl̩] 🎧 *Track 3825*
adj. 有利的，有營利的；獲利的
▶ The restaurant is a profitable business.
這間餐廳是個有賺錢的事業。

pro·gram [ˋprogræm] 🎧 *Track 3826*
=pro·gramme （英式英文）
n. 節目；節目單；計劃；方案；**v.** 為……安排節目；為（電腦）設計程式；為……制定計劃

pro·gress [prəˋgrɛs] 🎧 *Track 3827*
n. 前進；進步；進展；**v.** 前進；進步

pro·gres·sive [prəˋgrɛsɪv] 🎧 *Track 3828*
adj. 進步的，先進的；逐步的，發展中的；（醫）進行性的，越來越嚴重的
▶ ALS is a progressive fatal neurological disease, which is still incurable at present.
肌萎縮性脊髓側索硬化症是一種目前仍無法治癒，會逐漸惡化致死的神經系統疾病。

n. 進步分子；革新主義者；改革派
▶ Progressives wanted the government to take a more active role in regulating those big enterprises. 改革派人士希望政府在規範那些大企業上能扮演更主動的角色。

pro·hib·it [prəˋhɪbɪt] 🎧 *Track 3829*
v. （以法令）禁止；妨礙，阻止
▶ Smoking is prohibited in public places.
公共場所是禁止抽菸的。

proj·ect [ˋprɑdʒɛkt] 🎧 *Track 3830*
n. 計劃；企劃

prom·i·nent [ˋprɑmənənt] 🎧 *Track 3831*
adj. 傑出的
▶ He is a prominent baseball player.
他是一個優秀的棒球選手。

prom·ise [ˋprɑmɪs] 🎧 *Track 3832*
v. 承諾；答應；保證；**n.** 承諾；諾言

prom·is·ing [ˋprɑmɪsɪŋ] 🎧 *Track 3833*
adj. 有前途的，有希望的
▶ He is a very promising young man.
他是個很有前途的年輕人。

※灰色單字為英檢初級必備單字

pro·mote [prə`mot] 🎧 *Track 3834*
v. 擢昇，晉升
▶ He was promoted to the finance manager.
他被擢昇為財務經理。

pro·mo·tion [prə`moʃən] 🎧 *Track 3835*
n. 升遷；促銷
▶ He deserves the promotion.
他理當獲得升遷。

prompt [prɑmpt] 🎧 *Track 3836*
v. 促使；激勵；慫恿
▶ Her curiosity prompted her to check her boyfriend's cellphone.
好奇心促使她去檢查男友的手機。

n. 催促；提醒；提詞
▶ It is her job to give a prompt to anyone who forgets his lines on the stage. 她的工作就是要在有人在舞台上忘詞時負責提詞。

(補充片語)
give sb. a prompt 給某人提詞

adj. 敏捷的，及時的，迅速的
▶ I'm looking forward to your prompt reply.
期待您盡快給我回覆。

pro·nounce [prə`naʊns] 🎧 *Track 3837*
v. 發音

pro·nun·ci·a·tion 🎧 *Track 3838*
[prə‚nʌnsɪ`eʃən]
n. 發音，發音法
▶ The teacher corrected the student's pronunciation. 老師糾正學生的發音。

proof [pruf] 🎧 *Track 3839*
n. 證據，物證；證明
▶ There is no proof that he was involved in the death of the woman.
沒有證據可以證明他與女子的死有關。

adj. 不能穿透的，能抵擋的
▶ The fabric is proof against fire.
這款布料是可以防火的。

prop·er [`prɑpɚ] 🎧 *Track 3840*
adj. 適合的，適當的；合乎體統的，正派的

▶ My mother wanted me to stop fooling around and get a proper job.
我媽要我別再遊手好閒，並找份適合的工作。

(補充片語)
fool around 遊手好閒

prop·er·ly [`prɑpɚlɪ] 🎧 *Track 3841*
adv. 恰當地，正確地；理所當然地；體面地
▶ My girlfriend insisted that I should propose to her properly.
我女友堅持我應該要好好地向她求婚。

prop·er·ty [`prɑpɚtɪ] 🎧 *Track 3842*
n. 財產，資產，所有物
▶ It is intellectual property that really has value. 真正有價值的是智慧財產。

pro·por·tion [prə`porʃən] 🎧 *Track 3843*
n. 比例，比率；部分
▶ A large proportion of his salary is used to pay for his rent.
他的薪水有一大部分要拿來付房租。

(相關片語)
out of all proportion to 不成比例的
▶ It worries me that our expenditure is out of all proportion to our incomes.
我們的開銷與我們的收入完全不成比例，讓我非常憂心。

pro·pos·al [prə`pozl] 🎧 *Track 3844*
n. 計畫；建議；求婚
▶ Daniel asked Jenny to marry him, but she turned down his proposal. 丹尼爾請珍妮嫁給他，但她拒絕了他的求婚。

(補充片語)
turn down 拒絕

pro·pose [prə`poz] 🎧 *Track 3845*
v. 提議；建議；求婚

pros·pect [`prɑspɛkt] 🎧 *Track 3846*
n. （成功的）可能性；前景，前途
▶ Drug use ruined the future prospects of this promising actor. 使用毒品毀了這個有前途的演員未來成功的可能性。

pros·per [`prɑspɚ] 🎧 *Track 3847*
v. 使繁榮，繁榮

▶ I hope the country will prosper under the new government. 我希望在新政府的領導下，國家能夠繁榮起來。

pros·per·i·ty [prɑs`pɛrətɪ] 🎧 *Track 3848*
n. 繁榮
▶ He was amazed at the prosperity of this place when he first visited here. 當他第一次造訪此地時，對這兒的繁榮景象大為吃驚。

pros·per·ous [`prɑspərəs] 🎧 *Track 3849*
adj. 富有的，繁榮的，昌盛的
▶ Compared to many other cities in China, Shanghai is rather prosperous. 跟中國許多其他城市比起來，上海算是相當的繁榮。

pro·tect [prə`tɛkt] 🎧 *Track 3850*
v. 保護

pro·tec·tion [prə`tɛkʃən] 🎧 *Track 3851*
n. 保護；防護

pro·tec·tive [prə`tɛktɪv] 🎧 *Track 3852*
adj. 保護的
▶ I think you're a little too protective towards your son. 我覺得你有點太保護你的兒子了。

pro·tein [`protin] 🎧 *Track 3853*
n. 蛋白質
▶ You can obtain protein from meat or eggs. 你可以從肉或蛋中獲取蛋白質。

pro·test [prə`tɛst] 🎧 *Track 3854*
n. 抗議，異議，反對
▶ The demonstration is a protest against the import the American beef. 這次的示威運動是要反對美國牛肉的進口。

v. 抗議，反對；斷言，對……提出異議；聲明
▶ The man protested that he had never cheated on his wife. 男子聲明自己從未對妻子不忠。

proud [praʊd] 🎧 *Track 3855*
adj. 驕傲的；得意的

prove [pruv] 🎧 *Track 3856*
v. 證明

prov·erb [`prɑvɝb] 🎧 *Track 3857*
n. 諺語，俗語；眾所皆知的事
▶ "No pain, no gain" is a well-known proverb. 「一分耕耘一分收穫」是一句著名的諺語。

pro·vide [prə`vaɪd] 🎧 *Track 3858*
v. 提供

prov·ince [`prɑvɪns] 🎧 *Track 3859*
n. 省，州；（相較於大都市的）地方，鄉間；（學術）領域，（工作）部門，（職務）範圍
▶ Liaoning is a province in the northern China. 遼寧是中國北部的一省。

psy·cho·log·i·cal [ˌsaɪkə`lɑdʒɪkl] 🎧 *Track 3860*
adj. 心理的
▶ The domestic violence left the child a psychological scar. 家庭暴力在那孩子心中留下了心靈創傷。

psy·chol·o·gist [saɪ`kɑlədʒɪst] 🎧 *Track 3861*
n. 心理學家
▶ He is a famous psychologist. 他是一位著名的心理學家。

psy·chol·o·gy [saɪ`kɑlədʒɪ] 🎧 *Track 3862*
n. 心理學
▶ I majored in Psychology in college. 我大學時主修心理學。

pub [pʌb] 🎧 *Track 3863*
n. 酒吧
▶ Let's go to the pub and have a drink. 我們到酒吧去喝一杯吧。

pub·lic [`pʌblɪk] 🎧 *Track 3864*
adj. 大眾的；公共的；民眾的；**n.** 公眾；民眾

pub·li·ca·tion [ˌpʌblɪ`keʃən] 🎧 *Track 3865*
n. 出版，發行；出版物，刊物；發表，公布
▶ The fashion magazine ceased publication. 這份時尚雜誌已經停止發行。

※灰色單字為英檢初級必備單字

pub·lic·i·ty [pʌbˈlɪsətɪ] 🎧 *Track 3866*

n. 公眾的注意，名聲；宣傳；公開場合

▶ The man slapped the woman in the face in the full glare of publicity.
男子在眾目睽睽之下打了那女人一巴掌。

pub·lish [ˈpʌblɪʃ] 🎧 *Track 3867*

v. 出版

▶ When will your new book be published?
你的新書將於何時出版？

pub·lish·er [ˈpʌblɪʃə] 🎧 *Track 3868*

n. 出版社，出版商；出版或發行者；發行人

▶ The publisher went bankrupt.
那家出版社倒閉了。

pud·ding [ˈpʊdɪŋ] 🎧 *Track 3869*

n. 布丁

▶ I'm going to make pudding for dessert.
我要來做布丁當甜點。

puff [pʌf] 🎧 *Track 3870*

v. 一陣陣地吹；噴著煙移動；喘著氣走；腫脹；使氣急；使充氣

▶ The steam train puffed slowly into the tunnel. 蒸汽火車噴著煙慢慢地駛進了隧道。

n. （一）吹，噴；一陣，一股；（抽）一口煙；呼吸；膨脹；粉撲；泡芙

▶ Everyone was out of puff.
每個人都氣喘吁吁。

pull [pʊl] 🎧 *Track 3871*

v. 拉；拖；牽；拽；拔；**n.** 拉；拖；拉力

pump [pʌmp] 🎧 *Track 3872*

n. 泵，唧筒；抽吸；**v.** 用唧筒抽；打氣

pump·kin [ˈpʌmpkɪn] 🎧 *Track 3873*

n. 南瓜

punch [pʌntʃ] 🎧 *Track 3874*

n. 拳打

▶ He gave the man a punch in the face.
他朝他的臉打了一拳。

v. 用拳猛擊；用力按

▶ He punched the man in the face.
他往那男人臉上搗了一拳。

punc·tu·al [ˈpʌŋktʃʊəl] 🎧 *Track 3875*

adj. 嚴守時刻的，準時的；正確的，精確的

▶ My boss puts emphasis on being punctual.
我老闆很重視守時。

pun·ish [ˈpʌnɪʃ] 🎧 *Track 3876*

v. 處罰

pun·ish·ment [ˈpʌnɪʃmənt] 🎧 *Track 3877*

n. 懲罰

pu·pil [ˈpjupl̩] 🎧 *Track 3878*

n. 小學生，學生；未成年人

▶ There are nearly 3,000 pupils in this school.
這間學校有近三千名學生。

pup·pet [ˈpʌpɪt] 🎧 *Track 3879*

n. 木偶，玩偶；傀儡

▶ We enjoyed the puppet show very much.
我們都很喜歡看這場木偶戲。

pup·py [ˈpʌpɪ] 🎧 *Track 3880*

n. 小狗

pur·chase [ˈpɜtʃəs] 🎧 *Track 3881*

n. 購買；購買之物 **v.** 購買

pur·ple [ˈpɜpl̩] 🎧 *Track 3882*

adj. 紫色的；紫的；**n.** 紫色

pur·pose [ˈpɜpəs] 🎧 *Track 3883*

n. 目的；意圖；用途

purse [pɜs] 🎧 *Track 3884*

n. 錢包；女用手提包

push [pʊʃ] 🎧 *Track 3885*

v. 推；催促；**n.** 推進；努力；衝進

put [pʊt] 🎧 *Track 3886*

v. 放；擺；使處於⋯⋯狀態

puz·zle [ˈpʌzl̩] 🎧 *Track 3887*

n. 謎；難題；**v.** 迷惑；為難；使迷惑不解

Qq

通過中級英文檢定者的英文能力：

 聽 在日常生活中，能聽懂一般的會話；能大致聽懂公共場所廣播、氣象報告及廣告等。在工作時，能聽懂簡易的產品介紹與操作說明。能大致聽懂外籍人士的談話及詢問。

 讀 在日常生活中，能閱讀短文、故事、私人信件、廣告、傳單、簡介及使用說明等。在工作時，能閱讀工作須知、公告、操作手冊、例行的文件、傳真、電報等。

 寫 能寫簡單的書信、故事及心得等。對於熟悉且與個人經歷相關的主題，能以簡易的文字表達。

 說 在日常生活中，能以簡易英語交談或描述一般事物，能介紹自己的生活作息、工作、家庭、經歷等，並可對一般話題陳述看法。在工作時，能進行簡單的答詢，並與外籍人士交談溝通。

本書除包含官方公佈的中級4,947單字外，更精挑了近400個滿分必學的高手單字。同時，在片語的挑選、例句的使用上，皆依上述英檢官方公佈之能力範疇做設計，難度適中、不偏離考試主題。發音部分則是自然發音＆KK音標雙管齊下，搭配MP3以「分解／完整」方式錄音，給你最多元有效的學習手段，怎麼記都可以，想忘掉都好難！

---

quack [kwæk]　🎧 *Track 3888*

adj. 庸醫的；冒充內行醫病的；冒牌的；吹牛的；騙人的

▶ The quack doctor's inadequate treatment resulted in death of the patient.
那個庸醫的不當治療造成病人的死亡。

n. 庸醫，江湖醫生；冒充內行的人；騙子

▶ We should stop the quack from practicing medicine.
我們應該要阻止那個庸醫繼續行醫。

---

qual·i·fi·ca·tion　🎧 *Track 3889*
[ˌkwɑləfəˈkeʃən]

n. 資格，條件；限定性條件

▶ Although I didn't meet all the qualifications, I applied for the position anyway.
雖然我並沒有符合所有的資格，我還是提出了應徵職務的申請。

---

qual·i·fied [ˈkwɑləˌfaɪd]　🎧 *Track 3890*

adj. 符合資格的；具備必要條件的；合格的

▶ She soon proved herself qualified to undertake the challenge.
她很快地便證明自己有接受這份挑戰的資格。

---

qual·i·fy [ˈkwɑləˌfaɪ]　🎧 *Track 3891*

v. 使具有資格；使合格；取得資格；具備合格條件

▶ Three years of practical experience qualified him for the position.
三年的實務經驗使他具備勝任此職務的資格。

---

qual·i·ty [ˈkwɑlətɪ]　🎧 *Track 3892*
n. 品質

---

quan·ti·ty [ˈkwɑntətɪ]　🎧 *Track 3893*
n. 量；數量；分量；大量；音量

▶ How do we clean away such a large quantity of garbage on our own?
我們要怎麼自己清掉這麼大量的垃圾？

(補充片語)
clean away 清除、清掉；
on one's own 靠某人自己

quar·rel [`kwɔrəl]　🎧 *Track 3894*

n. 爭吵，不和，吵鬧

▶ I had a quarrel with my wife last night.
我昨晚跟老婆吵了一架。

v. 爭吵，不和；埋怨，責備

▶ She often quarrels with her husband over money.
她時常為了錢的事情跟老公起爭執。

quar·ter [`kwɔrtə-]　🎧 *Track 3895*

n. 四分之一；一刻鐘

queen [`kwin]　🎧 *Track 3896*

n. 皇后

queer [kwɪr]　🎧 *Track 3897*

adj. 古怪的，可疑的；不舒服的

▶ My husband's been acting very queer lately. 我先生最近的行為很可疑。

相關片語

queer fish 古怪的人，難以理解的人

▶ Mr. Robertson is quite a queer fish. He never socializes with his neighbors.
羅伯森先生是個相當古怪的人。他從不跟鄰居打交道。

quest [kwɛst]　🎧 *Track 3898*

v. 尋找，追求，探索；請求，要求

▶ He moved to the big city in quest of employment.
他搬到大城市去找工作了。

補充片語

in quest of 尋找，探尋

ques·tion [`kwɛstʃən]　🎧 *Track 3899*

n. 問題；詢問；**v.** 質疑；詢問

queue [kju]　🎧 *Track 3900*

n. （人或車輛的）隊伍，行列

▶ We had to wait three hours in the queue for a table in the restaurant.
我們排了三個小時的隊才等到餐廳的桌子。

v. 排隊，排隊等候

▶ We had to queue for the tickets.
我們得排隊買票。

相關片語

jump the queue 插隊

▶ I couldn't help shout at the man who tried to jump the queue.
我忍不住吼了那個試圖插隊的男人。

quick [kwɪk]　🎧 *Track 3901*

adj. 快的

qui·et [`kwaɪət]　🎧 *Track 3902*

adj. 安靜的

quilt [kwɪlt]　🎧 *Track 3903*

n. 被子，被褥

▶ You'll need a thicker quilt to keep you warm at night.
你晚上將會需要一條厚一點的被子來保暖。

quit [kwɪt]　🎧 *Track 3904*

v. 戒除；離開；退出；停止

quite [kwaɪt]　🎧 *Track 3905*

adv. 相當

quiz [kwɪz]　🎧 *Track 3906*

n. 測驗；隨堂小考

quote [kwot]　🎧 *Track 3907*

v. 引用，引述

▶ Mr. Cooper likes to quote Steve Jobs when making speeches. 庫伯先生在演講時喜歡引用史蒂夫‧賈伯斯的話。

n. 引文；引號；經典名言

▶ "Stay hungry, stay foolish" is one of Steve Jobs' best-known quotes.
「求知若飢，虛心若愚」是賈伯斯最為人所知的經典名言之一。

Rr

通過中級英文檢定者的英文能力：

 聽　在日常生活中，能聽懂一般的會話；能大致聽懂公共場所廣播、氣象報告及廣告等。在工作時，能聽懂簡易的產品介紹與操作說明。能大致聽懂外籍人士的談話及詢問。

 讀　在日常生活中，能閱讀短文、故事、私人信件、廣告、傳單、簡介及使用說明等。在工作時，能閱讀工作須知、公告、操作手冊、例行的文件、傳真、電報等。

 寫　能寫簡單的書信、故事及心得等。對於熟悉且與個人經歷相關的主題，能以簡易的文字表達。

 說　在日常生活中，能以簡易英語交談或描述一般事物，能介紹自己的生活作息、工作、家庭、經歷等，並可對一般話題陳述看法。在工作時，能進行簡單的答詢，並與外籍人士交談溝通。

本書除包含官方公佈的中級4,947單字外，更精挑了近400個滿分必學的高手單字。同時，在片語的挑選、例句的使用上，皆依上述英檢官方公佈之能力範疇做設計，難度適中、不偏離考試主題。發音部分則是自然發音＆KK音標雙管齊下，搭配MP3以「分解／完整」方式錄音，給你最多元有效的學習手段，怎麼記都可以，想忘掉都好難！

---

rab·bit [`ræbɪt]　🎧 *Track 3908*
n. 兔子

race [res]　🎧 *Track 3909*
v. 比速度；參加競賽；使全速行進；使疾走；**n.** 賽跑；競賽；人種；民族

ra·cial [`reʃəl]　🎧 *Track 3910*
adj. 人種的；種族的
▶ Racial discrimination still exists in many countries nowadays.
現在許多國家仍存在著種族歧視的問題。

ra·dar [`redɑr]　🎧 *Track 3911*
n. 雷達
▶ The airplane disappeared from radars twenty minutes after taking off from the airport.
這架飛機在從機場起飛20分鐘後，便從雷達上消失。

ra·di·a·tion [͵redɪ`eʃən]　🎧 *Track 3912*
n. 發光；輻射，輻射線

▶ The expert said that low levels of radiation exposure would not have any long-lasting health effects.
該專家表示，低劑量的輻射接觸對健康不會產生持久性的影響。

rad·i·cal [`rædɪkl]　🎧 *Track 3913*
adj. 根本的，基本的；與生俱來的；極端的
▶ He explained the necessity of radical organizational changes to the board of directors.
他向董事會解釋根本的組織改造的必要性。

n. 根部，基礎；（數）根號；激進分子
▶ Rumor has it that the radicals are planning for a revolt against the government. 謠傳激進分子正在策劃一場對抗政府的叛變行動。

ra·di·o [`redɪ͵o]　🎧 *Track 3914*
n. 收音機；無線電廣播

rage [redʒ]　🎧 *Track 3915*
n. （一陣）狂怒，盛怒；（風雨、火勢等）狂暴，肆虐；狂熱

▶The customer flew into a rage when he was told that his coupon was invalid. 那名顧客在被告知他的優惠券不能用時勃然大怒。

(補充片語)

fly into a rage 勃然大怒，暴怒

v. 發怒，怒斥；猖獗；肆虐
▶It's been three days, and the storm is still raging over the island.
已經三天了，暴風雨仍在這座島上肆虐。

rail·road [ˋrelˌrod]
=rail·way （英式英文）
🎧 *Track 3916*
n. 鐵路

rail·way [ˋrelˌwe]
🎧 *Track 3917*
n. 鐵路
▶We are planning a trip around Europe on the railways.
我們正在計劃一個坐火車遊歐洲的旅行。

rain [ren]
🎧 *Track 3918*
n. 雨；**v.** 下雨

rain·bow [ˋrenˌbo]
🎧 *Track 3919*
n. 彩虹

rain·coat [ˋrenˌkot]
🎧 *Track 3920*
n. 雨衣
▶He returned home soaked to the skin because he forgot his raincoat.
因為忘了帶雨衣，他回家時全身都濕透了。

(補充片語)

soaked to the skin 全身濕透

rain·fall [ˋrenˌfɔl]
🎧 *Track 3921*
n. 將與，下雨；降雨量
▶According to the weather forecast, there will be rainfall this afternoon.
根據氣象預報，今天下午會下雨。

rain·y [ˋrenɪ]
🎧 *Track 3922*
adj. 下雨的；多雨的

raise [rez]
🎧 *Track 3923*
v. 舉起；提高；養育；豎起；**n.** 加薪；提高

rai·sin [ˋrezn]
🎧 *Track 3924*
n. 葡萄乾

▶I like to add some raisins in my salad.
我喜歡在沙拉裡加一點葡萄乾。

ran·dom [ˋrændəm]
🎧 *Track 3925*
n. 任意行動，隨機過程
▶He picked a jacket at random and put it on.
他隨便挑了一條外套就把它穿在身上了。

(補充片語)

at random 隨便地，任意地

adj. 胡亂的，任意的
▶He made a random guess at the answer, and it was right.
他胡亂地猜了個答案，居然猜對了。

range [rendʒ]
🎧 *Track 3926*
n. 範圍；區域；**v.** 排列；使並列；把……分類；範圍涉及……

rank [ræŋk]
🎧 *Track 3927*
n. 等級；身份，地位；社會階層；行列，隊伍
▶Marco Pierre White is a chef of the first rank.
馬可皮耶‧懷特是一名一流的廚師。

(補充片語)

of the first rank 第一流的

v. 排列；分等級；把……評等；列隊
▶These restaurants were ranked according to their food as well as their services.
這些餐廳是依其食物及服務被評等的。

rap·id [ˋræpɪd]
🎧 *Track 3928*
adj. 快的；快速的

rare [rɛr]
🎧 *Track 3929*
adj. 很少的；罕見的

rare·ly [ˋrɛrlɪ]
🎧 *Track 3930*
adv. 很少，難得；異乎尋常地
▶She rarely interacts with her neighbors.
她很少跟鄰居互動。

rat [ræt]
🎧 *Track 3931*
n. 老鼠

rate [ret] 🎧 *Track 3932*
n. 比例，比率；費用，價格；等級
▶ This country's birth rate has been one of the lowest in the world in recent years.
這幾年，該國一直是全世界出生率最低的國家之一。

v. 對……估價；認為；列為；定……的速率；定……的費率
▶ This restaurant was rated as one of the best Italian restaurants in the city. 這間餐廳被認為是這個城市最棒的義大利餐廳之一。

ra·ther [ˋræðɚ] 🎧 *Track 3933*
adv. 相當；頗；寧可；倒不如

raw [rɔ] 🎧 *Track 3934*
adj. 生的
▶ I don't eat raw fish. 我不吃生的魚。

ray [re] 🎧 *Track 3935*
n. 光線；熱線；射線，輻射線
▶ Direct rays of sunlight may blind your eyes.
直射的太陽光線可能會讓你失明。

ra·zor [ˋrezɚ] 🎧 *Track 3936*
n. 剃刀
▶ He accidently cut his face while shaving with a razor.
他用剃刀刮臉時，不小心把臉割傷了。

reach [ritʃ] 🎧 *Track 3937*
v. 抵達；到達；伸手及到；與……取得聯繫；**n.** 可及的範圍

re·act [rɪˋækt] 🎧 *Track 3938*
v. 反應；影響；反抗；起作用
▶ When the accident occurred, she was in complete shock and didn't know how to react. 意外發生時，她整個人震驚得不知該如何反應。

re·ac·tion [rɪˋækʃən] 🎧 *Track 3939*
n. 反應，感應；【化】反作用
▶ I can't wait to see her reaction to the surprise party.
我等不及看她對這個驚喜派對的反應了。

read [rid] 🎧 *Track 3940*
v. 閱讀

read·er [ˋridɚ] 🎧 *Track 3941*
n. 讀者，愛好閱讀者；讀物，讀本
▶ I am a loyal reader of her blog.
我是她部落格的忠實讀者。

〔相關片語〕
mind reader 能讀人心思者
▶ My wife must be a mind reader; she always knows what's on my mind.
我太太一定是個能讀人心思的人，她總是知道我心裡在想什麼。

read·i·ly [ˋrɛdɪlɪ] 🎧 *Track 3942*
adv. 樂意地，欣然；立即；無困難地
▶ She readily accepted the job offer.
她欣然地接受了這個工作機會。

read·y [ˋrɛdɪ] 🎧 *Track 3943*
adj. 準備好的

real [ˋriəl] 🎧 *Track 3944*
adj. 真的；真實的

rea·lis·tic [rɪəˋlɪstɪk] 🎧 *Track 3945*
adj. 現實的，注重實際的，實際可行的
▶ Your plan sounds perfect, but it's not realistic.
你的計劃聽起來很完美，但卻不實際。

re·al·i·ty [rɪˋæləti] 🎧 *Track 3946*
n. 真實；現實
▶ Sooner or later he has to face the reality.
他遲早都要面對現實。

〔補充片語〕
sooner or later 遲早

rea·lize [ˋrɪəˏlaɪz] 🎧 *Track 3947*
=rea·lise （英式英文）
v. 領悟；理解

real·ly [ˋriəlɪ] 🎧 *Track 3948*
adv. 很；確實地；真的

rear [rɪr] 🎧 *Track 3949*
adj. 後面的

▶ Please get off the bus by the rear door.
請由後門下車。

n. 後部，後面
▶ My car was hit in the rear by a truck on my way to work this morning. 今天早上上班途中，我的車被一輛卡車從後面撞上了。

v. 撫養；栽培；栽種，飼養；建立
▶ He was reared by his grandmother after he lost his parents.
失去雙親後，他便由奶奶撫養長大。

rea·son [`rizn̩]　🎧 *Track 3950*
n. 理由；原因

rea·son·a·ble [`riznəbl̩]　🎧 *Track 3951*
adj. 通情達理的，有理智的；合乎情理的；適當的；公道的
▶ It is reasonable for your wife to attend her ex-husband's funeral. 你的妻子去參加她前夫的葬禮，是合情合理的。

reb·el [`rɛbl̩]　🎧 *Track 3952*
n. 造反者，反叛者
▶ The rebels were all under arrest.
造反者全都已經被逮捕了。

v. 造反，反叛，反抗
▶ It's time for us to rebel against the incapable government.
是我們該起來反抗這無能政府的時候了。

re·build [ri`bɪld]　🎧 *Track 3953*
v. 重建，改建；使恢復原貌
▶ No matter how long it's going to take, we will rebuild our beautiful homeland.
無論要花多久時間，我們都會重建我們美麗的家園。

re·call [rɪ`kɔl]　🎧 *Track 3954*
v. 回想，回憶起；召回；收回，撤銷
▶ Will you try to recall what happened last night?
你能試著回想昨晚發生了什麼事嗎？

n. 回想，回憶；召回；撤銷
▶ Our marriage is screwed, and I'm afraid it's beyond recall at this point.
我們的婚姻已經完蛋了，到了這個地步，恐怕已經無法挽回了。

(補充片語)
beyond recall 無法挽回

re·ceipt [rɪ`sit]　🎧 *Track 3955*
n. 收據
▶ You can't return your purchase without a receipt.
沒有收據是不能退貨的。

re·ceive [rɪ`siv]　🎧 *Track 3956*
v. 收到；獲得

re·ceiv·er [rɪ`sivɚ]　🎧 *Track 3957*
n. 受領人，收件人；接待者；聽筒，受話器
▶ The letter was sent back because the receiver's address was incorrect. 因為收件人的地址是錯的，所以信被退回來了。

re·cent [`risn̩t]　🎧 *Track 3958*
adj. 最近的；不久前的

re·cent·ly [`risn̩tlɪ]　🎧 *Track 3959*
adv. 最近；近來；不久前

re·cep·tion [rɪ`sɛpʃən]　🎧 *Track 3960*
n. 接待，接見；接待會，宴會；接待處
▶ The wedding reception will be held after the wedding ceremony.
婚宴會在婚禮後舉行。

(相關片語)
reception room 會客室
▶ A client is waiting for you in the reception room. 有個客戶正在會客室等你。

re·ces·sion [rɪ`sɛʃən]　🎧 *Track 3961*
n. 衰退，衰退期；後退，退回；退場
▶ His company went bankrupt during the period of economic recession.
他的公司在經濟衰退時期倒閉了。

(補充片語)
go bankrupt 倒閉

re·ci·pe [`rɛsəpɪ]　🎧 *Track 3962*
n. 食譜；烹飪法；訣竅
▶ Can I have your recipe for the beef stew?
你可以給我你燉牛肉的食譜嗎？

re·cite [rɪˋsaɪt] 🎧 *Track 3963*
v. 背誦
▶ The students are asked to recite Tang Poetry. 學生們被要求要背誦唐詩。

reck·less [ˋrɛklɪs] 🎧 *Track 3964*
adj. 不在乎的，魯莽的，不顧後果的
▶ The president's reckless remarks invited a lot of criticism.
總統魯莽的言論招致諸多批評。

rec·og·ni·tion 🎧 *Track 3965*
[ˏrɛkəgˋnɪʃən]
n. 認出，辨識；承認，認可
▶ Linda has changed beyond recognition since she had a plastic operation.
琳達自從整形後就變得讓人認不出來了。

(補充片語)
beyond recognition 無法認出

rec·og·nize [ˋrɛkəgˏnaɪz] 🎧 *Track 3966*
v. 認出，識別，認識；正式承認，認可
▶ You have changed so much that I could hardly recognize you.
你改變太多，我幾乎認不出你來了。

rec·om·mend 🎧 *Track 3967*
[ˏrɛkəˋmɛnd]
v. 推薦，介紹，建議
▶ I just finished the book you recommended.
我剛讀完你推薦的書。

rec·ord [ˋrɛkəd] 🎧 *Track 3968*
n. 記載；紀錄；前科紀錄；成績；最高紀錄；**v.** 記錄；錄音

re·cord·er [rɪˋkɔrdə] 🎧 *Track 3969*
n. 記錄器，錄音機；記錄者，書記員；錄音師
▶ Their conversation was taped by a hidden recorder.
他們的對話被一台隱藏式錄音機給錄下來了。

re·cov·er [rɪˋkʌvə] 🎧 *Track 3970*
v. 重新獲得；恢復（原狀）；挽回；彌補

re·cov·er·y [rɪˋkʌvərɪ] 🎧 *Track 3971*
n. 恢復，康復，復原

▶ He sent me a card to wish me a rapid recovery.
他寄了一張卡片給我，祝我早日康復。

rec·re·a·tion [ˏrɛkrɪˋeʃən] 🎧 *Track 3972*
n. 消遣，娛樂
▶ What do you usually do for recreation?
你通常做什麼消遣？

rec·tan·gle [ˋrɛktæŋgl̩] 🎧 *Track 3973*
n. 矩形；長方形

re·cy·cle [riˋsaɪkl̩] 🎧 *Track 3974*
v. 使再循環；使再利用；回收

red [rɛd] 🎧 *Track 3975*
adj. 紅的；紅色的；**n.** 紅；紅色；紅色的衣服

re·duce [rɪˋdjus] 🎧 *Track 3976*
v. 減少，縮小，降低
▶ We have to reduce our daily expenses in order to save for a car.
我們必須減少我們的日常開銷，才能存錢買車。

re·duc·tion [rɪˋdʌkʃən] 🎧 *Track 3977*
n. 減少，降低，削減，縮小
▶ A reduction in the unemployment rate is seen as the key to economic recovery.
失業率降低被視為經濟復甦的關鍵。

reef [rif] 🎧 *Track 3978*
n. 礁，礁脈；沙洲；暗礁；礦脈
▶ Those tourists were fined for damaging and collecting coral reefs.
那些遊客因為破壞及採集珊瑚礁而被處以罰鍰。

re·fer [rɪˋfɚ] 🎧 *Track 3979*
v. 把……歸因於；論及，談到
▶ He referred to his mother several times in his thankful speech.
他在致感謝詞中多次提到他的母親。

(補充片語)
refer to 提到，談論

ref·er·ence [ˋrɛfərəns] 🎧 *Track 3980*
n. 參考；參考文獻，出處；提及，涉及

※灰色單字為英檢初級必備單字

▶I have attached a document to this mail for your reference.
我隨函附上了一份供您參考的文件。

re·flect [rɪ`flɛkt] 🎧 *Track 3981*
v. 反射，照映出；表現，反映；反省；招致
▶As a parent, you should watch your words and deeds, because they will ultimately reflect on your children.
做為一名家長，你應該要注意自己的言行，因為它們最終都會反映在你的孩子身上。

re·flec·tion [rɪ`flɛkʃən] 🎧 *Track 3982*
n. 反射，回響；映像，倒影；深思，反省；想法，意見
▶Children's behavior is always a reflection on their parents.
小孩的行為是他們的父母的影子。

re·form [ˌrɪ`fɔrm] 🎧 *Track 3983*
n. 改革，革新，改良；革除弊端；改造
▶The presidential candidate promised to make a health care reform after he won the election.
該總統候選人承諾當選後會進行醫療改革。

v. 改革，革新；改過，改邪歸正
▶He has completely reformed after being in jail for 15 years. 他在牢裡被關了十五年之後，已經徹底改邪歸正了。

re·fresh [rɪ`frɛʃ] 🎧 *Track 3984*
v. 使清新；使重新提振精神；使得到補充；吃點心，喝飲料；補給
▶We had some snacks to refresh ourselves before we continued on our work.
在繼續工作之前，我們吃了些小點心提振精神。

re·fri·ge·ra·tor 🎧 *Track 3985*
[rɪ`frɪdʒəˌretə]
=fridge=ice·box
n. 冰箱

ref·u·gee [ˌrɛfjʊ`dʒi] 🎧 *Track 3986*
n. 難民
▶Germany took the lead in welcoming refugees from Syria.
德國帶頭歡迎來自敘利亞的難民。

(補充片語)
take the lead 帶頭，率先

re·fus·al [rɪ`fjuzl] 🎧 *Track 3987*
n. 拒絕
▶He made a refusal to attend the ceremony.
他拒絕出席那場典禮。

re·fuse [rɪ`fjuz] 🎧 *Track 3988*
n. 廢物，垃圾，渣滓
▶You will be fined if you dump your refuse here.
把垃圾倒在這裡，你可是會被罰錢的噢。

v. 拒絕
▶I refuse to comment on what you said.
我拒絕就你所説的發表評論。

re·gard [rɪ`gɑrd] 🎧 *Track 3989*
v. 把……看作；看待；注重；**n.** 注意；關心；問候；致意

re·gard·ing [rɪ`gɑrdɪŋ] 🎧 *Track 3990*
prep. 關於；就……而論
▶He refused to respond to any questions regarding his private life.
他拒絕回應任何有關他私生活的問題。

re·gard·less [rɪ`gɑrdlɪs] 🎧 *Track 3991*
adv. 不顧一切地，不管怎樣地，無論如何
▶The party will be held as scheduled regardless of the weather.
無論天氣如何，派對都會如期舉行。

re·gion [`ridʒən] 🎧 *Track 3992*
n. 地區；行政區域；部位；領域

re·gion·al [`ridʒənl] 🎧 *Track 3993*
adj. 地區的，局部的
▶He has been promoted to the regional manager.
他已經被升為區經理了。

re·gis·ter [`rɛdʒɪstə] 🎧 *Track 3994*
v. 登記，註冊
▶You need to register the birth of your baby no later than three months after his birth. 你們必須在寶寶出生後三個月內完成出生登記。

n. 登記，註冊；自動登錄機，收銀機

▶ No register of the child's birth was found.
查無該孩童的出生紀錄。

re·gis·tra·tion
🎧 *Track 3995*

[ˌrɛdʒɪ`streʃən]

n. 登記，註冊，掛號

▶ Now you can make a pre-registration online before you go to the hospital.
現在在你去醫院看醫生之前，可以在線上預先掛號。

(補充片語)

pre-registration 預先掛號

re·gret
[rɪ`grɛt]
🎧 *Track 3996*

v. 後悔；懊悔；感到遺憾；**n.** 遺憾，悔恨；哀悼

reg·u·lar
[`rɛgjələ]
🎧 *Track 3997*

adj. 固定的；規律的

reg·u·late
[`rɛgjəˌlet]
🎧 *Track 3998*

v. 管理，規範，控制

▶ The temperature in the fridge is regulated at 4℃.
冰箱的溫度是控制在攝氏4度。

reg·u·la·tion
🎧 *Track 3999*

[ˌrɛgjə`leʃən]

n. 規章，規定；條例；管理；調整，調節

▶ Dyeing hair is against the school regulations.
染頭髮是違反校規的。

re·hears·al
[rɪ`hɝsl]
🎧 *Track 4000*

n. 排練，試演，練習

▶ The wedding ceremony rehearsal will be conducted the day before the wedding.
結婚典禮的彩排會在婚禮前一天舉行。

re·hearse
[rɪ`hɝs]
🎧 *Track 4001*

v. 排練

▶ We have to rehearse several times before we perform on the stage.
在上台表演前我們得排練好幾次。

re·ject
[rɪ`dʒɛkt]
🎧 *Track 4002*

v. 拒絕；抵制；駁回；排斥

re·late
[rɪ`let]
🎧 *Track 4003*

v. 有關，涉及；使有聯繫；相處

▶ The newcomer doesn't seem to relate very well to his colleagues.
那位新進人員看起來似乎跟他的同事處得不是很好。

(補充片語)

relate well to sb. 與某人相處和睦

re·lat·ed
[rɪ`letɪd]
🎧 *Track 4004*

adj. 有關的

▶ I'll pass this information to related departments.
我會將此資訊傳遞給有關部門。

re·la·tion
[rɪ`leʃən]
🎧 *Track 4005*

n. 關係；關聯；血親關係；親屬

▶ This study is mainly about the relation between smoking and lung cancer.
這項研究主要是關於抽煙與肺癌之間的關聯。

re·la·tion·ship
🎧 *Track 4006*

[rɪ`leʃənˌʃɪp]

n. 關係；人際關係；親屬關係；婚姻關係；戀愛關係

▶ We both agree that it is best to end the relationship.
我們都同意結束這段關係是最好的決定。

(相關片語)

parent-child relationship 親子關係

▶ You can't expect a good parent-child relationship with your children if you spend all your time on work.
如果你把所有時間都花在工作上，就不能期待與你的孩子之間會有良好的親子關係。

rel·a·tive
[`rɛlətɪv]
🎧 *Track 4007*

adj. 相對的，比較的；與……有關的；**n.** 親戚；親屬

rel·a·tive·ly
[`rɛlətɪvlɪ]
🎧 *Track 4008*

adv. 相當，相對地，比較而言

▶ She plays the piano relatively well for a beginner.
就一個初學者來說，她鋼琴算彈得相對好了。

re·lax
[rɪ`læks]
🎧 *Track 4009*

v. 鬆弛；緩和；放鬆，休息

※灰色單字為英檢初級必備單字

Aa Bb Cc Dd Ee Ff Gg Hh Ii Jj Kk Ll Mm Nn Oo Pp Qq Rr Ss Tt Uu Vv Ww Xx Yy Zz

▶Why don't you take a hot bath and relax?
你為什麼不泡個熱水澡，放鬆一下呢？

re·lax·a·tion
[͵rilæks`eʃən] 🎧 Track 4010

n. 鬆弛；放鬆；休息，消遣，娛樂
▶This is the best holiday resort for you to enjoy complete relaxation.
這是能讓你享受全然放鬆的最佳度假勝地。

re·lease [rɪ`lis] 🎧 Track 4011

v. 釋放，放開；豁免；發行，發表
▶The hijacker agreed to release half of the hostages.
劫持犯同意釋放一半的人質。

n. 釋放，解放；豁免；發行，發表
▶Following the release of her latest album, the singer announced her retirement.
在最新的唱片發行之後，該歌手就宣布要退出歌壇。

re·li·a·ble [rɪ`laɪəbl] 🎧 Track 4012

adj. 可信賴的；可靠的；確實的
▶Not all of the information online is reliable and accurate.
並非所有網路上的資訊都是可靠及正確的。

re·lief [rɪ`lif] 🎧 Track 4013

n. （痛苦，負擔的）緩和，減輕；解除；寬心，慰藉；調劑
▶She breathed a sigh of relief when her son finally returned safe and sound.
當她兒子終於平安無事地回到家時，她如釋重負地鬆了口氣。

（補充片語）
breathe a sigh of relief 如釋重負地鬆一口氣；
safe and sound 平安無恙

re·lieve [rɪ`liv] 🎧 Track 4014

v. 減輕，緩和；解除
▶The birth allowance did more or less relieve our financial burden.
生育補助的確多少地減輕了我們的經濟負擔。

（補充片語）
birth allowance 生育補助；
more or less 多多少少

re·li·gion [rɪ`lɪdʒən] 🎧 Track 4015

n. 宗教，宗教信仰；宗教團體
▶I don't have a religion; Buddha or Jesus makes no difference to me. 我沒有宗教信仰；佛陀或耶穌對我來說沒有差別。

re·li·gious [rɪ`lɪdʒəs] 🎧 Track 4016

adj. 宗教的，篤信宗教的，虔誠的；修道的
▶Both of my parents are religious Catholics.
我的父母都是虔誠的天主教徒。

re·luc·tant [rɪ`lʌktənt] 🎧 Track 4017

adj. 不情願的；勉強的
▶She was reluctant to give up her career to be a full-time mother.
她不願意放棄自己的事業去當一個全職媽媽。

re·ly [rɪ`laɪ] 🎧 Track 4018

v. 依靠，依賴；信賴，指望
▶Her son is the only person that she can rely on. 她兒子是她唯一可以依靠的人。

re·main [rɪ`men] 🎧 Track 4019

v. 剩下；繼續存在；留下；保持；仍然是
▶The meeting has concluded, but many significant problems remained unsolved.
會議已經結束了，但是許多重大問題仍未獲得解決。

re·mark [rɪ`mɑrk] 🎧 Track 4020

n. 談論，評論，批評；注意，察覺
▶She was offended by his harsh remarks.
他嚴厲的批評激怒了她。

v. 談到，評論；言辭；注意，察覺
▶He remarked that his wife was a good cook. 他說他太太很會做菜。

re·mark·a·ble
[rɪ`mɑrkəbl] 🎧 Track 4021

adj. 值得注意的，傑出的，卓越非凡的
▶Gordon Ramsay is a remarkable chef.
高登・拉姆齊是個很傑出的廚師。

rem·e·dy [`rɛmədɪ] 🎧 Track 4022

n. 治療法；藥物；補救方法；補償
▶Herbal tea with honey is a good home remedy for coughs. 花草茶加蜂蜜是治療咳嗽的一個很好的居家療法。

v. 醫療，治療；補救，糾正

▶We should give him a chance to remedy his mistake.
我們應該給他一個補救自己錯誤的機會。

re·mem·ber [rɪ`mɛmbɚ] 🎧 *Track 4023*
v. 記得；記住

re·mind [rɪ`maɪnd] 🎧 *Track 4024*
v. 提醒；使記起

re·mind·er [rɪ`maɪndɚ] 🎧 *Track 4025*
n. 提醒者，提醒物；令人回憶的東西；（幫助記憶的）提示；催函

▶I received a credit card payment reminder from the bank today.
我今天收到銀行寄來的信用卡帳款催繳單。

re·mote [rɪ`mot] 🎧 *Track 4026*
adj. 遙遠的；偏僻的；關係疏遠的；（年代）久遠的；冷淡的，孤傲的；遙控的

▶She volunteered to teach in a remote village after graduation.
她畢業後自願到一個偏鄉去教書。

相關片語

remote control 遙控（器）

▶I cannot change the channels without the remote control. 沒有遙控器我無法轉台。

re·move [rɪ`muv] 🎧 *Track 4027*
v. 移動，搬開；去除；撤去，使離去；遷移

▶She used bleach to remove the ink stain from the white shirt.
她用漂白劑去除白襯衫上的墨漬。

re·new [rɪ`nju] 🎧 *Track 4028*
v. 更新，恢復；換新；重新開始；重申；續訂、續借

▶I'm not going to renew the apartment lease if my landlord raises my rent. 如果房東漲我的租金，我就不續公寓的租賃契約了。

rent [rɛnt] 🎧 *Track 4029*
n. 租；租借；租金；**v.** 租；租用

re·pair [rɪ`pɛr] 🎧 *Track 4030*
n. 修理；修補；修理工作；維修狀況；修理部位；**v.** 修理；修補；補救

re·peat [rɪ`pit] 🎧 *Track 4031*
v. 重複；重做；重讀

re·peat·ed·ly [rɪ`pitɪdlɪ] 🎧 *Track 4032*
adv. 一再，再三，多次

▶I've warned you repeatedly not to dump your trash here.
我已經再三警告你不要把垃圾丟在這裡。

rep·e·ti·tion [ˌrɛpɪ`tɪʃən] 🎧 *Track 4033*
n. 重複；反覆；重複的事物，複製品

▶Repetition is the mother of all learning.
重複是學習之母。

re·place [rɪ`ples] 🎧 *Track 4034*
v. 把……放回原處；取代，代替

▶It's urgent that we replace nuclear power with renewable energies.
以可再生能源取代核能是刻不容緩的一件事。

re·ply [rɪ`plaɪ] 🎧 *Track 4035*
v. 回答；答覆；回應；**n.** 回覆；答覆

re·port [rɪ`port] 🎧 *Track 4036*
n. 報告；報導；成績單；**v.** 報告；報導；告發

re·port·er [rɪ`portɚ] 🎧 *Track 4037*
n. 記者

re·port·ing [rɪ`portɪŋ] 🎧 *Track 4038*
n. 報導

▶The independent journalist insisted on providing impartial reporting.
這名獨立記者堅持要提供中立不偏倚的報導。

rep·re·sent [ˌrɛprɪ`zɛnt] 🎧 *Track 4039*
v. 象徵，表示；作為……的代表；意味著

▶Jack is going to represent his school at the National Spelling Competition.
傑克將代表他的學校參加全國拼字比賽。

rep·re·sen·ta·tion [ˌrɛprɪzɛn`teʃən] 🎧 *Track 4040*
n. 代表，代理；表示；陳述；抗議；演出

▶The company is seeking representation in Asia.
這家公司正在尋求亞洲地區的代理權。

※灰色單字為英檢初級必備單字

rep·re·sen·ta·tive 🎧 *Track 4041*
[ˌrɛprɪˈzɛntətɪv]

n. 代表物，典型；代表，代理人
▶ The representative of the United States objected against the proposal.
美國的代表反對了這項提案。

adj. 代表的，代表性的；代理的
▶ The 2016 Annual Representative Assembly will be held in Calgary in May.
2016年的年度代表大會將會在五月份於卡加利舉行。

re·pub·lic [rɪˈpʌblɪk] 🎧 *Track 4042*
n. 共和國，共和政體
▶ His nationality is the Central African Republic.
他的國籍是中非共和國。

re·pub·li·can 🎧 *Track 4043*
[rɪˈpʌblɪkən]

n. 共和黨人士；擁護共和政體者；共和主義者
▶ I am a Democrat rather than a Republican.
我是個民主黨人士，而不是共和黨人士。

adj. 共和國的；擁護共和政體的；共和主義的；共和黨的
▶ Donald Trump, the current Republican president, was inaugurated in 2017.
現任共和黨的總統唐納‧川普在2017年宣誓就職。

rep·u·ta·tion 🎧 *Track 4044*
[ˌrɛpjəˈteʃən]

n. 名譽，信譽；好名聲；聲望
▶ I will never risk my reputation to produce and sell tainted food.
我絕不會拿我的信譽做賭注，去製作並販售黑心商品。

re·quest [rɪˈkwɛst] 🎧 *Track 4045*
n. 要求
▶ The client made a request that we advance their shipment.
客戶要求我們提早交貨。

(補充片語)

advance shipment 提早交貨

v. 要求，請求；請求給予
▶ They had no choice but to request financial assistance.
他們不得不請求經濟支援。

re·quire [rɪˈkwaɪr] 🎧 *Track 4046*
v. 需要；要求；命令

re·quire·ment 🎧 *Track 4047*
[rɪˈkwaɪrmənt]

n. 需要；必需品；必要條件；要求
▶ David is the only person that meets all the requirements for the position.
大衛是唯一符合這職位需要的所有條件的人。

res·cue [ˈrɛskju] 🎧 *Track 4048*
n. 援救，營救
▶ Hundreds of climbers trapped in the mountains were still waiting for rescue.
數百名困在山區裡的登山客仍在等待救援。

v. 營救，救援
▶ The police rescued all the hostages from the hijackers.
警方從劫持犯那兒救出了所有的人質。

re·search [rɪˈsɝtʃ] 🎧 *Track 4049*
n. 研究，調查，探究
▶ The medical scientist has devoted himself to cancer research in genetic engineering. 這名醫學科學家專心致力基因工程的癌症研究。

v. 研究，探究；做學術研究；調查
▶ He is researching into causes, prevention, and treatments of colon cancer.
他正在研究大腸癌的起因、預防及治療方式。

re·search·er [rɪˈsɝtʃɚ] 🎧 *Track 4050*
n. 研究人員，調查者
▶ Medical researchers confirmed that Ebola virus could be transmitted through sexual contact. 醫學研究人員證實，伊波拉病毒可以透過性接觸傳遞。

re·sem·ble [rɪˈzɛmbl̩] 🎧 *Track 4051*
v. 類似，像
▶ The baby doesn't resemble his father at all. 這寶寶長得一點也不像他爸爸。

res·er·va·tion 🎧 Track 4052
[ˌrɛzə`veʃən]

n. 保留；自然保護區；預訂，預訂的房間（或座位）

▶ I have made a reservation at that restaurant for tonight.
我已經在那間餐廳預訂今晚的座位了。

re·serve [rɪ`zɝv] 🎧 Track 4053

n. 儲備物，儲備金；儲藏，保留；儲備；預備軍

▶ I will support you without reserve.
我會毫無保留地支持你。

(補充片語)

without reserve 毫無保留地

v. 保存，保留；預訂，預約

▶ Your table will only be reserved for ten minutes. 您的座位將只為您保留十分鐘。

res·i·dence [`rɛzədəns] 🎧 Track 4054

n. 居住，合法居住資格；住所

▶ My foreign husband is still applying for his permanent residence permit. 我的外籍老公現在仍在申請他的永久居留許可。

(補充片語)

permanent residence permit 永久居留許可

res·i·dent [`rɛzədənt] 🎧 Track 4055

n. 居民；定居者

▶ All residents were evacuated safely before the landslide buried their homes.
所有的居民都在土石流掩埋他們的家之前安全地撤離了。

adj. 居住的，定居的；固有的，內在的；常住的；住在任所的

▶ I hired a resident maid to take care of the household chores for me.
我請了一個住家女傭來幫我做家事。

re·sign [rɪ`zaɪn] 🎧 Track 4056

v. 放棄，辭去

▶ He resigned his job for no reason.
他無緣無故地辭去了工作。

res·ig·na·tion 🎧 Track 4057
[ˌrɛzɪg`neʃən]

n. 辭職

▶ I was shocked when I was informed of his resignation.
當我獲知他辭職的消息時，感到非常震驚。

re·sist [rɪ`zɪst] 🎧 Track 4058

v. 抵抗，反抗，抗拒；忍耐，忍住

▶ Stop resisting. You are under arrest.
不要抵抗。你已經被捕了。

re·sist·ance [rɪ`zɪstəns] 🎧 Track 4059

n. 抵抗；反抗；抵抗力

▶ I have no resistance to great food.
我對美食沒有抵抗力。

re·sis·tant [rɪ`zɪstənt] 🎧 Track 4060

adj. 抵抗的，抗……的

▶ Raincoats are usually made from water resistant fabrics.
雨衣通常是以防水布料製成的。

res·o·lu·tion [ˌrɛzə`luʃən] 🎧 Track 4061

n. 決心，決定；解答，解決

▶ He made a resolution to quit smoking.
他下決心要戒菸。

re·solve [rɪ`zalv] 🎧 Track 4062

v. 解決，解答；決心，決定；決議，作出正式決定；分解

▶ His answer resolved all my doubts.
他的回覆解決了我所有的疑慮。

re·source [rɪ`sors] 🎧 Track 4063

n. 資源；物力；財力

▶ This country lacks natural resources.
這個國家缺乏自然資源。

re·spect [rɪ`spɛkt] 🎧 Track 4064

n. 尊敬；尊重；注重；**v.** 尊敬；尊重

re·spond [rɪ`spand] 🎧 Track 4065

v. 作答，回應

▶ She hasn't responded to his proposal.
她還沒有對他的求婚做出回覆。

re·sponse [rɪ`spans] 🎧 Track 4066

n. 回應，回覆，回答

▶ I haven't received any response to my job application.
我的工作應徵函沒有得到任何回覆。

※灰色單字為英檢初級必備單字

in response to 作為對⋯⋯的回覆

▶ I got a letter from them in response to my request for help.
我收到他們回覆我請求幫助的信件。

re·spon·si·ble 🎧 *Track 4067*
[rɪˋspɑnsəbḷ]
adj. 有責任的；負責任的

re·spon·si·bil·i·ty 🎧 *Track 4068*
[rɪ͵spɑnsəˋbɪlətɪ]
n. 責任；職責；責任感

▶ I'll take full responsibility for your loss.
我會為您的損失負所有的責任。

take responsibility for 為⋯⋯負責

sense of responsibility 責任感

▶ The father has no sense of responsibility at all.
那個父親一點責任感都沒有。

rest [rɛst] 🎧 *Track 4069*
v./n. 休息

res·tau·rant [ˋrɛstərənt] 🎧 *Track 4070*
n. 餐廳

rest·less [ˋrɛstlɪs] 🎧 *Track 4071*
adj. 靜不下來的；永無安寧的；受打擾的；焦燥不安的；躁動的

▶ I felt extremely exhausted after a restless night.
我在輾轉反側了一夜之後覺得疲累不堪。

re·store [rɪˋstor] 🎧 *Track 4072*
v. 恢復，使復原；使恢復健康；修復；使復職

▶ Her health was completely restored after adequate rest.
她在充分的休息後已經完全康復了。

re·strict [rɪˋstrɪkt] 🎧 *Track 4073*
v. 限制，限定；約束

▶ The home party is restricted to the family members only.
這場家庭派對只限家庭成員參加。

re·stric·tion [rɪˋstrɪkʃən] 🎧 *Track 4074*
n. 限制；約束；限定；限制規定

▶ The library is open to everyone without restriction.
這圖書館開放給所有人使用，沒有任何限制。

rest·room [ˋrestrum] 🎧 *Track 4075*
n. 洗手間；廁所；盥洗室

re·sult [rɪˋzʌlt] 🎧 *Track 4076*
n. 結果；後果；**v.** 產生；發生；導致⋯⋯結果

re·tain [rɪˋten] 🎧 *Track 4077*
v. 保留，保持；留住；攔住；記住

▶ I tried to retain my composure when I got the sack.
當我被開除時，我試著保持鎮靜。

retain one's composure 保持鎮靜；
get the sack 被開除

re·tire [rɪˋtaɪr] 🎧 *Track 4078*
v. 退休

▶ It is his dream to travel around the world after he retires.
他的夢想是在退休後去環遊世界。

re·treat [rɪˋtrit] 🎧 *Track 4079*
n. 撤退；撤退信號；隱退

▶ The famous singer spent a year in retreat.
那位名歌手暫時退隱了一年。

v. 撤退；退避；退出

▶ We have to retreat before we run out of ammunition.
我們必須在彈藥用完之前盡快撤退。

re·turn [rɪˋtɝn] 🎧 *Track 4080*
v. 返回；歸；回復；歸還；**n.** 返回；歸；回報；報答

re·u·nite [͵rijuˋnaɪt] 🎧 *Track 4081*
v. 使再結合；使重聚

▶ The boy is looking forward to reuniting with his biological parents.
男孩很期待跟他的親生父母重聚。

re·veal [rɪ`vil] 🎧 *Track 4082*
v. 顯露出；揭示，揭露；暴露，洩露
▶ The secretary was fired for revealing the confidential information by accident.
秘書因為不小心洩漏機密情報而被開除了。

---

re·venge [rɪ`vɛndʒ] 🎧 *Track 4083*
n. 報復，復仇
▶ He was determined to take revenge on the man who murdered his father.
他決心要向那個殺害他父親的男人復仇。

(補充片語)
take revenge on sb. 對某人報復，向某人復仇

v. 報復，替……報仇
▶ He was determined to revenge his dead father by hook or by crook.
他決心要不擇手段為他死去的父親報仇。

(補充片語)
by hook or by crook 不擇手段，用各種手段

---

re·view [rɪ`vju] 🎧 *Track 4084*
n. 複習；溫習；再檢查；複審；評論；
v. 複習

---

re·vise [rɪ`vaɪz] 🎧 *Track 4085*
v. 修訂；校訂；修改

---

re·vi·sion [rɪ`vɪʒən] 🎧 *Track 4086*
n. 修訂，校訂；修訂版
▶ Your novel needs some revision before publication.
你的小說在出版之前需要修訂一下。

---

rev·o·lu·tion [ˌrɛvə`luʃən] 🎧 *Track 4087*
n. 革命
▶ The Industrial Revolution greatly changed the way people lived.
工業革命大大地改變了人們的生活方式。

---

rev·o·lu·tion·a·ry [ˌrɛvə`luʃənˌɛrɪ] 🎧 *Track 4088*
adj. 革命的
▶ The computer is one of the most revolutionary inventions in 20th century.
電腦是二十世紀最具革命性的發明之一。

---

re·ward [rɪ`wɔrd] 🎧 *Track 4089*
n. 報答，報償，賞金，酬金

▶ I will give you some money as a reward.
我會給你一些錢作為報答。

v. 報答，酬謝；報應，懲罰（壞人）
▶ I will reward you with a dinner.
我會回報你一頓晚餐。

---

re·write [rɪ`raɪt] 🎧 *Track 4090*
v. 重寫，改寫，加工編寫
▶ The chief editor asked me to rewrite this article.
總編要我改寫這篇文章。

n. 重寫，改寫（的文稿）；加工編寫的新聞稿
▶ My husband and I work as a team. He writes the first draft and I do the rewrites.
我先生和我是以團隊方式工作。他負責寫初稿，而我負責改編。

---

rhyme [raɪm] 🎧 *Track 4091*
v. 押韻；做押韻詩；把……寫成詩；用詩敘述
▶ Tang Poetry is easy to remember because it rhymes.
唐詩很容易背，是因為它有押韻。

n. 韻腳；押韻文，押韻詩
▶ This poem is not in rhymes.
這首詩沒有押韻。

---

rhyth·m [`rɪðəm] 🎧 *Track 4092*
n. 節奏，韻律
▶ A person with no sense of rhythm can't be a good drummer. 一個沒有節奏感的人是無法成為一名好鼓手的。

(補充片語)
sense of rhythm 節奏感，韻律感

---

rib·bon [`rɪbən] 🎧 *Track 4093*
n. 緞帶，飾帶，帶狀物；鋼捲尺；色帶；綬帶
▶ The whole room was decorated with colored ribbons for the party tonight.
整個房間為了今晚的派對用彩色的緞帶裝飾。

(相關片語)
blue ribbon 頭獎，藍勳帶
▶ He felt so proud of himself when he was awarded the blue ribbon.
當被授與藍勳帶時，他為自己感到相當驕傲。

※灰色單字為英檢初級必備單字

rice [raɪs] 🎧 *Track 4094*
n. 米；米飯

rich [rɪtʃ] 🎧 *Track 4095*
adj. 富裕的；豐富的；有錢的；**n.** 有錢人

rich·es [`rɪtʃɪz] 🎧 *Track 4096*
n. 財富，財產，富有，豐饒
▶ My grandfather's rags-to-riches story is the most inspirational one I've heard. 我爺爺由窮致富的故事是我聽過最鼓舞人心的。

(補充片語)

rags-to-riches 由窮致富的；白手起家的

(相關片語)

from rags to riches 由窮致富，白手起家
▶ Not being born into a wealthy family, he had to work very hard to go from rags to riches.
由於不是出生於富裕家庭，他得非常努力地工作，靠自己白手起家。

rid [rɪd] 🎧 *Track 4097*
v. 使免除，使擺脫，清除
▶ Smoking is a bad habit that you need to get rid of.
抽菸是一個你必須要戒除的壞習慣。

rid·dle [`rɪdl] 🎧 *Track 4098*
n. 謎，謎語；謎一般的人；莫名其妙的事情；難題
▶ I can never figure out this riddle.
我永遠解不開這個謎題。

v. 出謎，解謎；使困惑；打謎地說；佈滿，充滿
▶ Your article is riddled with grammatical errors. 你的文章充滿了文法錯誤。

ride [raɪd] 🎧 *Track 4099*
v. 騎馬；乘車；乘車旅行；乘坐；搭乘
n. 騎；乘坐；搭乘；乘車旅行；兜風

rid·er [`raɪdɚ] 🎧 *Track 4100*
n. 騎乘（馬或機車等）的人，搭乘（馬或車）的人
▶ I think all bicycle riders should be required to wear helmets. 我認為所有騎腳踏車的人都應該被要求戴安全帽。

ri·dic·u·lous [rɪ`dɪkjələs] 🎧 *Track 4101*
adj. 可笑的
▶ It is ridiculous that she thought she could do it by herself.
她認為能夠自己做這件事，真是太可笑了。

ri·fle [`raɪfl] 🎧 *Track 4102*
n. 步槍，來福槍
▶ The bank was robbed by a man armed with a rifle this morning.
該銀行在今日上午遭到一名持步槍的男子搶劫。

v. 用步槍射擊；洗劫，劫掠；快速翻找
▶ The burglar rifled through the house for cash and expensive things such as valuable jewelry.
盜賊為了找出現金和如貴重珠寶等昂貴的東西，翻遍了整個房子。

right [raɪt] 🎧 *Track 4103*
adj. 對的；正確的；右邊的；**adv.** 對；正確地；向右；**n.** 右邊；右側；權利

ring [rɪŋ] 🎧 *Track 4104*
v. 按鈴；敲鐘；打電話；（鐘或鈴）響
n. 戒指

ripe [raɪp] 🎧 *Track 4105*
adj. 成熟的
▶ The papaya is ripe enough to eat.
這木瓜已經熟得可以吃了。

rise [raɪz] 🎧 *Track 4106*
v. 上升；升起；上漲；增加；**n.** 增加；上漲；上升；提升；發跡

risk [rɪsk] 🎧 *Track 4107*
n. 風險，危險
▶ He invested all his money in it at the risk of going bankrupt.
他冒著破產的風險，將所有錢投資在這兒了。

v. 使遭受危險，以……做賭注
▶ Don't risk your life to try drugs out of curiosity.
不要拿自己的生命作賭注，出於好奇地去嘗試毒品。

ri·val [ˈraɪvl̩]
🎧 *Track 4108*

n. 競爭者，對手
▶ He's no rival of mine.
他不是我的對手。

adj. 競爭的
▶ We will manage to stay ahead of our rival companies.
我們將會設法保持領先我們的競爭公司。

v. 與……競爭，與……匹敵，比得上
▶ No one can rival my mother in making beef stew.
在做燉牛肉這方面，沒有人可以比得上我媽媽。

riv·er [ˈrɪvɚ]
🎧 *Track 4109*

n. 河；河流

roach [rotʃ]
🎧 *Track 4110*

n. 蟑螂

road [rod]
🎧 *Track 4111*

n. 馬路

roar [ror]
🎧 *Track 4112*

v. 吼叫，呼嘯；大聲狂笑，叫喊；喧嘩，喧鬧
▶ None of us were able to sleep because the wind roared all through the night. 我們沒有一個人能睡得著，因為風狂嘯了一整夜。

n. 呼嘯，怒號；轟鳴聲，喧鬧聲，大笑聲
▶ Being frightened by the roar of thunder, the baby started to cry.
寶寶被雷鳴嚇到，便開始大哭。

相關片語

roar oneself hoarse　喊得喉嚨沙啞
▶ All of us roared ourselves hoarse cheering for our team.
我們所有人為了幫我們的隊伍加油，個個喊得喉嚨沙啞。

roast [rost]
🎧 *Track 4113*

v. 烤；炙；烘
▶ My mother will roast a turkey on Thanksgiving.
我媽媽在感恩節那天會烤火雞。

adj. 烘烤的
▶ I'd like to have roast chicken for dinner.
我晚餐想吃烤雞。

n. 烘烤
▶ We will do a roast in the yard at noon.
我們中午要在庭院裡烤肉。

rob [rɑb]
🎧 *Track 4114*

v. 搶劫；盜取；非法剝奪

rob·ber [ˈrɑbɚ]
🎧 *Track 4115*

n. 搶劫者，強盜
▶ The bank robber escaped with two-million-dollars of cash.
銀行搶匪帶著兩百萬現金逃跑了。

rob·ber·y [ˈrɑbərɪ]
🎧 *Track 4116*

n. 搶劫，盜取，搶劫案；搶劫罪
▶ I happened to be in the bank when the bank robbery occurred.
銀行搶案發生時，我剛好就在銀行裡。

robe [rob]
🎧 *Track 4117*

n. 長袍；睡袍；浴袍
▶ It's very inappropriate to go out in just a robe.
只穿一件長袍出去非常不恰當。

ro·bot [ˈrobət]
🎧 *Track 4118*

n. 機器人

rock [rɑk]
🎧 *Track 4119*

n. 岩石；石塊；**v.** 搖動；使搖晃

rock·et [ˈrɑkɪt]
🎧 *Track 4120*

n. 飛彈，火箭，火箭彈
▶ They are going to launch the rocket into space. 他們即將要把火箭發射到太空去。

v. 用火箭運載；向前急衝；飛快進行；迅速上升
▶ It's unbelievable that the oil price has rocketed by 10% overnight. 油價一個晚上就上升了百分之十，真是令人難以置信。

rock·y [ˈrɑkɪ]
🎧 *Track 4121*

adj. 岩石的，多岩石的，岩石構成的

rod [rɑd]
🎧 *Track 4122*

n. 棒，竿，桿；枝條，藤條
▶ Spare the rod, spoil the child.
孩子不打不成器。（省了棍子，慣了孩子。）

※灰色單字為英檢初級必備單字

role [rol]   Track 4123
n. 角色；作用

roll [rol]   Track 4124
v. 滾動；轉動；搖擺；搖晃；**n.** 滾動；一捲；捲餅

ro·mance [ro`mæns]   Track 4125
n. 戀愛，風流韻事；愛情故事；羅曼蒂克氣氛，浪漫情調；羅曼語（拉丁系語言）
▶ Office romance is not allowed in our company.
我們公司不准我們發展辦公室戀情。

v. 寫傳奇，虛構故事；和……談戀愛，向……求愛，追求
▶ I don't romance with married men.
我不跟已婚男子談戀愛。

adj. 羅曼語的
▶ My great-grandmother is the only one that can speak the Romance dialect. 我曾祖母是唯一一個會說那個羅曼語方言的人。

ro·man·tic [rə`mæntɪk]   Track 4126
adj. 浪漫的，羅曼蒂克的；傳奇性的，富浪漫色彩的；虛構的；不切實際的
▶ We had a romantic candlelit dinner last night. 我們昨晚吃了一頓浪漫的燭光晚餐。

roof [ruf]   Track 4127
n. 屋頂

room [rum]   Track 4128
n. 房間；室；空間；場所

roost·er [`rustɚ]=**cock**   Track 4129
n. 公雞；狂妄自大的人
▶ The roosters crow as soon as the sun rises. 太陽一升起，公雞就開始啼了。

root [rut]   Track 4130
n. 根；根部；根基；根源；**v.** 使紮根；使固定；生根；根源於

rope [rop]   Track 4131
n. 繩子；繩索

rose [roz]   Track 4132
n. 玫瑰

rot [rɑt]   Track 4133
v. 腐爛，腐朽；腐壞，衰敗
▶ Meat rots easily if it's not frozen.
肉沒有冷凍起來很容易壞。

n. 腐爛，腐壞；腐敗，墮落；蠢話；蠢事
▶ The government has to stop the rot in its judicial system.
政府應該要阻止司法系統的敗壞。

rot·ten [`rɑtn]   Track 4134
adj. 腐爛的
▶ The meat will soon be rotten if you don't store it in the fridge. 如果你不把肉存放在冰箱，它很快就會腐臭了。

rough [rʌf]   Track 4135
adj. 粗糙的；粗製的；幹粗活的；粗俗的；狂暴的；艱難的
▶ He's been having a rough time since he lost his job. 自從他失業，日子就很不好過。

adv. 粗糙地；粗略地；粗暴地
▶ She has no patience with kids and often treats them rough.
她對小孩沒耐性，常常對他們很粗暴。

round [raʊnd]   Track 4136
adv. 環繞地；在周圍；在附近；到各處
prep. 環繞；在……周圍；去……四處；**n.** 一輪；一回合；循環；**adj.** 圓的；圓形的

route [rut]   Track 4137
n. 路線，路程；航線
▶ He didn't take his usual route today. 他今天沒有走他平常的路線。

v. 按規定路線走；安排……的路線或程序
▶ This tourist coach is routed to Taipei via Chiayi, Taichung and Taoyuan.
這輛遊覽車途經嘉義、台中和桃園開往臺北。

rou·tine [ru`tin]   Track 4138
n. 例行公事，日常工作，慣常程序
▶ She's busy with the office routine.
她忙著作辦公室的日常事務。

adj. 日行的，例行的，一般的
▶ It's just a routine procedure.
這只是一個例行程序。

row [raʊ] 　🎧 *Track 4139*
n. 一列；一排；**v.** 划船

roy·al [ˋrɔɪəl] 　🎧 *Track 4140*
adj. 王室的；皇家的

rub [rʌb] 　🎧 *Track 4141*
v. 擦；摩擦

rub·ber [ˋrʌbɚ] 　🎧 *Track 4142*
adj. 橡膠製成的；**n.** 橡膠

rub·bish [ˋrʌbɪʃ] 　🎧 *Track 4143*
n. 垃圾，廢物
▶You'd better clean the rubbish away.
　你最好把這垃圾清走。

adj. 垃圾的；糟透的
▶Please throw your garbage into the rubbish bin. 請把你的垃圾丟到垃圾桶裡。

rude [rud] 　🎧 *Track 4144*
adj. 魯莽的；無禮的

rug [rʌg] 　🎧 *Track 4145*
n. （鋪於室內的）小地毯；毛皮地毯
▶What a pretty rug. 真是個漂亮的地毯。

ru·in [ˋrʊɪn] 　🎧 *Track 4146*
n. 毀滅；毀壞；廢墟、遺跡；**v.** 毀壞

rule [rul] 　🎧 *Track 4147*
n. 規則；規定；慣例；**v.** 統治；管轄；支配

rul·er [ˋrulɚ] 　🎧 *Track 4148*
n. 尺；統治者

ru·mour [ˋrumɚ] 　🎧 *Track 4149*
=ru·mor
n. 謠言，謠傳
▶I don't believe the rumor.
　我不相信這個謠言。

run [rʌn] 　🎧 *Track 4150*
v. 跑；奔馳；經營；**n.** 跑；奔馳

run·ner [ˋrʌnɚ] 　🎧 *Track 4151*
n. 跑步者；賽跑者
▶He was far behind all the other runners.
　他遠遠地落後其他的跑者。

run·ning [ˋrʌnɪŋ] 　🎧 *Track 4152*
n. 跑步，賽跑；流出；（機器）運轉；（機構）管理
▶He practices running every day.
　他每天都練習跑步。

adj. 奔跑的；（水）流動的，流出的；（機器）運轉的；流鼻水的，出膿的
▶You need a good pair of running shoes.
　你需要一雙好的跑步鞋。

ru·ral [ˋrʊrəl] 　🎧 *Track 4153*
adj. 農村的，有鄉村風味的，田園的；生活於農村的；農業的
▶He likes peaceful rural life.
　他喜歡平靜的鄉村生活。

rush [rʌʃ] 　🎧 *Track 4154*
v. 衝；闖；趕緊；急速行動；**n.** 衝；奔；急速行動；匆忙；緊急

Rus·sia [ˋrʌʃə] 　🎧 *Track 4155*
n. 蘇俄

Rus·sian [ˋrʌʃən] 　🎧 *Track 4156*
adj. 蘇俄的；俄語的；**n.** 俄國人；俄語

rust [rʌst] 　🎧 *Track 4157*
n. 鏽，鐵鏽；（腦子）遲鈍；（能力）荒廢；鐵鏽色
▶There is rust on my bike.
　我的腳踏車上有鐵鏽。

v. 生鏽；（腦子）變遲鈍；（能力）荒廢；成鐵鏽色
▶His skills had rusted from disuse.
　他的技術因為太久沒用而荒廢了。

rust·y [ˋrʌstɪ] 　🎧 *Track 4158*
adj. 生鏽的；鐵鏽色的；褪色的，破舊的，過時的；荒廢的
▶His cooking skills are a bit rusty.
　他的烹飪技巧有些荒廢了。

Aa
Bb
Cc
Dd
Ee
Ff
Gg
Hh
Ii
Jj
Kk
Ll
Mm
Nn
Oo
Pp
Qq
Rr
Ss
Tt
Uu
Vv
Ww
Xx
Yy
Zz

※灰色單字為英檢初級必備單字

Ss

sack [sæk]　　🎧 *Track 4159*
v. 裝、入袋；（口）開除，解僱；洗劫
▶ Gary was sacked for personally attacking his boss. 蓋瑞因為對主管做人身攻擊而被解僱。

n. 粗布袋；睡袋
▶ He bought a sack of rice from the grocery store. 他在雜貨店買了一袋米。

相關片語

hit the sack 上床睡覺，就寢
▶ I fell asleep right after I hit the sack.
我一上床就睡著了。

sac·ri·fice [`sækrə,faɪs]　🎧 *Track 4160*
v. 犧牲；虧本出售
▶ I don't want to sacrifice my quality time with my family for work. 我不想為了工作犧牲我和家人相處的珍貴時間。

n. 牲禮，祭品；犧牲；犧牲的行為
▶ I am grateful for all the sacrifices my wife made for our children and me. 我很感謝妻子為我及我們的孩子所做的一切犧牲。

sad [sæd]　　🎧 *Track 4161*
adj. 悲傷的；悲哀的

sad·den [`sædn]　🎧 *Track 4162*
v. 使悲傷，使難過；悲哀，哀痛
▶ I was saddened to hear about your father's passing.
聽到你父親過世的消息讓我很難過。

safe [sef]　　🎧 *Track 4163*
adj. 安全的；平安的；**n.** 保險箱；冷藏櫃

safe·ly [`seflɪ]　🎧 *Track 4164*
adv. 安全地；可靠地，有把握的；穩固地
▶ I felt so relieved when the kids finally returned home safely. 當孩子們終於平安地回到家時，我才感到放心。

safe·ty [`seftɪ]　🎧 *Track 4165*
n. 安全；平安

sail [sel] 🎧 *Track 4166*
v. 航行；開船；駕駛（船）；**n.** 乘船航行；船隻；船帆

sail·ing [`selɪŋ] 🎧 *Track 4167*
n. 航海，航行；航班；帆船運動，帆船航行
▶ It's a perfect day for sailing.
今天是適合搭船航行的好天氣。

sail·or [`selɚ] 🎧 *Track 4168*
n. 船員；水手

sake [sek] 🎧 *Track 4169*
n. 目的；緣故
▶ You'd better quit smoking at once for your own sake.
為了你自己，你最好立刻戒菸。

sal·ad [`sæləd] 🎧 *Track 4170*
n. 沙拉

sal·a·ry [`sælərɪ] 🎧 *Track 4171*
n. 薪資
▶ He's going to job-hop to that country for better salary.
他將為了較高的薪水跳槽到那間公司去。

sale [sel] 🎧 *Track 4172*
n. 出售；銷售額；拍賣

sales·man [`selzmən] 🎧 *Track 4173*
n. 推銷員；男店員

sales·per·son [`selz͵pɝsn] 🎧 *Track 4174*
n. 店員；售貨員
▶ The salesperson talked her into buying the skirt. 店員説服她買那件裙子。

salt [sɔlt] 🎧 *Track 4175*
n. 鹽

salt·y [`sɔltɪ] 🎧 *Track 4176*
adj. 鹹的
▶ The soup is a bit too salty for me.
這湯對我來説有一點太鹹了。

same [sem] 🎧 *Track 4177*
pron. 相同的事物；**adj.** 一樣的；相同的

sam·ple [`sæmpl] 🎧 *Track 4178*
n. 樣品；試用品；例子；**v.** 抽樣檢查；品嘗；體驗

sanc·tion [`sæŋkʃən] 🎧 *Track 4179*
n. 認可，批准；贊許，支持；國際制裁
▶ The United Nations imposed strict economic sanctions on Iraq after the Gulf War. 聯合國對在波斯灣戰爭後，對伊拉克實施嚴厲的經濟制裁。

v. 認可，批准；支持，鼓勵；對……實施制裁
▶ Although death penalty is still sanctioned by law, it has not been practiced for decades in this country.
雖然法律仍然批准死刑，但是在這個國家已經有好幾十年沒有執行過了。

(補充片語)
death penalty 死刑

sand [sænd] 🎧 *Track 4180*
n. 沙

sand·wich [`sændwɪtʃ] 🎧 *Track 4181*
n. 三明治

sat·el·lite [`sætl͵aɪt] 🎧 *Track 4182*
n. 衛星，人造衛星
▶ The country is planning to launch another satellite in December.
該國正計劃在十二月發射另一枚人造衛星。

adj. 衛星的
▶ We have a satellite dish subscription to receive multiple channels. 我們有訂購衛星天線，可以收看很多的電視頻道。

(補充片語)
satellite dish 衛星碟形天線

sat·is·fac·tion 🎧 *Track 4183*
[͵sætɪs`fækʃən]
n. 滿足，滿意，稱心，樂事
▶ The baby fell asleep in satisfaction after getting enough milk.
寶寶在喝飽奶之後滿足地睡著了。

※灰色單字為英檢初級必備單字

sat·is·fac·to·ry 🎧 *Track 4184*
[ˌsætɪs`fæktərɪ]

adj. 令人滿意的，良好的，符合要求的

▶ The existing educational system is barely satisfactory.
現存的教育體系實在令人不滿意。

(補充片語)
barely satisfactory 差強人意

sat·is·fy [`sætɪs͵faɪ] 🎧 *Track 4185*

v. 使滿意；使滿足；滿足

Sat·ur·day [`sætə͵de] 🎧 *Track 4186*
=Sat.

n. 星期六

sauce [sɔs] 🎧 *Track 4187*

n. 醬；醬汁

▶ She mixed three egg yolks, butter and a spoon of lemon juice to make the sauce for the dish. 她將三顆蛋黃、奶油和一匙檸檬汁混合，來製作這道菜的醬汁。

sau·cer [`sɔsə] 🎧 *Track 4188*

n. 茶托；淺碟

saus·age [`sɔsɪdʒ] 🎧 *Track 4189*

n. 香腸，臘腸

▶ I had eggs, sausage and toast for breakfast this morning.
我今天早餐吃了蛋、香腸和烤吐司。

save [sev] 🎧 *Track 4190*

v. 救；挽救；節省；儲蓄；保留

sav·ing [`sevɪŋ] 🎧 *Track 4191*

n. 節約，節儉；救助；儲金，存款

▶ He had to live on his savings after he got the sack. 他被解雇後只能靠著儲金過活。

(補充片語)
get the sack 被解僱，被開除

saw [sɔ] 🎧 *Track 4192*

v. 鋸；鋸開

▶ The man sawed the dead branches off the tree. 男子將枯枝從樹上鋸下來。

n. 鋸子

▶ You should keep the saw out of reach of children. 你應該要把這把鋸子放在小孩子拿不到的地方。

say [se] 🎧 *Track 4193*

v. 說；講述

say·ing [`seɪŋ] 🎧 *Track 4194*

n. 說話，發表言論；話，格言；警語

▶ Saying is one thing, doing is another.
說是一回事，做又是另一回事。

(相關片語)
go without saying 不言而喻，不用說，毫無疑問地

▶ It goes without saying that we are both very proud of you.
不用說也知道我們都對你感到很驕傲。

scale [skel] 🎧 *Track 4195*

n. 刻度；比例；規模；磅秤

scan [skæn] 🎧 *Track 4196*

v. 細看，審視；粗略地看，瀏覽；掃描

▶ She scanned the catalog to see if there was anything interesting.
她瀏覽一下了目錄，看看有沒有有趣的內容。

n. 細看；瀏覽；掃描

▶ My doctor suggested that I had a brain scan. 我的醫生建議我做個腦部掃描。

scarce [skɛrs] 🎧 *Track 4197*

adj. 缺乏的，不足的；稀有的，珍貴的

▶ Natural resources are scarce in this country. 這個國家缺乏天然資源。

(相關片語)
make oneself scarce 離開，溜走

▶ The robber made himself scarce when he heard the police sirens.
搶匪一聽到警車鳴笛聲就溜了。

scarce·ly [`skɛrslɪ] 🎧 *Track 4198*

adv. 幾乎不，幾乎沒有；絕不；大概不

▶ He lives next to me but I scarcely see him. 他就住在我隔壁，但我幾乎很少看到他。

scare [skɛr] 🎧 *Track 4199*

v. 驚嚇，使恐懼；把……嚇跑

▶ The bomb explosion scared the residents.
炸彈爆炸把居民嚇壞了。

n. 驚嚇，驚恐；恐慌
▶ The sound of the thunder gave the kids a scare. 雷鳴的聲音讓孩子們嚇了一跳。

scared [skɛrd]　　🎧 *Track 4200*
adj. 害怕的；不敢的

scarf [skɑrf]　　🎧 *Track 4201*
n. 圍巾

scar·y [`skɛrɪ]　　🎧 *Track 4202*
adj. 引起驚慌的，可怕的
▶ The scary ghost story frightened all the kids. 那個可怕的鬼故事把所有孩子都嚇壞了。

scat·ter [`skætɚ]　　🎧 *Track 4203*
v. 使消散，使潰散；撒，散布；（砲火）散射
▶ Don't scatter your stuff all over the place.
不要把你的東西散落得整個地方都是。

n. 消散，分散，潰散；散播；零星散布
▶ There was only a scatter of houses in the suburbs. 郊區只有零零散散的幾棟房子。

scene [sin]　　🎧 *Track 4204*
n. 場面；景色；（事件發生的）地點；（戲劇的）場景

sce·ne·ry [`sinərɪ]　　🎧 *Track 4205*
n. 風景，景色；舞台布景
▶ We have to get up by four o'clock tomorrow morning to enjoy the beautiful sunrise scenery. 為了欣賞美麗的日出景色，我們明天早上必須四點前就起床。

sched·ule [`skɛdʒʊl]　　🎧 *Track 4206*
n. 時間表，日程表；時刻表；行程安排
▶ I have a very busy schedule next month.
我下個月的行程很滿。

v. 將……排入行程；將……列入計劃；安排，預定
▶ The launch of the new product is scheduled on September 15th.
新產品的上市時間是排定在九月十五日。

相關片語
behind schedule 比預定時間晚，落後原計劃
▶ I'm afraid I can't meet the deadline, because I am very behind schedule.
我恐怕沒辦法趕上最後期限，因為我現在進度落後很多。

scheme [skim]　　🎧 *Track 4207*
n. 計劃，方案；詭計，陰謀
▶ Their scheme to overthrow the government is impracticable.
他們要推翻政府的陰謀是行不通的。

v. 計劃，設計；密謀，策劃
▶ A stool pigeon revealed that the hooligan gang is scheming to rob the bank.
一位線民透露，那幫流氓正在密謀搶劫銀行。

補充片語
stool pigeon　（俚）線民，密探；
hooligan gang　一幫流氓

schol·ar [`skɑlɚ]　　🎧 *Track 4208*
n. 學者
▶ The scholar was invited to give a speech in our school. 該學者受邀到我們學校演講。

schol·ar·ship [`skɑlɚˌʃɪp]　　🎧 *Track 4209*
n. 獎學金
▶ He can't afford to go to the college without the scholarship. 沒有獎學金他就念不起大學。

school [skul]　　🎧 *Track 4210*
n. 學校

school·boy [`skulˌbɔɪ]　　🎧 *Track 4211*
n. 男學生
▶ The two schoolboys came to blows over a slight disagreement.
那兩個男學生一言不合就打起來了。

補充片語
come to blows over sth. 為某事打起來

school·mate [`skulˌmet]　　🎧 *Track 4212*
n. 同學
▶ I came across an old schoolmate in the department store today.
我今天在百貨公司遇到一位老同學。

sci·ence [`saɪəns]　🎧 *Track 4213*
n. 科學

sci·en·tif·ic [ˏsaɪən`tɪfɪk]　🎧 *Track 4214*
adj. 科學的；符合科學規律的；用於科學的；嚴謹的，有條理的
▶Can you give me a scientific explanation for things like ghosts? 你可以用科學的解釋說明如鬼魂這類的事物嗎？

sci·en·tist [`saɪəntɪst]　🎧 *Track 4215*
n. 科學家

scis·sors [`sɪzɚz]　🎧 *Track 4216*
n. 剪刀
▶Be careful with the scissors if you don't want to cut yourself.
如果你不想剪到自己，使用剪刀時就要小心。

scold [skold]　🎧 *Track 4217*
v. 責罵
▶He never scolds his children in the presence of others.
他從來不在別人面前責罵小孩。

scoop [skup]　🎧 *Track 4218*
v. 用勺舀，用鏟子鏟；舀空；挖空；挖出
▶She scooped some ice cream and put it on a cone.
她挖出一些冰淇淋，並把它放在冰淇淋筒上。
n. 勺子；戽斗；匙，勺；凹處；【口】最新獨家報導，最新內幕消息
▶He put a scoop of mashed potato on each plate. 他在每個盤子上放上一勺馬鈴薯泥。

scoot·er [`skutɚ]　🎧 *Track 4219*
n. 踏板車；小輪摩托車

score [skor]　🎧 *Track 4220*
v. 得分；**n.** 分數；比數

scout [skaʊt]　🎧 *Track 4221*
n. 偵察兵，偵察艦；偵查，搜查；球探、星探等發掘新人者
▶Jennifer was an ordinary high school student when she was discovered by a talent scout.
珍妮佛被一名星探發現時，只是一個普通的高中生。

（補充片語）
talent scout　星探
v. 偵查，搜查；（經過尋找）發現
▶The purpose of this reality TV show is to scout for potential fashion models.
這個電視實境秀的目的是要發現有潛力的時尚模特兒。

（補充片語）
reality TV show　電視實境秀

scratch [skrætʃ]　🎧 *Track 4222*
v. 搔，抓；抓破；劃傷；潦草地塗寫，亂畫
▶My back is itchy. Can you scratch it for me? 我的背好癢。可以幫我抓一下嗎？
n. 抓痕，擦傷；刮擦聲；亂塗
▶Is it possible to remove these deep scratches on my car?
有辦法把我車身上這些很深的刮痕弄掉嗎？

scream [skrim]　🎧 *Track 4223*
v. 尖叫；發出尖銳刺耳的聲音；大聲叫嚷地抗議
▶The woman saw the cockroach and started screaming. 女子看到蟑螂並開始尖叫。
n. 尖叫聲；尖銳刺耳的聲音
▶The sound of screams from the next door scared the baby.
隔壁傳來的陣陣尖叫聲把寶寶嚇壞了。

screen [skrin]　🎧 *Track 4224*
n. 屏；幕；簾；螢幕；紗窗、門；**v.** 遮蔽；掩護；放映（電影）

screw [skru]　🎧 *Track 4225*
v. 旋，擰；用螺絲固定，擰緊；扭歪（臉）；強迫，壓榨
▶Screwing the cabinet to the wall is a piece of cake for me. 把櫥櫃用螺絲固定在牆上，對我來說是小事一樁。
n. 螺絲，螺絲釘
▶You have to turn the screw in a counter-clockwise direction to loosen it.
要把螺絲鬆開，你得以反時針方向轉動它。
adj. 螺絲的，螺旋的
▶The first steamship in the world was driven by screw propellers.
世界上第一艘汽船是以螺旋槳驅動的。

have a screw loose （有根螺絲鬆了）有點不
正常，有毛病

▶Going for a walk at midnight? You must
have a screw loose.
大半夜的要去散步？你一定是腦筋有問題。

scrub [skrʌb]　🎧 Track 4226
v. 用力擦洗，刷洗；揉；擦掉；取消，中止
▶It took her two hours to scrub the mud off
the wall. 她花了兩小時才把牆上的泥巴刷掉。

n. 擦洗，擦淨；刷洗
▶The bathroom floor needs a good scrub.
浴室地板得好好刷一下。

sculp·ture [`skʌlptʃɚ]　🎧 Track 4227
n. 雕刻品，雕塑品，雕像
▶Rodin's "The Kiss" is one of the most
world-famous sculptures.
羅丹的《吻》是世界最知名的雕塑品之一。

sea [si]　🎧 Track 4228
n. 海

sea·food [`si,fud]　🎧 Track 4229
n. 海鮮
▶I'm allergic to seafood. 我對海鮮過敏。

sea·gull [`sigʌl]=gull　🎧 Track 4230
n. 海鷗
▶Other than fish, seagulls also eat insects,
spiders, small eggs, and small berries.
除了魚之外，海鷗也會吃昆蟲、蜘蛛、小蛋和
小莓菓。

seal [sil]　🎧 Track 4231
v. 密封；蓋章於，（以蓋章的方式）批准；
確定
▶Make sure all these document envelopes
are well sealed.
這些文件信封一定要確實地封好。

n. 印章；封印；封條
▶When I got the letter, the seal on the
envelope had already been torn open.
當我收到信時，信封的封口已經被撕開了。

search [sɝtʃ]　🎧 Track 4232
n. 搜查；搜尋；調查；**v.** 搜查；細看；探查

sea·side [`si,saɪd]　🎧 Track 4233
n. 海邊，海濱
▶They spent the whole summer at the
seaside. 他們一整個夏天都在海邊度過。

adj. 海邊的，海濱的
▶They enjoyed their dinner at a seaside
restaurant. 他們在一間海濱餐廳享用晚餐。

sea·son [`sizn]　🎧 Track 4234
v. 為……調味
▶The soup tastes plain. I must have
forgotten to season it.
這湯嚐起來沒有味道。我一定是忘記調味了。

seat [sit]　🎧 Track 4235
n. 座位；**v.** 就座

sec·ond [`sɛkənd]　🎧 Track 4236
n. 秒；瞬間；片刻；第二名；**adj.** 第二的；
次要的；**adv.** 其次；居次地

sec·ond·a·ry [`sɛkən,dɛrɪ]　🎧 Track 4237
adj. 第二的；中等的；次要的
▶I go to a secondary school in town.
我在城裡的一間中等學校上學。

sec·ond-hand [`sɛkəndhænd]　🎧 Track 4238
adj. 二手的，中古的
▶I can only afford a second-hand car.
我只買得起二手車。

adv. 間接地；做為舊貨
▶We learned of his death second-hand.
我們間接得知他的死訊。

se·cret [`sikrɪt]　🎧 Track 4239
adj. 秘密的；私下的；神秘的；**n.** 秘密

sec·re·ta·ry [`sɛkrə,tɛrɪ]　🎧 Track 4240
n. 秘書

sec·tion [`sɛkʃən]　🎧 Track 4241
n. 部分；地段；切下的部分

sec·tor [`sɛktɚ]　🎧 Track 4242
n. 地區，部門；區段；行業
▶Both my parents are engaged in the
banking sector. 我父母兩人都是從事銀行業。

Aa
Bb
Cc
Dd
Ee

Ff
Gg
Hh
Ii
Jj

Kk
Ll
Mm
Nn
Oo

Pp
Qq
Rr
Ss
Tt

Uu
Vv
Ww
Xx
Yy
Zz

※灰色單字為英檢初級必備單字

se·cure [sɪˋkjʊr]　🎧 *Track 4243*
v. 關緊；使安全；弄到
▶ Make sure your house is secured against the typhoon.
務必確保你的房子可以安全抵擋颱風的侵襲。

adj. 安全的；安心的；確定無疑的；穩固的
▶ I feel secure living next to the police station. 住在警察局隔壁讓我覺得很安心。

se·cu·ri·ty [sɪˋkjʊrətɪ]　🎧 *Track 4244*
n. 安全
▶ The man was stopped at the door by the security guard. 男子被保安人員擋在門口。
(補充片語)
security guard 保安人員

see [si]　🎧 *Track 4245*
v. 看到；看見；理解；將……看作；目睹

seed [sid]　🎧 *Track 4246*
n. 種子；籽；根源

seek [sik]　🎧 *Track 4247*
v. 尋找；探索；追求

seem [sim]　🎧 *Track 4248*
v. 看起來好像；似乎

see·saw [ˋsi͵sɔ]　🎧 *Track 4249*
n. 翹翹板

seize [siz]　🎧 *Track 4250*
v. 抓住；奪取；逮捕；沒收
▶ She seized the opportunity to work in London. 她抓住了那個去倫敦工作的機會。
(相關片語)
be seized with panic 驚慌失措
▶ He was seized with panic when the police questioned him about whether he was involved in the crime.
當警方訊問他是否與這宗犯罪案件有關時，他顯得相當驚慌失措。

sel·dom [ˋsɛldəm]　🎧 *Track 4251*
adv. 很少

se·lect [səˋlɛkt]　🎧 *Track 4252*
v. 挑選

se·lec·tion [səˋlɛkʃən]　🎧 *Track 4253*
n. 選擇；選拔；挑選
▶ There is a wide selection of main dishes on the menu. 菜單上有多的主菜可以選擇。

self [sɛlf]　🎧 *Track 4254*
n. 自身；自己；自我
▶ After getting rid of 20 kilos, I finally look like my old self again. 在減去20公斤之後，我終於又看起來像過去的自己了。

self·ish [ˋsɛlfɪʃ]　🎧 *Track 4255*
adj. 自私的

sell [sɛl]　🎧 *Track 4256*
v. 賣；出售

se·mes·ter [səˋmɛstə]　🎧 *Track 4257*
n. 學期

send [sɛnd]　🎧 *Track 4258*
v. 發送；派遣；寄

se·nior [ˋsinjə]　🎧 *Track 4259*
adj. 年長的，年紀較大的；地位較高的，較資深的；高級的；（大學）四年級的
▶ George is a senior engineer in our R&D Department.
喬治是我們研發部門的一位資深工程師。
(補充片語)
R&D Department=Research and Development Department 研發部門

n. 較年長者；前輩，上司，學長；（大學）四年級生
▶ My husband was my senior in college.
我老公是我的大學學長。

sense [sɛns]　🎧 *Track 4260*
n. 感覺；感官；意識；意義；**v.** 感覺到；意識到；了解

sen·si·ble [ˋsɛnsəbl]　🎧 *Track 4261*
adj. 明智的；察覺到的
▶ Are you sensible of the mistake you have made? 你察覺到你所犯下的錯誤了嗎？

sen·si·tive [ˋsɛnsətɪv]　🎧 *Track 4262*
adj. 敏感的，易怒的，易受傷害的，神經過敏的

▶He is sensitive about his previous marriage.
他對於自己前一段婚姻的事很敏感。

sen·tence [`sɛntəns] 🎧 *Track 4263*
n. 句子
▶There is a spelling mistake in this sentence.
這個句子中有個拼字錯誤。

n. 審判，宣判，判決
▶The families of the victims were resentful at the sentence because the murderer was sentenced only 10 years in prison.
受害者家屬對判決感到相當忿怒，因為那個殺人犯竟只被判坐十年牢。

v. 審判，判決
▶The kidnapper was sentenced to death.
綁架犯被判處死刑。

sep·a·rate [`sɛpə͵ret] 🎧 *Track 4264*
adj. 分開的；單獨的；個別的；**v.** 分割；分離

sep·a·ra·tion [͵sɛpə`reʃən] 🎧 *Track 4265*
n. 分開；分離
▶After three years' separation, they finally divorced each other.
在分居三年之後，他們終於離婚了。

Sep·tem·ber [sɛp`tɛmbɚ] =Sept. 🎧 *Track 4266*
n. 九月

se·ries [`siriz] 🎧 *Track 4267*
n. 系列；連續
▶J. K. Rowling is the author of the *Harry Potter* series.
J. K. 羅琳是《哈利波特》系列的作者。

se·ri·ous [`sɪrɪəs] 🎧 *Track 4268*
adj. 嚴重的；嚴肅的；認真的

ser·vant [`sɝvənt] 🎧 *Track 4269*
n. 僕人

serve [sɝv] 🎧 *Track 4270*
v. 為……服務；供應（飯菜）；端上；任職；服刑

ser·vice [`sɝ-VIS] 🎧 *Track 4271*
n. 服務

ses·sion [`sɛʃən] 🎧 *Track 4272*
n. 會議；（法院）開庭；會期，開庭期間；學期；講習班；授課時間
▶Several members of Parliament were caught nodding off during a parliamentary session.
有幾位國會議員被逮到在開會時上打瞌睡。

set [sɛt] 🎧 *Track 4273*
n. 一套；一組；一部；**v.** 放；置；設置；調整；**adj.** 固定的；下定決心的；準備好的

set·tle [`sɛtl] 🎧 *Track 4274*
v. 安頓；安排；安放；確定；使安下心來；解決
▶I'm glad that you finally settled down and have your own family. 我很高興你終於安定下來，並且有了自己的家庭。

set·tle·ment [`sɛtlmənt] 🎧 *Track 4275*
n. 解決；協議；安頓；安身
▶I hope we can reach a settlement of our differences this time.
我希望這次我們之間的分歧能獲得解決。

set·tler [`sɛtlɚ] 🎧 *Track 4276*
n. 移居者，開拓者；（糾紛的）解決者；（問題的）決定者
▶The ancestors of the Maori were believed to be the first settlers of New Zealand.
毛利人的祖先被認為是紐西蘭最早的開拓者。

set-up [`sɛt͵ʌp] 🎧 *Track 4277*
n. 【口】組織，機構；計劃，方案；（事情的）安排
▶The prank on the celebrities sounds like a set-up for public humiliation. 這次對名人惡作劇聽起來像是為了公開羞辱他們而做的安排。

sev·en [`sɛvn] 🎧 *Track 4278*
pron. 七個；**n.** 七；七歲；**adj.** 七的；七個的

sev·en·teen [͵sɛvn`tin] 🎧 *Track 4279*
pron. 十七個；**n.** 十七；**adj.** 十七的；十七個的

※灰色單字為英檢初級必備單字

sev·en·ty [ˈsɛvntɪ] 🎧 *Track 4280*
pron. 七十個；**n.** 七十；**adj.** 七十的；七十個的

sev·er·al [ˈsɛvərəl] 🎧 *Track 4281*
adj. 幾個的；**pron.** 幾個

se·vere [səˈvɪr] 🎧 *Track 4282*
adj. 嚴重的；嚴厲的；劇烈的；嚴格的
▶ He lost his wife in a severe storm.
他在一場嚴重的暴風雨中失去了他的妻子。

sew [so] 🎧 *Track 4283*
v. 縫補，縫合；縫製
▶ She is sewing socks for her baby.
她正在為她的寶寶縫製襪子。

sex [sɛks] 🎧 *Track 4284*
n. 性別，性；性行為
▶ Many parents nowadays still don't know how to talk to their kids about sex. 現在有很多父母仍不知道該怎麼跟孩子談論性這件事。

sex·u·al [ˈsɛkʃʊəl] 🎧 *Track 4285*
adj. 性的，性別的；關於性關係的
▶ Women should stand up against sexual harassment in the workplace.
婦女們應該挺身對抗職場上的性騷擾。

(補充片語)
stand up against 挺身對抗；
sexual harassment 性騷擾

sex·y [ˈsɛksɪ] 🎧 *Track 4286*
adj. 性感的
▶ Women don't have to be naked to be sexy.
女人不需要靠裸露身體也能性感。

shade [ʃed] 🎧 *Track 4287*
n. 蔭；陰涼處；陰暗
▶ We took a rest in the shade of a tree.
我們在樹蔭下休息。

v. 遮蔽，遮蔭
▶ I put on my sunglasses to shade my eyes against the sun.
我戴上太陽眼睛罩住眼睛，阻擋陽光。

shad·ow [ˈʃædo] 🎧 *Track 4288*
n. 影子，陰影，陰暗處；尾隨者；陰魂

▶ She follows her brother wherever he goes like a shadow. 無論她哥哥走到哪兒，她都影形不離地跟著他。

v. 遮蔽，投陰影於；使變暗；尾隨，盯梢
▶ A peaked cap shadowed his face.
一頂鴨舌帽遮住了他了臉。

adj. 非官方的，非正式的；影子內閣的
▶ The Shadow cabinet's responsibilities include intelligence gathering, criminal investigation and prosecution, etc.
影子內閣的職責包括了情報收集、犯罪調查及處決等等。

shad·y [ˈʃedɪ] 🎧 *Track 4289*
adj. 成蔭的，陰暗的；可疑的，靠不住的
▶ Let's find a quiet shady place to get some rest. 我們找個安靜陰涼的地方休息一下吧。

shake [ʃek] 🎧 *Track 4290*
v. 震動；搖動；動搖；**n.** 搖動；震動；握手；地震

shall [ʃæl] 🎧 *Track 4291*
aux. 將；會（用於第一人稱，亦可用於問句第一、三人稱）

shal·low [ˈʃælo] 🎧 *Track 4292*
adj. 淺的；淺薄的；膚淺的
▶ His shallow remarks didn't bother me at all. 他膚淺的言論一點也不困擾我。

shame [ʃem] 🎧 *Track 4293*
n. 羞恥（感）；羞辱；帶來恥辱的人或事；憾事
▶ His bad conduct brought shame on the whole family. 他的不良行為使整個家族蒙羞。
(補充片語)
bring shame on sb. 使某人蒙羞

v. 使感到羞恥，使蒙羞；使相形見絀
▶ Don't shame your husband in front of his family and friends.
不要在丈夫的家人和朋友面前讓他沒面子。

shame·ful [ˈʃemfəl] 🎧 *Track 4294*
adj. 可恥的，丟臉的
▶ I was so embarrassed by his shameful conduct. 他可恥的行為讓我感到很丟臉。

sham·poo [ʃæmˋpu] 🎧 *Track 4295*
n. 洗髮精
▶ We are running out of shampoo.
我們的洗髮精快用光了。

v. 洗（頭髮）
▶ How often do you shampoo your hair?
你多久洗一次頭？

shape [ʃep] 🎧 *Track 4296*
n. 形狀；形式；（健康的）情況；**v.** 形成；塑造；使成形

share [ʃɛr] 🎧 *Track 4297*
n. 一份；（分擔的）一部份；分攤；**v.** 分擔；分享

shark [ˋʃɑrk] 🎧 *Track 4298*
n. 鯊魚；貪婪狡猾的人；詐騙者

sharp [ʃɑrp] 🎧 *Track 4299*
adj. 尖銳的；鋒利的；急劇的；急轉的

sharp·en [ˋʃɑrpn] 🎧 *Track 4300*
v. 削尖，使變鋒利；加劇
▶ Can you sharpen my pencil for me?
可以幫我削尖鉛筆嗎？

shave [ʃev] 🎧 *Track 4301*
v. 刮（鬍子等）
▶ I shave my face every morning.
我每天早上都會刮鬍子。

shav·er [ˋʃevɚ] 🎧 *Track 4302*
n. 理髮師；剃鬍刀；小伙子
▶ An electric shaver can be a great Father's Day gift.
一支電動剃鬍刀是一份很棒的父親節禮物。

she [ʃi] 🎧 *Track 4303*
pron. 她

she'd [ʃid] 🎧 *Track 4304*
abbr. 她會、她已（she had或she would的縮寫）

sheep [ʃip] 🎧 *Track 4305*
n. 羊；綿羊

sheet [ʃit] 🎧 *Track 4306*
n. 床單；（一張）紙

shelf [ʃɛlf] 🎧 *Track 4307*
n. 架子；擱板

shell [ʃɛl] 🎧 *Track 4308*
n. 殼；外殼；甲殼
▶ Turtles have hard shells to protect them from harm.
海龜有堅硬的甲殼可以保護他們受到傷害。

she'll [ʃil] 🎧 *Track 4309*
abbr. 她會（she will的縮寫）

shel·ter [ˋʃɛltɚ] 🎧 *Track 4310*
n. 避難所；遮蔽物；庇護，掩蔽
▶ The big tree is a good shelter from sun.
這棵大樹是抵擋太陽的良好遮蔽物。

v. 掩蔽，遮蔽；庇護；避難
▶ We sheltered from the rain in the pavilion.
我們在涼亭裡避雨。

shep·herd [ˋʃɛpɚd] 🎧 *Track 4311*
n. 牧羊人
▶ "The Shepherd Boy Who Cried Wolf" is a well-known fable. 《喊狼來了的牧羊少年》是一個眾所周知的寓言故事。

v. 牧（羊）；指導，帶領；護送
▶ The woman shepherded the newcomers to the hall. 女子帶領新生們到大會堂去。

she's [ʃiz] 🎧 *Track 4312*
abbr. 她是（she is的縮寫）

shift [ʃɪft] 🎧 *Track 4313*
v. 轉移，替換；變換
▶ Don't try to shift your responsibility to someone else.
不要企圖把你的責任推卸給別人。

n. 轉換，轉移；輪班
▶ It's my turn to work on night shift this week. 這星期輪到我值晚班。

shine [ʃaɪn] 🎧 *Track 4314*
v. 發光；照耀

Aa
Bb
Cc
Dd
Ee
Ff
Gg
Hh
Ii
Jj
Kk
Ll
Mm
Nn
Oo
Pp
Qq
Rr
Ss
Tt
Uu
Vv
Ww
Xx
Yy
Zz

※灰色單字為英檢初級必備單字

shin·y [ˈʃaɪnɪ]　　🎧 *Track 4315*
adj. 發光的
▶Look at her shiny diamond ring!
　看看她閃閃發亮的鑽石戒指！

ship [ʃɪp]　　🎧 *Track 4316*
n. 船；**v.** 船運；運送

shirt [ʃɝt]　　🎧 *Track 4317*
n. 襯衫；男式襯衫

shock [ʃɑk]　　🎧 *Track 4318*
n. 衝擊；震驚；打擊；中風

shocked [ʃɑkt]　　🎧 *Track 4319*
v. 使震動；使震驚；使人感到震驚

shoe [ʃu]　　🎧 *Track 4320*
n. 鞋子

shoot [ʃut]　　🎧 *Track 4321*
v. 放射；開槍；射中；
n. 射擊；拍攝；狩獵會

shop [ʃɑp]＝**store**　　🎧 *Track 4322*
n. 商店；**v.** 購物；逛商店

shop·keep·er [ˈʃɑpˌkipɚ]　🎧 *Track 4323*
n. 店主，店經理
▶The shopkeeper caught the man stealing bread. 店主逮到男子偷麵包。

shop·ping [ˈʃɑpɪŋ]　　🎧 *Track 4324*
n. 買東西，購物
▶We do food shopping once a week.
　我們一個禮拜買一次菜。

shore [ʃor]　　🎧 *Track 4325*
n. 岸；濱

short [ʃɔrt]　　🎧 *Track 4326*
adj. 矮的；短的

short·age [ˈʃɔrtɪdʒ]　　🎧 *Track 4327*
n. 缺少，不足，匱乏
▶The labor shortage problem in this country is getting worse.
　這個國家的勞工短缺問題越來越嚴重了。

short·com·ing 　🎧 *Track 4328*
[ˈʃɔrtˌkʌmɪŋ]
n. 缺點，短處
▶No one is perfect. Everyone has shortcomings.
　沒有人是完美的。每個人都有缺點。

short·cut [ˈʃɔrtˌkʌt]　🎧 *Track 4329*
n. 捷徑；近路；快捷辦法
▶Let's take a shortcut to avoid the traffic jam. 我們抄個捷徑，避開交通壅塞吧。

(補充片語)
take a shortcut 抄近路

short·en [ˈʃɔrtn]　　🎧 *Track 4330*
v. 使變短，縮短，減少
▶The High Speed Rail has greatly shortened the traveling time between Taipei and Kaohsiung. 高速鐵路大大地縮短了臺北與高雄之間的交通時間。

short·ly [ˈʃɔrtlɪ]　　🎧 *Track 4331*
adv. 立刻，馬上，不久；簡短地；不耐煩地
▶He left shortly after she arrived.
　她到達後不久他就離開了。

shorts [ʃɔrts]　　🎧 *Track 4332*
n. 短褲；寬鬆運動短褲
▶If I were you, I wouldn't go to work in shorts. 如果我是你，我不會穿短褲去上班。

short-sight·ed 　🎧 *Track 4333*
[ˈʃɔrtˈsaɪtɪd]
adj. 近視的；目光短淺的
▶Over half of the students in my class are short-sighted.
　我班上有超過一半的學生是近視的。

shot [ʃɑt]　　🎧 *Track 4334*
n. 射擊；射門；嘗試

should [ʃʊd]　　🎧 *Track 4335*
aux. 應該

shoul·der [ˈʃoldɚ]　　🎧 *Track 4336*
n. 肩膀

should·n't [ˈʃʊdnt]　　🎧 *Track 4337*
abbr. 不該（should not的縮寫）

shout [ʃaʊt] 🎧 *Track 4338*
v. 呼喊；喊叫；**n.** 呼喊；喊叫聲

shov·el [ˈʃʌvl] 🎧 *Track 4339*
n. 鏟子；鐵鍬
▶ The farmer is working on the farm with a shovel. 農夫用鏟子在田裡幹活。

v. 用鏟子剷；用鐵鍬挖；用剷工作
▶ The worker is shoveling soil into the cart.
工人用鏟子把土剷進推車裡。

show [ʃo] 🎧 *Track 4340*
v. 顯示；顯露；展示；演出；出示；帶領
n. 展覽；表現；表演；演出節目；顯示

show·er [ˈʃaʊɚ] 🎧 *Track 4341*
n. 陣雨；淋浴；**v.** 下陣雨；沖澡

shrimp [ʃrɪmp] 🎧 *Track 4342*
n. 蝦

shrink [ʃrɪŋk] 🎧 *Track 4343*
v. 縮，縮小；退縮；變小；退縮
▶ 100% cotton clothes will shrink if you tumble-dry them. 如果你烘乾百分之百的棉質衣物，它們會縮小。

n. 收縮；畏縮；【俚】精神科醫生
▶ That crazy woman should go see a shrink.
那個瘋女人應該要去看個精神科醫生。

shrug [ʃrʌg] 🎧 *Track 4344*
v. 聳（肩）
▶ He shrugged at my question.
他對我的問題聳了聳肩。

n. 聳肩
▶ I asked him what he wanted eat for dinner and he responded with a shrug.
我問他晚餐想吃什麼，他聳了聳肩回應我。

(相關片語)
shrug off 不理
▶ She shrugged off the negative comments and kept doing what she thought was right. 她不理會那些負面評論，繼續做她認為對的事。

shut [ʃʌt] 🎧 *Track 4345*
v. 關閉

shut·tle [ˈʃʌtl] 🎧 *Track 4346*
n. 梭子；短程穿梭運行的車輛
▶ I'd like to reserve a hotel shuttle from the airport. 我想預約從機場出發的飯店接駁車。

v. 短程穿梭般運送；短程穿梭般往返
▶ The bus that shuttles between the airport and our hotel is free of charge.
往來機場與本飯店的公車是免費的。

shy [ʃaɪ] 🎧 *Track 4347*
adj. 害羞的；靦腆的

sick [sɪk] 🎧 *Track 4348*
adj. 病的；想吐的；對……厭煩的

sick·ness [ˈsɪknɪs] 🎧 *Track 4349*
n. 病，疾病；噁心，嘔吐
▶ Jerry is on sickness leave today.
傑瑞今天請病假。

(補充片語)
sickness leave 病假
(相關片語)
morning sickness 孕吐
▶ My wife suffered severe morning sickness during the first few months of her pregnancy.
我太太在懷孕頭幾個月經歷嚴重的孕吐。

side [saɪd] 🎧 *Track 4350*
n. 邊；面；一方

side·walk [ˈsaɪd͵wɔk] 🎧 *Track 4351*
=pave·ment （英式英文）
n. 人行道

sigh [saɪ] 🎧 *Track 4352*
v. 嘆息
▶ He didn't say anything but sighed.
他不發一語只是嘆氣。

n. 嘆息，嘆氣
▶ She breathed a sigh of relief when her son finally returned safe and sound.
當她兒子終於平安無事地回到家時，她如釋重負地嘆了口氣。

(補充片語)
breathe a sign of relief 如釋重負地鬆一口氣；
safe and sound 平安無恙

sight [saɪt]　🎧 *Track 4353*
n. 視覺；看見；視界

sight·see·ing [`saɪt͵siɪŋ]　🎧 *Track 4354*
n. 觀光；遊覽
▶ Sightseeing is the purpose of my visit this time. 觀光是我這次來旅行的目的。

sign [saɪn]　🎧 *Track 4355*
v. 簽名；**n.** 記號；標牌；手勢

sig·nal [`sɪgn̩]　🎧 *Track 4356*
n. 信號
▶ They tried to use smoke signal to ask for rescue. 他們嘗試用煙霧信號求救。

v. 用信號發出；打信號；以動作示意
▶ The teacher signaled the students to be quiet. 老師以動作示意，要學生安靜。

sig·na·ture [`sɪgnətʃə]　🎧 *Track 4357*
n. 簽名
▶ He faked my signature on the contract. 他在合約上仿造我的簽名。

sig·nif·i·cance [sɪg`nɪfəkəns]　🎧 *Track 4358*
n. 重要性；意義，含義
▶ Since we're running out of time, let's skip the issues of little significance. 既然我們快沒時間了，就略過那些不重要的議題吧。

sig·nif·i·cant [sɪg`nɪfəkənt]　🎧 *Track 4359*
adj. 有意義的；重要的
▶ The wedding ceremony is one of the most significant events in one's life. 婚禮是你人生中最重要的事件之一。

相關片語
significant other 另一半
▶ You are welcome to bring your significant other to the party. 歡迎帶你的另一半一起來參加派對。

si·lence [`saɪləns]　🎧 *Track 4360*
n. 沉默；無聲

si·lent [`saɪlənt]　🎧 *Track 4361*
adj. 沉默的；默不作聲的；寂靜無聲的

silk [sɪlk]　🎧 *Track 4362*
n. 絲
▶ This dress is very soft; it feels like silk. 這洋裝很柔軟，摸起來像是絲。

adj. 絲的；絲織的
▶ She wears a silk scarf. 她圍了一條絲巾。

sil·ly [`sɪlɪ]　🎧 *Track 4363*
adj. 糊塗的；愚蠢的

sil·ver [`sɪlvə]　🎧 *Track 4364*
n. 銀；銀色；銀牌；**adj.** 銀的；銀色的

sim·i·lar [`sɪmələ]　🎧 *Track 4365*
adj. 相似的；相像的

sim·i·lar·i·ty [͵sɪmə`lærətɪ]　🎧 *Track 4366*
n. 類似；相似
▶ The twin brothers don't have any similarities between them except their looks. 這對雙胞胎兄弟除了長相之外沒有任何相似之處。

sim·ple [`sɪmpl̩]　🎧 *Track 4367*
adj. 簡單的；簡樸的；單純的

sim·pli·fy [`sɪmplə͵faɪ]　🎧 *Track 4368*
v. 簡化，使單純
▶ The first step to simplify your life is to throw away what you don't need. 簡化生活的第一步，就是把你不需要的東西丟掉。

sim·ply [`sɪmplɪ]　🎧 *Track 4369*
adv. 簡單地；樸素地；僅僅；簡直

sin [sɪn]　🎧 *Track 4370*
n. （道德上的）罪孽，罪惡；（違反禮俗的）過錯
▶ It's a sin to cheat on your spouse. 欺騙配偶是一種罪惡。

v. 犯罪，違命；犯過失
▶ "I have sinned against the Lord," confessed the woman. 女子告解道：「我犯下了違抗主的罪」。

相關片語
as ugly as sin 非常醜陋，非常難看

▶ A mother will love her child even though he is as ugly as sin.
就算自己的寶寶再怎麼醜，母親也一樣愛他。

since [sɪns] 🎧 *Track 4371*
conj. 自從；既然；因為；**prep.** 自……以來；**adv.** 此後；之前

sin·cere [sɪn`sɪr] 🎧 *Track 4372*
adj. 誠摯的；衷心的

sin·cere·ly [sɪn`sɪrlɪ] 🎧 *Track 4373*
adv. 衷心地，誠摯地
▶ He sincerely congratulated his friend on his achievement. 他誠摯地恭賀朋友的成就。

sing [sɪŋ] 🎧 *Track 4374*
v. 唱；唱歌

Sing·a·pore [`sɪŋə͵por] 🎧 *Track 4375*
n. 新加坡

Sing·a·por·ean 🎧 *Track 4376*
[͵sɪŋə`pɔrɪən]
adj. 新加坡的，新加坡人的
▶ My new boss speaks English with a Singaporean accent.
我的新主管說的英文有新加坡腔。

n. 新加坡人
▶ Most Singaporeans speak fluent English.
大部分的新加坡人都會說流利的英語。

sing·er [`sɪŋɚ] 🎧 *Track 4377*
n. 歌手；歌唱家

sing·ing [`sɪŋɪŋ] 🎧 *Track 4378*
n. 唱歌
▶ The little girl has got talent in singing.
這小女孩對唱歌有天分。

sin·gle [`sɪŋgl̩] 🎧 *Track 4379*
adj. 單一的；單身的；**n.** 單個；單身者；單打比賽

sin·gu·lar [`sɪŋgjəlɚ] 🎧 *Track 4380*
adj. 單數的，單一的；非凡的，卓越的；異常的，奇異的

▶ The word "datum" is a singular noun.
「Datum」這個字是個單數名詞。

sink [sɪŋk] 🎧 *Track 4381*
n. 流理台；水槽；**v.** 下沉；沒落；下陷

sip [sɪp] 🎧 *Track 4382*
v. 小口喝
▶ She sipped at the tea while enjoying the lake view from her window.
她一邊從窗戶欣賞湖景，一邊小口喝著茶。

n. 啜飲
▶ The little girl took a sip of the coffee and spat it out right away.
小女孩啜了一口咖啡，便立刻吐了出來。

sir [sɝ] 🎧 *Track 4383*
n. 先生；老師；長官

sis·ter [`sɪstɚ] 🎧 *Track 4384*
n. 姐妹

sit [sɪt] 🎧 *Track 4385*
v. 坐

site [saɪt] 🎧 *Track 4386*
n. 地點，場所；舊址；部位
▶ Most popular camping sites are in the mountains. 許多受歡迎的營地都是在山上。

(補充片語)
camping site （露營）營地

sit·u·a·tion [͵sɪtʃʊ`eʃən] 🎧 *Track 4387*
n. 處境，境遇；情況，情形
▶ He never asks for help even when he's in a very difficult situation. 即使在相當艱難的處境下，他也從不要求幫助。

six [sɪks] 🎧 *Track 4388*
pron. 六個；**n.** 六；**adj.** 六的；六個的

six·teen [`sɪks`tin] 🎧 *Track 4389*
pron. 十六個；**n.** 十六；**adj.** 十六的；十六個的

six·ty [`sɪkstɪ] 🎧 *Track 4390*
pron. 六十；六十個；**n.** 六十；**adj.** 六十的；六十個的

※灰色單字為英檢初級必備單字

size [saɪz] 🎧 *Track 4391*
n. 尺寸；大小

skate [sket] 🎧 *Track 4392*
n. 冰鞋；四輪溜冰鞋；**v.** 溜冰

skat·ing [`sketɪŋ] 🎧 *Track 4393*
n. 溜冰，滑冰
▶ I enjoy ice skating a lot.
我非常喜歡溜冰。

sketch [skɛtʃ] 🎧 *Track 4394*
n. 速寫，素描；略圖，草稿
▶ He makes a living as a sketch artist.
他以當素描藝術家來謀生。

v. 寫生，速寫；為……畫草圖
▶ He makes a living by sketching people at the holiday market.
他靠在假日市集幫人畫素描維生。

ski [ski] 🎧 *Track 4395*
n. 滑雪板；**v.** 滑雪

ski·ing [`skiɪŋ] 🎧 *Track 4396*
n. 滑雪
▶ We are going skiing in Japan this winter.
我們今年冬天要去日本滑雪。

skill [`skɪl] 🎧 *Track 4397*
n. （專門）技術；技巧；技能

skilled [skɪld] 🎧 *Track 4398*
adj. 熟練的；有技能的

skill·ful [`skɪlfəl] 🎧 *Track 4399*
=skil·ful （英式英文）
adj. 有技術的；熟練的

skim [skɪm] 🎧 *Track 4400*
v. 撇去，去除；飛快地掠過；瀏覽，略讀
▶ He skimmed the magazine while waiting to board the plane.
他在等候登機時，瀏覽了雜誌。

n. 撇；撇去的東西；略過；表面層；脫脂牛奶
▶ He only had time for a quick skim through the book.
他的時間只夠快速地瀏覽過這本書。

skin [skɪn] 🎧 *Track 4401*
n. 皮；皮膚

skin·ny [`skɪnɪ] 🎧 *Track 4402*
adj. 皮的；皮包骨的、極瘦的

skip [skɪp] 🎧 *Track 4403*
v. 跳來跳去，跳躍；略過；快速處理
▶ Professor Brown will flunk students who skip his classes.
布朗教授會當掉翹他課的學生。

（補充片語）
skip class 翹課

n. 跳，蹦；省略
▶ He can recite the whole poem without a skip.
他可以從頭到尾一字不漏地背出整首詩。

（補充片語）
without a skip 從頭到尾不遺漏地

skirt [skɝt] 🎧 *Track 4404*
n. 裙；裙子；**v.** 位於……邊緣；繞過……的邊緣

sky [skaɪ] 🎧 *Track 4405*
n. 天空

sky·scrap·er 🎧 *Track 4406*
[`skaɪ͵skrepɚ]
n. 摩天大樓，參天高樓
▶ Skyscrapers have mushroomed all over the city.
整座城市的摩天大樓如雨後春筍般地出現。

slang [slæŋ] 🎧 *Track 4407*
n. 俚語
▶ Americans use a lot of slang in their daily conversations. 美國人在他們的日常會話中會使用大量的俚語。

slave [slev] 🎧 *Track 4408*
n. 奴隸
▶ I don't want to work like a slave to live like a millionaire.
我不想為了過百萬富翁般的生活而像個奴隸般地工作。

v. 奴隸般工作；苦幹

▶ I don't want to become a housewife who slaves over endless household chores day after day.
我不想成為一個日復一日辛苦忙於永遠做不完的家事的家庭主婦。

---

slav·e·ry [`slevərɪ] 🎧 *Track 4409*
n. 奴役，奴隸制度；奴隸身分
▶ The girl was sold into slavery when she was only ten.
這女孩在十歲時就被賣做奴隸。

---

sleep [slip] 🎧 *Track 4410*
v. 睡覺；**n.** 睡眠

---

sleep·y [`slipɪ] 🎧 *Track 4411*
adj. 昏昏欲睡的；想睡的

---

sleeve [sliv] 🎧 *Track 4412*
n. 袖子；袖套
▶ Roll up your sleeves and get down to work! 給我捲起袖子開始工作了！

(補充片語)
roll up one's sleeves （捲起袖子）準備行動，準備幹活

---

slen·der [`slɛndɚ] 🎧 *Track 4413*
adj. 修長的；苗條的；纖細的；微薄的

---

slice [slaɪs] 🎧 *Track 4414*
n. （一）薄片，片；部分，份
▶ I only had a slice of bread for breakfast, so I'm starving now.
我早餐只吃了一片麵包，所以我現在餓極了。

v. 把……切成薄片；切下，切開；把……分成部分
▶ She couldn't stop her tears while slicing the onion.
她在將洋蔥切片時，止不住自己的眼淚。

---

slide [slaɪd] 🎧 *Track 4415*
v. 滑；滑落；悄悄地走；**n.** 溜滑梯

---

slight [slaɪt] 🎧 *Track 4416*
adj. 輕微的；少量的；極不重要的
▶ I have a slight headache.
我的頭有一點痛。

v. 輕視；藐視；怠慢

▶ He never slights any of his opponents.
他從不輕視他任何一個對手。

n. 輕蔑，怠慢
▶ Mike suffered many slights from his stepmother. 麥可受到繼母諸多輕蔑。

相關片語
in the slightest 絲毫
▶ I don't care what people think about me in the slightest.
我絲毫一點都不在意別人是怎麼想我的。

---

slight·ly [`slaɪtlɪ] 🎧 *Track 4417*
adv. 輕微地，稍微地；嬌弱地，瘦小地
▶ I feel slightly under the weather today.
我今天稍微覺得有點不舒服。

補充片語
under the weather 身體不舒服

---

slim [slɪm] 🎧 *Track 4418*
adj. 苗條的；微薄的；少的

---

slip [slɪp] 🎧 *Track 4419*
v. 滑動；滑跤；滑落；溜；**n.** 滑動；下降；失足；意外事故

---

slip·pers [`slɪpɚz] 🎧 *Track 4420*
n. 室內便鞋；淺口拖鞋

---

slip·per·y [`slɪpərɪ] 🎧 *Track 4421*
adj. 滑的，容易滑的；油滑的，靠不住的；須小心對待的；不穩定的
▶ Be aware of that guy. He is as slippery as an eel. 小心那個傢伙。他跟泥鰍一樣狡猾。

補充片語
as slippery as an eel 滑如泥鰍；如泥鰍般狡猾

---

slo·gan [`slogən] 🎧 *Track 4422*
n. 口號；標語
▶ "Just do it" is a very famous slogan.
「做就對了」是一句非常有名的標語。

---

slope [slop] 🎧 *Track 4423*
n. 傾斜，坡度，斜面
▶ The children are having fun sliding down the grassy slope.
孩子們滑草坡滑得很開心。

v. 傾斜；使有坡度；【口】溜走

► He sloped off while his boss was in the meeting. 他趁主管在開會的時候溜走了。

(補充片語)

slope off 悄悄地溜走（以逃避工作）

slow [slo] 🎧 *Track 4424*
adj. 慢的；緩緩的；耗時的；慢了的；**v.** 放慢；使慢；變慢；**adv.** 慢了地；慢慢地

small [smɔl] 🎧 *Track 4425*
adj. 小的；少量的；瘦小的；低微的

smart [smɑrt] 🎧 *Track 4426*
adj. 聰明的

smell [smɛl] 🎧 *Track 4427*
n. 氣味；嗅覺；**v.** 聞；嗅；聞出；發出氣味；有氣味

smile [smaɪl] 🎧 *Track 4428*
v./n. 微笑

smog [smɑg] 🎧 *Track 4429*
n. 煙霧

► I can barely see anything further than ten meters because of the thick smog.
因為濃厚的煙霧，我幾乎看不到十公尺以外的任何東西。

smoke [smok] 🎧 *Track 4430*
n. 煙；煙霧；一口煙；**v.** 抽菸；冒煙；煙燻

smok·ing [`smokɪŋ] 🎧 *Track 4431*
n. 抽菸

► Smoking is prohibited in public places in Taiwan. 在台灣的公共場所是禁止抽菸的。

adj. 可抽菸的，冒煙的

► I'd like to reserve a table for two in the smoking area.
我想預約吸菸區一張兩個人的桌子。

smok·y [`smokɪ] 🎧 *Track 4432*
adj. 冒煙的，煙霧瀰漫的，冒氣的，有煙味的

► London used to be a smoky industrial city.
倫敦曾經是個煙霧瀰漫的工業城市。

smooth [smuð] 🎧 *Track 4433*
adj. 平滑的；平穩的；平坦的；流暢的，悅耳的；平和的，圓滑的；溫和的

► I wish you a smooth day at work.
祝你在工作上有個平順的一天。

v. 使平滑；使平坦；使優雅；變緩和；消除（皺紋、障礙、分歧等）

► This facial cream can keep your skin moist and smooth out wrinkles. 這款面霜能讓你的皮膚保持濕潤，並撫平皺紋。

snack [snæk] 🎧 *Track 4434*
n. 小吃；點心；**v.** 吃快餐；吃點心

snail [snel] 🎧 *Track 4435*
n. 蝸牛

snake [snek] 🎧 *Track 4436*
n. 蛇

snap [snæp] 🎧 *Track 4437*
v. 猛咬；突然折斷；啪地關上；用快照拍攝

► She flew into a rage when she found the paparazzi snapping her photo while she was swimming naked.
她在發現狗仔用快照拍她裸泳時勃然大怒。

(補充片語)

fly into a rage 勃然大怒

adj. 突然的，冷不防的

► He made a snap decision to marry the girl whom he just met.
他突然決定要跟那個他才剛認識的女孩結婚。

n. 猛撲；攫奪；突然折斷；劈啪聲；快照；輕鬆的工作；脆餅

► This cold snap was forecast to continue right up to the Lunar New Year.
這波寒流預計會一直持續到農曆春節。

(補充片語)

cold snap 乍寒，驟冷；寒流

sneak [snik] 🎧 *Track 4438*
v. 偷偷地走；偷偷地逃避

► Disguised as an old lady, the famous actress successfully sneaked out of the building. 這有名的女演員喬裝成一個老太太，成功地溜出了大樓。

sneak·ers [ˈsnikɚz]　🎧 *Track 4439*
n. 運動鞋

sneak·y [ˈsnikɪ]　🎧 *Track 4440*
adj. 鬼鬼祟祟的

sneeze [sniz]　🎧 *Track 4441*
v. 打噴嚏
▶ I can't stop sneezing whenever there are dogs around me.
只要有狗在我四周，我就會打噴嚏打個不停。

n. 噴嚏，噴嚏聲
▶ His loud sneeze gave me a scare.
他響亮的噴嚏聲讓我嚇了一跳。

相關片語
not to be sneezed at　不可輕視，不容小覷
▶ An award of US$50,000 is not to be sneezed at.　一筆五萬美金的獎金可不容小覷。

snow [sno]　🎧 *Track 4442*
n. 雪；**v.** 下雪

snow·man [ˈsnoˌmæn]　🎧 *Track 4443*
n. 雪人
▶ Let's build a snowman.
我們來做個雪人吧！

snow·y [ˈsnoɪ]　🎧 *Track 4444*
adj. 下雪的

so [so]　🎧 *Track 4445*
adv. 這麼；多麼；如此地；因此；**conj.** 所以；因此

soap [sop]　🎧 *Track 4446*
n. 肥皂；**v.** 用肥皂洗

sob [sab]　🎧 *Track 4447*
v. 嗚咽，啜泣，哭訴
▶ She sobbed herself to sleep every night after her husband died.
她丈夫死後，她每個晚上都哭著入睡。

補充片語
sob oneself to sleep　哭著入睡

n. 嗚咽聲，啜泣聲
▶ We hear soft sobs coming from her room every night.　我們每晚都能聽到她房間傳出來的輕微啜泣聲。

相關片語
sob one's heart out　哭得極傷心
▶ She sobbed her heart out after hearing of his death.
她在聽聞他的死訊後哭得極為傷心。

soc·cer [ˈsokɚ]　🎧 *Track 4448*
n. 足球；足球運動

so·cia·ble [ˈsoʃəbl]　🎧 *Track 4449*
adj. 好交際的，社交性的，友善的
▶ Mary is a very sociable person.
瑪麗是個非常擅長社交的人。

so·cial [ˈsoʃəl]　🎧 *Track 4450*
adj. 社會的；社交的

so·ci·e·ty [səˈsaɪətɪ]　🎧 *Track 4451*
n. 社會；社團；交際；交往

sock·et [ˈsakɪt]　🎧 *Track 4452*
n. 托座；插座；插口；（人體的）窩，槽，臼
▶ Don't touch an electric socket with your wet hands.　不要用濕濕的手去觸碰電插座。

socks [saks]　🎧 *Track 4453*
n. 襪子

so·da [ˈsodə]　🎧 *Track 4454*
n. 蘇打；蘇打水；汽水

so·fa [ˈsofə]　🎧 *Track 4455*
n. 沙發

soft [sɔft]　🎧 *Track 4456*
adj. 柔軟的；輕柔的；柔和的；不含酒精的

soft·ball [ˈsɔftˌbɔl]　🎧 *Track 4457*
n. 壘球，壘球運動
▶ David became a professional softball player at the age of 18.
大衛在十八歲時成了個職業壘球選手。

soft·ware [ˈsɔftˌwɛr]　🎧 *Track 4458*
n. （電腦）軟體
▶ You need to install an antivirus software on your computer.
你需要在你的電腦上安裝防毒軟體。

soil [sɔɪl]　🎧 *Track 4459*
n. 泥土，土壤；土地，領土；溫床；污物；糞便，肥料；墮落
▶ The soil in our garden is not rich enough for homegrown vegetables. 我們花園裡的土壤不夠肥沃，不能栽種自家蔬菜。

v. 弄髒，玷污；變髒
▶ The scandal soiled his reputation.
這起醜聞玷污了他的名聲。

so·lar [`solɚ]　🎧 *Track 4460*
adj. 太陽的，日光的；利用太陽的
▶ We can reduce our dependence on nuclear energy by using renewable sources such as solar energy. 我們可以藉著利用如太陽能等可再生資源，來減少我們對核能的依賴。

sol·dier [`soldʒɚ]　🎧 *Track 4461*
n. 軍人；士兵

sol·id [`salɪd]　🎧 *Track 4462*
adj. 固體的，實心的；純的；牢靠的，穩固的，可信賴的
▶ Uncle James and my father have developed a solid friendship since they were in college. 詹姆士叔叔和我父親從大學時代開始就建立了穩固的友誼。

n. 固體；立方體；固態物；固體食物
▶ I started feeding my baby solids when he was eight months old. 我在我的寶寶八個月大時開始餵他吃固體食物。

so·lu·tion [sə`luʃən]　🎧 *Track 4463*
n. 解答；解決辦法

solve [salv]　🎧 *Track 4464*
v. 解決

some [sʌm]　🎧 *Track 4465*
pron. 一些；**det.** 一些的

some·bod·y [`sʌm,badɪ]　🎧 *Track 4466*
=some·one
pron. 某人

some·bod·y's　🎧 *Track 4467*
[`sʌm,badɪz]
abbr. 某人的；某人是（somebody is的縮寫）

some·how [`sʌm,haʊ]　🎧 *Track 4468*
adv. 由於某種未知的原因
▶ Somehow I don't like Peter.
不知為什麼，我就是不喜歡彼得。

some·one [`sʌm,wʌn]　🎧 *Track 4469*
=some·bod·y
pron. 某人；有人

some·thing [`sʌmθɪŋ]　🎧 *Track 4470*
pron. 某事；某件事

some·times [`sʌm,taɪmz]　🎧 *Track 4471*
adv. 有時候

some·what [`sʌm,hwɑt]　🎧 *Track 4472*
adv. 有點；稍微
▶ I think the blue one is somewhat better.
我覺得藍色的稍微比較好看。

some·where [`sʌm,hwɛr]　🎧 *Track 4473*
adv. 某處；某個地方

son [sʌn]　🎧 *Track 4474*
n. 兒子

song [sɔŋ]　🎧 *Track 4475*
n. 歌曲；曲子

soon [sun]　🎧 *Track 4476*
adv. 馬上；立刻

sore [sor]　🎧 *Track 4477*
adj. 疼痛的；**n.**（身體或精神的）痛處；瘡；潰瘍

sor·row [`saro]　🎧 *Track 4478*
n. 悲痛；悲哀
▶ We feel sorrow for your loss.
我們為您所失去的感到悲傷。

sor·ry [`sarɪ]　🎧 *Track 4479*
adj. 抱歉的；難過的

sort [sɔrt]　🎧 *Track 4480*
n. 種類；類型；**v.** 將……分類；區分

soul [sol]　🎧 *Track 4481*
n. 靈魂；心靈

sound [saʊnd] 🎧 *Track 4482*
adj. 健康的，健全的，狀況良好的
▶ Don't worry. He will return safe and sound.
別擔心。他會平安無事地回來的。

(補充片語)
safe and sound 安然無恙地，平安無事地

soup [sup] 🎧 *Track 4483*
n. 湯

sour [`saʊr] 🎧 *Track 4484*
adj. 酸的；酸臭的

source [sors] 🎧 *Track 4485*
n. 源頭；根源；來源

south [saʊθ] 🎧 *Track 4486*
n. 南；南方；**adv.** 朝南；往南；向南
adj. 南方的；南部的

south·east [ˌsaʊθˋist] 🎧 *Track 4487*
n. 東南，東南方；東南部
▶ The wind is blowing from the southeast.
這風是從東南方吹過來的。

adv. 在東南，向東南，來自東南
▶ The ship is sailing southeast.
這船正往東南方航行。

adj. 東南的；向東南的；東南部的
▶ I haven't been to any countries in Southeast Asia.
我還沒去過東南亞的任何一個國家。

south·ern [`sʌðən] 🎧 *Track 4488*
adj. 在南方的；來自南方的；有南部特點的

south-west [ˌsaʊθˋwɛst] 🎧 *Track 4489*
n. 西南，西南方；西南部
▶ He comes from the southwest of the United States. 他來自美國的西南部。

adv. 在西南，向西南，來自西南
▶ The cold air mass is currently moving southwest.
這波冷氣團目前是往西南方移動。

adj. 西南的；向西南的；西南部的
▶ Southwest Taiwan consists of Tainan and Chiayi.
台灣西南部包含了台南與嘉義。

sou·ve·nir [`suvəˌnɪr] 🎧 *Track 4490*
n. 紀念品；紀念物；伴手禮
▶ She bought a T-shirt as a souvenir before she left London.
她離開倫敦前買了件T恤當作紀念品。

sow [so] 🎧 *Track 4491*
v. 播種；散布，傳播
▶ The farmers are busy sowing rice seeds in the soil.
農夫們正忙著將稻種播種在土壤裡。

相關片語
sow one's wild oats 生活放蕩
▶ He used to sow his wild oats in his youth.
他在年輕時日子過得很放蕩荒唐。

soy sauce [`sɔɪ-sɔs] 🎧 *Track 4492*
n. 醬油

soy·bean [`sɔɪbin] 🎧 *Track 4493*
=soy·a bean/soy
n. 大豆
▶ Would you like a glass of soybean milk?
你要不要來一杯豆漿？

(補充片語)
soybean milk 豆漿

space [spes] 🎧 *Track 4494*
n. 空間；場所；空地；宇宙、太空

space·craft [`spesˌkræft] 🎧 *Track 4495*
n. 太空船
▶ Another unmanned spacecraft was launched into space last month. 上個月又有一架無人駕駛的太空船被發射到太空去了。

spade [sped] 🎧 *Track 4496*
n. （撲克牌中的）黑桃
▶ Kevin always calls a spade a spade, even in front of his boss.
即使是在老闆面前，凱文也總是直言不諱。

(補充片語)
call a spade a spade 直言不諱，有話直說

spa·ghet·ti [spəˋgɛtɪ] 🎧 *Track 4497*
n. 義大利麵

※灰色單字為英檢初級必備單字

spare [spɛr]　🎧 Track 4498

adj. 多餘的，剩下的；備用的；節約的；少量的

▶ He spends his spare time volunteering at a local hospital. 他將他的業餘時間拿來在當地的一間醫院當志工。

(補充片語)

spare time　業餘時間，空暇時間

v. 分出；騰出（時間、人手）；節約，省用

▶ He spared no effort to help people who are in need. 他不遺餘力地幫助那些有需要的人。

(補充片語)

spare no effort　不遺餘力

n. 備用品；備用輪胎；備用零件

▶ We've got a flat tire. Do you have a spare in your car? 我們有個輪胎爆胎了。你車上有沒有備胎？

spark [spɑrk]　🎧 Track 4499

n. 火花，火星；生氣，活力；跡象，痕跡

▶ A single spark can start a prairie fire. 星星之火，可以燎原。

v. 發出火花；發動，點燃，激勵，鼓舞

▶ The experiment sparked his interest in science. 這個實驗點燃了他對科學的興趣。

spar·kle [`spɑrkl]　🎧 Track 4500

v. 發火光，閃耀；（才氣）煥發，活躍

▶ The little girl's eyes sparkled with excitement. 小女孩的眼睛興奮得發亮。

n. 火花，閃光；（才氣）煥發；活力，生氣

▶ There was a sparkle of mischief in the boy's eyes. 男孩的眼中閃著調皮的光芒。

spar·row [`spæro]　🎧 Track 4501

n. 麻雀

▶ Sparrows are a common bird in Taiwan. 麻雀是在台灣很常見的一種鳥類。

speak [spik]　🎧 Track 4502

v. 說；說話

speak·er [`spikɚ]　🎧 Track 4503

n. 說話者；說某種語言的人；演說家；擴音機

spear [spɪr]　🎧 Track 4504

n. 矛；魚叉

▶ All warriors were armed with spears. 所有的戰士都以長矛武裝著。

v. 用矛或魚叉刺、戳

▶ He speared a fish accurately. 他準確地刺中了一條魚。

spe·cial [`spɛʃəl]　🎧 Track 4505

adj. 特別的；**n.** 特別的東西；特刊；特餐

spe·cial·ized [`spɛʃəl‚aɪzd]　🎧 Track 4506

adj. 專門的；專科的；專業的；專業化的

▶ Our factory is specialized in producing computer components. 我們的工廠是專門生產電腦零件的。

spe·cies [`spiʃiz]　🎧 Track 4507

n. 種類；（生）種

▶ White rhinos are one of the endangered species in the world. 白犀牛是世界上瀕臨滅絕的物種之一。

spe·cif·ic [spɪ`sɪfɪk]　🎧 Track 4508

adj. 特殊的，特定的；明確的，具體的

▶ Do you have any specific requirements for your future husband? 你對你未來的丈夫有任何具體的要求條件嗎？

spec·ta·tor [spɛk`tetɚ]　🎧 Track 4509

n. （比賽等的）觀眾；旁觀者

▶ Compared with watching the game on TV, being present as a spectator is more exciting. 跟在電視上看比賽比起來，到現場觀賽更刺激。

(補充片語)

be present as a spectator　到現場觀賽

speech [spitʃ]　🎧 Track 4510

n. 演說；說話；致辭

speed [spid]　🎧 Track 4511

n. 速度；**v.** 迅速前進；加速

spell [spɛl]　🎧 Track 4512

n. 咒語；符咒；著魔

▶ The witch put a spell on the prince and turned him into an ugly frog. 巫婆對王子施了咒語，把他變成一隻醜陋的青蛙。

spell·ing [ˋspɛlɪŋ] 　🎧 *Track 4513*
n. 拼字；拼寫；拼法

spend [spɛnd] 　🎧 *Track 4514*
v. 花費（時間、金錢、精力）；度過

spice [spaɪs] 　🎧 *Track 4515*
n. 香料
▶ There are various kinds of spices in my kitchen. 我的廚房裡有各式各樣的香料。

v. 加香料於
▶ The soup is well spiced.
這湯的味道調得很好。

spic·y [ˋspaɪsɪ] 　🎧 *Track 4516*
adj. 加有香料的；辛辣的
▶ Thai curry is too spicy for me to eat.
泰式咖哩對我來說太辣了，我沒辦法吃。

spi·der [ˋspaɪdɚ] 　🎧 *Track 4517*
n. 蜘蛛

spill [spɪl] 　🎧 *Track 4518*
v. 使溢出，使濺出；洩漏（秘密）
▶ He spilt his coffee all over his desk.
他把咖啡灑得整張桌子都是。

n. 溢出；濺出；散落
▶ Can you get a rag to wipe off the spill?
你可以拿條抹布來把濺出來的東西擦掉嗎？

spin [spɪn] 　🎧 *Track 4519*
v. 紡；吐（絲），結（網）；旋轉；編造，虛構
▶ The woman spun us a yarn about her sufferings. 那女人對我們胡謅了一個有關她苦難經歷的故事。

（補充片語）
spin a yarn 胡謅，編故事

n. 旋轉；（車）疾馳；（飛機）盤旋下降；情緒低落；驚慌失措
▶ I've been in a flat spin trying to get the work done by the deadline.
我驚慌萬分地試著要在期限之前將工作完成。

spin·ach [ˋspɪnɪtʃ] 　🎧 *Track 4520*
n. 菠菜
▶ I'm going to make a salad with the fresh spinach. 我要用這新鮮的菠菜來做沙拉。

spir·it [ˋspɪrɪt] 　🎧 *Track 4521*
n. 精神；心靈；本意

spir·i·tu·al [ˋspɪrɪtʃʊəl] 　🎧 *Track 4522*
adj. 精神上的
▶ I can't give you financial support, but I can always provide you with spiritual comfort. 我無法給你經濟上的支援，但是我永遠可以給你精神上的慰藉。

spit [spɪt] 　🎧 *Track 4523*
v. 吐（口水、痰等）；口出（惡語）；點燃
▶ It's inappropriate to spit on the ground.
把痰吐在地上是很不合宜的行為。

n. 唾液，口水；微雨，小雪
▶ The way his spit flew as he talked really disgusted me.
他講話時一直噴口水讓我覺得很噁心。

spite [spaɪt] 　🎧 *Track 4524*
n. 惡意
▶ He humiliated her out of spite.
他出於惡意地羞辱她。

splash [splæʃ] 　🎧 *Track 4525*
v. 濺污；潑濕；使液體飛濺；【口】揮霍錢財
▶ The clumsy waitress accidentally splashed coffee on the customer's white skirt.
笨手笨腳的女服務生不小心把咖啡濺在顧客的白裙上。

n. 潑，灑，濺潑聲；濺上的污漬
▶ The kids jumped into the pool with a splash. 孩子們撲通一聲跳入了水池中。

（相關片語）
make/create a splash 引起轟動
▶ The ALS Ice Bucket Challenge made quite a splash throughout last year all over the world.
肌萎縮性脊髓側索硬化症冰桶挑戰，去年一整年在世界各地造成很大的轟動。

Aa Bb Cc Dd Ee Ff Gg Hh Ii Jj Kk Ll Mm Nn Oo Pp Qq Rr Ss Tt Uu Vv Ww Xx Yy Zz

splen·did [`splɛndɪd] 🎧 Track 4526
adj. 燦爛的；極令人滿意的
▶ We enjoyed a splendid concert last night.
我們昨晚欣賞了一場精彩的演唱會。

split [splɪt] 🎧 Track 4527
v. 劈開，切開，撕裂；分裂，斷絕關係
▶ They got married in 2009, but split up two years later.
他們在2009年結婚，但在兩年後就分開了。

n. 裂縫，裂痕；分裂；（舞蹈中的）劈腿
▶ The earthquake caused the splits in the walls. 地震造成牆壁的裂縫。

adj. 裂開的，劈開的；分裂的，分離的
▶ I asked my hair stylist to trim off my split ends.
我請我的髮型設計師修剪我分岔的髮尾。

(補充片語)
split ends 頭髮分岔的尾部

spoil [spɔɪl] 🎧 Track 4528
v. 寵壞；毀壞
▶ Too many cooks spoil the broth. 人多反倒誤事。（太多廚子，反而把湯給毀了。）

n. 戰略物，戰利品；競選勝利獲得的好處；獵物，贓物
▶ The police officer questioned the robbers about where they hid the spoils.
警察訊問搶匪將贓物藏在哪裡。

spokes·man [`spoksmən] 🎧 Track 4529
n. 發言人
▶ The Government spokesman said that the government would not allow any move to destroy national security.
政府發言人表示，政府絕不容許任何破壞國家安全的行動。

spon·sor [`spɑnsɚ] 🎧 Track 4530
v. 資助，支持，倡議；做……的保證人
▶ Sponsoring a child in need is good way to extend practical help. 資助一個貧困的孩童是給予實際幫助的好方法。

n. 發起人，主辦者；贊助者；保人
▶ Our company is one of the corporate sponsors of the charity bazaar.
我們公司是這場慈善義賣會的贊助企業之一。

(補充片語)
corporate sponsor 企業贊助者

spoon [spun] 🎧 Track 4531
n. 湯匙；一匙

sport [sport] 🎧 Track 4532
n. 運動

sports·man [`sportsmən] 🎧 Track 4533
n. 喜好運動的人、運動家；具運動家品格者
▶ A real sportsman doesn't care about winning or losing.
一個真正的運動家不會在乎輸贏。

sports·man·ship [`sportsmən ʃip] 🎧 Track 4534
n. 運動員精神
▶ It is sportsmanship that matters.
重要的是運動家精神。

spot [spɑt] 🎧 Track 4535
n. 斑點；污點；場所；職位；**v.** 玷污；弄髒；認出、發現

spray [spre] 🎧 Track 4536
n. 浪花，飛沫；噴霧，噴霧器
▶ Stop using hair sprays, because they can damage the Earth's ozone layer.
不要再使用頭髮噴霧了，因為他們會破壞地球的臭氧層。

v. 噴灑，噴
▶ He sprayed pesticide in order to kill harmful insects.
他為了殺死有害的昆蟲而噴灑殺蟲劑。

spread [sprɛd] 🎧 Track 4537
v. 使伸展；張開；塗、敷；散佈；**n.** 伸展；擴張；蔓延

sprin·kle [`sprɪŋkl] 🎧 Track 4538
v. 灑，噴淋；使成點狀分布；點綴；下毛毛雨
▶ She sprinkled some icing sugar on the top of the chocolate cake.
她在巧克力蛋糕頂部撒上一些糖粉做為點綴。

n. 毛毛雨；少量散步的東西；撒在表面的屑狀物

▶ She decorated her cake with some chocolate sprinkles.
她以一些巧克力碎片裝飾蛋糕。

spy [spaɪ] 🎧 *Track 4539*
n. 間諜，密探
▶ He was sent to their rival company to act as an industrial spy.
他被派去他們的競爭公司當商業間諜。

v. 當間諜；暗中監視；偵查；看見
▶ Once you become famous, there will be paparazzi everywhere spying into your private life. 一旦你出名了，就會到處有狗仔隊監視你的私生活。

相關片語
spy out the land 摸清情形
▶ We will take no further action before we spy out the land. 在摸清楚情況之前，我們不會採取進一步的行動。

square [skwɛr] 🎧 *Track 4540*
n. 正方形；方型廣場；**adj.** 正方形的；正直的；平方的；令人滿意的

squeeze [skwiz] 🎧 *Track 4541*
v. 榨，擠，壓；緊握；強取；壓縮；勉強得到
▶ He always tries to squeeze some time out of his busy schedule to exercise.
他總是試著從忙碌的行程中擠出一些時間來運動。

n. 壓榨；緊握；少量的榨汁；擁擠的一群；拮据
▶ She gave my hand a squeeze of appreciation. 她感激地緊握我的手。

相關片語
put the squeeze on sb. 對……施加壓力
▶ Soaring housing prices has put the squeeze on our youngsters. 不斷高漲的房價對我們的年輕人造成很大的壓力。

squir·rel [`skwɝəl] 🎧 *Track 4542*
n. 松鼠
▶ There is a squirrel eating nuts under the tree.
有隻松鼠在樹下吃堅果。

stab [stæb] 🎧 *Track 4543*
v. 刺，戳；刺入，刺傷
▶ The young woman was stabbed to death by her ex-boyfriend.
該年輕女子被她的前男友刺殺身亡。

n. 刺，戳；刺破的傷口；突發的一陣（驚奇或疼痛）；【口】嘗試
▶ She did take a stab at saving their marriage, but failed.
她的確有嘗試挽救他們的婚姻，但失敗了。

sta·ble [`stebl] 🎧 *Track 4544*
adj. 穩定的
▶ The patient's condition is stable now.
病人的情況現在已經穩定了。

n. 馬房，馬棚，馬槽
▶ It has long been believed that Jesus was born in a stable. 人們長久以來一直相信，耶穌是誕生在馬槽裡。

sta·di·um [`stedɪəm] 🎧 *Track 4545*
n. 體育場
▶ People crowed into the stadium for the baseball game.
人們為了看棒球賽湧進體育場。

staff [stæf] 🎧 *Track 4546*
n. （全體）職員，（全體）工作人員
▶ The cafeteria is open to our staff only.
員工餐廳只對本公司職員開放。

v. 給……配備職員
▶ Our Research and Development Department is staffed with 20 engineers.
我們的研發部門有二十名工程師。

stage [stedʒ] 🎧 *Track 4547*
n. 舞台

stair·case [`stɛrˌkes] 🎧 *Track 4548*
n. 樓梯
▶ Walking up and down the staircases is great exercise. 上下樓梯是很棒的運動。

相關片語
moving staircase 電梯
▶ The moving staircase is out of order at present. 電梯目前故障。

Aa
Bb
Cc
Dd
Ee
Ff
Gg
Hh
Ii
Jj
Kk
Ll
Mm
Nn
Oo
Pp
Qq
Rr
Ss
Tt
Uu
Vv
Ww
Xx
Yy
Zz

stairs [stɛrz]　　🎧 *Track 4549*
n. 樓梯

stake [stek]　　🎧 *Track 4550*
n. 樁，棍子；股本，利害關係；賭注，賭金；危險，風險
▶ We'd better hurry up and pull up stakes before the storm hits. 我們最好動作快一點，在暴風雨來襲之前拔樁撤帳。

(補充片語)
pull up stakes 拔樁撤帳篷；跳槽（離開工作很久的工作或住很久的房子）

v. 把……當賭注；拿……冒險；以樁支撐，以樁圍住
▶ He tried to persuade his parents to stake their savings on his business.
他試著說服他爸媽把他們的存款拿來賭在他的事業上。

stamp [stæmp]　　🎧 *Track 4551*
n. 郵票；**v.** 貼郵票於

stand [stænd]　　🎧 *Track 4552*
v. 站；站立；**n.** 站立；立場；攤子

stan·dard [`stændəd]　　🎧 *Track 4553*
n. 標準；水準；規格；**adj.** 標準的

star [stɑr]　　🎧 *Track 4554*
n. 星星；明星；**v.** 當明星；主演

stare [stɛr]　　🎧 *Track 4555*
v. 盯，凝視
▶ They stared at each other without saying a word. 他們不發一語地彼此凝視著。

n. 凝視，注視；瞪眼
▶ She was offended by his rude stare.
她被他無禮的瞪視給惹怒了。

(相關片語)
be staring sb. in the face 就在某人眼前；十分明顯
▶ Why waste your time searching for happiness when it's staring you in the face?
當幸福就在你眼前時，為何要浪費時間去尋找幸福呢？

start [stɑrt]　　🎧 *Track 4556*
v. 開始；**n.** 開始；開端

starv·a·tion [stɑr`veʃən]　　🎧 *Track 4557*
n. 飢餓；挨餓；餓死
▶ Statistics show that a child dies from starvation every 10 seconds. 統計數字顯示，每十秒鐘就有一個孩童死於饑餓。

starve [stɑrv]　　🎧 *Track 4558*
v. 餓死；挨餓；餓得慌；渴望，極需要
▶ She starved herself in order to lose some weight. 她為了減重讓自己餓肚子。

state [stet]　　🎧 *Track 4559*
n. 狀況，狀態；形態；情勢；國家，政府；身份，地位
▶ The country is currently in a state of chaos.
這個國家目前處於混亂的狀態。

adj. 正式的，官方的；國家的，政府的
▶ The U.S. president and his wife were invited to attend a state banquet held in Buckingham Palace. 美國總統及其夫人受邀出席在白金漢宮舉行的一場國宴。

(補充片語)
state banquet 國宴

v. 陳述；聲明；說明
▶ The victim stated that she had never seen the man who attacked her before.
受害者聲明自己以前從未見過攻擊她的男子。

state·ment [`stetmənt]　　🎧 *Track 4560*
n. 陳述；說明；正式聲明
▶ He denied having an affair with the woman in his statement.
他在他的正式聲明中否認與該女子有戀情。

sta·tion [`steʃən]　　🎧 *Track 4561*
n. 車站；站、局、所

sta·tion·e·ry [`steʃən͵ɛrɪ]　　🎧 *Track 4562*
n. 文具

stat·ue [`stætʃʊ]　　🎧 *Track 4563*
n. 雕像，塑像
▶ The Statue of Liberty in New York Harbor was a gift to the United States from France.
位在紐約港的自由女神像是法國送給美國的禮物。

sta·tus [`stetəs] 🎧 *Track 4564*
n. 地位；身分
▶ Women's social status has been improving over the years.
女人的社會地位在這些年來已經提升了。

stay [ste] 🎧 *Track 4565*
v. 停留；暫住；保持；止住；**n.** 停留；逗留

stead·y [`stɛdɪ] 🎧 *Track 4566*
adj. 穩固的，平穩的；鎮靜的，沉著的
▶ My boyfriend and I have been in a steady relationship, but we never thought of getting married. 我跟我男友的關係很穩定，但是我們從沒想過要結婚。

v. 使穩固；使鎮定；變穩，穩固
▶ Will you steady the ladder for me while I am reaching for the ball in the tree?
你可以在我要伸手拿樹上的球時，幫我扶穩梯子嗎？

steak [stek] 🎧 *Track 4567*
n. 牛排；肉排；魚排

steal [stil] 🎧 *Track 4568*
v. 偷；偷竊

steam [stim] 🎧 *Track 4569*
n. 蒸汽；水蒸汽；精力；氣力；**v.** 蒸煮；蒸發；用蒸汽開動

steel [stil] 🎧 *Track 4570*
n. 鋼；鋼鐵
▶ The pot is made of steel.
這鍋子是鋼做的。

v. 鋼化；使像鋼，使堅強，使下決心
▶ She has learned to steel her heart against disappointment.
她已經學會硬起心腸，不受失望影響。

steep [stip] 🎧 *Track 4571*
adj. 陡峭的；急劇升降的；（價格）過高的，不合理的
▶ I have problem driving up the steep slope in this old car.
我沒辦法將這輛舊車駛上這陡坡。

steer [stɪr] 🎧 *Track 4572*
v. 掌舵，駕駛；指導，帶領，操縱
▶ He felt nervous when the taxi driver steered into a dark alley.
當計程車司機把車子開進一條暗巷時，他感到十分緊張。

stem [stɛm] 🎧 *Track 4573*
v. 起源於；抽去……梗或莖；逆……而行
▶ His failure stems from a combination of his arrogance and bad luck.
他的失敗是他的自負加上運氣不好所造成的。

n. 莖，幹，柄；船頭；詞幹
▶ I didn't watch the movie from stem to stern.
我並沒有將這部電影從頭到尾地看完。

補充片語
from stem to stern 從（船）頭到（船）尾，完全

step [stɛp] 🎧 *Track 4574*
n. 腳步；一步的距離；步驟；**v.** 踏、跨步；踏（進）；踩

step·fa·ther [`stɛp͵faðɚ] 🎧 *Track 4575*
n. 繼父；後父
▶ My stepfather is a good man.
我的繼父是個好人。

step·moth·er [`stɛp͵mʌðɚ] 🎧 *Track 4576*
n. 繼母；後母
▶ My stepmother is younger than me.
我的繼母比我年輕。

ster·e·o [`stɛrɪo] 🎧 *Track 4577*
adj. 立體聲的，立體音響的
▶ A stereo system can make your music sound more powerful, clearer and more detailed.
一個立體音響系統能讓你的音樂聽起來更有力、更清楚且更精細。

n. 立體音響裝置；體視系統；立體電影
▶ The car stereo cost him nearly thirty thousand dollars.
這台車用立體音響裝置花了他近三萬元。

※灰色單字為英檢初級必備單字

stick [stɪk] 🎧 *Track 4578*
n. 枝條；棍棒；手杖；棒狀物；**v.** 釘住；黏貼；伸出

stick·y [ˋstɪkɪ] 🎧 *Track 4579*
adj. 黏的；泥濘的；濕熱的；棘手的
▶ Please don't touch anything in this room with your sticky hands. 請不要用你黏答答的手摸這房間裡的任何東西。

stiff [stɪf] 🎧 *Track 4580*
adj. 硬挺的；僵硬的；不靈活的
▶ My neck and shoulders always feel stiff after I work on my computer for a long day. 在我用電腦工作了長長的一天之後，我的頸間總是感到很僵硬。

adv. 僵硬地，堅硬地；完全地，極其
▶ He sat stiff on the sofa, not knowing what to say.
他僵硬地坐在沙發上，不知道該說些什麼。

still [stɪl] 🎧 *Track 4581*
adv. 仍然；還是；**adj.** 靜止的

stim·u·late [ˋstɪmjəˌlet] 🎧 *Track 4582*
v. 刺激，促使；起刺激作用
▶ A hot bath can stimulate blood flow.
一個熱水澡能促進血液循環。

sting [stɪŋ] 🎧 *Track 4583*
v. 刺，螫，叮；刺痛；傷害
▶ He was stung by a bee when he was trying to collect honey from the hives. 當他企圖從蜂窩收集蜂蜜時，被一隻蜜蜂螫了。

n. 螫針；（植物的）刺；刺痛；諷刺，挖苦
▶ The sharp sting in his criticism hurt her feelings.
他語帶尖銳諷刺的批評傷了她的感情。

stin·gy [ˋstɪndʒɪ] 🎧 *Track 4584*
adj. 吝嗇的；小氣的

stir [stɝ] 🎧 *Track 4585*
v. 攪拌；攪動
▶ You need to keep stirring the soup until it's done. 你要一直攪拌直到湯煮好為止。

n. 微動；騷動

▶ The diva's latest album caused quite a stir.
這天后的最新唱片專輯造成了相當大的轟動。

stitch [stɪtʃ] 🎧 *Track 4586*
n. 一針，針線；針法；一件衣服，一塊布
▶ He had five stitches in the wound on his left leg. 他右腿上的傷口縫了五針。

v. 縫，繡；縫合
▶ It took the doctor three hours to stitch up the wound on his head.
醫生花了三個小時才把他頭上的傷口縫合。

stock [stɑk] 🎧 *Track 4587*
n. 貯存，蓄積；庫存品，存貨；股票
▶ The bread machine you're looking for is currently out of stock.
你要找的那款麵包機現在沒貨了。

（補充片語）
out of stock 沒有庫存

v. 辦貨，進貨；貯存，庫存
▶ We'd better stock up enough food and drinking water before the typhoon.
我們最好在颱風前貯存足夠的食物和飲用水。

adj. 庫存的，現有的；平凡的，慣用的
▶ "No pain, no gain" is a stock saying.
「一分耕耘一分收穫」是一句老套的諺語。

stock·ing [ˋstɑkɪŋ] 🎧 *Track 4588*
n. 長襪
▶ The boy found gifts in his Christmas stocking on Christmas morning.
男孩在聖誕節早上發現了聖誕襪裡頭的禮物。

stom·ach [ˋstʌmək] 🎧 *Track 4589*
=tum·my
n. 胃；肚子；胃口

stom·ach·ache 🎧 *Track 4590*
[ˋstʌməkˌek]
n. 胃痛

stone [ston] 🎧 *Track 4591*
n. 石頭

stool [stul] 🎧 *Track 4592*
n. 凳子；馬桶；糞便

▶He stood on a high stool in order to get the book from the top shelf. 他站在一個高腳凳上，好拿最上層書架上的書。

相關片語

fall between two stools 兩頭落空
▶Henry tried to be both a good son and a good husband, but fell between two stools. 亨利想要同時當個好兒子和好老公，結果兩邊都做不好。

stop [stɑp] 🎧 *Track 4593*
v. 停；阻止；**n.** （車）站

store [stor] 🎧 *Track 4594*
n. 店；商店；**v.** 儲存；存放

sto·rey [ˋstorɪ] 🎧 *Track 4595*
=sto·ry（美式英文）
n. 樓層
▶We just bought a three-storey house in the suburbs.
我們剛在郊區買了棟三層樓的房子。

storm [stɔrm] 🎧 *Track 4596*
n. 暴風雨

storm·y [ˋstɔrmɪ] 🎧 *Track 4597*
adj. 暴風雨的

sto·ry [ˋstorɪ] 🎧 *Track 4598*
n. 故事

sto·ry·tell·er [ˋstorɪ͵tɛlɚ] 🎧 *Track 4599*
n. 講故事的人；說書人；短篇小說作家；【口】說謊者
▶Uncle James is a good storyteller.
詹姆士叔叔是個很會說故事的人。

stove [stov] 🎧 *Track 4600*
n. 火爐；爐灶

straight [stret] 🎧 *Track 4601*
adv. 直地；直接地；正直坦率地；**adj.** 筆直的；平直的；正直坦率的

strange [strendʒ] 🎧 *Track 4602*
adj. 奇怪的；奇妙的；陌生的；生疏的

strang·er [ˋstrendʒɚ] 🎧 *Track 4603*
n. 陌生人

strat·e·gy [ˋstrætədʒɪ] 🎧 *Track 4604*
n. 戰略，策略，計謀，對策
▶We need to come up with a great marketing strategy to sell our new product.
我們必須想出一個絕佳的行銷策略來銷售我們的新產品。

straw [strɔ] 🎧 *Track 4605*
n. 吸管

straw·ber·ry [ˋstrɔbɛrɪ] 🎧 *Track 4606*
n. 草莓

stream [strim] 🎧 *Track 4607*
n. 溪；溪流

street [strit] 🎧 *Track 4608*
n. 街道；馬路

strength [strɛŋθ] 🎧 *Track 4609*
n. 力；力量
▶We expect to see our business go from strength to strength.
我們希望能看到我們的事業日漸壯大。

補充片語

go from strength to strength 日益壯大

strength·en [ˋstrɛŋθən] 🎧 *Track 4610*
v. 加強，增強，鞏固
▶Good sleep, healthy food and regular exercise can help you strengthen your immune system. 良好的睡眠、健康的食物和規律的運動有助你增強免疫力。

補充片語

immune system 免疫系統

stress [strɛs] 🎧 *Track 4611*
v. 強調；著重；**n.** 壓力；著重；重要性

stretch [strɛtʃ] 🎧 *Track 4612*
v. 伸直；伸展；延伸
▶There is not enough space on the plane for you to stretch your legs.
在飛機上沒有足夠的空間可以讓你伸直雙腳。

n. 伸長，伸展；過度使用

※灰色單字為英檢初級必備單字

▶ I'll work at full stretch to get the work done by the deadline.
我會為了在期限前完成工作而全力以赴。

(補充片語)
at full stretch 竭盡全力，全力以赴

(相關片語)
stretch one's legs 散步，走動，遛遛腿
▶ We went out to stretch our legs after dinner. 我們晚餐後出去外頭走走。

strict [strɪkt] 🎧 *Track 4613*
adj. 嚴格的；嚴厲的
▶ He is very strict with his three kids.
他對他的三個孩子很嚴格。

strike [straɪk] 🎧 *Track 4614*
v. 打；擊；**n.** 打擊；攻擊；空襲；罷工

string [strɪŋ] 🎧 *Track 4615*
n. 細繩；線；一串
▶ He tied the letters up with a piece of string. 他用一條繩子把信綑起來。

v. （用線）串，綁，束，串起；上弦；伸展，拉直；使振奮；戲弄
▶ He has to have his guitar strung before he can play it. 他得先讓吉他上弦才能彈奏。

strip [strɪp] 🎧 *Track 4616*
n. 條，帶，細長片；一行，一列
▶ He cut the colored paper into strips and used them to decorate the party.
他將色紙剪成條狀，並用它們來佈置派對。

v. 剝去，剝奪；刪除；使成細條
▶ You can't strip your child of his right to education even if you're his father. 既便你是他的父親，也不能剝奪他受教育的權利。

strive [straɪv] 🎧 *Track 4617*
v. 努力；苦幹
▶ The workers are striving for better welfares. 工人們正在爭取更好的福利。

stroke [strok] 🎧 *Track 4618*
n. 打，擊，敲；（划船或游泳的）一划；（網球等）一抽；（病）突發；中風；突然的一擊，一下子

▶ The factory worker won the lottery in a huge stroke of luck. 這工廠工人在一次天大的意外好運中贏得了樂透。

(補充片語)
a stroke of luck 意外的好運

v. （用手）撫，摸，捻；踢，擊；輕拂
▶ He stroked the dog gently.
他輕輕地摸了摸狗。

(相關片語)
not do a stroke of work 什麼工作都不做
▶ I don't know why we hire him if he doesn't do a stroke of work. 如果他什麼活都不幹，我不知道我們為什麼要雇用他。

strong [strɔŋ] 🎧 *Track 4619*
adj. 強壯的；強健的；堅強的；濃烈的

struc·ture [ˋstrʌktʃɚ] 🎧 *Track 4620*
n. 結構，構造；組織；構造體
▶ Family structure in modern society has greatly changed over the last few decades. 現代社會的家庭結構在過去幾十年有很大的改變。

v. 構造，組織；安排；建造，使成體系
▶ He can't even structure his article, let alone write a novel. 他甚至連組織文章結構都不會，更別說是要寫一本小說了。

(補充片語)
let alone 更不必說

strug·gle [ˋstrʌgl] 🎧 *Track 4621*
n. 奮鬥；鬥爭；難事；**v.** 奮鬥；掙扎；艱難地行徑；對抗

stub·born [ˋstʌbɚn] 🎧 *Track 4622*
adj. 倔強的；頑固的
▶ He is very stubborn and won't change his mind easily. 他非常頑固，不會輕易改變心意。

stu·dent [ˋstjudnt] 🎧 *Track 4623*
n. 學生

stu·di·o [ˋstjudɪˏo] 🎧 *Track 4624*
n. （畫家等的）工作室；畫室
▶ We are going to interview the fashion designer in his studio.
我們要在服裝設計師的工作室訪問他。

stud·y [`stʌdɪ] 🎧 Track 4625
n. 學習；研究；課題；**v.** 學習；研究；用功

stuff [stʌf] 🎧 Track 4626
n. 東西，物品
▶ My landlord threw my stuff out of the apartment after I missed three months of rent. 在我三個月沒繳房租後，房東便把我的東西丟出公寓。

v. 裝，填，塞；把……裝滿；使……吃得過飽
▶ His nose is stuffed up. 他的鼻子塞住了。

stu·pid [`stjupɪd] 🎧 Track 4627
adj. 笨的；愚蠢的

style [staɪl] 🎧 Track 4628
n. 風格；文體；流行款式；式樣

sub·ject [`sʌbdʒɪkt] 🎧 Track 4629
adj. 易受……的；以……為條件的
▶ She has been subject to stomachaches in recent years. 她最近這幾年容易胃痛。

v. 使隸屬，使服從；使蒙受
▶ My grandfather speaks fluent Japanese because he was subjected to Japanese education when Taiwan was under Japanese rule. 我爺爺會說流利的日語，是因為他在台灣受日本統治時接受日本教育。

n. 主題
▶ What subject will we talk about today? 我們今天要談什麼主題？

sub·ma·rine [`sʌbmə‚rin] 🎧 Track 4630
n. 潛艇；海底生物；水下裝置
▶ One of our naval vessels was attacked by an enemy submarine. 我們有一艘軍艦遭到敵軍潛艇的襲擊。

adj. 海底的；水下的
▶ The mission to repair the damaged submarine cables is accomplished. 修復受損海底纜線的任務已經完成了。

相關片語
submarine sandwich 潛艇型三明治
▶ I'd like a beef submarine sandwich and large coke, please. 請給我一個牛肉潛艇堡，和一杯大杯可樂。

sub·stance [`sʌbstəns] 🎧 Track 4631
n. 物質，實質；本旨，要義；財產，財物
▶ A research shows that gutter oil contains poisonous substances that can lead to stomach and liver cancer. 一項研究顯示，地溝油含有會導致胃癌及肝癌的有毒物質。

sub·sti·tute [`sʌbstə‚tjut] 🎧 Track 4632
n. 代替人；代替物；代用品
▶ Honey is a good substitute for sugar. 蜂蜜是糖的良好替代品。

v. 用……代替；代替
▶ Jeremy will substitute as your supervisor while Mr. Chen is on leave. 陳主任休假期間，傑瑞米將會是你們的代任直屬主管。

相關片語
substitute teacher 代課老師
▶ I think our substitute teacher teaches better than Ms. Wang. 我覺得我們的代課老師教得比王老師好。

sub·tract [səb`trækt] 🎧 Track 4633
v. 減；減去
▶ If you subtract two from five, you will have three. 如果你將五減去二，就會得到三。

sub·urb [`sʌbɝb] 🎧 Track 4634
n. （城市周圍的）近郊住宅區（或村，鎮），郊區
▶ We can only afford a house in the suburbs. 我們只買得起郊區的房子。

sub·way [`sʌb‚we] 🎧 Track 4635
=un·der·ground
=tube (英式英語) =MRT=me·tro
n. 地下鐵

suc·ceed [sək`sid] 🎧 Track 4636
v. 成功；取得成功

suc·cess [sək`sɛs] 🎧 Track 4637
n. 成功

suc·cess·ful [sək`sɛsfəl] 🎧 Track 4638
adj. 成功的

※灰色單字為英檢初級必備單字

such [sʌtʃ] *Track 4639*
adj. 如此的

suck [sʌk] *Track 4640*
v. 吸;吮;啜
▶ Stop sucking your fingers. You're too old to do that. 別再吸手指了。你年紀已經大得不適合那麼做了。

相關片語

teach one's grandmother to suck eggs 班門弄斧
▶ Giving medical advice to a doctor is like teaching your grandmother to suck eggs. 給一個醫生醫學建議,簡直就是班門弄斧。

sud·den [`sʌdn] *Track 4641*
adj. 突然的

sud·den·ly [`sʌdnlɪ] *Track 4642*
adv. 忽然

suf·fer [`sʌfɚ] *Track 4643*
v. 遭受;經歷
▶ The country is suffering a cruel war. 這個國家正在經歷殘酷的戰爭。

suf·fer·ing [`sʌfərɪŋ] *Track 4644*
n. (身體或精神上的)痛苦;勞苦;苦難的經歷;令人痛苦的事
▶ Chemotherapy at end of life will cause great suffering for cancer patients. 生命末期的化療會為癌症病人帶來極大的痛苦。

suf·fi·cient [sə`fɪʃənt] *Track 4645*
adj. 足夠的,充分的;有充分能力的
▶ Make sure we have sufficient food for our guests. 我們務必要為賓客準備充足的食物。

sug·ar [`ʃʊgɚ] *Track 4646*
n. 糖

sug·gest [sə`dʒɛst] *Track 4647*
v. 建議

sug·ges·tion [sə`dʒɛstʃən] *Track 4648*
n. 建議;提議
▶ I will take your suggestion into consideration. 我會將你的建議納入考慮。

補充片語

take sth. into consideration 將某事納入考慮;考慮到某事

su·i·cide [`suə͵saɪd] *Track 4649*
n. 自殺
▶ She attemped suicide after her boyfriend left her. 在男友離開她後,她企圖自殺。

相關片語

commit suicide 自殺
▶ He believes that people who commit suicide will not go to heaven. 他認為自殺的人不能上天堂。

suit [sut] *Track 4650*
n. (一套)西裝;套;組;**v.** 適合;與……相配;使適合

suit·a·ble [`sutəbl] *Track 4651*
adj. 適當的
▶ I am looking for a suitable outfit for my job interview. 我正在找一套適合穿去工作面試的服裝。

suit·case [`sut͵kes] *Track 4652*
n. 小型行李箱,手提箱
▶ You have to check in this suitcase, because it's too big for the overhead compartment. 你必須託運這個行李箱,因為它太大了,沒辦法放進艙頂置物箱。

補充片語

overhead compartment (飛機上的)艙頂置物箱

sum [sʌm] *Track 4653*
n. 總數,總和;一筆(金額)
▶ He donated a large sum of money to charities. 他捐了一大筆錢給慈善機構。
v. 計算……的總和;總結,概括
▶ His annual salary sums up to two million NT dollars. 他的年薪總計有兩百萬新台幣。

補充片語

annual salary 年薪;
sum up 計算,總計

sum·mar·ize [`sʌmə͵raɪz] *Track 4654*
v. 總結,概括,概述

▶ The chairman summarized our discussion before he dismissed the meeting.
主席在散會前，總結了我們的討論內容。

sum·ma·ry [`sʌmərɪ] 🎧 Track 4655
n. 總結，摘要
▶ Here's the summary of our discussion.
這是我們討論的摘要內容。

sum·mer [`sʌmə] 🎧 Track 4656
n. 夏天

sum·mit [`sʌmɪt] 🎧 Track 4657
n. 尖峰，峰頂；最高官階，最高級會議
▶ This year's APEC summit will be held in Manila, Philippines.
今年的亞洲太平洋經濟合作組織高峰會將會在菲律賓的馬尼拉舉行。

(補充片語)
APEC= Asia-Pacific Economic Cooperation
亞洲太平洋經濟合作組織

sun [sʌn] 🎧 Track 4658
n. 太陽；日

sun·bathe [`sʌn‚beð] 🎧 Track 4659
v. 沐日光浴
▶ There are many nude people sunbathing on the beach.
海灘上有許多裸著身子的人在做日光浴。

Sun·day [`sʌnde] =Sun. 🎧 Track 4660
n. 星期天

sun·light [`sʌn‚laɪt] 🎧 Track 4661
n. 日光，陽光
▶ Let's go take a walk in the morning sunlight. 我們在清晨的陽光下散個步吧。

sun·ny [`sʌnɪ] 🎧 Track 4662
adj. 晴天的

sun·rise [`sʌn‚raɪz] 🎧 Track 4663
n. 日出；日出時間；日出景象
▶ They will depart at sunrise tomorrow.
他們明天日出時就會啟程離開。

sun·set [`sʌn‚sɛt] 🎧 Track 4664
n. 日落；日落時分；日落景象

▶ We sat on the beach and watched the sunset. 我們坐在海灘上欣賞日落。

su·per [`supə] 🎧 Track 4665
adj. 特級的；特佳的；極度的；**adv.** 非常；極度

su·perb [su`pɝb] 🎧 Track 4666
adj. 極好的，一流的
▶ Their performance was superb.
他們的表現一流。

su·pe·ri·or [sə`pɪrɪə] 🎧 Track 4667
adj. （在職位，地位等方面）較高的；較好的，較優秀的；高傲的，有優越感的
▶ Men are not necessarily superior to women in many ways.
男人在很多方面並不一定比女人強。

n. 上司；長輩；佔優勢者
▶ As a pianist, he has no superior in this country.
作為一個鋼琴家，國內沒有人比他厲害。

su·per·mar·ket [`supə‚markɪt] 🎧 Track 4668
n. 超級市場

su·per·vi·sor [‚supə`vaɪzə] 🎧 Track 4669
n. 監督人；管理人；指導者
▶ You can't take a leave without your supervisor's permission.
沒有直屬主管的同意，你不能休假。

sup·per [`sʌpə] =din·ner 🎧 Track 4670
n. 晚餐

sup·ply [sə`plaɪ] 🎧 Track 4671
n. 供應；供給；生活用品；補給品；**v.** 供應；提供

sup·port [sə`port] 🎧 Track 4672
n. 支持；**v.** 支持；資助；撫養

Aa
Bb
Cc
Dd
Ee
Ff
Gg
Hh
Ii
Jj
Kk
Ll
Mm
Nn
Oo
Pp
Qq
Rr
Ss
Tt
Uu
Vv
Ww
Xx
Yy
Zz

sup·port·er [sə`portɚ] 🎧 Track 4673
n. 支持者；擁護者；支援者；扶養者，贍養者
▶Both my husband and I are strong supporters of same-sex marriage.
我和我先生都是同性婚姻的支持者。

sup·pose [sə`poz] 🎧 Track 4674
v. 猜想
▶I suppose he is still single.
我猜他現在仍然是單身。

sup·posed [sə`pozd] 🎧 Track 4675
aux. 期望，認為必須
▶Parents are supposed to set good examples for their children.
父母應該要為孩子建立好榜樣。

adj. 假定的，假設的，想像的，被信以為真的
▶She married the man only because he was the supposed heir to his father's fortune. 她之所以嫁給那男人，僅是因為他是他父親財產的當然繼承人。

su·preme [sə`prim] 🎧 Track 4676
adj. 最高的，至上的；最大的，極度的
▶That is absolutely a decision of supreme stupidity. 那絕對是一個愚蠢至極的決定。

sure [ʃʊr] 🎧 Track 4677
adj. 確信的；一定的；**adv.** 的確；當然

sure·ly [`ʃʊrlɪ] 🎧 Track 4678
adv. 確實，無疑，一定；想必
▶The children surely had a great time at the beach.
孩子們肯定是在海灘玩得很開心。

surf [sɝf] 🎧 Track 4679
n. 拍岸浪花；**v.** 衝浪；在網路上或電視上搜索資料或快速地看

sur·face [`sɝfɪs] 🎧 Track 4680
n. 表面；外表

surf·ing [`sɝfɪŋ] 🎧 Track 4681
n. 作衝浪運動

▶Many people like to go surfing in the summer. 很多人夏天喜歡去衝浪。

sur·geon [`sɝdʒən] 🎧 Track 4682
n. 外科醫生
▶The dental surgeon suggested the man to have the top row of his teeth replaced with implants.
那名牙醫建議男子將他上排牙齒換成植牙。

（補充片語）
dental surgeon=dentist 牙醫

sur·ge·ry [`sɝdʒərɪ] 🎧 Track 4683
n. 外科；外科醫學
▶The surgeon suggested that he should have the brain surgery.
那名外科醫生建議他動腦部手術。

sur·prise [sə`praɪz] 🎧 Track 4684
n. 驚喜；驚訝；**v.** 使驚喜；使驚訝

sur·prised [sə`praɪzd] 🎧 Track 4685
adj. 感到驚喜的；感到驚訝的

sur·ren·der [sə`rɛndɚ] 🎧 Track 4686
v. 使投降，使自首；交出，放棄；屈服
▶The murderer's mother talked him into surrendering himself to the police.
殺人犯的母親勸他向警方自首。

（補充片語）
talk sb. into doing sth. 勸某人做某事；
surrender oneself to 自首，向……投降

n. 投降，屈服，自首
▶In order to reduce casualties, they decided to make an unconditional surrender.
為了減少傷亡，他們決定無條件投降。

sur·round [sə`raʊnd] 🎧 Track 4687
v. 圍繞，圍住；包圍；大量供給
▶The armed suspect has been surrounded by police.
該名持有武器的嫌犯已經遭到警方的包圍。

n. 圍繞物
▶I bought a silk blue tablecloth with white lace surround at the flea market.
我在跳蚤市場買了一張鑲有白色蕾絲邊的絲質藍色桌巾。

sur·round·ings
[sə`raʊndɪŋz]
🎧 *Track 4688*

n. 環境；周圍的事物，周圍的情況
▶ The man looked around at his surroundings. 男子看了看周圍的環境。

---

sur·vey [sə`ve]
🎧 *Track 4689*

n. 調查，調查報告；民意調查
▶ A recent survey reveals that nearly 45% of husbands in this country don't share housework with their wives.
最近一份調查報告顯示，這個國家內有近百分之四十五的丈夫不會跟妻子分擔家務。

v. 俯視，眺望，環視；全面考察；審視，檢驗；調查
▶ The authority will send someone to survey the typhoon damage today. 有關單位今天會派員過來調查颱風受損的情況。

---

sur·viv·al [sə`vaɪvl]
🎧 *Track 4690*

n. 倖存，殘存；倖存者
▶ The boy is the only survival of the car crash. 那個男孩是車禍唯一的倖存者。

---

sur·vive [sə`vaɪv]
🎧 *Track 4691*

v. 活下來；倖存

---

sus·pect [sə`spɛkt]
🎧 *Track 4692*

v. 察覺；懷疑
▶ The police suspected that the man murdered his neighbor.
警方懷疑該男子殺了他的鄰居。

n. 嫌疑犯，可疑分子
▶ It's a relief to know that the suspect is under arrest.
知道嫌犯已經被逮捕讓人鬆了一口氣。

adj. 可疑的，受到懷疑的，不可信的
▶ The man's words are suspect.
那男人所說的話很可疑。

---

sus·pend [sə`spɛnd]
🎧 *Track 4693*

v. 懸掛；使懸浮；中止；使暫停（職務、活動、學業等）；暫時取消
▶ His attorney's license will be suspended.
他的律師執照會被吊銷。

---

sus·pen·sion [sə`spɛnʃən]
🎧 *Track 4694*

n. 懸掛；暫停，中止；停職，停學；暫緩執行，暫停支付
▶ I was shocked when my son's school informed me about the suspension.
當我兒子的學校跟我聯絡，通知我有關停學的事時，我感到震驚不已。

---

sus·pi·cion [sə`spɪʃən]
🎧 *Track 4695*

n. 懷疑，疑心，猜疑
▶ I have a strong suspicion that my boyfriend is two-timing me.
我強烈懷疑我男友劈腿。

---

sus·pi·cious [sə`spɪʃəs]
🎧 *Track 4696*

adj. 猜疑的，疑心的，多疑的
▶ I am very suspicious of the stranger's intentions. 我非常懷疑那陌生人的意圖。

---

swal·low [`swɑlo]
🎧 *Track 4697*

n. 吞；嚥；**v.** 吞嚥；吞下；忍受

---

swan [swɑn]
🎧 *Track 4698*

n. 天鵝

---

swear [swɛr]
🎧 *Track 4699*

v. 發誓，宣誓；詛咒，罵髒話
▶ I swear that every single word I said was true. 我發誓我說的每句話都是真的。

---

sweat [swɛt]
🎧 *Track 4700*

v. 出汗；使幹苦活；焦慮；吃力對付；剝削
▶ I'm going to the gym to sweat off some weight. 我要去健身房出汗瘦身。

n. 汗，汗水；焦急不安；苦差事
▶ I was all of a sweat. 我滿身大汗。

---

sweat·er [`swɛtə]
🎧 *Track 4701*

n. 毛衣

---

sweep [swip]
🎧 *Track 4702*

v. 掃

---

sweet [swit]
🎧 *Track 4703*

adj. 甜的；**n.** 糖果

---

swell [swɛl]
🎧 *Track 4704*

v. 腫脹；（地）隆起；（水）上漲；增大，增強；情緒高漲；驕傲自大

▶His ankle swelled after he twisted it.
他的腳踝在他扭到後便腫了起來。

n. 鼓起，腫脹；增大，增強；隆起，洶湧
▶China used to enforce the one-child policy to stop the swell in its population.
中國曾經實施一胎化政策以阻止人口膨脹。

swift [swɪft] 🎧 *Track 4705*
adj. 快速的，立即的，（行動）快的
▶You need to make a swift decision.
你必須快速做決定。

n. 雨燕
▶He took the injured swift home.
他將那隻受傷的雨燕帶回家。

swim [swɪm] 🎧 *Track 4706*
v. 游泳

swim·ming [`swɪmɪŋ] 🎧 *Track 4707*
n. 游泳
▶It's important to warm up before swimming.
游泳前暖身是很重要的。

swim·suit [`swɪmsut] 🎧 *Track 4708*
n. 泳衣

swing [swɪŋ] 🎧 *Track 4709*
v. 搖擺；擺動；**n.** 搖擺；擺動；鞦韆

switch [swɪtʃ] 🎧 *Track 4710*
v. 打開或關掉（開關）；為……轉接（電話）；改變；調換，交換
▶Do you mind switching seats with me?
你介意跟我交換座位嗎？

n. 開關；轉轍器；變更，更改；調換，交換
▶He pressed the wrong switch.
他按到錯誤的開關。

sword [sord] 🎧 *Track 4711*
n. 刀，劍
▶The pen is mightier than the sword.
筆比劍更有力量。

syl·la·ble [`sɪləbl] 🎧 *Track 4712*
n. 音節
▶There are four syllables in the word "television". 「television」這個字有四個音節。

sym·bol [`sɪmbl] 🎧 *Track 4713*
n. 象徵；標誌；記號

sym·bol·ize [`sɪmbl͵aɪz] 🎧 *Track 4714*
v. 象徵，標誌；用符號表示
▶Dogs symbolize loyalty. 狗象徵忠心。

sym·pa·thet·ic [͵sɪmpə`θɛtɪk] 🎧 *Track 4715*
adj. 同情的，有同情心的；贊同的，支持的
▶She is sympathetic to those orphans.
她很同情那些孤兒。

sym·pa·thize [`sɪmpə͵θaɪz] 🎧 *Track 4716*
v. 同情，憐憫；體諒，支持
▶We sympathized with the boy.
我們十分同情那個男孩。

sym·pa·thy [`sɪmpəθɪ] 🎧 *Track 4717*
n. 同情，同情心；同感；慰問，弔唁
▶I have no sympathy for the liar at all.
我一點也不同情那個騙子。

sym·pho·ny [`sɪmfənɪ] 🎧 *Track 4718*
n. 交響樂，交響曲
▶My brother is in a symphony orchestra.
我哥哥在一個交響樂團裡。

symp·tom [`sɪmptəm] 🎧 *Track 4719*
n. 症狀；徵兆
▶The symptoms of dengue fever are similar to those of the flu.
登革熱的症狀跟流行性感冒的症狀很像。

syr·up [`sɪrəp] 🎧 *Track 4720*
n. 糖漿；果汁
▶I like to have pancakes with syrup.
我喜歡吃鬆餅沾糖漿。

sys·tem [`sɪstəm] 🎧 *Track 4721*
n. 系統；制度

sys·te·mat·ic [͵sɪstə`mætɪk] 🎧 *Track 4722*
adj. 有系統的；徹底的，有條理的
▶The reporter made a systematic research.
該記者做了徹底的研究。

Tt

通過中級英文檢定者的英文能力：

在日常生活中，能聽懂一般的會話；能大致聽懂公共場所廣播、氣象報告及廣告等。在工作時，能聽懂簡易的產品介紹與操作說明。能大致聽懂外籍人士的談話及詢問。

在日常生活中，能閱讀短文、故事、私人信件、廣告、傳單、簡介及使用說明等。在工作時，能閱讀工作須知、公告、操作手冊、例行的文件、傳真、電報等。

能寫簡單的書信、故事及心得等。對於熟悉且與個人經歷相關的主題，能以簡易的文字表達。

在日常生活中，能以簡易英語交談或描述一般事物，能介紹自己的生活作息、工作、家庭、經歷等，並可對一般話題陳述看法。在工作時，能進行簡單的答詢，並與外籍人士交談溝通。

本書除包含官方公佈的中級4,947單字外，更精挑了近400個滿分必學的高手單字。同時，在片語的挑選、例句的使用上，皆依上述英檢官方公佈之能力範疇做設計，難度適中、不偏離考試主題。發音部分則是自然發音＆KK音標雙管齊下，搭配MP3以「分解／完整」方式錄音，給你最多元有效的學習手段，怎麼記都可以，想忘掉都好難！

ta·ble [`tebl] 　　　　🎧 Track 4723
n. 桌子；餐桌

ta·ble·cloth [`tebl͵klɔθ] 🎧 Track 4724
n. 桌巾，桌布
▶ Coffee stained the tablecloth.
咖啡把桌布給弄髒了。

tab·let [`tæblɪt] 　　🎧 Track 4725
n. 藥片
▶ He took a sleeping tablet before going to bed. 他在上床睡覺前吃了顆安眠藥片。

相關片語
tablet computer　平板電腦
▶ He carries his tablet computer with him to work. 他帶著他的平板電腦去上班。

tack [tæk] 　　　　　　🎧 Track 4726
n. 大頭釘，圖釘；行動步驟，方針
▶ Our plan didn't work. We need to try a different tack.
我們的計劃行不通。我們得試試不同的辦法。

v. 用平頭釘釘
▶ He tacked the notice on the bulletin board. 他把公告用平頭釘釘在佈告欄上。

tag [tæg] 　　　　　　🎧 Track 4727
n. 牌子，標籤
▶ Any item with a yellow tag is 50% off today.
任何有黃色標籤的商品今日都是五折優惠。

v. 給……加標籤；添加，附加；給……加罪名
▶ The boy was tagged as a troublemaker.
這男孩被貼上麻煩製造者的標籤。

Tai·chung [`taɪ`tʃʊŋ] 🎧 Track 4728
n. 台中

tail [tel] 　　　　　　🎧 Track 4729
n. 尾巴；尾部；尾狀物

tai·lor [`telə] 　　　🎧 Track 4730
n. （男）裁縫師；服裝店
▶ The tailor decided to make his daughter's wedding dress by himself.
裁縫師決定自己製作女兒的結婚禮服。

v. 裁縫；做裁縫；修改
▶ The suit is well tailored. 這套西裝做得很好。

Tai·nan [ˋtaɪˋnɑn]　　　🎧 *Track 4731*
n. 台南

Tai·wan [ˋtaɪˋwɑn]　　　🎧 *Track 4732*
n. 台灣

Tai·wan·ese [ˌtaɪwɑˋniz]　🎧 *Track 4733*
adj. 台灣的；台灣人的；**n.** 台灣人；台灣話

take [tek]　　　　　🎧 *Track 4734*
v. 拿；取；帶去；接受；承擔；花費；占用

tale [tel]　　　　　🎧 *Track 4735*
n. 故事，傳說；謊話，捏造的話；閒話
▶ Prince Charming only exists in fairy tales.
白馬王子只會在童話故事裡出現。

（補充片語）

fairy tale 童話故事

tal·ent [ˋtælənt]　　　🎧 *Track 4736*
n. 天賦；能力

tal·ent·ed [ˋtæləntɪd]　　🎧 *Track 4737*
adj. 有天分的，有天才的；有才能的
▶ Jennifer is a talented violinist.
珍妮佛是個有天分的小提琴手。

talk [tɔk]　　　　　🎧 *Track 4738*
v. 說話；**n.** 談話；交談

talk·a·tive [ˋtɔkətɪv]　　🎧 *Track 4739*
adj. 喜歡說話的；多嘴的；健談的

tall [tɔl]　　　　　🎧 *Track 4740*
adj. 高的

tame [tem]　　　　　🎧 *Track 4741*
adj. 經過馴養的，馴服的；溫順的；
聽使喚的
▶ The dog is tame. He won't bite you.
這狗很溫馴。牠不會咬你的。

v. 馴化，馴服；制服，使順從
▶ He hired an expert to help him tame the fierce dog.
他請了一個專家來幫他馴服這隻兇猛的狗。

tan·ge·rine [ˋtændʒəˌrin]　🎧 *Track 4742*
n. 橘子

tank [tæŋk]　　　　🎧 *Track 4743*
n.（貯水、油、氣的）箱、櫃、槽

tap [tæp]　　　　　🎧 *Track 4744*
v. 裝上塞子；裝竊聽器；接通（電源或水源）
▶ He didn't know his telephone had been tapped. 他不知道他的電話被裝了竊聽器。

n. 龍頭，閥門；（酒桶的）塞子；竊聽器
▶ Don't drink the tap water unless it has been boiled. 不要喝沒有沸煮過的自來水。

（補充片語）

tap water 自來水

tape [tep]　　　　　🎧 *Track 4745*
n.（錄音或錄影）磁帶；膠布；膠帶；**v.** 用膠布貼牢；將⋯⋯錄音；將⋯⋯錄影

tar·get [ˋtɑrgɪt]　　　🎧 *Track 4746*
n.（欲達到的）目標；（攻擊、批評、嘲笑的）對象；**v.** 以⋯⋯為目標；以⋯⋯為對象

task [tæsk]　　　　　🎧 *Track 4747*
n. 任務；差事；作業

taste [test]　　　　🎧 *Track 4748*
n. 味覺；味道；滋味；一口；**v.** 嚐；嚐到；嚐起來；吃起來

tast·y [ˋtestɪ]　　　　🎧 *Track 4749*
adj. 美味的，可口的；高雅的，大方的；性感的，誘人的
▶ That is the tastiest peach pie I've ever had. 那真是我吃過最美味的桃子派。

tax [tæks]　　　　　🎧 *Track 4750*
n. 稅，稅金
▶ It is citizens' obligation to pay taxes.
納稅是公民的義務。

v. 向⋯⋯課稅；收費；使負
▶ Cigarettes are one of the most heavily taxed consumer goods in this country.
香菸是這個國家稅被課得最重的消費品之一。

（補充片語）

consumer goods 消費品

tax·i [ˋtæksɪ] 　🎧 *Track 4751*
=tax·i·cab=cab
n. 計程車

tea [ti] 　🎧 *Track 4752*
n. 茶

teach [titʃ] 　🎧 *Track 4753*
v. 教學；教導

teach·er [ˋtitʃɚ] 　🎧 *Track 4754*
n. 老師

Teach·er's Day 　🎧 *Track 4755*
[ˋtitʃɚz-de]
n. 教師節

team [tim] 　🎧 *Track 4756*
n. 隊；隊伍

tea·pot [ˋtiˏpɑt] 　🎧 *Track 4757*
n. 茶壺

tear [tɛr] 　🎧 *Track 4758*
n. 眼淚；**v.** 撕開；拔掉；扯破

tease [tiz] 　🎧 *Track 4759*
v. 戲弄，逗弄；取笑
▶My friends teased me about my new hair all day. 我朋友一整天都在取笑我的新髮型。

n. 戲弄，取笑；愛戲弄人的人；賣弄風騷的女孩
▶Don't be such a tease, tell me the answer to the riddle.
別這麼戲弄人，告訴我謎題的答案吧。

tech·ni·cal [ˋtɛknɪkl] 　🎧 *Track 4760*
adj. 技術的，科技的；專門的，技術性的
▶My son graduated from a local technical college. 我兒子畢業於本地的一間技術學院。

tech·ni·cian [tɛkˋnɪʃən] 　🎧 *Track 4761*
n. 技術人員，技師，技術精湛者
▶The technician is trying to fix the problem.
這個技術人員正嘗試著找出問題。

tech·no·lo·gi·cal 　🎧 *Track 4762*
[tɛknəˋlɑdʒɪkl]
adj. 技術（學）的，工藝（學）的；因新技術而造成的

▶The police have been investigating this highly technological crime for quite some time.
警方已經調查這起高科技犯罪案件相當長的一段時間了。

(補充片語)
highly technological crime 高科技犯罪

tech·nol·o·gy 　🎧 *Track 4763*
[tɛkˋnɑlədʒɪ]
n. 工藝，技術，科技
▶Modern technology has greatly affected our lives.
現代科技大大地影響了我們的生活。

teen [tin] 　🎧 *Track 4764*
n. 十幾歲；青少年
▶My three children are all in their teens.
我三個孩子現在都十幾歲了。

adj. 十幾歲的，十幾的；青少年的
▶The teen pop group is very popular at present.
這支青少年流行音樂團體現在非常受歡迎。

teen·age [ˋtinˏedʒ] 　🎧 *Track 4765*
adj. 十幾歲的；青春期的
▶Sometimes I have no idea how to communicate with my teenage son. 有時候我不知道該如何跟我青春期的兒子溝通。

teen·ag·er [ˋtinˏedʒɚ] 　🎧 *Track 4766*
n. 青少年

tel·e·gram [ˋtɛləˏgræm] 　🎧 *Track 4767*
n. 電報
▶I will dispatch a telegram to you as soon as I arrive there.
我一到那裡就打電報給你。

tel·e·phone [ˋtɛləˏfon] 　🎧 *Track 4768*
=phone
n. 電話；**v.** 打電話給；打電話告知

tel·e·scope [ˋtɛləˏskop] 　🎧 *Track 4769*
n. （單筒）望遠鏡
▶He watched the stars through his telescope.
他透過天文望遠鏡來觀星。

※灰色單字為英檢初級必備單字

tel·e·vise [ˈtɛləˌvaɪz] 🎧 *Track 4770*
v. 電視播送；播送電視節目
▶ The talk show will be televised live every Saturday night.
這個脫口秀節目將會於每個週六晚上在電視上播出。

tel·e·vi·sion [ˈtɛləˌvɪʒən] 🎧 *Track 4771*
=TV
n. 電視；電視機

tell [tɛl] 🎧 *Track 4772*
v. 告訴；講述；吩咐

tem·per [ˈtɛmpɚ] 🎧 *Track 4773*
n. 情緒；性情，脾氣
▶ My wife lost her temper easily during her pregnancy.
我太太在懷孕期間很容易發脾氣。

(補充片語)
lose one's temper 發脾氣

v. 鍛鍊；調和，捏和（黏土）；使溫和，使緩和
▶ The teacher tempered her criticism of the student's term paper by complimenting her effort.
老師藉由稱讚學生的努力，來緩和她對其學期研究報告的批評。

tem·pera·ture 🎧 *Track 4774*
[ˈtɛmprətʃɚ]
n. 溫度；氣溫；體溫

tem·ple [ˈtɛmpl̩] 🎧 *Track 4775*
n. 廟宇；寺廟；神殿；教堂；禮拜堂

tem·po·ra·ry 🎧 *Track 4776*
[ˈtɛmpəˌrɛrɪ]
adj. 臨時的；暫時的
▶ He earns his living as a temporary worker at a construction site.
他靠在工地當臨時工養活自己。

ten [tɛn] 🎧 *Track 4777*
pron. 十個；**n.** 十；十歲
adj. 十的；十個的

ten·ant [ˈtɛnənt] 🎧 *Track 4778*
n. 房客；承租人；住戶
▶ My tenant hasn't paid his rent for three months. 我的房客已經三個月沒有繳房租了。

tend [tɛnd] 🎧 *Track 4779*
v. 走向，去向；傾向，易於
▶ People who don't eat breakfast tend to get tired. 不吃早餐的人容易疲倦。

ten·den·cy [ˈtɛndənsɪ] 🎧 *Track 4780*
n. 傾向；性向；僻性；趨勢，潮流
▶ She didn't know that her husband has a violent tendency before they married.
她在婚前並不知道她丈夫有暴力傾向。

(補充片語)
violent tendency 暴力傾向

ten·der [ˈtɛndɚ] 🎧 *Track 4781*
adj. 嫩的；敏感的；溫柔的；幼弱的
▶ The mother spoke to her baby with a tender voice.
那個母親用溫柔的聲音跟她的寶寶說話。

ten·nis [ˈtɛnɪs] 🎧 *Track 4782*
n. 網球

tense [tɛns] 🎧 *Track 4783*
adj. 拉緊的，繃緊的
▶ The relationship between the two countries has become tenser.
這兩國之間的關係變得更緊張了。

v. 拉緊，繃緊，變得緊張
▶ His whole body tensed when the teacher called his name.
老師叫他的名字時，他全身都繃緊了。

ten·sion [ˈtɛnʃən] 🎧 *Track 4784*
n. 拉緊，繃緊；緊張，緊張局勢
▶ There is mounting tension between Israelis and Palestinians.
以色列與巴勒斯坦之間的緊張局勢日益升高。

tent [tɛnt] 🎧 *Track 4785*
n. 帳篷

term [tɝm] 🎧 *Track 4786*
n. 學期；任期；期限；條款；關係

ter·mi·nal [ˈtɝ·mənl] 🎧 *Track 4787*
n. 末端，終點，極限；總站；航空站，航廈
▶ My flight will depart from Terminal 2.
我的班機會從第二航廈出境。

adj. 末端的，終點的；末期的，晚期的；每期的
▶ He was awfully shocked when he was diagnosed with terminal liver cancer.
被診斷出罹患末期肝癌時，他震驚萬分。

ter·ri·ble [ˈtɛrəbl] 🎧 *Track 4788*
adj. 可怕的；嚇人的；令人不快的；極糟糕的

ter·rif·ic [təˈrɪfɪk] 🎧 *Track 4789*
adj. 可怕的；嚇人的；非常好的

ter·ri·fy [ˈtɛrəˌfaɪ] 🎧 *Track 4790*
v. 使害怕
▶ The scary-looking man terrified the little girl. 那個長相嚇人的男子嚇壞了小女孩。

ter·ri·to·ry [ˈtɛrəˌtorɪ] 🎧 *Track 4791*
n. 領土，版圖；（知識的）領域，（行動的）範圍
▶ Photography is totally outside my territory.
我對攝影領域完全是個外行。

（補充片語）
outside one's territory 不是某人的內行領域

ter·ror [ˈtɛrɚ] 🎧 *Track 4792*
n. 恐怖，驚駭；引起恐怖的人或事物；恐怖行動，恐怖統治；極討厭的人
▶ The man is the terror of the neighborhood.
那個男人是這附近地區的恐怖人物。

（相關片語）
anti-terror campaign 反恐活動，反恐戰役
▶ More and more countries publicly supported the anti-terror campaign.
越來越多國家公開支持這個反恐活動。

test [tɛst] 🎧 *Track 4793*
n. 試驗；測驗；小考；**v.** 測試；檢驗

text [tɛkst] 🎧 *Track 4794*
n. 正文；課文，課本；版本；文字；短信息
▶ The full text of the announcement is attached to the mail. 公告的全文已經隨函附上。

text·book [ˈtɛkstˌbʊk] 🎧 *Track 4795*
n. 課本；教科書

than [ðæn] 🎧 *Track 4796*
conj. 比；比較；與其；除了……之外
prep. 比起……；超過

thank [θæŋk] 🎧 *Track 4797*
v. 感謝；**n.** 感謝；謝意

thank·ful [ˈθæŋkfəl] 🎧 *Track 4798*
adj. 感謝的
▶ I'm very thankful for all you have done for me. 我非常感謝你為我所做的一切。

Thanks·giv·ing [ˌθæŋksˈgɪvɪŋ] 🎧 *Track 4799*
=Thanks·giv·ing Day
n. 感恩節

that [ðæt] 🎧 *Track 4800*
conj. 因為；由於；為了；引導名詞子句；
pron. 那個；那人；**adj.** 那個；**adv.** 那樣

that's [ðæts] 🎧 *Track 4801*
abbr. 那是（that is的縮寫）

the [ðə] 🎧 *Track 4802*
art. 這（些）；那（些）

the·at·er [ˈθɪətɚ] 🎧 *Track 4803*
=the·at·re （英式英語）
n. 劇場；電影院

theft [θɛft] 🎧 *Track 4804*
n. 偷竊，盜竊
▶ He was accused of theft and was sentenced to six months in prison.
他被控偷竊，並被判刑六個月監禁。

their [ðɛr] 🎧 *Track 4805*
det. 他們的

theirs [ðɛrz] 🎧 *Track 4806*
pron. 他們的（東西）
▶ You can give advice to your children, but the choice is theirs. 你可以給你的孩子們提供建議，但是選擇權是他們的。

※灰色單字為英檢初級必備單字

them [ðɛm] 🎧 *Track 4807*
pron. 他們

theme [θim] 🎧 *Track 4808*
n. 論題，話題；主題
▶ The theme of this party is love and sharing.
這次派對的主題是愛與分享。

them·selves [ðəmˋsɛlvz] 🎧 *Track 4809*
pron. 他們自己

then [ðɛn] 🎧 *Track 4810*
adv. 那時；然後；**adj.** 當時的

theo·ry [ˋθiərɪ] 🎧 *Track 4811*
n. 學說，理論；意見，揣測
▶ In theory, young children are particularly tough when they are around two years old. 理論上，小孩子在兩歲左右會特別難搞。

(補充片語)

in theory 理論上

ther·a·py [ˋθɛrəpɪ] 🎧 *Track 4812*
n. 治療，療法
▶ My father is undergoing a diet therapy to conquer his illness. 我父親為了戰勝疾病，正在接受一種飲食療法。

there [ðɛr] 🎧 *Track 4813*
adv. 在那裡；到那裡
pron. 那個地方；那裡

there·fore [ˋðɛrˏfor] 🎧 *Track 4814*
adv. 因此

there's [ðɛrz] 🎧 *Track 4815*
abbr. 那裡有（there is 的縮寫）

these [ðiz] 🎧 *Track 4816*
pron. 這些人；這些東西；**adj.** 這些的

they [ðe] 🎧 *Track 4817*
pron. 他們

they'd [ðed] 🎧 *Track 4818*
abbr. 他們會、他們已（they would、they had的縮寫）

they'll [ðel] 🎧 *Track 4819*
abbr. 他們會（they will的縮寫）

they're [ðer] 🎧 *Track 4820*
abbr. 他們是（they are的縮寫）

they've [ðev] 🎧 *Track 4821*
abbr. 他們已（they have 的縮寫）

thick [θɪk] 🎧 *Track 4822*
adj. 厚的；粗的；濃的

thief [θif] 🎧 *Track 4823*
n. 小偷

thin [θɪn] 🎧 *Track 4824*
adj. 瘦的；薄的；稀少的

thing [θɪŋ] 🎧 *Track 4825*
n. 事情；東西

think [θɪŋk] 🎧 *Track 4826*
v. 想；認為；想起；打算

think·ing [ˋθɪŋkɪŋ] 🎧 *Track 4827*
n. 思想，思考
▶ I need a few days to do some thinking.
我需要幾天思考一下。

adj. 思想的，有理性的，好思考的
▶ Any thinking person wouldn't give up such a good opportunity. 任何有腦子的人都不會放棄這樣的一個好機會。

third [θɝd] 🎧 *Track 4828*
adj. 第三的；三分之一；**adv.** 第三；**n.** 第三名；三分之一

thirst [θɝst] 🎧 *Track 4829*
n. 渴，口渴；渴望
▶ Bring some water with you if you don't want to die of thirst.
如果你不想渴死，就帶一些水在身上。

v. 口渴；渴望
▶ To me, those who thirst for wealth instead of health are very stupid.
對我來說，那些渴望財富而非健康的人，是非常愚蠢的。

thirst·y [`θɝstɪ] 🎧 *Track 4830*
adj. 渴的；口渴的；渴望的

thir·teen [`θɝˈtin] 🎧 *Track 4831*
pron. 十三個；**n.** 十三；十三個；十三歲；
adj. 十三的；十三個的

thir·ty [`θɝtɪ] 🎧 *Track 4832*
pron. 三十個；**n.** 三十；**adj.** 三十的

this [ðɪs] 🎧 *Track 4833*
pron. 這個；**adj.** 這個
adv. 這麼；像這樣地

thor·ough [`θɝo] 🎧 *Track 4834*
adj. 徹底的
▶ The doctor suggested that he should have a thorough health examination.
醫生建議他做個徹底的健康檢查。

those [ðoz] 🎧 *Track 4835*
pron. 那些；**adj.** 那些的

though [ðo] 🎧 *Track 4836*
conj. 雖然；儘管；**adv.** 然而；還是

thought [θɔt] 🎧 *Track 4837*
n. 思維；想法；考慮

thought·ful [`θɔtfəl] 🎧 *Track 4838*
adj. 深思的，沉思的；經認真思考的；細心的，體貼周到的
▶ It was very thoughtful of you to do so.
你這麼做真的是很體貼周到。

thou·sand [`θaʊznd] 🎧 *Track 4839*
pron. 千個；**n.** 一千；一千個；**adj.** 一千的；成千的；無數的

thread [θrɛd] 🎧 *Track 4840*
n. 線，線狀物；頭緒
▶ I will not give up as long as there is a thread of hope. 只要有一線希望，我就不會放棄。
v. 穿（針線），把……穿成一串；通過，穿透過
▶ My grandmother has very poor eyesight, so she is unable to thread the needle by herself. 我奶奶視力很差，沒辦法自己穿針。

threat [θrɛt] 🎧 *Track 4841*
n. 威脅，恐嚇；構成威脅的人或事物
▶ He betrayed his country under the threat of death.
他在死亡的威脅下出賣了自己的國家。

threat·en [`θrɛtn] 🎧 *Track 4842*
v. 威脅，恐嚇，揚言要……
▶ My girlfriend threatens to break up with me all the time.
我的女友老是威脅要跟我分手。

three [θri] 🎧 *Track 4843*
pron. 三個；**n.** 三；三個；**adj.** 三的；三個的

throat [θrot] 🎧 *Track 4844*
n. 喉嚨

through [θru] 🎧 *Track 4845*
prep. 穿過；通過；**adv.** 穿過；通過；從頭到尾

through·out [θruˈaʊt] 🎧 *Track 4846*
prep. 遍佈；從頭到尾；貫穿

throw [θro] 🎧 *Track 4847*
v. 丟

thumb [θʌm] 🎧 *Track 4848*
n. 拇指

thun·der [`θʌndɚ] 🎧 *Track 4849*
n. 雷聲；雷；**v.** 打雷；發出雷般聲響；大聲斥責

thun·der·storm 🎧 *Track 4850*
[`θʌndɚˌstɔrm]
n. 大雷雨
▶ He insisted on going fishing regardless of the thunderstorm.
他不管外頭下著大雷雨，堅持要去釣魚。

Thurs·day [`θɝzde] 🎧 *Track 4851*
=Thurs./Thur.
n. 星期四

thus [ðʌs] 🎧 *Track 4852*
adv. 因此

Aa
Bb
Cc
Dd
Ee
Ff
Gg
Hh
Ii
Jj
Kk
Ll
Mm
Nn
Oo
Pp
Qq
Rr
Ss
Tt
Uu
Vv
Ww
Xx
Yy
Zz

tick·et [ˋtɪkɪt]　　🎧 *Track 4853*
n. 票

tick·le [ˋtɪkl]　　🎧 *Track 4854*
v. 呵癢，使發癢；使發笑；觸，撥，彈
▶She tickled his belly to make him laugh.
她搔他肚子，惹他笑。

tide [taɪd]　　🎧 *Track 4855*
n. 潮汐
▶This piece of land disappears when the tide comes in. 漲潮的時候這塊土地就會消失。

ti·dy [ˋtaɪdɪ]　　🎧 *Track 4856*
adj. 整齊的；井然有序的；**v.** 收拾；使整齊

tie [taɪ]　　🎧 *Track 4857*
n. 領帶；聯繫；束縛；**v.** 繫；綁；打結；結為夫妻

ti·ger [ˋtaɪgɚ]　　🎧 *Track 4858*
n. 虎

tight [taɪt]　　🎧 *Track 4859*
adj. 緊的；緊貼的；密封的；（比賽）勢均力敵的
▶I have a very tight schedule next week.
我下星期的行程很緊。

adv. 緊緊地，牢牢地
▶He tied his necktie too tight.
他的領帶打得太緊了。

tight·en [ˋtaɪtn]　　🎧 *Track 4860*
v. 使變緊，使繃緊
▶He had to tighten his belt before he found a job.
在找到工作之前，他得勒緊腰帶，省吃儉用。

（補充片語）
tighten one's belt 束緊腰帶過日

till [tɪl]=**un·til**　　🎧 *Track 4861*
prep. 直到⋯⋯才；**conj.** 直到⋯⋯為止

tim·ber [ˋtɪmbɚ]　　🎧 *Track 4862*
n. 木材，木料
▶The bridge is built of timber.
這座橋是木造的。

time [taɪm]　　🎧 *Track 4863*
n. 時間；**v.** 為⋯⋯計時；預定⋯⋯的時間

time·ta·ble [ˋtaɪmˌtebl]　　🎧 *Track 4864*
n. （車次的）時刻表；時間表，課程表
▶According to the timetable, his train will arrive at 6:05 p.m. 根據時刻表，他的火車會在下午六點零五分抵達。

v. 把⋯⋯排入時間表；把⋯⋯排入時刻表；把⋯⋯列入課程表
▶The flight is timetabled to depart at 8:45 a.m. 班機定於上午八點四十五分起飛。

tim·id [ˋtɪmɪd]　　🎧 *Track 4865*
adj. 膽小的，易受驚的，羞怯的
▶He likes the girl but is too timid to talk to her. 他很喜歡那女孩，但太害羞了，不敢跟她說話。

tin [tɪn]　　🎧 *Track 4866*
n. 錫；馬口鐵，鍍錫鐵皮；罐頭
▶Tin cans are recyclable.
錫罐是可回收再利用的。

ti·ny [ˋtaɪnɪ]　　🎧 *Track 4867*
adj. 極小的；微小的

tip [tɪp]　　🎧 *Track 4868*
n. 小費；**v.** 給⋯⋯小費

tip·toe [ˋtɪpˌto]　　🎧 *Track 4869*
v. 踮著腳；踮起腳走；躡手躡腳地走
▶She tiptoed quietly into the bedroom.
她躡手躡腳地安靜走進房間。

n. 腳尖
▶She walked on tiptoe to avoid waking anybody.
她踮著腳走路，以免吵醒任何人。

（補充片語）
on tiptoe 踮著腳

tire [taɪr]=**tyre**（英式英文）🎧 *Track 4870*
n. 輪胎
▶I think we've got a flat tire.
我想我們的車爆胎了。

（補充片語）
flat tire 爆胎

v. 使疲倦，使厭煩
▶ Endless housework tires me.
做不完的家事讓我疲憊不堪。

tired [taɪrd]　🎧 Track 4871
adj. 疲累的；厭倦的

tire·some [`taɪrsəm]　🎧 Track 4872
adj. 令人疲勞的，使人厭倦的；討厭的，煩人的
▶ Doing the same job day after day is pretty tiresome.
日復一日地做著一樣的工作相當令人厭倦。

tir·ing [`taɪrɪŋ]　🎧 Track 4873
adj. 累人的，令人疲倦的；麻煩的，無聊的
▶ After a long tiring day, all I want is a hot bath. 在漫長累人的一天之後，我只想要泡一個熱水澡。

tis·sue [`tɪʃʊ]　🎧 Track 4874
n. 面紙、衛生紙；薄織物；（動植物）組織
▶ We're running out of toilet tissues.
我們的廁紙快用完了。

(補充片語)

run out of 用完；toilet tissue 廁紙

ti·tle [`taɪtl̩]　🎧 Track 4875
n. 標題；書名；頭銜；名稱

to [tu]　🎧 Track 4876
prep. 向；往；到；**inf.** 不定詞

toast [tost]　🎧 Track 4877
n. 吐司；烤麵包片；**v.** 烤（麵包）；烘（手或腳）

to·bac·co [tə`bæko]　🎧 Track 4878
n. 菸草，菸草製品；抽菸
▶ My husband is a heavy smoker who can't live without tobacco.
我先生是個大菸槍，他沒菸活不下去。

to·day [tə`de]　🎧 Track 4879
adv. 今天；**n.** 今天

toe [to]　🎧 Track 4880
n. 腳趾；足尖

to·fu [`tofu] =bean curd　🎧 Track 4881
n. 豆腐

to·geth·er [tə`gɛðə]　🎧 Track 4882
adv. 一起；合起來

toi·let [`tɔɪlɪt]　🎧 Track 4883
n. 馬桶；廁所、洗手間

tol·e·ra·ble [`talərəbl̩]　🎧 Track 4884
adj. 可忍受的
▶ The pay is not as good as I expected, but tolerable.
工資沒我期望得高，但是還能接受。

tol·e·rance [`talərəns]　🎧 Track 4885
n. 寬容
▶ My parents have no tolerance for lies.
我的父母對謊言絲毫不寬待。

tol·e·rant [`talərənt]　🎧 Track 4886
adj. 忍受的，容忍的，寬恕的；有耐性的；有耐藥力的
▶ How can you be so tolerant of your neighbors? They're so noisy! 你怎麼能對你的鄰居如此寬容？他們那麼吵耶！

tol·e·rate [`talə,ret]　🎧 Track 4887
v. 忍受，寬容
▶ She doesn't tolerate dishonesty in her house.
她不容許家裡有不誠實的事情。

to·ma·to [tə`meto]　🎧 Track 4888
n. 番茄

tomb [tum]　🎧 Track 4889
n. 墓碑
▶ The battlefield was his tomb.
戰場就是他的葬身之地。

相關片語

Tomb-sweeping Day 清明掃墓節

to·mor·row [tə`mɔro]　🎧 Track 4890
adv. 明天；**n.** 明天

ton [tʌn]　🎧 Track 4891
n. 噸；公噸；大量，許多

※灰色單字為英檢初級必備單字

▶We eat tons of ice cream every summer.
每年夏天我們都會吃很多冰淇淋。

相關片語

weigh a ton 非常沈重
▶What did you pack in your luggage? It weighs a ton!
你在行李裡裝了什麼呀？它好重！

tone [ton] 　　🎧 *Track 4892*
n. 色調；音調；腔調；氣氛
▶He spoke to his son in an angry tone.
他用生氣的口吻跟他兒子說話。

v. 調音；為⋯⋯定調；裝腔作勢地說；增強，提高
▶Cycling to work every day has toned up my legs.
每天騎腳踏車去上班讓我的腳變得強健了。

補充片語

tone up 強化，提高

tongue [tʌŋ] 　　🎧 *Track 4893*
n. 舌頭；說話方式；語言

to·night [tə`naɪt] 　　🎧 *Track 4894*
adv./n. 今晚

too [tu] 　　🎧 *Track 4895*
adv. 太；也

tool [tul] 　　🎧 *Track 4896*
n. 工具；方法；手段

tooth [tuθ] 　　🎧 *Track 4897*
n. 牙齒

tooth·ache [`tuθ͵ek] 　　🎧 *Track 4898*
n. 牙痛

tooth·brush [`tuθ͵brʌʃ] 　　🎧 *Track 4899*
n. 牙刷

tooth·paste [`tuθ͵pest] 　　🎧 *Track 4900*
n. 牙膏
▶I don't like the smell of toothpaste.
我不喜歡牙膏的味道。

top [tɑp] 　　🎧 *Track 4901*
n. 頂端；頂部；上方；頂點；**adj.** 頂上的；最高的；居首位的；**v.** 給⋯⋯加蓋；達到⋯⋯的頂部；高於

top·ic [`tɑpɪk] 　　🎧 *Track 4902*
n. 題目；話題；標題

torch [tɔrtʃ] 　　🎧 *Track 4903*
n. 火炬，火把；手電筒；（文化、知識的）光；（對某人的）愛火
▶The Buddhist temple was put to the torch. 那間佛寺已經付之一炬了。

補充片語

put to the torch 付之一炬；燒掉

v. 縱火
▶The suspect confessed that he had torched 15 cars in the past two months.
嫌犯坦承他在過去兩個月縱火燒掉了十五輛車。

tor·na·do [tɔr`nedo] 　　🎧 *Track 4904*
n. 龍捲風，旋風，颶風
▶The massive tornado killed 24 people and caused an estimated $2 billion in property damage.
這個巨大的龍捲風造成24人死亡，及估計二十億的財物損失。

tor·toise [`tɔrtəs] 　　🎧 *Track 4905*
n. 烏龜，陸龜；行動遲緩的人
▶A tortoise can live over 200 years.
一隻烏龜可以活超過兩百年。

toss [tɔs] 　　🎧 *Track 4906*
v. 拋，扔，投；突然抬起；擲幣打賭；甩頭離去
▶Let's toss a coin to decide who should do the dishes. 我們來拋錢幣決定誰該洗碗。

n. 拋，扔，投；投擲的距離；擲幣決定
▶You can't decide everything on the toss of a coin. 你不能靠擲幣來決定每件事。

相關片語

not give a toss 毫不在乎
▶I don't give a toss what they say about me. 我毫不在乎他們怎麼說我。

to·tal [`totl`] 🎧 *Track 4907*
adj. 總記的；全體的；**n.** 總數；**v.** 合計為；總計

touch [tʌtʃ] 🎧 *Track 4908*
v. 摸；觸碰；**n.** 觸覺；觸感；接觸；聯繫

tough [tʌf] 🎧 *Track 4909*
adj. 堅韌的；強硬的；不屈不撓的；不幸的；棘手的；嚴格的
▶ This client is a tough nut to crack.
這個客戶很難應付。

(補充片語)

a tough nut to crack 難以應付的人或事物

n. 粗暴的人；暴徒；惡棍
▶ The man was attacked by a gang of toughs. 該男子遭到一幫惡棍襲擊。

v. 堅毅地抵抗
▶ Even if everything seems to go against you, you have to be strong and tough it out.
即使一切似乎都不如你的意，你仍必須堅強地堅決面對。

tour [tʊr] 🎧 *Track 4910*
n. 旅行；旅遊；巡迴演出；**v.** 旅行；在……旅遊

tour·is·m [`tʊrɪzəm] 🎧 *Track 4911*
n. 旅遊，觀光；旅遊業，觀光業
▶ Tourism makes a major contribution to this country's economy.
觀光業為這個國家的經濟帶來很大的貢獻。

tour·ist [`tʊrɪst] 🎧 *Track 4912*
n. 旅遊者；旅客，觀光客
▶ Every year, tens of thousands of tourists from all over the world flock to Japan during the cherry blossom season.
每一年，數以萬計來自世界各地的遊客會在櫻花季時湧入日本。

(相關片語)

tourist attraction 觀光勝地，旅遊勝地
▶ Sun Moon Lake has always been a popular tourist attraction in Taiwan.
日月潭一直是台灣的一個受歡迎的旅遊勝地。

tow [to] 🎧 *Track 4913*
v. 拉，拖，牽引
▶ Your car will be towed if you park it in front of the store.
如果你把車停在店門口，車子會被拖吊。

n. 拉，拖，牽引
▶ My car has run out of gas. Could you please give it a tow?
我的車沒油了。可以請你幫我拖個車嗎？

(補充片語)

run out of 用完

to·ward [tə`wɔrd] =to·wards 🎧 *Track 4914*
prep. 朝；向
▶ She walked toward the painting and took a close look at it.
她朝那幅畫走過去，就近端詳。

tow·el [`taʊəl] 🎧 *Track 4915*
n. 毛巾

tow·er [`taʊɚ] 🎧 *Track 4916*
n. 塔；高樓

town [taʊn] 🎧 *Track 4917*
n. 城鎮

toy [tɔɪ] 🎧 *Track 4918*
n. 玩具

trace [tres] 🎧 *Track 4919*
v. 追蹤；**n.** 蹤跡

track [træk] 🎧 *Track 4920*
n. 行蹤；軌道；小徑；**v.** 跟蹤；追蹤

trade [tred] 🎧 *Track 4921*
n. 交易；貿易；**v.** 進行交易；交換；做買賣

trade·mark [`tred͵mɑrk] 🎧 *Track 4922*
n. 商標；（人或物的）標記，特徵
▶ Don't forget to file a patent for your trademark.
別忘了幫你的商標申請專利。

(補充片語)

file a patent 提出專利權的申請

trad·er [`tredɚ] 🎧 *Track 4923*
n. 商人，商船；交易人
▶ I bought a hand-made Qing dynasty cabinet from an antique trader.
我跟一個古董商買了一個手工的清朝櫥櫃。

tra·di·tion [trə`dɪʃən] 🎧 *Track 4924*
n. 傳統；慣例

tra·di·tion·al [trə`dɪʃənl] 🎧 *Track 4925*
adj. 傳統的；慣例的

traf·fic [`træfɪk] 🎧 *Track 4926*
n. 交通

tra·ge·dy [`trædʒədɪ] 🎧 *Track 4927*
n. 悲劇；悲劇性事件，慘案，災難
▶ It's a real tragedy that the man was killed by his own son.
男子被自己的兒子給殺害，這真是一場悲劇。

tra·gic [`trædʒɪk] 🎧 *Track 4928*
adj. 悲劇的；悲慘的，不幸的；悲痛的
▶ The tsunami that occurred in South Asia in 2004 was a tragic natural disaster.
2004年發生在南亞的海嘯是一個不幸的天災。

trail [trel] 🎧 *Track 4929*
n. 痕跡
▶ The hunter found the trail of the bear in the woods. 獵人在森林裡發現了熊的足跡。
v. 拖曳；跟蹤；追獵；蔓生
▶ The police trailed the drug dealer and discovered the drug den.
警方跟蹤藥頭，並發現了毒窟。

(補充片語)
drug dealer 販毒者，藥頭；drug den 毒窟

train [tren] 🎧 *Track 4930*
n. 火車；**v.** 訓練；培養；接受訓練；鍛鍊

train·ing [`trenɪŋ] 🎧 *Track 4931*
n. 訓練，培養
▶ We provide effective on-the-job training for our employees to help them acquire new skills and enhance their knowledge.
我們為員工提供有效的在職訓練，以幫助他們獲得新技能，並提升他們的知識。

(補充片語)
on-the-job training 在職訓練

trans·fer [træns`fɝ] 🎧 *Track 4932*
n. 遷移，移交，轉讓
▶ Carl has applied for a transfer to Sales Department.
卡爾已經申請轉調到業務部門了。
v. 搬，轉換，調動；換車，轉學；轉讓，讓渡
▶ Mike will be transferred to our London branch next month.
麥可下個月就要被調到我們倫敦的分公司了。

trans·form [træns`fɔrm] 🎧 *Track 4933*
v. 使改變；轉換；改造
▶ A caterpillar will transform into a butterfly.
毛毛蟲會變成蝴蝶。

tran·sit [`trænsɪt] 🎧 *Track 4934*
n. 運輸；公共交通運輸系統

trans·late [træns`let] 🎧 *Track 4935*
v. 翻譯，轉譯；（以不同的說法）解釋，說明
▶ Can you translate this English letter into Chinese?
你可以把這封英文信件翻譯成中文嗎？

trans·la·tion 🎧 *Track 4936*
[træns`leʃən]
n. 翻譯；譯文，譯本
▶ A Chinese translation of this French novel will be published next month.
這本法文小說的中文譯本下個月就會出版了。

trans·la·tor [træns`letɚ] 🎧 *Track 4937*
n. 譯者，譯員，翻譯；翻譯家；翻譯機
▶ An automatic language translator may come in handy while we're travelling abroad.
一台自動語言翻譯機在我們到國外旅遊時可能會用得著。

(補充片語)
automatic language translator 自動語言翻譯機；come in handy 遲早有用，用得著

trans·plant [træns`plænt] 🎧 *Track 4938*

n. 移植；移植器官
▶ The patient needs a liver transplant to live.
這病人需要肝臟移植才能活命。

v. 移植；移種；移居
▶ We are going to transplant this tree to our backyard.
我們將會把這棵樹移植到後院去。

trans·port [`træns,port] 🎧 *Track 4939*

n. 運輸；交通工具；交通運輸系統
▶ You can't go anywhere in this obscure village without your own transport.
在這窮鄉僻壤，沒有自己的交通工具你便哪兒也去不了。

（補充片語）
obscure village 偏僻村莊，窮鄉僻壤

v. 運送，運輸；搬運
▶ Your commodities will be transported to you by freight.
你的貨品會以貨運方式運送給你。

trans·por·ta·tion 🎧 *Track 4940*
[,trænspə`teʃən]

n. 運輸，輸送；運輸工具，交通工具；旅費，交通費
▶ The public transportation system of the city is well designed.
這城市的大眾運輸系統設計良好。

（補充片語）
public transportation system 公共運輸系統

trap [træp] 🎧 *Track 4941*

v. 設陷阱捕捉；使落入圈套；堵塞；**n.** 陷阱；圈套

trash [træʃ] 🎧 *Track 4942*

n. 垃圾；廢物；無用的人

trav·el [`trævl] 🎧 *Track 4943*

v. 旅行；移動
n. 旅行；遊歷；旅遊業；移動

trav·el·er [`trævlə]
=travel·ler （英式英文） 🎧 *Track 4944*

n. 旅行者，旅客

▶ The youth hostel is popular among young travellers. 青年旅社很受年輕旅客歡迎。

trave·ling [`trævlɪŋ]
=travel·ling （英式英文） 🎧 *Track 4945*

adj. 流動的；旅行用的；旅行的
▶ My husband and I love traveling around and he is a wonderful traveling companion.
我跟我先生喜歡到處旅行，而他是個很棒的旅行同伴。

tray [tre] 🎧 *Track 4946*

n. 盤子、托盤，文件盒
▶ The waiter put all the dirty plates on the tray. 服務生將所有髒盤子放在托盤上。

trea·sure [`trɛʒə] 🎧 *Track 4947*

n. 金銀財寶；貴重物品；**v.** 珍惜；珍視

treat [trit] 🎧 *Track 4948*

v. 對待；處理；治療；款待、請客；**n.** 請客

treat·ment [`tritmənt] 🎧 *Track 4949*

n. 對待；處理；治療；療法

treat·y [`tritɪ] 🎧 *Track 4950*

n. 條約，協定，契約，協議
▶ The Qing government was compelled to sign the unequal treaty with Western powers.
滿清政府被迫與西方政權簽署不平等條約。

tree [tri] 🎧 *Track 4951*

n. 樹

trem·ble [`trɛmbl] 🎧 *Track 4952*

v. 發抖，顫震；搖晃；擔憂
▶ The little girl's voice trembled with fear.
小女孩的聲音因恐懼而顫抖。

n. 震顫，發抖；震動
▶ He denied having been involved in the affair with a tremble in his voice.
他語帶顫抖地否認與這件事有關。

tre·men·dous 🎧 *Track 4953*
[trɪ`mɛndəs]

adj. 巨大的，極大的；極度的，驚人的；很棒的

※灰色單字為英檢初級必備單字

► My working holiday experience has made a tremendous change in my life.
打工度假的經歷讓我的人生有了極大的改變。

trend [trɛnd] 🎧 Track 4954
n. 走向，趨勢；傾向，時尚
► Even though there was no chance for us to win, we decided to buck the trend.
既使我們沒有機會獲勝，但我們依然決定要逆勢而行。

（補充片語）
buck the trend 逆勢而行

tri·al [`traɪəl] 🎧 Track 4955
n. 試用；試驗；棘手的事；審問、審判

tri·an·gle [`traɪ͵æŋgl̩] 🎧 Track 4956
n. 三角形

tribe [traɪb] 🎧 Track 4957
n. 部落，種族；一幫，一夥；緊密聯繫的群體
► We encountered some people from an indigenous tribe.
我們遇到了一些來自土著部落的人。

trick [trɪk] 🎧 Track 4958
n. 詭計；花招；竅門；手法；戲法；特技
v. 哄騙；戲弄

trick·y [`trɪkɪ] 🎧 Track 4959
adj. 狡猾的；機警的，足智多謀的；困難的，棘手的
► I need a helping hand to deal with this tricky problem with me. 我需要一個幫手來跟我一起處理這個棘手的問題。

trip [trɪp] 🎧 Track 4960
n. 旅行；行程

tri·umph [`traɪəmf] 🎧 Track 4961
n. 勝利；成功；因為勝利而帶來的喜悅
► His rival congratulated him on his triumph in the election.
他的對手恭喜他競選勝利。

v. 獲得勝利；歡慶勝利
► The patient hopes to triumph over his illness. 病人希望能夠戰勝病魔。

（補充片語）
triumph over 打敗，戰勝

troub·le [`trʌbl̩] 🎧 Track 4962
n. 麻煩；困境；費事；騷亂；**v.** 麻煩；使憂慮；使疼痛；費心

trou·sers [`traʊzɚz] 🎧 Track 4963
=pants （美式英文）
n. 褲子

truck [trʌk] 🎧 Track 4964
n. 卡車

true [tru] 🎧 Track 4965
adj. 真的

trum·pet [`trʌmpɪt] 🎧 Track 4966
n. 喇叭；小號

trust [trʌst] 🎧 Track 4967
n. 信任；信賴；**v.** 相信；信賴；依靠

truth [truθ] 🎧 Track 4968
n. 真相；實情

try [traɪ] 🎧 Track 4969
v. 嘗試；試圖；努力；**n.** 嘗試；努力

T-shirt [`ti͵ʃɝt] 🎧 Track 4970
=tee-shirt
n. T恤；短袖圓領汗衫

tub [tʌb] 🎧 Track 4971
n. 盆；桶；浴缸；（放冰淇淋的）杯

tube [tjub] 🎧 Track 4972
=un·der·ground rail·way
n. （英）地下鐵
► In London, traveling by tube is more convenient than traveling by cab.
在倫敦，搭地鐵比搭計程車方便。

Tues·day [`tjuzde] 🎧 Track 4973
=Tues./Tue.
n. 星期二

tum·my [ˋtʌmɪ] 🎧 *Track 4974*
=sto·mach
n. 胃；肚子；啤酒肚

tun·nel [ˋtʌnl̩] 🎧 *Track 4975*
n. 隧道；地道

tur·key [ˋtɝkɪ] 🎧 *Track 4976*
n. 火雞；火雞肉

turn [tɝn] 🎧 *Track 4977*
v. 轉；翻轉；轉向；轉身；變化；**n.** 轉向；
依次輪流的機會

tur·tle [ˋtɝtl̩] 🎧 *Track 4978*
n. 海龜；龜肉

TV [ti-vi] 🎧 *Track 4979*
n. 電視

twelve [twɛlv] 🎧 *Track 4980*
pron. 十二個；**n.** 十二；**adj.** 十二的

twen·ty [ˋtwɛntɪ] 🎧 *Track 4981*
pron. 二十個；**n.** 二十；**adj.** 二十的

twice [twaɪs] 🎧 *Track 4982*
adv. 兩次

two [tu] 🎧 *Track 4983*
pron. 兩個；**n.** 二；兩歲；兩點；**adj.** 二
的；兩個的

type [taɪp] 🎧 *Track 4984*
v. 打字；用打字機打；**n.** 類型；型式；樣式

ty·phoon [taɪˋfun] 🎧 *Track 4985*
n. 颱風

👑 Note

Aa
Bb
Cc
Dd
Ee
Ff
Gg
Hh
Ii
Jj
Kk
Ll
Mm
Nn
Oo
Pp
Qq
Rr
Ss
Tt
Uu
Vv
Ww
Xx
Yy
Zz

※灰色單字為英檢初級必備單字

Uu

通過中級英文檢定者的英文能力：

 聽
在日常生活中，能聽懂一般的會話；能大致聽懂公共場所廣播、氣象報告及廣告等。在工作時，能聽懂簡易的產品介紹與操作說明。能大致聽懂外籍人士的談話及詢問。

 讀
在日常生活中，能閱讀短文、故事、私人信件、廣告、傳單、簡介及使用說明等。在工作時，能閱讀工作須知、公告、操作手冊、例行的文件、傳真、電報等。

 寫
能寫簡單的書信、故事及心得等。對於熟悉且與個人經歷相關的主題，能以簡易的文字表達。

 說
在日常生活中，能以簡易英語交談或描述一般事物，能介紹自己的生活作息、工作、家庭、經歷等，並可對一般話題陳述看法。在工作時，能進行簡單的答詢，並與外籍人士交談溝通。

本書除包含官方公佈的中級4,947單字外，更精挑了近400個滿分必學的高手單字。同時，在片語的挑選、例句的使用上，皆依上述英檢官方公佈之能力範疇做設計，難度適中、不偏離考試主題。發音部分則是自然發音＆KK音標雙管齊下，搭配MP3以「分解／完整」方式錄音，給你最多元有效的學習手段，怎麼記都可以，想忘掉都好難！

---

ug·ly [ˋʌglɪ] 　🎧 *Track 4986*
adj. 醜的；難看的；可怕的

um·brel·la [ʌmˋbrɛlə] 　🎧 *Track 4987*
n. 雨傘

un·a·ble [ʌnˋebl̩] 　🎧 *Track 4988*
adj. 不能的，不會的；無能力的，無法勝任的
▶ Because of his injured shoulder, he will be unable to play basketball for a while. 因為他受傷的肩膀，他將有一陣子不能夠打籃球。

un·a·ware [ʌnəˋwɛr] 　🎧 *Track 4989*
adj. 不知道的，未察覺的
▶ The woman was unaware that she was being followed.
那女子沒有察覺到自己已經被跟蹤了。

un·be·liev·a·ble 　🎧 *Track 4990*
[ˏʌnbɪˋlivəbl̩]
adj. 難以相信的；不可相信的；非常驚人的
▶ It is unbelievable that you turned down such a great job offer. 你竟然拒絕這麼好的一個工作機會，真是令人難以相信。

un·cle [ˋʌŋkl̩] 　🎧 *Track 4991*
n. 叔叔；舅舅；伯伯；姑丈；姨父等對年長男子的稱呼

un·con·scious 　🎧 *Track 4992*
[ʌnˋkɑnʃəs]
adj. 不省人事的，失去知覺的；未發覺的；無意識的
▶ The man remained unconscious for a week after the brain surgery. 男子在腦部手術之後，有一個星期的時間是不省人事的。

un·der [ˋʌndɚ] 　🎧 *Track 4993*
prep. 在……下；**adv.** 在下方；在下面

un·der·ground 　🎧 *Track 4994*
[ˋʌndɚˏgraʊnd]
adj. 地面下的；秘密的，不公開的
▶ There's an underground passage that leads to the other office building.
有一條地下通道可以到另一間辦公大樓。

adv. 在地下
▶ A dog was found buried underground alive. 一隻狗經人發現被活埋在地底下。

n. 地面下層；（英）地下鐵；地下組織；

▶In London, you can travel to almost anywhere in the city by the Underground. 在倫敦，你可以搭地下鐵到這城市的幾乎任何一個地方。

un·der·line [ˌʌndəˈlaɪn] 🎧 *Track 4995*
v. 在下面劃線

un·der·pass [ˈʌndəˌpæs] 🎧 *Track 4996*
n. 地下道

un·der·stand
[ˌʌndəˈstænd] 🎧 *Track 4997*
v. 理解；明白

un·der·stand·ing 🎧 *Track 4998*
[ˌʌndəˈstændɪŋ]
n. 了解，領會；理解力；諒解，同感；共識

▶Thank you for your understanding and sorry for the inconvenience we've caused you. 感謝您的諒解，同時對我們對您造成的不便感到很抱歉。

adj. 了解的，能諒解的，寬容的；有理解力的，聰明的

▶My boss is a very understanding person. I'm sure he will grant my leave. 我老闆是個非常通情達理的人，我相信他會准我休假的。

un·der·take [ˌʌndəˈtek] 🎧 *Track 4999*
v. 著手做，進行；從事；承擔，接受；答應，保證

▶We will undertake the job of decorating the apartment immediately. 我們將會立刻著手進行公寓裝潢的工作。

un·der·wa·ter 🎧 *Track 5000*
[ˈʌndəˌwɔtə]
adv. 在水中，在水下

▶She can hold her breath underwater for as long as five minutes. 她可以在水中閉氣長達五分鐘。

（補充片語）

hold one's breath 閉氣，忍住呼吸

adj. 水中的，水面下的

▶He brought an underwater camera with him when going skin diving. 他去浮潛時，隨身攜帶了一個水底照相機。

un·der·wear [ˈʌndəˌwɛr] 🎧 *Track 5001*
n. 內衣

un·der·weight 🎧 *Track 5002*
[ˈʌndəˌwet]
adj. 重量不足的，體重不足的

▶The child was apparently undernourished because she was ten kilos underweight. 這孩子明顯是營養不良，因為她比正常體重輕了十公斤。

un·ex·pect·ed 🎧 *Track 5003*
[ˌʌnɪkˈspɛktɪd]
adj. 想不到的，突如其來的，意外的

▶She was thrilled when she got an unexpected promotion. 當她獲得意外晉升時，簡直欣喜若狂。

un·for·tu·nate 🎧 *Track 5004*
[ʌnˈfɔrtʃənɪt]
adj. 不幸的，倒霉的；可惜的，令人遺憾的

▶A natural disaster like a tsunami always results in unfortunate consequences. 像海嘯這樣的一個天災，往往造成令人遺憾的不幸後果。

un·for·tu·nate·ly 🎧 *Track 5005*
[ʌnˈfɔrtʃənɪtlɪ]
adv. 不幸地；遺憾地，可惜地

▶We did our best to save him, but unfortunately, he didn't make it. 我們盡了最大努力去救他，但是很不幸地，他沒有撐過來。

un·friend·ly [ʌnˈfrɛndlɪ] 🎧 *Track 5006*
adj. 不友善的，有敵意的

▶People here seem very unfriendly to foreigners. 這裡的人似乎對外國人非常不友善。

un·hap·py [ʌnˈhæpɪ] 🎧 *Track 5007*
adj. 不高興的；不幸的；對⋯⋯不滿意的

u·ni·form [ˈjunəˌfɔrm] 🎧 *Track 5008*
n. 制服；**adj.** 相同的；一致的

u·nion [ˈjunjən] 🎧 *Track 5009*
n. 結合；合而為一；聯盟；工會，聯合會；結婚；（大學）社團

▶Your marriage is a perfect union. Congratulations! 你們的婚姻是完美的結合！恭喜！

labor union 工會

▶It is estimated that there will be more than 10,000 labor union members joining the strike. 據估計，將會有超過一萬名工會成員參加這次罷工行動。

u·nique [juˋnik] 🎧 *Track 5010*
adj. 獨一無二的；唯一的

u·nit [ˋjunɪt] 🎧 *Track 5011*
n. 單位；單元；一組；一個；一套

u·nite [juˋnaɪt] 🎧 *Track 5012*
v. 使聯合，統一，使團結；使結婚；混合
▶We should unite to fight against terrorism.
我們應該團結起來對抗恐怖主義。

補充片語

fight against 抵抗，與……作戰

u·nit·ed [juˋnaɪtɪd] 🎧 *Track 5013*
adj. 聯合的，統一的；團結的，一致的
▶The United Nations headquarters is located in New York City, USA.
聯合國總部位於美國紐約。

u·ni·ty [ˋjunətɪ] 🎧 *Track 5014*
n. 單一性，一致性；團結，聯合，統一；和諧，融洽
▶Unity is strength. 團結就是力量。

u·ni·ver·sal [͵junəˋvɝsl] 🎧 *Track 5015*
adj. 全體的，普遍的；宇宙的，全世界的；萬能的，通用的
▶English is a universal language.
英語是個全世界通用的語言。

n. 普通性，普遍現象，通用原則
▶Family, language, and religion are three human universals that can be found in all cultures. 家庭、語言及宗教信仰，是在所有文化裡都能發現的三個人類共通現象。

u·ni·verse [ˋjunə͵vɝs] 🎧 *Track 5016*
n. 宇宙；全人類；全世界

u·ni·ver·si·ty [͵junəˋvɝsətɪ] 🎧 *Track 5017*
n. 大學

un·known [ʌnˋnon] 🎧 *Track 5018*
adj. 未知的；默默無聞的；不知道的
▶She used to be an unknown pianist before she won the international Frederic Chopin piano competition.
在贏得國際蕭邦鋼琴比賽之前，她曾經是個默默無聞的鋼琴家。

un·less [ʌnˋlɛs] 🎧 *Track 5019*
conj. 除非
▶I won't leave unless I get my money.
除非拿到我的錢，不然我不離開。

un·like [ʌnˋlaɪk] 🎧 *Track 5020*
prep. 不像，和……不同，與……相反
▶Unlike his sisters, Jamie is a very thoughtful kid.
不像他姊姊們，傑米是個非常貼心的孩子。

un·like·ly [ʌnˋlaɪklɪ] 🎧 *Track 5021*
adj. 不太可能的，不可能發生的，不像是真的
▶My boss is unlikely to grant my personal leave for seven days.
我老闆不太可能答應讓我請七天的事假。

un·til [ənˋtɪl] 🎧 *Track 5022*
conj. 直到……時；在……之前；**prep.** 直到……時，直到；在……之前

un·touched [ʌnˋtʌtʃt] 🎧 *Track 5023*
adj. 未觸動過的；原樣的；未受損傷的；無動於衷的
▶She returned his gift untouched.
她將他的禮物原封不動地退回來。

un·u·su·al [ʌnˋjuʒʊəl] 🎧 *Track 5024*
adj. 不尋常的；稀有的；獨特的
▶It is unusual for him to help with the housework actively.
他會主動幫忙做家事，是很難得的。

up [ʌp] 🎧 *Track 5025*
adv. 向上；增加；上揚；**prep.** 向……上；在……上；**adj.** 向上的；上行的；起床的

up·on [əˋpɑn] 🎧 *Track 5026*
prep. 在……之上；在……之後立即……

up·per [`ʌpɚ]　🎧 *Track 5027*
adj. 較高的；上層的；上游的；**n.** 鞋幫；上舖；安非他命

up·set [ʌp`sɛt]　🎧 *Track 5028*
adj. 翻倒的，翻覆的；心煩的，苦惱的
▶ They were upset about their father's health condition.
父親的健康狀況使他們感到心煩意亂。

n. 翻倒，混亂；心煩意亂；（腸胃）不舒服；吵架
▶ I have been having stomach upsets for two weeks.
我腸胃不舒服已經有兩星期了。

v. 弄翻，打亂；意外擊敗；使心煩意亂，使生氣；使（腸胃）不適
▶ Not being invited to the party upsets her a lot.
沒有獲邀參加派對讓她很不開心。

up·stairs [`ʌp`stɛrz]　🎧 *Track 5029*
adv. 在樓上；往樓上；**adj.** 樓上的；**n.** 樓上

up·ward [`ʌpwɚd]　🎧 *Track 5030*
adj. 往上的，向上的，升高的，趨好的
▶ After a short break, they proceeded with the steep upward climb. 在短暫的休息之後，他們繼續沿著陡峭的山路往上爬。

ur·ban [`ɝbən]　🎧 *Track 5031*
adj. 城市的；居住在城市的
▶ Houses in urban areas are usually more costly. 城區的房子通常比較貴。

urge [ɝdʒ]　🎧 *Track 5032*
v. 催促；激勵，力勸；慫恿；極力主張
▶ His parents urged him to get married and have children. 他的父母催促他結婚生子。

n. 衝動，迫切要求；強烈慾望
▶ It's so hot today, and I have an urge to go swimming at the beach.
今天好熱，我好想去海邊游泳。

ur·gent [`ɝdʒənt]　🎧 *Track 5033*
adj. 緊急的，急迫的
▶ Don't call me during the weekend unless there's something urgent. 除非有緊急的事情，否則週末不要打電話給我。

us [ʌs]　🎧 *Track 5034*
pron. 我們

USA [ju-ɛs-e]　🎧 *Track 5035*
n. 美利堅合眾國；美國

us·age [`jusɪdʒ]　🎧 *Track 5036*
n. 使用，用法；習慣，習俗；慣用法
▶ Besides definitions of the most common English words, this dictionary also provides additional usage information of each word.
除了最常用的英文單字解釋之外，這本字典也為每個單字提供額外的使用資訊。

use [juz]　🎧 *Track 5037*
v./n. 使用；利用

used [juzd]　🎧 *Track 5038*
adj. 舊了的；用舊了的；**v.** 曾經

use·ful [`jusfəl]　🎧 *Track 5039*
adj. 有用的；有幫助的；有助益的

use·less [`juslɪs]　🎧 *Track 5040*
adj. 無用的，無效的，無價值的；（人）無能的
▶ He realized that the knowledge he learned from school is completely useless in this situation. 他發現他在學校裡學到的知識，在這個情況下完全派不上用場。

us·er [`juzɚ]　🎧 *Track 5041*
n. 使用者；用戶

u·su·al [`juʒʊəl]　🎧 *Track 5042*
adj. 平常的；慣常的

u·su·al·ly [`juʒʊəlɪ]　🎧 *Track 5043*
adv. 慣常地；通常地

Aa Bb Cc Dd Ee Ff Gg Hh Ii Jj Kk Ll Mm Nn Oo Pp Qq Rr Ss Tt Uu Vv Ww Xx Yy Zz

※灰色單字為英檢初級必備單字

Vv

通過中級英文檢定者的英文能力：

 在日常生活中，能聽懂一般的會話；能大致聽懂公共場所廣播、氣象報告及廣告等。在工作時，能聽懂簡易的產品介紹與操作說明。能大致聽懂外籍人士的談話及詢問。

 在日常生活中，能閱讀短文、故事、私人信件、廣告、傳單、簡介及使用說明等。在工作時，能閱讀工作須知、公告、操作手冊、例行的文件、傳真、電報等。

 能寫簡單的書信、故事及心得等。對於熟悉且與個人經歷相關的主題，能以簡易的文字表達。

 在日常生活中，能以簡易英語交談或描述一般事物，能介紹自己的生活作息、工作、家庭、經歷等，並可對一般話題陳述看法。在工作時，能進行簡單的答詢，並與外籍人士交談溝通。

本書除包含官方公佈的中級4,947單字外，更精挑了近400個滿分必學的高手單字。同時，在片語的挑選、例句的使用上，皆依上述英檢官方公佈之能力範疇做設計，難度適中、不偏離考試主題。發音部分則是自然發音＆KK音標雙管齊下，搭配MP3以「分解／完整」方式錄音，給你最多元有效的學習手段，怎麼記都可以，想忘掉都好難！

---

va·cant [ˋvekənt] 🎧 *Track 5044*
adj. 空的；未被佔用的；空缺的；空閒的；（心靈）空虛的
▶The lavatory is now vacant.
廁所現在沒人在用。

va·ca·tion [veˋkeʃən] 🎧 *Track 5045*
n. 假期；休假

vague [veg] 🎧 *Track 5046*
adj. 模糊不清的，朦朧的；不明確的，曖昧含糊的
▶I don't remember the exact location, but I have a vague idea where it is. 我不記得確實的地點，但我大概知道它在哪裡。

vain [ven] 🎧 *Track 5047*
adj. 無益的；徒然的；虛榮的
▶I hope that our efforts were not in vain.
希望我們的努力沒有白費。

(補充片語)
in vain 徒勞，無結果

Val·en·tine's Day 🎧 *Track 5048*
[ˋvæləntaɪnz-de]
n. 情人節

val·ley [ˋvælɪ] 🎧 *Track 5049*
n. 山谷；溪谷

val·u·a·ble [ˋvæljʊəbl] 🎧 *Track 5050*
adj. 值錢的，貴重的；有價值的，有用的
▶There's nothing valuable in this house.
屋子裡沒什麼值錢的東西。

val·ue [ˋvælju] 🎧 *Track 5051*
n. 價值；重要性；價值觀；**v.** 估價；重視；珍視

van [væn] 🎧 *Track 5052*
n. 有蓋小貨車；廂型車
▶We have to pack everything before the moving van arrives.
我們得在搬家貨車來之前，把所有東西都打包好。

moving van　傢俱搬運車

van·ish [`vænɪʃ] 🎧 *Track 5053*
v. 消失，突然不見
▶ When I returned, the man had already vanished with my wallet and cellphone.
當我回來時，那男人早就已經帶著我的錢包和手機消失不見了。

va·por [`vepɚ] 🎧 *Track 5054*
=va·pour （英式英文）
n. 水汽，蒸汽；煙霧；無實質之物，幻想
▶ The science teacher is explaining how evaporation turns liquid water into water vapor to the students.
自然老師正在向學生解釋液態的水是如何蒸發而轉化成水蒸汽。

va·ri·e·ty [və`raɪətɪ] 🎧 *Track 5055*
n. 多樣化，變化；種種
▶ Sleep problems can be caused by a variety of factors.
睡眠問題可能是由各種不同的原因所造成的。

var·i·ous [`vɛrɪəs] 🎧 *Track 5056*
adj. 不同的，各種各樣的，形形色色的
▶ Many young people choose not to get married for various reasons.
很多年輕人由於各種不同的原因而選擇不婚。

var·y [`vɛrɪ] 🎧 *Track 5057*
v. 使不同；改變；使多樣化；偏離，違反
▶ Opinions on this political issue vary from person to person.
對這個政治議題的看法，每個人都不同。

vary from person to person　因人而異

vase [ves] 🎧 *Track 5058*
n. 花瓶
▶ The antique vase she bought turned out to be a fake.
她買的那個古董花瓶，結果證明是個贗品。

vast [væst] 🎧 *Track 5059*
adj. 廣闊的，浩瀚的；龐大的，巨額的；【口】莫大的

▶ There is a vast difference between Japanese food and Chinese food.
日式料理和中式料理有很大的差別。

VCR [vi-si-ɑr] 🎧 *Track 5060*
=vid·e·o cas·sette re·cord·er
n. 卡式錄放影機

veg·e·ta·ble [`vɛdʒətəbl] 🎧 *Track 5061*
n. 蔬菜；青菜；**adj.** 蔬菜的；植物的

veg·e·tar·i·an [ˌvɛdʒə`tɛrɪən] 🎧 *Track 5062*
adj. 素食的；吃素的
▶ She usually dines at that vegetarian restaurant. 她常常在那間素食餐廳用餐。

n. 素食者；草食動物
▶ Many people choose to be vegetarians for their health.
很多人為了健康，選擇成為素食者。

ve·hi·cle [`viɪkl] 🎧 *Track 5063*
n. 運載工具；車輛；飛行器；傳播媒介，工具，手段
▶ Compared with the big cities, there aren't so many vehicles in the village.
跟大城市比起來，村子裡沒有那麼多的汽車。

vend·or [`vɛndɚ] 🎧 *Track 5064*
n. 攤販；小販；叫賣者

ven·ture [`vɛntʃɚ] 🎧 *Track 5065*
n. 冒險；冒險事業，投機活動
▶ No venture, no success.
不入虎穴，焉得虎子。（不敢冒險，何以成功。）

v. 使冒險；以……作賭注；大膽提出（或說出）；敢於
▶ They ventured to explore the underground cave. 他們冒險地去探索地底下的洞穴。

verb [vɝb] 🎧 *Track 5066*
n. 動詞
▶ The word "book" can be used as noun as well as a verb. 「book」這個字可以當名詞用，也可以當動詞用。

verse [vɝs] 🎧 *Track 5067*
n. 詩，韻文，詩句，詩作；（聖經的）節

Aa
Bb
Cc
Dd
Ee
Ff
Gg
Hh
Ii
Jj
Kk
Ll
Mm
Nn
Oo
Pp
Qq
Rr
Ss
Tt
Uu
Vv
Ww
Xx
Yy
Zz

※灰色單字為英檢初級必備單字

▶This poem is written in free verse.
這首詩是以自由詩的方式寫成的。

相關片語

chapter and verse 確切依據，準確依據

▶I can tell you everything, chapter and verse. 我可以確切地把一切都告訴你。

ver·sion [ˈvɝʒən]　　🎧 *Track 5068*
n. 譯文，譯本；描述，說法；變化形式；改編形式，改寫本；版本

▶The Chinese version of this Spanish novel will be published next month.
這本西班牙小說的中譯本將在下個月出版。

ve·ry [ˈvɛrɪ]　　🎧 *Track 5069*
adv. 非常；**adj.** 正是；恰好是

ves·sel [ˈvɛsl̩]　　🎧 *Track 5070*
n. 船；艦

▶The vessel has a capacity of a thousand passengers. 這條船可以容納一千名乘客。

相關片語

blood vessel 血管

▶Regular exercise helps to keep your blood vessels flexible and healthy.
規律的運動幫助你保持血管彈性和健康。

vest [vɛst]　　🎧 *Track 5071*
n. 背心；汗衫；內衣

vic·tim [ˈvɪktɪm]　　🎧 *Track 5072*
n. 犧牲者；受害者

▶She is one the victims of the war.
她是戰爭的受害者之一。

vic·to·ry [ˈvɪktərɪ]　　🎧 *Track 5073*
n. 勝利

vid·e·o [ˈvɪdɪˌo]　　🎧 *Track 5074*
n. 錄影節目；電視；**v.** 錄像；錄製

vid·e·o·tape [ˈvɪdɪoˌtep]　🎧 *Track 5075*
n. 錄影帶，錄像帶

▶I transferred the videotape to digital form in order to share it on the Internet. 我把錄影帶轉成數位形式，以便在網路上分享。

v. 將……錄到帶子上

▶Our wedding ceremony was videotaped from start to finish.
我們的婚禮從頭到尾都有錄下來。

view [vju]　　🎧 *Track 5076*
n. 景色；看法；**v.** 觀看；看待；將……視為

vig·or [ˈvɪgɚ]　　🎧 *Track 5077*
=vig·our （英式英文）
n. 體力，精力，活力；強健，茁壯；氣勢，魄力

▶Our tour guide was a young lady full of vigor and enthusiasm.
我們的導遊是個充滿活力及熱忱的年輕小姐。

vig·o·rous [ˈvɪgərəs]　　🎧 *Track 5078*
adj. 精力充沛的，強健的；強而有力的

▶If you want your wound to heal faster, avoid vigorous exercise for a few weeks.
如果你希望傷口痊癒得快一點，這幾週就先避免做劇烈運動。

vil·lage [ˈvɪlɪdʒ]　　🎧 *Track 5079*
n. 村；村落；村莊；村民

vin·e·gar [ˈvɪnɪgɚ]　　🎧 *Track 5080*
n. 醋

vi·o·late [ˈvaɪəˌlet]　　🎧 *Track 5081*
v. 違背，違反；侵犯，妨礙；褻瀆；（對婦女）施暴

▶A good doctor will do nothing that violates medical ethics.
一個好醫師絕不會做出違反醫德的事。

vi·o·la·tion [ˌvaɪəˈleʃən]　🎧 *Track 5082*
n. 違背，違反；違反行為

▶His driver's license was suspended for violation of traffic regulations.
他因為違反交通規則而被吊銷駕照。

vi·o·lence [ˈvaɪələns]　　🎧 *Track 5083*
n. 暴力

▶The woman has been suffering from domestic violence for years.
那女子已經被家暴好幾年了。

補充片語

domestic violence 家庭暴力

vi·o·lent [`vaɪələnt］ 🎧 Track 5084
adj. 猛烈的；暴力的
▶ Not until he started beating her did she know that he had violent tendencies.
一直到他開始揍她，她才知道他有暴力傾向。

vi·o·let [`vaɪəlɪt］ 🎧 Track 5085
n. 紫羅蘭，紫羅蘭花，紫羅蘭色；羞怯的人
▶ The violets in our garden are in full blossom. 我們花園裡的紫羅蘭花都盛開了。

adj. 紫蘿蘭的；紫蘿蘭色的，紫色的
▶ I'm wearing a violet dress.
我穿著一件紫色的洋裝。

【相關片語】
shrinking violet 非常害羞的人；會怯場的人
▶ She is a shrinking violet. She won't agree to give a speech at your wedding.
她是如此害羞的人，一定不會答應在你的婚禮上致辭的。

vi·o·lin [ˌvaɪə`lɪn］ 🎧 Track 5086
n. 小提琴

vi·o·lin·ist [ˌvaɪə`lɪnɪst］ 🎧 Track 5087
n. 小提琴家，小提琴手
▶ Joshua Bell is one of the greatest violinists of the time.
約書亞‧貝爾是當代最偉大的小提琴家之一。

【補充片語】
of the time 當代

vir·gin [`vɝdʒɪn］ 🎧 Track 5088
n. 處女，未婚女子；童男
▶ It makes no difference to me whether my future wife is a virgin or not.
我未來的妻子是否個處女，對我來說並沒有差別。

adj. 處女的；貞潔的；未玷污的；未開發的；未加工的，初榨的
▶ After the gutter oil scandal, they only use extra virgin olive oil for cooking.
在地溝油醜聞爆發之後，他們只用特級初榨橄欖油來做烹調。

【補充片語】
extra virgin olive oil 特級初榨橄欖油

vir·tue [`vɝtʃu］ 🎧 Track 5089
n. 美德
▶ Virtue is its own reward.
美德本身就是最好的回報。

vi·rus [`vaɪrəs］ 🎧 Track 5090
n. 病毒
▶ The Ebola virus cannot be spread through the air, by water, or by food.
伊波拉病毒不會透過空氣、水或食物散播。

vis·i·ble [`vɪzəbl］ 🎧 Track 5091
adj. 可看見的
▶ Germs are not visible to the naked eyes.
細菌是肉眼看不見的。

vi·sion [`vɪʒən］ 🎧 Track 5092
n. 視力；所見事物；洞察力，眼光
▶ I have twenty-twenty vision, so there's no need for me to wear glasses.
我的視力正常，所以沒有需要戴眼鏡。

【補充片語】
twenty-twenty vision 正常視力

vis·it [`vɪzɪt］ 🎧 Track 5093
v. 參觀；拜訪；**n.** 參觀；拜訪；暫住；逗留

vis·it·or [`vɪzɪtə］ 🎧 Track 5094
n. 訪客；遊客

vi·su·al [`vɪʒuəl］ 🎧 Track 5095
adj. 視力的，視覺的；光學的；靠目視的
▶ An airline pilot can't have any visual defects. 一個航空飛行員是不能有任何視力缺陷的。

vi·tal [`vaɪtl］ 🎧 Track 5096
adj. 生命的；維持生命所必需的；充滿活力的；極其重要的，必不可少的
▶ The man had no vital signs when he was sent to the hospital.
男子被送到醫院時已經沒有生命徵象了。

【補充片語】
vital signs 生命徵象（呼吸、心跳、血壓、體溫等）

vit·a·min [`vaɪtəmɪn］ 🎧 Track 5097
n. 維他命
▶ Guavas are a fruit rich in vitamin C.
芭樂是富含維他命C的一種水果。

※灰色單字為英檢初級必備單字

Aa Bb Cc Dd Ee Ff Gg Hh Ii Jj Kk Ll Mm Nn Oo Pp Qq Rr Ss Tt Uu Vv Ww Xx Yy Zz

viv·id [ˋvɪvɪd] 🎧 *Track 5098*

adj. 強烈的，（色彩）鮮艷的；有生氣的，活潑的；生動的，逼真的

▶ It is inappropriate to wear an outfit of vivid colors to a funeral.
穿著顏色鮮艷的衣服參加葬禮是不合宜的。

vo·cab·u·la·ry 🎧 *Track 5099*
[vəˋkæbjəˏlɛrɪ]

n. 字彙；詞彙

voice [vɔɪs] 🎧 *Track 5100*

n. 聲音

vol·ca·no [vɑlˋkeno] 🎧 *Track 5101*

n. 火山

▶ There are more than 100 active volcanoes in Japan, including Fuji Mountain.
日本有超過一百座活火山，包括富士山。

vol·ley·ball [ˋvɑlɪˏbɔl] 🎧 *Track 5102*

n. 排球；排球運動

vol·ume [ˋvɑljəm] 🎧 *Track 5103*

n. 冊；卷；音量

vol·un·ta·ry [ˋvɑlənˏtɛrɪ] 🎧 *Track 5104*

adj. 自願的，志願的；故意的；自發的，自覺的

▶ The man was charged with voluntary manslaughter. 男子被控蓄意謀殺。

vol·un·teer [ˏvɑlənˋtɪr] 🎧 *Track 5105*

n. 自願者，義工，志願兵

▶ Mr. Lee has been a hospital volunteer since he retired.
李先生自從退休後就一直是醫院的志工。

（補充片語）

hospital volunteer 醫院志工

v. 自願做，自願提供，自願服務

▶ She volunteered to babysit her little brother while her parents were out.
她自願在爸媽出門時，當弟弟的臨時保姆。

vote [vot] 🎧 *Track 5106*

n. 選舉；投票；選票；**v.** 投票；表決；投票決定

vot·er [ˋvotɚ] 🎧 *Track 5107*

n. 選舉人；投票人

vow·el [ˋvaʊəl] 🎧 *Track 5108*

n. 母音

▶ The letter "a" is a vowel while the letter "b" is a consonant.
英文字母「a」是個母音，而字母「b」則是個子音。

voy·age [ˋvɔɪɪdʒ] 🎧 *Track 5109*

n. 航海，航行；乘船旅遊

▶ He is planning to make a solo voyage across the Pacific Ocean.
他正計劃要獨自橫渡太平洋。

v. 航空，航海，航行，旅行；飛過，渡過

▶ How long does it take to voyage across the Atlantic Ocean?
橫渡大西洋要多久的時間？

Ww · Xx

通過中級英文檢定者的英文能力：

 聽
在日常生活中，能聽懂一般的會話；能大致聽懂公共場所廣播、氣象報告及廣告等。在工作時，能聽懂簡易的產品介紹與操作說明。能大致聽懂外籍人士的談話及詢問。

 讀
在日常生活中，能閱讀短文、故事、私人信件、廣告、傳單、簡介及使用說明等。在工作時，能閱讀工作須知、公告、操作手冊、例行的文件、傳真、電報等。

 寫
能寫簡單的書信、故事及心得等。對於熟悉且與個人經歷相關的主題，能以簡易的文字表達。

 說
在日常生活中，能以簡易英語交談或描述一般事物，能介紹自己的生活作息、工作、家庭、經歷等，並可對一般話題陳述看法。在工作時，能進行簡單的答詢，並與外籍人士交談溝通。

本書除包含官方公佈的中級4,947單字外，更精挑了近400個滿分必學的高手單字。同時，在片語的挑選、例句的使用上，皆依上述英檢官方公佈之能力範疇做設計，難度適中、不偏離考試主題。發音部分則是自然發音＆KK音標雙管齊下，搭配MP3以「分解／完整」方式錄音，給你最多元有效的學習手段，怎麼記都可以，想忘掉都好難！

---

wage [wedʒ] 　🎧 Track 5110
n. 工資，薪水，報酬
▶ The minimum wage has been raised to twenty thousand dollars a month.
法定最低工資已經提高到一個月兩萬元。

（補充片語）

minimum wage　法定最低工資

v. 進行，從事，發動
▶ The country waged a war against its neighboring country for oil.
該國為了石油，對鄰國發動戰爭。

（相關片語）

wage slave　薪水奴隸
▶ He decided to start his own business, because he didn't want to be a wage slave. 他決定自己創業，因為他不想當個領薪水的奴隸。

---

wag·on [`wægən] 　🎧 Track 5111
n. 運貨馬車
▶ The workers are busy loading the wagon train with the daily supplies.
工人忙著把日常用品裝上運貨馬車。

---

waist [west] 　🎧 Track 5112
n. 腰；腰部

---

wait [wet] 　🎧 Track 5113
v. 等；等候；等待

---

wait·er [`wetɚ] 　🎧 Track 5114
n. 侍者；服務生

---

wait·ress [`wetrɪs] 　🎧 Track 5115
n. 女侍者；女服務生

---

wake [wek] 　🎧 Track 5116
v. 醒來；覺醒；喚醒；弄醒

---

wak·en [`wekn] 　🎧 Track 5117
v. 醒來；喚醒，弄醒；覺醒；激發
▶ A loud scream wakened me at midnight last night.
昨晚半夜一聲響亮的尖叫聲把我吵醒。

walk [wɔk] 　🎧 *Track 5118*
v. 走；散步；陪……走；**n.** 走；步行；散步

Walk·man [`wɔkmən] 　🎧 *Track 5119*
n. 隨身聽

wall [wɔl] 　🎧 *Track 5120*
n. 牆；牆壁

wal·let [`wɑlɪt] 　🎧 *Track 5121*
n. 皮夾；錢包

waltz [wɔlts] 　🎧 *Track 5122*
n. 華爾滋舞，華爾滋舞曲
▶ My parents are both good at dancing the waltz. 我爸媽都很會跳華爾滋。

v. 跳華爾滋舞；輕快地走動；旋轉；輕鬆順利地前進
▶ Mark waltzed into the office an hour late this morning. 馬克今天早上晚了一小時才慢吞吞地走進辦公室。

〔相關片語〕
waltz off with sth. 偷走某物；輕易贏得某事物
▶ Joshua waltzed off with the championship in the national swimming competition. 約書亞在全國游泳競賽中輕而易舉地贏得冠軍。

wan·der [`wɑndɚ] 　🎧 *Track 5123*
v. 閒逛，漫遊，徘徊於……；偏離正道；迷路；失神
▶ Instead of going home right away, the boy wandered on the streets after school. 男孩放學後沒有馬上回家，反而是在街上閒晃。

want [wɑnt] 　🎧 *Track 5124*
v. 想要

war [wɔr] 　🎧 *Track 5125*
n. 戰爭；競賽；對抗

ward [wɔrd] 　🎧 *Track 5126*
n. 病房；牢房；行政區；受監護的人；看護，監禁，拘留
▶ Patients infected with Ebola were put in separate wards to prevent the spread of the infectious disease. 感染伊波拉的病人被安排住在單人病房，以避免該傳染性疾病的擴散。

v. 避開，擋開，避免
▶ He takes vitamin C every day to ward off common colds. 他每天都服用維他命C以避免感冒。

war·fare [`wɔr͵fɛr] 　🎧 *Track 5127*
n. 戰爭，衝突，交戰狀態
▶ The police have stepped up preparations for a probable outbreak of gang warfare. 警方為了一場可能發生的幫派衝突暴動，已經加強戒備。

warm [wɔrm] 　🎧 *Track 5128*
adj. 溫暖的；暖和的；**v.** 使溫暖；使暖和

warm·ing [`wɔrmɪŋ] 　🎧 *Track 5129*
adj. 讓人感到暖和的

warmth [wɔrmθ] 　🎧 *Track 5130*
n. 溫暖，親切；熱情
▶ The landlady welcomed us with warmth. 女主人熱情地歡迎我們。

warn [wɔrn] 　🎧 *Track 5131*
v. 警告，告誡，提醒
▶ He warned the man to stay away from his family. 他警告那男子離他家人遠一點。

warn·ing [`wɔrnɪŋ] 　🎧 *Track 5132*
n. 警告，告誡，先兆，徵候
▶ He got the sack without any warning. 他在毫無預警的情況下被開除了。

〔補充片語〕
get the sack 被開除
adj. 警告的，告誡的，引以為戒的
▶ Blood in the stool is an important warning sign of colon cancer. 血便是大腸癌的首要的警告徵兆。

war·ship [`wɔr͵ʃɪp] 　🎧 *Track 5133*
n. 軍艦
▶ The warship sank to the bottom of the sea after their enemy fired a missile at it. 軍艦在遭到敵軍發射飛彈後，便沈入海底。

wash [wɑʃ] 　🎧 *Track 5134*
v. 洗；沖洗

wash·ing [`wɑʃɪŋ］ 🎧 *Track 5135*
n. 洗滌，洗漱；洗好或待洗的衣物；洗滌劑
▶ Sunday is my washing day.
星期天是我洗衣服的日子。

相關片語

washing powder 洗衣粉
▶ Can I borrow some washing powder? Mine ran out. 我可以跟你借點洗衣粉嗎？我的用完了。

was·n't [`wɑznt] 🎧 *Track 5136*
abbr. （過去式）不是、還沒（**was not**的縮寫）

waste [west] 🎧 *Track 5137*
n./v. 浪費

watch [wɑtʃ] 🎧 *Track 5138*
n. 手錶；看守；監視；警戒；**v.** 看

watch·man [`wɑtʃmən] 🎧 *Track 5139*
n. 夜間看守人，巡夜者；警備員
▶ We hired a few watchmen to guard the building at night by turns. 我們請了幾位看守人在夜間輪流守衛這棟大樓。

wa·ter [`wɑtɚ] 🎧 *Track 5140*
n. 水；**v.** 澆水；給水

wa·ter·fall [`wɑtɚ͵fɔl] 🎧 *Track 5141*
n. 瀑布

wa·ter·mel·on [`wɑtɚ͵mɛlən] 🎧 *Track 5142*
n. 西瓜

wa·ter·proof [`wɑtɚ͵pruf] 🎧 *Track 5143*
adj. 防水的
▶ The coat is waterproof. 這件外套是防水的。

n. 防水材料，防水布；【英】雨衣
▶ He put on his waterproof when it started to drizzle. 當天空開始下起毛毛雨時，他便穿上了他的雨衣。

v. 使防水
▶ They invented a new technique for waterproofing the cellphones.
他們發明了一種使手機防水的新技術。

wave [wev] 🎧 *Track 5144*
n. 波浪；浪潮；揮手；捲髮；**v.** 對……揮手；揮動；使形成波浪

wax [wæks] 🎧 *Track 5145*
n. 蠟
▶ He sealed the letter with hot wax.
他用熱蠟把信封好。

adj. 蠟製的
▶ This is just a wax figure. 這只是個蠟像。

v. 打蠟
▶ The worker will wax the floor this afternoon. 工人下午要幫地板打蠟。

way [we] 🎧 *Track 5146*
adv. 非常，大大地（加強語氣）
▶ The man is way too old for you. Are you sure you're marrying him? 那男人對你來說年紀也太大了吧。你確定你要嫁給他嗎？

we [wi] 🎧 *Track 5147*
pron. 我們

weak [wik] 🎧 *Track 5148*
adj. 虛弱的；柔弱的；衰弱的

weak·en [`wikən] 🎧 *Track 5149*
v. 削弱，減弱，減少；變虛弱
▶ Whatever happens, a mother's love for her children never weakens.
不論發生什麼事，一個母親對孩子的愛是絕不會減少的。

wealth [wɛlθ] 🎧 *Track 5150*
n. 財富
▶ To me, health is more important than wealth. 對我來說，健康比財富要來得重要。

wealth·y [`wɛlθɪ] 🎧 *Track 5151*
adj. 富裕的
▶ The girl was born into a wealthy family.
這女孩出生在一個富裕的家庭。

weap·on [`wɛpən] 🎧 *Track 5152*
n. 武器；兇器

wear [wɛr] 🎧 *Track 5153*
v. 穿；戴；**n.** 穿；配戴；服裝

Aa Bb Cc Dd Ee Ff Gg Hh Ii Jj Kk Ll Mm Nn Oo Pp Qq Rr Ss Tt Uu Vv **Ww** Xx Yy Zz

※灰色單字為英檢初級必備單字

weath·er [ˈwɛðɚ]　🎧 *Track 5154*
n. 天氣

weave [wiv]　🎧 *Track 5155*
v. 編織，編製；編造；結網；迂迴行進
▶My mother weaved this blanket for me before I was born.
我媽媽在我出生前就為我編織了這條毯子。

n. 織法，編法；編織式樣；織物
▶This loose weave rug is the bestseller in our store.
這個以寬鬆編織法織成的毯子是我們店裡的暢銷商品。

web [wɛb]　🎧 *Track 5156*
n. 網；網路；蜘蛛網
▶What he said was a web of lies. Don't buy it. 他說的是一套謊言。別相信。

(補充片語)
a web of lies 編織成網的謊言，一套謊言

wed [wɛd]　🎧 *Track 5157*
v. 嫁；娶；與……結婚

we'd [wid]　🎧 *Track 5158*
abbr. 我們已、我們會（we had、we would 的縮寫）

wed·ding [ˈwɛdɪŋ]　🎧 *Track 5159*
n. 婚禮

Wednes·day [ˈwɛnzde]　🎧 *Track 5160*
=Wed., Weds.
n. 星期三

weed [wid]　🎧 *Track 5161*
n. 雜草，野草；香菸，煙草；軟弱無用的人，廢物
▶There are weeds all over our backyard.
我們的後院雜草叢生。

v. 除掉（雜草）；清除廢物，淘汰
▶The judges had to weed out less talented contestants before the competition.
評審必須在比賽開始前，淘汰掉比較沒有天分的參賽者。

week [wik]　🎧 *Track 5162*
n. 星期；週

week·day [ˈwik‚de]　🎧 *Track 5163*
n. 平日；工作日

week·end [ˈwikˈɛnd]　🎧 *Track 5164*
n. 週末

week·ly [ˈwiklɪ]　🎧 *Track 5165*
adj. 每週的；一週一次的；週刊的；**adv.** 每週地；每週一次；**n.** 週刊；週報

weep [wip]　🎧 *Track 5166*
v. 哭泣，流淚；悲歎，哀悼
▶They stood up for a minute's silence to weep for the dead.
他們起立靜默一分鐘，為死者哀悼。

n. 哭泣；眼淚
▶Have a good weep, and you'll feel better.
好好地哭一場，會讓你感到舒坦一些。

weigh [we]　🎧 *Track 5167*
v. 秤重；有……重量；考慮；權衡
▶An adult male elephant can weigh up to 16000 pounds. 一隻成年公象可能重達16000磅。

weight [wet]　🎧 *Track 5168*
n. 體重

wel·come [ˈwɛlkəm]　🎧 *Track 5169*
v. 歡迎；**adj.** 受歡迎的；被允許的；可隨意使用的；**n.** 歡迎；款待

wel·fare [ˈwɛl‚fɛr]　🎧 *Track 5170*
n. 福利；福祉；福利事業，救濟事業
▶I'll job-hop to that company for better employee welfare.
我會為了更好的員工福利跳槽到那家公司。

adj. 福利的；福利事業的；接受社會救濟的
▶Besides teaching, Kelly is also an animal welfare volunteer. 除了教書之外，凱莉還是個從事動物救濟的志工。

well [wɛl]　🎧 *Track 5171*
n. 井；水井；油井；來源，源泉
▶This well provides water to the villagers all year round.
這口井一整年都為村民供水。

(補充片語)
all year round 終年，一年到頭

we'll [wil]　🎧 *Track 5172*
abbr. 我們會（we will的縮寫）

well-known [`wɛl`non]　🎧 *Track 5173*
adj. 眾所周知的，出名
▶Tainan is well-known for its traditional snacks.
台南因傳統小吃而出名。

we're [wɪr]　🎧 *Track 5174*
abbr. 我們是（we are的縮寫）

weren't [wɜnt]　🎧 *Track 5175*
abbr. （過去式）不是（were not的縮寫）

west [wɛst]　🎧 *Track 5176*
n. 西邊；西方；**adv.** 向西；往西；自西；**adj.** 西部的；向西的；由西邊來的

west·ern [`wɛstən]　🎧 *Track 5177*
adj. 西部的；朝西的；西方的；歐美的；**n.** 西方人；歐美國家的人；西部片

west·ern·er [`wɛstənə]　🎧 *Track 5178*
n. 西方人，歐美人
▶Many westerners find it difficult to eat with chopsticks.
許多西方人都覺得用筷子吃東西很困難。

wet [wɛt]　🎧 *Track 5179*
adj. 濕的；**v.** 弄濕

we've [wiv]　🎧 *Track 5180*
abbr. 我們已（we have的縮寫）

whale [hwel]　🎧 *Track 5181*
n. 鯨魚

what [hwɑt]　🎧 *Track 5182*
pron. 什麼；**adj.** 什麼；何等

what·ev·er [hwɑt`ɛvə]　🎧 *Track 5183*
pron. 無論什麼；**adj.** 無論什麼的；不管什麼樣的

what's [hwɑts]　🎧 *Track 5184*
abbr. 是什麼（what is的縮寫）

wheat [hwit]　🎧 *Track 5185*
n. 小麥

▶Wheat flour is the main ingredient of our hand-made noodles.
我們的手工麵條的主要原料是小麥粉。

相關片語

separate the wheat from the chaff 鑑別優劣，分辨好壞，去蕪存菁
▶We will give our applicants a test to help us separate the wheat from the chaff. 我們將會讓我們的應徵者做個測驗，以做個篩選。

wheel [hwil]　🎧 *Track 5186*
n. 輪子；車輪；方向盤

when [hwɛn]　🎧 *Track 5187*
conj. 在……的時候；**adv.** 何時；**pron.** 何時

when·ev·er [hwɛn`ɛvə]　🎧 *Track 5188*
adv. 無論何時；究竟何時
▶Whenever will you give my money back?
你究竟什麼時候才要還我錢？

conj. 每當；無論何時
▶I will be there for you whenever you need me.
無論何時你需要我，我都會在出現在你身邊。

when's [hwɛnz]　🎧 *Track 5189*
abbr. 是什麼時候（when is的縮寫）

where [hwɛr]　🎧 *Track 5190*
adv. 哪裡；**conj.** 在……的地方

where's [hwɛrz]　🎧 *Track 5191*
abbr. 在哪裡（where is的縮寫）

wher·ev·er [hwɛr`ɛvə]　🎧 *Track 5192*
adv. 無論在何地；究竟在何處
▶Wherever have you been hiding all these years?
你這些年究竟躲到哪裡去了？

conj. 無論在哪裡；無論到哪裡；無論在什麼情況下
▶I'll follow you wherever you go.
無論你到哪裡，我都會跟著你。

wheth·er [`hwɛðə]　🎧 *Track 5193*
conj. 是否

which [hwɪtʃ]　🎧 *Track 5194*
pron./conj./adj. 哪一個；哪一些

which·ev·er [hwɪtʃ`ɛvə]　🎧 *Track 5195*

※灰色單字為英檢初級必備單字

det. 無論哪個，無論哪些
▶Whichever dish you order, you have to finish it.無論你點了哪一道菜，你都要把它吃完。

pron. 無論哪一個；究竟哪個
▶Whichever you choose makes no difference to me.不論你選哪一個，對我都沒差別。

while [hwaɪl] 🎧 *Track 5196*
conj. 當……的時候；**n.** 一會兒；一段時間

whip [hwɪp] 🎧 *Track 5197*
n. 鞭子；抽打；攪拌器
▶The brutal man whipped his dog to death.
那個殘忍的男人把他的狗抽打致死。

v. 鞭笞，抽打；攪打；煽動；急走；徹底擊敗
▶She is whipping the egg whites and sugar to make a cake.
她為了做蛋糕，正攪打著蛋白和糖。

whis·per [ˋhwɪspɚ] 🎧 *Track 5198*
n. 耳語；私語；傳聞、流言
▶The girls are talking in whispers.
女孩們在竊竊私語。

v. 低語；私下說；低聲說
▶It's impolite to whisper in front of others.
在別人面前竊竊私語是不禮貌的。

whis·tle [ˋhwɪsl] 🎧 *Track 5199*
v. 吹口哨，吹哨子；呼嘯；吹口哨示意
▶Henry always whistles while taking a shower when he is in a good mood.
當亨利心情很好的時候，總是會一邊淋浴一邊吹口哨。

n. 口哨，警笛；哨音
▶A passer-by blew the whistle on the robber by calling the police.
一名路人打電話報警，阻止了那個搶匪。

(補充片語)
blow the whistle on 告密，阻止，使……停下

white [hwaɪt] 🎧 *Track 5200*
adj. 白的；白色的；**n.** 白色

who [hu] 🎧 *Track 5201*
pron. 誰；什麼人
conj. （關係代名詞）……的人

who'd [hud] 🎧 *Track 5202*
abbr. 誰會、誰已（who would、who had 的縮寫）

who·ev·er [huˋɛvɚ] 🎧 *Track 5203*
=whom·ev·er
pron. 無論誰；到底是誰
▶Whoever finds my dog, please contact me as soon as possible.
無論是誰找到我的狗，請立刻與我聯繫。

conj. 無論誰
▶I will give a prize to whoever finds my dog.
無論誰找到我的狗，我都會給他一筆獎金。

whole [hol] 🎧 *Track 5204*
adj. 全部的；整個的；所有的；**n.** 全部；全體

whom [hum] 🎧 *Track 5205*
pron. 誰；任何人；**conj.** 誰

who's [huz] 🎧 *Track 5206*
abbr. 是誰（who is的縮寫）

whose [huz] 🎧 *Track 5207*
det./conj. 誰的

why [hwaɪ] 🎧 *Track 5208*
adv. 為什麼；**conj.** ……的原因；為何

wick·ed [ˋwɪkɪd] 🎧 *Track 5209*
adj. 邪惡的，缺德的；頑皮的；惡劣的，有害的；過分的；很棒的
▶How could you do such a wicked thing to me? 你怎麼能對我做這麼缺德的事？

wide [waɪd] 🎧 *Track 5210*
adj. 寬的；寬鬆的；廣泛的

wid·en [ˋwaɪdn] 🎧 *Track 5211*
v. 放寬；加大；擴大

wide·spread [ˋwaɪdˏsprɛd] 🎧 *Track 5212*
adj. 普遍的，廣泛的；分布廣的
▶Poor health services and child malnutrition in India are two major factors that lead to widespread poverty.
印度貧乏的醫療服務及孩童營養失調是導致普遍貧窮的兩個主要因素。

width [wɪdθ] 　　*Track 5213*
n. 寬度

wife [waɪf] 　　*Track 5214*
n. 妻子；太太；夫人

wild [waɪld] 　　*Track 5215*
adj. 野生的；未被馴養的；粗野的；瘋狂的；猛烈的；**n.** 荒野；未被開發之地

wil·der·ness [`wɪldɚnɪs] 　*Track 5216*
n. 荒漠，無人煙處；不受控制的狀態
▶ He finally returned to power after two years in the wilderness.
在消沉了兩年之後，他總算東山再起了。

(補充片語)

return to power 東山再起；
in the wilderness （政治上）不再處於重要地位或具影響力

wild·life [`waɪld͵laɪf] 　*Track 5217*
n. 野生生物，野生動物
▶ We were so so excited when we spotted a pink dolphin, a very rare type of wildlife in the Amazon River. 當我們無意間看到一隻粉紅海豚這種在亞馬遜河中非常珍稀的野生生物時，真的是興奮極了。

wild·ly [`waɪldlɪ] 　*Track 5218*
adv. 野生地；失控地；粗暴地；瘋狂地
▶ My heart was beating wildly when they were going to announce the result of the game.
當他們要宣布比賽結果時，我的心狂跳不已。

will [wɪl] 　　*Track 5219*
n. 意志，毅力；心願，目的；遺囑
▶ The patient has a strong will to live.
這病人有很強的求生意志。

(補充片語)

will to live 求生意志

will·ing [`wɪlɪŋ] 　*Track 5220*
adj. 願意的

wil·low [`wɪlo] 　*Track 5221*
n. 柳，柳樹
▶ We had our picnic under the willow by the lake.
我們在湖邊的柳樹下野餐。

win [wɪn] 　　*Track 5222*
v. 贏；獲勝；**n.** 獲勝；成功

wind [wɪnd] 　　*Track 5223*
n. 風

win·dow [`wɪndo] 　*Track 5224*
n. 窗戶

wind·y [`wɪndɪ] 　*Track 5225*
adj. 颱風的；多風的

wine [waɪn] 　　*Track 5226*
n. 酒，葡萄酒；水果酒

wing [wɪŋ] 　　*Track 5227*
n. 翅膀

wink [wɪŋk] 　　*Track 5228*
v. 眨眼；使眼色，眨眼示意；假裝無視；閃爍
▶ She winked a warning at me when I was about to make a slip of the tongue.
就在我快說溜嘴時，她使眼色警告我。

(補充片語)

make a slip of the tongue 說溜嘴

n. 眨眼，眼色；閃爍，閃耀；瞬間，霎時
▶ In the wink of an eye, my baby boy has grown into a handsome young man.
才一眨眼的時間，我的寶貝兒子已經長大成為一個年輕帥小子了。

(補充片語)

in the wink of an eye 一瞬間，一眨眼的時間

(相關片語)

sleep a wink 打個盹，闔一下眼
▶ I didn't sleep a wink last night because my husband snored all night long. 我昨晚一夜都沒闔眼，因為我老公整晚打鼾打個不停。

win·ner [`wɪnɚ] 　*Track 5229*
n. 贏家；獲勝者；優勝者

win·ter [`wɪntɚ] 　*Track 5230*
n. 冬天

wipe [waɪp] 　　*Track 5231*
v. 擦，擦乾，擦去，抹
▶ The bad news wiped the smile off everyone's face.

※灰色單字為英檢初級必備單字

這壞消息抹去了每個人臉上的笑容。

(補充片語)

wipe the smile off one's face　讓人笑不出來；掃某人的興

n. 擦，揩

▶ The table is so dirty that it needs a good wipe. 這桌子好髒，需要好好擦一擦。

(相關片語)

wipe the floor with　完全打敗，使潰敗

▶ Jerry wiped the floor with all his opponents in the election.
傑瑞在這場選舉中大敗所有對手。

wire [waɪr]　🎧 *Track 5232*
n. 金屬線；電纜；電話線

▶ Ms. Chen is on the wire now.
陳小姐現在正在講電話。

(補充片語)

on the wire　使用電話中；正在講電話

v. 用金屬線綁、連接、加固；給……裝電線；用電報發送，拍電報

▶ He wired the flowerpots to the fence.
他用金屬線將花盆綁在籬笆上。

wis·dom [`wɪzdəm]　🎧 *Track 5233*
n. 智慧，才智；知識，學問；古人名訓

▶ My grandma might lack education, but she showed great wisdom in her words and deeds.
我奶奶也許沒受過教育，但她的言行在在顯露出非凡的智慧。

(補充片語)

words and deeds　言行

(相關片語)

wisdom tooth　智齒

▶ Is it really necessary to have my wisdom tooth taken out?
真的有必要拔掉我的智齒嗎？

wise [waɪz]　🎧 *Track 5234*
adj. 有智慧的；明智的

wish [wɪʃ]　🎧 *Track 5235*
v. 希望；但願；**n.** 願望；心願；祝福

wit [wɪt]　🎧 *Track 5236*
n. 智力；機智；智慧；富有智慧的人

▶ His quick wit has gotten him out of trouble many times.
他的腦筋轉得快，因此避開了不少麻煩。

(相關片語)

have one's wits about one　保持警覺，時刻警覺

▶ You have to have your wits about you when you're on duty.
值班時，你必須隨時保持警覺。

witch [wɪtʃ]　🎧 *Track 5237*
n. 女巫

▶ The witch put a spell on the princess and made her sleep forever.
巫婆對公主施了咒語，讓她永遠沉睡。

with [wɪð]　🎧 *Track 5238*
prep. 和……一起

with·draw [wɪð`drɔ]　🎧 *Track 5239*
v. 抽回，收回；提領；撤銷；離開；退出

▶ The player was compelled to withdraw from the race because of his leg injury.
因為腳傷，該選手被迫退出比賽。

with·in [wɪ`ðɪn]　🎧 *Track 5240*
prep. 在……範圍內；不超過；在……內部；**adv.** 在裡面；在內部

with·out [wɪ`ðaʊt]　🎧 *Track 5241*
prep. 沒有

wit·ness [`wɪtnɪs]　🎧 *Track 5242*
n. 目擊者，見證人；證詞；證據

▶ He is the only witness to the traffic accident.
他是那場交通意外的唯一目擊者。

v. 目擊；證明；為……作證

▶ He was the only person that witnessed the murder. 他是唯一目擊那場兇殺案的人。

wiz·ard [`wɪzəd]　🎧 *Track 5243*
n. 巫師

▶ Harry Potter is a young wizard.
哈利波特是一名年輕巫師。

wok [wɑk]　🎧 *Track 5244*
n. 鑊；中式炒菜鍋

wolf [wʊlf]　🎧 *Track 5245*
n. 狼

wom·an [ˋwʊmən]　🎧 *Track 5246*
n. 女人；婦女

won·der [ˋwʌndɚ]　🎧 *Track 5247*
v. 納悶；想知道；**n.** 驚奇；驚歎；奇觀、奇事

won·der·ful [ˋwʌndɚfəl]　🎧 *Track 5248*
adj. 美好的；神奇的；極好的

won't [wont]　🎧 *Track 5249*
abbr. 不會（will not的縮寫）

wood [wʊd]　🎧 *Track 5250*
n. 木頭、木材；森林、樹林

wood·en [ˋwʊdn]　🎧 *Track 5251*
adj. 木製的；僵硬的

wool [wʊl]　🎧 *Track 5252*
n. 羊毛；毛線；毛織品
▶ She wears a wool sweater today.
她今天穿著一件羊毛毛衣。

相關片語

lose one's wool　發怒；發火
▶ He lost his wool when his son talked back to him.
當他兒子跟他頂嘴時，他發了頓脾氣。

word [wɝd]　🎧 *Track 5253*
n. 字；一句話；言辭；談話

work [wɝk]　🎧 *Track 5254*
n. 工作；事；職務；**v.** 工作；幹活；（機器）運轉

work·book [ˋwɝkˏbʊk]　🎧 *Track 5255*
n. 習題簿，練習簿；業務手冊，工作筆記本
▶ He couldn't do his school assignment because he left his workbook at school.
他沒辦法做學校作業，因為他把習題本留在學校了。

work·er [ˋwɝkɚ]　🎧 *Track 5256*
n. 工人；勞工；勞動者；工作者

work·ing [ˋwɝkɪŋ]　🎧 *Track 5257*
adj. 工作的；有效的；操作的；有工作的
▶ It is a challenge to find balance between work and family for a working mother.
對一個上班的媽媽來說，要在工作和家庭間找到平衡點是一項挑戰。

n. 工作，勞動；運轉；經營，操縱
▶ The teacher used illustrations to explain the workings of the human brain to the students.
老師利用圖示向學生說明人類大腦的活動。

相關片語

working holiday　打工度假
▶ Donna will go to Australia for a working holiday after graduation.
唐娜在畢業後將會到澳洲打工度假。

work·shop [ˋwɝkˏʃɑp]　🎧 *Track 5258*
n. 工作坊，小工廠；研討會，專題討論會
▶ She is planning to create a reader's workshop for the kids in the neighborhood. 她正在計劃為附近的孩子們創設一個讀書工作坊。

world [wɝld]　🎧 *Track 5259*
n. 世界；**adj.** 世界的

world·wide [ˋwɝldˏwaɪd]　🎧 *Track 5260*
adv. 在世界各地；在全世界
▶ The experts warned that the Ebola virus could spread worldwide. 專家警告，伊波拉病毒可能會散播到世界各地。

adj. 遍及全球的，全球性的
▶ Selfies have become a worldwide phenomenon.自拍已經成為一個全球性現象。

worm [wɝm]　🎧 *Track 5261*
n. 蟲，蠕蟲，蛀蟲；可憐蟲，懦夫
▶ The early bird catches the worm.
早起的鳥兒有蟲兒吃。

v. 使蠕動；使緩慢前進；潛行，潛入；擺脫困境
▶ It was not easy but she still managed to worm out of difficulties.
這不容易，但她仍設法擺脫了困難。

補充片語

worm out　擺脫；刺探出

※灰色單字為英檢初級必備單字

a can of worms 複雜的問題
▶He volunteered to open the can of worms.
他自願著手處理這個棘手的問題。

worn [worn] 🎧 *Track 5262*
adj. 用舊的，磨壞的；精疲力盡的，憔悴的
▶They were worn out after a long day's work. 他們在工作了漫長的一天之後，已經精疲力竭了。

補充片語

worn out 疲累不堪

wor·ried [`wɝɪd] 🎧 *Track 5263*
adj. 擔憂的，擔心的
▶The missing girl's parents were worried about her safety.
失蹤女童的父母親很擔心她的安危。

wor·ry [`wɝɪ] 🎧 *Track 5264*
v. 擔心；擔憂；**n.** 擔心；憂慮；令人擔憂的事

worse [wɝs] 🎧 *Track 5265*
adj. 更差的；更壞的；更糟糕的；（並）更重的
▶Things are getting worse.
情況變得更糟了。

adv. 更糟；更壞；更惡化
▶My husband treats me worse than he treats everyone else.
我先生對待我比他對待任何人的態度更糟。

n. 更糟的狀況
▶Things have gone from bad to worse.
事情已經越變越糟糕了。

補充片語

go from bad to worse 越來越糟

worst [wɝst] 🎧 *Track 5266*
adj. 最差的；最壞的；**adv.** 最壞地；最惡劣地；最不利地；**n.** 最壞的狀況

worth [wɝθ] 🎧 *Track 5267*
adj. 有……的價值；值……；**n.** 價值；值一定金額的數量

worth·less [`wɝθlɪs] 🎧 *Track 5268*
adj. 無價值的，無用的；不中用的

▶His room is piled up with worthless pieces of junk.
他的房間堆滿了無用的垃圾。

worth·while [`wɝθ`hwaɪl] 🎧 *Track 5269*
adj. 值得花費時間（或金錢）的，值得做的；有真實價值的
▶She finds it worthwhile to quit her job to be a full-time mother.
她認為辭去工作當全職媽媽是值得的。

wor·thy [`wɝðɪ] 🎧 *Track 5270*
adj. 有價值的；值得的，配得上的；足以……的
▶His proposal is worthy of consideration.
他的提案值得考慮。

n. 知名人士，傑出人士
▶The local worthies are all invited to the opening ceremony.
知名的地方人士都獲邀出席開幕典禮。

would [wʊd] 🎧 *Track 5271*
aux. 會；將；要；願意

would·n't [`wʊdnt] 🎧 *Track 5272*
abbr. （過去式）不會（would not的縮寫）

wound [wund] 🎧 *Track 5273*
n. 傷口；創傷；**v.** 使受傷；傷害

wow [waʊ] 🎧 *Track 5274*
interj. （表示驚訝，欣喜或痛苦的叫聲）哇，噢
▶You did this all by yourselves? Wow!
這全是你們自己做的？哇！

v. 使驚訝，使驚艷
▶The dish was good, but it didn't wow me.
這道菜很好吃，但是並沒有讓我驚艷。

wrap [ræp] 🎧 *Track 5275*
v. 包，裹；穿外衣，披圍巾；偽裝；使全神貫注
▶I'd like this book to be wrapped as a gift.
請幫我把這本書包成禮物。

n. 包裹物，覆蓋物；外衣，圍巾，披肩；墨西哥捲
▶I'd like to have some tortilla wraps for lunch.
我午餐想要吃墨西哥捲。

wrap·ping [ˋræpɪŋ] 🎧 *Track 5276*

n. 包裝紙，包裝材料
▶ Excessive wrappings are wasteful.
過度的包裝是浪費的。

---

wreck [rɛk] 🎧 *Track 5277*

n. 失事，遇難；（失事的）殘骸；破壞
▶ The rescue team finally found the wreck of the flight.搜救隊終於找到了飛機的殘骸。

v. 使失事，遇難；損害
▶ Excessive drinking will wreck your life.
酗酒會毀了你的人生。

---

wrin·kle [ˋrɪŋkl] 🎧 *Track 5278*

n. 皺紋；難題
▶ Is it possible to remove the wrinkles from my neck naturally?
有可能以自然的方式除去我頸部的皺紋嗎？

v. 使起皺紋；皺起來
▶ I want to buy shirts that don't wrinkle.
我想要買不會起皺的襯衫。

---

wrist [rɪst] 🎧 *Track 5279*

n. 腕；腕部；腕關節

---

write [raɪt] 🎧 *Track 5280*

v. 寫

---

writ·er [ˋraɪtɚ] 🎧 *Track 5281*

n. 作家；作者；撰稿人

---

writ·ing [ˋraɪtɪŋ] 🎧 *Track 5282*

n. 書寫，寫作；筆跡；文學作品；文件
▶ Many students take writing classes to improve their writing skills for their school studies and exams.
很多學生為了學校的課業及測驗，參加寫作班以增強寫作技巧。

相關片語
the writing on the wall 凶兆，不祥之兆
▶ The increase in oil price is the writing on the wall for taxi drivers.
油價調漲對計程車業者來說是個不祥之兆。

---

wrong [rɔŋ] 🎧 *Track 5283*

adj. 錯誤的；不對的；出毛病的；**adv.** 錯誤地；不正當地；**n.** 錯誤

X-ray [ˋɛksˋre] 🎧 *Track 5284*

n. X光；X光檢查；X光照片
▶ The doctor looked at the X-ray of his lungs and saw a white spot.
醫生看著他肺部的X光照片，看到了一個白點。

v. 用X光檢查
▶ The doctor X-rayed his lungs to see whether they were normal.
醫生用X光檢查他的肺部，看看他的肺部是否正常。

---

xe·rox [ˋzɪrɑks] 🎧 *Track 5285*

n. 靜電複印機；影印機

v. 靜電複印；影印

Aa
Bb
Cc
Dd
Ee

Ff
Gg
Hh
Ii
Jj

Kk
Ll
Mm
Nn
Oo

Pp
Qq
Rr
Ss
Tt

Uu
Vv
Ww
Xx
Yy
Zz

※灰色單字為英檢初級必備單字

Yy·Zz

通過中級英文檢定者的英文能力：

在日常生活中，能聽懂一般的會話；能大致聽懂公共場所廣播、氣象報告及廣告等。在工作時，能聽懂簡易的產品介紹與操作說明。能大致聽懂外籍人士的談話及詢問。

在日常生活中，能閱讀短文、故事、私人信件、廣告、傳單、簡介及使用說明等。在工作時，能閱讀工作須知、公告、操作手冊、例行的文件、傳真、電報等。

能寫簡單的書信、故事及心得等。對於熟悉且與個人經歷相關的主題，能以簡易的文字表達。

說

在日常生活中，能以簡易英語交談或描述一般事物，能介紹自己的生活作息、工作、家庭、經歷等，並可對一般話題陳述看法。在工作時，能進行簡單的答詢，並與外籍人士交談溝通。

本書除包含官方公佈的中級4,947單字外，更精挑了近400個滿分必學的高手單字。同時，在片語的挑選、例句的使用上，皆依上述英檢官方公佈之能力範疇做設計，難度適中、不偏離考試主題。發音部分則是自然發音＆KK音標雙管齊下，搭配MP3以「分解／完整」方式錄音，給你最多元有效的學習手段，怎麼記都可以，想忘掉都好難！

---

yam [jæm]　🎧 *Track 5286*
=sweet po·ta·to
n. 山芋類植物（如山藥、甘藷、馬鈴薯等）
▶ I usually make myself yam salad for an easy lunch. 我經常為自己做山芋沙拉，當做一頓簡單的午餐。

yard [jɑrd]　🎧 *Track 5287*
n. 院子；庭院

yawn [jɔn]　🎧 *Track 5288*
v. 打呵欠
▶ It's quite rude to yawn when someone is speaking to you.
在某人跟你說話時打呵欠是非常失禮的事情。

n. 呵欠；乏味的人或事物
▶ He gave a big yawn and said goodnight.
他打了一個大呵欠，然後說晚安。

yeah [jɛə]　🎧 *Track 5289*
interj. 對啊！好啊！

year [jɪr]　🎧 *Track 5290*
n. 年

year·ly [`jɪrlɪ]　🎧 *Track 5291*
adv. 每年；一年一度

yell [jɛl]　🎧 *Track 5292*
v. 叫喊；吼叫著說
▶ Don't yell at me. 別對我吼叫。

n. 叫喊聲；吼叫聲
▶ Did you hear the yell from next door?
你有聽到隔壁傳來的叫喊聲嗎？

yel·low [`jɛlo]　🎧 *Track 5293*
adj. 黃的；黃色的；**n.** 黃；黃色；黃色的衣服

yes [jɛs]**=yeah**　🎧 *Track 5294*
interj. 好極了；真的；**adv.** 是；是的

yes·ter·day [`jɛstɚde]　🎧 *Track 5295*
n./adv. 昨天

yet [jɛt] 🎧 *Track 5296*
adv. （用於否定句）還沒；已經
conj. 然而；卻

yo‧gurt [ˋjogɚt] 🎧 *Track 5297*
=yo‧ghurt
n. 酸奶；酸乳酪；優格
▶You can replace salad dressing with yogurt if you're on a diet.
　如果你在節食的話，可以用優格取代沙拉醬。

yolk [jok] 🎧 *Track 5298*
n. 蛋黃
▶He ate the yolk and left the egg white on his plate. 他吃了蛋黃，把蛋白留在盤子上。

you [ju] 🎧 *Track 5299*
pron. 你

you'd [jud] 🎧 *Track 5300*
abbr. 你會、你已（**you had**、**you would** 的縮寫）

you'll [jul] 🎧 *Track 5301*
abbr. 你會（**you will**的縮寫）

young [jʌŋ] 🎧 *Track 5302*
adj. 年輕的；年幼的；**n.** 年輕人們；青年們

young‧ster [ˋjʌŋstɚ] 🎧 *Track 5303*
n. 小孩、兒童；年輕人
▶Youngsters under 12 must be accompanied by an adult.
　十二歲以下的孩童必須由一位成人陪同。

your [jʊɚ] 🎧 *Track 5304*
det. 你的；你們的

you're [jʊɚ] 🎧 *Track 5305*
abbr. 你是（**you are**的縮寫）

yours [jʊrz] 🎧 *Track 5306*
pron. 你的（事物）；你們的（事物）

your‧self [jʊɚˋsɛlf] 🎧 *Track 5307*
pron. 你自己；你們自己

youth [juθ] 🎧 *Track 5308*
n. 青春時代；青年；年輕；青春

youth‧ful [ˋjuθfəl] 🎧 *Track 5309*
adj. 年輕的；富青春活力的；朝氣蓬勃的
▶She's youthful despite her age.
　儘管上了年紀，她仍然很有青春活力。

you've [juv] 🎧 *Track 5310*
abbr. 你已（**you have**的縮寫）

yuck‧y [ˋjʌkɪ] 🎧 *Track 5311*
adj. 討人厭的；難以下嚥的；難聞的

yum‧my [ˋjʌmɪ] 🎧 *Track 5312*
adj. 好吃的；美味的

ze‧bra [ˋzibrə] 🎧 *Track 5313*
n. 斑馬

ze‧ro [ˋzɪro] 🎧 *Track 5314*
n. 零；零號；零度；無；烏有；**adj.** 零的；全無的

zone [zon] 🎧 *Track 5315*
n. 地帶；地區
▶Singapore and Taiwan are in the same time zone.
　新加坡與台灣是在同一個時區。
（補充片語）
time zone 時區
v. 劃區；使分成區或地帶
▶This area has been zoned for industrial land use.
　這地區已經被劃為工業用地。

zoo [zu] 🎧 *Track 5316*
n. 動物園

Aa
Bb
Cc
Dd
Ee
Ff
Gg
Hh
Ii
Jj
Kk
Ll
Mm
Nn
Oo
Pp
Qq
Rr
Ss
Tt
Uu
Vv
Ww
Xx
Yy
Zz

※灰色單字為英檢初級必備單字

原來如此 系列 *E187*

100%符合考試要求　110%收錄考試關鍵單字　3000%的模擬訓練量

GEPT全民英檢中級單字╳一擊必殺

英檢官方指定+教育部公告必學+名師試場嚴選=英檢中級單字聖經！

作　　　者	李宇凡
顧　　　問	曾文旭
社　　　長	王毓芳
編輯統籌	耿文國、黃璽宇
總　　　編	吳靜宜
執行主編	潘妍潔
執行編輯	詹雲翔、楊雲慶、嚴晟珈
美術編輯	王桂芳、張嘉容
法律顧問	北辰著作權事務所　蕭雄淋律師、幸秋妙律師

初　　　版	2018年05月
	2024年初版12刷
出　　　版	捷徑文化出版事業有限公司
電　　　話	（02）2752-5618
傳　　　真	（02）2752-5619

定　　　價	新台幣420元／港幣140元
產品內容	1書+單字音檔+實戰試題檔案

總 經 銷	采舍國際有限公司
地　　　址	235 新北市中和區中山路二段366巷10號3樓
電　　　話	（02）8245-8786
傳　　　真	（02）8245-8718

港澳地區總經銷	和平圖書有限公司
地　　　址	香港柴灣嘉業街12號百樂門大廈17樓
電　　　話	（852）2804-6687
傳　　　真	（852）2804-6409

捷徑 Book站

國家圖書館出版品預行編目資料

GEPT全民英檢中級單字╳一擊必殺 / 李宇凡
著. -- 初版. -- 臺北市：捷徑文化, 2018.05
　　面；　公分（原來如此：E187）

ISBN 978-957-8904-34-7(平裝)

1. 英語　2. 詞彙

805.1892　　　　　　　　　　107007644